SCOURGED

TAY ROSE

SCOURGED

THE SOLSTICE CYCLE
BOOK TWO

TAY ROSE

LUEXRITH
EVERHEIM MOUNT
ANTORIS
KHENTO
KASIA
KINGDOM OF
ONIT
XARA'S ROAD
ANDBURGH
IVORY FOREST
KREAH
TOLONA
IDRIX
VATHA
ONITA & S

ETTERVAN
MIRRORED
SEA
BAY OF NRIA
VERITH
KIZAR ISLANDS
ATTLEHON MOUNTAINS
SACALE
RRITORIES

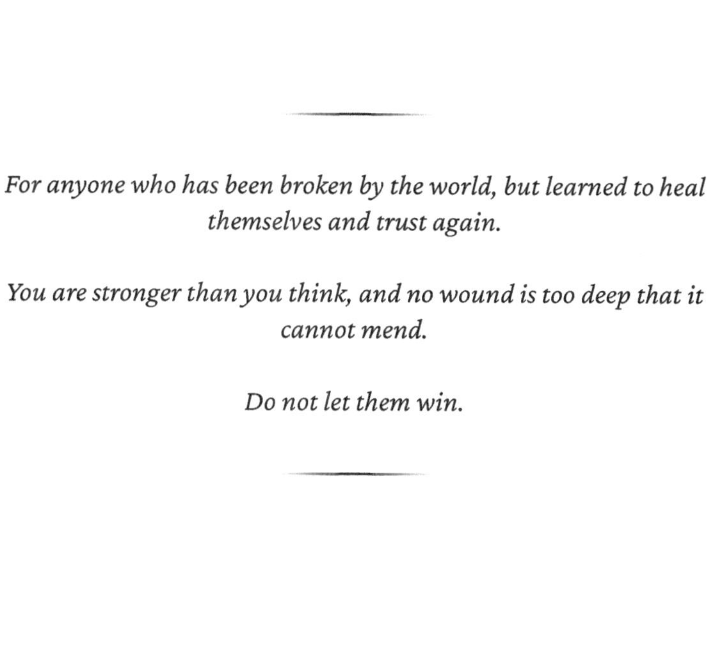

For anyone who has been broken by the world, but learned to heal themselves and trust again.

You are stronger than you think, and no wound is too deep that it cannot mend.

Do not let them win.

AUTHOR'S NOTE

Scourged is an adult fantasy romance containing content which may not be suitable or appropriate for all readers.

Sensitive content includes the graphic torture of a main character, perceived cheating, on-page sexual assault of a main character with vague descriptions, violence, gore, death of a family member, suicidal ideations, anxiety and panic attacks, and forgiving an abuser.

Scourged also contains adult content, such as cursing, strong or offensive language, and sexual content.

Reader discretion is advised, and please, always take care of yourself.

This is book two in an ongoing four-book series, and is the sequel to *Threaded.* It ends on a cliffhanger.

PROLOGUE

The cold, aching rip in his chest dragged Sebastian from the clutches of sleep.

The bridge that lived there—the one binding him to his queen, woven by her miraculous magic of light and life—had only just started to feel like a part of him. But now it was cracking and crumbling as if a great, ancient beast were hurling dark stones upon its brilliance.

He lurched from his bed, feet hitting the cold floor, clutching at his bare chest. He gasped for air, tears streaming down his face, the sudden pain wracking him with a ferocious intensity.

Sebastian's entire world stood still, then tilted violently on its axis.

He threw himself toward a chair, snatching a discarded pair of trousers from the back and sliding them up his legs, hands shaking. His breathing labored as he found a rumpled cotton shirt, tugging it over his head. He grabbed his sword from the wall, belting it around his waist as he staggered into the hall.

Sebastian was unsurprised to find he was not alone.

Drystan leaned heavily against his door frame, longsword unsheathed, Feran by his side, gripping his Kreah short swords with tense, white knuckles. Quentin, wild red hair in disarray and a manic gleam in his eye rushed into the hall, baldric strapped across his chest as he palmed a throwing knife in each hand. Matheo and Trefor were close on Quentin's heels, bows and arrows notched, and more weapons strapped to their sides.

The only one not present … was Andrian. The hair on Sebastian's arms rose.

In a single movement, their panic threading together through the air, Mariah's Armature turned to Mariah's door.

Sebastian didn't think, didn't hesitate. He leaped into motion, rushing down the hall and slamming his body against the heavy white and gold oak door. The lock snapped, a few pieces of splintered wood skittering across the marble floor, the door crashing off the wall.

The silence that greeted him was the loudest.

He rushed into his queen's suite, the others behind him. The balcony doors were closed, the hearths burned out. Mariah's things were scattered around the space—a pair of discarded boots in the corner, two short swords from the palace armory on the island, blankets and sweaters strewn over the back of the plush couches.

It was perfectly normal … save for the silence.

Sebastian turned slowly to the right, to Mariah's bedroom door.

Her *open* door.

Fear gripped him close and held him to its chest as he moved closer to the entrance, peering inside.

It was dark, the bed rumpled. Slept in, but …

Sebastian pushed the door open wider and flipped a *lunestair* switch on the wall. Drystan stepped to his side as the room blazed with illuminating, silver-gold light.

Revealing the empty bed.

Swift inhales of breath and shocked murmurs echoed behind Sebastian, but his eyes had latched onto something that filled him with more fear than even that empty room could.

Drystan cursed, low and savage, metal clanking as he rushed past Sebastian into the room. He halted beside the bed, hands clenching into fists, before half-turning to Sebastian. "She's not here."

Sebastian didn't answer him. Couldn't move, still held captive by what lay discarded on Mariah's nightstand.

"Sebastian?" Matheo's earnest question loosened Sebastian's feet. With more jolting steps, he shuffled forward to that nightstand.

He picked up the object of his attention, holding it in his hands with a pained, blank expression. Turning sluggishly to face the others, his movements slowed by his fear, Sebastian watched his shock and horror slowly reflect themselves across the other's faces.

His hands tightened around the worn leather hilt of Mariah's dragon-winged dagger. The dagger she never went anywhere without.

The dagger she would've *never* left here ... unless she truly believed she wouldn't need it.

Or ... Sebastian swallowed.

Or if she'd been forced to leave it.

Sebastian couldn't stop his mind from snagging on one person. One person who could have made her feel that safety. One person who was also horribly, maddeningly, sickeningly missing.

"We have to find her," Sebastian said, voice low and thick. "And Andrian. Something has happened. Search the palace— *now.*"

MARIAH'S ARMATURE snapped into action at Sebastian's order. Matheo raced for Ryenne's wing to alert Kalen and Ryenne's Armature. The others split into two pairs: Trefor and Quentin were to sweep the palace from the north, Drystan and Feran from the south, and they would meet in the center at the throne room.

Sebastian would meet up with whoever he found first, after he roused the rest of Mariah's court.

He stood outside an unassuming brown door in the wing

neighboring Mariah's, desperately clawing for control of his racing heart and roiling stomach. With a shaky inhale, he twisted the unlocked handle and rushed inside.

He shot past the small kitchenette and quaint table he knew overflowed with clothes and jewelry, heading straight for the bed at the back of the room. Through the dim light filtering in from the open door, Sebastian could just make out Ciana's sleeping shape, curly blonde hair strewn about her blush-colored sheets. Lunging to her side, Sebastian gripped her shoulders, gently squeezing and shaking, ignoring her soft skin beneath his calloused palms.

"Ciana," he croaked, voice hoarse from his panic. He cleared it, trying again. "Ciana, wake up. Something has happened."

Ciana twitched in his grip. "Go away," she grumbled, shifting and burying her face deeper into her pillow.

Sebastian swore softly, giving her another shake. "Ciana," he hissed, his panic leeching into his voice. He released her, reaching for the lamp beside her bed. He flipped the switch, washing the room with light before giving her another shake. "*Wake up.*"

Finally, she roused herself from sleep, brushing off his hand as she rolled onto her back. When she cracked open her eyes, meeting his stare, she shot up, nearly knocking her forehead against his.

"Sebastian? What in Enfara are you doing here?" Her voice was groggy, but her amber eyes were sharp.

Sebastian stood from her bed, backing away a step. He tried to keep his gaze locked on hers, to not let it drop to the scoop of her low-cut maroon nightdress. As if she could read his thoughts, Ciana reached for her silk sheets, pulling them up around her chin.

"Sebastian?" she repeated, and Sebastian swallowed, trying to control the agony of what still raced through him.

"Something has happened," he finally whispered. "To Mariah. We can't find her."

Ciana froze. Her hands released her sheet, the silk falling back around her hips. Her brow crinkled for a moment as if processing Sebastian's words while shaking off the clutches of sleep.

Her eyes widened. "Last night, she told me that Andrian was going to bond with her. That he'd finally agreed to it and was planning something special. She was to meet him in one of the courtyards at the starlight hour."

Sebastian was tired of taking these blows.

Andrian. Agreeing to take the bond. Immediately after a difficult meeting with his father and Lord Shawth. One that had sent him back to the city, leaving Mariah alone and in need of him.

The starlight hour, that last hour just before dawn, had just passed. It was the last chance to catch the moon and stars before they disappeared beneath the light of the sun. A glance out of Ciana's window, which opened to the Bay of Nria, revealed the first rays of dawn spreading tendrils across the sky.

Sebastian truly worried, at that moment, that he might be sick. His failure coursed through him with each pounding beat of his heart, shredding him apart from the inside out.

"Get dressed," he told Ciana. "We need to wake Delaynie. And then … we must find that courtyard."

Ciana didn't hesitate; she jumped out of bed and sprinted into her bathroom in search of her closet. Sebastian again did his best to avert his stare as she ran past him in that short nightdress, full thighs on display. His eyes lingered on her closed bathroom door for a long moment, savoring the blankness in his mind, when a clatter and a curse on the other side shattered his reprieve. He shook his head, running a hand through his hair, before stepping back into the hall, fingers tracing anxious patterns around the worn leather pommel of his sword.

His whole life, he'd been perfect. The perfect son, the perfect Marked trainee, the perfect soldier. The perfect Armature.

The perfect Armature … who had failed to keep track of his queen.

The perfect Armature who'd let something happen to her as he'd slept peacefully in his bed.

Crippling self-loathing and novel self-hatred reared up like a wave around him.

The door behind him opened just before it could crash down and sweep him away. Ciana stepped into the hall, glancing at him with a tempest in her amber eyes as she stormed across the hall and pounded her fist on the door.

"Delaynie!" she barked. She didn't wait for a response before bursting through the door, the other girl's yelp of surprise ringing into the hall.

And once again, Sebastian was left alone with his consuming, debilitating failure.

He closed his eyes, drawing in a deep breath. No. He might've failed once, but letting these feelings crush him … it would only be failing again. Failing further. Something he simply couldn't allow to happen.

They *would* find Mariah. There was simply no other option.

It wasn't long before Delaynie's door opened, and the two women strode into the hall.

Ciana's eyes were hard and she wore a determined set to her brow. "I might know which courtyard."

The silence in the hall was crushing and thick.

"Well?" Sebastian demanded, voice heavy with his impatience. "Which one?"

Ciana blinked. "One of the lower ones, by the stables. It has the best view of the stars. Mariah mentioned it last night, briefly. I think that's where Andrian told her to meet."

Sebastian's stomach dropped. A part of him still refused to believe that Andrian—a man he'd known for most of his life, a man he truly considered a brother—had anything to do with this.

And yet …

And yet, that courtyard was closest to the stables. Closest to the palace exits. Closest to the easiest way to sneak in or out of the massive fortress.

Sebastian would know. They used to use the tunnel just below that courtyard all the time when they were young and stupid, used it to sneak away from their master-at-arms and into the market district for a night of idiotic frivolity.

Andrian used to use those tunnels, too.

Sebastian swallowed down the bile creeping up his throat. "Let's go."

They raced through the halls, winding down staircases and bursting through doors. They passed Quentin and Trefor on their way to the courtyard, who saw their urgent pace and fell into step behind them without a word.

The moment they emerged into the open air, with songbirds singing in the early dawn and the light of the rising sun filling the stone courtyard, all lingering hope fled Sebastian's chest.

The courtyard was empty. Not a trace of Mariah or Andrian, or if a bonding had occurred there that night.

More footsteps rang out behind them, and Drystan and Feran hurried into the sunlight, followed closely by Matheo and Kalen. Sebastian turned to them all, chest heaving as he struggled to maintain his composure.

Struggled to fight back that rising tide of failure, mounting again around him. Inescapable, dauntless, and ruthless.

"Lock down the palace. Lock down the city. No one comes or goes through those gates without us knowing." Sebastian met Drystan's stare, knowing the golden-haired warrior would see it done.

A muscle twitched in Drystan's jaw and he nodded before striding away, Feran and Matheo falling into step behind him.

Sebastian turned back to the courtyard, a dull buzzing filling his ears. He scanned the space, eyes snagging on something familiar.

There, concealed in the shadows, was that old trapdoor. With a shuddering breath, he stalked forward, knees threatening to buckle with each step. Lighter footsteps followed as Ciana moved with him, her beautiful golden features twisted and stricken.

Sebastian knelt beside the trapdoor. His fingers brushed across the floor, feeling for the expected signs of disuse—dust, dirt, rust.

That wasn't what he found.

His fingers brushed against fresh cuts in the stone, the ground around it clean.

This door had been opened. Very recently.

The last bit of light in his chest he'd held onto so tightly slipped through his fingers, vanishing through that trapdoor and chasing after his missing queen. Betrayal took its place, sweeping up along with his failure.

After all, he's the one who'd told her to trust Andrian, all those many weeks ago.

Sebastian turned to Ciana, meeting her wide-eyed stare with a blank one of his own.

"She's gone," he whispered. "Andrian, too. He—someone took her. She's gone."

PART 1

CAGED

The beasts of old are caged beneath the ground,
catacombs of might and power.
They locked themselves away to bind the darkest evil,
and do not intend to taste freedom again.

—Exerpt from the Ginnelevé diary, dated 524 years after the reign of Xara. Author unknown.

CHAPTER 1

ix Weeks Later

BETRAYAL WAS A POISONOUS, curious thing.

Many believed it a devouring force, a sickening that drained the soul and ate away at all things good and happy.

But they were wrong. Betrayal did not devour; it nurtured. Fostered a sour growth, a sickly tumor to take hold and fester in the heart, guaranteeing no light would ever shine again.

The growth of betrayal in Mariah Salis's chest—right where her heart should be—shifted and pressed against her lungs. She rolled from her back to her side, the coils of the flimsy mattress digging into her shoulder as the metal frame creaked.

She had no pillow, but her arm sufficed, body curling around itself as she pulled up her legs and tucked into a ball, desperate to fight off the chill of the dark, disgusting cell.

It was so, so cold. An iciness that greeted the betrayal beneath her ribs like an old companion, a friend welcomed home after a long journey away.

She should be used to it by now, this ever-permeating cold. A trapped victim of her naivety for six weeks, if the routine of stale meals delivered once a day to her cell were any indicator. But deep underground, in the bowels of what had to be a castle, with no source of light—from either the sun or the moons—to help Mariah track the days, she was all but blind to the time slipping away.

The loss of light … With each wasted hour, it was another thing that fed the betrayal in Mariah's chest. Like a piece of her had been amputated, losing those once-familiar, brilliant threads of silver and gold that had twined and twisted in her soul had left her empty and hollow.

Lifting her hand, Mariah glared at the slender black and gold shackles clamped around her wrists. She'd scratched desperately at the stone for each of those long weeks she'd been trapped there, her wrists raw and chafing, the skin raised and red and unhealing with blisters that burned despite the frigid temperatures in the dungeon.

She wasn't quite sure how she hadn't fallen sick yet. Why her body held out against the cold and infection clearly taking root in her wrists.

While she spent most of her time fighting and raging … there were still times when she wished the chill would snake into her lungs, when infection would wrap around her heart and pull taut until it stopped.

Mariah settled heavily back into her anger and shifted again on her thin, disgusting mattress. Everything she'd come to cherish in the past few months was just … gone. In a flash of hands and stinging betrayal, power and bonds she'd learned to lean on were snuffed out, leaving behind an empty, shadowed hollowness where light once blazed. Her magic and power had whispered away before she could so much as think, before she could do so much as convey a single warning to those six minds who'd shared a bridge with her own.

A shiver raced up her rag-covered body, and she curled tighter around herself. If she was right, and six weeks had indeed passed, then the new year had long since come and gone. They were now creeping up on the first hints of spring. Flowers would soon start pushing through the frost-cracked ground into the still-frigid air.

Her faith in the gods had fled, but she still prayed the six brave, good men who'd once been bound to her were not still searching.

They would be, despite her prayer. Sebastian, especially, would not be one to let her disappearance go forgotten. A quiet, broken part of her still hoped that despite their desperation, they could recognize all she wanted was for them to ensure the advances she'd made on the Winter Solstice weren't in vain. That the surge of magic and brilliantly lit *lunestair* beside the throne would be enough to guard her city, her kingdom, from whatever threats might linger in the far reaches of the continent.

That slowly, more and more women across the kingdom would come to realize their power in this world that strove to keep them weak.

In the cold darkness, it was easier to focus on dreams of what could be rather than where she currently was—frozen and bleeding and starving in a dirty cell with nothing but a rock-solid mattress and a waste bucket to keep her company.

Mariah released a heavy sigh, breath frosting around her face. She uncurled herself enough to slide her palm to the mattress, pushing into the metal springs. The muscles in her arms tremored, straining under her meager weight, and she groaned with effort as she forced herself upright.

Her neglect in this place was palpable. The single, disgusting meal each day offered her no real sustenance, and in the darkness, her toned muscles had atrophied past the point of recognition. Her arms and legs were weak, her ribs now visible beneath pallid and sickly skin.

Mariah brushed a shaky hand across her collarbones, scratching her dirty skin and moving the tangles of her hair. Once long silky strands of the deepest brown brushing her lower back, her hair was now a matted and tattered mess around her head. Clumps had begun to fall from her scalp, after she'd tried to brush her fingers through the knots, so she'd stopped trying.

She might be heartbroken and damaged, but she refused to let herself go fucking *bald*.

Despite it all, Mariah could tolerate the neglect. It meant she was forgotten here, in this miserable darkness. And for that, she was grateful.

"Too cold for even the rats," Mariah mumbled to herself. It was something she'd found herself doing increasingly more often as the days passed. Her croaks echoed around the cramped space, her only companion in the dark.

She eyed the threadbare blanket knotted at the foot of her mattress, and with another low groan, reached out and wrapped it up around her shoulders.

One other thing her gracious hosts were kind enough to bestow upon her. A mattress, a single daily meal, a shit bucket ... and a too-thin blanket.

"But at least there's no rats," she whispered into the shadows.

Not long after the only man she'd ever been weak enough to love had snapped cold shackles around her wrists and thrown a burlap sack over her head, Mariah had come to terms with the reality that she would likely die here, in this small cell, surrounded by bitter cold and the smell of her excrement.

And she'd once dared to call herself *Queen*.

In the distance, a door slammed, followed by heavy, booted steps.

A sound she hadn't heard in weeks, not since she'd been hauled into her miserable prison, abandoned and forgotten and left to wither away.

The servants who brought her meals were always female, shuffling in and out on quiet feet like dutiful mice.

These steps ... they did not belong to a servant.

The steps grew louder, and the hallway beyond her iron-grated cell door filled with the silver-gold light of an *allume* lamp. Three tall shapes emerged, keys clinking as they neared.

Dread pulsed deep in her gut in time with the light, right alongside her hunger and betrayal. After weeks of solitude and isolation ... why was she receiving a visit *now*?

Whatever the reason, it couldn't be good.

She may be weak and starved and cut off from her magic, but she still had some fight in her. If these men were brave enough to see what they could scrape from a destitute, fallen queen, she was prepared to fight.

They'd likely win, but she'd make it clear that no matter how much they abused her body, they would never touch her soul.

Never again would she be so weak.

The moment the light shifted to touch the faces of the approaching men, all her resolve vanished like smoke on a breeze, carried into the clouds to dance with the gods who'd forgotten their chosen.

Two of the men were strangers, faces cut into harsh lines and dressed in the red and black livery of House Shawth. But the third … he was so achingly, painfully familiar. His onyx hair was longer than before and fell into characteristic loose, errant waves over his eyes, brow slightly arched as his lips tilted into that devastatingly beautiful smirk he wore so well.

His eyes, though—those brilliant, wild, magnificent tanzanite eyes—held an edge of madness to them, something unreadable dancing in their depths.

Andrian Laurent, the only man she'd ever loved, stepped to the bars of her cell, eyes gleaming brighter.

A guard slid a key into the lock, pushing the door open on squealing hinges.

Andrian's smirk morphed fully into a smile.

"My, my, princess. I must say, you've never looked better."

CHAPTER 2

Andrian's grip on her right arm was both foreign and familiar.

The calluses on his hand were the same. Even in just a few short months, the feel of his skin against hers had become ingrained into her psyche, her very soul. But now, there was something ... *different* about his touch. Something strange. Something possessive and wicked and frightening.

While Andrian had, at one point, been—or tried to be—all those things ... his touch never had. He may have hidden his feelings behind a wall of ice, but his hands always gave him away.

Until now.

Mariah was dragged down the hall, her weak legs barely able to take lurching steps. Her stumble earned her a sneer from the guard on her left and a firm shove to her shoulder by the one at her back.

That same awful, gleeful smile still stretched across Andrian's face. "What's the matter, princess? Having trouble keeping up? Don't tell us you haven't been enjoying our hospitality here in Khento these past few weeks."

The guards snickered.

Mariah only gritted her teeth, straightened her spine, and

forced back the growl of fury and defeat crawling its way slowly up her throat.

Andrian led them down a long tunnel, a thin layer of melting ice coating the uneven floor. The tunnel ended at a steep, narrow staircase, the stone slippery and dripping with moisture. Andrian released her arm, taking the first few steps up the stairs in a graceful leap, not deigning to see if she followed. The first guard followed him, and the other, the one who'd shoved her before, brusquely hit her again, pain blooming in her weakened shoulder.

"Climb," he ordered, humorless distaste dripping from his voice.

Mariah narrowed her eyes at the staircase but held her tongue as she took her first few steps.

The stairs weren't extraordinarily high; it wasn't more than thirty steps to the top. But the sudden, forced exertion quickly proved too much on Mariah's starved and atrophied body. Eighteen steps up, chest heaving, she faltered, bare feet slipping on slick stone, sending her careening forward. Her knee crashed against the stone, the sharp edge of a step slicing the bare skin of her forearm.

Her entire body barked in agony. She hissed, blood already welling to her skin.

The guard grabbed her again, his grip on her arm bruising, and dragged her to her feet and up the remaining steps. "Pathetic," he jeered in her ear. "Can't even handle a few fucking stairs."

At least he wasn't holding her where she now bled freely, ruby-red droplets dotting the ground. Small blessings, she supposed.

With a grunt, the guard threw her to the ground in the corridor at the top of the stairs. Mariah landed heavily on her injured knee and arm, letting out a yelp of pain, vision spotting. She closed her eyes and clenched her teeth, gasping for breath on the cold floor, scraping the very dredges of what little fight she had left.

She forced a deep inhale through her nose, exhaling through her mouth. The trembling in her body slowed, just enough for her to crack open her eyes, even as blood continued to drip down her forearm and streak her hands.

Two booted feet filled her vision, spotted with scarlet. They shifted, and a large, familiar hand gripped her chin, twisting her head to meet his crushing blue stare.

"Stand up, princess. You need to be on your feet when you greet our Royal hosts."

THE LIGHTS of the room were blinding, a fierce, burning reminder of the darkness Mariah had dwelled in for the past several weeks.

She blinked blearily against the brightness—it wasn't sunlight, but was instead the warm glow of *allume*, the magic harvested twice a year on the Solstices that powered light and technology throughout Onita. It's normally comforting, magical glow was now harsh and unforgiving, and her eyes adjusted slowly.

She was exhausted and weak and defeated, but that didn't stop the anger from sparking low and warm in her stomach, pushing into her fingers and toes, burning against the black and gold stone shackles on her wrists as she took in her surroundings.

It was a throne room. Or, perhaps, a mockery of one.

The aisles were clear, the black stone floor empty except for Mariah and her escorts. Gathered in raised galleries flanking either side of the open space were lords and ladies, the wealthy and privileged of Onita. Clothed in their richest velvets and rarest furs, they watched the girl who was supposed to be their future queen be paraded out of a dark tunnel wearing nothing more than dirty, shredded rags. Their leers and murmurs grated against Mariah's raw skin, pulling out what remained of her pride and raking it across the inky marble floor.

But she paid those lords and ladies and merchants no heed. Her focus turned to the man sitting in a chair upon a raised dais, his thinning blond hair dull in the light of the *allume*, face bearing a familiar sneer. Behind him stood a second figure, also blond but with scorching golden eyes set into a face devoid of any warmth.

Heads of two of the six Royal Houses of Onita: Lord Victor Shawth, the man whose grasp on power was threatened by Mariah's very existence, and Lord Julian Laurent, Andrian's father, who had once promised to end her reign—and her life—if Andrian ever bonded with her.

At least she didn't have to worry about that second part anymore. Silver linings.

Andrian peeled away from her side to stand beside the dais, a dark shadow wearing an ambivalent expression. The foul-tempered guard behind Mariah gave her one final shove, forcing her to her knees. Sharp pain speared through her as a bleeding knee met the black marble with a wet thud. Even as she bit her cheek to swallow her cry, Mariah did not pull her glare away from the lords on the dais.

She may not have her magic, but she still had her soul. And despite the brokenness she felt inside, she would not let these men bear witness to it.

Shawth lifted an eyebrow, lips twitching and watery blue eyes shining. With a cavalier wave of his hand, the crowd fell silent, filling the room with an eager expectancy. Shawth stood slowly from his seat, hands shoved in his pockets as he gazed down at Mariah, smile widening.

"Well, Miss Salis. What a difference a month or so can make. One moment, you're the most beautiful creature in the kingdom, and the next, you're … well … this."

Chuckles and laughs sounded from the galleries.

Mariah clenched her jaw, sparks of hatred and rage igniting in her gut. She stared up at Shawth, letting her wrath fill her eyes, baring her teeth in a vicious, animalistic grin.

"I may not be much to look at right now, Shawth, but I can promise you still have no fucking chance." Her voice cracked from disuse and dehydration, but she forced the words out regardless, thankful for a moment to throw back some of the hate festering in her chest.

Shawth only chuckled. "Chance? A chance at what? To fuck you?" More laughs from the galleries. "My dear, if I wanted to fuck you, I would have done so already."

A growl surged up her throat, bitter and hollow. Laurent rose from his seat and stepped to Shawth's side, and the rumble in Mariah's chest died when she caught the cruel glint in Laurent's eyes.

Her blood ran cold when he turned that cruel stare upon his son. Andrian had stood still, immobile, but his spine straightened with that look from his father, his own lips tilting up in a smirk.

Mariah's bravado faded quickly as her eyes lurched from Andrian, bounding between Shawth and Laurent. Her strength washed away like rushing water, her anger settling into tired resignation.

Shawth sighed before stepping down one level of the dais. "No, my dear. Contrary to what you might believe, I do not want to harm you. In fact, I have brought you here, before the people who truly rule this kingdom, to offer you a choice."

Mariah cocked her head, the matted length of her hair shifting across her back. "A choice?" She scoffed. "I can tell you right now, I'm not interested in any *choice* you offer."

Shawth grinned again. "Oh, but I think you might be interested in this one. I could give you everything you've always wanted. I could give you *freedom*."

Mariah's heart gave an unsteady lurch in her chest, sweat breaking out beneath her palms. He couldn't possibly know that about her; couldn't possibly know the one thing she'd always craved. Only a few people on the continent—in the entire world—knew what she'd most deeply desired, knew the true reason she'd attended the Choosing all those months ago.

Mariah wouldn't entertain the possibility that Shawth had learned that about her from anyone close to her. She glanced, one more time, at Andrian, pain striking her gut with every beat of her heart.

He wasn't looking at her, but the rot of betrayal wound its roots deeper into her blood.

Her instincts had led her so astray. She couldn't equate the man who'd once been unable to tear his attention from her to this stranger with a strangling, empty ambivalence.

With a heavy swallow, desperate for moisture in her parched, burning mouth, Mariah slowly turned her attention back to Shawth. "What, exactly, do you mean?"

Shawth hmphed, taking another step down the dais, pulling one hand from his pocket to scratch his scraggly beard. "It's quite simple. Give me what I want, and I will set you free."

"And what is it you want?" she asked, voice quiet and withdrawn. She held her wariness and alarm close to her pounding heart and fixed a mask of boredom on her face. Her blood still dripped down her forearm to the black marble beneath her, the sound like a pounding drum to the fraying fear clawing down her limbs.

Shawth's grin widened, taking the last few steps. He now stood so close that she had to tilt her head back to meet his stare. The smell of his too-strong cologne burned her throat and turned her stomach as she held his bitter sneer.

"Your *power*, Mariah. The power of the queen. Give me that, and I will set you free."

Everything inside Mariah stood still. Her insides boiled and froze in a constant, repetitive loop of anger and fear and thrashing distress. Her hands shook, and even her magic, though locked far from her reach, snarled at Shawth as it fought against its chains.

Mariah took another grimacing swallow and gritted her teeth. "I ... I can't do that."

"Of course you can! For whatever reason, the Goddess gave that power to you, and you can just as easily give it back." Shawth slowly knelt, lowering his face to hers. The barest hint of power-drunk madness swam behind his eyes, an insanity brought on after too many years of exerting ultimate control over more deserving people. "Abdicate your power and your magic, and I will set you free. I promise it."

Mariah's gagged magic clawed desperately against the walls of its prison, scrounging for purchase, a caged silver-gold beast thrashing against the lord's so-called offer. She leaned into it, desperate for even the barest of connections to the piece of her that had been silent and missing for too long, using the anger of her dampened magic and the fuel it fed her battered soul.

"Fuck. No." Her voice was laced with everything she couldn't do with her body, all the hate and anger and anguish and terror and heartbreak and betrayal she'd dwelled on those past six weeks.

These men could take everything from her: her home, her magic, her dignity. But they could never have her power. Could never take something so ingrained in her soul, it wasn't even hers to give. She didn't know if what Shawth asked was possible, and she had no inkling of desire to find out.

Even with her firm, confident resolve flushing her skin with her racing heartbeat ... she did not miss the flicker of excitement warming Shawth's gaze at her defiance. As if he was expecting, even *hoping*, for this response from her. There was no anger or fear, only a subtle glee that would've terrified her if she hadn't been so fucking *angry*.

Shawth exhaled a dramatic mockery of a sigh, leaning back on his heels and rising to his feet. He stared at her for a few more beats before turning on his heel and returning to his makeshift throne. "What a shame."

On the dais, Laurent's jaw was tight, eyes blazing. Flames, a gift of elemental magic he didn't deserve, danced on his fingertips and in his pupils. Shawth gave him the barest of nods that cooled a portion of Mariah's rage, icy fear beginning to prickle once again beneath her skin.

Laurent's face spread into a shallow grin, straightening the lapels of his jacket. He quelled his flames and walked down the steps, heading to an alcove beside the galleries. He bent down, retrieving an object, then strode back and halted beside his son.

"Andrian," Lord Laurent said, a cruel smile twisting his voice. "Why don't you show our guest a little ... *hospitality?* Something that might shift her spirits in our favor."

The guards behind Mariah gripped her shoulders and upper

arms, locking her behind them and pinning her knees to the marble floors, her battered skin screaming in protest.

She struggled weakly in their grasp, twisting just enough to see Laurent and Andrian, her fingertips digging into the skin of her thighs beneath her tattered leggings. Everything in her froze in abject, muted horror as she saw what Laurent pushed into his son's hands.

It was a whip. A coiled length of leather, its end tipped in something dark and glittering.

Mariah's limbs slackened, and she sagged against the guards. True dread, oily and vile, now crawled through her like sludge.

"Ellis, Konnor, if you would please make our guest comfortable," Shawth said, his tone conversational, as if merely discussing the weather.

Mariah heard a blade slide free from its sheath, then felt the bite of cool metal against the small of her back.

But it was not there to cut her. No, with an easy slice upward, the sharp edge only slashed through the fabric of her ragged sweater before snapping the elastic of her underclothes. In a matter of seconds, the two men pinned her between them, Shawth's greedy, watery eyes drinking in her exposed chest as her clothes dropped to the ground. Jeering and raucous calls filled the throne room.

"The whore queen!"

"On her knees, where she belongs!"

Shawth raised his hand, and the cheers fell silent.

"Seven lashes should be sufficient, Andrian. We only need to change her mind. Break her spirit, just a touch."

The command was far away from Mariah's ears. At the sight of the whip, at the shredding of her clothes, and the calls from the crowd, she began pulling back all of herself, retreating into the deepest and darkest parts of her soul. She wanted to find those threads of silver and gold, to cower with them away from what awaited her, but she still only felt that familiar place within her, walled in by vile black and gold stone.

Mariah simply laid her mind against that wall, curling into it, and waited for the pain to come.

She felt him at her back. She would always feel connected to him, as much as she might despise it. His presence wrapped around her, choking out her hope.

The whip uncoiling was like the sound of a million broken hearts whispering through the stars.

The first strike was the worst.

Her skin split and sundered, blazing agony ripping through her body and piercing straight to her soul, where she still hid against that wall of onyx and gold adamant. She bit her tongue so hard she tasted blood. But she did not cry out.

The second strike had her digging her fingers into the still-bleeding wound on her arm, her ears sharpening onto the sound of dripping blood on black marble floors.

The third and fourth strikes dropped her to all fours, tugging her out of the guards' grip, panting heavily, the sound of more raucous calls filling her ears, but even as she was hauled back up, she did not cry out.

The fifth and sixth were the easiest. Her back was now numb. She focused only on the pool of blood dripping under her right hand, on the way the ruby liquid vanished against the black stone.

But she did not cry out.

When the seventh and final blow came, it hit directly over a previous strike.

That was when a sound finally broke past her lips, when she could no longer swallow the pain. When the agony dragged her up, kicking and screaming, from where she'd hidden herself in the corners of her mind.

It was a barely audible whisper, a faint brush of air through clenched teeth, but she heard it.

She knew Andrian heard it, too. Her body trembled, and she panted, but a fresh wave of fear forced her to go rigid, muscles pulling against ruined flesh. Waiting for him to react, for her punishment to come.

But … it never did. He remained motionless behind her, dropping the whip to the floor with a sickening, wet thump.

"*Seven!*" the crowd cheered, ruthless laughs echoing around the room.

Shawth clapped his hands with merry excitement. Laurent was full of calculating cruelness, eyes narrowed first on Mariah before shifting over her shoulder, to his son.

Mariah met their glares with the very last dregs of her hate, holding herself together with a desperation wrought only from utter hopelessness.

"Andrian," Laurent said, icy voice strong above the din of the crowd. "Take our little friend back to her … room. Make sure she knows to think long about her decision today and how much easier things could be for her if she simply obliged our request."

Hands grabbed Mariah's arms—not the hands of the guards, but familiar hands, calloused hands, wickedly gentle hands—and pulled her to her feet.

Andrian dragged Mariah back through the throne room, pulling her towards one of the dark hallways. He tugged her down the steep staircase, her body involuntarily sagging against his as her consciousness dipped and wavered. His skin felt too hot against hers, too grating, too poisoned, but she was too weak to pull away. He was emotionless, a stranger who half-carried her through the dark, winding hallways.

The further they moved, the more her vision spotted. She bled excessively, her life draining from her starved and weakened body through the wounds on her back. Her heartbeat pounded in her ears, breathing heavy and labored.

Somewhere in her haze, she let herself be pushed against the cool stone wall. She latched onto its icy stability with all her strength, fighting against her mind to keep from sliding down to the ground. Andrian left her there, and she focused her entire being on pulling air into her lungs and strength into her shaking legs.

Something was thrust into her face, something that felt like coarse cloth.

"Put this on." Andrian's voice was flat, mechanical.

Somehow, somewhat dazedly, Mariah remembered her torso was still bare, the chill stone of the wall a salve against the burning of her skin.

With a tremor that wracked through her damaged body, Mariah heaved off the wall, grasping the linen tunic Andrian offered her in a shaking, bloody hand. Her vision again peppered, fighting against the rising tide of exhaustion and pain. She slowly pushed her hands into the tunic, snaking them out through the sleeves.

Andrian watched her with that empty look. She released a hiss as the tunic fell around her ruined flesh. It was thin, barely covering her, and it immediately clung to her back where her wounds had so far failed to clot. The foreign touch washed a renewed bout of nauseating agony across her skin.

She rocked for a moment, panting.

Before she was ready, Andrian resumed his grip on her arm and dragged her the rest of the way to her cold, dark, disgusting cell. He unlocked the door with a small skeleton key he pulled from his pocket before roughly pushing her back into captivity.

Mariah caught herself against her soiled mattress, hair falling around her face. Her cell door clicked closed behind her, the lock sliding into place with a quiet *snick*. Only then did she lift her head, using the last dredges of her strength to meet his stare.

She remembered a time, not long ago, when that stare had looked at her with so much love. Enough that would have stopped hearts and ended worlds.

Now it was empty. Void of all emotion. Absent of everything that had once made him so much more than the unworthy villain he'd long believed himself to be.

Her voice was soft, but despite her failing body, it was not weak. "This is not you."

Something finally flickered in those flat blue eyes. Something like shadow and ice and seething flame.

As fast as it flickered, it vanished.

That same unfamiliar, cruel grin spread across the face of the one she loved most.

"You don't recognize me, princess? Of course, it's me. This has always been me."

He turned on his heel and left her, bloody and weak and alone.

Mariah latched onto the glimmer of life she'd seen in his eyes, ignoring his words, as she finally fell unconscious.

CHAPTER 3

Andrian dragged his heavy, dulled training sword back to the rack. The blisters on his palms were painful and throbbing, his seven-year-old body weighted with bruises and soreness and exhaustion.

"May I go, Master Borus?" he asked, voice shaking with weariness.

The Antoris master-at-arms didn't answer immediately, instead taking the training blade from Andrian's hands, setting it back against the rack.

Andrian looked up at the elderly man, wrinkled face hidden behind a scraggly white beard. Something in his expression confused Andrian. It was a bit like sympathy, something Andrian had seen in so many of the castle staff's faces, but just a little harsher.

Master Borus opened his mouth like he was about to speak but then glanced over Andrian's shoulder and closed his mouth with a firm snap. Andrian turned, following the master-at-arms's stare.

He just barely caught the disappearing shape of his father, the Lord of Antoris, stalking back towards the main gates of the keep. Even through his exhaustion, the sting of disappointment and rejection hit him like a dulled blade.

He'd tried; he really had. He'd only been on the training pitch for a *year, and the swords still didn't fit in his hands. But Father had told him to be perfect. It hurt Andrian that he wasn't.*

Shoulder's slumping, he turned back to the master-at-arms. "Master Borus?"

The older man dropped his gaze back to Andrian, lips turned down and dark eyes tired. "Yes, my boy. My apologies. Of course, you are dismissed. I will see you again tomorrow."

Andrian dipped his head before trudging toward the main keep of Antoris, the same way his father had gone.

Inside, it was warm; the permeating northern cold chased away by a roaring hearth in the great hall. Andrian's father was nowhere to be seen, but Andrian didn't mind. He marched, as best he could with his aching muscles, straight to the blazing fire. He stuck his numb hands out to the flames, not even feeling the blood and blisters coating his palms.

After all, these weren't his first blisters. Those had come last year when he'd turned six.

A flurry of movement rustled behind him, just before gentle hands gripped his shoulders and whirled him away from the flames. Andrian blinked heavily, exhaustion weighing his eyelids as he met his mother's shimmering amethyst eyes.

"Oh, my sweet Andrian. Look at your hands." She tsked, kneeling in front of him. Her movement was slow, awkward, her balance upset by her massive belly.

She'd let him touch her swollen stomach once when the baby inside her was moving and kicking. Andrian hadn't quite understood what it all meant—how was a baby in her stomach? Had she eaten it? And why was it growing?—but he'd kept his questions to himself, content to share his mother's excitement and the joy that lit up her lovely, cherished face.

It was so rare that Andrian saw her happy and smiling. Most of the time, she was so quiet, so empty-looking.

But she came alive in these moments when she was alone with him, her entire demeanor shifting into something vibrant and joyous.

She clucked her tongue, inspecting his palms. "These won't do. Come with me, and I'll fix you right up." She heaved back to her feet, dropping Andrian's hands before ushering him away from the fire, murmuring lilting words after him.

Andrian loved the way she talked. It was so different from his father or from anyone else in the keep. He'd heard someone call it an accent, a way of speaking she'd kept from her homeland of Leuxrith. It was cadenced and soothing as if she were singing every word she uttered.

She pushed him down the halls, and even though he was so, so tired, he managed to take each step towards his rooms. They arrived at his bathing chamber, a cozy room with a fire already burning in one corner and a great claw-foot tub fed by allume-heated water. His mother turned on the faucet, the basin beginning to fill, giving him another glowing smile before leaving him to his bath.

Once he was bathed and changed, his mother led him into his sleeping chamber, sitting him in front of yet another fire. She laid out various healing tools and materials, pulling them from a basket woven through with black and gold threads. A healer stepped into the room at one point, offering to take over for the lady of the keep, but his mother shooed her away.

"Thank you for the offer, but I will be the one to care for my son, as I always have." She turned her amethyst eyes to Andrian. "As I always will."

Andrian couldn't stop the warmth that spread through his chest. He loved the idea of staying here, in this room, with her, forever.

As she set to work on his hands, he made a simple request, one of his favorites.

"Can you tell me a story?"

Something unreadable flickered in his mother's purple eyes.

"I will tell you something better than a story, my love. I will tell you an old folktale from my people." Her hands stilled. "Do you know what a folktale is, Andrian?"

He shook his head. He knew what a tale was, but a folktale? That was not something he'd read in his history books.

His mother smiled before resuming her work. "They are stories, passed down from generation to generation, but never written. It is said they tell us certain truths, things that explain the unexplainable, and they are made better by each new generation who tell them. They are meant to bring us closer—both to the world we share and to each other."

Andrian thought about her words, watching her delicate fingers deftly clean and bind the wounds on his palms before nodding. "Yes. I understand. Can you tell me a folktale, then?"

His mother flashed him a brilliant smile. "Of course, my love. There are many that my people still share, but this one ... this one is about the dragons."

Andrian's eyes widened. Of all the things he'd read about in his books, it was the dragons that intrigued him the most.

"My people—your people—still whisper that the dragons are not gone, as many in Onita believe," his mother continued. "They say the dragons simply exist now in a form we cannot see but are still very much alive.

"It is promised that one day, the dragons will return. On the day we need them most, they will crack forth from the earth and the sky and join us again to defeat all evil and set the world back upon the path of light."

Andrian listened in rapt fascination as his mother continued with her story of dragons and magic and darkness and victory, the pain and exhaustion in his body and hands forgotten.

A QUIET, deadly voice snaked out of the void of darkness, a prison crafted by invisible black and gold shackles.

"Your mother was a very smart woman," the voice whispered. *"She knew more than most and was so committed to seeing a world freed from darkness."*

Andrian sank deeper into the abyss, lost to time and memories and pain and sadness.

"It is such a shame she is dead."

CHAPTER 4

The sweat-drenched chills wracking Mariah's frame were the first sign that something was very, very wrong.

She could hardly keep her eyes open as she lay helplessly on her stiff mattress, unsure if it was her sweat or her blood that clung the threadbare blanket to her skin. The wounds from the flogging were deep; her memories, her nightmares, were consumed by the feeling of sharp stone flaying her skin, scourging deep rivets in her flesh as pain scorched and burned.

Without a healer's touch, and in this disgusting cell, she'd quickly fall prey to infection. The fester of her wounds would spread rapidly in her malnourished body, her weakened state unable to stave off the onslaught.

The rot seeped into her blood, and as death brushed against her back, she didn't even have the strength to feel afraid. Nausea rolled through her gut, a ship lost at sea, before her eyelids fluttered shut, and she slipped back into unconsciousness.

Was this part of the lords' plan? They wanted her power; she knew that now. And while they had obviously tried to break it out of her, perhaps they'd now resorted to letting her die.

Ryenne's lessons flashed through her fever-hazed mind. A queen had never died outside of an ascension ceremony. If Mariah died now, would her magic find a new host? Or would the cycle end, the queen's magic returning to Qhohena's waiting hands?

Perhaps the lords had decided they wanted that power vacuum. No more queens meant an empty throne, ripe for their taking.

Mariah didn't know if days or hours or minutes passed before she opened her eyes again, only to be blinded by a raging, burning silver light.

It hurt her eyes, just for a single fleeting second, before it receded to reveal a familiar female shape, dark skin and silver hair outlined by incandescence.

Mariah tried to speak, to greet the Goddess of Death. She wanted something, *anything,* to stop the rotting pain wracking her body. Her mouth opened, lips parched and cracking, and she tried to push words from her throat.

She failed.

Zadione floated closer, a somber look on her unnervingly beautiful and ageless face. "Do not try to speak, Mariah. I can hear you, regardless of your words." Her silver eyes roamed over Mariah's emaciated body, her ravaged back. When she returned her attention to Mariah's face, her expression was wrought with dark fury and depthless sadness. They were not the emotions of a mortal life but an immortal goddess who'd seen too many try to achieve all their desires and fail catastrophically every time.

"I tried to warn you. Love ... it is always a weakness. But I suppose it is impossible to change what was always meant to pass." Zadione's words were not scolding but tragically empathetic, the emotion washing from her to Mariah enough to cut through even the thick haze of sickness.

Was this one of the gifts of the Goddess of Death? That in these final moments, it was only her voice and her presence that could be felt clearly?

If this was the way Mariah was to go, with this goddess to keep her company, then perhaps it wouldn't be so bad. Her friends were strong; they would face the lords without her. Mariah, though ... she was so, so tired. She just wanted to rest.

But Zadione took a floating step closer. Reached out a hand. Rested her luminescent palm on Mariah's skin. Even through the warped shadow of her fever, the goddess's touch was like being kissed by the brightest moonlight on a winter night, gentle and caressing but also harsh in its revealing light.

"It is not your time, Mariah. We are bound, you and I, in ways you cannot yet fathom. Your work on this earth is not yet finished."

Mariah's eyes snapped back open, meeting the goddess's mercurial gaze.

"Am I ... Am I dreaming?" Mariah's voice was jilted and rough, her throat sore from disuse and sickness, but they were pulled from her by the deity's touch and the otherworldly glow washing through the room.

Zadione smiled another agelessly sad smile. "No. No, unfortunately, this is all very much real. For both of us." Her hand left Mariah's cheek to rest against the side of her head as she shifted closer, sitting beside Mariah on the thin, stained mattress. Sadness still clung to the goddess's face, so out of place on her star-bright features, so at odds with the macabre animal bones woven into her unbound silver hair. "So young and already enduring so much. Here, allow me to inspect your wounds."

Mariah obeyed, rolling onto her stomach, breath hissing between her teeth. Zadione peeled up the soiled tunic, sticky and cracked with Mariah's blood, bunching it at the base of Mariah's neck. Mariah closed her eyes as the goddess's hands roved across her skin, clenching her teeth against the anticipated pain.

But ... that pain never came. She still felt Zadione's gentle touches, but where her fingers met Mariah's skin, there was only a steady, soothing tingling, a numbness that alighted across her skin and loosened the vice around her chest.

"I had love. Once, a long, long time ago."

Mariah's breathing stilled, her entire body freezing at the goddess's words.

"He was ... everything to me. We burned brighter and hotter together than should be permitted." Mariah could almost hear the smile in Zadione's voice. "But sometimes, the things that burn the brightest are what hurt us the most."

Beneath the blessed numbness, Mariah felt a twinge in her back, the odd feeling of skin knitting together. More warmth bloomed along her spine, from the base of her hips to her shoulder blades.

"I have always valued my freedom. The wilds of the world were my home. But he ... he did not understand that. He desired to have me to himself, to keep me locked away by his side. That desire drove him to madness. He decided his brightness made him remarkable, even amongst the gods, and would rather plunge the world into darkness than treat us as equals. We—and humanity—could either bow to him ... or die." While Zadione spoke with the steadiness of one telling a story long since passed, there was a sort of quiet resignation to her voice, a sadness that stretched farther than the gaps between the stars.

"It was *Flétrir*, wasn't it? The Scourge?" Mariah's question tumbled from her mouth. Myths and stories were blending with truths in her mind, and as the pain eased, her thoughts raced.

Zadione halted. Her palms were still warm, and Mariah could feel the goddess's power sweeping across her skin. Somewhere, locked away deep in her soul, she felt silver threads of light struggle against the walls of a gold and onyx prison, desperate to greet their mistress.

And even though she couldn't see Zadione's face, she knew the goddess was staring at Mariah's wrists. At the stone cuffs shackling that power away.

"He went by a different name then. But, yes, when I refused to submit to him, that is who he became. When the *world* refused to submit to him."

The goddess resumed her work, Mariah pondering her final words. If *Flétrir* had once been known by a different name ... were there any besides the gods who remembered it? Her mind flitted for a moment to her mother's journal, the diary of the *Ginnelevé* family that had been passed down from mother to daughter for thousands of years and enchanted with a small trace of Zadione's magic to preserve it against the annals of time. Had one of her ancestors known the truth? What other secrets did that little gray book contain, secrets lost to lazy, forgotten history?

The mattress shifted as the goddess stood.

"You have further injuries. Sit," Zadione commanded, silver robes rustling around her feet.

Mariah gave a small nod, pushing herself up, a sudden wave of breathless energy surging across her skin. Her tunic fell back around her torso as she rolled her shoulders, the fresh, healed skin of her back tight. She glanced at her right forearm, the deep slice there clotting but warm with infection.

Zadione knelt, wrapping her hands around Mariah's arm, and that soothing warmth enveloped her once again, illuminating where their skin touched. Mariah watched, eyes wide.

She could hardly comprehend how Zadione felt so ... *real*. Not like an other-worldly being, but someone *alive*.

Before she could ask, Zadione withdrew her hands. Mariah twisted her arm, inspecting where the wound was.

All that was left was a pale, thin scar, the surrounding skin puckered and jagged but healed.

Zadione stood. "I have done what I can. You had an injury to your knee, as well, but it mended itself when I cleared your body of the infection. Your wounds were deep, but you are no longer in danger from them." The goddess hesitated, her eyes flaring a touch brighter. "I fear there is nothing I can do about the scars. Those you will bear forever."

Mariah shifted again, adjusting herself to her new skin. "How?"

Zadione smiled. "Why do you think your mother and the women of your line have always been so talented at healing? That magic was *my* gift."

It made such perfect sense. Of course, the Goddess of Death would also be one of healing, of injury and sickness, of the deathbed that ushered lives from this plane into the next.

Mariah swallowed. "Thank you."

The goddess's silver eyes hardened and flashed. She'd been so solid a moment before but was fading into the shadows of the cell, her light dimming with each pound of Mariah's heart.

"Your love used to be a weakness, Mariah. But now that you have fallen, you must find a way to make it your retribution." The goddess's parting words were soft, barely audible, but they brushed across Mariah's skin like the final rattle of life in a dying creature's lungs.

Zadione winked out of the cell in a burst of starlight, and Mariah was left alone in the darkness, confused and wondering.

CHAPTER 5

*A*t eight years old, Andrian learned how to be a man.

At least, that's what his father told him. In addition to the daily training with Master Borus, Andrian was expected to follow Lord Laurent throughout the day, joining him in every meeting and learning from each encounter.

"Do you know what it means to be heir to House Laurent, Andrian?" His father's words were kind enough, but Andrian knew them to be a test.

They were always a test. And when Andrian failed them—as he often did—he was lucky if the worst punishment he received was a stinging lash of fire magic across his knuckles. Not enough to leave burns, but enough to draw tears.

Sometimes, he wasn't as lucky.

"It means that one day, I'll be you … right?" The hesitancy forced its way into his voice, fear making him desperate for reassurance from a man who'd never give it.

His father narrowed his gleaming, golden eyes. "You will always be you. You will never be me. But it does mean that you are my firstborn son. And one day, you will sit in my seat in the great hall, and you will do the job that I now do. Do you understand?"

Andrian was confused—why would he do his father's job if Father could just do it better?—but he knew better than to say anything other than, "yes, Father."

Lord Laurent regarded his son with a look so cold it should be impossible for one with fires in his blood. He opened his mouth, ready to say something, when a bustle of movement at the door to his study drew away his frigid attention. A rare, exuberant smile spread across his face.

"Ah! There's my boy!"

Andrian twisted in his chair to see Nadya, the nursemaid, standing in the entry of his father's office, a giggling, blond-haired baby boy bouncing on her full hips. Behind them walked Andrian's mother, dark hair coiled primly around her neck.

"Mama!" Andrian leaped from his seat and rushed into his mother's embrace. He heard his father's disapproving grunt, but he didn't care. His mother was here.

She stroked his hair, pushing it out of his eyes. "You need a haircut, Andrian."

He perked up. "Will you give me one?"

She smiled. "Yes. Of course." She glanced behind him. Andrian released his hold on her, turning around and standing at her side. His father had taken Andrian's baby brother, Gabriel, from Nadya, and the three stood beside Lord Laurent's massive desk, smiling and laughing.

"My Lord," his mother said meekly. "If I may have a moment of your attention."

His father hardly spared her a glance, still bouncing Gabriel on his hip. "What is it?"

Something in his dismissive tone sparked a feeling deep in Andrian's chest. He had a sudden urge to stand up for his mother, to defend her from his father's coldness. He straightened his spine, opening his mouth to speak, before his mother's hand on his shoulder washed the fight from him.

She was stopping him because they both knew that challenging Father never went well. He would receive something far worse than little singeing lashes to his fingers. Something that would upset Mother much more than just the way Father spoke to her.

"I would like to give our son a haircut." His mother kept his hand on his shoulder as she spoke.

His father hmphed. "Yes, alright. I will have Nadya return Gabriel to you shortly."

Andrian's mother dipped her head. "Thank you, My Lord." She grabbed Andrian's hand and led him out of the office.

They walked through drafty hallways toward the wing housing his mother's rooms. Andrian was nearly giddy, doing everything he could to not skip along beside her, trying desperately to stay dignified and ... lord-like.

That's what his father would want. And, somehow, Lord Laurent was always watching.

It didn't take them long to reach his mother's wing, her spaces not far from those of his father. She slipped them through the door into her receiving room, depositing Andrian on a cushioned stool in front of an old vanity mirror before quickly starting a fire in the grate against the wall.

Every room in Antoris always needed a blaze roaring in the hearth.

Once the flames caught, Andrian's mother rummaged through a drawer in her vanity, withdrawing a pair of small, sharp shears, the kind perfect for trimming hair.

"Sit back and sit straight. And don't move, or else you might lose an ear."

The words were slightly morbid, but Andrian saw his mother's smile and smiled too. He did as he was asked, straightening his back on the stool, planting his feet on the ground.

His mother brushed through his black hair, the same shade as her own, with a fine-toothed comb she'd also pulled from the drawer. She sighed, a quiet sound, before making the first delicate snips.

"Teach me new words," he blurted, staring at her in the mirror. She looked so sad, and ... he wanted her to be happy. "I love it when you teach me your words."

Her hands stilled, shears held suspended above his head. "You know your father does not approve of me teaching you my language."

Andrian frowned. "Why?" It was something he'd never understood. His father was always talking about understanding his Onitan *heritage. Why was it so bad to learn about the other half? To learn about where his mother came from, about her history and traditions?*

His mother sighed again. "It is ... complicated. But I suppose a few more words couldn't hurt." She met his gaze in the mirror, something mischievous shining in her amethyst eyes. "It can become our special language, just for you and me."

Andrian smiled wider, nodding. He liked the sound of that.

His mother returned to his haircut. "What word would you like to know first?"

Andrian pondered for a moment. "How about ... 'magnificent.'"

She laughed softly. "'Magnificent?' Where did you even learn to say that in Onitan?"

"I read it in a book to describe one of the past queens." Andrian shrugged. "I liked it. I want to add it to our special language."

His mother continued to snip and snip away at his hair, a small smile on her lips. "Reisligr."

"Reisligr." Andrian tested the word on his tongue, the strange vowels and syllables rolling easier than he'd expected. "I love it. Better than magnificent."

"I told you; do not teach the boy that filth." Lord Laurent's disgusted voice filled the room. "He should only know the language of his people."

Andrian jolted on his stool; he'd been so consumed by the feeling of his mother's hands in his hair and the new word on his tongue that he hadn't heard the receiving room door open, his father's presence filling the space. His mother stiffened, her fingers leaving Andrian's head, and Andrian twisted to meet his father's glare.

"Please, Father. Don't get mad at Mother. I asked her to teach me. It was my fault."

Julian narrowed his eyes at his son, flames dancing in their cold depths. "You are far too much like her; I hardly see any of myself in you. It is time to grow out of this dependence and become a man." The Lord of Antoris whirled on his heel, storming from the room, the door closing behind him with a shuddering slam. Distantly, Andrian could hear a baby fussing, Nadya's cooing words of adoration as she soothed Gabriel.

"Turn back around, Andrian. I am not yet done with your haircut."

Slowly, Andrian twisted back. He refused to meet his mother's stare in the mirror, instead focusing on the blaze in the fireplace. His mother resumed, pieces of his thick, dark waves falling into his lap.

"I will teach you one more word," she said quietly. His eyes snapped to the mirror, to see her watching him. "It is a very special word. But I can only share it if you promise not to mention it to your father."

Andrian sat up straighter. "Of course, Mother. Our secret language, remember?"

She smiled. "Yes. Our secret language." She trimmed a few more pieces around his face. His hair was much shorter, now neat and tidy, where it was once errant and messy.

"What is the word?" Andrian couldn't mask his impatience.

His mother snipped one last lock of hair, running a comb through it with her fingers, before walking around his stool. She knelt in front of him, lifting a hand to his face, and cupped his cheek. Her amethyst eyes shone with a sadness Andrian didn't understand.

"'Nio.'"

---

*"H*OW SENTIMENTAL OF YOU.*" A voice rang through Andrian's subconsciousness. "Funny how you once thought you could use that word as an insult ... but even you knew that never would have worked. So interesting to see how much the little queen means to you.*

"How much she has always meant to you."

CHAPTER 6

The stone battlement rattled, splintered shards of ice raining from above. Sebastian cursed under his breath, diving for cover under the parapet overhang.

Drystan slammed into the wall beside him, blond hair that had escaped from the low knot at the base of his neck plastered to his face. "Feran!"

The third warrior stood at the edge of the battlement, a longbow in his hands, arrow drawn. Feran's arms were steady despite the tremors echoing through the tower. He loosed the arrow, even as sharp pieces of ice fell over his skin.

A distant cry, heard over even the cacophony of battle, told Sebastian the arrow found its mark.

"Feran!" Sebastian called, echoing Drystan.

Feran whirled, dark braids swinging with him.

Sebastian pushed off the wall, muscles barking. "We have to get the trebuchets reloaded. You take the east towers." Sebastian turned. "Drystan, take the west."

Both men didn't even spare Sebastian a nod before sprinting down the battlements. Sebastian watched them leave before turning back to the edge of the wall, stepping up to the stone rail.

The fleet from the Kizar Islands squatting in the Bay of Nria filled him with as much dread as it had when it first appeared, six weeks ago.

They arrived the day after Mariah's disappearance, black sails filling the horizon as the sun crested in the sky. Frantic with his missing queen, his oldest friend's betrayal, and his failure, Sebastian had ignored the approaching problem, trusting in the wards to hold as they formed parties to search for Mariah.

And at first, the wards had protected them. The fleet had halted just beyond the Bay, a contingent of City Guards and Royal Infantry watching them from the same battlements on which Sebastian now stood. Sebastian had led the Armature and other select officers from both the Guard and the Infantry as they scoured the city and surrounding area for any sign of where Mariah might have been taken.

They were just about to venture further from Verith, to start expeditions to the other keeps and strongholds of Onita, when the lights began to flicker.

In all his thirty-one years of life, Sebastian had never seen the lights flicker. *Allume* was always present, always powerful, never weakened. Even when the *lunestair* pillars beside the throne were dull, still the *allume* was there, spreading heat and warmth and energy across the kingdom.

And those pillars still blazed bright with magic, but ... the lights had flickered.

The same day the lights sputtered, the wards began to fail.

Sebastian stared down at the nearest ship. "Shit."

A group of men—pirates—had gathered on the prow, hands weaving and working as one. A great ball of water rose from the Bay, spinning and swirling until it hung over the ship. The men slowed their hands, holding the globe suspended, and slowly, it hardened into ice.

Apparently, the pirates of the Kizar Islands didn't just have a vast armada at their disposal.

They possessed water magic.

Sebastian hadn't believed the reports that arrived the day the wards slipped. Still wrought in his desperation, his failure, he'd dismissed them as a distraction to pull them away from their task.

Until Quentin and Matheo had visited the contingent on the battlements along the Bay. They dragged Sebastian with them that next day.

Sebastian still didn't quite believe it—and he certainly didn't understand it. But this was his reality now. A failure of an Armature, forced to abandon his search for his missing queen to protect her city. Facing an enemy that wielded water like a fifth limb as the wards weakened and the lights guttered.

The ball of ice on the ship below was nearly solid now. The pirates set it gently on the deck of the ship, rolling it to the giant siege machines mounted there. Like Verith's own trebuchets, but smaller and more nimble, perfect for attacks by sea.

Sebastian whirled, glancing at the cliff above him. A boulder was loaded into the west trebuchet, Drystan barking orders at the Guardsmen as they heaved the leavers. Their trebuchets were powerful but ancient. Decrepit, outdated contraptions that took precious minutes to reload, requiring a full squad of men to load and fire.

"*Incoming!*" The Guardsman's roar over the chaos of battle pulled Sebastian back to the Bay below.

Just in time to see the giant sphere of ice launched from the nearest ship careening toward Sebastian.

He was rooted to the ground as it spun through the air. He'd seen this happen enough that he knew what came next.

It twisted and turned, the world slowing as Sebastian watched the deadly, stone-solid ice fly. Two hundred feet from the battlements, though, the sphere met something invisible. The ice shuddered midair, its opacity dripping off it with the droplets of water it shed. In a matter of seconds, it turned transparent, now a perfect, shimmering ball of glass rather than a deadly globe of ice.

Sebastian didn't flinch as the glass struck the stone, shattering on impact with a boom. But that was the most damage it inflicted.

The wards were malfunctioning, but … they still worked, in a way. If they ever fell completely, those spheres of ice would blast the battlement towers from the coast. As it were, the wards worked just enough to weaken the ice into a nuisance.

Their dance had become one of traded blows. The Kizar pirates seemed content to remain there, sending their spheres of ice into the battlements, as long as Verith fought back. Never sailing closer, but never going home, either.

A week after the attacks had begun, Sebastian had decided to ignore this ridiculous game. He'd ordered Mariah's Armature and the chief officers to let the pirates launch their harmless attack; they would return to their search for Mariah and Andrian.

Sebastian hadn't realized that the pirates weren't sailing any further by *choice*. That the wards only kept out magical attacks, not physical crossings.

The blood of the people who'd been on the docks that day now stained his hands, adding to the long tally of his failures.

He'd failed those innocent people by not protecting this city.

He'd failed Mariah by urging her to trust an untrustworthy man.

He'd failed his queen by not saving her from a fate that haunted his nightmares.

Sebastian's rage—at Andrian, at these fucking pirates' obnoxious games, at his failure—swept over him as he turned, meeting Drystan's stare. Crystalline shards still rained around them, shattered globes reminding them why they stood here and fought. His lip curled back from his teeth as he raised his hand.

"*Fire!*" he roared, voice ringing off the cliffs. Twisting, he echoed the command to Feran.

In perfect tandem, the two trebuchets launched massive stone boulders into the Bay.

Sebastian's eyes tracked the stone from Feran's trebuchet. It arched through the sky before plummeting down, down, down.

Right into the deck of the nearest ship, wood splintering into the water with a shattering boom. The mast cracked in half, men diving into the blue-green waters and swimming for their sister vessels. Cheers from the battlements filled the late afternoon skies.

But Sebastian knew how this game was played.

In the center of the fleet sat a ship larger than the others. Sebastian trained his attention on that ship, waiting.

Sure enough, there was movement on the deck. Then, a massive white flag was attached to a central mast, hoisted up into the sky. The dance was done for the day.

That was all it took. Sink a ship, and the pirates would retreat to lick their wounds. Sometimes, it took days for the ancient trebuchets to land a shot. The longest it had taken was a week, the fighting raging day and night. The Armature took battlement duty in shifts, sinking into exhausted slumber and shoveling food down before it was their turn to return to the lines, to keep the morale of the Guards and Infantry high.

They got lucky this time. This battle had only started at sunrise. Sebastian had been here since it started.

It was a short one, but he knew it wouldn't last. The pirates would be back.

"Sebastian!" Drystan's voice rang out over the battlements, cutting through the cheers.

Sebastian turned, seeing Drystan and Feran standing on the battlement above him, exhaustion written plainly on their faces.

Feran slung his longbow across his back, rolling his shoulders. "It's over for the day. Let's go home."

Sebastian spared one final look out at the black-sailed ships retreating from the Bay of Nria. With a sigh, he nodded, hanging his head.

"Let's go home."

THE *ALLUME* SCONCES on the walls flickered. Darkness guttered around them, peppering the marble floor with shadows.

Sebastian's bones were leaden as he trudged down the hall, flanked by Drystan and Feran. None of them so much as flinched at the wavering lights; after five weeks, they'd become all but accustomed to it.

Accustomed, but not accepting. Sebastian would never accept this as their eternal fate.

They had to get Mariah back.

Sebastian knew this game for what it was; the timing was too coincidental. The pirates arrived, toying with them on the coast, a mere week before the wards began to fail. And there was no reason for the wards to fail; nothing had changed. The pillars burned bright, the magic was not running low, and Ryenne had no answers.

The only thing different about Verith was Mariah's absence. The connection was obvious.

Whoever had orchestrated her abduction was connected to the pirates and their arrival. And it was all an effort to keep Mariah's Armature distracted, to keep them from searching for their queen.

They rounded a corner, stalking toward a spiraling staircase. They ascended the floors, heading higher to the top floors of the palace. A heavy, tired silence hung around them as they walked down a long hallway lined with black oak doors, not stopping until they stood before the one set of doors that differed.

Sebastian paused outside the white painted wood, golden paneling mocking in its brilliance.

The others preferred to meet here because it gave them hope. To be reminded of her—of her scent, her possessions, her glowing aura—kept them going each time the pirates launched a new attack, each day they had to forgo their search to protect this city.

To him, though, it was his punishment to meet here. A reminder of his failure, of all the ways he'd trusted the wrong man, of the ultimate betrayal that had happened under his watch.

As Sebastian placed his hand on the heavy gold handle and

pushed open the now-repaired door he'd splintered on that fateful night six weeks ago, he made a vow.

If—*when*—they found Mariah, and if Andrian was with her … he would *never* forgive him.

"You're back!" A bright voice, like tinkling wind-chimes, greeted Sebastian as he stepped into the foyer of Mariah's suite, Drystan and Feran following through behind him. There was a flash of golden curls, and then Ciana was there, tossing her hands around his neck. He grunted but couldn't stop the small smile that crept across his lips as he was wrapped in her honeysuckle and lilac scent.

"Hi, Cee," he murmured, her curls tickling his cheek.

She peeled off him, settling on the balls of her feet as she looked him over, nose crinkling. "You smell awful."

"Yes, well." Sebastian ran a hand through his hair. "Dealing with those pirates since dawn isn't exactly a day at the spa."

Quentin stood from the couch, flipping a knife over his fingers. "Are they, then? Dealt with? For the day, at least."

"For today, they are." Drystan brushed past Sebastian, walking to the island in the center of Mariah's kitchen. There was a full bounty of food and drink spread there, likely prepared by Mikael and a few other chefs earlier in the day. Sebastian's stomach grumbled as Drystan picked up a loaf of bread and a pitcher of water before turning back to them.

"Feran made the hit this time," he said quietly, lifting his pitcher as he shot the other man a casual grin.

Feran merely shrugged. "It was a lucky shot." But he, too, was smiling as he filled a plate, downing half a pitcher of water in a single gulp.

Sebastian glanced down at Ciana, still standing in front of him, wearing a vaguely amused expression on her face. Gently, he grabbed her hands from where they still gripped his arms, placing them back by her sides. The contact jolted her, and she flushed as she stepped away.

"Sorry," she murmured.

Sebastian gave her a soft smile. "It's fine. Just hungry." She nodded, and he strode to the island, his hunger taking the reins from his exhaustion.

A few minutes—and several pitchers of water—later, they all sat strewn about Mariah's couches, silent and staring.

This was how they so often were now. Trapped in a game, waiting for something to change and free them. Empty and hopeless.

The lights flickered again as if to emphasize the point.

Quentin blew out a heavy breath and shoved back further into the couch. "I'm getting so fucking tired of those lights."

Matheo nodded. "I think I could tolerate the lights, if only the wards worked."

"The wards don't even matter. Those pirates would sail to the docks, regardless," Trefor quipped, pale blond hair messy. He sipped from his mug of ale.

"They could do that right now." Sebastian's voice cut through the conversation, low and hollow. "They could sail right past us every single day, but as long as we are on those battlements, they don't."

Drystan growled, a frustrated, angry sound. "It just doesn't make *sense*. If they're here to sack the city, then just sack the fucking city."

"They're not here to sack the city, Drystan, and you know that." Feran's response was quiet and measured. "They're here to keep us distracted."

Sebastian nodded, as did the rest of them.

This was how this conversation always went; they'd made this realization weeks ago, after all those lives on the docks were lost. This wasn't about the city; it was about *them*. Mariah's Armature, and the other members of the City Guard and Royal Infantry who were loyal to her.

"We need Mariah back."

Sebastian's head snapped to the figure sitting at the far end of the couch. Beautiful, delicate, clothed in a baby blue gown, but with ice blue eyes glowing with inner fire. Delaynie locked her gaze on Sebastian. "The magic is failing because Mariah is gone. I know it, you know it, Ryenne knows it … we *all* know it. We need to get her back."

Sebastian held her fierce stare. "Trust me, Delaynie. I know how bad we need her back. But …" He swallowed, shame and failure clogging his words in his throat. "But we can't sacrifice innocent lives for that. Mariah wouldn't want that."

Delaynie's eyes narrowed at him before she pursed her lips and stared out the wall of windows lining the living space.

Ciana cleared her throat. "Maybe … maybe I could help. Both Delaynie and me. We have our obligations here, but with the pirates, those meetings are few and far between. Maybe, when we can, we can organize searches, start focusing on finding Mariah—"

"*No*." Sebastian's interruption was harsher than he intended. But the fear that swallowed him as Ciana spoke, the desperation that clenched around his chest, was unbearable.

He hadn't been able to keep Mariah safe. He would rather damn his soul to Enfara than risk Ciana, too.

Ciana blinked at him in surprise, before her brow twisted, amber eyes sparking. "Excuse me?"

Bodies shifted uncomfortably around the room. Sebastian cleared his throat, sitting up straighter. "It's not safe outside the palace, Ciana. And none of us can be spared to go with you. You know what happens when we try."

"None of you need to go with us. There are plenty of Marked in the Guard and Infantry; not all of them are needed on the Bay. Let them go with us—"

"I said no, Ciana." Sebastian was so tired. He needed her here, safe, so he could focus on defending this city. Why didn't she understand that?

The tension in the room was thick as Ciana glared at him, breathing heavily before shoving to her feet.

"Mariah was taken from inside the palace, you know. If you think it's any safer in here than it is out there, then you're more lost than I thought." She whirled away, storming toward the exit.

The door slammed behind them, the pressure in the room swirling like a tempest.

Sebastian could only stare at the spot on the couch where she'd been, her words drawing out all the feelings of failure and fear and rage and dropping them heavily on his chest.

They needed Mariah back, or he feared more than just this city would fall.

But he was utterly lost on how to find her.

CHAPTER 7

A week had passed, and Mariah was still rocked by the miraculous healing of her wounds.

Well, perhaps less miraculous and more divine.

The infection had retreated, the fever no longer clawing hot fingers down her spine or squeezing her heart too tight. The deep ridges left by the whip's spiked metal tip were healed, still occasionally tingling and itching, but Mariah didn't mind.

It reminded her she would not die today.

Mariah picked at the plate on the ground in front of her. It was pathetic, as it always was: a meager portion of half-frozen, moldy bread and a cup of tepid water. The bread was like sawdust, but she did what she could to wash down the taste, grimacing as it hit her empty stomach like lead.

She sometimes felt like she'd dreamed the encounter with Zadione. Everything was so hazy—the goddess wreathed in silver, Mariah's fever threatening to burn her away from this cold, dark cell. The story of an epic love that razed and destroyed far more than it built and grew. She wasn't sure how the goddess's appearance, if it had all been real, was even possible; she was no expert on the gods, but they didn't just appear on the earth in physical forms like the one Zadione had taken.

Mariah didn't ponder the puzzle for long. Somehow, she was healed; that's all that mattered. She now bore some nasty scars on her back and forearm, but ... she was proud of that.

Let them see what they've done to her. What they've made.

Zadione's words, while hazy as a rapidly fading dream, still rang through her mind.

"Your love used to be a weakness, Mariah. But now that you have fallen, you must find a way to make it your retribution."

Mariah liked the sound of that.

Love was her weakness, but it would also be her retribution.

The low, unexpected echo of footsteps from the hall beyond her cell chilled her far more than the stone floor against her skin.

The fresh scars on her back itched as the light of an *allume* lamp seeped into the hall, illuminating two familiar guards and a pair of tanzanite eyes that had her sinking further into the floor.

Her physical wounds had healed, but to forgive the hand that dealt them ... even if he'd meant more to her than her own life, she was far from being strong enough for that.

Make love your retribution.

She straightened her spine, leaning against the rickety frame of her bed. She searched Andrian's expression for a flash of that familiar fire she'd sworn she'd glimpsed the last time she'd seen him.

Nothing lingered in his eyes but emptiness. Bottomless and cruel.

She watched him with a mirroring hollowness as he pulled a key from his pocket and unlocked her cell door. The two guards swept in around him.

"Stand up," the foul-tempered one—Ellis—said, his beady, hate-filled eyes narrowed.

Mariah wanted to fight the command.

But she could feel Andrian's empty stare on her, and her fury was pulled away. She deflated, withering into herself as violent memories of a metal-tipped whip whistling through the air dragged against freshly mended scars. The words from the goddess had enlightened her, empowered her with renewed vigor ... but it had only lasted for a moment.

She quietly unfolded her legs, hands still cuffed and raw in that sickening black and gold stone, and stood. The guards grabbed her arms roughly, pulled her through the cell door, and halted before the tall figure lurking in the shadows.

Andrian eyed her with muted disinterest. "You're looking better than we anticipated."

Mariah didn't answer. Only stared up at him, desperately trying to rationalize this stranger with the man who'd shared his face. He shrugged, turning, and only then did she find her voice.

"Where are we going?"

There was silence for a moment as the guards pushed her after him down the hall, towards the treacherous stairs leading to that makeshift throne room.

"You've been invited to join the Royals for dinner. As their *honored* guest." Andrian's flat voice answered, and only her desire to move and keep warm kept her limbs from locking up, from collapsing to the ground.

THIS INVITATION WASN'T one she would've ever wanted.

Instead of being welcomed into the dining room, offered a chair at the table, she was pushed into a corner. The guards made quick work of forcing her to her knees, of binding her arms behind her back, of tying those binds to her ankles so she couldn't move or fight.

The gag was the worst of it. Once she was bound, they shoved a strip of cloth in her mouth and wrapped it around her head. It was foul-tasting and dirty, and she coughed and choked the moment it touched her tongue.

The guards only laughed.

"I thought you had experience being gagged?" Ellis said, his grin baring yellowed teeth, his eyes too meandering.

"You forget, El. She's only okay being gagged by a cock." The other one—Konnor—chimed in before kneeling before her, eyes bearing a similar dark gleam. "If that's what the little whore queen wants, though, perhaps after the feast, we can indulge her."

"Ellis, Konnor, leave our guest alone and join us."

Mariah knew Andrian's voice was too dull and emotionless to be any sort of rescue on her behalf, but a sick, pathetic part of her couldn't help but feel grateful for it.

The two guards glanced over their shoulders before rising to their feet. "Maybe next time, little whore," Ellis sneered in farewell before sauntering off, joining the rest of the Royals and their guests at the table.

Leaving Mariah blessedly alone. Uncomfortable, sure. But alone and forgotten was, again, the best she could hope for in a situation like this.

So she sat. Forced to listen and watch as the wealthy around her ate and drank and indulged, the delicacies splayed across the table a picture of tantalizing excess.

And because she had not eaten a real meal in weeks—months, even—her stomach panged angrily against the walls of her ribs, her too-thin frame shaking with hunger.

But she did not ask for food. Nor was she offered any, but that was no surprise.

"Miss Salis!" Shawth's raucous voice rang out across the hall, pulling everyone's attention first to him, then to her.

Mariah lifted her chin to meet his watery gaze, the familiar slimy smile across his face.

He stood from his chair, filling up a plate with food, before stepping around the table and meandering over to her. "Are you hungry, my dear? I hear they fed you tonight, but I imagine it wasn't quite up to your standards. We have so much delicious food we would love to share with you!"

Mariah only kept her eyes on him, watchful and wary and furious.

Soon, too soon, he stood before her, that plate overflowing with food clutched in his meaty hands. He knelt, grunting with the effort, a few clumps of rice falling from the plate. The smell struck Mariah in the face like a punch, desperation for the nourishment roaring and raging inside her.

She bit down on the gag in her mouth to stop from groaning.

Shawth eyed her, curiosity written across his face. "You look … quite well, considering the state I last saw you in. Did someone heal you?"

Mariah forced every last ounce of hatred and rage into her stare, hoping it was enough to burn him where he stood. He watched her, brows furrowed, before he sighed and shook his head.

"It is no matter. Surely, you must be hungry?" A glint returned to his eyes. "I will promise you this." He lifted the plate, bringing it closer to her face, wafting it under her nose. Her eyes watered with starvation. "We'll let you join us for this feast—let you eat as much as your heart desires. On one condition."

As much as Mariah didn't want to hear it, she already knew what the condition would be.

A darkness entered Shawth's blue eyes. "Abdicate your power, and the food is yours. All of it, as much as you want. And everything we offered you earlier as well. Your freedom, your independence, your health. You can have it all … if you just abdicate."

For a brief, fleeting moment, Mariah wavered.

Why would it be so bad to give up her power? She didn't think it was possible to do what Shawth asked, but what if it was? She would have everything she'd ever wanted—money, freedom, the ability to go anywhere and be anyone she wanted. To remake her life into what she wanted it to be, not what some man or goddess decided it would be for her.

She allowed her resolve to waver there for those moments. Allowed herself to be desperate, weak, and selfish, just for a heartbeat.

Then the promises she'd made came rushing back. Her promise to Ciana, to girls all over the kingdom just like her best friend. Victims of a society that didn't appreciate them and would never change without something drastic to force it.

Promises to her mother to always stay strong, to never lose who she was—a fighter.

Promises to her goddess to stay the path, to listen. To fight the war that none could see, but Mariah could feel brewing, even if she didn't yet know who was responsible.

With those promises, she remembered why she'd gone to the courtyard that night in the first place. It hadn't just been to see Andrian.

It had been to become *Queen*.

Mariah lifted her head, the flickers of her magic locked away in her soul stinging against the stone on her wrist, and she knew that despite the suppression, silver-gold flashed in her eyes, her fury gleaming.

She couldn't speak, not with the gag in her mouth, so she simply growled, the sound low and hardly human. A sound that shocked even her.

A beast stirred beneath her skin, roaring awake.

Something—fear, curiosity, horror—flickered in Shawth's eyes. Wavered and then went out, replaced by his usual dead, hateful stare.

"Do you have something you wish to say, my dear?" He handed the plate of food to a guard behind him before pulling the gag from her mouth, his hands resting too long on her cheeks.

Disgust raced through her as she spat on the floor the moment the gag was free, coughing and desperate to clear her mouth of the vile taste.

"Well?" Shawth's tone was expectant, excited.

Gods, Mariah really shouldn't say what she was about to. But holding her tongue wasn't one of her strengths.

"I do have something to say." Her voice was hoarse from disuse, but the room still fell silent, even the whispered side conversations of the ladies ceasing in expectation. Shawth lifted an eyebrow as Mariah met his stare.

"I will ..." She coughed again, throat still raw. "I will pray to the goddess that you get fucked up the ass by your horse before being drowned in the depths of the Mirrored Sea."

Mariah wasn't sure what sort of reaction she expected from her words, but it certainly wasn't the one she got.

The room erupted into raucous, roaring laughter. Shawth grinned merrily before rising from his crouch.

"What a pity." He glanced at his guards. "Replace her gag."

The scrap of fabric was just as disgusting as the first time as it slid back between her teeth.

"It seems our little whore queen still has a bit of a mouth on her. Nice to know we haven't broken her spirit ... yet." Shawth laughed, eyes glimmering with dark maliciousness. Mariah's blood ran cold as he gazed down at her.

"Enjoy the rest of your evening, Mariah."

THE LORDS LEFT Mariah there in the corner, bound and gagged and starved, as they continued to eat and drink and enjoy an evening of squawking merriment.

Mariah did her best to tune it out. Did her best to ignore them, to pretend she was the only one in that room. To pretend the lack of attention from a dark-haired son seated at the end of the table didn't shred her already broken heart into smaller, twisted pieces.

Not that she would prefer his attention. That had proven to be just as damaging. Her scars itched.

Perhaps the glimmer she'd seen in his remarkable eyes had been an illusion, a play in the dim light, a sick joke from her crippled mind. It cracked something inside her further open, but a part of her had suspected that this was the truth all along, that she'd been fooled as easily as they mocked her for.

She was lost in the dark ocean of those thoughts when movement caught her attention. Mariah's eyes darted up to see a pretty, dark-haired girl close to her age sauntering out from the crowd, a sneer twisting her features.

Mariah inspected the girl as she neared. She was shorter than Mariah, skin pale from a lifetime spent within castle walls. Long, chocolate tresses draped across her shoulders, her honey-brown eyes set in a regal face glimmering with superiority.

She was beautiful, and well-bred, and obviously sent to torment Mariah. But Mariah had spent her whole life dealing with girls like this.

Mariah lifted her head, a hint of a challenge.

The girl paused a few feet from Mariah, gripping a chair and sliding it away from a small table nearby. She placed it beside Mariah but just out of arms-reach, sitting down primly, smoothing down the folds of her rich red gown.

"I thought it was time to introduce myself. You don't know me, but I certainly know you." Her eyes did a sweeping pass of Mariah's bound and filthy form, lip curling. "Hard to say I'm impressed. This image you paint here is just pathetic. Hardly suitable for a queen." She swept her dark hair off her shoulder, settling in the chair.

"My name is Anniliese Hareth, daughter of Royal Lord Hareth," the girl—Anniliese—continued, before locking her brown gaze on Mariah, angry, vengeful fire dancing in their depths. "And I should've been Chosen as the next queen; not you."

Everything in Mariah went too-still. She hardly thought she was breathing. She realized that while this girl looked unassuming enough, she had more reason than most in that room to hate her.

Which was certainly saying something.

"Everyone thought it would be me. I was born at the right time, I come from a Royal house, and I do not have magic. When I received Queen Ryenne's summons, a great celebration was held in Ettervan. I'd been bred and raised to take the throne, and I was ready." Her delicate hands tightened into fists, smooth brows furrowing.

"Until the day of the Choosing, when the magic, for whatever reason, slipped over my head and chose you instead." Anniliese's voice was low, almost a whisper, as she stared out at the room. Blood flushed into her cheeks. "You, a mere *commoner*, with no training or respect or dignity. Nothing more than a whore from the crossroads."

Mariah was surprised the girl didn't turn and spit at her, just to get the point across. Though she didn't feel any anger at Anniliese's words. Perhaps she was too tired, too hungry, to care. She'd been called so much worse just in the last hour; nothing Anniliese said was original.

Anniliese shifted in her chair. "I don't understand why they even bother keeping you alive. We all thought you would have been taken care of a week ago. I say they should just kill you now. Only a few months have passed since the Choosing; I know the magic would flow to me. Where it belongs. And I'll get what I was always meant to have."

Her words were impassioned and manic, but Mariah heard something lost and broken in them.

For a moment, Mariah felt sorry for Anniliese. She was just like Ciana, like so many other girls in Onita, in so many ways. Told to be only one thing her entire life, molded to fit the needs and desires of men who didn't truly care for her.

She hated herself for feeling it.

"But, if you die … I wonder what happens to your Armature?"

That streak of sympathy vanished in a flash of anger and fear.

Every muscle in Mariah's body tensed. She clenched her already sore jaw tighter around the gag, fingernails digging into her palms so hard she was sure she broke the skin.

When Mariah saw Anniliese's eyes take on a dark glint as they focused on where Andrian sat at the table beside her father, everything in her mind went blank.

"Well … at the very least, I'm glad *he* isn't bonded to you. No need to worry that far, then." Anniliese turned back to Mariah, her eyes cold and assessing. "He is quite nice to look at, isn't he? I've known him my whole life. Every time I visited Verith with my father, I would visit Andrian, too. Despite our age difference, we shared a special bond—because we were both Royal, of course. I do hope that no matter what ends up happening to you, I'll be allowed to keep him. This is simply where he belongs."

The emptiness Mariah felt made it easy to keep her emotions from her face. Everything was cold and dark, and she was vacant.

There must've been something there that Anniliese saw. Something that made her brown eyes flash with victory, something that made her pretty lips twist into an evil grin.

Mariah supposed brokenness and heartbreak, no matter how empty they made you feel, never quite left the eyes.

"He never loved you, you know. He only played his part so deliciously well," Anniliese purred, leaning closer. "He fed you exactly what you wanted to hear, and you ate it up like the desperate little slut you are." She rose to her feet, glancing once more at Andrian before looking down her nose at Mariah, kneeling at her feet.

"Why don't I prove it to you?" Anniliese hummed, sweet and sinister.

With that same wicked grin, Anniliese strode away, her path leading her to where Andrian lounged, casual and devastating, beside his father.

As much as Mariah wanted to look away, to not watch whatever was about to happen ... she couldn't. She was frozen in place, the ice that held her sliding over the beating of her heart, forced to watch the scene unfold before her.

Anniliese ambled behind Andrian, running her long-nailed fingers along his shoulders and into his thick, dark hair. His answering smile was as empty and hollow as his eyes. She bent, whispering into his ear. His shoulders tensed, a shadow flickering across his features, a shadow that was quickly shuttered as he returned that hollow smile to Anniliese with an answering chuckle.

The lords around them grinned and snickered, their attention shifting away to continue their meaningless discussions.

But Mariah did not look away.

She did not look away as Anniliese settled herself across Andrian's hips, pushing up her heavy red skirts as she straddled his muscular thighs.

She did not look away as Andrian's hands settled on those thighs, on the creamy skin peeking out from beneath the fabric.

Did not look away as Anniliese purred into Andrian's ear, as she ran her hands through his hair, mussing it in a way that was reminiscent of the day he'd surprised Mariah in a forgotten palace gallery. She'd thought his hair had looked much the same way—like possessive hands had been run through it too many times.

Did not look away, even as Anniliese lowered her mouth to his, capturing his lips in a hungry kiss.

Everything in Mariah flooded and broke and drowned. Every piece of her washed away, hopelessness and despair both emptying and filling her.

How could she have been so blinded? So wrong?

Zadione had tried to warn her. Tried to help her avoid making the same mistakes the goddess herself had once made.

And Mariah hadn't listened. Now she was here, watching her first love, her only love, kiss another woman like Mariah never existed.

As if she'd called his name, Andrian's eyes snapped open, the blue clashing with hers across the room. He yanked away from Anniliese, chest heaving as waves of raw, heavy emotion warred and raged across his face.

But Mariah was too empty to contemplate his changed expression or what thoughts might battle behind his walls of ice. It was too late for her. She'd been drowned, and she was lost to the emptiness of her pain.

Despite the hollowness, she held Andrian's stare until Ellis approached, roughly undoing her binds. The gag was yanked from her mouth, and she was pushed out of the dining room, back down the stairs to her dungeons.

It was only once the lock had *snicked* into place and the light of the *allume* lamp had faded from view that her tears fell.

CHAPTER 8

I t had been three years since the Mark of the next queen appeared on Andrian's chest, and he still wasn't quite used to calling Verith home.

It was easy to pretend during the day. They—he and the other nineteen boys who'd been Marked with him—spent their days training with the best weapons masters in the kingdom, the same commanders who trained the most elite of Onita's military. When they weren't on the training pitch, they were in the classroom, continuing their education and learning the pieces of history that would be most valuable to a potential member of a queen's Armature. Those history lessons, as they'd always been, were a solace to Andrian.

It was the nights when things became difficult.

He was always driven awake by a panic and fear that he could never quite place. Images would flash through his mind—the faces of his father and younger brother, Gabriel. His mother, crying quietly as she said goodbye to him through the closing door of a carriage. There were more ... flashes and glimpses of a small dark-haired girl he didn't know, teetering wildly through a lush forest of trees dripping with leaves like emeralds.

Tonight was no exception.

The dreams dissipated from his mind as he woke with a jolt,

stomach in knots. A sensation coiled deep in his gut, the feeling of something yanking and grabbing at his skin before pulling pieces of him away. It felt like the night he'd been Marked but without the pain. No, this feeling didn't hurt, but it also didn't feel right.

His fear deepened when a hand gripped his skin, fingers digging into his arm as it roughly shook him into consciousness.

"Andrian! Wake up!" A voice whispered urgently in his ear.

It was Sebastian. Despite Andrian's general proclivity to being a recluse, he and the boy had become friends since their arrival in the capital. They were the closest in age, the oldest amongst their group, and their companionship had come easy.

There was nothing friendly in Sebastian's voice now, though. All Andrian heard was panic, weak and desperate.

"Andrian, seriously. Can you see us? We're trying to turn the lights on, but it's so dark. Ryland hit the lunestair *panel, but nothing happened. We need to get Cedoric or even Kalen—"*

Andrian's eyes flew open as he shot from bed, a startled Sebastian falling back with a yelp. "Andrian, what in Enfara—"

"I—I think I know what's wrong." Andrian's voice was calm, even though he felt anything but. He also saw the inky darkness spreading around them, so pitch black it was as if the depths of the pit had leaked into the world, right into their barracks.

But it wasn't something from Enfara.

Not that it made it any less cursed.

For despite the darkness, he could still see. Not with his eyes—not exactly—but with his other senses. A new *sense. The thing that seeped off his skin and coiled in his gut. Everything the darkness touched, he could feel and see and recognize.*

Because the darkness was him.

A memory tickled the back of his mind, a page from a dusty textbook he'd read no more than a year ago. A book so old and worn, it was a marvel that it still existed—especially considering the dark piece of Leuxrithian history it described.

"It's me," he whispered, voice flat, fear and understanding still raging a war. With an instinct as natural as breathing, he pulled those shadows back into his skin.

They withdrew from the corners of the room, slowly revealing the allume *lamps and lights that were all switched on during the desperate quest for illumination. When the last wisp of darkness vanished beneath his skin, Andrian faced Sebastian. The other boy sat on the edge of Andrian's cot, eyes wide and face filled with confusion and disbelief. The rest of the boys in the room wore similar expressions as they slowly inched closer.*

Andrian's frustration burst through him like a ray of sunlight, melting his usual iciness. He wasn't some circus trick to be marveled at. And he definitely *didn't want to be scrutinized by a room full of curious boys who he had to live with for the next eighteen years.*

But even with his anger ... these boys were still all he had left. Something had just happened to him. Something he didn't understand and was terrified to face.

"You're a reykr. *One of the shadow-wielders. I didn't ... I didn't think they still existed. I thought shadow magic was a myth," Sebastian whispered, a soft statement that confirmed what Andrian had read on that page not long ago.*

Andrian's irritation fizzled out, ice sliding back in.

Everything in him went cold. He'd known the truth the moment he'd reached out and touched the darkness with his mind, pulling it beneath his skin. It was a power found only in the northern kingdom, the kingdom of his mother's people. A power that had been extinct for nearly a thousand years, the legends of it rooted in a bloody and violent past. Shadow magic was a bedtime story meant to terrify children. And, besides that ... Andrian lifted his head to meet his friend's stare.

"It's ... that's impossible, right? I'm Onitan." He glanced back down at his empty palms, as if he could still see the magic swirling in his blood, just beneath. "No one on the continent has shadow magic. Not anymore."

Even as he said it, he knew he was wrong. Despite the cold shock, he felt no denial; something in his soul had cracked open, and those shadows spilled out. As much as his mind snapped about in lashing anger, it was tempered by his heart.

Whatever this was, it was a part of him. Something that was always there, just buried beneath the surface until he was old enough to set it free. As simple to understand as the breath in his lungs or the beat of his heart. It wasn't something he could understand, and at thirteen years old, he wasn't inclined to.

"You're right," a soft-spoken boy with golden hair—Drystan— said. "There's never been a reykr *reported in Onita before. But you said your mother was from Leuxrith, didn't you?"*

Andrian gulped. His mother had shared so much about her culture, her people, but she'd never shared this. And those history books, the ones that spoke of the reykr *... none of them were kind to those who wielded shadows. The opposite of the light magic that fueled Onita, some historians even considered it an abomination, a dark perversion of the gods' gifts born in the shadows of the cold northern mountains.*

"Does ... does this mean I'm evil?" Something was quiet and broken in his question. A boy who'd only ever wanted to be accepted but faced yet another burden that would just make him more different.

"Andrian, no." Sebastian gripped his forearm, meeting his stare. "You're not evil. The history books are not always right; you know that better than any of us. Maybe ... maybe we just don't know everything there is to know about magic. But we'll learn what this is and what it means. We'll help you."

The mumbled words of affirmation from the group of boys who'd become like brothers were the last things Andrian heard before floating into a void of shadow and starlight.

<hr>

THE MEMORY SHOOK something free within Andrian's soul. Those feelings of brotherhood reminded him, for just a moment, who he really was. Clawing desperately for purchase, he felt his binds briefly slip free as he jolted awake.

Or ... partially awake. Free from the eternal vacuum of his thoughts and memories, he still had no control, but he had awareness. Feelings. Sensations.

With a world-tilting suddenness, he became cognizant of a feminine body in his lap, of dark hair tangled in his hands. He felt lips on his but knew instantly it wasn't *her.*

Her scent was wrong. He would search for that smell of eucalyptus and jasmine, hinted with cedarwood, even in death. And he knew that even if this was the afterlife, even if he was no more, he still would know that this girl in his lap with her lips on his was *wrong*.

The realization was enough for him to push past whatever power held him. He struggled, desperate to stop the feeling of wrongness. But he stopped, horror dripping through even his paralyzed soul as he saw a pair of forest-green eyes staring at him across a banquet hall.

Her face was so achingly, painfully, beautifully familiar. But it was also ... changed. Her skin had lost its bright pallor, no longer capable of that flush he loved so much, her cheeks gaunt and her expression haunted and broken. Her mouth was gagged, and her clothes were torn and filthy, her body bound and tied in a kneeling position on the cold marble floor.

She became all he saw. The center of his entire being. He pushed against his binds with an internal roar that might've ripped his soul in two.

If he even had a soul left to cleave.

But just like that, with hardly a whisper of effort, the wave of shadow and darkness that had held him captive for what could've been an eternity washed over him again, dragging him back deep beneath the surface and wiping the images of the broken girl with dull green eyes from his consciousness.

"Your little queen is nothing to you, and the more you fight me, the more I shall prove it."

The parting words, spoken in a masculine voice as dark and eternal as the shadows stretched by the sun at dusk, chased him into oblivion.

CHAPTER 9

"I would be glad to arrange an extra shipment of grain to the capital, My Lady," the merchant droned, "however, my clients will require assurances that the threats to the city will not result in an uncompensated loss to their crops."

Ciana nearly rolled her eyes. *Yes, let's allow an entire city under siege to starve. Wouldn't want to record a loss on this season's books.*

"We can assure you, sir." Delaynie sat forward at the table. "All steps are being taken to protect the city and its occupants. Whatever guarantees your clients need, we would be happy to make them."

Ciana drummed a finger against her leg. At least Delaynie had her wits about her today.

"Yes," she finally said, grabbing her fidgeting hand with the other. She forced a smile as she met the merchant's stare. His dark eyes narrowed at the two women. "Whatever is necessary. We only want to keep the people of the city fed during this time of turmoil."

The merchant regarded them both before he sniffed. "There are rumors floating about that the Queen Apparent is no longer in the city, abandoning Verith at its time of greatest need."

Ciana stiffened, a whirlwind sweeping through her chest.

It wasn't the first time one of these fat merchants had made suggestions about Mariah's disappearance. It came up now in nearly every conversation, however few and far between they'd become.

And Delaynie, ever the practiced politician, gave the same answer every time.

"Rumors certainly spread like wildfire, good sir. But Queen Apparent Mariah is not yet coronated, and Queen Ryenne is more than capable of securing the city, as is her responsibility until the ascension occurs." She gave the merchant a cool smile as icy as her tone.

The merchant grunted. "And why hasn't the Queen Apparent been coronated? This must be one of the longest transitions Onita has seen." He scratched his chin. "The people are anxious to see a strong queen on the throne once again. That they haven't, well ... many have begun to worry if there is an issue. With suitability." He smiled wildly, revealing teeth stained by a life of excess.

"What are you suggesting?" Ciana demanded. The maelstrom in her heart spun faster, and she almost stood from her seat, almost leaped across the table.

She fucking *hated* these men and their *opinions*.

"I am sure the good sir is not suggesting anything untoward about our Queen Apparent. He wouldn't dare be so brazen before members of Her Highness's court." Delaynie pinned him with her sharp, cutting stare. "Would he?"

The merchant lifted his hands in mock surrender but still wore his sour smile. "Of course, My Lady. I'm simply alerting you both to what is said amongst the common folk. I imagine it is stuffy up here, tucked away in your mountain palace, and I view it as an obligation to keep you informed."

"Thank you for the gesture, sir," Ciana ground out, not meaning a single word.

The merchant grinned wider and pushed back from the table.

"Well." He rose from his seat, Ciana and Delaynie following

suit. "It is always a pleasure meeting with you lovely young ladies. I must return to my offices. Expect correspondence from me in the next few days, detailing the amount of grain available and what securities we will require importing it to Verith."

With one more greasy smile and nod, the merchant shuffled from the room, followed by the Guardsman who'd been stationed by the door, heavy oak slamming shut behind him.

Delaynie collapsed back into her chair with a huff, slouching into the seat, the perfect lady vanished. "I fucking *hate* that man."

Ciana choked a meager laugh. "Just when you think they can't get any worse." She remained standing, twisting her hands, that cyclone in her gut beginning to spread into her limbs.

"Hey," Delaynie murmured. Ciana turned to her friend, finding Delaynie's ice-blue stare locked on her. "You okay?"

"Yes. No. I ... I don't know." Ciana slumped, returning to her chair and dropping her head into her hands. "I just hate this. *All* of this. This entire fucked up situation."

Delaynie was silent for a moment. "Are you still upset with Sebastian?"

Sebastian. Gods, yes, Ciana was still furious with him. Her best friend—next to Mariah—and the person who perhaps knew her best, but he still had the audacity to tell her what to do and where to go.

He may be in command, but he didn't command *her*. No man ever would again.

A soft hand touched Ciana's shoulder. She peeked at Delaynie through her mass of curly hair.

"You should talk to him. He should be back from the Bay by now. You're going crazy in this palace." Delaynie glanced at the door, where the merchant had just vanished. "And I, for one, would relish a chance to get out and see the city again. If for the sole reason of seeing if the rumors that man spoke of really are running around out there."

Ciana nodded. "I just feel so ... useless here. I can't force myself to care about everything else, when Mariah ..." She inhaled a shaky breath. "When Mariah is still missing." She clenched her jaw, fighting back the rush of frantic desperation.

She would give anything to be out there, searching for Mariah. To be anywhere but in this old, cavernous palace, wasting her days as the weeks turned to months.

Every day, the sense of comfort and safety she'd found there slipped further away. She'd never known those things before arriving in Verith; her entire life until that point had been filled with fear and suppressed trauma, evilness haunting her at every corner. Mariah gave her a home, a place to finally be herself and feel safe.

But with Mariah gone, the darkness of Ciana's past had seeped in around the edges of her world. Shadows haunted her in the ancient halls, and her demons inched closer with each terrifying flicker of the lights.

Delaynie squeezed her again. "Talk to him again, Cee. Alone, this time. Make him see that we can do so much more out there than we can in here. That we aren't helpless, and the risk is worth it if it means we can get Mariah back."

Ciana met her friend's fierce stare. She and Delaynie had grown so much closer these past weeks, leaning heavily on each other as the world grew darker.

Ciana nodded. "I'll talk to him."

Ciana rapped her knuckles on the black oak door.

"Who is it?" A deep voice echoed through the wood, a voice thick with exhaustion and defeat.

"It's me. Ciana. It's Ciana." She sighed. *Smooth.*

A pause answered her. Then footsteps. The door swung open, revealing a rather uncharacteristically haggard-looking Sebastian, brown hair tussled, weary dark circles under his hazel eyes.

He leaned heavily against the doorframe, running a hand through his hair. "Is everything alright?"

Ciana nodded. "Yes, everything's fine. It's just—" She looked around him. "Can I come in? I want to talk."

"Of course." He opened the door wider as he stepped back.

She brushed past him, catching the faintest scent of leather and whiskey. Her eyes settled on the half-full glass on his counter, at the uncorked decanter beside it.

She couldn't say she blamed him.

Sebastian walked past her, picking up his glass. He shot her a sheepish look, just before taking a sip. "I'd offer you some, but I know you don't like it."

Ciana crinkled her nose. "It tastes like shoe leather."

"Sweet, vanilla-flavored shoe leather. There's a difference." Sebastian's lip twitched up into the faintest of smiles, and Ciana relaxed. Just a touch.

She took a deep breath. "I—"

"I wanted to apologize. For the way I spoke to you the other day. That was out of line, and I'm sorry."

Ciana blinked. "Thank you for apologizing. I know it's hard right now. With ... everything."

He nodded, deflating. "I just want one fucking break, for one thing to go right. I want to get back to searching for Mariah. But I can't abandon the city. And it's tearing me apart, making that decision."

"Well ..." Ciana took a step closer, resting her hands on the counter. "That's actually what I wanted to talk to you about." She took another deep inhale. "You and the others have to guard the Bay. But Delaynie and I ... we hardly have any meetings anymore, and most days, we're just standing around, waiting for the worst to happen. We are going *insane*, and we can help. Besides, there are rumors spreading in the city—about Mariah—and we think it could be helpful if we learned what those are and if they might lead to—"

"Ciana." Sebastian's tone was quiet but firm. His face had fallen as she'd been speaking, his mouth now set in a grim, tired line. "Just because I apologized doesn't mean my answer has changed. It's not safe."

Anger lit up Ciana's chest, whipping through her blood. She straightened her spine, hands tightening into fists.

"You can't tell me what is or isn't safe. You don't get to tell me what to do." Her voice grew louder as she spoke, tears threatening behind her eyes. "*No one* gets to tell me what to do, not anymore. If I have to spend one more second in this palace, standing about like a helpless idiot, I ... I ..." Her hands shook, and she sniffed, a frustrated choke catching in her throat.

"You're my best friend, Sebastian. You know how much I need to do this. *Please*." Her voice cracked. "Please don't lock me in here. Please let me help."

Sebastian watched her, expression unreadable, the silence spreading between them thick and heavy. Ciana heaved her breaths, tears still running tracks down her cheeks. Sebastian released one long, tortured exhale, hanging his head, hair falling forward to hide his face.

"I'm not having this conversation again, Ciana. I'm not changing my mind."

Ciana exploded.

"You have *given up*!" She stormed forward, shoving his chest. He took a stunned step back, nearly knocking over his glass. "At least let those of us who still care do something *useful*, instead of locking us up just so you can feel better!"

The second those words left her lips, Ciana knew she was wrong to say them. She didn't believe them, not really. But she was so *angry*, and by the gods, he needed to see it.

Sebastian's stare hardened. "I know how hard all of this has been on you, so I'm going to forgive you for that. But don't you ever dare accuse me of not caring. You know I'm doing everything I can with what I'm dealt."

"Not everything. You're being a coward."

"I refuse to be reckless. That's what they want."

Ciana whirled away from him, marching to the door. She yanked open the heavy wood.

She couldn't speak. Her words were clogged by her anger. She needed to leave.

"Don't leave the palace, Ciana. Please."

"Fuck you." The door slammed behind her, rattling the walls.

CIANA STORMED THROUGH THE HALLS, her steps kept company by her fuming mutterings.

A part of her, deep down, knew she was being irrational and self-centered. They were all coping with an unimaginable loss and an impossible situation, and Sebastian was doing the best he could.

Unfortunately, Sebastian's best was forcing Ciana into her worst. She felt trapped, scared, vulnerable. This anger, this self-ishness ... it was all she could do, too.

Her steps took her winding through the gilded halls. She'd meant to head to her rooms, but she'd only peered down the brightly lit hallway and strode past it without hesitation.

Stagnation would be the worst possible thing for her now.

Ciana wound down a spiraling staircase, brushing her hand along the gilded walls before reaching the bottom and bursting into a lower courtyard.

And freezing in her steps.

Queen Ryenne stood alone in the courtyard, none of her Armature or ladies in sight, staring at Ciana as if she'd been waiting for her.

"Queen Ryenne," Ciana said slowly, chest still heaving from her panicked flee through the palace. "I ... I'm sorry to intrude."

The aging queen smiled, skin crinkling around her ocean-blue eyes. "You are not intruding, Lady Visseau."

Ciana shifted awkwardly. "I will ... I'll leave you alone, forgive me—"

"You misunderstand, Lady Visseau. I do not wish to be left alone. I was waiting for you."

Ciana lifted a brow. "Waiting ... for me? Here?" The courtyard was one of the ones with a domed glass ceiling, trapping in heat and moisture and keeping out the brisk late winter air. Plants and trees with great leaves in the shape of massive fronds arched and brushed the glass and stone, flowering vines crawling up their trunks. "I wasn't ... I didn't even mean to come here."

Ryenne smiled. "You might not have meant to come, but I knew you would, regardless."

This is very strange. "I'm not sure I understand, Your Majesty."

"I may be old, Lady Visseau, and my magic may be all but gone, but I have a few tricks left to me still." The old queen turned, gesturing to Ciana with a pale, splotched hand. "Come. Sit with me."

Ciana obeyed, her rage now replaced by interested confusion. She'd never really interacted with Ryenne before, not beyond the few shared moments with Mariah and the others of Ryenne's court. Ryenne was also absent from any governance meetings, leaving most of Ciana's dealings, however fleeting, with Ryenne's ladies instead of the queen herself.

Ryenne settled on a marble bench beneath a rich green frond, the shading dappling her pale gray hair. Ciana sat hesitantly beside her, twisting her hands in her lap as she stared at a pile of golden stones stacked by the spiraled trunk of a tree several feet away.

They sat there in silence for a long moment, Ciana daring hidden glances beneath her lashes at Ryenne. The queen was still, her blue eyes misty, gazing across the courtyard at nothing.

"I have been doing much thinking, these past several weeks. About my reign ... and about how it shall end," Ryenne said after what felt like an impossible eternity.

Ciana's hands paused their anxious twisting. She slowly turned to face the queen; her shock written across her face.

"I don't think I understand ... Nothing can happen to you until there is a coronation, right?" Ciana hadn't been the best in schooling—far from it, actually—but she remembered that there was some final, secret ceremony that happened at a new Queen's coronation, some last transfer that conferred all Qhohena's magic and carried the old queen to the afterlife.

Ryenne smiled sadly. "To my body, yes. I will linger on this earth until Mariah has made her seventh bond and is ready to ascend. But the formal transfer of power is not what I speak of." She inhaled deeply. Her hands shook, brushing across the crushed velvet of her gown. "All of this ... this entire situation we now find ourselves in. It is not what I planned, what I foresaw, but perhaps I should have." Ryenne ducked her head, a curtain of grayed golden hair falling around her face, but not before Ciana caught what gleamed in the edges of her ocean-blue eyes.

Tears. The queen was crying.

Ciana hesitated.

For one fleeting moment, one in which Ciana was nothing more than a scared little girl afraid of the big world that had tried so hard to break her, she thought about running. It was what she was best at.

Then, the image of her best friend, her queen, leaped into her mind. The picture of Mariah on the Winter Solstice, pressing her bleeding palms to the panel of *lunestair* behind the throne, bridging ropes of silver-gold light from twin pillars together to form a dazzling display of power and magic. The feeling of *allume* thrumming through the earth, a knife slicing into Ciana's palm, her own blood feeding the beautiful, cacophonous magic.

Ciana reached out a hand, resting it gently atop Ryenne's. The queen stiffened, and with a shuddering inhale, straightened her shoulders.

But she did not wipe the tears from her eyes.

"All of this. The Royals and their reluctance to give up power, Ksee's rejection of Qhohena's will, Mariah's capture, the faltering *allume*, the Kizar pirates playing their games ... all of it is my fault. There would not be such strife if I had simply been strong enough to hold on to my power all those centuries ago. But I was not, and now here we are. A Chosen stolen, our lights and wards failing, our people in danger. Mariah's reign shall begin with blood and pain, and it is all my fault."

Ciana was silent for a moment. Not that she disagreed with the queen's words; she would never voice the thought aloud, but from the second she'd heard from Mariah what Ryenne had done with her power, she'd felt betrayed and furious and shocked.

But Ciana had known that information for a long time now. Had been able to dwell on her feelings and think through what it truly meant.

"You know," Ciana began, her hand still atop Ryenne's. "A few months ago, I might've agreed with you. I would've told you that this *was* all your fault." She inhaled deeply, expelling the air through her lungs. "But now ... now I think it's more complicated than that. I think whatever is happening, whatever led to Mariah's kidnapping and the failing magic and the arrival of the pirates, has been brewing for a very, very long time. I don't think the propensity of men—and some women—to take things they don't deserve was born overnight. This is a malignancy that has festered for ... well, maybe even since Xara's time. Hidden, but still there, just beneath the surface, waiting for a chance to burn its way out."

Ryenne shifted her gaze to Ciana as the young woman spoke, a curious expression spreading across her face. Ciana blinked once in surprise at the queen's attention.

"You have known great pain in your life for someone so bright."

Ciana started, her lungs freezing with her shock. She'd only told the stories of her past to three people: Mariah, Delaynie, and Sebastian. She didn't believe one of them capable of sharing that history with Ryenne, but ...

The queen chuckled. "Relax, Ciana. I do not know the details of your past. But I can see it—feel it in you. And the way you speak about an evilness that has always lurked beneath the surface ... I have lived enough life to know when words are spoken from personal knowledge and not mere observation." The queen turned to the sky. It was still day, but the sun was beginning its descent towards the horizon, shifting into the late afternoon.

"Mariah needs you. Even the Chosen of a goddess has her limits, and I worry what might happen if she reaches hers."

Ciana followed Ryenne's stare to the sky. "I want to find her. But ..." She swallowed. "But Sebastian ..."

"Let me guess. That Armature won't let you leave the palace." The queen turned. "They mean well. They are Marked, trained, and Selected to be protectors. But sometimes, there are things more important than our safety, and they struggle to see that." Her blue eyes flashed. "Don't be afraid to disobey. They can defend the city; you must find your queen."

Ciana liked the sound of that.

CHAPTER 10

The temporary war room in one of the many palace conference spaces smelled of coffee and sweat and frustration.

"I told you: if we can convince one of the wealthier merchants to use a few of their ships, we can sail out to the Kizar fleet and surprise them—"

"Which merchants? Do you really think any of those greedy oafs would let us use their precious vessels?" Matheo snorted. "You're brave, Ryland, but be realistic. Even if we garnered a few ships, what then? The Kizar fleet is larger, faster, and better equipped than any Onitan ship. They'd sink us in a matter of minutes—even with the element of surprise on our side."

Ryland, a younger Marked City Guard captain and one of the men who'd been raised with Sebastian and the others but were not Selected by Mariah to her Armature, deflated. "I was just trying to offer an idea that might put an end to this mess."

Sebastian slumped further in his chair, barely listening. He was ... so tired. Their latest skirmish had ended yesterday after a lengthy three-day stand-off, and despite his body craving a much-needed night of sleep, rest had avoided him.

Dark, aching nightmares had wrenched him awake in the

middle of the night. Feelings of sorrow and pain and loneliness bellowed into his mind, worming their way into his subconscious.

By the haunted looks in his fellow Armature's eyes, he knew they'd endured the same. The implication of them all experiencing a shared dream set them on edge, driven sharper by exhaustion.

"Perhaps, once this mess is over … it might be time to consider reforming the Onitan Navy. There are records of one existing long ago, nearly as mighty as the Kizar fleet. If it existed once, it could exist again," General Emer, Royal Infantry insignia emblazoned on his chest, rumbled from the end of the table, scratching his full gray beard.

Across the table, Feran chuckled.

"Let me get this straight, General Emer," Feran said, voice low as he slowly stood. "After nearly two decades of teaching us that, and I quote, 'Onita needs no navy because our magic and technology are so far advanced from any neighboring threats it would simply be a waste of resources to maintain,' you are now changing your mind?"

The General glared at Feran. "The circumstances have changed, boy. I taught you to adapt when the times called for it."

"Or, perhaps, you are simply trying to save face after being proven *wrong*," Feran seethed.

Sebastian sat up straighter in his chair, eyes darting between the two men as they leaned closer over the table.

"I asked you these questions eighteen years ago. Do you know what we could have accomplished in eighteen years? We could have ships in that bay right now, ships that could face the Kizar fleet and defend the city while we do the job we swore and bound our souls to do: *protect our queen*." Feran's fingers dug into the wood, lips pulled back in a snarl.

The aging General blinked his shock, stepping back.

It was bad when even Feran—even-tempered, observant Feran—was ready to draw blood from a man they'd known for over half their lives.

Sebastian rose to his feet. "You've made your point, Feran."

Feran's dark, fury-filled stare snapped to his. Drystan stepped to Feran's side, resting a hand on his shoulder. Feran held Sebastian's gaze for a second longer before loosing a heavy exhale and collapsing back into his chair.

Sebastian nodded to him. Feran simply fixed his stare on a swirl in the wood, scratching at the table with a finger.

"Perhaps"—Trefor glanced warily between Feran, Sebastian, and Emer—"there are improvements we can make to the trebuchets? Ones that might increase loading speed and distance? I found a few interesting notes in the library ..."

Sebastian lowered himself back into his seat as the tension slowly dissipated, replaced by Trefor's thoughts and a few interjections by other Armature, City Guard Captains, and Royal Infantry Commanders. He had nothing to offer—not anything they weren't already discussing—so his mind wandered.

The conversation he'd had with Ciana the night before, after he'd returned from the battlements ... It still didn't sit right with him. How it had happened, the things she'd said, the things *he'd* said.

The way it had ended.

Why didn't she understand? They were fighting for their lives just to keep the city from being overrun. The last thing he needed was to be worried about whether she was safe.

Even if the Kizar pirate's magic broke past the wards, it was still a long distance from the Bay to the palace. And Sebastian *desperately* needed that distance between the pirates and Ciana to exist.

He wouldn't lose any more best friends to the darkness of this cursed city.

Her words intruded into his thoughts, unimpeded.

"If you think it's any safer in here than it is out there, then you're more lost than I thought."

Perhaps she was right; maybe he was lost.

That didn't change his opinion, though. They would find another way to search for Mariah, one that didn't require Ciana leaving the most fortified place in the city.

Besides ... Ciana's point no longer stood. They *were* safer here in the palace. It wasn't this location that had been Mariah's downfall, but the actions of the one Armature who'd gone missing with her.

Sebastian's fist tightened. If Andrian really was behind Mariah's disappearance ...

It didn't matter how long Sebastian had known him. He'd kill Andrian himself.

"We can likely start implementing some of these changes this week," Orryn, a Marked City Guard captain said. "It may take some time to find craftsmen suited to the task, but—"

The lights around them flickered.

And then went out.

Sebastian shot to his feet, the room around him deadly quiet. They stood there, waiting, counting in the dark.

One. Two.

The darkness grew louder.

Three.

Sebastian's hands reached for his sword, the empty place in his soul where the bond had been cracking open.

Four.

Steel clinked as warriors shifted on their feet.

Five.

The lights returned, flooding the room with warm illuminance. Sebastian saw his dread, his anguish, and his fear reflected on the faces of the other men around him.

Quentin stepped forward, expression uncharacteristically hard and serious, a knife poised between his fingers. "They've never gone all the way out before."

Sebastian grimaced. "No. They haven't."

Quentin's green eyes blazed. "If the magic fails completely, no changes we make to the trebuchets will matter. The wards will be gone, and the pirates will wipe out the battlements in a matter of minutes."

"Are you suggesting a solution, Quentin? Or just pointing out the obvious?" Sebastian's patience wore thin. He was exhausted and felt his sanity slipping further and further from his reach.

"We can't abandon the battlements," Quentin said, "but we need our *queen* back. Or else it won't matter."

Sebastian opened his mouth, about to thank Quentin for the reminder, when the doors swung open. Delaynie, auburn hair hanging loose around her face, burst through, cheeks flushed a rosy pink. Quentin whirled, and Delaynie's eyes landed on the red-haired warrior first before jumping to Sebastian.

"We have some new arrivals. You need to meet them. Now."

<hr>

Two women stood in the cavernous throne room, a City Guard beside them, clothed in draping, paneled garb.

Sebastian halted at the sight of them. He instantly recognized them, memories from the *Porofirat*—Mariah's presentation ball—flashing through his mind. "I know you."

Their eyes had already sharpened on him, flashing his direction the moment he stepped into the room. One of them, her flowing skirts a pristine white, gold jewelry clinking softly, stepped forward, inclining her head. "And we know you, Armature."

"What are you doing here?" His feet finally unrooted, and he took several steps forward, Quentin and Delaynie on his heels. The rest of the Armature followed, and out of the corner of his eye Sebastian saw Ciana rush out of a hallway, hair wild about her head.

The woman smiled. "We are here to help."

"I'm sorry," Ciana said, a little breathless as she approached. She fixed a hard stare on the newcomers. "Who are you?"

Sebastian was about to answer but was too slow.

"My name is Kiira," said the woman in white and gold, brushing a dark-skinned hand down her chest as she again dipped her head. "And this is my twin sister, Rylla." The other woman—Rylla—was nearly identical to her sister, quirked her lips into a half-smile. She crossed her arms, dark gray paneled skirts swirling and silver jewelry tinkling.

"We are the youngest daughters of Ambassador Enoch, the first Kreah Ambassador to Onita in nearly one thousand years," Rylla said proudly. "We met Queen Ryenne—and your queen, Mariah—at the *Porofirat*. Queen Ryenne granted us permission to explore Verith and Onita while on our travels, and we decided to remain in Verith and experience the largest city on the continent for ourselves." She glanced once at her sister before meeting Sebastian's stare.

"It was in the city that we heard … rumors."

"Rumors of what?" Ciana snapped, her tone urgent. Sebastian whipped his head to her but she dutifully ignored him.

"Rumors," Kiira answered, "surrounding the new problem with the pirates from the Kizar Islands. Rumors that they are only here, plaguing your people, because your queen is not."

Sebastian's veins flushed with ice.

He hadn't given much thought to the beliefs and opinions of the common people these past few weeks. He was dedicated to protecting them, to keeping this city and its occupants safe from the threat on the Bay. But how they interpreted that threat, what they believed caused it, and why their queen—or queen apparent—wasn't out there, helping to defend them or broker peace … those weren't things that had crossed Sebastian's mind.

He should have considered how it would look, what rumors might run rampant.

"What are the people saying?" he gritted out, chest heaving with effort.

"I already know," Ciana said, lifting her chin. She still ignored him, directing that rich, amber gaze at Kiira. "The people are saying that Mariah has abandoned them. That the queen apparent has fled the city and has no intentions of saving them."

Kiira and Rylla shared a grim look. That was the only confirmation Sebastian needed. He didn't know how Ciana had learned of such rumors. But truthfully, that was the least of his concerns.

The people knew Mariah was gone.

And, worse, they believed she'd abandoned them. Vanished into the night, leaving them to suffer and die.

"I take it," he said, forcing the words through clenched teeth, "that you are not inclined to believe those rumors."

Kiira shook her head. "We have only met your queen twice, but the moment we heard the people talking ... we knew this was not the truth. We knew there was more to the story."

A pregnant pause followed Kiira's words. The Kreah sisters waited for information, and Mariah's court just ... waited.

Sebastian was the decision-maker. The leader. But at that moment, he didn't know what to do. He was paralyzed by his choices, by his mistakes, by his failures. The weight of all he'd lost and all he'd destroyed rested on his shoulders, wrapping around his ribs, and he worried he'd crumple right there on the marble throne room floor.

"Mariah didn't abandon the city."

Ciana's golden blonde hair was still wild about her, her freckled cheeks still flushed rosy-pink, but her small frame had straightened, amber eyes clear.

It was only then that she turned his way. Not seeking permission, but ... telling him she would share the truth. She would make this decision when he could not.

He simply inclined his head, and she turned back to the Kreah sisters.

"Mariah didn't abandon the city," Ciana repeated, "because she was taken. She has been missing for nearly eight weeks."

Kiira blinked in shock, and Rylla's brow furrowed.

"What do you mean," Rylla said slowly, "that she was taken?"

"She vanished, early one morning, along with one of her Armature. Her only *unbonded* Armature," Quentin interjected. He toyed with the knives strapped in his baldric as he stepped up beside Sebastian.

Kiira and Rylla shared a look. "And what steps have you taken to find her?"

Sebastian grimaced. "We were about to search when the pirates arrived."

"So … you have done nothing." Kiira's words sounded harsh in her Kreah accent, an accusation that pierced Sebastian's flesh.

"If you're here to offer help," Ciana said, "then we won't turn you away."

The sisters shared a glance.

"We will help you," Kiira declared.

"Besides," Rylla said, a sly smile spreading across her face, "we have certain skills which might prove helpful."

Delaynie crept forward cautiously. "What do you mean, certain skills?"

Rylla shifted on her feet. "You Onitan's have your magic—not just the energy you call *allume*, but gifts that can control the elements of fire or wind. Or the gift of light borne by your queen." Her smile widened. "Us in Kreah have similar gifts. And our goddess is most generous with them."

Sebastian's alarmed confusion slammed into him. "Your goddess? What goddess—"

Pale blue light, as bright and vibrant as the day sky, flashed through the throne room, and Sebastian's mind emptied.

Rylla was gone, and in her place stood a great black cat, hazel eyes gleaming as its tail swished through the air. The hint of fangs peeked out from beneath its jaw, its paws as large as a human hand.

"Oh, my gods …" Ciana breathed out. She stepped closer to the rest of them, hand covering her mouth.

This was impossible. This magic … it did not exist in Onita.

At least, not recorded.

"There is nothing to fear," Kiira said, a smile in her voice. "She may have changed forms, but it is still my sister." The black cat beside her sat back on its haunches. "This is the magic of Kreah."

"Wait," Ciana said. "Having Kreah magic … makes you *shifters*?"

Kiira nodded. "It is symbolic of our goddess, Rulene."

Sebastian's head spun, caught in a vortex. He considered himself read, but never in his over three decades of life had he read such things.

"If this is true," he said, "than this would be the best kept secret on the continent."

"It is not the end of the secrets kept from Onita, I fear." Kiira grimaced. "But not by choice. Many thousand years ago, Onita decided to isolate from the rest of the continent. No knowledge would enter or leave. The memories of the other magic, of the other gods, was quickly lost to time."

Drystan crossed his arms over his chest. "Then how do your people remember?"

Kiira narrowed her near-black stare. "Our people never forgot."

"I believe them," Ciana whispered. Everyone again turned their attention to her, Sebastian's mouth hanging agape once again.

Ciana swallowed. "Before the Winter Solstice, we met a woman from Leuxrith. She said she was a priestess of Callamus and told us of the other gods. I remember her mentioning Rulene, the patron goddess of Kreah." She glanced at them all, stare lingering on Sebastian. "If this is what it takes to get Mariah back, then we don't have any choice *but* to trust them."

Sebastian clenched his fists, more shock and misplaced anger rushing through him.

Ciana had known about this ... and had not told him. She had kept this secret from him, this information that changed everything about what they knew of their world. And for that, he was *furious*.

But ... he also knew she was right.

With a clipped nod to Ciana, he shifted to Kiira and Rylla, the latter's hazel feline gaze sharp and unnerving as it prickled his skin.

"If you truly can help find our queen ... then your aid is what we desperately need."

CHAPTER 11

Mariah had thought she knew what it felt like to shatter.

She'd thought she'd known true pain. But really, she had no idea, not until she saw the hands of the man she loved wrapped around the body of a girl who wasn't her. Saw his lips pressed against hers, saw something spark in his eyes that she'd thought had once been just for her.

She was such a fucking *fool*.

The cell, already cold, dark, and wet, had fallen into further decay. Hope and any chance of leaving its captivity seeped from the walls along with Mariah's tears. The moisture on her face had long since dried, but that didn't mean she didn't still feel it, right there behind her eyes, clawing for a way out they couldn't find.

Just like she felt.

"I always warned you to remember your place, Mariah."

She hadn't even heard the approach of her latest tormentor. If she had anything left in her heart that could allow her to care, Mariah would've felt a streak of anger, of outrage, at Ksee's voice echoing against the walls of her prison. Instead, all she felt was a slight surprise that faded into learned, defeated silence.

She was hardly shocked Ksee had chosen this moment, when

Mariah was at her most broken and defeated, to show her face. To reveal where she'd disappeared to since the night she'd taken her priestesses and fled the city, days before the Winter Solstice.

To finally flaunt her victory over Mariah.

Mariah turned a vacant look to the high priestess, meeting her molten brown eyes, a soft ember of fire—a reminder of the magic that had exalted Ksee to her position—resting in her open palm. The faint flare cast the priestess and her golden robes with a sickly glow. Ksee knelt, holding her robes from the dirty, wet floor with one hand, lifting her other with the light, sneering at Mariah.

"And this ... this is what happens when you forget."

Mariah only stared at the priestess. There was no response on the tip of her tongue, no desire to rise to Ksee's challenge.

That girl had died the day Andrian had locked the foul stone cuffs around her wrists and was buried no more than a few hours before when his lips met another's.

"You probably still think your little Solstice was a success, don't you?"

Ksee's words awoke something. Not fully, but enough to spark the most subtle of flickers, faint shifts of light deep in Mariah's soul.

Mariah blinked, a slow fading of light as her eyelids dropped and lifted. "What do you mean?" Even her voice was raw, scarred, maimed.

Ksee's lip lifted further. "Did you really think we would let you get away with that ... that *defilement*?"

Another slow blink. "What defilement?" But a memory flashed into her mind. Of the day after the Solstice, when she'd placed a hand upon the pillar and reveled in the power and luminosity of the *allume* that her magic—her *people*—had generated the night before. It was a forbidden thing, to touch those pillars. Yet that hadn't stopped her from binding the magic in her blood to them during the Solstice, nor had it stopped her from basking in her success the day after.

She also remembered that feeling she'd sensed beneath all the light. The one of twisted darkness, a black reeking of anger and fear and the pain of those who were innocent and couldn't protect themselves. All the feelings Mariah had once set out to eradicate from her kingdom, coiled amidst her sweet light.

What a fool's dream that was, to believe she could bring such change.

"You created an abomination," Ksee whined shrilly. She lifted her chin, staring down her pointed nose. "Tainted the pure magic of our goddess. So, we turned to another to help correct your mistake. We were left with no choice."

Something about Ksee's words made Mariah's blood run cold. Made the sparks of light in her chest beat a little harder against her heart. She sat just a little straighter, cocking her head slightly. "Another ... who?"

"Another *god*, you stupid brat. The Consort God, Priam himself. He does not fault the choices of his Consort—he would never do such a thing—but he knows you were always a mistake. A mockery. A *trick*."

If it weren't for the shifting threads deep in her soul, threads that made the stone on her wrists burn and sting her skin, Mariah would've believed Ksee's words. Would have collapsed back in on herself like a dying star, content to let the vacuum of her imprisonment consume her, body, mind, and soul.

But because of those threads, a presence she'd only felt in moments of significance those past weeks, she focused on what they whispered to her from behind the walls of their prison.

Wrong. Something, everything was *wrong*.

"What did you do?" Mariah asked, her voice quiet and confident in a curious, contained sort of way.

Her father had taught her to heed her instincts—something she'd forgotten in the face of love. She wouldn't forget again.

Mariah had stood in the Antechamber of Priam. She recalled the presence she'd felt there: warm, comforting, something solid to guide the souls of the dead crossing into the realm of the gods for their final rest. There was no judgment to be meted out, no coups to be staged, no questions against the Goddess of Life to be asked.

"What did *I* do?" Ksee snorted, oblivious to the shift in Mariah. "Just a cleansing ritual. I have heard and learned more from Priam since the Solstice than I ever had from Qhohena." A tinge of bitterness seeped into Ksee's tone, something angry and wanting.

Mariah did not miss it, though. "But aren't you a priestess of Qhohena?"

"I am," Ksee snapped. "Or ... I was. But with you, with your Choosing, I have lost my faith in my goddess. I still follow the gods, but I will do whatever it takes—listen to whatever deity honors me with their guidance, whether that be Qhohena or Priam—to protect Onita from vileness like you."

She rose from her crouch, movement brisk, robes swishing down around the floor as she released them from her grip. With a scathing look, a final parting glare meant to strip Mariah down, Ksee turned on her heel and strode from the cell, taking the flame of light in her palm with her. The space plunged back into cold, bleak darkness.

But Mariah was awake and beginning to feel quite at home in the darkness.

CHAPTER 12

Even with Ksee's words, Mariah knew she needed to sleep when she could. Somehow, despite the cold, despite everything, she fell into a fitful slumber, the mattress rock-solid but comforting beneath her shoulder blades.

A crawling along her skin pulled her from the clutches of consciousness, alerting her to the presence of another, standing in her cell and watching as she dozed.

Her body tensed, but she didn't open her eyes. Instead, she opened her other senses—her smell, her hearing, the last dregs of supernatural power she could barely scratch with the shackles locked around her wrists. She couldn't hear anything, but there was a scent in the air, something familiar and perfect and heart-breaking—

With rain and sandalwood flooding her senses, she slowly lifted her eyelids, meeting a gaze of brilliant blue.

Andrian stood just inside her cell, the heavy door open, his posture rigid. His arms hung by his sides, but his hands were clutched into tight fists, the veins in his forearms as prominent as the whites of his knuckles.

A quip was on the tip of her tongue, ready to lash out at him, the pain from the previous evening still raw and heaving in her aching heart. But ... something in his posture, in his expression, had her pausing, assessing, watching. Something about him was off, even more so than usual. It was as if he struggled with an invisible enemy, an internal war being waged inside his mind. Flashes of a battle sparked in his eyes, and his hair was messier and more tousled than usual.

It was so far from the emptiness he'd worn since that night in the courtyard. He was ... changed. Mariah had endured enough to not feel hopeful, but she couldn't help the prickles of curiosity against her skin.

After all, she'd resolved to make love her retribution.

"Is there something I can help you with?" Her voice was cold, dead, empty. Much like how she felt.

He jolted at her words as if surprised she was awake. His arms and shoulders tensed tighter, his head dipping to stare at his feet for just a moment before he lifted his eyes, boring into hers with bizarre curiosity.

Never in a thousand years could Mariah have guessed the next words that would leave his lips.

"Your eyes ... they are very strange."

Mariah stilled before pushing herself up into a sitting position. She swung her legs around so her feet were planted firmly on the cold door, letting the familiar chill ground her and offer comfort.

"My ... eyes?" she repeated, words falling flat, but the question laced with confusion.

His gaze intensified, morphing into a burning violet-blue flame. "Yes. They look green, but there's brown and gold and blue and gray there, too. All the colors of the forest."

Her confusion warped brighter, sliding around her lungs and wrapping around her heart.

"It's too dark in here for you to see my eyes." She wasn't in the mood for these games, for whatever he was trying to drag out of her. She'd been hurt enough. No more.

He didn't answer despite her harsh tone. Just stared, expression confused and vacant, like a lost child who was far from home and didn't know his way back.

She couldn't let herself fall victim to that again, though.

"Is that all?" So cold. The temperature of the floors and the walls had become a part of her.

Another pause, another lapse without a response, as he watched her.

"What color are *my* eyes?" His question was even softer than the first, voice barely more than a hoarse whisper.

Mariah blinked. And blinked again. Her shock was eating at her. Strange feelings she hadn't felt in so long burned at the back of her throat. She swallowed some of them down, pushing them past the lump forming in her chest before she played along. She met his stare, the rawness in his expression palpable and broken.

"Do you know what tanzanite is?"

His face twisted with slight confusion, as if searching his memories. Then he relaxed and nodded. "A stone. From the mountains. Bright blue with a touch of violet."

Mariah nodded. "That's what color your eyes are. Just like the stone from the mountains.

They stared at each other, the moment stretching past the point of comfort. It could have been minutes or hours that passed as they watched each other. He felt so different than he had the past weeks, so different than he'd felt before. It was as if he'd regressed in age, so it was no longer the thirty-one-year-old man she knew and had tragically fallen in love with but the boy he'd been decades ago. Before he'd been Marked with the symbol of her reign, before he'd left his family for Verith. Before his mother had died, leaving him feeling more alone than he ever had before.

Without warning, something snapped. The softness calcified back into icy stone. His eyes resumed their dark, wicked glint, stranger's eyes that reveled in her decrepit state. He roved that foreign glare over her body before pulling his lips back into a sneer.

"You are disgusting. Pathetic. A disgrace. Just thought you needed a reminder."

Mariah hardly heard his words as he spun on his heel and strode from her cell, the door slamming shut behind him. Her mind was caught in a maelstrom, thoughts spinning and swirling around each other as she relived their conversation, the strangeness of it. It all left her wondering.

Wondering if who he'd been just before he left, with his snide insults, was not the man she'd fallen in love with.

Wondering if maybe, just maybe, that man was still in there, just as trapped as she was. If his prison was one of flesh, while hers was of stone and steel.

CHAPTER 13

"Thank you, sir. We much appreciate the information." Delaynie dipped her head to the scowling man, a pleasant smile on her pink-hued lips.

The man grunted, shrugging his coat farther around his shoulders, before storming off down the quiet market district street.

It took everything in Ciana not to roll her eyes at the man's disappearing form. "Well, he was ..."

"An ass? I agree."

Ciana whipped her head to Delaynie, a look of mock outrage on her face. "Lady Albellane! How unbecoming. We are representatives of the palace court!"

Delaynie grinned. "And what were *you* about to say?"

Ciana shifted in her saddle. "That he was ... quite a disagreeable gentleman."

Delaynie snorted. Ciana sighed. "Fine. He was a prick. A foul-tempered, useless prick."

It was how most of the people they'd spoken to that day were. They'd tried to stop as many city residents they could on every street they'd turned down, searching for something, *anything* that might be helpful to them.

And each time, they were met with distrusting looks. Suspicious glares at the twin crescent moon sigil on their horses' saddle blankets. Short, single word responses when they felt sufficiently trapped by Delaynie's sweet yet terrifyingly insistent questioning.

All the while, as Ciana, Delaynie, Kiira, and Rylla ventured farther from the palace, the knot in Ciana's stomach grew. Her glances back over her shoulder grew more frequent, alternated with gazes toward the Bay of Nria.

At the battle she knew raged there.

"It's just as we told you this morning." Kiira sidled her gelding up beside Ciana's gray mare, Keely. "If it is rumors about the palace and the queen that we seek, then taking horses bearing palace tack will surely drive all gossip away. No one wants to speak ill about a monarch to members of her own court."

Ciana sighed again, glancing up and down the empty street. It had been busy when they'd arrived, but the second they started asking their questions, the doors had slammed shut, the windows boarded, and the alleys deserted. "I know you're right. I just ...." She twisted her hands around the leather reins. "I just didn't realize they would be this negative."

"They feel abandoned by their queen and her court," Rylla said from where she lingered behind them. "Many lost family and friends when the pirates stormed the docks. They won't forget easily."

"We are doing the best that we can," Delaynie snapped, ice blue eyes flashing. "You are new here, so perhaps you don't know the full truth of what has occurred in this city. We are all sacrificing things to keep this city afloat and its occupants safe and fed—"

"My sister meant no offense, Delaynie," Kiira murmured. "All we mean is that this approach of questioning people in the streets ... it won't get you the information you seek."

A small bead of anxiety formed in the pit of Ciana's stomach. She wasn't nervous about the two Kreah sisters—even though they were shifters, something she'd thought impossible only a day ago. She somehow trusted them. Mariah had, too, at her presentment ball. And if Mariah trusted them, then Ciana could find it in herself to do the same.

That morning, after Sebastian, Matheo, Trefor, and Quentin left for the latest skirmish on the Bay of Nria, Ciana and Delaynie had roused themselves quickly and met the Kreah sisters in the stables. They'd planned it all last night: tired of waiting in the palace for news to come to them, they would go and seek information of their own.

Rylla had led the charge. Ciana turned in her saddle and faced her, hazel eyes—now human, and not feline—sharp and alert, the dark gray of her clothing melding seamlessly with the rich, cool umber of her skin and the silver jewelry braided into her hair.

"Does it hurt?"

Rylla snapped that sharp stare to Ciana. "Does what hurt?"

Ciana tightened her hands around her reins. "Shifting. When you shift, does it hurt?"

Rylla smiled. "No, Ciana. It does not hurt. Maybe it did, at first. But now it feels as natural as breathing."

"Perhaps even more natural sometimes." Kirra grinned, sharing a look at her sister. The dark-eyed twin had revealed her second form to them all last night, as well: a great tawny cat with rings black as midnight dotting her fur. A leopard, Rylla had explained, while Rylla's own pitch-black feline was what they called a panther.

Of course, that had prompted Quentin to ask about the famed desert sphinx's of Kreah. To which Kiira had blanched and instructed Quentin to never go seeking a sphinx, lest he go in search of a most terrible fate.

Which had only made Quentin grin wickedly. Ciana had almost been able to see the plans of adventure forming in his mind.

"You know what needs to be done if you wish to find out any useful information." Kiira's accented voice tugged Ciana back to the empty city streets.

Ciana swallowed. "You promise you won't eat anyone?"

"As long as they don't strike first."

Kiira shot her sister a glare. "We told you," she said. "We may change forms, but we remain human, in all the ways that count."

Delaynie's pale blue eyes watched the Kreah sisters, her brow wrinkled.

"What do you think, Del?" Ciana asked.

Delaynie was silent for a moment, before turning to Ciana. "I don't like the idea of giant cats roaming the streets, but ... they're right. We're accomplishing nothing this way. If it means we might learn something useful, then perhaps we should try."

Kiira nodded, a short bob of her head. "I'm glad you both got to venture into the city, though," she said. "You needed to see what it was like down here. How the people are feeling. It is impossible to govern without knowing such things."

"Try telling that to Sebastian," Ciana mumbled under her breath.

She hadn't meant to say it, not really. But the thought slipped past her lips unimpeded, just loud enough for Kiira to lift her lips in a gentle smile.

"Don't fault the Armature too much," Kiira said. "He is good at what he does, but they are not rulers; they are guardians. And sometimes, a ruler must place herself in danger for the betterment of the realm."

"I'm not a ruler," Ciana said. That ball of anxiety was back and building, a weight on her chest constricting her lungs and hammering in her heart.

Was that what she was to become if they couldn't get Mariah back? A regent over a failing kingdom, waiting desperately for twenty-one years to pass so a new queen could rise? And if the magic failed before then, if they lost everything...

Ciana had thought the idea of grappling with the loss of her best friend, her queen, terrible enough. She couldn't stomach thinking about this sort of ruinous fate, too.

Kiira leaned out of her saddle, placing a hand on Ciana's arm. "Of course, you're not a ruler, Ciana. And gods willing, you never will have to be. But this city needs you now, and when she is back, your queen will need you, too." The Kreah woman removed her hand from Ciana and slid from her saddle. She handed the reins to Ciana, just as Rylla handed hers to Delaynie.

"Do not panic if we are not back tonight. Sometimes, the best information is only learned at night. Trust that if we learn something, you will be the first we tell."

Ciana and Delaynie nodded in unison, just as a flash of pale blue light filled the afternoon street.

On massive, silent paws, the two cats—one black, one spotted gold—melted off into the shadows of the city, vanishing from view.

"I don't think I'll ever get used to that." Delaynie ran a hand over her auburn hair, smoothing the sleek waves before fidgeting with a delicate necklace at her throat.

Me, neither. Ciana rolled her shoulders, forcing the tension in her gut to settle. She again glanced towards the Bay, and then back to the castle.

She'd been trying to avoid it all day, but ... gods, Sebastian would be furious with them for leaving.

But they had to try. To see for themselves. To do something more than just sit around the palace in their cashmere sweaters, waiting for a miracle.

Ciana gripped the reins of Kiira's horse before pressing her heels against Keely's flank. The gray mare started into a walk, slowly heading back the way they'd come. The steady clop of hooves behind her told her that Delaynie followed.

Neither girl spoke as they meandered back up the streets. Inquisitive and suspicious eyes from behind curtained windows pricked at Ciana's skin. Her hands grew clammy, and sweat beaded her brow as they wandered up the streets.

Exposed. Vulnerable. That was how she felt. They'd slipped out without a City Guard to accompany them—mostly to avoid alerting Sebastian—but now Ciana wished desperately for that feeling of safety a guard would have offered.

Feeling vulnerable reminded Ciana of how she used to feel in that terrible house, where her stepbrother used to play his games. And she hated it.

The brown cobblestones of the market district gave way to the gold sandstone of the mountain district. The buildings shifted from shops into residences, vendor shops replaced by taverns and inns.

One such inn caught Ciana's eye. She'd noticed it on their way down, and seeing the reminder now settled some of the turmoil in her gut, calming a bit of her racing heart.

She turned to Delaynie. "In the mood for a drink?"

Delaynie started before glancing past Ciana at the inn on the corner. A knowing look filled her expression as she read the sign, smiling softly as she nodded. "A drink sounds great."

So, the two girls deposited the four horses with a ruddy-faced stable hand and pushed through the solid birch doors of The Silver Moon.

THE TAVERN WAS WARM, a fire roaring in the great hearth, and was entirely empty.

Empty ... save for the silver-haired barkeep standing behind a polished and waxed mahogany bar, fastidiously wiping a glass with a cloth rag.

A bell jangled above them as the door closed, and the barkeep glanced up, surprise on her comely face.

"Sorry," Ciana stammered, twisting her hands. "I thought ... if you're closed, we can come back--"

"Nonsense!" The barkeep set her glass on the ledge behind her. "The hours before shift change are always slow, but I'm very much open. Please, come in."

Hanging their coats on the rack by the door, Ciana and Delaynie strode to the bar, perching themselves on two cushioned stools. Their host leaned against the bar, peering at them both with sharp gray eyes only a shade darker than her hair.

"What can I get you ladies? Perhaps some warm mulled wine to ward away the chill?"

"Do you have gin?" Ciana blurted. She loved mulled wine, but ... for some reason, she craved her favorite liquor. Wanted something that would burn the entire way down, like it was cleansing her from the inside out.

The barkeep nodded. "Certainly." She pulled a bottle from beneath the bar, uncorking it and emptying a finger of its clear contents into a glass. She glanced at Delaynie. "And for you?"

"Just wine, please. White, if you have it." Del folded her hands in her lap, looking entirely out of place in the dark, rustic tavern.

"Of course." The barkeep poured the wine, pushing it across the bar, before affixing that sharp-eyed stare back on them.

"Why don't you drink with us?" Ciana toyed with the rim of her glass. She didn't know why she asked it; only that the woman's stare was too bright, like she knew something Ciana did not, but wanted to.

The barkeep looked around her tavern. "Normally, I'd say no. But ... seeing as it is quite the slow day, I suppose I could." She turned, pushing a mug beneath a tap and pulling the lever. Rich amber ale filled the glass, a frosty white foam forming at the top. The barkeep returned to them, smacking her lips.

"I'd been craving an ale all day." She raised the glass to her mouth, taking a long sip. Setting it back on the bar, she extended her hand to Ciana.

"I don't drink with strangers, so ... the name's Beva. Owner of this establishment."

Ciana clasped Beva's offered hand. "I'm Ciana. And this is Delaynie."

She gestured to her friend, who watched behind glimmering blue eyes as she politely inclined her head.

"It is a pleasure to meet you, Ciana and Delaynie." Beva took another sip from her ale. "Now that we're no longer strangers, why don't you tell me what two ladies from the Queen Apparent's court are doing drinking at a tavern away from the palace?"

Ciana's mouth popped open, clammy hands slipping on her

glass of gin. Despite her own frantic surprise, Delaynie still held that practiced neutral expression, watching the barkeep with renewed interest.

Ciana raised her glass to her lips, hands shaking slightly. She sipped the gin, the burning liquor carving a path through her chest before landing in her gut. She coughed slightly, then cleared her throat.

"We aren't sure we understand what you mean, Beva." Play dumb. That's what she'd decided. Feigned ignorance.

Beva chuckled. "I saw those horses you rode up on. It's hard to miss palace insignia when they put it everywhere."

Ciana opened her mouth, searching for an excuse.

"You're right. We are Mariah's ladies."

Ciana's mouth snapped closed as she whipped her head to Delaynie, who took a delicate sip of her white wine.

Beva hmphed. "That's what I thought." Her gray eyes danced with warm humor between Ciana and Delaynie. "You are looking for something?"

"Information. We want to know what the city folk are talking about," Delaynie said evenly.

"Let me guess," Beva said, "the people you met today haven't exactly been forthcoming."

Ciana narrowed her eyes and shook her head. "We don't understand. We only wish to help."

"Certainly. I believe you do. But they don't know that." Beva sipped her ale. "They hardly know their new queen-to-be, and when they heard she'd absconded in the middle of the night, just before pirates attacked the city ... well, surely you can imagine their distrust."

"That isn't what happened!" Ciana blurted. Delaynie shot her a warning glare, and Ciana's cheeks flushed. She reached for her glass, downing a gulp, before wringing her hands in her lap.

Beva watched her shrewdly, taking another sip. "I know, child. Not a single piece of me believes that Mariah Salis willingly abandoned this city or her friends."

"You speak as if you know her," Delaynie murmured.

Beva smiled. "In a way, I suppose I do." Her gray eyes took on a far-away look. "I met her once, before the Choosing. But it's her parents who I know the best. Wex and Lisabel Salis met in this very bar, when we were all young and terribly naïve."

The barkeep shook her head. "All that is a story from another lifetime. But I know Wex Salis's daughter would never willingly abandon her post or those she cares about."

Ciana was slack-jawed. What were the odds that this woman, the owner of a small, quiet tavern off the main city streets, knew Mariah's parents? "You ... knew ... what?"

Delaynie rested a hand on Ciana's arm. "We're thankful for your faith in our queen. And perhaps a bit jealous that you know a piece about her life that we don't. Yet." She smiled at the barkeep, who smiled back.

"You know." Beva drained the rest of her ale and turning to the tap. "If information is what you two seek ... I may know a thing or two." The tap groaned as amber liquid poured from the silver spout. "After all, there's no one people like to complain to more than a bartender."

Ciana, finally able to unclench her hands, reached for her gin, taking a quick sip. "Please. We'll take anything at this point."

"Well ..." Beva leaned against the bar. "There was a particularly interesting rumor going around the day after our dear Queen Apparent vanished. Some people said they spotted a group of seven figures riding away from the city, all lead by a handsome dark-haired man with blue eyes."

Ciana and Delaynie both froze. They shared a glance, and the pain and fear racing through Ciana was reflected in her friend's expression.

"I take it," Beva said, "that this means something to you."

Ciana released her breath, pushing it between her teeth. "Sebastian is going to be *so* pissed." She took another sip of her gin. She was pissed, too, of course. But she still clung to the hope that there was more to this than it appeared.

Mariah had just found love and was so happy. Ciana had to believe that meant something, for her best friend's sake.

Beva eyed them with confused interest. "You know, this rumor has been circling for weeks now. You would have learned it much sooner if this wasn't the first time you were venturing past the palace gates."

"Trust us, if we'd had our way, we would've been down here weeks ago."

"This sounds like a story." Beva grinned. "Come, complain to your bartender. This is what I live for, remember?"

Ciana's shoulders sagged. "Okay. Fine. We weren't allowed to leave the palace; we're still not, but today, we decided enough was enough and snuck out."

Beva nodded knowingly. "Men forget that us women can take care of ourselves. Especially"— her gray eyes glinted—"when they love us."

Heat rushed to Ciana's face and roared in her ears.

This was ridiculous. Sebastian was a friend. A friend who was the first man she'd ever felt truly safe with, and who made her laugh even when his protectiveness infuriated her ...

"Sebastian does not love me. He loves his queen. I'm simply the queen's best friend." Ciana washed down her mumbled words with the burn of gin.

Delaynie and Beva shared a grin. "Bring him here one day, when the chaos has settled. Let me be the judge for what he feels."

"C'mon, Cee." Delaynie bumped her shoulder into Ciana's. "I know you're pissed at him now, but please. We all see those dreamy glances the two of you share—"

"I don't think you want to talk about dreamy glances, Del. How long have you been secretly pining after a certain redhead?" This was now war. Ciana was determined to pull out all the tricks.

Delaynie flushed a deep, rich red, nearly the color of her hair. "I don't know what you're talking about," she mumbled into her wine glass and then drained the rest of its contents.

Ciana did the same, a smile stretching across her face, feeling something blossom in her chest that she hadn't dared feel in weeks.

Hope.

CHAPTER 14

In the darkness, Mariah had no way of knowing what day it was, but she estimated at least three days had passed since Andrian's strange visit.

And she hadn't been fed once.

After what she'd believed to be the first day, her stomach had settled into its familiar pangs, the discomfort like an old friend. The few sips of tepid water she'd been given calmed her throat but sat heavy in the emptiness of her gut.

By the second day, Mariah was feeling weaker. Exhausted. She grew light-headed, and her thoughts floated idly through her mind. She couldn't sleep; her stomach shriveled into a tight ball that panged angrily against the hollow walls of her abdomen.

The third day, she thought she might be on the verge of madness. The water had stopped, and her thirst added to her hunger. Everything was shrinking, shriveling, drying from the inside out. Her eyelids were heavy, her tongue was thick, and every bone and muscle in her body hurt.

Mariah had always thought starvation would feel like a wasting sickness. But really, it was consuming her, devouring her until she feared there would be nothing left.

She was so lost to her hunger and thirst that she didn't notice the servant arrive. Not until Ellis's soft snicker broke the monotonous silence. The guard smiled cruelly at her as the servant shuffled forward, bearing a tray, a glass of water, and a pitcher of wine.

When the scent hit her, all humanity left her.

The aroma was rich, warm, and savory as it wrapped around her, running devilish claws through her mind and down the empty walls of her stomach. Instinct consumed her: a drive for food, for water, for *anything* to abate the ravenous pain wracking her famished body. She lurched forward, off her cot, a feral growl rumbling low from the back of her throat.

She'd always been a bit of a caged, starved beast.

Now it was just far more literal.

Ellis unlocked her cell door with a sneer, waving the servant in. She bent down, placing the tray on the floor, and hastily retreated.

The moment the door closed, Mariah launched herself at the tray of food, nearly knocking the liquids over in her desperate haste.

"Pathetic," Ellis muttered through the bars of her cell, then followed the servant and stalked a few paces down the hall. Mariah paid them no heed.

The meal was delectable. Roast mutton, mashed potatoes, a mound of vegetables sauteed in a sauce that was both salty and sweet. The water washed down her shoveling bites, and the wine burned her throat with welcomed pain.

"There are no gifts here. Do not fall for this. Stay the course, stay strong."

Somewhere, in the part of her mind that had not yet succumbed to pure instinct, a goddess whispered to her.

But Mariah ignored the voice, in no mood to listen. Not when her stomach clenched around something other than itself, when her palette tasted of herbs and spices and her nose was filled with the scent of cooked lamb.

The plate was empty within minutes. Mariah had to force herself from licking the last of the sauces and scraps from the porcelain. The water was now empty, and the wine slowly seeped into her veins with molten contentedness. She sat back, reveling in the bloat to her stomach, resting a hand on her chest as she breathed deeply.

As she sat and breathed … the molten flow of her blood thickened into sludge.

Into something far more noxious.

Mariah's eyes flew open just as her conscious mind processed the warning that had flitted through her moments ago.

There were no gifts here.

The binds wrapped around her like a sudden vise. Her limbs fell away from her control, her mind locked into a steel trap as surely as her magic was by the black and gold cuffs around her wrists. Realization spawned through her, rash and wild and angry, as the paralysis settled into her bones.

She'd been drugged.

Her mind was very much awake, but everything else was sealed away. Terror gripped her in its clutches as footsteps and voices echoed in the hall.

"She was starving. I'm sure she's eaten it all by now. Shawth said it wouldn't take more than a few minutes for it to take effect."

The guards, Ellis and Konnor, appeared in the dim hallway, Konnor carrying his usual *allume* lamp. Ellis unlocked the door, standing in the frame. "Stand."

The command tore through Mariah. Her mind screamed and kicked and fought and scratched, but it was no use. Her body was no longer hers to control. She felt her legs unfold, her arms pushing her up. Once she was standing, she turned to face her captors, hoping and praying to the goddesses who'd tried to stop this from happening that those men would see the rage boiling inside her irises, like a forest set ablaze.

The idle amusement on Ellis's face told her that her prayers were ignored. Just as she'd ignored the warning.

She couldn't say she blamed Zadione and her sister. They'd tried to help, and she ignored them. As she tended to do.

Ellis turned and snapped his fingers. Two servant girls, eyes wide and set into youthful faces no more than sixteen years old, melted out from the shadows.

"Take her upstairs, to where we showed you. Ensure she's bathed and dressed. The lords expect her at dinner tonight." Ellis faced Mariah. "Go with them and do whatever they tell you."

Mariah obeyed, screaming in her mind the entire time, but she knew her face was slack and her eyes were empty.

———

THE GIRLS who bathed and dressed her were gentle, and Mariah couldn't deny it was nice to feel clean for the first time in weeks. Her hair was washed, skin scrubbed and shaved, her face brightened with powder, and her eyes lined with kohl.

Any feelings of thankfulness dissipated when she caught her first glimpse of what they planned to clothe her in.

Mariah had worn plenty of what others might deem to be scandalous articles of clothing in her life. She'd even worn no more than lingerie to her own Winter Solstice, her body on display for hundreds to see.

But that had always been on her *own* terms, and she'd worn those clothes as a tribute to her power. This ... this was a mockery. A clear attempt to devalue her, debase her, to ensure she felt as worthless as they wanted her to believe she was.

One of the servant girls picked up the scrap of fabric, a flimsy, see-through thing layered with tulle and lined with feathers and lace. "Step forward, please," she said meekly, keeping her eyes downcast.

With the drugs pumping through her, Mariah had no choice but to obey. The two girls slid the dress up her body, turning her to face the mirror in the corner.

When she saw her reflection, her mind crumpled. Collapsed inward like a dying star. With just a glance, she knew what this night had in store for her.

Mariah had lost so much weight in the passing weeks, but she knew she was still beautiful; just not in the way she'd always loved. Gone were her curves, the muscles that filled out her shoulders and arms and legs. Instead, she was all sharp angles, pale skin, and straight lines.

The barely there garment she wore just brushed the skin of her upper thighs, and with a pang in her chest she knew that mere weeks ago, she wouldn't have fit in such a scrap of material. She wore no underwear, too aware of how bare she was under the light pink lace and tulle.

Everything about her appearance was an attack on who she was, on the power she'd tried to reclaim for women across the kingdom.

Tonight, dressed this way, she would belong to the men around her.

She no longer belonged to herself.

Mariah retreated further into the dark recesses of her mind as Ellis reappeared in the chamber doorway, perusing her form as a look that made Mariah shrink flickered across his face.

"You girls are dismissed. Mariah—you come with me."

Mariah begged and pleaded for her feet to stay rooted to the ground, for the drugs pulsing through her system to dissipate and grant her back her autonomy.

Nothing worked. She turned, leaving the image of the empty, dark-haired doll clothed in blush-pink fabric in the mirror as she stepped after the guard and into the hall.

Her feet were bare, and she felt every touch of the cold stone on her soles. Mariah trailed behind Ellis, her body rigid and tight and not hers. The guard stopped, stepping to the side to watch as she continued padding forward.

Of course, she didn't stop. No more than an automation, a statue given life.

He didn't touch her until she'd drawn up beside him.

"Stop," he commanded, his voice carrying a tinge of something that made her want to whimper if she could.

She halted.

Ellis circled her like a shark that dwelled in the Mirrored Sea, a finger pressed against his lips, eyes too hungry.

"I've waited many, many weeks for them to make you fair game to us," he said, low and cruel. The finger against his lips reached out to her chest, pulling at the lace and tulle around her cleavage. "A bit thin for my taste, but …" His hand slid around her body, grasping her ass, pulling her flush against him. He smelled of sweat and alcohol and hatred, and the bulge of his erection had her stomach roiling with the beginnings of a gag.

She couldn't react. Her face was frozen as her body revolted against the touch, the beast within clawing for a way out.

But that was the problem with beasts in chains. Those chains often held, and the beast stayed in its cage.

"I suppose I'll look past it for a chance at some Goddess-blessed pussy." His voice was as thick as blood in her hair.

"Sir Ellis!" a shrill, feminine voice echoed down the hallway. The guard released Mariah with a frustrated growl, stepping back and whirling to meet the newcomer.

"Lady Anniliese. How can I help you?"

If Mariah could feel anything other than lifelessness and disgust, she would've been swept away by burning rage at the sight of the pretty, dark-haired girl rounding the corner, clothed in an elegant gown of cobalt blue.

But that rage was doused when Anniliese halted in the hallway, visceral shock, surprise, and horror flowing across her features. A flush crept into her cheeks as she took in Mariah's starved frame, the limp drapery of her hair, the obnoxious doll-pink dress.

"What …" Anniliese swallowed, looking back at Ellis. "What are you doing with our … guest?"

"That does not concern you, Lady Anniliese," Ellis said gruffly. "Is there something I can help you with?"

Anniliese did not seem satisfied with Ellis's response. Her brow twisted, gathering her skirts in her hands. "She is not supposed to leave her cell. Lord Shawth commanded it."

"Lord Shawth demanded that she join the other lords for their cocktail hour this evening. I suggest you stand aside, Lady Anniliese. This does not concern you."

Anniliese's honey-brown stare lingered on Mariah. Beneath the heavy weight of the drug, Mariah struggled—she fought for something to reach her eyes, for her lips to twitch, for her brows to contract. Something to show the other girl this was evil, to beg her to help. Anything.

She doubted Anniliese would do anything, even if she knew, but Mariah had to try. If for no other reason than to extend a plea between two women.

And for a moment, she thought it had worked. Anniliese opened her mouth, brow still twisted.

"Don't do something stupid, girl. Your father can only protect you for so long." Anniliese blanched, her blush leaking from her face, as Ellis grinned. "Now, excuse us. Lord Shawth doesn't like to be kept waiting." With a rough-handed grip, Ellis dragged Mariah forward.

Mariah latched onto the terrified pity in Anniliese's honey-brown eyes, if for no other reason than to remind her that at least one person in this castle hadn't yet lost their humanity.

Rounding a corner, Ellis released Mariah's arm. "Keep moving."

And she did.

They approached a familiar set of doors at the end of the hallway, and everything in Mariah screamed to fight back, to run away, to not cross that threshold.

It was useless, of course.

Ellis pushed open the doors, and a cacophony of drunkenness and boredom greeted Mariah.

A deadly combination for a woman without her power.

"Ah, there she is!" A familiar, slimy voice rose above the rest.

The room quieted, many faces and eyes swinging to her. To soak her in, to take everything she didn't want to give, to reduce her to nothing more than ashes and dust.

Mariah withdrew fully inside herself, hiding amongst the ruins of her soul and the scraps of her magic that she could just barely touch, just barely reach if she stretched her fingers past that black and gold wall. The silver and gold brushed against her, no more than a whisper, not enough to act but enough to lend the strength of the goddesses they'd once belonged to.

We are here. You are not alone. You can withstand this.

You will not break.

Mariah was not so sure, but she let herself sink into those thoughts.

Shawth rose from his seat, glass of wine nearly overflowing. His eyes held a dark merriment as they swept down her ridiculous clothing and the body it did nothing to hide.

"Our little whore queen, come to join us for drinks." Chuckles echoed off the walls. Shawth sipped his wine, the red staining his lips like blood. "And finally dressed appropriately. Maybe she'll be able to offer a *real* service to her kingdom tonight."

Somewhere, deep inside the hiding place in her soul, Mariah felt a small swell of nauseousness. She clenched tighter to the wall where her magic was held captive, dropping further into numbing darkness.

Shawth set his wine glass down on the table before stepping out from his chair.

"Come here," he said, voice low.

Mariah's feet moved. One slow, barefoot step after the other. She walked around the table of lords, their hands grazing her exposed skin just as their eyes ripped her apart. They were a pack of wolves, and she was nothing more than a fawn, wounded and helpless as they barked and yipped and bit. Soon, she stood before Shawth, his face wearing that same hungry look she'd quickly come to know as something to be feared.

She wasn't familiar with fear. At least, she hadn't been before this place, when a family who meant more to her than her own happiness had sheltered and nurtured her.

Now, it was an old companion, holding her close against the true evilness of her world.

Shawth reached out his hand. Touched her cheek, ran it down her neck. Cupped her breast, the meaty flesh of his palm stinging.

"You are much better like this," he muttered, still grinning. "So ... compliant." He glanced at the watching lords. "Now, why don't you be a good girl for us all and *kneel*." His command was louder, echoing around the hall.

As Mariah dropped to the floor, the captive part of her sobbed.

She knew this command was intentional. That, somehow, they knew Andrian had said words so very similar not long ago in the shadowy stacks of the palace library. Perhaps he'd been forced to share those details with them himself.

His image, lost and broken and confused as he stood in her cell's doorway, flashed through her mind.

She didn't know what to believe when it came to him. Confusion and warring instincts joined her fear, settling beside her in the hollow crevices of her soul.

"Well done, Lord Shawth!" boomed a boisterous voice. A voice that thought it commanded attention, believed itself powerful, but was just empty and full of malicious, useless feelings of inferiority.

The voice of the Lord of Andburgh, the Crossroad City. Mariah's home before a letter from the queen started her life anew.

Her mind fled to her family, still residing in Andburgh. What could Donnet's presence here mean for them?

Two pairs of boots filled her vision. Heavy hands gripped her hair.

"Stand up, pretty girl."

She stood. Lord Donnet stared at her with too much possession.

"How did you do it, Lord Shawth? Her compliance is truly remarkable."

Shawth grinned. "We got her starving, then laced some *uxosil* in her food. I always knew she was more animal than woman; she didn't even think twice about it. Who knew it would be so easy to fell a *queen?*" More laughter echoed as he sneered the word.

"I'd heard rumors about the drug but had no idea it would be so potent." Shawth's grin faltered slightly, brow twisting in contemplation. "Unfortunately, I think it will only work to break her spirit. We can't force her to abdicate like this; she must do that willingly. That queen magic is stubborn and too tightly bound to her—only she can coax it out. But I imagine we can try to spark a ... change of heart from her, don't you think?"

Donnet's expression turned curious. "So she is conscious?"

Shawth nodded. "Yes. Fully conscious and aware of us, but unable to move her body on her own or speak for herself. It will not last long, but ..." Those hands reached back out. Drew her too close to him. Pressed his body against hers. "For now, it's absolutely perfect."

He released her, pushing her toward the table of lords with a slap to her ass. The material of her short dress fluttered, and she knew too much skin flashed.

"Now go. Be a good girl and show our lords a good night."

Her world blurred.

Hands were on her skin. Lips were on her neck. Hot, putrid breath touched her mouth and nose. Her eyes were open, but she did not see any of it; she stayed curled and hidden and safe against her wall, with her magic, letting her body get swept away. Bodies could be healed and cleaned, but her soul, her spirit ... that would always belong to her, and she wouldn't let them have it.

"I could've had her before, back in Andburgh, you know," Donnet's loud voice boasted, filtering through her haze. "I knew which taverns she frequented. But I just didn't think it appropriate to lower myself like that, you know?"

"And yet you lower yourself now?" The answering voice was softer, deadlier, and achingly familiar.

Donnet snorted. "Hardly. Plenty fine to touch, but I think all of us agree that fucking a girl like that will foul you forever."

More laughter. But not from that voice.

"Well, I suppose I'm just as dirty as her."

Mariah was aware of the pause in the conversation. How the hands on her thighs stopped circling, how the fingers in her hair withdrew. Donnet floundered.

"You know that's not what I meant, my boy—"

"We know, Lord Donnet." Lord Laurent's cool voice echoed

around the room. "But perhaps you and my son both make a good point." Laurent leveled his golden stare on Mariah.

"Go to my son," he commanded.

Mariah rose, turned to the man with onyx hair and gemstone blue eyes, and walked. His gaze tracked her, and she could sense something off about him. That same unsettledness that was in him the other day, when he'd visited her in the cell.

Something familiar and awake flickered in his cobalt irises.

When she stood before him, he shifted in his seat, opening his thighs.

"Sit," Andrian said without breaking her stare.

Mariah wasn't sure at that moment if it was the drugs, or just him, that compelled her to obey. To settle her legs on either side of his, the pose so familiar and so painful she could hardly breathe.

The second their skin touched, however, something happened. That familiar charge, that lightning of power that had graced them only a few times before when they'd taken a step that would alter their lives. It whipped and curled around her, lancing across her skin and into the coiled ball where she'd curled herself. She knew he felt it, too: could feel his body go rigid, could see his pupils widen and dilate. Everything about him shifted, no longer hidden by a layer of confusion and shadow. He looked awake and alert, his eyes darting across her face, her body, and the room.

"Well, go on then, Andrian." Shawth's voice spliced the magnetic energy between them in two. "Looks like you've got our little guest all to yourself tonight." The evil insinuation dripped off Shawth's tongue like knives and venom.

Andrian's eyes hardened, but he didn't look away from Mariah's face. Instead, he pulled her closer before he leaned forward and stood, her legs wrapped around his torso.

Mariah shivered, deep inside, at how familiar it all was. A distortion of what was once a moment they'd shared when they'd needed each other the most.

"I don't fuck in public. I'll take my prize in private if you don't mind." He dipped his head to Shawth and his father. "My Lords."

With a tightening in his jaw, he strode toward the exit of the dining hall, Mariah still pressed tightly against his chest. The calls and whistles from lords who'd indulged in too much wine and unearned power chased them away.

Andrian's steps were steady and even at first. But the further they grew from the hall, the closer they drew to the downward stairs and the cells beyond, the more they faltered. Mariah still didn't have control of her body, but she tried to convey to him that he could put her down, that she could carry herself.

Nothing caught his attention.

Soon, they were outside her cell. He was pushing open the door and stepping inside. He deposited her on her cot made of stone, casting one last confused, broken glance at her, before walking back to the door of the cell.

Mariah only watched him, bewilderment and something else stirring in her belly.

Just before he walked from the cell, Andrian paused. Reached into a pocket. Withdrew a sharp, wicked looking paring knife clearly meant for slicing thick roasts of meat.

He tossed the knife at Mariah's feet before pushing from the cell, locking the door, and disappearing down the hall.

Mariah stared after him for a moment before glancing down at the knife. The handle was gold, and the blade tempered steel. It was not meant for killing, but it was beautiful, nevertheless. She picked it up, her movements slow and jerking as she fought against the fading drugs still tearing through her system.

She tucked the blade under the mattress, wedging it between the cot and the wall, and was filled with foreign certainty.

Everything since the courtyard was a lie.

Her Andrian was still in there, just as trapped as she was.

And she had to get him out.

CHAPTER 15

Andrian was sixteen, eating in the mess hall where he and the rest of the Marked took their meals, when a letter arrived from Antoris.

In ten years, it was the first letter from his previous life he'd ever received.

The moment he saw the familiar scrawling script of his father, his blood ran cold. Shadows raced through his veins as he tore open the seal and flipped open the pieces of parchment.

The words written there shattered his entire world, clothing it in loathsome darkness.

Andrian,

I write with sad news. Your mother took a terrible fall in the kitchens. Unfortunately, she did not survive. May Priam guide her soul.

Cordially,

Lord Julian Laurent

So short. So emotionless. So cold.

Andrian was left feeling ... everything. His world narrowed, sharpened, focused on the only words that mattered.

Unfortunately, she did not survive.

His mother—that kind, gentle woman who'd taught him words in the tongue of her people, sharing with him a secret language that they held close, a secret between just them. The only person who'd made him feel less like an outcast, less like a stranger in that massive northern castle where his dark hair and violet-blue eyes set him apart more than made him feel like he was at home.

He knew her marriage to his father was one of convenience; the two had never shared any real bond. But to hear her passing described so dispassionately ...

Andrian remembered her shuddering sobs when he was Marked. When he'd packed up his belongings and set out for Verith. He'd always thought she simply grieved the loss of her eldest son, the boy who looked the most like her people carrying a piece of her soul with him.

But now, he wondered if she had simply voiced her fears at being left alone in that cold castle with a man whose fires could never melt the layer of ice encasing his soul.

"Andrian? Are you alright?"

He blinked, his attention focusing on Trefor's sea-green gaze. The boy wore a hesitant look upon his face, his expression open but worried.

Andrian didn't want that. Didn't want any of that.

There was one thing he needed. One thing that could distract him from the hatred and anger and loss swirling through him on a maelstrom of ice and shadow and blood.

He turned on his heel and shouldered his way from the mess hall, heading for the game park nestled behind the palace.

THE DEAD OAK *tree did not deserve his savagery, but he didn't care.*

He didn't deserve his mother's death.

Or ... perhaps he did.

But his mother certainly hadn't.

Andrian swung again. The sharp edge of his two-handed

broadsword burrowed deep in the bark, splintering the wood. With a low growl, he yanked it out and continued to swing.

The clearing was of his own design and was a haven he'd created. With the help of the other Marked, they'd dragged in logs to serve as dummies and targets and weapon racks of all kinds. They'd marked off a section of the grass for sparring and dug a pit, filling it with sand for hand-to-hand training. It was quiet, more secluded than the training rings at the barracks, and the perfect place for boys to go when they were learning how to become men.

It was also the perfect place for a boy who'd just lost the only source of love and affection he'd ever known.

He swung again. The tree shuddered, dropping a few more dull brown leaves. Ropes of shadows curled around his arms and legs, whipping and snapping in the air. A reflection of the fracturing, angry soul within.

His mother.

Not his mother.

Another swing of his sword.

He knew there were steps behind him. Knew that two others had joined him in that clearing. Someone cleared their throat.

"Andrian?"

Andrian's sword embedded once again in the soft flesh of the tree. This time, he let it stay as his chest heaved, lungs desperate for air.

The breeze that brushed his face and the chill it brought, whispering softly against the moistness on his cheeks, shocked him.

He was crying. He couldn't remember the last time he'd cried. The revelation made something inside him go numb, shuttering closed. His left his sword buried in the tree trunk, like a steel mockery of a limb. He wiped his face and turned.

Sebastian and Quentin stood warily at the edge of the clearing, watching with too many questions in their eyes. They were, perhaps, his closest friends—if he had such things. Sebastian was a natural leader, a strong supporter of everyone around him. It was impossible to not eventually call him a friend.

Quentin mostly just made for a fun drinking companion.

Andrian met their stares. If they had the gall to ask him what was *wrong ... he would tell them. But he wasn't one for idle chit-chat and did not volunteer information without first being asked.*

At least, not unless he had a very, very good reason.

Sebastian cleared his throat again. "Andrian," he repeated. "Is ... is everything okay?"

Andrian's jaw clenched. He shoved his hand into his pocket, balling up the piece of parchment. He withdrew his hand and tossed it to the other boys with all the carelessness one might throw a piece of trash.

Quentin caught the note, flattening it out. Sebastian leaned over his shoulder and read it with him.

Andrian watched them with icy numbness. Slowly, they lifted their eyes back to his, shock and horror and despair written on their faces.

They were always so much better at wearing their emotions than he was. Everyone was.

"I think he did it." Andrian spoke with all the cold darkness of the shadows that ran through his blood, the last gift of his mother he had left.

They both blinked in surprise. "Who did what?" Quentin's voice was unusually subdued but curious.

"My father. I think he did it." Andrian turned away to stare up at the peaks of the Attlehons towering above the valley of the game park. "He always despised her for sullying his bloodline. For creating me. Something more Leuxrithian than Onitan."

"Andrian," Sebastian said, insistent. Andrian glanced back. "You are just as much Onitan as the rest of us. And ... we are here for you." Sebastian looked at Quentin, who nodded. "All of us."

Andrian cocked his head.

"Thank you." But he didn't mean it. He couldn't mean anything anymore, not when he felt so empty inside. Hollow and worn.

CHAPTER 16

Mariah wasn't stupid enough to pull the slender, sharp paring knife out from between the mattress and the stone wall of her cell.

But her mind spun around it, nevertheless.

It started the moment her skin had touched Andrian's in the dining hall. At the bolt of energy that shot between them.

She swore she saw something flicker in his eyes, something haunted and familiar and real. It had wavered, in and out, as he'd spoken to the lords, excused them from the table, walked her back to her cell.

There was a moment of utter clarity, when the haze had cleared from his eyes, leaving only the gleaming richness of tanzanite, as he'd tossed the knife at her feet.

Even with all her thinking, she couldn't figure out *why*. Why this was what he'd chosen as his singular act of defiance before he'd slipped back away into his prison of flesh and shadow.

Mariah was still lost in those thoughts when, once again, steps sounded from down the dark, lonely hall leading to her cell. She sat up straighter, leaning her rigid back against the cold stone, focusing on the soft thump of approaching footfalls.

She noted they were light, delicate feet garbed in slippers

instead of boots. They weren't the footfalls of a man. They were the steps of a woman, dressed in finery, who had no idea how to move without alerting others of her approach.

The faint gold glow of *allume* appeared around the corner, and Mariah schooled her expression into neutrality as Anniliese Hareth strode from the darkness, dark hair pinned into a mass atop her head, her creamy neck bared and framed by a gown of rich fuchsia.

All the money in the world, and this girl chose to dress in fucking flower pink.

The sight of Anniliese roused something dark in Mariah's blood, pulling out her anger despite her current defeat. Her jaw clenched, hands tightening around her threadbare blanket. She forced glittering knives into her stare.

Just like the knife now hidden below her bed.

But when the other girl came to a halt outside the heavy iron door of Mariah's cell, peering through the bars, her rage faltered. Still hot, still burning, but tempered. Doused with a mist of cool water.

Despite her polished appearance, Anniliese's honey-brown eyes were rimmed in red. As she stared at Mariah, who still wore the ugly, demeaning monstrosity from the night before, something in her expression dimmed.

"Why are you still putting yourself through this?" Anniliese's voice was soft and muted.

Mariah kept her expression still, even as confusion raced through her. "Putting myself through what?"

Anniliese gathered her skirts in her hand, setting down the *allume* lamp. She rose again, still holding Mariah's gaze.

"All ... this." She gestured with a pale hand at the cell, the mattress, the clothing on Mariah's back. "You could put an end to it all, so easily."

"Oh? I could?" A note of incredulity crept into Mariah's voice.

Anniliese nodded. "Yes. My father told me that if you give up, if you agree to abdicate your power, all this will end. They will let you leave here with your life and dignity intact."

Mariah couldn't stop the dull, lifeless snort that escaped her lips. "You can't honestly be that stupid."

Anniliese stiffened. "I trust my father. The other lords can be … difficult, but my father—"

"Your father had his hands up my skirts last night, pawing at me like an animal, just like the rest of them. He treats you well, certainly, but you're his daughter. It's how a man treats the other women in his life, the ones who have less value to him, that show his true nature."

Anniliese's mouth gaped open and closed, gasping like a fish. Mariah would've laughed.

Would have. If she'd been anywhere else, not trapped and defiled in a rotting cell below the earth.

To her shock, the other girl's cheeks flushed pink. She hung her head, a few curls falling around her face.

"I'm sorry," she whispered. "I didn't—I didn't know. What they were going to do to you. I wanted to stop it, but—" Anniliese breathed a shaky inhale, still hiding her eyes.

Mariah watched her, curiosity settling like stones. "You're afraid of them." It was just a guess, but Mariah didn't ask it as a question. There was something about the other girl that now felt so empty, so defeated.

Like Anniliese, too, was trapped in a prison. One that wrapped velvet and tulle around her neck and wrists, corseted bodices worn like chains.

Anniliese sniffed, wiping a quick finger beneath her eyes, before lifting her head.

"Why would I be afraid of them," she said evenly. "They are my family, and they care for me. They will always protect me."

"If you truly believed that, you would've stopped them last night."

Anniliese raised her chin higher. "I said I didn't know what they would do and that I was sorry. I didn't say I had any wish to help you or protect you."

Mariah smiled at her, somewhat sadly. "Then it's quite a good thing I don't need your help or protection."

Anniliese blinked, before shaking her head. "Why do you do this? Why are you letting them break you?" Her fingers flew to her thin neck, toying with a delicate necklace lying there.

"Why are you suddenly so concerned about them breaking me, Anniliese?" Mariah narrowed her eyes. "You certainly didn't have any reservations before about tormenting me."

Anniliese released a frustrated groan. "That … that wasn't my *choice*. They made me. They told me the faster you broke, the sooner I could become queen. I did what they asked, and I hated every minute of it."

The air around Mariah stilled. Water dripped down the damp stone walls, collecting in frozen pools at the back of her cell. She shifted, her tangled hair brushing across her too-thin arms.

"What are you talking about?" she asked, no more than a deadly-quiet whisper.

Anniliese's eyes widened, face leeching of color. "I—nothing. I was … nothing. I was talking to myself."

The silence between the two women stretched into the sky somewhere high above, where the moons cast their longing rays upon the earth and the stars cried out for something to hope for.

"I want you to promise me something, Anniliese Hareth." Mariah's voice was still quiet, but there was strength behind her words. Strength she hadn't felt in many long, cold weeks.

Anniliese regarded her cautiously. "I will not free you."

"That's not what I want from you." Mariah shifted forward on her cot, placing her feet flat on the stone.

"Stop playing for your father. For men who will never appreciate a woman's worth. Find it in yourself to start making your own choices. Do things not because they tell you to do them, but because it's what *you* want for yourself."

Something on Anniliese's face cracked just a little bit further. A hint of the tortured soul beneath shone through, bright and raw and desperate for freedom.

Before it was shuddered away behind the mask of a Royal princess. She lifted her chin, staring down the bridge of her nose.

"Tell me what Qhohena's magic feels like."

Mariah cocked her head. Part of her wanted to push back against this spoiled puppet, but she couldn't shake that brief, honest look she'd pulled from Anniliese. Something tugged Mariah toward a different response. Her own extension of honesty, a step towards the change some squashed part of her still longed for. She inhaled once, breathing in the cold air, letting it settle her before she opened her mouth to speak.

"It feels—felt"—she winced, the correction burning her throat—"like threads. Woven into my soul. A part of me."

Anniliese nodded, some of that superiority falling away. "And what does it do?"

Mariah smiled sadly. She rubbed idly at the slender black and gold cuffs on her wrists. "I think I had only barely learned the true extent of it. So, I don't think I can offer you a proper answer." She met Anniliese's honey stare, finding a reflection staring back at her.

Another broken soul, caged and thirsty for freedom. This girl had been used just as much as Mariah.

She just didn't know it.

Anniliese watched her for a few more moments before bending down and picking up her *allume* lamp. "You're never going to abdicate, are you?"

Mariah chuckled, shaking her head. "Don't you understand? I can't."

Anniliese only watched her.

Mariah sighed. "The lords think themselves all-knowing, but they're ignorant fools. A queen has no power over her own abdication, no more than she has power over her Choosing."

Anniliese's face hardened, mask slipping back into place until it settled into a scowl. "You're wrong. High Priestess Ksee has told us it's possible. She says everything you say is a lie."

"Is it?" Mariah snorted. "Yes, trust Ksee. I don't think she's held communion with her goddess in over a decade."

Anniliese huffed. "You're a disrespectful animal."

"A title I bear proudly." Mariah flashed a grin. "Anything else I can do for you, Anniliese?"

The girl sniffed. "I have tried to help you. I felt sorry for you, and I tried. But it seems you'd prefer to remain here, in what is as good as Enfara."

"At least it's quiet."

Anniliese let out a final, frustrated humph before turning on her slippered feet and striding away down the hall, the light bobbing away with her steps.

The second the light vanished, Mariah dove for the space between her mattress and the wall. Her fingers slid across cool metal, grasping gently to avoid the sharp edge of the blade.

Several thoughts struck her at once as she withdrew the paring knife.

First, she felt the spark of life reignite in her belly. Glimpsing who Anniliese truly was, the girl trapped beneath the pretty shell, had awoken the raw desperation that burned through Mariah. She had a chance to change everything—her life, the life of *everyone*—if she were to be freed.

Second, talking about her magic had reminded her of what lived in her soul. There was a reason these lords hadn't wanted her to ascend, why they'd taken her before the rite of coronation could be completed. There was a reason Lord Laurent had told his son that a bond with her would result in a forfeit to her life.

Perhaps it was just a threat, but it had worked: if Andrian hadn't been so afraid, if there hadn't been such a delay, then maybe, right now, she wouldn't be here.

Third, she realized exactly what she had to do if she ever wanted to escape this place.

Her fingers clenched tighter around the handle, and for the first time in weeks, Mariah drifted to sleep with a smile on her face.

CHAPTER 17

The version of Andrian who strode down the dungeon hallway was the cruel stranger, the coldness behind his eyes nothing like the ice Mariah had learned how to melt.

"Of course, you're still dressed like a little whore. How fitting." His lips lifted from his teeth in a sneer.

Mariah held his stare. "Have I had much of a choice? I don't see many other options for me down here."

"You could simply wear nothing. You're basically there now."

She tilted her head, assessing him. Andrian—or whatever beast wore Andrian's skin—leaned against the wall across from her cell, arms crossed and posture ambivalent. But she couldn't help noticing that despite this not being *her* Andrian, despite the mask being one she didn't recognize, it seemed there was no reason for his visit other than to taunt her. It was almost like ... like he couldn't stay away, like he was drawn to her for reasons the beast in his skin did not understand.

It made Mariah's chest flutter with a fool's hope. A hope born from the few flickering looks in his eyes, a hope fueled by the knife tucked beneath her mattress. A hope that now grew with the realization that perhaps it wasn't the beast within that drew him down into the depths of the dungeons of Khento.

Perhaps, that was just … *him*. The pull between them was as difficult to ignore as it was when they'd both been adamant on fighting it.

That's when her resolve settled, when her decision was reached.

She shifted forward on the cot, hiding the movement of her hand behind her body. She touched the cool handle of the paring knife as she tilted her head and morphed her expression, features relaxing into a mask she'd donned many times when she needed a man to obey her without him knowing.

Even if a man didn't react well to power … they always responded to sex.

"Is that a suggestion, or an order?" she purred, voice low as she crossed her legs, doing what she knew best despite the lost muscle and pallid skin.

Andrian's eyes flashed to her bare legs, and when they returned to hers, they were blazing.

He pushed off the wall and took the two steps to the bars of her cell. His expression was hungry, and it curled hatred in her gut for whatever it was inside him that dared to look at her like that.

But Mariah choked down on those feelings. She had a goal. She would do whatever it took to accomplish it.

"Come here," he ordered, voice low and flat, but his eyes still burned.

Mariah, with a slow movement meant to flash more skin and allow her to hide the knife in her hand behind her back, rose from the cot. She took the few short steps to the cell door, holding that careful beguiling mask. She stopped just shy of his reach, blinking up through her lashes.

"Is this close enough?"

He growled, low and impatient. Shoving a hand in his pocket, he withdrew a familiar ring of skeleton keys. He shoved one of them into the lock of the cell, pulling it open with enough force for it to clang against the cell beside hers.

Andrian stormed through the door and was on her.

She let him paw and grab and pull her to him, hands possessive and foreign. His face buried into her hair, inhaling deeply from the skin of her neck.

"You even *smell* like her," he whispered, low and dark and with a voice that raised the hair on Mariah's arms.

She swallowed the last of her pride and disgust and continued playing the part she'd unknowingly practiced for years.

Arching her back, she slid her free hand up his chest, halting just below his collarbone. She leaned forward, whispering into his ear on a breathless exhale that wasn't entirely forced.

"I can be whatever you want me to be."

The answering growl against her felt hardly human. She was clutched harder, pushed toward the back wall of her cell until her spine hit cool stone, pinning her knife between it and her back.

Which was fine. Easier to hide as she continued to work.

The beast inside Andrian licked and smelled and tasted her skin, and she let him. He was distracted by her, by whatever it was about her that set him on edge in the same way it did her. She used it to her advantage to undo the first button of his shirt.

Then the next. And the next.

Down the line of his chest, until the skin below was visible. Until she was able to push the black material off his left shoulder, revealing the Mark tattooed on his skin by the hand of a god, the maw of a dragon wrapped around itself roaring and vengeful.

Mariah surged forward against him, freeing the hand behind her back. She took a moment to steady herself, clutching the knife by her side, focusing on the ground beneath her feet and the air filling her lungs. She dropped her right hand from his chest, flipped the knife in her left, and sliced a shallow, clean cut across the skin of her right palm. She leaned forward again, her lips brushing the shell of Andrian's ear.

"If you're in there, Andrian ... I'm coming."

With the last of her strength, she shoved him back, just enough for her knife to arch up to his chest.

Fueled by desperation, her aim was true. The sharp paring knife sliced a thin cut right over the line bisecting the dragon-shaped Mark. Ruby blood welled to the surface, beading around the black ink.

Before he could move, she lifted her bleeding palm and slammed it against his chest.

Andrian tensed, his body going rigid. They were both frozen, breathing heavily as they were suspended in time, breaths stirring the strands of the other's hair. Mariah steeled herself, readying to descend into that ethereal region of light and darkness and magic that would bind their souls.

Until the seconds ticked by … and nothing happened.

Slowly—so, painstakingly slow—Andrian pulled back from her. Her hand was still pressed to his bleeding chest, their mingled blood running thin rivulets down his skin. With the gap between them widened, Mariah was able to glance at her hand, at her wrist. Her blood went cold as she realized her mistake.

The bond was missing the most important piece: her magic. Her eyes settled on the black and gold cuff encircling her wrist, searing the skin that was now covered in blood.

With defeat settling in her gut, she lifted her gaze from her shackles into his eyes.

They were so cold. So furious.

But not as cold and furious as she was expecting.

"You *bitch*," he spat, wrapping his hand around her wrist and pulling it from his chest. He shoved her back into the wall, his steps faltering as he stumbled away from her.

Mariah did not miss how his hands shook. How his face had drained of blood. He looked down at his chest, at the cut there and the stain of both their blood. His brow twisted, and he raised his attention back to her.

Mariah held herself utterly still, not even daring to breathe.

So many emotions flashed through his beautiful eyes. Confusion, shock, anger, horror, grief, rage. A cycling loop, a raging war in the ocean of violet blue.

He staggered back another step, lurching toward the open cell door. Bracing himself against it, he glared at her, chest still heaving.

"You ... you will fucking *pay* for that." His shaking hand pressed to his chest, smearing the red like war paint.

Mariah held her tongue, content to watch.

With another tremor, he stepped out of her cell. Fumbled for the keys in his pocket. Closed and locked the door before staggering down the hall, forgetting his *allume* lamp on the damp hallway floor.

Mariah stood there in the pale gold light, watching the shadows flicker around her. She eventually moved forward, reaching a hand through the bars of her cell to flip off the lamp. She sighed in relief as she was plunged back into darkness.

She perched herself atop the cold-hard edge of her cot. Opening her right palm, she stared at the thin, slowly clotting cut.

In her left palm, she still clutched the golden paring knife. It dripped with both hers and Andrian's blood.

Then, there was the foul black and gold stone ringing her wrists. She felt the block it had erected in her mind, made of the same material, an impassable barrier to her magic.

She needed that magic back. And to get that magic back, she needed those cuffs removed from her wrist.

A feeling she didn't dare acknowledge tugged at her gut as she wiped and cleaned her palm as best she could. As she wiped the polished edge of the blade and stored it back between her cot and the wall of her cell. As she settled herself into bed, pulling the threadbare sheet around her shoulders in search of some semblance of comfort.

She didn't name that feeling until she sank into a cold, heartless, dreamless slumber.

Defeat.

CHAPTER 18

When Andrian came back to consciousness, he stood in what must be his rooms.

He felt as if he was in a daze, no clue as to how he'd gotten there. Like he was half-asleep or perhaps still caught in a dream, dropped into the world with some semblance of a past, but no idea how he'd arrived.

He focused on the image in front of him. Another person—a man—stood there, shirt unbuttoned, messy black hair falling errantly into too-bright eyes as blood dripped down his chest.

Not a man. His reflection. He stood in front of a mirror.

Andrian cocked his head in curiosity as he stared at the image of himself in the glass. His reflection staring back at him was just as perplexed.

His shirt and black trousers were dirty, as if he'd fallen and pushed himself up more than once. Etched on his chest, just over his heart, was his Mark, the roaring dragon with flames leaping from its maw. At the center of the tattoo, just over where a solid black line had once bisected the Mark, was a shallow cut—the source of the blood staining his clothes and smeared across his skin.

The longer he stared at that tattoo, the more those feelings of being only partly there grew and intensified. His attention focused on the cut. He didn't know how it had happened, but he felt as if the memory lingered, just out of reach. He pushed against the wall, stretching out his mind, grasping for more ... but nothing. Only whispers of a half-forgotten dream, tinged with the scent of eucalyptus and jasmine.

As far as he knew, dreams could only harm the mind. Never the body.

An acquainted darkness crept up within him, its talons and claws tearing at the other half of his mind. That darkness was all he'd known while trapped in his dreams, a lingering malevolence he was unable to escape.

Perhaps that was what had given him the cut. Nightmare turned flesh for just a moment.

The beast in his mind clawed at him, even as Andrian sharpened his focus on his chest, on the Mark that adorned it, on the blood that spilled from it. The raging of his living nightmares faded to a dull roar, and he watched a bead of blood well to the surface of his skin. It cut a track down his chest, dripping to the floor.

When it splashed against the tiles beneath his feet, he felt something else stir.

It wasn't the horror that had kept him trapped for as long as he could remember, locking him in memories of a life he couldn't recall or was even sure was his. It was still dark, still wreathed in the shadows of the world, but it was familiar. Comforting, even. Something in his blood that made him feel at home, that made him feel less like an amalgamation of memories and more like *himself.*

Whoever that was.

The comforting darkness spread through him as he watched his reflection in the mirror. Slowly, tendrils of shadows pushed from his shoulders, weaving through his unbuttoned shirt. They formed into ropes of shade, twisting and dancing in the air above his head.

The sinister presence in his mind thrashed. But something

had clicked, shifted. Andrian could keep that monster locked down, shut out, as he watched the shadows of his soul weave a tapestry in the mirror's reflection.

Without warning, the delicate strands of darkness plunged back beneath his skin, wrapping themselves around his heart, his pulse stuttering. His vision sharpened, tongue going dry as adrenaline and whatever else flooded his system.

For the first time in weeks—for as long as he could remember —he felt alive.

Andrian inhaled a gasping breath, taking a shuddering step forward and bracing himself against the mirror. He lifted his head again, meeting his stare for three more heartbeats, before the shadows—his shadows—moved again.

They unwound themselves from his heart and again jumped from his skin. This time, instead of drifting in the air, they pulled him toward the door with a gentle tug on his ribs. Andrian tapped his chest, his fingers smearing the blood.

He turned and followed his shadows to the door.

The monster screamed. He ignored it.

His shadows led him to a cavernous, unfamiliar hallway. Turned him left, pulling him down long, dark, winding corridors. There was a lingering chill in the air, and the air smelled sickly sweet, as if too much perfume and cologne had been sprayed to mask the scent of death and decay and despair.

Andrian wasn't sure what this place was, but he hated it.

The shadows took him to a steep staircase, tugging him down the treacherous steps. Fangs dragged against his mind as the monster grew desperate.

Andrian took the first step down the stairs, knees shaking.

At the bottom of the steps, several *allume* lamps hung from the walls, plugged in by their *lunestair* chains. He took a lurching step toward them, but the tug in his chest halted his movement. He turned to where his shadows lingered, urgent and restless, a few feet in front of him.

With a jolt, he realized he could see, even without the light of the *allume* lamps. He could somehow feel where the shadows touched, could sense everything they enveloped. He was far from blind—in fact, he felt far more aware than he ever had before.

Andrian followed his shadows forward, deeper into darkness.

It was even colder here, even fouler. A thick layer of pain and sadness hung heavy in the air. With those strange senses he was just remembering, he felt another, there in the bowels of their prison.

It was a girl. A woman. Curled tightly on a disgusting mattress, desperate for any warmth she could create for herself.

His steps quickened as he chased his shadows through the dungeons toward the woman held captive, miserable and alone.

He saw her in a cell, one of many in a long line. Her dark hair fanned around her head, body concealed by a thin, stained blanket.

She must've sensed his arrival. Her body shifted, going rigid, and she shot up in bed just as her eyes blinked open.

Even in the dark, the glowing, brilliant forest green hit him like a hammer, knocking the breath from his lungs and nearly sinking him to his knees. The only things that kept him standing were his shadows at his back, pushing him toward the cell door, and the vicious creature tearing a hole in his mind. He could feel it pushing in, desperate to take back the control he'd somehow wrested in his mockery of a nightmare.

Andrian stared at the woman. She stared at him. His hands shook, clenched into fists.

His shadows wrapped around his wrists, pulling them into the pockets of his trousers. His fingers grazed cool metal.

He withdrew the keys. The woman did not break her gaze from his.

Still guided by his shadows, Andrian selected a thick skeleton key from the ring. Inserted it into the lock of the cell door. Twisted until the lock clicked.

The woman did not move as he stepped into the cell, his shadows pulling him with renewed desperation.

The creature in his mind lurched forward, and this time nearly reached him. He couldn't stop from staggering forward, from dropping to his knee, pain fracturing up his leg as bone made impact with the icy stone. His palm landed beside his knee, bracing himself in the darkness.

There was a soft movement, a subtle shift in front of him. The woman stood from her cot, wearing nothing more than a short pink dress made of shredded lace and tulle. She didn't flinch as her bare feet touched the cold ground. Andrian gritted his teeth and lifted himself up, staying in his half-kneel as she took a few more cautious steps toward him.

His shadows tugged his hands again, their urgency palpable. He could almost taste the fear—if shadows could feel such things.

His fingers moved to a new key. A small key, black and delicate. What could it possibly open, if he'd already opened the door to the woman's cell?

But his eyes snagged on the woman's wrists. On the delicate black and gold bands encircling them, the foulness permeating from them forcing his shadows to retract, cowering beneath his skin.

His fingers tightened on the small black key. The woman stiffened. Her eyes, somehow just as familiar in the dark as his own, darted down to the cuffs, then the key gripped in his hand, before rising to his face.

Despite the urgency raking down his spine, despite the evil screaming, biting, and tearing at his mind, he couldn't stop the breath rushing from his lungs. If he hadn't already been on his knees, he would've fallen to them all over again.

Even bruised and cold and dirty, she was the most beautiful woman he'd ever seen. Perhaps his memories were limited, but he was confident he would never see anyone more perfect for the rest of his life, even if the Goddess herself returned to the earth to walk among her people.

Fuck, for all he knew, this was that goddess, and he was about to set her free.

He raised his hands, extending the black key to her. She stilled, for just a heartbeat, something unreadable flashing through those hypnotizing green eyes, before reaching her wrists out to him, palms up.

The key holes were there, nearly invisible. With shaking hands, tremors caused by her and the effort it took to hold back the force that was almost there, mere minutes from snatching back control, he pushed the key into the hole in the cuff on her right wrist. The snick was silent, but that was all it took. The cuff fell from her wrist, landing on the floor with a clatter. He repeated the movement on the other side until both cuffs were on the floor. With a disgusted look, the woman kicked them viciously out of her sight. They clanged against the bars of her cell.

Andrian barely heard it. He was fading, whatever barrier that had granted him this reprieve weakening. Staggering to his feet, something primal urging him to get far, far away from this place before he lost control. He lurched to the cell door, stumbling through, turning back once. Just for one final look at that perfect face, broken confusion written across the features of a goddess.

Her mouth opened as if to speak, but before any words could slip past her full lips, he'd launched into a sprint down the hallway, clawing his way back up the stairs and scrambling down as many winding hallways as he could.

His heartbeat thundered and his breath rasped as he collapsed into a pile of freshly fallen snow outside the castle, the darkness of the beast taking him back once more.

He remembered nothing of that day.

CHAPTER 19

The clouds floating in the sky high above Ciana's window mirrored the way her thoughts floated through her mind. Partially formed, mostly fleeting, and never sure if they would lead to sun or rain or snow or a thunderstorm.

Thank the gods she at least had wine to keep her company. She took another long sip from the glass of mulled red—she'd been craving it since meeting Beva—the bite of cinnamon warming her tongue against the lingering winter chill. She swirled her glass; this winter had lasted longer than most. The cold should break into the early hints of spring soon.

Which meant Mariah had been gone for almost two months. Two months vanished into mist and they had no more idea where she might be than they did on that terror-filled morning when she'd gone missing.

Ciana could handle thinking about all the other issues plaguing them. She didn't mind stewing over the pirates' arrival, or the flickering magic, or the way Sebastian had been *furious* with her after learning she'd disobeyed him and ventured into the city with Delaynie.

She couldn't handle thinking about her best friend. Of where she might be. How she might be suffering. Some thoughts were too dark for even the most tormented of minds.

Sighing heavily, Ciana leaned back on her comfortable cream suede couch, legs propped on the gold and marble coffee table. A fire roared in the hearth, but since Ciana was nothing if not a constant contradiction, her balcony door was also slightly ajar, a cool breeze blowing in from the Bay of Nria. Ciana's rooms were one of the few in the palace that faced the city and the Bay.

She was one of the first to notice the black sails creeping in on that terrible morning, and was often kept awake at night by the sounds of the battle along the coastal cliffs, the crashing of stone striking waves.

It was quiet today. They'd landed a hit last night, and the pirates still retreated. Their reprieve wouldn't last long, but the pause was appreciated.

Especially when the lights had failed completely again that morning. This time, they remained off for six terror-filled minutes.

Despite his anger with her, Ciana would endure endless days of Sebastian's scolding if it meant they could get their queen back. Not just for her; but for everyone.

This world needed Mariah Salis, despite the way it hated her.

Ciana took another long pull from her wine, savoring the burn down her throat.

She missed her best friend so fucking much. There was a woman-sized hole cut into the tissue of her heart, bleeding out with every beat. Mariah looked like she'd been wrought from darkness, and Ciana from sunlight, but it had always been the light in Mariah's soul that had filled the shade in Ciana's.

Her hands shook when she lifted the glass back to her lips, desperate for the burn to quell the ache in her heart.

A voice echoed from beyond her door. It *almost* sounded like her name, reverberating off the palace hallway.

That voice was Ciana's only warning before a fist pounded on the wood.

Ciana groaned. "Good Goddess, it's unlocked! Don't go breaking my door down."

She didn't bother turning as the door slammed open. Footsteps echoed and two figures appeared before her, blocking her view of the Bay.

Her eyebrows shot to her hairline at a particularly frazzled-looking Delaynie and an uncharacteristically serious Quentin as they stared down at her, nestled into her couch.

"What is it?" Ciana dropped her feet from her table, setting down her glass as she stood. She first met Quentin's stare, then shifted to Delaynie, the blue gray of her friend's eyes wild.

"Kiira and Rylla found someone," Delaynie said, breathless. "They found her in the city, asking for a way into the palace. I think you need to hear what she has to say."

"They ... found someone? Already? Who?" Ciana nearly knocked her wine over as she leapt over her coffee table, shoving her feet into a pair of slippers. She paused when Delaynie didn't answer right away, turning slowly back to see the hesitation on her face.

Ciana narrowed her eyes. "Delaynie ... what is it?"

"You just need to hear for yourself." Quentin crossed his arms. "She's in the throne room; everyone's there already."

"Well, you could've led with the fact that I'm late," Ciana grumbled, already moving to the door.

"I didn't think that would be enough to separate you from your wine."

Ciana shot a venomous look over her shoulder at Quentin, his familiar grin faint on his lips, just as Delaynie swatted him across the back of his head. He ducked, feigning injury as he glanced under his arm at Delaynie.

"Ow," he mouthed, rubbing his head. "That wasn't very nice, little wolf."

Little wolf?

"Don't call me that," Delaynie snapped. "Besides, if Ciana wants to have a glass of mulled wine, I don't think any of us could blame her." She met Quentin's stare before flushing a brilliant shade of red and glancing away. "In fact, I think most of us would want to join her."

Quentin chuckled. "Alright, alright. You win. I would kill for some mulled wine right now."

Ciana watched their exchange, curiosity and amusement twitching at her mouth. "If that's all," she said, "I thought you both said this was urgent."

"Yes. Right. It is." Delaynie's already-red cheeks flared a bit brighter as she brushed past Quentin and Ciana, storming into the hall. "Come!"

Ciana turned slowly to Quentin, the mulled wine in her belly pulling her lips into a grin, despite the urgent tenor that dragged them toward the throne room.

"'Little wolf'?"

Quentin stiffened for a heartbeat too long before stepping past her. "Jealous, Cee?"

Ciana laughed. "Hardly."

She followed Quentin through her door and after Delaynie, her friend's dark auburn hair swaying with her urgent steps as her hands gripped her full, traditional skirts. Delaynie had dressed down during their outing into the city, but that was a rare occasion; on all other days, she dressed like the lady of the court that she was. Ciana noticed how Quentin's eyes tracked Delaynie with a recognizable intensity and remembered the teasing conversation they'd shared with Beva a few days ago.

Ciana hesitated before parting her lips. "If you hurt her ..."

"You'll chop my balls off?" Quentin grinned at her again. "Trust me; I know. Especially once Mariah is back."

The mention of their queen's name dropped the temperature in the hallway by at least ten degrees. As if on cue, the *allume* sconces on the walls flickered. Ciana swallowed, pushing her steps faster.

"Besides," Quentin said, "it's nothing. I'm just teasing her. She's tougher than she looks."

"Yes," Ciana said, just before they caught up to Delaynie. "Yes, she is."

They burst through the gold and white doors into the cavernous, glass-ceilinged throne room.

Mariah's Armature were gathered before the great golden throne, brilliant pillars of *lunestair* gleaming with mocking brightness. They turned as one to face Ciana, Delaynie, and Quentin as they rushed across the marble floor. Rylla, in her human form, peeled out of the shadows, clasping her hands.

"What's happened?" Ciana twisted her hands behind her back. A familiar, nervous tick. "Is there someone …"

Another figure stepped out of the shadows, Kiira beside her. It was a young woman—a stranger—her pale strawberry blonde hair piled piously atop her head. But it wasn't anything about her hair or her skin that had Ciana tensing, had her vision flooding with anger, had something wild and strange racing through her.

It was the pale gold robes the girl wore. The robes of a priestess of Qhohena.

"What the *fuck* is she doing here." Ciana's voice was cold as ice, the ends of her blonde curls barely shifting on a phantom wind.

"Ciana," a low, male voice said from beside her.

Ciana snapped her attention to Sebastian, his hazel eyes guarded.

The prior night, when he'd caught her walking in the stables … she didn't think she'd ever seen him that angry. Sebastian did not yell, but his face had taken on a foreign, bitter coldness as he'd quietly asked her where she'd gone.

He'd warmed, just a touch, when she told him about the rumors from Beva, but had still stormed away with a harsh set to his jaw. She hadn't seen him since.

Until now.

He swallowed. "Just … listen to her. Please."

"Just *listen to her*?" Ciana took a step closer to him, incredulity dripping from her tongue, amber eyes scorching. "She's a *priestess*. A follower of that bitch, Ksee, who we all know is not innocent in whatever the *fuck* happened here after the Solstice." She whirled to the priestess, fury blazing through her veins, gnashing its teeth like a monstrous maelstrom.

"Ksee is the reason the *allume* is failing, isn't she?" Ciana stormed closer, Rylla watching her with a curious expression. "You priestesses are behind *all* of this. Everything."

The girl blanched, taking a step back. "I don't—I didn't—"

Kiira stepped in front of the priestess, forcing Ciana back with a jump of surprise. "Let the girl speak before you pass your judgments. We know you will want to hear what she has to say." Kiira glanced over Ciana's shoulder at the rest of Mariah's court. "We know all of you will want to hear what she has to say."

Ciana closed her eyes, forcing a shaky inhale. Tremors wracked her body—frustration at Sebastian, fury at the priestess, fear for her queen, all blending to form a terrifyingly potent cocktail.

When she finally opened them, she was surprised to find that the priestess had peeked around Kiira, watching Ciana with a similarly curious expression.

Ciana's leash on her self-control pulled taut, just before a hesitant hand met her shoulder. She snapped her gaze to Sebastian, still wearing that guarded expression, but now a bit more pleading.

"You went into the city to find Mariah," he whispered, just for her. "And I fucking hate that you did that, but ... what if this is what we've been waiting for? What if this is the information we need?"

Ciana slowly looked back at the priestess. "What did you do with my queen?"

The priestess quaked like a leaf, skin paling even further. "I didn't ...I didn't do anything. But I might know who did."

That strange, foreign feeling filled Ciana at the priestess's words. *Hope.*

Ciana took a step back to give the priestess space, brushing Sebastian's arm. He moved with her, standing beside her in her retreat. She refused to look at him—she was still furious—but somewhere, buried deep down, she was grateful he was there.

He was right. What if this *was* what they'd been looking for? Endless weeks of fighting pirates whose only interest was to keep them occupied, to keep them from finding their queen, and with some twist of luck an answer might have stumbled onto their doorstep.

Ciana lifted her chin, inhaling a steadying breath. "Tell us what you know, priestess."

The priestess glanced at Kiira, who nodded reassuringly to her. With a shallow bob to her head, the girl cleared her throat.

"Shortly before the Winter Solstice, we were ordered to leave the city and our temple by the High Priestess. We were told that the Queen Apparent was planning something horrible, and that we would be celebrating the Solstice far from her reach."

Something horrible. Ciana remembered all that horror: the throne room filled with so much magic and light and life, it was nearly blinding.

"Many of my sisters were all too excited to leave," the priestess continued, twisting her hands in her robes. "They were blinded by the High Priestess's words, and ... many were jealous. Jealous that a commoner was Chosen as queen, while they were simply dragged into temple servitude. They questioned nothing.

"But I ..." The girl swallowed again, meeting Ciana's stare. "I *felt* what happened on the Solstice. Even away from the palace, I felt it. Never in my life have I felt such raw power and magic. Something changed in the earth that night, and it was powerful, and blessed, and *good*." Conviction shone in her eyes. "I felt the queen's power, and I knew it was real. I knew I couldn't defy her without also defying my goddess."

Ciana and the rest stood in stunned silence, staring at the priestess. They'd known that what Mariah had done on the Solstice was earth-shattering, soul-shaking, but Ciana hadn't expected it to be felt outside the city, even by those simply participating in their own muted version of the celebrations.

But was it enough to convince a timid, young priestess to

commit an act of rebellion? The girl's tale certainly seemed genuine and believable. But, then again, Ciana knew well that an innocent face was more than capable of masking deception.

She narrowed her eyes at the priestess, trying to pierce beneath any façade. The girl was clearly still terrified, face washed of color, but she held Ciana's stare without wavering. Her body trembled, hands clenched around her pale robes, but she did not falter.

A towering, golden-haired figure stepped to Ciana's right. "Why now, priestess?" Drystan asked, voice soft and gentle. "Why flee your sisters and come back to the city now?"

The girl darted her eyes around the room, pupils wide, before settling again on Ciana. "The High Priestess visited us recently."

"Visited?" Ciana asked. "Ksee hasn't been with you?"

The priestess shook her head. "She was with us for the Solstice but then left. We haven't seen her in some time, not until about a week ago. We didn't know where she'd gone, but she didn't look well." There was a nervousness in the girl's voice, a hesitation that Ciana knew was born from fear.

"Tell them what you learned when Ksee visited you," Kiira prompted, accented voice soothing.

The girl nodded. "I ... overheard some things." She flushed. "I shouldn't have been eavesdropping, but the High Priestess was saying such strange things. I owed it to my goddess to learn more."

"Priestess," Ciana warned. "What did you learn?"

A flush again rose to her cheeks. "The Royals have the Queen Apparent. They captured her with the help of one of her Armature, and have been keeping her imprisoned in Khento, at Lord Shawth's keep."

The bottom of Ciana's world fell out beneath her feet. She reached for Sebastian on instinct, grasping his arm, digging her nails into his skin. Curses echoed around her.

"There's more, isn't there?" Feran had approached, standing beside Drystan, voice deadly soft.

The priestess nodded. "That was why I ran. I had to get here, to you. They—the Royals and Ksee—are planning something. A ritual, or ... I don't know. But they plan to involve the Queen Apparent in it somehow, and ... I don't think they mean for her to survive." She glanced pleadingly around her, meeting the stares of each of Mariah's court.

Minus one, of course. But Ciana couldn't bring herself to focus on that. Not yet.

"Queen Mariah is in Khento, and if you don't save her, I don't think she'll survive the next week."

CHAPTER 20

The solitude was her companion. The cold, her friend. The anger, her ally.

And the confusion ... her nemesis.

Mariah stewed over the strange encounter with Andrian the night before. Everything about it was ... bizarre. Not only his appearance—shirtless, bleeding, haggard—but even his steps were jilted, expression twisted yet blank, eyes shadowed yet manic. None of what he'd done made sense. From the moment he'd unlocked the door to her cell, then stepped closer to her with that small black key in his hand.

When he'd unlocked the shackles around her wrists, the stone falling to the ground at their feet, before rushing from her cell like some sort of man possessed.

She'd been left dumbfounded ... until her gaze had landed on the cuffs, now lying on the ground. Elation had soared around her, and she'd braced herself against the onslaught of her magic, joyously freed from its binds.

An onslaught ... that never came.

When the cuffs fell from her wrists, she'd felt nothing but empty nothingness. Not a whisper of those threads wound through her, not a single one stirred.

She'd spent the entire night reaching and grasping for it, sloughing through the trenches of her shattered soul.

Several hours later, and Mariah could finally summon enough light to give a faint glow to her skin. Just a single, delicate thread.

She watched that thread, a meager morsel trailing sluggishly around her finger. Tried to search for more from it—more spark, more fire, more warmth. Clawed into the oblivion of her mind for the six bridges of silver and gold that once existed there. Her bonds with her Armature felt like missing limbs she'd forgotten in the many weeks she'd been trapped in the miserable dark of this cell.

Lost in her thoughts, she almost missed the other light that began to grow at the end of the hallway. Was almost too slow at pulling back that paltry thread, hiding it back beneath her skin. Mariah buried her hands in her thin blanket, shielding her now-bare wrists from view.

She was beyond glad for her intuition as Shawth appeared in the hallway, his strides slow, face wearing his usual twisted, sour grin. He stopped in front of her cell, peering at her through the iron bars.

"Once again, I am shocked by your beauty, Mariah. Captivity truly does suit you."

"To what do I owe this visit, Shawth?" Mariah kept her face expressionless as she leaned back against the wall, seeking its cold companionship.

Shawth regarded her with a thoughtful twist to his brow, just for a moment, before pulling a stool from the shadows of the hallway. He placed it in front of her cell, teetering himself on the wood as he rested his *allume* lamp on the ground.

"I must admit." He scratched his chin. "You are stronger than I'd thought."

Mariah narrowed her eyes at him but said nothing.

Shawth sighed, leaning back on his stool. "At first, once we realized we couldn't control you, we thought we could just kill you. Do it quickly and silently. Sure, we would have to wait another twenty-one years for a new queen, but what of it? Things would be as they should, without some bratty little slut snatching our power away.

"That Uroborus ..." He heaved a sigh. "You have no *idea* the lengths we went to obtain one of those. And for you to just *kill* it, with nothing more than a simple dagger ..." He scoffed, folding his arms over his chest. "It shouldn't have been possible. That was when we changed tactics. If we could do something public, make it seem like the people had plotted and were rejecting you, we'd have more success."

Mariah's breath was caught in her throat.

None of this was a surprise to her; she'd always suspected the Royals were behind the attempts on her life.

But to hear him admit to it, so casually, as if discussing the weather ...

"Cedoric," she whispered, hands clenched as more threads of her magic were roused from their slumber. "You failed to kill me, but you killed a member of Queen Ryenne's Armature. He was a good man." Her voice rose from a whisper to a growl. "An *innocent* man."

Shawth gave her a quizzical look. "You hardly knew him. Why do you care?"

She ground her teeth. "I *care* because his death forced me into ruling far sooner than any of us wanted, you swine."

"Oh, my dear." Shawth chuckled, leaning back. "Don't pretend that you weren't looking for a way to grab control. Besides, there are no innocent losses in our quests for power. There are few sacrifices that are not worth it.

"Which is what led us to our new benefactor. He has shown us a new path. An easier path." He grinned at her, yellow teeth glowing in the light. "We learned your death would not be necessary for us to get what we want—at least, not yet. Rather, keeping you alive would be in our best interests. All we had to do was break you."

Mariah's blood chilled, before heating again on a rush of fire through her belly.

Her capture. Her abandonment in the darkness of the dungeons for six weeks.

The metal-tipped flog.

Anniliese and Andrian.

The drugged food. The hands on her skin.

"That's truly what this has all been about? Breaking me?" Memories—brutal, painful, terrible memories—swam through her as she clung to her bravado with every shred of herself that she had left.

She'd been ripped apart, body and soul, but as she met Shawth's pale blue gaze, she vowed that *nothing* these men could do would shake the light from her veins.

Shawth scoffed. "Well, there is a bit more to it, but for the most part, yes." The stool creaked as he shifted. "We thought it would be easy. When we sent Andrian to collect you, we had six other guards go with him. Not because we thought he would need that much support; what could you do, unarmed and without magic?" He chuckled. "We wanted you to think that your Armature had turned against you."

Mariah didn't even flinch. She'd dwelled on this exact coincidence during the early days of her captivity as the madness of solitude crept in. Her captors were veiled and hooded, faces obscured from sight, but even in the darkness of her thoughts, she never truly believed them to be her Armature. She'd walked with their souls, and a piece of herself stayed with them.

"But you weren't the least bit perturbed." Shawth uncrossed his arms, leaning forward. "So, we turned to ... other means."

"Yes," Mariah whispered. "You certainly did." She loaded as much of her rage and anger and pain into her stare. The scars scourged on her soul rumbled awake, more threads of newly freed magic shaking loose and unraveling in her gut.

Instead of cowering before her, he simply smiled. "I suppose I underestimated you. You truly care very little for your well-being. Even after everything, you still have that ridiculously defiant look." He sighed, smile broadening.

"I had hoped the fun we had with the *uxosil* might finally do it. Tricky to obtain, but Lord Cordaro had a connection in Idrix. Quite skilled with poisons, those southerners. Perhaps, once this is all over, it might be time to lift the embargo and open the borders. I'd like to learn more about such magics."

Embargo? "I think I would be interested in the same. If only to make sure every last drop of that *shit* is wiped from the earth." Her voice was distant to her ears, holding a confidence she did not feel.

Shawth huffed a chuckle again, before meeting her stare and scratching his chin. They watched each other, pompous lord and ragged prisoner, his stare sliding over her grimy skin and too-thin body.

"You could end it all, right now, you know." His voice was quiet, and ... almost genuine.

She'd be a fucking fool if she believed it.

"After that confession? Knowing that you wanted me dead, before my reign even began, and all the things that came after? I think we're just getting started, Lord Shawth," she said hollowly. "I've told you that I never wanted this. If I wanted to get rid of this magic and get myself out of this miserable prison, I would've done so already. I would've done it after the fucking *Choosing*." She snarled the last word, forgotten frustrations spilling all too easily from her tongue.

"Well, you see, my dear, I simply do not believe that." Shawth's voice carried a hint of sadness. "You cannot lie to me. The magic would not have Chosen you if you had not wanted it. The Goddess, or whoever else pulls our strings, must have seen your ambition."

Whoever else pulls our strings? Mariah was reminded of Shawth's mention of a new benefactor, and Ksee's words describing something similar. She fully believed they'd abandoned Qhohena, led astray by ... something.

"Ambition?" She clenched her fists beneath her blanket. "I remember coming to you and Laurent for your help in running the kingdom because I knew I couldn't do it alone. It wasn't the same deal you had with Ryenne, but you still would've had power."

"Power? It would have been a mockery to call you Queen." He propped his feet out in front of him. "Power is the only currency that matters in this world, and if you still possessed more than me —you, some little slut from the hovels of Andburgh—that simply would never do."

"That is truly all you care about? Power?"

He laughed. "Don't lie and tell me you do not feel the same! I can see the same drive in you, the same hunger. It's how you have lasted this long, and it's why we simply cannot allow you to remain on the throne."

Mariah hated that he was right. She hadn't wanted this life—not at first—but no, she thirsted for that strength. The ability to change the world required power, and she had no desire to give it up.

"What of the other lords?" she asked. "You come to me seeking power, and I've never known you to be a man willing to share it. Do they support you in this little vendetta?" She supposed at least three of them did. Laurent had been instrumental in her capture, Hareth had offered his daughter as part of her emotional torture, and Cordaro had helped secure the *uxosil*. But she still had to ask the question.

Anything to sow seeds of discontent. That was the only game she had left.

Shawth's eyes glinted in the pale gold light. "Despite what they say, you certainly are a smart little witch." He rubbed a hand across his chest. "The other lords are weak and soft. So long as they may remain the masters of their castles, they care very little about the politics of the continent. Except, of course, Lord Laurent ... But his allegiance has been bought in other ways," he said, a gleeful and malevolent grin spreading across his face.

The hair along Mariah's arms rose.

"What do you mean?"

Shawth scoffed. "Oh, come now, Mariah! As if I would share those delicious morsels with you. I think I've shared more than enough with you tonight. Rest assured, though—when the veil is lifted, I cannot *wait* to see what he has planned for you."

Mariah's spine locked as the temperature in her blood dropped. "He? Your new ... benefactor?"

"You were paying attention." Shawth chuckled. "Good. For now, let's just say he is very, *very* excited to meet you."

Fuck.

"Shawth, listen to me." She pressed her palms into the mattress, leaning forward with a sudden, desperate urgency. "I cannot transfer the magic. It's not a decision that's up to me. And even if it was, you can't force a new queen; the magic will choose who it chooses. You could be stuck with someone even worse than me." She forced air into her lungs and filled herself with all the pleading she could muster. "But I promise, right now. I swear, in Qhohena's name. I'm done fighting. It's over. You've won. I'll ... I'll be the figurehead that Ryenne was. I keep my crown, but you would rule."

As the words left her lips, she begged desperately that her silent prayer be heard. That he would believe her, would call off his mad pursuit that would only end poorly for them both. She would find another way to change the world. There would be plenty of opportunities to undermine him, and even then, her life would last centuries, while he had only a few decades left.

Shawth's grin stretched wider across his sallow face, blue eyes festering. "What pretty words you say, little queen. Such a shame I do not believe them." He rose from his stool and dragged it back against the wall, away from her cell.

She must've prayed to the wrong goddess.

Mariah's jaw hung open with her disbelief. "Why come, then? Why bother, even when I offer what you say you want?"

Shawth's hand rested on the wall, and he turned back to Mariah with a wide smile that failed to reach his eyes and showed too many cracked, yellowed teeth.

"Sleep well, Your Majesty. I look forward to seeing all he has planned for you." He picked up his *allume* lamp and sauntered off down the dungeon hallway, whistling an off-key song.

The terror and rage in Mariah's blood sank lower, settling through her veins. Her magic pushed out through her skin, just a bit stronger than before. Her fingers grazed the hilt of the paring knife still tucked between her mattress and the wall.

She had no intention of ever meeting this mysterious benefactor. Had no intention of being trapped here, at less than her full power, when she now had everything she needed to unleash her light upon this castle.

Mariah would wait for her moment, then she would get the *fuck* out of this place.

CHAPTER 21

The stables and courtyard were a flurry of ordered chaos, the sort of urgent structure found only in the moments that existed before things went to shit.

Sebastian knelt beside the great statue of Qhohena, the steady roar of the fountain soothing against his frayed senses. He finished the final lacings on his boots before standing, picking up his leather bracers from the ground, and sliding them onto his forearms.

Horses were being readied at the stables, stable hands running to and fro. Feran worked with the stable hands, tightening cinches, fitting bridles, securing saddlebags filled with supplies. They had a three-day journey ahead to the northern castle of Khento, and it would be a hard ride for both the men and the horses. Sebastian trusted Feran to ensure they were well-prepared.

Drystan stood closer to the barracks that sat between the stables and the castle itself, directing Matheo and Trefor as they organized weapons, sifting through the stockpile of broadswords and rapiers and bows and daggers. Drystan himself was already dripping with steel, but still secured several additional weapons to his blood bay gelding. Matheo slung a bow and quiver of arrows to Sebastian's gray mare; his brother knew Sebastian's proclivity for the weapon.

That didn't mean Sebastian didn't still have daggers sheathed at his hip or a longsword already tucked into his saddle. Having options was always the preference.

"Quentin, do you mind making yourself at least moderately useful?" Drystan's voice rang across the courtyard, pulling Sebastian's attention with it.

Quentin, who stood before several stacked bales of hay, loosed another dagger into the target he'd roughly secured to the fodder. He shot a venomous glare at Drystan, before pulling another knife from his baldric and repeating the throw.

Sebastian huffed a chuckle, starting forward. "Leave him to it, Drystan. You know how he gets." Drystan glowered for a moment at Quentin, before sighing and turning back to the weapons pile. Sebastian strode toward them, finishing up the lacings on his bracers as he walked.

"Sebastian!"

He paused mid-stride, turning back halfway. "Ryland? What is it?"

The City Guard captain jogged across the courtyard, breathless as he halted before Sebastian. He was one of the Marked who hadn't been Selected, and Sebastian had known him since boyhood. Ryland glanced around at the flurry of movement, concern on his face.

"Are you … are you sure this is a good idea? What if the pirates storm the docks again?"

Sebastian grimaced. "Then your Guardsmen best be prepared to defend the city, as they are sworn to do." In truth, he felt Ryland's fears; they'd kept him up all night. The implications their leaving the city would mean for the resident's safety.

Sebastian still heard the screams from the last time they'd abandoned their post in favor of searching for their queen.

He sighed, stepping forward to grasp Ryland by the shoulder. "I understand your worries. But you heard what the priestess said. If our queen's life is truly in jeopardy, we have no real choice. We must try to save her ... or die trying."

"But do you all have to go? The men will feel your absence. At least have a few of you stay; Drystan, or Feran, perhaps."

Sebastian had debated it; only asking a few of Mariah's Armature to go on this mission. But as he'd thought about it and met the looks in his brother's eyes, he knew he could never ask any of them to stay behind. They had just as much of a right to see her safely home as he did.

He bore the blood of enough innocents; he could tolerate a bit more if it meant Mariah was home.

The one thing he *hadn't* thought much about was what they'd do if they found Andrian there. With her. Sebastian's fury had already burned too hot for him to dwell on that for long.

"I can't ask that of them." He forced a smile, releasing Ryland. "It will only be for a few days; a week, at most. You have the queen's Mark, too; I have faith you will protect this city."

Ryland's mouth opened and conflict warred across his face, as if he wanted to say something further. Ultimately, though, he set his mouth in a grim line and nodded.

"Safe travels." With a tense set to his shoulders, he turned, striding towards the barracks.

Sebastian sighed, his gaze drifting idly over the activity of the courtyard ... before it stopped.

Ciana and Rylla padded out from the tunnel leading to the palace side entrance. Ciana was dressed comfortably, a red sweater bundled around her to fight off the spring chill, glowing golden curls blowing around her face in the slight breeze.

Gods, he'd been so furious with her when he'd found out about her little foray into the city. He still was; why couldn't she understand the panic it had caused him? There was so much to be fearful of, and of course, she had to choose to create more.

But without her insistence, without her pushing, without her defiance, they might not have learned what they did. Maybe Rylla and Kiira would've found the priestess without Ciana leading them all out that day into the city, but ... maybe not.

Sebastian knew—gods, did he know—that Ciana cared so deeply and so brightly for those she loved. He'd asked her to stay at the palace for *him*, for his peace of mind. He was still mad, but he was realizing that what he'd asked of her was something she never would've obeyed. Not forever.

Her amber gaze landed on him. She twisted her hands nervously in front of her before giving him a hesitant smile.

He returned it—perhaps a touch more enthusiastically. Ciana unclasped her hands and turned to walk to him. Rylla peeled away from her side, heading to join the preparing Armature.

Rylla, who was in her black panther form, her sleek black coat shimmering in the morning sunlight. They'd decided that while Kiira would remain behind with Ciana and Delaynie, Rylla would join the Armature. As strange as it was to be confronted with the existence of shifters in their world, Sebastian couldn't deny that her particular skills would prove invaluable for this type of mission. The horses knickered at her, ears pricking as they pawed at the ground, but they relaxed as she slowly wound her way between them.

"It's quite strange, isn't it?"

Ciana stood a few paces in front of him, blinking in the sunlight. Her amber eyes were wide as they tracked Rylla's movement between the horses, and her cheeks flushed a delicate shade of pink, freckles stark against her skin.

He swallowed. "Strange?"

Ciana nodded at Rylla. "I mean, we know she's human. We've spoken to her and we've seen her shift. But seeing her like that …" She sighed. "I don't know. It just reminds me of how little we really know about the world. How much has been kept from us."

Sebastian watched her before slowly nodding. "I agree. It makes me wonder what else might be out there."

She hummed in response but said nothing further. He cleared his throat, shifting slightly.

"I've … been meaning to apologize."

Her attention snapped to him. "You? Apologize?" She scoffed.

"I never thought I'd see the day." Her eyes carried a guarded look, but she still lifted an eyebrow. A cautious, playful gesture.

He exhaled. "I know. It's been ... It's been a difficult few weeks." He ran a hand through his hair, glancing at the ground. "And I'm sorry. For the things I said to you. And the way I treated you. I wanted you safe, but I know why you had to get out."

Ciana took a step forward, now only a foot from him. He met her bright eyes, the way a golden curl blew across her face.

He was struck by a sudden urge to reach out and tuck the errant strand behind her ear.

"I'm still pissed at you for not listening to me," she said before he could move. "But I understand your reasons. And I appreciate you saying sorry."

He chuckled. "I'm still pissed at you, too."

Just as he said it, the sparkle in her eyes snuffed out.

Fuck. What was it about her? It was like she made him forget himself. Forget how to say the right things, forget how to do what was best. Forget how to be perfect.

She made him feel ... human.

"Wait, that's not what I meant." He reached desperately for the right words. "I only meant—I'm still mad that you didn't listen to me and went into the city. But I'm far more thankful to you that you did." He took a step forward, reaching for her hand. Her skin was smooth and soft as he clutched it in his, her gaze rising again to meet his.

"If you continued to listen to my stupid rules, then we wouldn't know what we know. We wouldn't be leaving now, about to bring home our queen. When we save Mariah, it will be because of *you*."

Her fingers twitched against his palm. She sniffed, lifting her chin. "Next time, don't tell me what I can and can't do. I spent enough of my life trapped by men. And I know you are nothing like those monsters, but I refuse to spend a single more second feeling like a captive."

Sebastian felt the blood leave his face, his eyes going wide. The idea that through his commands he had made her feel such things. That it had bothered her enough to even *make* such a comparison ...

He was struggling with his failures, to be sure, but to be mentioned in the same sentence as the animals who'd once hurt her ... he thought he might be sick.

He released her hand, stepping back. "Ciana ... I am so, so sorry. I never meant—I never should have—"

A finger against his lips immobilized him. Amber eyes glimmered in front of him.

"Even at your worst, Sebastian, you could never be anything like them. Ever." She dropped her hand, a hint of a smile touching her lips. "I might know a way you can make it up to me, though."

He tilted his head hesitantly. "How?"

She cracked, truly smiling. "You get a beer with me." Her brightness dimmed, just a touch, as she swallowed. "You bring our girl home, and you bring yourself home. Don't you dare leave me in this city alone; I will never forgive you and will haunt your soul once my time is spent. And then, once you—and Mariah—are back, you'll get a beer with me."

So many emotions burned behind Sebastian's eyes, in the back of his throat. Sadness, and fear, and hope, and happiness, all melting together and dripping through him like scalding fire. He swallowed, forcing an inhale.

With a slow, measured movement, he reached out a hand and rested it against Ciana's cheek, sinking his fingers into her thick golden curls. She leaned so subtly into his hand, and every part of him burned with something new and indescribable and terrifying.

"I promise, Cee. I *will* bring her home. For both of us. And then ..." His throat closed, the wind brushing her hair across his skin, alighting him like the rays of his very own, personal sunshine. A sunshine he swore to carry with him north, into the cold shadows of Khento.

"And then, we'll get that beer."

CHAPTER 22

Mariah had never seen the servant girl before.

Every day, like clockwork, the same mute servant brought her a single paltry meal. Her hair was always up, and her face shrouded. She never once said a word to Mariah, only simply opening the small grate at the bottom of Mariah's door, slipping in the tray, and vanishing back into darkness.

Today's girl, though ... today's girl was different.

She had long, ash blonde hair, and her rags were torn and stained. A kitchen maid, most likely, given the flour dusting her hollow cheeks and the burn scars on her hands. She carried an *allume* lamp, eyes darting like a nervous mouse as she stumbled gracelessly down the hall. She halted outside Mariah's cell, clumsily fumbling for her keys.

Instinct alone had Mariah rising from her cot. She still wore her ridiculous pink dress—now stained and tattered, but still just as demeaning—but she ignored the brush of tulle against her thighs as she gripped her paring knife behind her back.

The girl awkwardly balanced the tray on her hip as she slid a key into the iron lock to Mariah's cell.

The door. Not the small grate at the bottom.

"I look forward to seeing all he has planned for you."

No. Mariah would not sit idly by to find out what Shawth meant.

She dove into herself, into the part of her soul that was still too dark and shadowed. Her threads had slowly come back to life, but they were still weak, only a glimmer of what they once were. But she latched onto them, wrapping around them and drawing them to the surface.

They seemed to grumble against her, almost lethargically, but they obeyed. Mariah could have sighed with relief.

The moment the girl opened the cell, still trying to balance that tray of frozen, nutritionless food on her hip, Mariah exploded.

Light shot from her free hand like coiled vines, striking the girl in the chest. She stumbled back with a cry, hitting the far wall, the tray crashing to the ground and the cell door clanging open.

"No—wait! Stop!" the girl yelled hoarsely as light rippled off Mariah. She lunged for the exit, pausing for a flash of a heartbeat at the threshold. Her light still held the girl pinned to the wall, her struggles weak as she sobbed.

The girl was innocent in this. And she might die for her failure.

But Mariah was too broken to care about all those she couldn't save.

"I'm sorry," Mariah said in a sad whisper, before she sprinted down the corridor, leaving the servant girl there, whimpering and terrified. Her light snapped back under her skin, leaving a faint, luminescent glow as she reached those steep, slick stairs.

And began to climb.

Mariah's heart was pounding in her ears, atrophied muscles in her legs holding her up only through the flood of adrenaline pouring through her veins. When she reached the landing, stumbling out into the cold, quiet hallways of Khento, she paused, panting heavily. Her body trembled, and her mind was focused on one singular goal.

Escape. Escape. Escape.

The word thrashed and hammered through her skull, lurching

her frozen feet back into motion. They led her through the halls, kept company only by the soft patter of her footfalls, the heavy wheezes of her lungs, the faint glow of her skin.

Mariah didn't know how long she ran. Only that if she stopped, it would all be over.

A pair of massive oak doors loomed at the end of the hall. She stumbled, steps faltering, but kept pushing forward. Slamming into the wood, she fumbled for the handle. With a final shudder, her hand found metal, and she wrenched it down as she pushed with all the strength she had left.

The door swung open with a too-loud groan, and Mariah stumbled outside into a decadent garden spotted with late winter snow.

And above her head shone the moons. Two slender slivers—one silver, one gold—that seemed to pulse brighter as Mariah stepped into their light, taking in a deep, sobbing, choking inhale.

Her cheeks chilled as tears tracked down her skin. Those moons were almost gone; the Spring Equinox was almost here. But they had not vanished yet, and she took a moment to revel in their light, her magic dancing with more life and joy than it had in weeks.

It wasn't enough to chase away the darkness, but light needed the dark to shine its brightest.

A branch snapped, no more than a few feet away. Mariah's skin pulsed with magic, gripping her knife with all her meager strength.

A figure, seated on a stone garden bench, shifted in the soft moonlight. Silver and gold reflected off black hair, and the weight of the universe slammed into her as she met a brilliant, haunted gemstone blue gaze.

Eons stretched between them, as Mariah held Andrian's stare in the dim light of her magic and the moons.

"I know you," he murmured into the quiet, and it was like time restarted.

Her fingers twitched around her dagger. She'd wanted to simply escape, to flee into the darkness. But her magic was still not strong enough; there was still a gaping hole trying to refill. If the lords caught her, she'd be finished.

There might be one very simple way to ensure her safety.

Not just her own. No, there was another held captive here in this evil castle, and he was seated no more than a few feet from her, beautiful and broken in the moonlight.

Memories of shattered pain haunted her, but her soul still loved his. And if she could free them both from this evilness, she had to try.

She took a single, hesitant, fateful step forward. "And I know you," she whispered back, voice hoarse in the cold.

The silence between them pressed against her skull, heart pounding in her chest like the beats of a war drum.

"How ... how do I know you?" He looked like he'd been ripped from his bed, not at all dressed for the cold gardens. Black cotton trousers and a black shirt, unbuttoned and slung carelessly around his shoulders. With another step forward she could see his Mark, stark against his skin, the still-healing cut down its center scabbed and raw. The cool, flat-edge side of her knife pressing into her forearm burned.

Staring at his Mark, with his question ringing between them, she was frozen. Paralyzed by a sudden realization that despite her magic now freed, this still might not work. Nothing else that made a normal bonding ceremony was here—no candles, no sweetly spoken swears, and they were far more clothed than she'd been for other ceremonies. Even the knife she gripped was nothing more than a simple paring knife from a dining set, nothing like the decorative blade normally used.

She gritted her teeth. Took a deep inhale, holding it in her lungs until it burned, before exhaling in a long, steady breath.

This *would* work. Those things, those other elements ... they weren't what was most important to the bond. She hesitated to call it all part of another antiquated ritual, but in her soul, she knew what was important.

Mariah had her sparkling magic, her blood, and the light of the moons.

Andrian had his Mark and his shadow-wreathed soul.

That was *all* that mattered.

This would work.

She took the final step to him, standing in front of his legs, her bare skin grazing the material of his trousers. He tilted back his head, something desperately profound shining in his eyes.

"You know me from another life. One I hope to find you in again." They were the first words she found, carrying softly on the night breeze, and her soul thrashed in pain at how much she meant them.

She flipped her knife in her hand, wrapping her palm around the blade, ready to slice through soft skin.

"You have very beautiful eyes."

Mariah stiffened. Forced herself to look closer at him, as if she could peer into his soul.

She swore she saw him there—the *real* him. Not the one who'd been paraded around this castle for the last few weeks, who hurled vile words at her at every opportunity. Not the one who'd flayed her skin or shredded her heart.

She saw the broken man who'd made himself her greatest weakness. Her consort. Her King.

Mariah smiled, thickness clogging her throat. A strange, foreign half-smile danced across her lips.

"You do, too, *Rhoi*."

Andrian cocked his head to the side—a small, child-like movement. "I've seen your eyes before, and I think about them more than I think about anything else. I see them in my dreams. They haunt my nightmares." His eyes flickered. "Are you a demon? Or a goddess?" he finished in a whisper.

Mariah's heart thundered against her ribs. He sat deathly still as she moved even closer to him. Lifted a leg, settling it on the side of his. Lowered herself onto his lap.

His skin was hot and feverish against her, despite the chill of the night air. A line of sweat dampened his brow. She leaned in, forehead pressing against his, his heat consuming her ever-present chill as their noses brushed.

"I am neither," she whispered against his skin. "I am your retribution."

Shadows flickered across his face, dulling the manic brightness in his eyes. Shadows that made her heart race in excitement and soar with the idea of hope.

She knew those shadows. She *welcomed* those shadows. They called to her magic, as much as the day called to the night and the darkness called to the light.

The threads in her soul leapt and twined through her blood. Mariah sank herself into it, wrapping herself around as many of them as she could muster. Both silver and gold answered her, spinning together in a glorious maelstrom of light and power.

She clenched her left hand tightly around the blade of her knife, hardly registering the faint sting as the steel cut her skin. Blood welling to the surface, she loosened her grip, switching the knife to her right hand, swinging it up around her body. The blade glinted with the ruby droplets of her blood as she lowered it to his still-healing chest, to the line bisecting her dragon-shaped Mark, maw roaring and devouring.

Andrian's eyes blinked with shock, clarity winning for a moment. He looked at her—*into* her—then down to his chest.

When he returned his stare to hers, something new shone there.

Determination. Devotion.

Love.

He nodded to her, and that was all she needed.

Mariah sliced her simple paring knife through his Mark.

When she slammed her bleeding palm to his chest, when her blood laced with silver and gold light met his, the earth beneath their feet trembled and quaked.

CHAPTER 23

Mariah was falling.

Light and shadows flashed around her. She was nothing more than a mass of brilliant, burning light, both as cold as death and hot as life. She screamed into the void, but there was no one there to hear her.

Until something rose out from that void. Or perhaps they broke from her shoulder blades, something huge and solid and blindingly bright. She couldn't be sure, but she felt her descent halting, her wild path through the darkness pulled short.

Spindles of silver and gold had spread from her being, winding together as they formed something solid beneath her. She alighted atop the shimmering surface, moving across it as it spanned the cavernous space.

Somewhere in this void, she felt other bridges. All made of silver or gold and other colors, all reigniting after being dormant for far too long. A part of her, a part she'd forgotten and neglected, leaped in joy. Fear and happiness and anger and elation slammed into her from those bridges, and for a moment they wrapped around her, all six making her soul leap and dance in splendid exaltation.

She knew what it meant that those six consciousnesses now

brushed against her own. But she couldn't dwell on it for long; bliss permeated her being for a moment longer before she closed those connections, sending back her own feelings of happiness and hope.

Mariah's attention refocused on the bridge being built beneath her. The silver and gold threads of magic wove together until they were one, all but indistinguishable from each other. It was so bright—brighter than the others had been—and with each weave, she felt the tugs of fate burning brighter. She welcomed it, reveled in it. Fighting this destiny had forced her into darkness, wallowing in her weakness.

Not now. No more.

She progressed across the forming bridge, fixing her stare on the void beyond. Excitement raced through her like a million torches, lighting her soul ablaze.

Until the bridge stopped forming, and nothing was there to greet her.

Only a mass of writhing, twisted darkness.

She reached a piece of herself toward the void and instantly recoiled. This wasn't something she knew.

This was something malignant and filled with festering hate, a dark tumor infecting the mind of the one whom she loved.

Somewhere, in a decadent moonlit garden on a different plane of existence, she bared her teeth in a snarl.

The evilness stilled, watching Mariah just as she watched it back. She pulled everything she possessed to her, ropes and weapons of silver and gold coiling like a mass of twisting, winding serpents.

She remembered a time when serpents had almost ended her life. Those were demons of the darkness.

She was a warrior of the light, and she would not be intimidated. She would wield what had once been used in an attempt on her life to exact the retribution singing in her soul.

With that final thought, she unleashed her light upon the darkness.

There was no sound in this void, this plane that existed somewhere between sleep and waking, life and death, the heavens and the earth. But Mariah could feel the battle raging, could feel the darkness clawing back at her light as she blasted and burned and scourged the evil from this place.

Slowly—in what could have taken an eternity, or only a few fleeting moments—the darkness retreated, chased away by creatures of light, an army fashioned from the most feral and vengeful part of her soul.

With one final surge, the wall of darkness snapped and sundered, dissipating like morning mist.

Mariah's form sagged, exhaustion crumpling her as the last bits of her light chased away the few lingering tendrils of darkness.

With the other side of the chasm cleared, she could see who waited for her at the foot of her bridge of silver and gold.

Another form made of shadows, but these ones were familiar. Comforting.

Home.

Streaks of tanzanite danced within the shadows, the gemstone blue shining brilliantly against the void between their souls.

Happiness cleaved her soul as she raced toward him. Her light refracted off his shadows, a myriad of colors and brilliance arching across this eternal place.

It was beautiful.

She wove two threads of light—one silver, one gold. They wound together until they formed a single rope, a solid mass that could be seen from the heavens far above, in a place that resembled the one of their minds but that they could not yet truly comprehend.

On a swell of power, Mariah pushed that coiled rope of light into the being of shadow and tanzanite. It twisted into him, around him, melding into the very fabric of his being.

Soaring with euphoria, she turned back to the bridge, now spanning between their minds, and sprinted across it, desperate for the touch of the one whose soul she'd now seen. Had now touched.

Whose soul she now knew perfectly reflected her own.

MARIAH SLAMMED BACK into her body with a gasping breath, her hand still pressed to Andrian's chest, palm slick and sticky with their mingled blood.

She opened her eyes and was greeted by a clear, unclouded gemstone blue. Not a hint of darkness or confusion or emptiness dwelled in their depths. Shadows snapped in the air above their heads, shadows that danced with corded silver-gold light.

She met that brilliant stare, and the world tilted.

"*Mariah*." Her name spilled from his tongue, and the stars pulsed.

It was a whisper. A prayer. A desperate call for salvation. She'd heard her name said like that only once before, just before the Winter Solstice.

He was back.

Andrian was *back*.

It had *worked*.

"*Andrian*," she choked, her voice a sobbing murmur. She wrenched her hand from his chest, grabbing his face, blood smearing across his jaw. Her fingers curled into his hair, long and unkempt after their weeks in this gods-cursed castle.

And then she kissed him.

Moons waxed and waned. Stars rose and fell. Waves crashed against a cliffy shore, the wind whipped across wild plains, and plants pushed forth from the earth before wilting and returning. The sun tracked a blinding path across the sky, shadows forming and disappearing in its wake.

The heavens themselves fissured around them.

Mariah gasped against his lips as his hands tightened on her hips, so warm and heavy and familiar. With the magic coursing through her veins, scorching her soul, she forgot the agonies she'd endured those past weeks. Forgot what they'd tried to take from her. Fire lit her blood, settling low in her core, cataclysmically unbearable.

Until a single, broken thought wandered in, unwanted and unbidden.

His hands had hurt her, too.

She wrenched herself away from him with a sudden jerk. His lips were swollen, and his eyes were wide, his face filled with a clarity she'd not seen in a long time.

But that did not forgive the reminder that had sprung to her mind. No matter how much her body wanted this, how much her soul reveled in the bond now stretching between them, a brilliant bridge of silver and gold and shadows.

Some wounds simply cut too deep.

The scars on her back, while healed, itched under the weight of his stare. The feeling of his hands on her hips had her recoiling, a reminder of possessive touches that had sought to demean her. To make her feel less than human.

She pushed off his lap, staggering to her feet, movements jerky and stilted. Her chest heaved as her feet burned against the ice covering the ground, as the sickly sweet smell of late winter jasmine and early spring crocus burned her nose. Andrian's eyes widened in a strange mix of shock and surprise, blinking rapidly as if to expel a haze, before finally glancing around at his surroundings.

The baffled confusion that filled his too-handsome face dragged her battered soul through shards of glass.

She remembered *everything* that had been done to her. But he … he remembered nothing.

Even the things that his hands had done, the new scars he'd inflicted. She knew, she felt, she remembered. But Andrian was blind, helpless in the dark.

Mariah didn't know which was worse. Which caused her more pain.

He was free, but she was still trapped. Perhaps would be forever. A new, atrocious curse.

Andrian slowly rose from the stone bench, expression still open and cautious and filled with pure, unadulterated hope. Unfiltered hope. Hope that made Mariah want to crumple to the ground.

"Mariah—"

"If you take a single step closer to her, Armature, then these gardens will become your grave."

CHAPTER 24

"Tf you take a single step closer to her, Armature, then these gardens will become your grave."

The cool tip of metal grazed Andrian's throat. He recognized the voice. It was one he'd grown up with, one who'd been there to offer him steadfast companionship after all the worst moments of his life. A voice he knew better than even his brother by blood.

"Sebastian, it's me." He swallowed. "Please."

A wave struck him, a washing glow of panic and confusion and fear and joy. He nearly stumbled, gasping, before he locked on a pair of glowing forest green eyes.

That wave ... it wasn't coming from him. It belonged to *her*.

Gods, he could *feel* her. He could feel everything. He didn't know if she was aware of how vibrant this connection between them was, or if she was accustomed to it. If this was how every bond felt.

That thought made him grind his teeth, a foreign feeling of jealousy washing through him with a ferocity that terrified him. He momentarily forgot the dagger at his throat, clawing for some semblance of his self-control.

"Mariah," he whispered, lurching for her.

Her flinch as he moved for her tore him apart with more confusion than any piece of steel ever could.

Was she ... afraid of him?

That dagger bit into his skin. "If you think I won't do it, then you are poorly mistaken."

Andrian almost growled. Almost swung, lashing out with shadows and limbs.

Until a choking sob shattered his world. More hope and grief crashed into him, drowning him out.

"Sebastian?" Mariah's voice was a soft shudder, thick and clouded with all the same emotions he felt.

Or ... that *she* felt. It had all become the same to Andrian, so much raging magic surrounding him that he wasn't sure where he ended, and she began.

The dagger lifted from his neck, just a touch. "Yes. We're here, My Queen. We're getting you out."

Mariah trembled again, before rushing forward. Andrian's heart leaped with joy—

—Until she brushed past him and leapt into Sebastian's open embrace. The dagger finally left his throat, and Andrian turned as Sebastian clutched Mariah to him, face burrowed in her neck.

"We're here," he repeated. "It's us."

Andrian gritted his teeth at Sebastian's crooning words.

Mariah sniffed and stepped back, staring up at Sebastian. "Us?'"

The wind shifted as five more shapes melted from the shadows of the gardens, all armed to the teeth, faces wearing mixed expressions of exuberant joy ... and terrible rage.

The latter seemed to be mostly directed at him. He shifted his stance, uneasy as they circled him. He knew these men but did not know the way they stared at him.

Like he was an enemy.

Mariah, though, didn't seem to notice. She sobbed again, before launching herself at Feran, Drystan, and Trefor. She turned finally to Matheo, tears tracking down her cheeks, and was about to wrap her arms around him when she halted.

A sixth shape had melted from the moonlit shadows. Instinct alone sent Andrian lurching forward, grasping for Mariah's hand. He ignored the hissed warnings from the other Armature, just as he shoved back the sting as she flinched away from him again.

It was a huge cat, black as the night around them, stalking into the aura of Mariah's glowing skin. Its hazel eyes gleamed as bright as the wicked claws peeking from its paws, its glistening fangs flashing as its maw lifted into a snarl.

Matheo cast a glance at the giant cat before turning back to Mariah and Andrian, a grin on his face. "Relax," he said, much too calmly as the predator stalked closer, glowing eyes evaluating its prey.

"Relax? That's a fucking *panther*," Mariah whispered, words strained and scratched with fear.

Andrian had never heard terror in her voice like that.

Matheo hadn't, either, because he paused as well, eyes going wide as his smile softened. "Yes, but it's also a friend. She'll explain when we get out of here, but it seems there's more to our old friends from Kreah than they first let on."

Kreah? Andrian gaped at Matheo before looking again at the panther. It had dropped the snarl, sitting back on its haunches as its tail swished across the pebbled garden path.

What the actual fuck was going on?

"We can chat and catch up about everything later. It's been a long nine weeks. We need to leave." Sebastian's voice was low and rough, and the others shifted into movement. "It's way too open out here. Which ... how did you even get out here, Mariah?"

But Andrian's mind had caught on to Sebastian's earlier words. He whirled to Sebastian before Mariah could answer.

"Did you just say nine *weeks*?"

He didn't care about Sebastian's frustrated curse at him. Didn't care about the others circling them, trying to herd them into shelter. His mind was blank as he turned to Mariah.

She glanced at him once, quickly, before shuttering her stare and stepping away. Letting herself get swept up by Sebastian and

Drystan and that massive black cat watching them with unnerving alertness.

He made himself look around him. At where they were. Made himself look at *her*.

He'd noticed the gardens after he'd first slammed into consciousness, the bond freshly formed and roaring between them. But in the haze, he'd only focused on Mariah's presence, on the bridge now thrumming between their souls. He hadn't looked closely at her appearance, or at the castle rising out of the gardens.

He did now, though.

She wore a pale pink dress, short and brushing her thighs, the tulle dirty and torn. Her long, dark hair hung in limp tangled knots down her back, and her skin was too pale, too dirty. Its golden glow was gone, replaced by a sickly sheen.

When she looked at him again over her shoulder, he noticed how gaunt her face was. How frail she was. Mariah had always been a force of nature, formidable in both a ballgown and in the training ring.

Now, she just looked ... weak. Starved. *Broken*.

"Yes, Andrian," she said, voice still muted. "It's been nine weeks. Nine weeks, I—we have been trapped here."

He was paralyzed, rooted to the ground, blocks of ice thick around his feet. "I don't remember any of it."

An emotion filled her face—not quite sadness, or pity. But true, raw heartbreak.

"I know."

A rustling across the gardens, where the dark castle pierced the sky, shattered the moment. A heartbeat later, Quentin burst into view, panting lightly as his red hair was in tossed disarray. His expression lit up when he saw Mariah, and he shoved past Drystan and Sebastian to pick her up in another great hug.

Quentin set her back down as quickly as he'd raced in, shooting a look at the rest of them, eyes lingering for a moment too long on Andrian with shock, anger, and distrust. "I think word is spreading about a commotion in the gardens. We need to get the fuck out of here. *Now*."

"I know." Sebastian nodded and glanced at Mariah. He then shifted to Andrian, expression hardening as his mouth opened to say something else.

"Sebastian, no." Mariah reached out a hand, resting it on his arm. "Stop. He's coming with us. I'll explain everything when we're out, I promise. But I was not the only one held prisoner in this place."

Sebastian stood still as a statue for a few heavy heartbeats, his stare never breaking from Andrian's, before he nodded. "As you wish." He twisted on his heel, about to lead them away from the castle and to the dark safety of the trees beyond.

"Is ... is someone there?"

Everyone froze as the faint, feminine voice rang across the quiet gardens.

"*Shit*," Quentin whispered. "We need to move."

"No, wait." Mariah raised a steadying hand.

Andrian watched them all, expression and mind vacant.

Nine weeks. Nine weeks, missing from memory, trapped in a black bit of despair and unfamiliar darkness.

Mariah stepped around him, peering into the shadows. Hesitancy raced from her through their fresh, aching bond.

"Anniliese?" she called softly into the dimness.

A dark-haired woman stepped out from around a willow tree, dressed in a fine jade robe, face powdered and hair pressed.

A Royal. Somewhere, in a far distant memory, Andrian recognized her. Some spoiled daughter of another lord he'd met once or twice.

"What ... what is this?" The girl's voice was high-pitched and clearly terrified, eyes widening as she observed the group of men bearing more weapons than was ever reasonable.

The panther lurking behind Matheo certainly didn't help.

"Anniliese," Mariah repeated, this time far gentler than Andrian would've ever expected. "We're leaving. Now. You should come with us."

The girl—Anniliese—cast them all a wild glance. "Leaving? To where?"

"Verith," Drystan answered quickly, steady voice like an anchor.

Anniliese shook her head. "You'll never make it. They'll catch you."

"Not if we move now. We will make it." Mariah's voice trembled, just once, but she held her head high. Andrian could feel her fear but noticed how she refused to let it touch her body.

Anniliese's fingers toyed with a silk ribbon on her robe. "I … I cannot go with you. I belong here, with my father." She turned to Mariah, pinning her with a stare that made Andrian's hackles rise.

"I couldn't sleep tonight and thought I would take a walk through the gardens to calm my head. I had been thinking about what you said, and maybe it's fate we met again." She drew in a breath. "I still do not accept you. I likely never will. But I understand what you told me, and I believe you. You can't give up your crown, even if you wanted to. Even if I still believe the Goddess made the wrong choice."

Drystan loosened a low growl, and Quentin palmed his knives. Andrian's shadows twitched around his fingers, but a raised hand from Mariah had them all falling still.

"Will you turn us in, then? Will you alert the guards, or will you let us go?" Mariah was calmer than a summer's day, but a hidden danger lurked beneath her words. Andrian shifted and knew his brothers did the same.

They had no desire to harm an unarmed woman, but they would do what they must to protect their queen.

Anniliese turned to them again, a swallow traveling down the thin column of her throat. Her gaze lingered on Andrian for a moment, a darkness shuttering behind her light brown eyes. She took another shaky inhale and looked back at Mariah.

"No. I won't. I will be committing treason to my host, but … I won't tell them you've gone, or that I saw you."

Mariah cocked her head as if studying the young woman.

Sebastian fidgeted nervously beside her. "Mariah—"

"Thank you, Lady Anniliese," Mariah said and turned on her heel. She pushed back Sebastian, moving to Drystan and Quentin's side before she paused and glanced once more over her shoulder.

"I understand why you feel you must stay. But stop letting these men run your life as if it wasn't your own. You know, deep down, that isn't what you want."

Anniliese blinked, something like shame and surprise flashing across her face, before nodding once and turning with a twirl to her skirts, walking away to the castle.

The rest of them turned to face Mariah, who stood at their center. The star around which they orbited, the anchor holding them to earth. She had her face turned up to the sky, and Sebastian shifted, before darting a burning glare at Andrian.

He searched his mind, again, and was met only by blackness.

His queen might have stood her ground for him, but he feared his fellow Armature would be far harder to convince.

Mariah sighed, dropping her eyes from the sky. She turned to the forest, to the freedom and hope that awaited them there.

"Let's go home, Armature."

PART 2

SCARRED

Strength is found amongst the scarred,
And forged amongst the broken.

— Excerpt from the Ginnelevé diary, dated 1,002 years after the reign of Xara. Authored by Elara Ginnelevé during the second Idrixian Civil War.

CHAPTER 25

They snuck across the frost-covered ground, the bare pads of Mariah's feet burning against the chill, and all she could think was that they would be spotted. That Anniliese had lied.

That any moment, this happy reunion would come crashing down in a wave of blood and despair.

But her fears never came to fruition. Somehow, they reached the trees, Sebastian ushering them all into the cover of the thick brush. They ran several yards deeper, the impenetrable canopy above blocking the moonlight; Mariah tripped twice on a twisted tree root, caught both times by Quentin's outstretched arms. They were guided only by instinct, intuition, and training.

And Rylla, the black cat's shining hazel eyes seeing far better than theirs in the dark. Numb shock had rocked Mariah when Sebastian whispered an order to the feline, dull recognition sweeping through her.

After a few wild minutes, they stood in a small glade, panting into the cold night air.

Mariah waited for the horns and alarms to pierce the quiet darkness.

When they didn't come, she began to worry.

That apprehension only grew as they walked deeper into the forest, the sound of the woods at night offering her little comfort. The glade opened into a full clearing, early wildflowers pushing up past the frost to dance in the moonlight. Seven horses waited there, saddled and ready. Mariah's Armature leaped into action, checking cinches and swinging into saddles. Mariah lingered a few feet away, staring at the seventh and final horse.

And Andrian, who stood beside it.

She was aware of him. Achingly, *painfully* aware of him. It was like it always was after the bond, but exponentially heightened. She didn't know if it was because their bond was so new or if it was something she would not—could not—think about, but energy pulsed and raced between them on a current that made the hair on her arms stand on end.

Staring at that final horse, and despite the deep, ripping pull coursing through her veins ... she couldn't do it.

Every part of her body wanted to be near him, to touch him ... but her battered soul screamed in agony at the thought.

Her magic snapped and bit beneath her skin, but with gritted teeth, she turned herself away from him. Walked in the other direction, to the other side of the clearing.

Where Feran stood beside his horse, his open face watching her with a curious, heartbreakingly sympathetic expression. She stopped in front of him, meeting his dark stare.

"Can I ride with you?"

He blinked and nodded. "Of course."

With that, she climbed into the saddle, Feran settling in behind her. Across the clearing, Andrian mounted the seventh horse.

It took every fiber of her being to ignore the burning itch of his stare as they rode into the night.

A BREEZE PUSHED in from the north, and Mariah wrapped the wool cloak tighter, shifting deeper into the saddle. Feran's warmth seeped into her bones, the gentle rocking of the horse between her thighs comforting and familiar.

They'd been riding for some time under the cover of darkness, the steady clip of the horses' hooves beating a soothing melody against the forest trail. Their pace was swift, Sebastian leading them with his quiet urgency.

The trail dipped down a gentle bank, and the tinkling of a clear, starlit stream could be heard over the nocturnal woods. They crossed it without stopping, the water lit with silver-gold moonlight reaching the knees of Feran's gelding. It splashed Mariah's legs, bitingly cold. So cold Feran took a sharp intake of breath behind her.

But she didn't even flinch. She'd learned how to find comfort in the chill.

Rylla was last to cross, shaking water from her sleek fur as she raced ahead, droplets raining around her like fallen stars. She slowed when she reached Sebastian, glancing up as he looked down. He pulled his horse to a halt, scanning the small clearing walled in by a towering copse of pine trees.

"We'll rest here for a few hours—at least until sunrise. We're far enough away, and we haven't been followed." Sebastian looked again at Rylla, and she nodded her head as if in confirmation.

Strange. The existence of shifters was ... Mariah hadn't yet been able to rationalize that to herself. It was extraordinary but certainly useful.

Sebastian slid from his mare's back, concerned gaze landing on Mariah. "Trefor, Feran, you take first watch. Drystan and Matheo will relieve you. Quentin and I will take the final shift."

At his command, Mariah's Armature set about making camp, pulling pallets and bedrolls from saddles and clearing forest underbrush to create some semblance of comfort. Rylla retreated to the edges of the glade, near the banks of the stream, grooming her still-damp fur before drinking straight from the crystal-clear water.

Feran swung himself from his horse, offering a hand to

Mariah with a patient smile. She tightened the cloak around her shoulders, taking his hand and sliding from the gelding's back.

She tried to fight the pull.

But it was futile.

Her eyes locked on a dark figure over Feran's shoulder. Tracked him as he dismounted his horse and walked with hesitant steps toward Sebastian.

"I can take a watch, too." Andrian's voice was low, but it still echoed around the clearing.

Everyone paused. Mariah's heartbeat was in her throat.

Sebastian turned slowly, a strange, uncharacteristic fury written across his face. "You are lucky you're not in *chains*, Armature," he growled. "The only reason you're not is because my queen commanded we let you travel with us. You will sleep where we can watch you, but Enfara will freeze over before I place our safety—*her* safety—in your hands again."

"Sebastian, that's enough." The surge of protectiveness that washed over Mariah shocked her, pulling words from her throat before she could stop them. But deep down, she knew why.

She had no desire to see Andrian in chains. Not again.

She especially didn't want Sebastian to be the one to place them there.

"No, it's fine. Really," Andrian said, voice unusually soft, carrying with it a hint of unfamiliar defeat. Mariah darted a glance at him and wished she hadn't.

He stared at her with utter anguish. Other emotions lingered on his face, too. Emotions she'd once acknowledged and given herself.

Never again.

Love is a weakness ... but also your retribution.

"It's fine," she echoed Andrian as she turned back to Sebastian, exhaustion suddenly settling into the depths of her bones. "Let's just focus on getting home. Then we can figure out ... everything else."

She didn't linger on what *everything else* meant. Instead, she watched her Armature settle into their temporary camp, enjoying something she never thought she'd know again.

Safety.

She still couldn't believe it was real. That they were all *here*. Anxiety still twisted in her gut, a nauseating worm, at the thought that this was all a dream. That she would lay her head down to rest, and tomorrow she would wake up in that cold, dark, terrible cell and find this was all just some new trick invented by the lords to torment her.

She couldn't get over how it had all been so *easy*. From the new servant girl to the lack of guards patrolling the halls to the absence of alarms, it had all lined up so perfectly.

Every lord in Onita, every member of the aristocracy, was in Khento, and it seemed as if they'd just ... let her go.

The threads of her magic bubbled around her, feeling her drifting panic. She toyed with one between her fingers, the soft glow of the light and the brush of magic against her skin weaving a soothing pattern.

She let the magic dissipate into the air as she curled herself onto a bed roll, nestled into the soft forest floor between Sebastian and Matheo. Despite the frayed disquiet of her mind, her exhaustion won.

CHAPTER 26

Mariah hadn't woken when Sebastian and Matheo roused for their respective watch shifts.

She hadn't woken when the sun crested the horizon or when the songbirds rang through the thick canopy overhead.

It was only when the twin crescent moons finally slipped from the sky that her eyelids fluttered open as if her body craved every moment of rest beneath their light. There were rustles and muted conversations as her Armature cleaned the camp and ate a meager breakfast. A horse nickered a few yards away, pawing at the earth.

But all those sounds faded away as she opened her eyes, adjusting to the morning light.

A black butterfly rested on the forest floor beside her, ebony wings slowly opening and closing. Its antennae twitched as she exhaled, breath rustling its delicate wings.

As she watched the butterfly, she had the distinct feeling the butterfly watched her back. Something threaded through her gut—something gold and silver and familiar, reaching desperately for the small creature sharing her waking space. She slowly lifted her arm, giving into instinct as she reached for the insect.

The desperation to touch it, to confirm it was *real*, consumed her.

But before her fingers could brush its silken wings, the butterfly took flight, fluttering as it hovered just over her head. Mariah rolled onto her back as she watched the butterfly dance in the air, her hand still lifted, tracing its pattern. It was a shadow dappling the morning light, a ghost playing in the sun.

"Mariah?" A familiar, gentle male voice pulled her from her reverie. Her attention snapped from the onyx insect, meeting a concerned set of hazel eyes.

"Good morning, Seb." She pushed to her feet, taking the blanket she'd wrapped around herself in the night with her. She still only wore that awful, disgusting monstrosity of pink tulle, along with the warm wool cloak. As she stood, she winced; the skin between her thighs had been rubbed raw during their desperate flee. Everything burned and scalded.

She needed this dress off her. Now. Needed to feel *human* again.

Sebastian still watched her as he bridled his horse a few paces away. He paused, taking a hesitant step toward her. "How are you? Do you need anything?"

Mariah gritted her teeth. Pulled an inhale through parted lips. Her hands shook as she clutched the blanket to her tighter.

"Clothes. I need clothes."

Sebastian's eyes widened. "Shit, I—of course. I'm so sorry." He glanced over her shoulder. "Matheo!" he called, before looking back at Mariah. "Ciana packed you some. Matheo is carrying them. I'll help you—"

"No. It's okay. Thank you." She didn't need his help. And the mention of Ciana ...

Goddess, she missed her best friend.

Mariah turned, and on aching feet, crossed the clearing to Matheo.

Halfway across, a dark shape emerged from the shadows of the trees, and Mariah paused. She met Rylla's gaze, recognizable hazel eyes gleaming in the morning light.

They watched each other—for how long, Mariah didn't know. But something settled in her, and she released a sigh. The cat blinked, tail swishing.

"Thank you, Rylla." The panther's tail twitched again. "It seems we have much to catch up on once we arrive back in Verith. But, in the meantime ... thank you."

The panther dipped its head, just once, before melting back into the shadows.

"Mariah? You okay?"

Mariah swallowed, turning to Matheo. He held his horse's reins, watching her with raw concern.

She forced a smile to her face, and on shaky legs, walked to meet him.

"Morning, Matheo." She reached out a hand, but not to him. Stepping to his horse's side, she ran a hand down the chestnut mare's neck before scratching her just below her mane. The mare swung her head to Mariah, brown eyes taking her in as her warm breath huffed against her arm.

The brush of the mare's muzzle against her skin turned her smile just a bit more genuine. Made her forget the burning of the torn tulle on her skin. Grounded her on this earth, just a bit more.

She missed her buckskin gelding, Kodie. And for the first time in so long, she allowed herself to be excited to see him again.

"What's her name?" she asked Matheo, voice quiet as she continued scratching the mare's neck.

"This is Ruby."

Mariah huffed a laugh—a faint, weak chuckle, but a laugh, nonetheless. "Ruby?" She turned to Matheo, finding him wearing a broad smile. "Couldn't have come up with something a bit more creative?"

He shrugged. "I didn't name her, but I think it fits. She certainly is a gem for me."

"You're lucky indeed to have earned the trust and affection of a red mare." Mariah ran her hand lightly down Ruby's face, over the wide white blaze, as her smile faltered. "I need—I need clothes." She tripped over the request, and as heat flooded her cheeks, she knew she was flushed.

Gods, she hated that blush.

Matheo's smile softened. "Of course." He turned, reaching into one of the saddlebags tied to Ruby's saddle. He pulled out a rolled-up pair of cotton leggings, underclothes, and a wool sweater.

So much—gratitude, joy, sadness, homesickness—welled up in Mariah as he handed them to her. Tears burned behind her cheeks, and her chest heaved and cracked.

She still waited for the dream to shatter, for the nightmare to claw back in.

With a heavy inhale, she clutched the clothes to her chest, and started for the trees and the stream they'd crossed the night before.

A rustling that followed her had her pausing. She glanced over her shoulder to see Matheo following.

"What are you doing?"

Matheo flushed. "Sebastian would kill me if I let you go wandering off alone."

Mariah frowned. "I need to change. I'd like a moment of privacy to do so."

"I know, but—" Matheo glanced over her shoulder. He snapped his mouth closed before giving her a tight-lipped smile and stepping back. "That'll work. Thanks, Rylla."

Mariah whirled to see the black cat again lurking in the shadows, hazel stare pinned on Matheo. As if in warning.

She couldn't stop the laugh that bubbled out of her. It was faint, and weak, but still ... she laughed. She continued into the trees, whispering to Rylla as she passed.

"These boys mean well, but sometimes a girl needs some space."

The panther's tail brushed her legs as she walked to the stream.

———

THE WATER WAS SO cold it burned.

Mariah had tossed her shredded, filthy pink rags on the bank before plunging in, desperate to wash even just a single layer of the hell she'd endured from her skin. Rylla lingered downstream, far enough to give her privacy, but close enough to be the watchful eyes that eased her Armature's worries.

She lingered in the water as long as possible, scrubbing and scrubbing and scrubbing, sitting on the smooth pebbled bottom. It was only when her teeth chattered that she finally emerged from the stream, finding a small, folded travel towel placed beside her clothes. Mariah smiled at the disappearing wisp of black fur, before drying herself and slipping into her once familiar clothes.

The warmth that encompassed her was instant. And unfamiliar. The clothes hung loose on her thin frame, but they were *hers*. And the way it felt, having that much softness touching so much of her raw, damaged, tortured skin ...

Her hand flew to her mouth as she sunk to her knees in the soft moss along the banks of that babbling, lively stream. A sob choked up her throat, anguish shredding delicate threads.

Mariah remained like that for what could have been a century. Trying to hold herself together, even as the fraying edges slipped and unraveled and burned, pain and despair rising around her.

Until she saw it.

The black butterfly hovered before her, dipping and swaying in the light breeze brushing through the canopy. It wove a delicate dance, and as Mariah's eyes tracked its movement, her own soul lifted, taking flight. Dancing in the morning light with the onyx insect.

The butterfly shot up into the trees and disappeared from Mariah's sight. She stood for a few more moments, staring at where it had disappeared, before she took a deep, steadying inhale and strode back up the hill towards the camp.

When she arrived, it was no longer a camp. Everything was packed and readied, her Armature standing beside their horses. Feran held a pair of boots and socks in his hand, greeting her with a gentle smile. She returned it, bare feet crunching the icy ground.

"Are you alright, *nio*?" The too-familiar voice fixed her in place. A voice that had her soul singing and sent fear and panic racing through her limbs.

She turned, slowly, to face Andrian. That nickname, one she hadn't heard in many long, tortuous weeks, twisted a knife further into her gut. All the pain, all the heartbreak she felt was etched plainly across her face.

The entire clearing fell silent.

Mariah held Andrian's gaze for seven long, tortuous heartbeats, before she found her words amongst the shreds of her soul.

"You never told me what that means. What it meant."

Andrian blinked in shock. "It was stupid of me to lie to you, that day in the library. But ... you never asked again."

Mariah squeezed her eyes closed. It was too much. She knew he recalled none of what had happened, but she had no idea how far back that went. How much of what they'd shared was real, and how much was just the work of a nameless darkness that had kept Andrian shrouded and wreathed in a mental prison as strong as her iron cage.

"I did. I asked again. The same night I lost you, I asked." She opened her eyes to meet his stare once more.

"But now, I don't think I want to know anymore."

She turned, striding to Feran with as much purpose as she could muster. She could feel the pain between their bond snap and sunder her soul, knew it would be etched on his heartbreakingly beautiful face. But she did not let it buckle her, did not let it show beyond the slight tremor to her hands as she took her socks and boots from Feran and slid them onto her feet.

She kept it all bottled up, even as she settled on Feran's horse. Even as his warmth wrapped around her.

As they rode from the clearing, through the forested foothills of northern Onita, only one thing kept her from tumbling head-first into the bottomless despair of her thoughts.

Delicate, white snowbell blossoms had pushed past the last of the winter frost, their arched shape hanging over green stems. The symbol adorning the queen's crown, representing the rejuvenative magic of Qhohena and how, despite all hardship, life always emerged victorious.

Passing field after field of the beautiful white flowers, none of them speaking into the cold quiet, Mariah wondered if they had it all wrong.

Maybe life never won; it was just death donning a prettier face.

CHAPTER 27

They arrived back in Verith much the same way Mariah had left it: quietly and cloaked in darkness.

Except this time, Mariah returned surrounded by those who'd risked everything to save her. The only constant, of course, was a single man who trailed the group, eyes downcast and shrouded in shadow.

But Mariah did not want to focus on the similarities. Instead, she wanted to focus on how her return was different.

She wanted to focus on where she would go from here.

The entrance through the city wall was worn and rusted, iron creaking as the gate was lifted by two heavy chains. They passed beneath the ancient stone and emerged on the other side, somewhere in the center of the city. The twinkling lights of the mountain district rose above them, just as the brighter vibrancy of the market district down below glowed against the early spring night. The Bay was empty and quiet, and she released a soft sigh of relief.

Feran had filled her in on what had happened since she was taken. About the threat of the Kizar Islanders as they'd pummeled the coasts, keeping her Armature distracted and preoccupied. She still had many more questions but wanted to see the city for herself before deciding what to do next.

Feran shifted behind her, adjusting the reins and leaning close to her ear. "Welcome home."

Home.

The word clattered through her.

The nagging feeling that it was all a dream again crept up on her. It was a spiral she'd fallen into often during their days of travel. If tomorrow, she would simply wake again in that cold, dark cell, all hope of freedom and happiness washed away in the night. She was so hesitant to let herself feel joy, to feel happiness at being back in Verith. And she knew exactly why.

In those weeks, she'd gotten to know Shawth quite well. He would not be one to simply give her up in such a way.

Not unless he was sure it would result in something he could use to get what he wanted.

All those dark thoughts followed Mariah like a cloud as they marched steadily up the hills of the mountain district, their path leading to the great golden palace, resplendent and vibrant even at night as it rose into view. A beat of annoyance raced through her; not only had nine weeks of her life been stolen from her, but she could not even enjoy being home.

"Home," she finally whispered back to Feran.

It pulsed through her like a drum, reverberating around her aching and traumatized mind.

She couldn't remember when this place had become her home. When her life had shifted fully and she'd stopped referring to a quiet cabin in the woods on the outskirts of a crossroad town as *home*.

The surprise she felt at the wave of homesickness for that perfect place was sudden, and foreign, and struck her like a punch to the gut.

She had no lost love for Andburgh. Her memories of that town and the people who resided there, for the man who called himself its lord, were far from happy. But there were three people in that town who she did miss, more than anything. Once, not long ago, her family was the only thing that kept her chin high. The only thing that kept hope in her veins was that one day, she would find a better future for herself than the one the other girls of Andburgh had before them.

Mixed with the homesickness and the surprise was something else: guilt. So much *guilt*. Mariah dropped her chin to her chest to hide the tears burning behind her eyes, more shock and sadness pounding through her veins until she feared she might drown in it.

She had forgotten her family. Had completely forgotten about her brother, Ellan, and his annoying knack for being kind when the people around him didn't deserve it. Had forgotten about her father, Wex, and his soft yet fierce protectiveness, his determination to raise a daughter who wouldn't be crushed by what this world did to so many women who didn't have anyone to teach them to stand on their own.

She'd forgotten about her mother, Lisabel, and her gentle healer hands and veiled golden eyes which held so much love and so many secrets. Mariah was so swept up in the excitement of her new life that she'd forgotten the one who'd made her who she was, who'd gifted her with what she'd needed to turn a situation she'd never expected to find herself in into one where she could make a difference.

Mariah was so lost in her thoughts she hardly noticed as they passed through the palace gates. It wasn't until they passed beneath the statue of Qhohena, shimmering even in the dim waxing moonlight, that she blinked and pulled herself from where she'd drifted. She stared at the goddess's serene face, arms open and outspread.

Your sister has spoken to me many times. So, why haven't you?

When her only answer was her slow heartbeat and sound of water falling from the fountain's outstretched arms, Mariah didn't know why she felt so sad.

The horses stopped outside the stables, half-asleep stable hands rushing from the shadows to grab the reins of the weary beasts. Feran swung himself from their horse, landing firmly before offering a hand to Mariah. She took it, body stiff and sore and exhausted. He looked at her as she landed beside him, eyes dark and warm.

"Where do you want to go?" He asked gently, releasing her hand.

She wrapped her arms around herself, answering on instinct.

"My rooms. I want a bath."

THE WATER RAN from the faucet, filling the massive porcelain bath with steaming, scalding water.

It would likely strip her skin raw the moment she stepped into it.

It wasn't hot enough.

She wanted it to burn everything from her, to cleanse her to her bones. And even then, she feared it wouldn't be enough.

It might never be enough.

The bathroom was unchanged. Her entire suite was unchanged—lived in, obviously used by her court during her absence, but that didn't change the feeling of familiarity that washed over her the second she'd passed through those white doors gilded with a map of Onita.

Despite that feeling, these rooms still felt like those of a stranger. Of a person she'd once known before trauma shaped and forged her into someone new. Someone who did not enjoy baths because of how relaxing they were, but because they offered a chance to soak away the past. A simple means to a complicated end.

Mariah turned from the still-filling tub to meet her reflection in her bathroom mirrors. She had disrobed, leaving the sweater and leggings from her travels in a pile by the door.

A sudden wave of recognition washed over her as she stared at herself in those mirrors.

She felt like that butterfly she'd seen on the road. A being capable of complete metamorphosis. Not long ago, she'd been nothing more than a simple commoner, the outcast daughter of a healer and a soldier. Her life was uprooted, and she'd transformed into a queen apparent who wore resplendent gowns and attended balls with members of the continent's elite.

She'd now undergone yet another metamorphosis. From royalty … to wraith.

For that was what stared back at her in the polished, floor-length mirrors. A wraith, her once-tanned skin now pale and sickly, cheeks sunken and eyes ringed in dark shadows. Her hair hung in limp, matted strands down her back, and her bones poked uncomfortably beneath her skin. Her collarbones were too prominent, ribs too visible. Even the generous, muscular curve of her hips and thighs had wasted away, leaving nothing more than a ghostly skeleton in its wake.

The only part of her that still looked familiar were her eyes, the forest-green ringed by dense grey and glowing with faint silver-gold light.

She was glad that even though her body no longer felt like her own, she still had her eyes.

Mariah stared at her reflection for many long moments, unmoving as the bath behind her filled and filled. The room became wreathed in steam, and she tore herself from the stranger in her reflection to turn off the faucets as the water neared the lip of the tub. She sank thankfully into the near-scalding water with an audible sigh. As expected, the water burned her skin, but she welcomed it.

She wanted all traces of the past nine weeks, all traces of those hands that had touched and taken and tried to break her wiped clean. Even if that meant she had to rip off the layer she had, to allow it to be replaced by something new.

CHAPTER 28

The palace looked just the same as it did in Andrian's last memories—massive, imposing, and mocking.

He had bits and pieces of other recollections, blurred images fading in and out, like remembering a dream or a nightmare. But one of the last real moments he remembered before he was woken by the silver-gold bond burning through his soul was him furiously spurring his stallion out of the palace gates and down the gold-cobbled streets. Straight to the city manor of House Laurent to confront his father.

After that ... it was all darkness and shadow.

Andrian watched Feran pull his horse to a halt, Mariah seated in front of him. Watched as they both dismounted, as she took lurching steps toward the palace.

Every single instinct in his chest, in his heart, in his soul screamed at him to follow, to go to her. To be near her.

But the beats of frustration and anger and sadness flowing from her down that freshly forged bond held him firmly in place.

That new bond ... it was so much. *Too* much. He didn't know if she felt the same, or if this was how all the bonds felt. If this was something she was simply accustomed to. Perhaps she was still so closed off by whatever had happened to her back in that hellish castle. But all he craved was her nearness, her touch, her smell and taste and the feel of her on his skin.

He urged his horse forward with a grimace. A stableboy scampered out from the shadows, hair still mussed from sleep. The boy grabbed hold of the horse's reins as Andrian dismounted. He had no possessions—the horse had carried nothing beyond a meager change of clothes, probably intended for one of the other Armature. He was filthy and tired and knew he smelled, but none of that mattered to him.

He'd just taken a single step after Mariah when a familiar figure blocked his path. A second stalked up to the first's side, and Andrian could only watch in frustration and a pang of longing as Mariah disappeared around the side of the stables to the rear entrance of the palace, Feran beside her.

"Not so fast, Armature." Sebastian's voice was low and rigid, his posture just as tense. Quentin stood beside him, palming the knives strapped to his chest, chaos dancing in his eyes.

"What? I'm tired," Andrian said, his defensiveness rising like hackles along with his magic.

Quentin's fingers twitched. Sebastian's lips pressed into a hard line.

"There are some questions you need to answer for us first. Before we can decide what to do with you."

"Decide what to *do* with me?" Andrian glared at Quentin and Sebastian, before looking quickly at Drystan, who had sidled up beside Quentin. "Are you sure you have the authority to do that?"

The men stared at each other for several tense heartbeats before Sebastian rested his hand on the hilt of his sword.

Andrian didn't miss the threat.

"Just come with us." Sebastian turned on his heels, leaving Andrian glaring darkly, Quentin grinning, and Drystan watching Andrian with a contemplative expression. Quentin broke first, following after Sebastian.

"Put his mind at ease. Please." Andrian glanced at Drystan. The man was always so calm, so level-headed. It often was a comfort to the group, Andrian included, especially knowing the man was a deadly warrior—the best among them—when he needed to be.

Right now, though, his words achieved nothing beside pissing Andrian off. There was only one thing Andrian wanted to do, and it was not humoring Sebastian in whatever power-play this was about to be.

But as he held Drystan's stare, familiar doubt and self-loathing twisted in, cooling his anger. His friend was right. He'd been gone for nine weeks, taken the same night as Mariah. He would suspect himself, too, were the roles reversed.

Fuck, if he were them, he would've likely killed himself on sight. The fact that they had superior levels of self-control than he did was not lost on him. Besides, he'd grown up with these men. They knew him, as well as anyone.

"Fine," he growled. With steady steps, he followed Sebastian and Quentin, trailed by Drystan as they strode into the familiar, gilded palace halls.

Sebastian led them not to their usual wing, but to an older, quieter area of the palace, one reserved for guests but hadn't been used in years. He pushed his way into one of the many rooms lining the corridor, Quentin on his heels. Andrian went next, and Drystan closed the door behind them with a *snick*.

The room was clean, if not a bit stale. There was a modest dining table, a bed, and a door on the left that must lead to the bathing room. Andrian took a step toward the table, wanting to take a seat on the dark wood chair, when something cool and sharp against his neck froze him in place. He glanced at Quentin, grin back on his face, a blade that was the twin to the one against Andrian's neck clutched in his left hand.

"Give us one gods-damned reason we shouldn't kill you right now." Sebastian's cool voice rang through the small, quiet room.

Drystan stepped around Andrian. "Sebastian—"

"No, Drystan. I need to hear his answer."

"My *answer*?" Andrian's response was a growl. He could feel his shadows in turmoil, the blade against his throat making them beg for freedom, pushing off his shoulders and reaching desperately for Quentin and that dagger. He held them back … for now.

"What fucking answer do you want? That I remember nothing, that I was as much a prisoner there as she was? I never fucking *touched* her, Sebastian. The last thing I remember was riding to confront my father about my mother's death. After that, it's all darkness and nightmares until the bond. The end."

"'*The end.*'" Quentin pressed the dagger further into Andrian's throat. "Do you honestly expect us to believe that? How is it that she'd planned to bond with you the very night you both went missing?"

Andrian blinked. "What … what the fuck are you talking about?"

Sebastian stepped forward, brows pushed together over dark eyes. "Oh, don't pretend to be ignorant now. You returned from wherever you went after your meeting with your father and Shawth and told her you were ready to take the bond. She said as much to Ciana before she went to bed that night." Sebastian's voice guttered, anger hardening his hazel stare into stone. "She was so happy. And now she's a ghost of herself."

Andrian gaped, jaw slackening. His chin touched the cool metal of the dagger against his throat, but he didn't care. "I … I don't remember. I don't remember *any* of that. That *wasn't me*."

"Then who the fuck was it? Because it looked and sounded enough like you that it fooled even her."

Andrian didn't have an answer for Sebastian. He simply stared at his friend, his brother, forcing his shadows and his rage away, burying them deep. Back into the twisted and tattered ruins of his soul, where they belonged.

Quentin must've seen the defeat humming off him; he pulled the dagger from Andrian's jugular, taking a step away. He didn't sheath it, though.

Andrian swallowed, his mouth dry, his throat dry. He was so tired, yet filled with a strange, disorganized energy, whirling and vibrating just beneath his skin. It was something new and foreign, but also welcome and familiar.

As much a conundrum as the dark-haired woman who he expected was its source.

"I don't know," he whispered, not bothering to hide his fear. His rage. His exhaustion and frustration. The three men raised their brows, their postures relaxing. Quentin finally slipped his dagger back into his baldric, while something like pity wrote itself across Drystan's face.

Andrian suspected this was the first time any of them had heard—truly heard—that much raw emotion in his voice.

"I don't know what it was. I only remember bits and pieces. Nightmares, mostly. Nightmares shrouded as memories. And a voice whispering to me everything I've always known that was broken with me." He met Sebastian's gaze. If anyone would hear him now, it was him.

"There were moments when I could glimpse the world around me, but I was so locked away that I couldn't understand what it meant. My senses governed in those moments—smell, touch, bits and flashes of color. But beyond that, everything was shadow and darkness, a never-ending hellscape that felt a bit too much like Enfara for my liking."

They watched him in silence as he spoke. Sebastian took a small step back as Drystan shifted on his feet.

"You're different," Quentin murmured. "Changed."

Andrian scoffed. "No shit."

"No, I mean ... you've *changed*." Quentin cocked a head, like a bird of prey working through a puzzle. "The old you would've never been so open about what he felt. Either Mariah has really managed to get through to you, or ..." He unsheathed a new dagger and twisted it in his hand.

"Or what?" The Andrian of a few months ago would've been annoyed. Irate, even, at this ridiculous line of questioning.

The Andrian of today, though, was only tired.

"Or this isn't you, and you're still wearing the same disguise you were when you stole her from us the first time."

That was the final straw. Shadows broke from Andrian's shoulders, and he clenched his hands into fists as he snarled back at Quentin. "You little fucking *prick*—"

"That's enough." Drystan moved, placing himself firmly between Andrian and Quentin. The latter had settled into a fighting stance, an eager grin on his face as he palmed his knives. Drystan glared hard at him.

"We're not making any decisions or accusations here tonight. None of us knows what truly happened, and it's not for us to decide what happens next."

"We can't just let him go back to his rooms, Drystan." Sebastian's voice was quiet, controlled. It grated against Andrian's skin, pulling his teeth further back into a snarl.

His control was waning thin, and he was craving a little blood and chaos.

"You're right." Drystan swung his firm golden stare to Andrian. "We can't. But we also can't lock him up anywhere, either. I propose he stay here, in these rooms. They're comfortable and clean, and he can go about his days in the palace without too much risk of crossing paths with Mariah." Drystan turned back to Sebastian and Quentin. "Since, I'm assuming, that's what you're both so concerned about? You just want to keep him away from her until she decides what to do with him?"

As Sebastian and Quentin shared a contemplative look, Andrian felt his chest go tight. Felt his shadows withdraw back below his skin, his rage dissipating as it was replaced with something ... else. Something cold and painful and lonely.

For some stupid, self-indulgent reason, he hadn't realized that his fate would be decided by his queen. Yes, he was bonded to her. But a part of him whispered that this bond was a means to an end for her, nothing more than a method of survival. That maybe she had no desire to be close to him, and simply needed the strength his connection would give her to escape.

That revelation stung and twisted his heart more than he knew was possible.

Especially with the last words she'd left him with, the last look she'd tossed his way.

He'd called her *nio*, and her response had nearly split him in two.

"*I don't think I want to know anymore.*"

"I agree with Drystan, I'll stay here. And … and I'll stay out of the way. I promise to leave her be until she's ready to decide what to do with me." Andrian's voice was filled with the same quiet defeat and desperation he felt.

She might not feel the same about him anymore, but he still meant every word he'd said to her that night before the Solstice.

He still loved her. She was still the reason his heart beat, the reason he felt alive. She was the answer to every one of his questions.

And if she wanted him gone, he would leave. Because he loved her far more than he would ever love himself.

CHAPTER 29

ariah stumbled from her bath when the water grew cold and stagnant, toweling off before slipping into an oversized tunic. She shuffled to her bed, collapsing into the down.

She'd forgotten this bed. How comfortable it was. Her lingering worry and panic and fear simmered below the surface, but the familiar quiet wrapped around her. So much had changed, so quickly, but that silence was still her companion.

Sleep pulled her down quickly, and she let herself fall.

Mariah awoke early in the morning, faint sunlight streaming through her window, dark matted hair splayed across the silk pillows.

She sat up with a jolt, chest heaving and tight, panicked breaths laboring as she shoved back the comforter. Comfortable, at ease. *Trapped.* The way the heavy blankets wrapped around her like a vice, drowning her in greedy, foreign opulence.

She was safe, but her mind had yet to catch up.

Mariah closed her eyes, forced her breathing to slow, for her heart to stop racing. Shaking slightly, she swung her legs off the bed, touching the soles of her feet to the soft rug below. Her feet were still bruised and scabbed from her time in the dungeons and had just started to heal after being swaddled in socks and proper shoes for the past few days. They ached dully, but Mariah didn't mind.

She'd spent so much time barefoot in those cells, she'd forgotten what it was like to not have her toes cold and numb.

She stood fully from bed and padded across the rug until her feet found cool marble.

The cold was much more familiar. More welcome. She savored it, just for a moment.

Drawing a breath, she cracked open her bedroom door, peering into the living room of her suites.

They were just as she remembered, just as she'd seen them last night. Just as empty, just as familiar, just as strange. The spring sunrise lit the Attlehon Mountains in an ethereal glow, and as she walked to the balcony door and opened it on its silent hinges, she smelled the snowbell blossoms blooming, could hear the wingbeats of the eagles echoing off the mountains.

Another inhale. An exhale. A rumble of her stomach.

Mariah turned, leaving the door open, and strode with a sudden purpose toward a cabinet beside the stove. She wasn't sure how good of an idea this was, but she wanted to make something. Create something that would bring her just a sliver of that past joy she once felt, a happiness she could remember but no longer felt.

Swinging open the cabinet, she spotted the familiar cast iron device, clean and seasoned. She squatted, rocking back on her heels, knees and ankles and the wasted muscles of her thighs screaming.

She wrapped her hands around the sides of the waffle iron. And lifted.

Or ... tried to lift. But her arms gave out, and so did her balance, and she collapsed backward. She fell on her tailbone, back slamming into the island behind her.

Her scars itched and pulsed.

Mariah stared hard at that waffle iron. Looked down at her

hands, at her arms. At how weak and thin they were, how unfamiliar they felt.

Tears pricked behind her eyes. Another unfamiliar feeling, but one she couldn't suppress for much longer.

"Mariah? Are you … are you awake?"

Mariah sobbed at the familiar sing-song voice that called out, hesitant yet still filled with hope. She turned just as Ciana burst into the kitchen, appearing around the island, a wave of shock flashing over her bright golden features.

The shock didn't last long. It was quickly replaced by undiluted joy, the kind of happiness that made Mariah's heart jump into her throat.

Somehow, she pushed out two words.

"Hi, Cee."

Ciana answered with a sob of her own before throwing herself forward, straight to the floor, and wrapping her arms around her queen. Around her best friend.

"Oh, thank the Goddess. You're alright. You're alright." Ciana kept repeating those words, pressing harder into Mariah. Mariah's back dug further into the island, scars rubbing, but she didn't mind. Ciana's sweet lilac scent wrapped around her, the first familiarity that didn't carry with it a sting of what she'd lost.

"The boys made me wait until the morning before coming to see you. I couldn't find Sebastian, but Feran and Trefor told me you needed to rest. I told them I would come see you as soon as the sun was up, so that's what I did."

Mariah smiled. It felt unnatural, but also … right. "I'm glad you did. I missed you so much, Cee."

"I missed you too, M. Don't you *ever* fucking do something like that to me again."

"I promise. Never again." Mariah heard the coldness that crept into her voice. She didn't try to hide it. And Ciana didn't miss it.

Her golden-haired friend leaned away, peeling off Mariah. Her bright amber eyes scanned Mariah more closely, and she could only imagine what Ciana saw.

A ghost. A wraith. A shadow of herself.

Someone who …

"You look like shit."

That … wasn't what she'd expected to come from Ciana. It shocked Mariah, but also made her feel, for the first time, at home.

Mariah smiled a second time. "Yes, well … a stint in a dungeon will do that to a girl."

Ciana's face fell, and she pushed further from Mariah, but not out of fear or worry. What Mariah saw on Ciana's face was complicated. Contemplative. Observant. A look into the brilliant, tortured mind lurking behind those shining smiles and light-hearted jokes.

Ciana watched Mariah, then darted her eyes to the open cabinet. To what was inside. Her golden brow twisted. "What were you just trying to do? Before I came in?"

Mariah couldn't help it. She was so tired, so broken, so defeated. And this was her best friend, something she'd never had before in her life.

Tears sprang into her eyes, and another sob shuddered through her. She took a deep, cleansing inhale before she could steady herself and meet Ciana's amber gaze.

"I-I just wanted to do one thing. One thing, for me, on my own." Her voice wavered and shook.

"I just wanted … wanted waffles. You know—I loved waffles." She didn't correct her use of the past tense. The girl she used to be loved waffles.

But this girl? Mariah didn't know. She'd wanted to find out, but her own body had betrayed her.

"I know. I love waffles too," Ciana murmured, voice gentle. "Why couldn't you?"

Mariah stared at the iron, pouring venom into her gaze. "I couldn't lift it."

Those words settled in the air for several heartbeats, neither woman moving.

"Do you still want them? The waffles, I mean."

Mariah shook her head. She was hungry, but it hadn't been about the food—not really.

Ciana drew in a breath. "Okay. Mikael will be here in a little bit, anyways. He'll cook us something." She shifted onto her knees, forcing Mariah to meet her stare.

"What do you *really* want?"

Mariah met that amber gaze unflinchingly. She knew what Ciana was asking, and for once in her life, she wasn't afraid to be vulnerable.

"I want to be strong again. I want to *feel* strong again."

Ciana nodded, a single, brisk movement. "Okay. We can do that. Where should we start?"

That had Mariah pausing. She glanced down at her hands resting in her lap. In doing so, she glimpsed her hair, the matted layers nearly reaching her hip. She lifted her head to look back at Ciana.

"A haircut. I need a haircut."

"Oh, thank the *Goddess*, I was worried you'd never admit that." Ciana pushed to her feet, reaching a hand down to Mariah.

Mariah took it. She was inches taller than her friend, but in that moment, Ciana felt like the unmovable force, the unstoppable object. Mariah was simply floating in her orbit.

Her friend gripped both her hands tightly.

"You *will* be strong again. You *will* heal. And you *will* take your vengeance. But you don't have to do any of those things right now. Right now, you can focus on what you *can* control. And that just so happens to be a haircut."

Tears fell freely down Mariah's cheeks, and she didn't bother stopping them. Ciana only smiled, before pulling her gently from the kitchen, back into Mariah's bedroom, and into the bathroom. She pulled out the vanity seat, tapping the back.

"Sit."

Mariah sat.

From somewhere—a drawer, maybe—Ciana withdrew a hairbrush and a pair of slender shears, the kind reserved for hair. Mariah twisted in her chair.

"Have you ever done this before?"

"What, given my best friend and queen a haircut after her nine-week imprisonment in the dungeon of a villainous, power-hungry lord? Surprisingly, no."

Mariah blinked, unamused. Ciana grinned.

"Calm down. Yes, I've given people haircuts before. Girls are expected to know all things about beauty and caring for a household, remember?" Her words were thick with bitter memories. Ciana gestured at the mirror. "Now, turn back around and let me work my magic."

At the beginning, Ciana tried to comb out as many of the matts as she could. Tried to salvage as much of the once-beautiful ebony curtain that had dripped down Mariah's back like streaks of painted night.

It soon became apparent, though, that it couldn't be saved. So Ciana took a steely gulp and made the first cut, just above where the matts began.

Mariah watched on, mute and emotionless, as her hair fell to the ground.

When Ciana was done, Mariah's hair brushed her collarbones, just barely past her shoulders. She felt naked and exposed ... but she also felt new. Yet another metamorphosis, another transformation.

She was lighter. Cleaner. Less like herself, but more like someone she wanted to become.

Hair would only get in the way of her vengeance.

CHAPTER 30

Queen Ryenne Shawth, tenth Queen of Onita, felt so very, very old.

She could feel the age in her bones, in her skin, in her veins. In the tissues and sinews holding her body together. Each one was weakening, stretching thin, slowly losing a piece of life with each strenuous beat of her heart.

She ambled down the hallway, one side of her body leaning heavily on her cane, the other leaning on Kalen. But he, too, was old, the many centuries of their lives racing up to them with a ferocity that terrified her.

Her entire Armature had grown as old as her, frail and tired and ready for the peace that awaited them. However, besides Cedoric, she hadn't lost any others; their life forces were still tied to hers, and they were bound to the earth until the last of her tasks were complete. When it would finally be time for the Goddess to welcome them home.

Ryenne's breath rattled in her lungs as she ascended the wide stairs, cane clicking on the marble.

The wound in her heart left by Cedoric's death was still raw, but she took comfort knowing that soon, she would join him again. That Priam would soon usher them into the afterlife, to join the stars sparkling in the sky as the world held its bated breath at what her successor would do next.

They reached the landing at the top of the stairs, and Ryenne's heart squeezed as they turned down the familiar hallway leading to the queen's chambers. She'd been kept informed by members of Mariah's court about what had happened—what they'd learned, who'd taken her. Where she'd been found.

Once, a long, long time ago, she'd wandered the grounds of Khento, a delicate blonde-haired girl with pigtails and ocean blue eyes. Most of the year it was so cold there in the north, but it had been her home. The place she'd grown from girl to woman, before leaving to become Queen.

Before she'd made any of the mistakes that had all but doomed her country. Mistakes that now had their *allume* faltering, had Kizar Pirates in their bay for the first time in centuries. Mistakes that forced another young woman through so much agony endured within the same hallowed halls where she'd once known joy.

Even with her body failing, the way she'd failed Onita—the way she'd failed Mariah—made her sick.

A hand squeezed hers, and she tilted her head to meet Kalen's warm brown gaze. His face was sagging and aged, handsome skin now worn with wrinkles and pockmarks. But he was still beautiful to her, everything she never knew she needed. Even after these centuries, he never ceased to surprise her, to make her laugh. To bring her light when she felt most lost in the dark.

"Your thoughts consume you today, Rey," he whispered to her, voice cracked and hoarse.

She squeezed him back, shuffling forward. "Just nervous. To see her. To see what I did to her."

"You did not do this to her. This was all the doing of those lords."

"I know you always mean well, Kalen," she said. "But do not lie to me. Not now."

He didn't respond. Only squeezed her hand again.

They turned down the final curve to the queen's suites. The corridor—one Ryenne knew very well, as she'd called it her home for many, many years—smelled of fire and wind as if several hearths had been lit, and then all the windows opened to the mountain air.

Their slow steps took them to just outside Mariah's doors. Matheo stood there, posture relaxed but eyes alert. Ryenne disentangled herself from Kalen, putting more weight on her cane, giving the young warrior a soft smile.

"Is she awake?"

Matheo nodded, returning her smile. "Yes, Your Majesty." He turned, knocking twice on the door.

"Mariah, Queen Ryenne is here."

"Let her in, Matheo." The feminine voice was muffled behind the wood. It was a voice that once was so strong, so vibrant, and full of fire and life. But now it was dull, carrying an emptiness that twisted Ryenne's gut into further knots.

She steeled herself. She knew Mariah well, about as well as she knew herself. The last thing she would want to see was pity, even if it wasn't directed toward her. So Ryenne shoved down her guilt and pushed through the carved gold and white doors.

The foyer was much the same—white and clean, with the glass doors to the parlor study on the right. The study was dusty and unused, which was a bit of a surprise to Ryenne, given the excitement that had danced in Mariah's eyes when she'd first seen these rooms those many months ago.

But when Ryenne turned back to face the main living area of the suites, when her eyes rested on a woman with a forest in her eyes, she realized that the similarities between this woman and the one who had looked at the study with light in her expression ended with those eyes.

Mariah's hair was still near black, but what once were long strands spilling down her back was now a blunt bob, just brushing the tops of her collarbones. Collarbones, which were now much too prominent, made clearer by the hollowness of

Mariah's cheeks, the paleness of her skin, the gauntness of her frame. The girl who once was a force of her own, a creature exuding as much strength and power as the men who surrounded her, was now no more than a waif. A shell of her former self.

And it was all Ryenne's fault.

The click of Ryenne's cane was the only sound as she hobbled forward, Kalen steady and patient at her side.

Ciana stood rigidly beside the dining table, gaze darting between Mariah and Ryenne. She remembered her decorum at the last moment, dipping her head to Ryenne and dropping into a lackluster curtsy.

It was that same protectiveness Ryenne had seen the day of the Choosing. The same protectiveness that knew, innately, that Ciana and Mariah were destined for each other, in the way only best friends could be.

Ryenne's heart squeezed as she remembered the first lady of her own court. She'd left Ryenne, many long years ago, but Ryenne still carried her memory with her all these centuries later. That was another person Ryenne was eager to see once her journey on this earth was complete.

But when she looked at Mariah, she knew it would be a bit more time before her successor would be ready to take that final step.

Ryenne swallowed heavily.

"It is good to see you, Mariah."

Mariah's throat bobbed. "It's good to see you too, Ryenne."

Ryenne. Not *My Queen.* Tears pricked behind Ryenne's eyes. Despite everything, all this girl must have endured, she was still, at her core, the true queen in that room.

And they all knew it.

Ryenne hobbled another step forward, moving until she stood before Mariah, bending her stiff neck back to meet those glowing green eyes.

Even though Mariah's body was weak, her magic still pulsed around her. Ryenne couldn't remember a time when her eyes had glowed like that, when the magic was so eager to be a part of her that it had danced in her vision.

She lifted a hand, resting it on Mariah's arm. Squeezed once, gently. "I am so, so sorry—"

"Please, Ryenne," Mariah interrupted. There was something else in her expression, something that pulled a tear free from Ryenne's eyes.

Pain.

"I don't want you to apologize," Mariah continued. "I don't want to talk about the past or what happened. I only want to talk about the future. About what comes next. Where we go from here."

More of Ryenne's tears fell, and she didn't bother to catch them. *Qhohena*, she prayed silently, *this girl has been tested enough. Do not force her to prove herself more.*

"Of course," Ryenne whispered. "Let us talk about what comes next, then. On the balcony?"

Mariah nodded, expression stoic.

Ryenne removed her hand from Mariah's arm and wiped her eyes. Kalen's fingers brushed hers, and he pushed a handkerchief into her hand. She turned to give him a brief smile before dabbing her eyes with the soft cotton.

Her consort always knew what she needed, often before she did.

Composing herself, she tucked the handkerchief into the pocket of her full velvet gown. "Help an old woman? I am not as spry as I once was."

To Ryenne's delight, that pulled a faint, ghostly smile to Mariah's lips. She dipped her head, hair falling forward into her eyes, before tucking the ends behind her ears and extending an arm to Ryenne. Together, they walked slowly to the balcony doors, Mariah opening the heavy glass with enough effort to squeeze Ryenne's chest again.

The two queens—one young, one old—stood on the balcony, breathing in the morning spring air.

"This is my favorite time of year." Ryenne tilted her head to the sky, closing her eyes. "The smell of the snowbells on the breeze. The eagles nesting in the mountains. Their chicks will hatch soon, and in a few months, we'll hear their cries as they begin their first flying lessons."

"Have you seen them?" Mariah asked softly. Ryenne cracked her lids and glanced at the young woman, who watched the sky. "The Attlehon eagles? I've heard their wingbeats, but I've never actually seen them flying. I've often wondered if it's just a figment of my imagination, something I knew I should hear because I learned of their existence in school but never *really* heard."

Ryenne smiled. "Of course, I have seen them. I've lived here for over three centuries. But they are hard to spot."

Mariah turned, head tilting. "Why? I thought they were gold, easy to see."

Ryenne shook her head. "They are gold when they nest and when they land. But their feathers carry a magic of their own. They refract the light—both that of the sun and the moons—and when they fly, they become all but invisible. The only way you can see them is on an Equinox night—or if they *want* you to see them."

Mariah's brow furrowed. "How do you make them want you to see them?"

"You don't." Ryenne brushed a lock of gray hair from her face. "But one day, you will, and it will be the greatest moment of your life."

Mariah was silent for a moment. "That would be ... nice." She stared at the mountains as if listening for those wingbeats. "I think I would like that," she murmured.

Ryenne watched Mariah for a few more heartbeats, breathing into the air. "So, the future. No matter what we discuss, I want you to know that there is no timeline. We can take whatever time you need."

Mariah's chest rose and fell with a breath. Her hair swirled around her face, eyes darting across the sky, still searching for those invisible eagles in the air.

"I want vengeance. Retribution." She said the second word

with a snarl, a twist to her lips. She turned to meet Ryenne's gaze. "I never told you about the other side of the magic I carry. About the other goddess who blessed me before I was born."

Everything stilled inside Ryenne. Her lungs froze, weighed down by the years of her life. Her heart struggled to keep beating, her mind fighting to process Mariah's words.

"Zadione?" Ryenne whispered. When Mariah nodded, she clasped a hand over her mouth. *Impossible.*

"The only goddess who has ever spoken to me, who has ever answered my prayers, is the goddess of death. My mother and her family trace their lineages to an ancient line of priestesses—priestesses who worshipped and were blessed by Zadione. My mother carried some of that magic with her; it's what made her an exceptional healer. And I ... I got the equivalent to whatever Qhohena blessed Xara with, long ago. But instead of gold, those threads burn silver, cold as death but wild as the life that leads to it."

Ryenne was stunned. She almost didn't believe it, not really. Zadione had locked herself away in Enfara with the Scourge, a self-inflicted banishment for the death and destruction she'd caused to the continent during the First War. All Onitans knew this story.

But as she stared at Mariah, as she watched the light shining in her eyes, she realized ... it was *true.* For it wasn't just threads of gold that shimmered in her forest depths. There was silver there, too, so vibrant that Ryenne felt like a fool for missing it before.

"That is ..." She exhaled heavily, still staring at those eyes.

"I know," Mariah whispered. "But it's true. And you know it."

Ryenne closed her eyes. Breathed again. And nodded.

"I do. I do know it." She reopened her eyes. "Do you know what it means? To carry the magic of the goddess of life and the goddess of death?"

"No." Mariah turned back to the mountains. "Do you?" There was a subtle, hopeful note to her question. As if she truly believed Ryenne might have the answers she sought. The answers to who she was and why she existed.

But Ryenne could not lie to her. Not now, not anymore.

"I am sorry, Mariah. I do not."

The two women stood on that balcony for several minutes in silence, lost in their thoughts and the impossibility of the future that now stared back at them.

"I want to discuss my coronation." Mariah's voice, hoarse and tired, broke the silence.

Ryenne again rested her hand on Mariah's arm. "Whenever you are ready, so am I." Another pause. "The final bond happened … there, didn't it?"

Out of the corner of her eye, she saw Mariah's nod. She didn't pry further; there was no need. She could feel the magic, could feel the change in her very aura.

"I carry one final drop of magic with me. At the coronation, it will become yours. And it will be done. My connection to the earth will end, and my Armature and I will be at rest. Onita will be yours until Qhohena wills it otherwise."

"Until Qhohena wills it otherwise," Mariah echoed, still staring at the mountains.

A sound burst through the doors behind them. Something exuberant, and filled with tears, and carrying the faint scent of saffron and cinnamon and cloves.

"Lassie!" Mikael's bright voice echoed across the balcony, and Mariah whirled. Tears leaped into her eyes, and with more emotion than Ryenne had seen from her, she jolted forward, straight into the cook's arms.

"*Mikael*," Mariah choked out through sobs. "I am so fucking happy to see you."

"Oh my, dearie," Mikael said, his tears streaming down his freckled face, his usual brown band of leather holding his unruly shock of orange hair from his face. "If you were that hungry, all you had to do was send for me earlier."

As Ryenne watched the merry reunion, and then joined them for a full breakfast, as she watched Mariah shovel food into her mouth with a desperation that twisted her heart, she wondered how many more mornings like this she would have.

With Mariah, Ciana, Mikael, and Kalen engaged in happy conversation, Ryenne glanced out the balcony window. A smile touched her lips at the golden Attlehon eagle perched upon the railing, watching the festivities within. It met her gaze, blinking once, before lifting into the sky, visible for a few moments until its feathers shifted it into the brightness of morning.

CHAPTER 31

Mariah's gaze swept her bedroom, Ciana's tinkling laugh as she said goodbye to Mikael slipping past the closed door.

She'd excused herself a few minutes ago after Ryenne and Kalen had left. As she'd finished in the bathroom, she meant to rejoin them, but something held her back.

She hadn't yet had a moment to herself within these four walls. She'd bathed, then slept, but there'd been no lingering. Not a second to pause and breathe and try to figure out who she used to be, before everything. Who she was now.

The plush white rug beneath the massive, quilted bed. The arching window, with a cushioned seat below. The marble floors and gilded walls, shimmering with royal, ancient decadence.

Ten queens before her had called this room home. What gave her the right to reside here, too? Despite her confident words to Ryenne, she was no queen.

Not yet.

Her feet moved to her nightstand of their own accord. Her fingers wrapped around the leather pommel, sliding the silver blade from its red leather sheath. The dragon wings on the cross guard gleamed in the pale *allume* light.

Mariah remembered the night she'd taken this dagger. How she'd scaled the walls of Lord Donnet's keep, slipping into a poorly guarded room, plundering his trove, and taking her fill before leaving that town forever.

That sack of stolen gold still lay beneath her bed. Right next to …

Mariah strapped the dagger to her thigh, its weight the first welcomed familiarity, before dropping to all fours and peering under her bed.

Sure enough, there was that burlap bag, still bulging and heavy. But her hands didn't reach for the gold.

She instead reached for the small, silver leather book beside it, somehow free of dust and dirt and anything else that should've accumulated there as it lay forgotten beneath her bed.

Mariah sat back, crossing her legs, as she turned over the book, reading the cover.

Ginnelevé. Her mother's name. The name of every woman in their line, dating back to Zadione's first priestess during the First War.

Mariah's name. The last Ginnelevé priestess.

She almost snorted. Far more than priestess, in truth, but she supposed that was just a matter of semantics.

Her fingers fanned the pages, the centuries—millennia— worth of entries breezing past her eyes. The book was so small, but it seemed to grow in her hands as the pages buzzed past. As if the magic that preserved it also hid its true depth of knowledge. Despite all those entries, there were still empty pages at the back.

Right after the final entry. The letter written not on the pages of the journal, but on a single sheet of her paper. Her mother's elegant script stared up at her as Mariah brushed the creamy page.

Fear burst through her, unannounced. Ever since things with the Royals started to decline, Mariah had sworn to keep her family out of her mess. When she'd blinded Lord Campion— who must have passed, replaced by his son in Khento—and killed Lord Beauchamp, she'd known she couldn't return to them. Not until her position was more secure and a trip would be safe.

Now, though ... Lord Donnet had been there, in Khento, with the rest of them. And Donnet *knew*. He knew all about her past, and her family, and where they lived in their small, perfect house at the edge of town.

If the lords wanted to strike at her, all they'd have to do was get to her family.

She forced a deep breath—in through her nose, out through her mouth. Like her father had taught her.

Her father. Wex would keep his family safe. Mariah had no doubt that if he had even the slightest feeling of something amiss, he would take Lisabel and Ellan and get out of town. They could ride, hunt, and fight; there were many small towns they could escape to and lie low in until the danger passed.

She'd learned all that she knew from her family. There was nothing she could do at present for them; going after them now would most definitely raise suspicion. She had to trust they could manage for themselves, at least for a little while longer.

Mariah snapped the book closed, staring at the cover. She felt that drop of magic woven into its core, ancient and wild and so like her silver light. Her fingers again brushed the leather.

"*If—when—you ever feel lost, truly lost, when you need a reminder of who you are and what you are capable of ... that book will tell you everything you need to know.*"

Her mother's words, shared so long ago beside a roaring fire, blazed through her mind. The hair on her arms stood on end.

Could her mother have known what awaited her? Perhaps she knew her trip to Verith would lead to a greater destiny, but everything that had happened after ...

Mariah swallowed. No. Her mother hadn't known what evil would be committed against her daughter. Perhaps she knew Mariah would feel lost, but there's no way she could've known just how truly adrift her daughter would be.

"If you have help to offer me," Mariah whispered to the silver journal, "I'll take it now."

She fanned the pages again, stopping on a page near the beginning.

And began to read.

They are coming. They move in the night under the cover of their wicked shadows. They mask the light of the moons, hiding our goddess from sight. Abominations, monsters, evil crafted from the darkest corners of the heavens. It is not known if the reykr are born soulless or if they are turned that way.

It does not matter. No light has ever burned out their darkness. The most we can hope is that they pass us over, that they continue on with whatever unholy task their fallen god charges them with—

Mariah's chest heaved as she slammed the book shut, tears choking her throat as her heart pounded in her ears and beat against her chest. She threw the journal across the floor, a sob shuddering out of her as she scrambled away from it.

Shadows ... abominations ... monsters ... evil ... soulless.

Reykr.

She pressed her hands against her ears, trying to stop the pounding.

She'd *felt* that darkness. During the bond. She'd chased it out with her light, leaving only the soul behind.

The *reykr* soul behind.

No light has ever burned out their darkness.

Mariah whimpered.

Three times. *Three times* she'd given that journal a chance, and each time, it had stripped her soul from her body and left her raw and bleeding on the floor.

Her bedroom door slammed open. Small, soft hands gripped her forearms, pulling them away from her ears. Wide, concerned amber eyes filled her vision.

"Mariah! Mariah, what's wrong? What happened?" Ciana's voice was muffled as if Mariah were trapped underwater. "Matheo! Get in here!"

Mariah still hid against her nightstand, shuddering and sobbing and far away, as Matheo raced in, sliding to a halt when he saw her. He knelt beside Ciana, gentle hands gripping her, silver and sky bond tugging in her gut.

"Mariah? Are you alright? Just breathe, it's okay. You're safe. We're here, you're home, and you're safe." A tug on their bond punctuated each word he said.

And with each tug, Mariah felt herself rising to the surface. Far enough for her to shudder a breath, gasping, and managing two words.

"*Take it.*"

Ciana and Matheo shared a glance. "Take what?"

Mariah lifted a shaking hand, pointing at the journal lying a few feet away.

"Take it," she repeated, still whispering. "Keep it hidden and safe, but get it *away* from me."

Ciana leaned away from Mariah, taking the journal. She looked at it curiously, reading the name on the cover. "I remember this. Your mother's journal?"

"Said it would help me," Mariah forced out, chest still heaving. "But all it does is cause pain."

"What did you read in it, Mariah?" Matheo's question was gentle, but his curiosity carried an edge.

Mariah swallowed, meeting his hazel stare.

"*Reykr*," she whispered. More tears burned in her eyes, clogging her throat.

Gods, she was tired of this. Of being so fucking *afraid*. Her heart was telling her one thing—that everything she'd just read was the dramatic ramblings of some old, ancient relative. That *her* shadow-wielder was not like that, that she had burned out whatever darkness was planted in him, and now his familiar shadows sang only for her.

But her body remembered the crack of a metal-tipped whip,

the fire as her skin was split. Her mind remembered the image of his lips meeting another's. Her skin remembered greedy hands stealing her humanity from her, piece by piece.

"Hey. Mariah. Look at me." Ciana was back, gripping either side of Mariah's head.

"Whatever you just read, it isn't true. You said so yourself; this is just a journal from the women in your family. Mostly gibberish. You are *safe* here. And you are *strong*. Trust yourself, trust your heart, and fuck all the rest."

Mariah couldn't speak. Only nodded, refusing to break from Ciana's stare, latching onto that warm amber like it was her last lifeline at sea.

"I will take the book. I'll keep it safe and hidden. If you want to see it again, all you must do is ask. But right now, I need you to forget. Focus on the future. The past is done, and we're leaving it there."Ciana released Mariah, stepping back with Matheo to give Mariah space.

Mariah just kept breathing. Inhale. Exhale. Inhale. Her heart slowly stopped pounding in her ears, her blood no longer rushing through her veins. Her magic had remained unusually quiet, curled in her belly and watching her with slitted eyes.

"You should get some rest," Matheo murmured.

But Mariah was already standing. Her knees still shook, but she forced herself upright. Ciana gave her a quick nod, clutching the journal to her chest before she spun and left the room in a flurry of golden curls.

Mariah turned to her window and the cushioned seat. "Can you get Trefor?"

"Trefor? Uh, sure." Matheo shifted as Mariah settled at the window. "Mariah, are you okay?"

"Just want some sun," she said softly, staring out her bedroom window. "I need a moment. And to speak to Trefor."

Matheo lingered for a moment, hesitating, before he finally heaved a sigh. "Of course. I'll be right back. Quentin will be outside if you need anything."

Mariah nodded absently, not looking back as he left the room.

She felt a little guilty for being so cold, but she didn't have it in her to put on a mask. She would apologize to Matheo later and give him a healthy thanks. For being there and pulling her back from the abyss.

Right now, though ... her fingers toyed with the winged cross-guard of her dagger.

Right now, she just needed the sun.

CHAPTER 32

The familiar woods that lay between the palace and the Attlehon Mountains smelled of spring, rebirth, change, and new beginnings.

They differed from the Ivory Forest Mariah had grown up in. The way the rustling of the leaves brushed her ears was less comforting, the birds chirping in the branches above less soothing. But they were still woods, and it was grounding to be surrounded by the wilds once again.

Which was great, since nothing in her life truly grounded her. Not anymore.

Especially not after yesterday. Her resolve had shifted and steadied as she'd sat in her window, soaking in the sun as it crossed over the mountains, watching for eagles.

It was now late morning as Mariah walked briskly down the forest path. Trefor walking beside her, the sun dappling through the trees warm against her too-pale skin. Her clothes were loose on her frame, her hair was too short to be braided, and her lungs already burned with the effort of the walk, but to her surprise, those things didn't bother her.

They only served to remind her that she had survived. That she was stronger now.

That she would become strong again and she would find her vengeance.

Her *retribution*.

Something flitted at the edge of her vision. She froze, a bolt of surprise racing through her, as a black butterfly darted out of the trees and danced its way down below the canopy. It landed on a branch just off the path, near her head, watching her much the same way it had before.

Beside her, Trefor paused. "Mariah? You okay?"

She hushed her blond-haired Armature, attention still fixed on the insect.

There was no way it was the same butterfly she'd seen on the journey from Khento. That would be impossible.

Yet something in her cocked its head at the insect. Her magic pushed its way up from her gut and into her veins. Those threads of silver-gold light slipped free from her skin, dancing to the butterfly.

The second her magic touched its delicate black wings, an image slammed into her skull, shoving her back with a gasping step. Trefor's hands gripped her shoulders and her magic pulled back into her, coiling around her soul with a wild protectiveness.

"M! What's wrong?"

Mariah couldn't answer Trefor, not yet. Not with an image burned into her skull. When she closed her eyes, she could see it, clear as the day.

It was a dragon, maw parted in a great roar, massive wings stretched wide, taloned claws digging into soft earth.

And its color ... its color was unlike anything she'd ever seen.

Not a color—not exactly. At first, it was black with flickering streaks of gold. Then, that black shifted to silver, but the gold remained. It kept morphing, back and forth, from black to silver, dark to light. Only gold remained, but hardly made the image any clearer.

Mariah's eyes flew open, chest heaving as she stared back at where the butterfly had been.

Of course, it was gone.

"N-nothing." She shook off Trefor's hands, forcing herself to stand straight. "I'm fine. Just ... trying to get used to my magic again. That's all." She tried her best to ignore the tremor in her voice.

The image was fading, but she was still filled with an emotion she'd become far too acquainted with those past few months.

She was terrified.

Mariah gulped deep, steadying breaths as she stood there on the forest path, Trefor's concerned stare grazing her cheek. She let her heart rate settle, let the image fade fully from her mind.

A trick of her imagination, nothing more. Brought on by an actual night's sleep, one that followed too many restless, cold, terrified ones.

Once her hands had stopped shaking, and she felt as normal as she ever did now, she turned to Trefor. She forced a smile when she met his worried sea-green gaze. "I'm sorry. I'm fine, I promise. Let's keep going."

He gave her a wary, tight nod, pale hair shifting in the breeze. They continued down the path, and she inhaled deep breaths of his sea salt and citrus scent, like the groves of the trees that grew along the northern coast.

His wariness fell away, giving way to an excited energy, as they pushed past a line of hedges and into the training clearing hidden deep within the confines of the forest game park. That energy spilled into her, and she couldn't stop the smile that spread across her face.

She'd made it out. She would be strong again.

Trefor darted from her side, already pulling out equipment and arranging it around the clearing. Mariah didn't quite know why she'd asked Trefor to be the one to train with her that morning. Perhaps it was because he'd been recently injured, struck by an arrow meant for Mariah herself, and had just retrained himself.

Or perhaps, of all her Armature, she knew him the least, but something in her needed his vibrant, excited energy, right at this moment.

She'd only failed to listen to her gut once. And it had resulted in her leaving her dagger on her nightstand and strolling into captivity, unarmed and defenseless. She had no intention of ignoring those instincts again.

Her fingers toyed idly with the hilt of her dragon-winged dagger, strapped once again to its familiar place on her thigh. She'd run from some things since returning home but swore to never let that blade leave her side again.

"You sure you don't want to talk about what happened on the trail?" Trefor was still watching her with concerned curiosity. "How are you feeling?"

She couldn't blame him for his worry; they'd only returned two nights ago, after all. And before that, it had been three days of hard riding through the harshest of Onita's northern terrain. It would make sense if she weren't feeling up to training yet.

While her body certainly protested, her soul cringed at that idea. Idle rest meant stagnation, and if she let herself sit, she feared her wounds would fester.

So, she'd opted for movement.

"It was nothing. And I'm tired," she admitted, "but ready to train."

Trefor's smile faltered. "You know, you don't have to. You should get some rest—"

"Please, Trefor," she pleaded. "I don't want to rest. Not now. I want to train." She hoped he read her desperation, her burning desire to no longer feel as she did. To regain everything that was stripped from her, to come back stronger than before.

After a few heartbeats, he nodded. "Okay. Then let's train."

MARIAH'S BOOTS clicked down the marble hallway, feeling lighter than she had in months.

Her muscles ached. Every inch of her was sore. She had shed the tunic she'd worn down to the game park, now dressed only in a thin-strapped camisole and cooling underclothes. Her skin was coated in a thin sheen of sweat, but she reveled in it: this feeling of being alive, and in control, and a bit more like herself than she had that morning.

"I need to grab some lunch," Trefor said, running a hand through his hair. They paused at the landing of a descending staircase, one that would lead down into the palace kitchens. "Do you want to join me?"

Mariah considered it for a moment. She was hungry, but the thought of being around so many, of being the focus of every set of eyes in those tunnels …

She swallowed.

"I'm okay. I'm sure Mikael made something before he left this morning." She turned, facing Trefor fully, and let a real smile spread across her face.

"Thank you for this morning. I needed it. More than you'll ever know."

Trefor smiled back. "Of course. Same time tomorrow?"

She lifted her chin. "Earlier."

With a crooked grin, he pulled her into a lopsided hug, pressing a quick kiss into her hair.

"We're so happy to have you back," he whispered. "You have no idea."

She fought back tears as she stepped away from him, tugging lightly on their bond, the one that shimmered like a golden citrus sea. "You have no idea how happy I am to be back."

He squeezed her one more time before releasing her and jogging toward the stairs, descending into the lower palace levels. She watched him until he vanished from sight, smile lingering across her lips as she turned back down the hall.

She wanted a shower. Desperately.

Mariah took the stairs that would take her to her rooms one at a time, muscles protesting every step. Reaching the landing, she meandered down the white and gold marble hall. Her fingers grazed the gilded walls as she basked in the daylight streaming in through the windows. Something in her soul continued to lift as she walked, stretching before her, pulling her along into brighter days.

She rounded the final corner to find a man wearing clothes as black as his hair, tanzanite eyes widening with surprise.

The bond between them crackled and sparked in the air, an invisible pulse of energy. It was like that day so long ago, before the Choosing, when the world had shrunk to encompass just them. Only this time, with their souls now bridged, it was so much stronger, a powerful vibrancy that nearly buckled her already-shaking legs.

One day apart, and her soul was crying out for him. *Begging* for him.

But her mind and body still recoiled from that thought, and despite the pull between them, she felt herself freezing, rooting to the ground. Unable to take another step closer.

The slam of the box he'd been carrying hitting the floor echoed through the hallway.

"Mariah." His voice was a low, strangled sound that sunk into her blood and settled into her bones. A knife through her stomach. He took a staggering step toward her, closing the distance.

And though her soul screamed to move closer, her body took a step back.

He stopped. Pain twisted his face.

"Please," he said. He sounded so much like he had that day before the Solstice, when he'd confessed to her everything she hadn't known she'd been desperate to hear.

Those words were too perfect. Had they even come from him?

The scars on her back tingled.

"I can't," she forced out through her teeth, entire body vibrating with emotions that warred and clashed.

"You can't *what?*" he pleaded. This time, there was a flash of anger in his blue gaze. He took another step forward, shrinking the space between them, and she stayed rooted to the spot. Rooted by a feeling.

Fear.

He didn't stop until he was within arms-length. His chest rose and fell with heavy breaths, and something desperate and wild danced in his eyes. His shoulders were wreathed in tendrils of shadows, another sign that he was frustrated and confused and angry.

"Why are you avoiding me? No one can give me a straight answer. You are the *only* one who knows what happened back there in that Enfara-damned place. Yet you won't share it with anyone. I told you—I was just as much a prisoner there as you were, and I think you know that."

"I do know that," she whispered, surprising herself with her interruption.

He leaned back as if he'd been slapped, some of the rage fading from his eyes. His shadows softened, drifting closer to his body.

"I know that you were a prisoner there. I saw it ... *you* ... many times." The words burned as she forced those memories from her mind. She was not prepared to relive that—not now, not here.

"But ... Andrian, don't make me do this."

"Do *what*?" His words leaked of desperation. "Tell me why you can barely look me in the eye? Why you flinch every time you hear my voice?" His voice cracked, and he paused.

"Mariah, I don't care what happened. I am yours, and I *love*—"

"Don't say it. Say *that*. Please." Tears burned in her eyes.

Andrian blinked again in shock. "Just ... give me a chance again. Please. Let me prove to you that no matter what happened, this is still me."

Tears fell, spilling down her cheeks. "I can't do that."

"Can't, or won't?"

"Does it matter?" A sob clogged her throat. "I'm not the girl I was on the Solstice. Too much has happened, too much has changed. *I've* changed, so many times that I don't even know who I am anymore. And you ..." She couldn't complete that sentence. Couldn't even complete the thought.

"And I ... what? Tell me, Mariah. Let me be there for you. Let me *help* you."

"I'm sorry, Andrian. But you can't help me." With those final words, her voice still a choked whisper, she moved around him, staying just out of his reach. Every instinct in her screamed, thrashed, pulled her back, but despite her resolve to listen to those instincts, she ignored them.

Mariah couldn't give in to them now. Not with this.

His eyes tracked her. But he didn't try to reach for her, to stop her.

Until his sharp inhale hit her like a drop of lead in her stomach. New emotions raced down their bond—horror, unfiltered and unmasked. And then rage, monstrous in its depth.

Her back was to him now. And in the camisole she wore, the skin of her shoulder blades was bare. Deep, roughly healed scars were on full display.

"Who the *fuck* did that to you?"

His voice was quiet, a shadow of a sound, but filled with an endless, eternal rage. She could've sworn the temperature in the hallway plummeted several degrees, that unearthly shadows dimmed the sunlight outside.

Time froze. The world stood still. Mariah clenched her hands together so hard, she felt her nails pierce the skin of her palm. A trickle of blood dripped to the white marble floors, its splash echoing like a torrent down the hallway.

She gave herself to the pain as she turned slightly, looking back at him over her shoulder. He looked like a dark, avenging god, ready to tear the world apart once she confessed the identity of her torturer.

She swallowed thickly, blinking away the tears. So many tears. She was tired of them.

Her voice croaked, low and hoarse, when she answered him.

"You did."

CHAPTER 33

Mariah was a ghost for the rest of the day, refusing to leave her rooms.

She took her shower, washing the sweat from her skin. Changed into a cotton tunic and butter-soft trousers. Then sat on her balcony, staring at the mountains, listening desperately for the wingbeats of eagles as the sun arched its way across the sky.

Mikael came and went, too, preparing a quick dinner that he left in front of her before leaving with a sad smile on his face. She ate the food, not feeling enough to taste it. Her hunger had vanished, but her body was still starved, and she now valued food far more than she ever thought she would.

Every time she blinked, she saw the look on Andrian's face as she told him how she'd received her scars.

And each time her eyes closed, she hated herself a little more. Because while those scars on her back were caused by his hand, she knew—*knew*—he hadn't been the one to hurt her.

But she'd decided to hurt him back, anyways.

When the sun set and the stars twinkled in the sky, she moved from the balcony to her bed, settling herself into the silk sheets and down comforter. She fell freely into her despair and misery, like a star falling from the heavens.

But instead of falling into the vast emptiness of sleep, she awoke in a crystalline meadow, snowdrop blossoms blooming around her, the entire scenery awash in a vibrant, golden glow.

Despite the color, it didn't feel like sunlight. This light was less harsh, more subdued, more subtle. The way it brushed her skin was calming and almost ... feminine. Somehow, impossibly, the setting pulled a certain peacefulness through Mariah, something she hadn't felt in far too long.

A figure stepped into the clearing. The light receded, revealing a woman. Golden hair, golden skin, golden eyes. Even her robes were gold, spilling around her. Much as they did in the statue of her likeness adorning the palace courtyard built in her honor.

Mariah pushed to her feet, toes curling into the cushiony grass. When she spoke, her voice was low, inadvertently reverent. A reaction she couldn't help.

"Qhohena."

She also realized she was dreaming.

The goddess smiled, face glowing and beautiful. While her sister was the picture of death, everything about Qhohena embodied life. Flowers were woven into her hair, and golden vines wrapped up her arms and down her legs. Her hair was a cascading rivulet of gold, like a gilded waterfall down her back. On her fingers twinkled rings of precious gemstones, and her full figure embraced feminine virility in its truest form.

Qhohena turned her lovely, youthful face to Mariah and smiled. It was like being touched by eternal life itself, nearly knocking Mariah off her feet with its potency.

"Mariah, my daughter. It is so good to meet you."

Mariah knew her mouth gaped. Knew she was stunned by the goddess's presence, a mystical figure she'd grown up hearing about, but a part of herself had doubted even existed.

It was hard to believe in a goddess who never answered your prayers.

Mariah hardened. Her mouth snapped shut, jaw clenching, fingers balling into fists.

All this time. After everything that had happened. Every bit of abuse and torment she'd endured, and Qhohena hadn't come once. But now, when Mariah was safely home and healing, of course, the goddess would lift her veil.

Qhohena's Chosen, her ass.

"Why are you here? Why have you come?" Mariah's voice was cold, flat. Emotionless.

This may be a goddess, but she'd never groveled once in her life. She didn't intend to start now.

Qhohena halted, surprise illuminating her too-bright features. "You are … upset?" The goddess sounded confused as if she could not comprehend Mariah's frustration. Her pain.

Mariah answered with silence. She wasn't sure she could trust her voice to speak for her.

The goddess stared at her open palms. Her feet were bare, and the grasses of the glade wound their way up her feet as if claiming her back into the earth.

"I am sorry," the goddess whispered, as gentle as a night breeze. She raised her eyes, and Mariah saw them lined with droplets of gold.

Qhohena was crying.

"It has been many, many millennia since I have interacted with humans. Your lives are so short, and you endure so much pain that I no longer know when I need to interfere. Because if I were to help every time someone cried out for me, I would fade away into the universe, my powers spent."

Mariah's brow furrowed. "But … you are a goddess. Your powers are infinite. Are they not?"

Qhohena smiled sadly. "They may seem endless, but I assure you, they are far from it. Like all things in nature, we have our limits. And as the years—centuries—have passed, I find myself wasting away. Especially without the grace I gave away long ago."

The golden threads, deep in Mariah's gut, stirred in response. "That grace. It's the queen's magic, isn't it?"

The goddess nodded, hair shifting like molten gold. "It is. I feel it in you. And while I do miss that part of myself ... it belongs to you now. To Onita."

They stood in silence, Mariah's mind spinning over Qhohena's confession. She tilted her head to the side, expression softening as she regarded the goddess.

"You didn't answer my question."

Qhohena smiled again. "You wonder why I am here. Why I have come." She turned, lifting a golden arm. She spun her hand in a circle, and from it fell golden threads of light. The light settled on the ground and moved, weaving and winding until soon, a great golden boulder rested in the center of the meadow. Qhohena lifted her skirts and settled herself atop the boulder, her movements delicate and graceful. She looked back to Mariah, resting a hand on the stone.

"Sit with me, daughter. Let me try to explain what I can."

Mariah hesitated before striding through the meadow. She hoisted herself onto the boulder, far less gracefully than Qhohena, nearly sliding off the smooth stone. But the rock was warm, and she was instantly surrounded by the goddess's scent: honeysuckle and snowdrops and moonlight.

"My little sister," Qhohena began, "is far more cynical than I am. She always feared for you and how the weakness of your human heart might one day be used against you. Perhaps because even she, despite not being human, fell victim to that weakness." The goddess sighed. "I tried to remind her that love is not always a weakness, but ... you have met her. You know how persuasive she can be."

Mariah remembered a half-forgotten dream, one obscured by exuberant joy and incapacitating pain. "It was Zadione," she breathed. "Zadione was the one whispering to me all those years. Warning me that love is a weakness."

"Yes. She wanted to ensure you were warned. That you felt prepared for whatever your life might bring. I told her that no matter what she did, you would still make your own choices, and she could not stop you."

Mariah soaked in the boulder's warmth. An inky streak of misery wormed its way through her, and it pulled the next words from her throat.

"I should have listened to her."

"Mariah." Qhohena's voice was firmer now, no longer the same melodic softness as before. Mariah looked at the goddess and shrank away from the fire and heat roaring in her golden eyes.

"Your love does not make you weak. It never did. It was always your destiny to feel as you do, and it was wrong of my sister to interfere with that. She will never admit to it, but she knows it now, as well as I do."

Mariah blanched. "What do you mean, I was always destined to fall in love?"

Qhohena held her stare, eyes blazing. "The stories of our world are always destined to repeat themselves."

Mariah opened her mouth, about to ask what the goddess meant, but snapped her lips shut. She could tell, from the look on Qhohena's face, that she would not get more on that subject tonight.

So she turned away, looking out instead across the clearing. She swallowed past the lump in her throat, annoyed that it was there.

"But ..." Another swallow. A lift of her chin to drain the emotions away. "Why him?"

She felt Qhohena's demeanor shift. She glanced to find the goddess now slightly slumped, regarding Mariah with so much sadness.

"We do not get to choose these things, my daughter. Not even the gods."

"If not the gods, then who?"

Qhohena blinked, slowly, before turning away to stare at the sky. Her form flickered. She didn't answer.

Mariah watched her intently, brow furrowing, before asking another question lurking in her mind.

"Why are you here, in my dreams? And why was Zadione able to visit me in the flesh?"

Qhohena's body solidified again. "Our bond with you is built through trust. Mutual trust. Zadione has been visiting you for a long time. You inherently trust her more than you trust me. Which is understandable, and I do not fault you for that." Qhohena steeled a breath. "However ... I hope to change that. So next time I might visit you outside of this plane. We can never appear to anyone other than you, but we want you to know that we will always be here for you. To guide, and to offer strength."

Mariah held her tongue at the surge of frustration. The goddess could promise such things all she wanted, but she'd still let Mariah be captured, abused, broken.

Qhohena saw it all.

"While I wish my sister had waited to visit you ... I want you to know that I am glad she did. She could save you in that place because of it. I wanted to help. Please believe that. But you were not ready for me, and the support of my sister was more than enough to get you out."

Mariah stared down at her hands, wringing themselves in her lap. Qhohena's revelations changed nothing ... Didn't they? How hard was it for Mariah to believe that the goddesses were strengthened only through trust, and without it, their actions were limited? It was a convenient truth, to be sure. But did its convenience make it a fallacy?

"I forgive you." Mariah's words were breathed out on a gentle, honeysuckle breeze.

Qhohena's light pulsed, as if with relief. "Thank you, daughter—"

"But I want to know," Mariah said. "Why now? What changed? Why not let Zadione continue to be the one to speak to me?"

Qhohena lips parted, her brow scrunched, before lifting a golden hand. It reached for Mariah, sweeping a strand of night-dark hair away from her face. The goddess rested her fingertips on Mariah's cheek, and Mariah drew in a sharp inhale at the touch. It was like being touched by life itself. Invigorating. Exalting. Like drinking an elixir of immortality.

"Because you are hurting, my daughter. Not physically—my sister tended to those wounds, as is her specialty. But your conflicted emotions about the *reykr* are tearing you apart. Breaking you, from the inside out, more than what you endured in that place ever could. I am here with you tonight because I needed to remind you of who you are. This world needs you—all of you—now, more than ever.

Mariah gulped, hesitating to ask her next question, but knowing she had to.

"And what does *he* have to do with reminding me who I am?"

Qhohena smiled. "Because he is your past, your present, and your future. There are forces at play that are far greater than us gods, and as I said, all things in nature eventually repeat themselves."

The meadow was beginning to shrink, the surrounding light dimming. Qhohena's touch on Mariah's face increased in pressure, even as her body faded.

"You will not find yourself until you learn to trust him again."

The goddess's voice faded into a whisper on the wind as Mariah slammed back into her body, gasping in her bed.

"Make that love your retribution, Mariah."

CHAPTER 34

Mariah woke to the sound of screaming.

The words from the goddess still burned in her mind as she flew from her bed, feet carrying her to her bedroom window. She pushed open the panes and leaned into the crisp morning air. The wind wrapped around her, carrying the scent of melting snow and early blooms.

The screams drifted past on that sweet-smelling breeze.

A pounding knock boomed from the entrance to her suites. "*Mariah!*"

She shoved herself away, racing out of her bedroom and to the door. A wild-eyed Trefor stood there, Drystan and Feran appearing over his shoulder, Sebastian bursting into the hall.

"What's going on?" Her heart raced in her chest, but her voice was surprisingly ... calm. Shrieks echoed off the palace, but her mind was still flooded with life-giving, golden magic.

"I—do you not notice it?"

"Notice what?" Mariah scanned the dark hallway, opening her senses, letting her magic spill from a finger. It blazed around her, too-bright—far brighter than it should've been.

Her stomach dropped when the realization hit.

"The lights. Why are the lights off?"

That's why it was so dark, why her magic was so bright. The sconces on the walls, the ones usually illuminated with *allume*, had gone dark.

And Mariah had spent so much time recently in the dark, she hadn't even noticed it.

"The whole city has gone dark," Feran murmured. Beside him, Drystan nodded. "All the lights are off. And ... the wards are gone."

The wards. They hadn't meant much to her before—besides a few off-hand comments made by the lords during her early meetings, she'd hardly even acknowledged their presence—but she'd learned how the pirates had wormed their way out of the Kizar Islands, launching great stones of ice at her city. How they'd stormed the docks, just once—as if to make a point—and innocents on the port had lost their lives.

Those wards were the only thing that saved the battlements lining the Bay. Without them, the pirates' ice would've destroyed their defenses in one fell swoop, and the Bay of Nria would've turned red with blood.

"Is the Bay secure?" Her words were clipped as she whirled, striding for her room. Feran followed her, waiting outside her bedroom as she pawed through a drawer, pulling out her favored black leggings and a tawny long-sleeve shirt.

"There's been no sign of the pirate lords, if that's what you're asking," Feran answered from the doorway as she slipped out of her oversized tunic and into the clothes. "The Bay appears to be safe. But without *allume* ... I think our most pressing concern is chaos in the city."

"The screaming, I take it." Mariah shoved her feet into her boots.

Feran huffed. "Yes. The screaming. The people don't like it when their reliable magic goes out."

Mariah paused for a moment, turning slowly to face Feran. "This has happened before, hasn't it?"

Feran, faintly illuminated by Mariah's magic, shifted uncomfortably. "A few times. Only once has it gone out completely." He tilted his head, dark braids falling across his shoulders. "They never flickered in Khento?"

Something inside her shuddered closed, and Feran winced. "I'm sorry, I shouldn't have—"

"I never saw them flicker. But I was kept in the dark most of the time. If it happened, I wouldn't have known." Her voice had gone cold. She snatched her grandfather's dagger from her nightstand, strapping it to her thigh before brushing past Feran.

"Let's go. I think I know how to fix this."

MARIAH HAD ULTIMATELY CONVINCED MOST of her Armature not to follow her, instead sending them into the city to help the City Guard with calming the residents. Sebastian had insisted that one of them remain with her, however, so Feran strode at her side, silent and watchful.

Their hurried steps took them down the winding hallways and arching staircases, emerging into the great, cavernous throne room. Mariah paused in the shadows, tilting her head up to see the stars twinkling above the glass ceiling. It was early morning, in the hour just before dawn, when even the night had gone to sleep.

The starlight hour. The same time of night when she'd met Andrian in that courtyard, so many weeks ago.

She swallowed, eyes still searching the skies. "The Spring Equinox is soon, isn't it?"

Feran's arm brushed hers. "In three weeks, yes."

There. Mariah finally found those twin moons, nothing more than pale crescents in the night sky.

She still could hardly believe the passage of time. She'd gone underground when those moons were bright and blazing amongst the stars and emerged with them quartered, their light dimmed with her own.

No. She was not dimmed. The moons came and went, their

natural cycle as eternal as the tides they pulled along the shores of the Mirrored Sea. They would burn bright again.

Just as she would, too.

Mariah dropped her gaze from the sky, levying it on the *lunestair* pillars flanking the great golden throne. Despite the darkness of the palace and the city, those pillars still glowed with ethereal light, the milky white stone illuminated from within.

But as Mariah watched, she saw it.

A twisting mass of darkness snaked across the glow of the stone, carving a piece of the light away. It crawled like a serpent, too-alike the Uroborus that had once tried to claim her life.

She remembered what she'd felt when she'd rested her palm on those pillars the day after the Solstice. The way the magic had pulsed and burned, so full of power and life ... but hidden beneath it, buried deep, was a knotted mass of cruel darkness. A blackness born of pain and suffering and deceit, not the joy and life she'd tried to instill throughout the kingdom that night.

Mariah gritted her teeth and stalked toward the pillars, magic uncoiling around her fingers.

The pillars pulsed, even as the lights stayed dark. The darkness seemed to seep from them, spilling across the marble, a poison in the air.

"Mariah, what are you—"

"It's okay, Feran," she murmured, not turning as she climbed the dais, before repeating, "I can fix this."

He didn't answer as she halted before the nearest pillar. Her entire being had focused on the glowing moonstone, on the snaking shadows within it.

With her magic pulsing in her chest, she pressed her hand against the cool stone.

The *allume* snapped and sang through her, recognizing her from that fateful Solstice. It danced and twirled and sparked, so much light it was blinding.

That was when Mariah felt the darkness.

Just as before, it crawled out of the depths of the light, a wickedness whispering the terrible things that usually lived only in her nightmares.

She'd felt this darkness before. Not just when she'd last touched this pillar after the Solstice. No, this was the same darkness she'd felt inside Andrian, the same one she chased away as she wove her soul with his.

As if reminded, that bond roared to life, wrapping around her and pulling with a vicious ferocity. Mariah gasped, twisting her lips into a snarl.

She knew she'd neglected that bond. But she wasn't yet ready to face it, no matter how much it might grab at her, demanding her attention.

"Mariah, I'm not sure if this is a good idea—"

Ignoring Feran, she closed her eyes and speared her mind into the pillar.

At first, all was quiet. It was only Mariah, her magic, and the wild energy of the *allume*, familiar yet untamed. She relaxed for a moment, the power wrapping around her.

The darkness slammed into her with an animal's ferocity.

It wrapped around her like serpents, biting and squeezing. It was suffocating, this darkness. Burning and consuming and devouring, and it would leave nothing but pain and ashes in its wake. It ate at her light like a starved beast, hungry for more power to fuel its wicked, senseless rage.

Mariah shuddered. Somewhere, she might have released a scream. So much pain drove the darkness. So much empty suffering, terrible and vile and wrought with the wrong kind of desperation.

Deep in her chest, beneath where even her magic lived, something ancient rustled awake. It rumbled through her, growling in annoyance as the darkness around her balked.

Mariah didn't hesitate. She gasped her breath as the serpents released her before unspooling her magic through her mind. She hissed into the void within the pillar, vengeful and tired and broken.

"This place is mine. And it's time you got the fuck *out."*

Her threads of light grew claws as she unleashed them on the darkness.

It was over in an instant. As quickly as the darkness had emerged, it burned away, shredded and consumed by silver-gold light. The moment it was gone, the *allume* settled, returning to its gentle state of wild, thrumming power.

Mariah slammed back into her body, drenched in sweat, chest heaving. Feran caught her as she stumbled away from the pillar, her weak and sore body shaking.

"Fucking Enfara, Mariah. What was that? What did you do?"

Mariah didn't answer him. Instead, she stared at the lights lining the throne room walls, at the pillars blazing beside the throne.

Lights that were on, glowing bright, not a hint of a flicker. The *lunestair* glowed with familiar pale light, not a whisper of darkness marring its depths.

Mariah sagged in Feran's arms. "I told you. It's fixed." She stared again at the pillar. "I fixed the *allume*. It won't go out again."

Feran's exhale grazed her cheek. "Next time, give me a heads-up."

She chuckled. "Let's hope there won't *be* a next time."

Carefully, he released her, steadying her with a hand under her arm. Mariah rolled her shoulders, standing straight, and was about to step down the dais when a flash of movement caught her eye.

Timidly, hesitantly, a delicate shape emerged from the shadows. Short and wrapped in billowing, pale gold robes, but obviously female. Her hood was pushed back from her face, youthful features open, strawberry blonde hair twisted atop her head in a conservative coronet.

Mariah knew those robes.

Her back went rigid as she lifted her chin, forgetting her exhaustion as magic stirred back to life in her chest and illuminated the tips of her fingers. Mariah released Feran's arm as she stared the young woman down, her throne at her back. No longer would she be fearful and intimidated here, in her own palace.

In her home.

The girl's doe eyes were wide as her mouth gaped.

"That … was incredible, Your Majesty. I have … I have never felt so close to my goddess." With a furious blush, the girl gathered her pale robes in her hand and sank to her knees, the material pooling around her. "I am so sorry for not announcing my presence sooner. I woke when the *allume* went out and came to see if there was anything I could do. Please forgive my intrusion."

Mariah glanced at Feran, fury fading slightly into confusion. He smiled at her before stepping back with a nod, retreating down the dais steps and into the shadows at the other end of the throne room.

What?

Mariah slowly turned back to the girl, still kneeling on the marble. "Who are you?"

The girl's body dipped as if she was releasing a deeply held breath. "My name is Liliane, Your Majesty." She still didn't lift her face, voice quiet and subdued, shaking slightly. "I am—was—a priestess of Qhohena, one of the worshippers who used to call this place home."

Mariah was quiet for a moment, still catching her breath and calming her racing heart. Her magic slowly receded back beneath her skin and came to rest in its familiar place within her soul. "You told my court where they took me. You gave them what they needed to find me."

Liliane peeked up shyly from beneath her bangs. "Yes, Your Majesty. But it was no trouble. I would do it all over again if I could."

"You would stand against your High Priestess again? Betray her to those she declared enemies of her faith?"

The girl pressed her lips into a firm line before nodding. "Yes. I would. Because even though Ksee is High Priestess, beloved of Qhohena … you are her Chosen. You wield her magic in your veins. I just saw as much myself, only a few moments ago. To me, to betray you is to betray my goddess."

Mariah was silent for a moment, watching the girl. And to her surprise, the girl watched back.

"Stand up, Liliane."

The girl tilted her chin up further, rising to her feet, hesitation slowing her movement. Mariah stepped slowly down from the dais, striding past Liliane to one of the benches lining the throne room. She sat, brushing a hand over the smooth marble.

"Sit," Mariah commanded.

Liliane paused before a smile stretched across her youthful face. She gathered her skirts and settled beside Mariah, the smell of incense and candle wax moving with her.

Mariah turned to the still-dark morning, visible through the glass ceiling. And sighed.

"How old are you, Liliane?"

The girl twisted her hands in her lap. "Nineteen, Your Majesty."

Mariah's heart clenched. Sure, only two years younger than herself, but those two years felt like an eternity.

"And when did you ... join the temple?"

A pause. "When I was twelve," Liliane said, quietly. "My family is from here—Verith. I grew up in the market district. My father works for a merchant, always working down on the docks. My mother wove nets and baskets and sold them in our little stall near the Bay." She took a breath. Mariah kept her gaze fixed on the fading stars.

"One day, I wanted to leave the stall to go down to the docks to see my father and the ships as they came in. There was this ... girl." Mariah risked a glance and saw Liliane's cheeks flushed a rosy pink in the starlight. A smile tugged at her lips, but she kept silent.

"Her father also worked for a merchant, just as mine did. We liked to sit on the docks in the mornings and watch the ships pull into the Bay of Nria, guessing where each might have come from. Of course, only the Onitan trading vessels could make port at the docks, but we could see the other ships dropping anchor in the Bay.

"That day, she'd told me to meet her at the docks. New ships were coming in, she'd said, and she wanted to watch with me. But ..." Liliane swallowed audibly. "But Father had to work a double shift and Mother said no, she needed my help at the stall."

Tears now rimmed Liliane's brown eyes. "I got so mad," she continued. "I screamed and cried and threw a tantrum, like a child. I felt something boiling up with my anger, and before I knew it, flames were leaping from my fingertips, and my family's stall was going up in smoke. All those baskets and nets that my mother spent hours weaving until her fingers bled ... all gone, just because I wanted to see a girl when instead I owed my family a single day."

Mariah furrowed her brow. She searched the girl's face, a little surprised at how much of herself she saw there. A hunger for a life different from what she'd been born into. A thirst to forge a new path, one just for herself.

Liliane wiped away a tear before resting her hands back in her lap, recomposing herself into the perfect, poised priestess. "I couldn't look my family in the eyes after that. Not after such shame. So when the priestesses came for me the next day, I went with them gladly."

They sat there in silence for a few more minutes, the cavernous throne room silent and still, even with Feran lingering across from them against a pillar.

"Thank you," Mariah said, "for sharing. I'm sorry your first experience at magic had to be like that."

"It's nothing," Liliane rushed. "It was a long time ago."

Seven years is hardly a long time, Mariah thought, but held her tongue.

"Liliane," Mariah said instead. "I have a more ... serious question for you. And if you don't want to answer, just tell me. I won't be offended."

Liliane turned to her, brown eyes wide, and nodded. "Okay. I mean—yes, Your Majesty. Of course."

Mariah smiled. "You can call me Mariah if you want."

The girl smiled hesitantly but said nothing further.

Mariah sighed. "What did Ksee do for the Solstice?"

The question had been plaguing her long before she confronted that darkness in the *lunestair* pillars. It had lurked menacingly in the corner of her mind, ever since Ksee had visited her in her cell in Khento. The things Ksee had said ... it seemed to Mariah that the priestess had done something. Something that might have tried to counteract all the progress Mariah had made on her own.

The noxious sludge of the darkness that poisoned the *allume* slithered through her. She felt weak and tired, drained from the confrontation. It had felt like a dream, but one that chased her into the waking world. Her senses told her it was gone, but her instincts ...

Mariah shivered.

Liliane swallowed, twisting her hands between her pale robes. "I wasn't permitted near it or allowed to know. I'm too low in the ranks." She turned to face Mariah. "But ... they did something. I'm sure of it. I felt your magic that night, but I also felt something *else*. Whatever they did."

Mariah's lips dropped into a grim frown, and she nodded.

Liliane might not know what had happened that night, how her beautiful magic had been polluted. But Mariah was determined to find out.

"Thank you, Liliane. I'm glad my court listened to you."

Liliane's shoulders relaxed, palms lying flat on her legs. "I'm glad they did, too, Your Majesty." She frowned then, her brow twisting. "Were you ever in danger, there in Khento? Were they really about to do something terrible to you, something you wouldn't survive?"

Mariah blinked in surprise. "What are you talking about?"

Liliane blanched. "I'd heard—that's why I came here when I did. I heard a rumor that they were planning something terrible for you."

Mariah was quiet for a moment, her thoughts turning dark.

As they always did, when confronted with memories of that place.

"I wasn't aware of anything. I was far from safe, and plenty of terrible things were done to me, but they weren't to the point of killing me. Not yet, anyways."

Liliane's eyes had blown wide. "I'm so sorry, Your Majesty." she said meekly. "I didn't know. They keep so much from us—I should have come sooner."

Mariah closed her eyes, forcing a breath. The panic of those dark memories slowly abated, washing back into the scarred and shadowed part of her. "You have nothing to apologize for, Liliane. None of it is your fault, and I am grateful you came at all. And seriously—call me Mariah."

Liliane relaxed as she nodded again. "Okay." The priestess gripped her robes, about to rise from her bench, before she hesitated, turning back to Mariah.

"Your—Mariah." She stumbled over her words, blushing again. "I ... I also have a slight request."

Mariah sat up with interest. "Which is?"

Liliane cast her eyes down. "I wished to see if I could resume the weekly services in Qhohena's temple here in the palace. They can be run by any robed priestess, and I think it could be good for the people to get back to something normal. Especially after so many weeks of chaos."

Mariah knew these services. She'd been once or twice, back in Andburgh, dragged along by her mother for some rare special occasion. Onita celebrated no holidays beyond the Solstice, but there were other events that sometimes demanded a trip to temple: a birth, a marriage, or a death.

"I will need to check with my Armature," Mariah began slowly, "and I can't promise I'll ever attend. My relationship with Qhohena is ... interesting, to put it lightly." Flashes of a golden meadow peppered the backs of her eyes. "But I see no reason to say no. I agree it would be good for the people who want it."

Liliane's face lit up like a torch, her flames—the same ones that had gifted her those robes—lighting up her soft brown eyes.

"Thank you, Your—Mariah. I think this will be just what the city needs." Her smile softened. "Even after everything you suffered … thank you for letting me stay. This city has been my home my entire life, and the temple since I was twelve. I'm grateful to be allowed to call it my home again."

Mariah stood from the bench, taking a small step forward to stand before the priestess. She was taller than the girl, and after a moment's hesitation rested a hand on Liliane's shoulder. The girl started, lips parting in surprise as Mariah did something that shocked even her.

She smiled, full and genuine.

"You are always welcome here, priestess. Thank you for reminding me that just because one or two have been corrupted … most are just as lost as the rest of us."

Liliane smiled. "You hardly seem lost, My Queen."

Mariah dropped her hand and stepped back, smile falling. The light faded from Liliane's eyes at the change.

"Don't let the starlight fool you, Liliane. The darkness plays tricks with our eyes, but it wouldn't exist without the light."

CHAPTER 35

Sebastian blinked as the *allume* street lamps blazed to life, flooding the market district street with pale silver-gold light.

"What—is the magic back?"

"Oh, thank the goddess—"

"What if it goes out again? Are the wards back, too?"

Chatter filled the air as Sebastian sagged slightly against his horse. When the magic had snuffed out and chaos had erupted in the city, he'd rushed down into the streets with Quentin, Matheo, Drystan, and Trefor. Feran stayed behind with Mariah, who'd worn a determined look on her face as she murmured something about knowing how to fix it.

It seems she'd been successful. At least, Sebastian hoped that was the case.

Night workers on the docks had started the screaming that had woken them all in the early hours of the morning. Their lanterns had flickered out, and the darkness drove them into a sudden panic. They'd raced through the streets, shouting the alarm, afraid that with the wards now down, the pirates would come storming back.

But even in the weak moonlight, no black sails dotted the

horizon, and Sebastian and the Armature's task had been to calm the hysteria raised by those workers. It would serve no one if the city descended into needless madness.

"Sir? What happened? Are we safe?"

Sebastian lifted his head. A young woman, flanked closely by a man near her age—her husband, he presumed—stood a few paces away, her brow pushed together with worry.

He forced a smile. "There was a short *allume* outage, but there is nothing to worry about. The city is safe."

The woman shared a glance with her husband. "Is it … is it fixed? Will it go out again?"

"The queen herself fixed it," Sebastian answered. He didn't know for sure, but he was confident in Mariah. When she said she could, he believed her.

"The queen?" The woman's husband gripped his wife's arm. "Queen Ryenne?"

Sebastian paused. "No," he said slowly. "Queen Mariah."

"I—Oh." The husband's eyes widened. "I'm sorry. I forgot—"

"Has she been coronated? Do we have a new queen?" the woman interrupted her husband, suspicion flashing through her eyes.

Sebastian narrowed his. "No. Not yet. But she will be, any day now. And even still, she is Onita's Queen, in all the ways that matter." He gestured with his chin. "You can return home now. Dawn is approaching soon, and the city is safe."

The couple eyed him again, that unnerving suspicion still rife in their stares, before nodding and retreating down the street.

Sebastian released an exhale, running a hand through his hair.

He hated that suspicion, that distrust these people carried. Not for him—he could stomach that, considering how much he deserved it—but for Mariah. She'd only been back for three days and needed a chance to recover and heal. But the people needed a queen, if only for the sense of stability it offered.

Sebastian's stomach knotted with worry. The way Mariah had looked when they'd found her in those cold castle gardens—

clothes torn and tattered, hair hanging in clumps down her back, frame starved and weak—haunted his sleepless nights. He knew she'd immediately started training with Trefor, which he didn't particularly like, but he understood her reasoning.

She just looked so ... *weak*. Sebastian wished she would focus on resting and recovering, but supposed she, too, had her own demons she needed to fight.

He'd also heard from Quentin that Andrian had crossed paths with her in the hall outside of her suites as he was grabbing some of his belongings. Sebastian ground his teeth as he watched more city-folk meander back to their homes, staring blearily up at the illuminated street lamps.

Gods, it made him fucking *angry*. He'd given Andrian one instruction: stay away from Mariah. And not only had Andrian broken that his second day back, but he'd then *questioned* her.

As if he had any fucking right to her thoughts or experiences. Not when he was the reason she looked so changed and broken.

The fact that Andrian had since committed to holing up in his rooms ever since was the only good to come from any of it.

"Seb, we should head back." Drystan appeared on the other side of Sebastian's horse, blond hair hanging around his face. "I think things have calmed down. Sunrise isn't far off, and I'd like to at least get a little more sleep."

Sebastian sighed and nodded. "Yeah, you're right." He turned, tightening his saddle.

As he was about to swing up into the seat, a figure strode into the street.

It wasn't that there was a person still out at that hour that made Sebastian pause. It was the strange red cloak the figure wore, the color of a blood-stained sunset, and the way it completely concealed the stranger's face.

Sebastian held himself utterly still as the man walked straight for him, not stopping until he stood so close that he shared Sebastian's breath. The man appeared unarmed, but Sebastian's hand tightened around his sword tucked beneath his saddle.

The man leaned in closer, and Sebastian glimpsed his eyes

beneath the hood. They were fevered and wild as if struck with some insanity.

"Tonight was just the beginning," the man whispered roughly, voice like ground coals. "The moons are setting, and the sun will soon rise."

Sebastian stumbled back, pulling his blade from its sheath in a single, smooth movement. He leveled it at the stranger, just as a manic grin spread on his face beneath the hood.

"What did you say?"

But the man was already backing away, eyes still gleaming with madness. He turned, raising his arms to the street.

"*The sun will rise!*" he shouted into the pre-dawn air, the few people still lingering on the streets turning with curiosity before he sprinted down the nearest alley.

"Oh, fuck this—" Quentin lunged past Sebastian, about to pursue the stranger into the belly of the city. But Sebastian caught his arm, hauling him back.

"No, Quentin. Let him go."

Quentin whirled. "What? He's *mad*. What the fuck was that about?"

"Exactly." Sebastian glanced down the alley where the man had vanished. "He's mad. Let it be. The last thing we need is for a member of Mariah's Armature to be seen dragging an unarmed civilian through the street. You saw how they were tonight."

Quentin growled, green eyes flashing, but dropped his hand from his baldric. "Fine. What did he even say to you? Before he shouted the sun thing."

Sebastian glanced away again, inspecting a crack in the cobblestones beneath them.

The moons are setting, and the sun will soon rise.

"Nothing," he said finally, turning to his horse. He could feel Quentin's eyes on him still but did his best to shrug it off. "It was gibberish, nonsensical. Like you said, he was obviously mad. Or just had a too-late night at a tavern nearby."

Quentin grunted. "Weird fucking night, I swear. I hope the goddess at least lets me nap some today."

Sebastian murmured agreement but wasn't truly listening. The man's words, while nonsense, still raced through his head.

It was all likely nothing, truly just the words of a drunk or a madman. But Sebastian couldn't ignore the nagging feeling that it felt a bit like a threat.

He would tell Mariah about it, he vowed to himself. Not tomorrow; she was still recovering, and after whatever she did tonight to fix the *allume* would likely need even more rest. But eventually, when she was ready, he would tell her.

And until then, there was no need to tell anyone else.

CHAPTER 36

The sun rose over the Attlehon Mountains, and Mariah looked for the golden eagles. For the first time in a long time, she felt at peace.

The morning spring air was chilly, but she didn't bother with a blanket. She inhaled the smell of the mountains and the sea, the rays of the sun soaking into her pale skin. Her mind lingered on the conversation she'd shared with Liliane, on what she confronted in the *lunestair* pillars, on the visit she'd had from Qhohena the night before.

That visit from the goddess ... it felt so different from the visits with Zadione. Less urgent, warmer. Which, she supposed was no surprise—it was a human reaction to be slightly unnerved by the goddess of death.

But there was a part of her, deep down, that couldn't deny the strange feeling that grew every day.

Something inside of her wasn't quite human.

She shrugged away the thought. Of course, she wouldn't feel like a typical human; not anymore. She was only one step away from ascending into power that would grant her near-immortality. Her body was changing, her spirit expanding to accommodate a life far longer than the one she thought she was born into.

A slap of wings pushed wind across her face. Mariah whipped her head, scouring the skies with narrowed eyes.

She sighed heavily. Nothing.

She would never get to see those damn eagles.

A clamor behind her sent her shooting from her chair, palming the hilt of the dragon-winged dagger at her thigh.

She relaxed when a head of golden curls strode into her sitting room, bearing a heavily laden silver platter. Mariah felt a genuine smile spread unimpeded across her face as her hand relaxed around her dagger. She took a step toward the balcony door just in time to see Delaynie, Kiira, and Rylla follow Ciana in, all bearing identical silver trays.

"Get over here, Your Royal Majesty! We brought breakfast food!"

Ciana's clear voice rang through the living room, and Mariah's grin widened as she pushed through the balcony doors. The other four women turned to her, all answering her grin with smiles of their own.

"Mariah!" Delaynie gracefully set her platter on the island before gathering her skirts, rushing to meet Mariah, her practiced poised momentarily abandoned. They collided in an embrace, tears springing into Mariah's eyes.

"Hi, Del," Mariah whispered, squeezing her friend tight. She'd been back for three days, but she hadn't yet seen the second lady of her court. Someone had to keep the kingdom running, and Delaynie had placed her duty above her feelings. And for that, Mariah was grateful.

Delaynie squeezed back tighter. "I missed you."

"I missed you, too." With a bit of reluctance, Mariah pulled away, meeting Delaynie's crystal blue gaze. "Thank you for keeping this kingdom running while I was ... gone."

Delaynie smiled, tears falling down her pale cheeks. "Of course. Always."

Kiira, Rylla, and Ciana waited beside the island, uncovering the trays of food and arranging them around the white marble. Mariah's mouth salivated at the eggs, bacon, ham, winter pomegranates, and several loaves of fresh-baked bread. There was even a tray loaded with waffles, the pastries accompanied by warmed maple syrup and whipped cream. Mariah looked at Ciana, who met her glance with a smile and a slight nod before turning back to the food.

For the first time since arriving home, Mariah didn't look at that food as a means to an end. A requirement to get strong again.

She looked at it with a desire to simply *enjoy* it.

A piece of Mariah's broken soul clicked back into place.

"Grab the plates, will you, Cee?"

Mariah leaned her head on the pillow behind her, a soft groan spilling from her lips.

"Gods, that was so good." She pressed a hand to her bloated stomach, the food settling there like lead. She probably shouldn't have eaten so much, not when she was still recovering and adjusting to being fed again.

But with her friends around her and the breakfast looking so tantalizing, she'd indulged herself. Just this once.

"With that, I would have to agree," Ciana murmured from the floor below Mariah, her head tipped back against the couch, feet stretched in front of her. Delaynie sat as poised as possible at the other end of the couch, and around the bend of the plush furniture lounged Kiira, her eyes closed. Rylla sprawled face down on the pillows beside her sister. She carefully pushed herself up to her elbows, turning to the side.

And belched. Loudly.

"*Bhagini!*" Kiira grabbed a discarded pillow from the floor, chucking it at her grinning sister. "That was disgusting! Apologize!"

Rylla opened her mouth, but a sound cut her off.

Not just any sound. A laugh like spilling water, a dam breaking.

Mariah was laughing. It was not a soft chuckle or a light

giggle. But true, deep laughter, the kind that started in her stomach and worked its way up her chest until tears streamed down her face and she couldn't breathe.

The sound made everyone in the room freeze before breaking into laughter of their own. Joy peeled through the room of marble and glass, and before long, they were all wheezing and snorting and gasping for air. Mariah doubled over, slipping off the edge of the couch, her hand landing on Ciana's shaking shoulder. Even Delaynie had tucked into a ball, holding her side as she dissolved into stitches.

Eventually, the laughter slowed and eased down to a few lingering chuckles and giggles and hiccups. Mariah wiped the tears from her eyes, cheeks burning from how long she'd held that smile.

"I am sorry," Rylla said, her accented voice still carrying a hint of merriment. "That was rude of me."

"No," Mariah said with a shake of her head. "Please, don't apologize. I haven't laughed that hard in ... well, I don't think I've ever laughed that hard."

The other women shared a glance, amusement still on their faces, but the joy dulled from their eyes. Just a touch. Mariah backtracked.

"No, please, don't look at me like that." She chuckled again, rolling onto her back. "I just mean ... even before that happened, before I even came here, I never really had friends. At least, not the kind who would just have breakfast with me." She looked around the room, meeting each of their gazes, and smiled.

"It's nice."

Ciana twisted, looking at her with those sharp amber eyes, and rested her hand on Mariah's. "I never really had friends, either. But I'm glad we all have each other."

Murmurs of agreement swept around the room. Mariah smiled at Ciana before turning her attention to the Kreah sisters who lazed upon the couch, much like the big cats who shared their skin.

Which, speaking of ...

"So," Mariah started, "shifters?"

Kiira and Rylla both snapped their gazes to her, one brown and one hazel. And nodded.

Mariah watched them shrewdly. "I've seen a lot of what I used to consider impossible these past few months. Had a lot of world views shifted. But I'm going to need a bit more of an explanation than that."

Kiira looked at Rylla, who pushed herself off her stomach and sat up on the couch, her legs still curled beneath her. Mariah could almost picture the black tail of the cat beneath her skin swishing idly around her legs, the feline comparison to the movement so uncanny.

"Yes, we are shifters," Rylla said. "In Kreah, we do not have magic of the elements like you do here in Onita. Also, not just our men are blessed with such gifts." Rylla cut a glance at Ciana for a split-second, so fast Mariah almost missed it. "Not everyone is gifted, but it is equal. Men and women."

"And the magic—it's from their goddess, Rulene!" Ciana interjected excitedly, turning up to look at Mariah, who couldn't stop her grin.

"I've heard of Rulene," Mariah said, nodding. "A priestess from Leuxrith once told me of the continent's other gods."

Kiira cocked her head. "A Leuxrithian priestess? By the skies, what was she doing in Onita?"

Mariah's smile hardened. "Let's just say she wasn't exactly supposed to be here."

"Do you know where she went? Is she still here?" Rylla asked.

Mariah glanced toward the balcony, frowning slightly. "No ... no, I don't think so. I have no idea where she went." She turned back to Rylla. "Tell me more about your magic and your goddess."

"Well," Rylla started, adjusting her feet. "Rulene is the Goddess of the Day Sky. And the day sky changes more than any other—sometimes clear and blue, sometimes dark and gray. She blessed Kreah with her magic of change, mixing with its people. We were brought closer to nature, and with it ... the power to shift."

"Are you all ... leopards and panthers? Or cats?" Mariah's curiosity was insatiable.

Rylla smiled. "No. We are not all leopards and panthers. Some of us are felines; others are wolves and foxes. Some are bears, or horses, or even great birds of prey. But no matter what form we take, we are all blessed with a shared connection to the sky above our heads, the earth beneath our feet, and the steady pulse of nature around us all."

Ciana sighed. "I want to visit Kreah someday." Delaynie hummed in agreement.

Kiira nodded, lips tipping up in a faint smile. "You are always welcome. All of you."

They fell silent for a moment, watching each other. Mariah sat up straighter, planting her feet on the ground, running her palms along her thighs.

"I ... I wanted to thank you both. For ... everything." She swallowed, twisting her hands together, fighting off the memories of darkness and cold and fear. "You have no obligation to this court or to me, and you didn't have to risk your lives like that. So ... thank you." Her words felt weak, not adequate to convey what she felt, but they were the best she could do.

Kiira and Rylla glanced at each other, a shared look between sisters, before turning back to Mariah with a curious gleam in their eyes.

"Did you know," Kiira started, "that Kreah has no queen or king?"

Mariah furrowed her brow. "What do you mean?"

A smile brightened Kiira's smooth, ebony skin. "I mean, Kreah is not ruled by a monarch. There is no single person who holds all the power. Instead, we are governed by a Council of Elders who make decisions for the nation amongst themselves. There is a High Counsellor, but they simply preside over the Council; they do not rule. The Elders are chosen by each *ksetra*, or region, and serve for their whole lives or until their *ksetra* decides they are no longer able.

"The second—and third, and fourth, and fifth—children of

each family are permitted to roam the world. *Encouraged* to. To see other lands, to learn other cultures, to share the livelihood of Kreah with others. Many journey and eventually return to their homeland. But some choose to stay and are free to choose a loyalty beyond that of the Elders or their *ksetra*.

"Many have settled in Leuxrith, in Idrix, in Vatha. Some even made homes in the Kizar Islands, and even more have sailed beyond the Mirrored Sea for whatever lies beyond. But ... none have settled in Onita."

"Because Onita's borders have always been closed," Mariah murmured, her mind whirling.

Kiira nodded. "Yes. For so long, Onita kept its borders shut. While there were some who snuck across, no one was formally allowed to visit, and even trading ships had to stay far from port and unload by ferry. But with your *Porofirat*, suddenly Queen Ryenne opened the borders. To allow delegations from the other countries to attend, to see Onita for the first time in thousands of years. Onita has certainly progressed, technologically." Kiira glanced around the room, at the *allume* chandelier above, the modern kitchen, the panels of *lunestair* on the walls. "But in other ways ... Onita has fallen behind. Lost its way."

Mariah couldn't disagree. She merely nodded, her lips pressing into a firm line as Kiira continued.

"Lost its way ... until you."

Mariah straightened. Ciana did, too, and Delaynie folded her hands in her lap. An instinct prickled at the back of Mariah's neck.

"You pushed back against some of Onita's antiquated ways. That despite all their power, they were still so lost, so weak. We saw it in you, that very first day in the stables. And we saw it again at the *Porofirat*. When Ryenne invited us to stay—something that has never happened to a Kreah citizen, not in modern memory—we knew we had to remain close. We'd made a choice but needed to wait until we were needed before making it known."

Something in Mariah's blood stirred, her magic waking in her veins. It reached the tips of her fingers as she said, "What choice did you make?"

"My sister told you that we, as fourth and fifth daughters, are free to choose a leader to follow," Rylla said, this time with a wide smile. "Someone who deserves our undying loyalty, the leader of a nation we wish to call home."

Everything in the room stilled. Mariah didn't even dare a breath.

"You are not our queen by birth, Mariah," Kiira said, her voice soft and low. "But you are the queen we choose. If you'll have us."

As one, the Kreah sisters stood from the couch. They wore Onitan clothing—familiar black leggings and soft wool sweaters—but Kiira still had gold jewelry woven into her braids, and Rylla's silver necklace and bangles tinkled as she moved. Together, they sank to their knees on the plush rug, heads bowing and hands clenching into fists over their hearts.

Mariah's heart raced, magic flowing unimpeded into the air around her. Ciana, her amber eyes wide, hurriedly stood and moved to sit beside Delaynie, whose blue gaze was warm and bright with emotion.

Mariah grounded her toes into the rug as she stood. She cleared her throat, finding the right words.

"Stand, Kiira and Rylla, daughters of Kreah, beloved of Rulene, Goddess of the Day Sky."

They rose together. Two sets of eyes—one brown, one hazel—leveled expectantly at Mariah.

She hadn't felt much like a queen since her return. Had felt too cowering, too meek. Too quiet and damaged.

But with those Kreah warrior shifters watching her the way they did, with the words of the Goddess fresh on her mind from the previous night, how it had felt to cleanse the magic of that awful, tainted darkness ...

Something in Mariah remembered the taste of power.

"You are both always welcome in my country. May this forever be a home to you." Mariah paused, just a breath. "I have a question for you, as well."

The Kreah sisters stayed silent. Waiting.

"You risked your lives for me. As Kreah, you know far more about the continent than I ever will. Because of that ..." Mariah drew in a breath. "I would like to ask you both if you'd like to join my court. As ladies, to serve by my side. To counsel me in my rule for the rest of your time on this earth."

Behind her, Ciana sobbed. Delaynie whispered a *shush*. A smile twitched on Mariah's lips.

Slowly, smiles spread across Kiira and Rylla's faces. Kiira stepped forward first.

"It would be our absolute honor, Your Majesty."

With laughing sobs and sounds of delight, the five women surrounded each other, enjoying a friendship they each never knew they would find and were too stunned to believe they'd been blessed with.

On the balcony railing, a golden eagle watched, sharp aureate eyes watching the shared moment before lifting from her perch and disappearing into the sky above.

CHAPTER 37

The sitting room walls were painted white and covered with resplendent paintings, each set in a similarly rich plated gold frame. They were signs of opulence and wealth, power emanating throughout the room. All the way down to the stiff chair upholstered in maroon suede, where Anniliese Hareth sat in her lilac gown, clutching a cup of tea and wondering how bad the bruises from her corset would be tomorrow.

She daintily sipped the warm liquid, chamomile and vanilla tickling her throat. Across from her sat Lady Florithe Beauchamp, the youngest of the lord's wives. Anniliese's father had instructed her to take tea with the other young woman, to foster a friendship.

What her father hadn't mentioned was how dreadfully boring and drab the lady was. Pretty enough, as Anniliese eyed her honeycomb hair and milky skin, but as empty as the decorative vase sitting between them on the marble coffee table.

"I suppose as we move into the spring and summer, we can fill the space with peonies and tulips. But I fear the pollen might upset my allergies! How dreadful, to be sneezing all over. Simply would not do."

"Yes," Anniliese said dryly then drained the rest of her tea.

"Goddess forbid the men remember we are human with a sneeze."

Lady Beauchamp went rigid.

Oops. She definitely hadn't meant to say that out loud. She'd been raised better than that. Was bred better than that.

"I only mean," Anniliese tacked on hastily, "that it is simply not lady-like! The men work too hard; they deserve our best, always."

That assuaged Lady Beauchamp, her posture relaxing as a smile filled her smooth and empty face. "Yes, you are absolutely right. To please our lords is our greatest honor in life."

Anniliese smiled back, but it didn't reach her eyes. She'd had tea with Lady Beauchamp before—plenty of times, actually. And while the lady certainly was as simple as they came, these afternoons never used to grind on Anniliese the way they did now.

She'd always been happy with her station in life, content knowing she was blessed to have been born into one of the six Royal houses. Growing up knowing of the high possibility she would be Chosen as Ryenne's successor, would move into the palace, would continue her life of wealth and opulence and comfort.

Even when that future was snatched from her, she'd still been relatively content. Still happy with her dresses and tea, the flowers and pastries and jewels.

Until the lords brought in the new queen, and Anniliese was forced to confront everything she'd lost. Everything that was given to another so beneath her, so *unworthy*.

The worst part was that by the end, she wasn't sure if she even still hated Mariah.

Anniliese set her teacup on the table with a clink. "Well," she said, standing and pressing out the front of her skirts as her corset pulled tight across her chest. "I fear I must be going. I am to have dinner with my father and our hosts this evening; can't be late for such an honor!"

Lady Beauchamp nearly dropped her cup before bustling to her feet. "Oh, my! No, you absolutely cannot. I do hope I have not kept you. As always, it was such a pleasure to take tea with you, Lady Anniliese. Let's meet again soon!"

Anniliese smiled, another fake, forced thing. "Of course. These meetings for tea are always the highlight of my week."

Lady Beauchamp beamed, and with a sigh of relief, Anniliese stepped from the room on her delicate, slippered feet.

The air about the great keep at Khento was light and relaxed, the thick haze of celebration and comfort evident in every room. The lords gathered in the great hall and feasted every night, their raucous laughter echoing down the hallways. It was only in her rooms, situated in a comfortable guest wing of the castle, where Anniliese could find any peace.

The merriment that filled the keep was … bizarre, to put it mildly. Anniliese hardly knew what to make of it all. A little over a week ago, Mariah had escaped with the help of her Armature, and ever since, the lords had behaved as if this was a cause for celebration. As far as Anniliese knew, no attempts were made to search for the young queen or to follow and bring them back to the keep. How any part of the situation could be good for the lords was an unwelcome mystery.

The only lord who seemed at least mildly perturbed was Lord Laurent. Anniliese twisted her thin necklace, a *debutante* gift from her father, around the column of her throat as she padded around a corner and up a flight of stairs. The foul-tempered Lord of Antoris was even pricklier than usual, his mood worsening after it was discovered Andrian had fled back to Verith with Mariah.

Clamminess washed over Anniliese's skin, the air too hot. She remembered the part she'd been asked to play. Even at the beginning, when she was all too eager to rub her victory in Mariah's face … something had never settled right in her stomach. She swallowed past a lump in her throat, remembering Andrian's empty stare and blind obedience, only shaken when in the presence of the young queen.

Anniliese would never tell Mariah, but that night she'd kissed Andrian at her father's behest, she'd raced to her room, sick for hours. She'd sat in the shower until her handmaids had to drag her out, desperate to wash the disgust and shame from her skin.

She shook her head, delicately clearing her throat. She'd done what she had to do to support her family. Just as she'd always done.

Anniliese wound her way down the upper-level halls, inching closer to her rooms in the west wing. She strode past the northern hallways, a part of the castle reserved for the members of House Shawth. It housed not only their residential rooms but their family coffers and troves.

Her steps quickened.

She did not fear House Shawth. They were the most powerful of the Royal families and had led Onita with strength and dignity for centuries. As their gracious hosts, her family was indebted to them for leading this battalion against the unworthy claimant to the throne.

But she couldn't stop the shiver of fear scraping down her spine each time she walked by this section of the castle. How an air of darkness, of misery, of fate, seemed to reach out with clawed talons, wanting to reach itself around her and draw her down into the whispering deep.

It was a figment of her imagination; Anniliese was sure of it. She just wasn't used to living in a castle so large and ancient. She'd spent nights in the palace, certainly, but that was the palace. A place she'd thought to one day call her home.

She was just unfamiliar with this place, that was all.

But each day, it became harder and harder to deny how the darkness grew in force and strength. How it cried out to her with increasing fervor, a dangerous temptation that scared her far more than it intrigued her.

And today, it was almost unbearable. She was nearly running by the time she reached the end of the hallway, fleeing from whatever invisible force chased her and called to her at the same time. She rounded a final corner and kept running.

Anniliese halted when she reached her guest wing and slumped against the wall, catching her breath as her mind churned. It had never been so bad before. She wondered if anyone else noticed, if the castle staff who ventured there could feel it. It was now past the point of her imagination; what she'd felt just then was undeniably real and terrifying.

Mariah's words to her before she'd fled the castle gardens with her Armature in tow, flashed through her mind.

"I understand why you feel you must stay. But stop letting these men run your life as if it wasn't your own. You know, deep down, that isn't what you want."

Anniliese straightened.

She certainly felt no affection for the young queen. Mariah was brash and rude and unpolished, all the things Anniliese was not. But, for whatever reason, when Mariah had asked Anniliese to abandon her family and go with them ... she'd hesitated. And then, even when she'd said no, Anniliese had turned her back and made for the castle without sounding the alarm.

She hadn't said a word about that night to anyone. And still, she didn't know why. A weakness had sprouted that night, one she hadn't been able to overcome.

However, there was something about those last words that lingered. Some truth in them. Anniliese pushed her head higher and made her way to her chamber doors. A handmaid greeted her, having already drawn a bath and laid out her evening gown.

As she was cleaned and primped and dressed, she resolved to ask their gracious host about the darkness she'd felt. She was, after all, a lady of a great house.

She deserved answers about the place where she currently rested her head. And answers she would get.

***

ANNILIESE SAT beside her father in the private dining chamber, picking daintily at the lemon tart she'd been served for dessert. A glass of sparkling wine also sat in front of her, untouched.

She wanted her wits about her tonight as she asked her question.

Across the table sat Lady Shawth, her silver-streaked auburn hair coiled into a crown atop her head, her hazy eyes empty and emotionless. The Lady of Khento was quiet, but of just the right breeding to bear Lord Shawth's sons. Those sons were too young to join them at the table, but Lady Shawth seemed ambivalent to the absence of her children.

She seemed ambivalent to most things, actually.

Her husband sat beside her, whiskey tumbler in hand, leaning back in his chair as he jested with Anniliese's father, Lord Hareth. Anniliese speared a piece of her tart with her fork as Lord Shawth roared with laughter, her father chuckling forcefully in answer.

Anniliese felt sorry for her father sometimes. He was a widower—her mother had died many years ago, leaving him alone with a daughter, a castle in Ettervan, and no male heirs. Anniliese had a baby brother once, very briefly. But that baby brother was the same life that took her mother from the world before following her quietly into the afterlife a few days later.

She chewed on her tart, the bitter sweetness pleasant on her tongue, remembering those early days after her mother and brother had passed. It had made her Choosing even more critical. The Royals had all been informed of Ryenne's abdication, and the future of Anniliese's very house hinged on her ascension to the throne.

That was what her father had told her every single day as she'd grown up. She had to be perfect, the ideal image of Onitan Royalty. One who the magic could not possibly pass up.

Then Mariah had stolen that from her, and she'd returned to her father with her head bowed and an apology on her lips. All their plans slashed to pieces.

Anniliese's fork clattered to her plate. Lord Shawth paused in his animated storytelling, and her father shot her a frustrated look. Even Lady Shawth's dead eyes flickered away from her glass of wine.

Flames licked up Anniliese's cheeks. "Apologies, My Lords."

She felt her father's attention linger on her for a few more moments before he turned back to Lord Shawth.

Lord Hareth was a quiet man, content to follow behind those with greater ambitions than his own, but Anniliese didn't think he would ever forgive her for her failure at the Choosing.

"Did you enjoy your meal, Lady Anniliese?"

Well, at least she no longer had to sit here in boredom, picking at her lemon tart.

"Yes, Lord Shawth," she answered, softly clearing her throat. "Thank you, again, for your hospitality and the wonderful meal." She dipped her head to him, then turned to his wife. "And my thanks to you as well, My Lady."

The empty woman just smiled back.

"So," Shawth said, swirling his whiskey. "Have you enjoyed your stay here in Khento? I am sure it is nothing compared to the cliffs of Ettervan, but I do hope you have found it comfortable enough for your liking."

This is my chance.

"Yes, My Lord. You keep a very beautiful and splendid home. I —we—are honored to have joined you as guests these past months."

Lord Shawth smiled, nodding once, and leaned back in his chair. He turned back to her father, about to return to their conversation.

"However," Anniliese said, "there is ... something. Just a small inquiry, something that could make things more comfortable for myself. If that's not too much to ask." Her father stiffened. Ladies didn't ask for favors from their hosts. Ladies only offered compliments, only smiled, never spoke out of turn.

For the first time in her life, Anniliese ignored her father, focusing on the Lord of Khento. Shawth's pale blue eyes had gone cold and calculating, and he took a slow sip from his whiskey.

"Of course, Lady Anniliese. After all, we certainly want all our guests to be comfortable." The last word was a sneer, but Anniliese chose to ignore it. She swallowed once before pressing on.

"Is there something my father and I should know about the castle? Sometimes when I walk by the northern corridors, something feels ... strange. Dark. Malevolent, even. Perhaps I might be permitted to inspect it myself? I'm sure it's nothing, but I must always be concerned about our safety. I pray you understand."

The second she heard the words leave her mouth, she knew she shouldn't have said them. They were improper, intrusive, and accusatory. *What am I thinking?*

She expected Lord Shawth to explode into a fit of rage at her impropriety.

Instead, he simply set down his glass and smiled. A cold, terrifying smile, his eyes trailing down her body.

"So curious about my private wing, aren't you, Lady Anniliese? Do you wish to visit my bed? To assist your family by sleeping your way through the lords? I will give it to you—you are a pretty little thing." He licked his thin lips, and something in Anniliese's stomach turned. "And with your mild resemblance to our little whore queen, I imagine you would fetch quite a price." Lord Shawth turned to her father, who wore an expression of horror and indignity.

"Would you sell your daughter to save your family, Lord Hareth? Was this your plan? Seems a little desperate, even for you."

Anniliese wasn't even sure where to look. At Lord Shawth, with his hungry, vile expression. At her father, his eyes blown wide with panic and mouth stuttering like a floundering fish. Or at Lady Shawth, empty as ever, her eyes glazed as she watched her husband invite another woman to his bed.

"Please, My Lord," her father said, choking on his words. "Please forgive my daughter. She is young and curious and forgets her place." He glared at Anniliese, rage and fear in his eyes. "She will apologize. And from now on, she will remember her manners and hold her tongue before inquiring into the privacy of others."

Anniliese gaped. Not only had her father declined to defend her from Shawth's despicable words, but he *reprimanded* her. There. In front of Shawth and his wife.

Her cheeks burned, her stomach twisting into knots, as she

turned to Lord Shawth, her eyes downcast and tears burning behind her lids.

"I apologize, My Lord," she whispered. "I ... I was out of turn. Please forgive me and do not pin my mistakes on my family."

Lord Shawth tsked. "You are forgiven, Lady Anniliese. But from now on, perhaps you should not invite yourself to places or start conversations you have no intent of seeing through."

Anniliese dropped her head further, a curtain of dark hair hiding her face from view as she stared at her lap. A single tear fell, landing on her folded hands.

"Stop letting these men run your life as if it wasn't your own." Mariah's words again flitted through her mind.

Not only had she let them do just that, but she was no closer to learning what monstrous nightmare might inhabit the castle with her and her father.

The shame that washed over her and lingered in her mouth for the next week tasted like flame and ash.

CHAPTER 38

Andrian had always prided himself on being emotionless. On locking everything away so squarely behind a block of ice, leaving only his rage and apathy free.

Then, a dark-haired woman had stepped into his life, melting that ice and uprooting everything about himself he'd held dear. She had become the thing he valued most. It didn't matter what he felt, or what he did, or who he was. As long as it was all for her.

But he'd seen those scars on her back. Once smooth, glowing skin, now marred with deep rivets of torn flesh. Only a wicked weapon could cause those—an iron-tipped whip, wielded with the intent to cause maximum pain and destruction.

"Who the fuck did that to you?" He could still hear the anger and rage and fear ringing in his voice, like a nightmare he couldn't shake.

But it wasn't nearly as awful as her answer.

"You did."

He hadn't thought it possible to hate himself more than he did.

He was so very, very wrong.

Three days had passed since those simple words drifted through the air back to him, falling from Mariah's lips like shards of ice. Three days, and he couldn't remember the last time he'd slept or bathed. He was still in those secluded rooms, far away in a seldom-used guest wing of the palace, a forced isolation that had quickly become self-imposed.

At least he'd had time to grab the most important of his belongings. Which, of course, meant he'd been able to snag his stash of liquor from his rooms.

Andrian's head thumped against the wall behind him as he swirled the glass of whiskey. He tracked the streaks left on the cloudy glass before lifting it to his mouth, dumping the contents down his throat. It burned, and he grimaced, but he reveled in the pain and the immediate numbness that followed.

The whiskey was a peaty blend, aged and distilled in Sacale, just south of Verith and nestled in the Attlehon Mountains on the coast. It was his favorite, and he'd been hoarding bottles of it each time he saw a new shipment arriving in the market district.

He was a miserable fucking idiot most of the time, but at least he was smart enough for that. Leaning forward on the couch, he refilled his glass from the half-empty bottle on the table, vision swimming slightly.

His world was blurred, fuzzy, dulled. It was the only way he could tolerate ... everything.

He was sure he'd eaten. He must have—too many days had passed, and he wasn't dead yet.

He just didn't remember. Just as he couldn't remember his hands lifting that whip, couldn't remember the way he'd scourged her back. He couldn't remember any of the pain he knew she'd suffered at his unworthy hands. All he remembered was unending darkness, flashes of malevolent nightmares bursting through his mind each time he closed his eyes.

Andrian tried to recover those lost memories. Every night, he would lie awake, peeling back the layers of his subconscious, trying desperately to see through his eyes while he'd been locked away. But it was as if they simply didn't exist; his memories were only of that lightless prison, the occasional flash of color peppering his dreams.

It was like the events happening in *this* world were done by another entity, someone whose memories Andrian had no access to because they never belonged to him.

He didn't know if he should be thankful ... or terrified.

A part of him wished he could go back to forgetting, to fall back into the void of despair he didn't deserve to be rescued from.

Andrian raised the now-full glass back to his lips, movement a little jilted, and was about to take a sip when a booming knock rattled the door to the quaint room.

His eyes narrowed on the door. He sat still for five, ten heartbeats. Maybe he'd imagined it.

When there was only silence, he shrugged and lifted his glass again.

The knock rang out a second time.

Andrian let loose a low growl. "Go away."

Someone shuffled on the other side of the door, and the handle twisted. The door swung wide, and Drystan spilled into the space, his golden shoulder-length hair slightly rumpled. His aureate eyes blazed as he took in Andrian and the room, nose wrinkling in disgust.

Honestly, he was being dramatic. Andrian didn't think it was that bad in here. The asshole needed to keep his judgment to himself.

"Good to see you're still alive." Drystan's voice was dry and flat, carrying no traces of amusement.

Andrian grunted. "I said," he growled before taking another sip of the fiery liquor. "Go the *fuck away.*"

"No. I don't think I will." Drystan closed the door behind him with a soft click. He tapped the *lunestair* panel on the wall, the shimmering stone illuminating faintly before the lights set into recessed alcoves in the ceiling blazed to life.

The light fucking *burned.* Andrian hissed, eyes flickering closed as he threw his free hand over his face.

"Turn those fucking lights back off."

"No," Drystan repeated. Andrian cracked open an eye as Drystan sniffed a tray of half-forgotten food left on the dining table before pulling out a chair, swinging it around to sit facing Andrian.

He guessed he had eaten, after all.

Drystan clasped his hands, watching Andrian.

"You look terrible."

Andrian grumbled. "I honestly couldn't give two shits what I look like."

"Oh, trust me. That much is apparent." Drystan's golden eyes surveyed him uncomfortably close, as if peeling back the layers Andrian would rather keep buried beneath his skin and his whiskey. "What I'm not getting is what changed."

Andrian glowered at him. "What do you mean, 'what changed?'"

"When we first told you to move into these rooms, you were resigned, but you were accepting of it. You understood. You were hardly distraught. This, though ..." Drystan tsked. "Something else caused *this*."

"Nothing happened." Andrian glared. "I don't want to talk about it."

"Nothing happened, or you don't want to talk about it?"

Andrian groaned. His head hurt. He closed his eyes and rested his hand back over his lids to block out the light.

He heard Drystan shift. "I'll tell you what," he said. "You come with me, get out of this disgusting room, let the staff do some basic cleaning, and I won't take your entire stash of whiskey and leave you empty."

Andrian's eyes snapped open, the light burning. "You wouldn't fucking dare."

Except it seemed Drystan really *would* fucking dare. Because the noise Andrian had heard wasn't Drystan shifting in his chair; it was Drystan standing from his seat, inching to the coffee table, and snatching up Andrian's bottle of Sacalan whiskey. He clutched it to his chest like one of the hide balls they used to play with in the clearing as boys.

Andrian's voice was low, a warning. "Give that back."

Drystan dangled it in the air. "Come with me and bring your glass, and I'll pour you another."

It was a clash of wills: eyes of bleary, dulled tanzanite battling with blazing gold.

The pounding in Andrian's head pushed him to relent. He dropped his hands into his lap, slumping forward with a groan.

"Fine," he said. "But bring food, too. I'm hungry."

THEY SAT in a quiet glade in the game park. Not the training clearing, but one just a little smaller, a little more open, a little less familiar.

And as promised, Drystan had brought the decanter of whiskey. Andrian swirled it again in his refilled glass, smiling slightly before tossing it down his throat.

Gods, he was drunk. But that was how he preferred to spend his days now, anyway.

Drystan had also somehow secured several loaves of freshly baked bread, cheeses, and a roast. Andrian was annoyed at how good it all looked. He grew even more annoyed as he devoured it, knowing it would likely reduce the happy lightness from the whiskey he'd only just started feeling.

On his third slice of bread, Drystan cleared his throat.

"So," he said, perched atop a boulder a few paces from where Andrian rested against a stump of his own. "You going to tell me what the fuck is going on with you? Other than the usual, of course?"

Andrian glowered up at him, still chewing. He washed it down with another deep sip of whiskey, grimacing against the burn.

"I told you. I don't want to talk about it."

"That's too bad. There's too much going on for us to be constantly worried about if you're taking care of yourself. So, we're going to sit here until you tell me what's bothering you, or else you're going to find it very difficult to find a refill of that whiskey bottle once you finish it."

Andrian seethed, the world swirling around him. *Fuck*, Drystan was clever.

The threat of losing his whiskey was, in all truth, the only thing that would've ever gotten him to open up. From anyone else, that threat would've been meaningless. But from Drystan ...

From Drystan, Andrian knew to take it seriously. Too many blurry memories swam through his mind; memories of Drystan besting him in every sparring match, winning at too many games of chess played on bored nights around a fire.

If any of the Armature could follow through on a threat, it was Drystan.

Andrian dropped his head into his hands, running his fingers through his hair. He needed a haircut. It was too long and too thick, too messy, and in his eyes.

The thought of a haircut cracked something in his chest. Loosened the ice that had formed, allowed sadness and grief and anger and rage to spill into its spaces. His mother and Mariah were nothing alike, but in a way, he'd been the one to hurt them both.

The first woman he'd loved and the last. Bound by a common thread: him and the way he'd hurt them.

He would never, *never* let Mariah suffer the same fate his mother had.

He lifted his head from his hands, meeting Drystan's stare, and knew that tears lined his eyes.

"I hurt her." His voice was so quiet, he wasn't sure it would be heard.

Drystan leaned forward. "What? I can't hear you. It's just me here; no one else has to know."

Andrian drew in a shaky breath before voicing his sins into the glade.

"I *hurt* her."

Drystan stilled.

"What do you mean," he began slowly, "you *hurt* her? Do you remember something?"

Andrian shook his head, grief tight in his chest. His hands shook as he lifted his glass to his lips, as he forced down another gulp. "I remember nothing, but I ... I ... I saw her back. Her scars. And when I asked her who did that to her ..." Andrian choked on the next words, unable to force them free. He closed his eyes, inhaling deeply, before turning his head to the sky.

"I asked her who did that to her. And she said *me*."

The clearing was silent, but for the barely there whisper of the spring breeze through the trees. It was a mild day, as was typical for the early vernal season in Verith, the smell of salt on the wind from the bay mingling with the crisp scent of mountain snowdrops.

After several long moments, Andrian opened his eyes and dropped his head, finding Drystan watching him with an expression that shocked him to his core.

The golden-haired man wasn't angry, or scared, or anything that Andrian might've expected.

Instead, he simply looked ... sad. Devastated.

"Do you remember?" Drystan asked quietly. "Any of it?"

Again, Andrian shook his head. "Even after she told me, I still remember nothing. It's all just dark memories and nightmares. Besides," he said, looking at his whiskey glass, tightening his fingers so his knuckles turned white. "Do you think I would still be here in the palace if I did?"

"No. You wouldn't be. I think you would have tossed yourself into the Bay of Nria with lead tied to your ankles."

Andrian grimaced but didn't respond. They both knew Drystan was right.

They sat like that again, in silence, just the wind around them. With another swallow and a clench of his teeth, Andrian spoke.

"She can hardly look at me."

Drystan's brow furrowed in contemplation. "Are you sure of that?"

"Of course, I'm fucking sure. She couldn't even look me in the eyes."

"Yes, three days ago. Much can happen in three days."

Andrian snorted. "I'm not sure those sorts of wounds are going to heal in three days."

Drystan turned away, looking at the trees. "We all love her. Would fall on our swords and die for her. Would sacrifice ourselves and the entire world for her." He exhaled heavily through his nose. "But you, Andrian ... you *love* her. More than just an Armature loves his queen. I've seen you look at her like she is a moon and you are the sun, chasing each other across the skies."

"How sentimental of you." Andrian sloshed another sip of whiskey to drown the burning in his chest.

"Don't be an ass. You know I'm right." Drystan turned back to face him. "Aren't I?"

Andrian blinked once, then deflated. He sagged against the stump, his empty whiskey tumbler hitting the ground.

"Yes. You're right." He hung his head. "I love her, and I've lost her."

Drystan shook his head. "See, you believe that, but I don't think it's true."

"Did you not just hear me? I hurt her. I fucking *wrecked* her. In what realm will she ever be able to trust me again?"

"It wasn't you, though. I know that and you know that. And, most importantly, *she* knows that. It was something that wore your skin, that looked like you. But she's not an idiot, Andrian. Don't insult her intelligence by claiming she doesn't know the difference. She just needs time. And she will need *you*."

Andrian lifted his chin and snarled. "You don't have to tell me how smart she is, dickhead."

Drystan grinned. "That's more like it."

Andrian's anger burned quickly, then ran out. He looked at his hands, the tumbler and bottle of whiskey forgotten.

"I used to believe I could live without her. That I could stumble through this life from afar, could do my duty to this court and kingdom without getting caught up in her. But I was always lying to myself."

Drystan nodded. "I know you were."

Andrian clenched his fists. "I need her, Drystan. But she doesn't need me."

"I think she does."

The two men were silent for a long moment, the birds chirping in the trees and the breeze shifting the fresh green leaves. Andrian lost himself in his sorrow and misery, let himself drown in it.

Enough.

He hauled himself to the surface with a shaky breath, his mind gasping as he broke through the onslaught of despair and self-loathing.

He turned to Drystan with determination in his heart.

"How do I get her back?"

Drystan grinned, a spark in his golden eyes.

"You remind her who *you* are. What it felt like to be loved by you, and how you intend to love her for the rest of your life."

Andrian let his friend's words settle over him, and with a gentle, naïve burse of hope in his chest, he smiled back.

CHAPTER 39

The knock on Ciana's door was soft—a gentle rap on the solid wood.

She shuffled across her room, butterflies dancing in her stomach. Gripping the brassy knob, she opened the door with a flourish.

In the doorway stood Sebastian, dressed comfortably in a deep green cotton t-shirt and brown pants, an easy smile on his lips and a veil of hesitation in his hazel eyes.

Ciana stared at him, mind emptying, even though she'd been expecting him. "Hi," she said a little dumbly.

"Hi," he murmured back. His brown hair was short and neat, his hands slipped too casually into his pockets. Through his shirt, she could see the lines of the warrior's body hiding beneath his polished, studious exterior, his stance too solid to be anything other than that of a man trained to be always on alert.

Gods, he was handsome. All the men in Mariah's Armature were attractive, but something about Sebastian tugged at Ciana's gut in an uncomfortable, unfamiliar way. The way he was kind, but strong and smart and masculine ...

Heat burned in her cheeks. What was she thinking? This was her friend.

Just her friend.

Just her kind, handsome friend with dark hair, a sweet smile, and great abs.

Ciana had been used by men all her life. She was still plagued by nightmares and mourned the loss of her childhood and innocence. Men had never made her comfortable, and she'd long resigned herself to a life on her own.

The thought of feeling anything genuine toward a man was like a silly little fantasy. Trust one of those monsters? Never.

But there she stood, smiling like an idiot up at a man she'd learned to trust over a few too many late nights while sharing the finest bottles of palace wine. A man who had listened as she shared all her dark, poisonous secrets. Who'd helped her adjust to a new life and had never once shied away from the things she shared. Had never once made her feel anything less than *her.*

Not that anything more than friendship would—could—ever happen between them. Despite whatever bond they built, Sebastian was still Mariah's. His soul was bonded to hers for eternity. He would live hundreds of years by her side, forever young and strong, while Ciana would grow old and eventually leave this earth the same way she'd entered it.

Alone.

Sebastian chuckled softly and she blinked up at him in surprise. He pushed off the door frame, straightening his shoulders.

"Ready to get that beer?"

"How, exactly, did you find this place?"

Ciana tossed her head, golden ringlets spilling around her shoulders. The sun was out and shining today, and she reveled in the warmth on her skin, her dour thoughts from earlier long suppressed behind her familiar radiant mask.

"It's a long story. Maybe one for another day." She shot Sebastian a glance, tossing him a wink. "Or perhaps, after I have that beer in front of me."

A grin tugged at Sebastian's lips. "It's quite an interesting name. Unusual for an establishment in the golden city to be called The Silver Moon."

Ciana nodded, somewhat absently. She'd remembered thinking the same thing the day she and Delaynie first stumbled upon this place.

So much had changed since then, and yet so much was the same. Mariah was back, and she was safe, but things still felt so uncertain. Not only with the *allume* issues causing hysteria in the city, but the angry conversations she'd shared with Sebastian. About the way a wall still felt like it existed between them despite his relaxed demeanor.

She forced a bright smile. "The ale is the best in the city. The name is just a bonus." She grabbed Sebastian's forearm, trying not to think about the way the muscles there tensed and flexed under his skin or the way heat coursed through her from where they touched, and pulled him toward the awning and through the door.

The tavern was much the same as she'd remembered it— bright and warm, *allume* lights overhead illuminating the polished bar and long rows of tables. However, unlike the last time she'd been here, the tavern was packed nearly to the brim with off-duty soldiers and other city patrons alike, the loudness of their comfortable chatter wrapping around her like an old friend.

"Girl!" a female voice rang out over the din.

Beva stood behind the bar with a broad grin stretched across her warm face, four full pints of ale in her hands, and two dish-towels slung across her shoulders. The barkeep set the mugs down, pushing them toward the patrons, before waving Ciana towards the other end of the bar. Ciana followed her pointing and spotted two stools tucked neatly at the end, the last open spots.

"C'mon," she said brightly to Sebastian, sliding her hand down his forearm and latching onto his hand. She once again tried not to think about the way her cheeks flushed and her core burned a touch hotter when his fingers curled around hers as he let her drag him through the throngs of boisterous patrons.

It only took a few moments of maneuvering before Ciana was pulling herself into one of the open stools, dropping—somewhat unwillingly—Sebastian's hand in the process. She forced herself to fold them neatly on the bar, waiting for Beva to finish her round. Sebastian settled onto the stool beside her, his thigh brushing hers.

The silence between them was a little awkward, but just as Ciana was about to turn to Sebastian, Beva appeared.

"I was wondering when I'd see you again, blondie! Should I pour you the good gin, same as before?"

Ciana ignored the look Sebastian shot her, eyebrows raised. She smiled sweetly at the barkeep, fingers drumming on the polished wood.

"Not today, Beva. We're here for a few pints of your coldest ale."

Beva's attention turned to Sebastian, surveying him with that same sharp, too-perceptive stare. "Is this him? The boy?"

This time, it was embarrassment that made Ciana's cheeks flush with burning heat. She was sure even the tips of her ears turned scarlet and was glad they were hidden beneath her full-bodied curls.

"'The boy?'" Sebastian repeated, turning to Ciana with a shit-eating grin. "Is that what I am now?"

"Beva," Ciana squeaked, swallowing past her embarrassment. "This is Sebastian. Sebastian, this is Beva, the owner of The Silver Moon." She refused to look at him but could feel his grin widen.

"Pleasure to meet you, Beva," Sebastian said warmly, extending his hand to the barkeep. Beva gripped it, shaking firmly, the way only a businesswoman who'd spent her whole life catering to soldiers would know how.

"Seems much busier than last time, Beva! Did we miss an invite to something?" Ciana asked, desperate to change the subject.

Beva grinned. "Shift change, dearie. Just have to learn when the guards rotate their watches, that's all."

Ciana relaxed slightly into her stool. "I wasn't sure you would remember me."

"Oh, I never forget a face, girl. Especially one belonging to Her Majesty's court." She tossed Ciana a wink. "Let me get you two those ales." She left them, pausing along the way as she was flagged down by a few other patrons.

It took Ciana a few moments before she felt the warmth of Sebastian's gaze. She tilted her head to find him studying her intently.

"She knows who you are." His words were light, but the question in them was clear.

Ciana glanced at her hands resting on the bar. "A few weeks ago, when ..." She took a deep breath. "When Delaynie and I went with Kiira and Rylla into the city to look for signs of Mariah, we got frustrated with how the residents were refusing to talk to us. Kiira and Rylla suggested they go off on their own, and Del and I ... well, we decided we needed a drink."

Ciana braced herself for Sebastian's familiar anger that always sparked when her brazen trip to the city was mentioned. This time, however, he was silent, watching her with a slight furrow to his brow.

"And is that when you told her who you were?"

Ciana snorted, relief rushing through her like a broken dam. "Gods, no. She just ... guessed. Said she saw my palace horse, and since not many were allowed to freely come and go from the palace, she put the two together. And," Ciana said with a smile, "she said she knew Mariah's *parents.*"

"That I did, my dear," chimed that familiar feminine voice. Beva set two full pints of amber ale on the bar top, gray eyes sparkling. "I have known Wex and Lisabel for many years, ever since they were barely older than teenagers. I'm glad to hear our young queen has returned safe."

Ciana stiffened. Mariah's disappearance and return were no

secret—it couldn't be—but Sebastian was more protective of that information than any of them.

But, to her surprise, Sebastian only tipped his head graciously. "We are glad as well, Beva. I'll be sure to give Mariah your kind words," he said.

Beva nodded, glancing one more time at Ciana, before walking away to see to the other patrons.

Chest squeezing at Sebastian's calmness, Ciana leaned forward and took a deep, long drink from her ale. It was crisp and cold, the rich flavors of malt and barley and honey exploding across her tongue. She groaned slightly before licking her lips and setting down the mug, now close to half-empty.

Sebastian was acting like how he'd been *before*. Before Mariah was taken. Before he blamed himself. And for just a moment, Ciana forced her worries from her mind.

When she turned to Sebastian, he was smiling, but there was the touch of a shadow across his handsome features.

She furrowed her brow. "What?"

He shook his head. "Nothing." He sipped his ale, then stared down at the mug. "Gods, that's good."

Ciana chuckled. "You're welcome."

He set down his glass. "Actually," he began, running a finger down the side of the glass. She tracked his movement, swallowing heavily. He turned to face her.

"I wanted to apologize to you. For real, this time."

She flushed again and looked away. "You already apologized."

"Not in the way I wanted to. I—I had no right to say the things I said or to keep you locked up in the palace. I never should have dismissed you like that. I'm sorry, and I hope you can forgive me."

Ciana refused to look at him. Instead, she slid her fingers along the cold rim of her glass, the beads of moisture coating her hands. "You just ... you have no idea how *trapped* I felt. I was scared and vulnerable, and instead of letting me help and do something, you locked me up behind those pretty doors. Just like

...” She sniffed, quickly wiping a hand across her cheek and glaring at her glass. “Just like *they* used to do.”

Even though the tavern was boisterously loud, the silence between them stretched thick and heavy. Ciana's emotions—all that pain and trauma and terror she'd grown up knowing as her companion—exploded wildly through her chest, and she grasped desperately for control to keep the tears from spilling down her face. She took another sip from her ale, and just as she placed it back on the bar, a large hand wrapped around her own.

“Ciana.”

She pulled her gaze to Sebastian's, and her stomach dropped at the way he looked at her.

He looked ... devastated.

His thumb stroked idly across the back of her hand, and she gulped, some of the ache in her chest fading at the touch.

“I am ... so sorry,” he murmured, holding her gaze with so much intensity she thought her heart would burst. “For how I was. I was just so hopeless, and I felt like ... like a failure. But I was selfish about it, because even though I wasn't the only one who felt that way, I acted like I was. I lost sight of myself, and if you never forgive me for that, I'll understand.” He sighed, his thumb still tracing maddening circles across her skin. “It wasn't fair of me to take any of it out on you, or to remind you of those monsters. Mariah may be my queen, but you will always be my friend.”

More tears prickled behind Ciana's eyes, and with a sniff she again wiped them away with the back of her hand.

“You're a softy, you know that?”

Sebastian grinned, loosening a light chuckle. “I prefer to think of myself as ‘emotionally available.’”

“Alright, that's too far. No need to indulge in that sort of flattery.”

His smile widened, so brilliant that something in her chest cracked. His beauty was radiant, and it was unfair that his heart shined just as bright.

Too bad it would never work between them. For thousands and thousands of reasons.

She pulled her hand from his, reluctance straining her movement, and reached for her ale. They both took a few sips, watching the crowds around them in companionable silence before she steeled herself and turned to him again.

"There's something else I wanted to talk to you about."

He glanced at her through his thick lashes. "Oh?"

She tightened her jaw and lifted her chin. "When are you going to stop punishing Andrian for something we all know he didn't do?"

In an instant, the warmth vanished from his eyes. The mask of the cool commander slid over his face, hardening everything about him. "We don't know for certain it wasn't him."

Ciana scoffed. "I know you're not an idiot, Sebastian. You've known Andrian longer than any of us. He's an ass, sure, and I know we were all a bit worried there in the beginning, but I am willing to bet that Enfara itself would freeze over before he would ever willingly hurt her."

"He's the one who took her, Cee."

"And he claims he was just as trapped as she was." She glared back at him. "You've called him your brother before. I didn't know being family meant turning your back on someone the second those loyalties are tested."

Sebastian was tense and angry, scowling as he held her stare. Then, as if a breeze washed through the tavern, his mood lifted, a thundercloud vanishing on a morning wind. He loosened a great exhale and sagged.

"You're right," he said. "I just ... I need to do something. I can't just sit here as she's in pain."

This time, it was Ciana who reached out a hand to him, resting it lightly on his broad shoulder. "I understand," she said. "But ... you can't protect her from everything. And this decision? What to do with a member of her own Armature, *especially* him? She needs to be the one to decide. Not you."

He looked at her, then at the hand on his shoulder, then back at her. With another breath, he deflated further, leaning forward to rest his forearms on the bar.

Beva reappeared, two fresh mugs full of ale in her hands.

"We looked like we needed a refill down here." She set the pints on the bar, swiping away the now-empty glasses. Ciana reached for hers just as Sebastian did. She turned to him, glass lifted.

"Cheers," she said, "to having our queen home and not knowing what the fuck happens next."

With a spark of hope and glee in her heart, Sebastian turned to her, lifting his own ale. A smile spread across his handsome face.

"Now that, I'll cheers to."

As their glasses clinked and Ciana lost herself in the mug and in Sebastian's friendship, she felt genuine happiness.

CHAPTER 40

Mariah lay on her back in a small clearing in the game park woods; eyes closed as she soaked up the warm spring sun. The soft grass tickled her bare arms as her fingers curled around the delicate strands.

As she lay there, her mind drifted.

And as her mind drifted, she forced herself to *feel*.

She started with the sun. Then turned to the blades of grass. With some reluctance, she turned inward, toward her soul.

That wrecked, broken little soul of hers, curled in the hollow space beneath her ribs. A soul that once wished desperately for escape, for adventure and freedom, but now only craved safety. Comfort. Familiarity.

Things it would never know again. Things that were cleaved from her with the lash of a steel-studded whip and by the touch of unwanted, taking hands. Things that were stolen from her by starvation and betrayal and feelings too confusing and twisted to process.

A coiled and gnarled mass of panic burst through her body, roots that burrowed deep and strangled her lungs. She wanted to run from those things. To retreat into her surface-level self, to lose herself to a run or a fight or a bottle of wine. It was what she'd always been good at: using the world around her to create a life she could live with.

But something forced her to stay.

It wasn't anything she recognized. Not a force she could name or one she'd known before. But it filtered in and held her there within herself, forcing her to lie with the smoking ruins of her soul.

And as she stayed, her heart stopped hammering so heavily beneath her ribs, and her lungs stopped squeezing the air from her chest. Her hands unfurled, clumps of grass falling out as her fingers loosened, bits of dirt buried beneath her nails.

She allowed herself to sit with her brokenness and did not run from it.

Mariah didn't know how much time passed as she lay there beneath the rustling trees. Birds sang in the canopy above; a cricket chirped from its place in a bramble bush; a curious rabbit peeked its nose out from behind a fallen log, its heartbeat racing, sending vibrations through the forest floor. Her pain and grief and rage wrapped around all that she heard, and her panic and fear slowly and slowly ebbed away.

"M? Are you ... are you *sleeping*?"

A familiar voice cut through her reverie. Mariah pulled herself from those deepest parts of herself, her mouth spreading into an easy smile as she cracked open her eyes. Bright light blinded her, but she knew who'd disturbed her peace.

"Well, Quentin, if I *was*, I'm definitely not anymore."

She'd heard his footsteps start a few minutes before he spoke, felt the steadily increasing tremors beneath her hands. She had opened their bond, just a fracture, guiding him to her little clearing.

She'd had enough of being alone.

"Oh, please. I'm quiet as a mouse." Quentin grinned, his movements easy and casual as he slipped his baldric from his chest. He cavalierly tossed the leather leaden with throwing knifes to the side before sliding to the ground a few feet from

Mariah. He leaned back against the trunk of a smooth birch tree, kicking out his feet before him.

Mariah huffed a chuckle. "Yeah, sure," she quipped, sitting up and leaning back on her hands. "If mice were the size of an Idrixian Ephalant."

Quentin barked a laugh. "Gods, M." His bottle green eyes shone with mirth. "Do you think the Ephalant's are real? I always thought they were just myths, but I also didn't think shifters could exist, so ..."

"I don't know," Mariah said with her own answering laugh. "But I think it would be fun to find out for sure one day, don't you think?"

"If this is you telling me I get to go to Idrix, then say no more."

Mariah picked at a single blade of grass, still smiling, but her humor settled in her chest. "Maybe one day." She turned to the sky. "Onita has spent so long in solitude, who's to say what the world is really like beyond its borders?"

Quentin didn't answer her right away. Some of their early lightheartedness faded, washing away with Mariah's question. Instead, he studied her, head cocking to the side, an errant strand of wild ginger hair falling across his freckled forehead.

"Have I ever told you about where I came from? Where I was ... before I was Marked?"

Mariah whipped her head to Quentin. He'd lost the usual blithe gleam in his eye, replaced by an uncharacteristic seriousness. She blinked at him once, slowly, before shaking her head, straightening her back, and crossing her legs in the soft grass.

He shifted against the tree, clearing his throat. "Well, I was born here, in Verith. But not in the shiny streets of the mountain district." He picked at his fingers. "My mother ... she worked at a brothel. Told me my father was a rich pirate lord from the Kizar Islands who had slipped past the blockades and made it to shore. Which, come to think of it, *fuck* those pirates." His fist met his leg as a frustrated sound tore from his throat. Quentin breathed deeply, rolling his neck.

"I lived with her, for a time ... until a few men decided they didn't want to pay for the goods and took from her instead. They left her there in that dirty alleyway for me to find. She was so pretty, with her honey hair and crystal blue eyes ... but whenever I try to recall her face, all I can picture is the way she looked on the day she died. Bloody and bruised and broken."

All the sounds of the forest faded away. Mariah stared at her brave and fierce Armature, usually so full of exuberant fire, and saw who he really was, hidden beneath it all.

Someone who wasn't much different from who she was now. Someone damaged and starved and broken. Someone who'd seen the worst in humanity but had come out on the other side stronger for it.

"Quentin ..."

"After that," he forged on, ignoring her and reaching for his baldric, "I was left to the streets. Not a great place for a five-year-old boy, but we make do with the hands we are dealt." He withdrew one of the knives and flipped it over in his fingers.

"That first night, I found a drunkard, passed out on the side of the street. He was covered in vomit and piss, but he also had a dagger on his belt. I stole it and used it to keep myself alive and fed for the next few years. I ..." He swallowed, flipping the knife again. "I did some things I'm not proud of. But, one day, when I was eight, I was woken up by the Mark. Someone told me to go straight to the palace, and the rest is history."

One final flip before he re-sheathed the blade into its leather holster.

Mariah gaped at him, her mind reeling.

"Quentin," she repeated. He lifted his gaze to her, the pain from his memories still flickering in the bottle green. "You ... *five-years-old*, Quentin. You were a *child*. A boy. I am ... I am so sorry for what you—"

"Why? Why are you sorry? You didn't cause my piece of shit father, whoever he was, to fuck my mom and then abandon us. You weren't those men who dragged her out into an alley, raped her, then beat her to death when they were finished with her." He leaned forward, urgency bright in his expression. "You, Mariah, *you* were the one who saved me. Your Mark got me out, got me into a gods-damned palace. Even if you had never Selected me, I would've been forever in your debt. There is nothing more you could ever do for me."

Mariah didn't know she was crying until Quentin smiled softly, reached across the distance between them, and wiped the tears from her cheek. She sniffed, brushing the back of her hands across her face.

"Why?" she asked. "Why tell me this?"

"Besides the fact that you are my queen, and I thought it was about time you knew?" He shrugged, growing serious once more. "I know you likely went through some things back there in that hellhole. I know it was no vacation, and I know what it's like to have to trade your life for your soul. What it's like to do anything you must to survive, even if it means changing yourself irrevocably. And I wanted you to know that if you ever need someone to talk to, I'm here."

Mariah stared at him, at one of these men that she'd somehow been blessed enough to have bound to her for the rest of her life. They were all strong, just not in the same ways.

She'd always thought Quentin was chosen for her—by Zadione's magic, no less—because Mariah needed his light-heartedness.

Now, she knew that was but one facet. Somehow, those beautiful threads of magic saw the broken soul beneath the fire and knew Mariah would need its heat to reforge her own.

She planted her hands in the grass, pushing up and scooching over until she sat beside him against the tree. She extended a hand and he placed his baldric in her waiting palm. With deft fingers, Mariah withdrew one of the sharp silver knives, gripping it tight.

"How did you survive it? How did you move past it?"

"Time. Time was the greatest healer. But I never moved past it. I simply decided, after coming to the palace, that what I had done was a part of me, but it didn't have to define me. I alone was the master of my fate, and only I could decide what was next for me."

Mariah flipped the dagger in her hand. "Who knew you were such a poet, Quentin."

He chuckled, shoulder brushing hers. "Yeah, well, don't get used to it. After this conversation, I'll be sucked dry of wisdom for the next year."

Mariah couldn't help herself. She raised an eyebrow, turning her head just slightly to meet Quentin's gaze.

And then burst out laughing, Quentin's hysterics echoing her own.

Mariah wiped a tear from her eye as her laughter slowly died. "Well, Quentin, I'm happy to *suck you dry* of wisdom any day." She tossed him a wink, slipping the dagger back into its sheath. Quentin nearly choked, before he roared in laughter again.

"I know you're joking, but on the off chance you're not ..."

Mariah slapped his arm, chuckling again, before shoving to her feet. "C'mon," she said. "I want to train. Join me?"

Quentin grinned before jumping to his feet and slipping his baldric back over his chest. "I thought you'd never ask."

CHAPTER 41

The arrow thrummed through the air, the weapon still vibrating in Sebastian's hands.

Thwonk.

"That was terrible."

Sebastian frowned. "Thank you, Matheo. Encouraging as always."

Matheo shrugged. "You missed the target by six inches." He raised his weapon, drawing the string as he took aim. His shoulders lifted on an inhale, and as they dropped, he loosed his arrow.

It struck the center of their target ... six inches below Sebastian's arrow, buried in the same tree trunk.

"You're distracted, Seb." Matheo slung his bow over his back as he strode for the tree. He ripped the arrows from the soft wood before facing Sebastian with an expectant grin.

Sometimes, Sebastian really couldn't stand having his actual blood brother bound to be his brother-in-arms for life.

"There are a lot of distractions right now." Sebastian ignored Matheo's raised brow and notched a new arrow. "Things are very ... distracting." He gritted his teeth. His arms burned as he drew back the string, an exhale whistling between his teeth as he released the arrow.

It missed the tree entirely, soaring past the wide oak and disappearing into the brush.

Sebastian groaned. "*Fuck.*"

"I've never seen you this bad, brother." Matheo clasped a hand on his shoulder. "And what distractions? The pirates are gone, the *allume* seems to be fixed, and most importantly, Mariah is back. Things should be easier for you now, not harder."

Matheo was right, in a way. The issues that had plagued them just a few weeks ago were gone.

But that didn't mean Sebastian no longer had anything to worry about.

Sebastian also wasn't in the mood to discuss any of it with his brother.

"Just take your shot so I can go find my arrow."

It was a game they'd played since they were boys, running wild around their parents' manor house in Sacale. They each had a single arrow, and whoever shot poorly enough to lose their arrow first had to do the other's laundry for a week.

It was how they'd each become so skilled with a bow. It didn't take long for most matches to end in stalemates, their games called off only when their mother summoned them for dinner.

The game was much the same now, except it was their duties summoning them away instead of their kindhearted mother.

"*If* you can find your arrow." Matheo smirked as he notched his bow. "My laundry desperately needs attention. It's getting warmer out, and my socks are getting particularly ripe." His bow snapped, and the arrow, again, struck the center of the target.

Sebastian groaned. "You're disgusting."

"I learned from the best." Matheo propped his bow against his hip. Sebastian set his own weapon down, unhooking his leather bracers.

He had to find that fucking arrow.

"I'll make you a deal."

Sebastian glanced up at Matheo. "A deal?"

"Yeah," his brother said. "I'll let you off the hook from laundry duty ... if you tell me what's *really* going on. Particularly with a certain blonde-haired lady."

Sebastian stilled. He'd ventured into the city with Ciana yesterday, joining her for that beer he'd promised her. But was that really the reason he was so distracted?

"There's nothing going on," he answered gruffly, dropping a bracer on the ground. "She's just a friend and wanted to grab a beer. That's all."

"Right." Matheo drew out the word, mischief twinkling in his hazel eyes. "That's why you're blushing. Because you got beer with your *friend*."

"I am not *blushing*, you asshole." The heat burning down his neck called him on his lies.

Matheo's grin widened.

Sebastian sighed, slumping against a nearby tree. "Alright. Fine. Whatever. It was nice to get out of the palace for a bit and do something *other* than be an Armature." He slipped off his other bracer, and it landed on the grass next to the first with a dull thud. "She makes me feel ... I don't know, normal. Like I don't have to be perfect all the time and can just be *me*."

His brother made a low noise before turning and striding to their target tree. He pulled his arrow free, tossing it between his hands as he walked back.

"You don't, you know." Matheo leaned against the tree beside Sebastian. "Have to be perfect, I mean. No one expects that—you should know that by now."

"*I* expect it of me," Sebastian murmured. He glanced up as the wind brushed through the trees, rustling the branches overhead.

That strive to be perfect ... It had always been his struggle. It came so naturally to him as a boy and as a young man, especially when all he had to do was follow orders and obey.

But now that he was the one giving them? His stomach twisted into knots.

He'd failed his biggest test as an Armature. And even though Mariah was back, he still wasn't sure he could forgive himself.

"I'm happy for you, brother." Sebastian dropped his gaze to

Matheo. "I'm happy you have someone you feel normal with." Matheo's lips twitched. "Are you interested in her being maybe more than just your friend?"

Sebastian's heart plummeted from his chest to rest beside his bracers in the grass.

Of course, he'd thought about it. From the moment she'd stepped foot through the palace gates, Ciana had been a ray of sunshine—warm and vibrant and full of life. It was impossible not to feel drawn to her, even when she stood beside the planetary force that was their queen.

But ...

"She wouldn't want that. Not from me. Nor am I interested in her in that way, either." He tacked on his last sentence hastily.

He loved his brother, but Matheo was the biggest gossip of them all. And the last thing Sebastian would ever want was word of this conversation to reach Ciana.

Because beneath all that sunshine dwelled monsters darker than the shadows of Enfara. He couldn't put that sort of pressure on her, not like that. Her words from the bar flashed back through his mind. How the way he'd controlled her had reminded her of her nightmares. He refused to ever again be compared to those evil men from her past.

Despite his words, Matheo still grinned at him conspiratorially. "Alright then, brother. Whatever you say." He slid his arrow into his quiver. "Is there anything else? Didn't I hear you had an odd confrontation with a crazy man down in the city on the night the *allume* went out?"

Sebastian really needed his brother to stop asking questions he didn't want to answer.

"Oh ... yeah." He shrugged, doing his best to feign nonchalance. "Like you said—he was crazy. Yelling nonsense about the sun. It was gibberish."

Thankfully, Matheo didn't push it. He merely answered with a shrug of his own. "Bizarre. Wish I had been there." Picking up his arrow and quiver, he nodded to Sebastian. "Alright—that was enough. I'll let you off laundry duty this time. But get your shit together, brother! We can't have a Riqueti man wandering through Onita unable to hit a simple target on a tree. What an embarrassment."

As they laughed together, walking back through the game park to the palace, Sebastian couldn't stop thinking.

Not only about Ciana but the words that man had said to him.

"The moons are setting, and the sun will rise."

He'd told himself he would share it with Mariah, but he hadn't. He hadn't shared the truth with anyone.

And he still wasn't quite sure why.

"Alright, brother. It's your turn."

Matheo turned to Sebastian, brows lifted. "My turn? For *what*?"

Sebastian grinned, stepping over a branch on the forest path as he adjusted his bow across his back. "I shared a bit about Ciana. Now it's your turn. Is there anyone who happens to be on your mind?"

"You *shared*? You hardly gave me anything!" Matheo scowled, even as blood slowly filled his cheeks.

Sebastian's smile widened.

"Oh, c'mon, Matheo." He bumped his brother with his shoulder, earning him another glare. "There has to be someone."

Matheo shrugged. "Honestly … no, not really. But I'm okay with that. I like my life of training and fighting and guarding. I don't really want any complications."

Complications. Sebastian's smile faltered. He'd never once viewed Ciana—or Mariah, for that matter—as a complication, but in a way, he supposed it was true.

Before their court, life had been simpler. More monotonous and repetitive, but predictable. But for Matheo to prefer that life?

"I always thought you craved a bit of adventure. You were always the one inventing wild stories of heroics while I refused to leave the libraries."

Matheo smiled sadly. "Did you ever pay attention to the roles I gave myself in those campaigns?"

Sebastian hesitated, sifting through his memories. But for some reason, he came up short.

Matheo shifted his bow. "I was always the warrior. The guardian. The knight. While you read about great adventures and imagined yourself as the prince or the king or the captain, I was busy playing in the yard as the protector who served without hesitation." His fingers clenched around the rowan of his bow. "I was the second son. Never cared about leading or about adventure. I just wanted to belong."

The blood rushed from Sebastian's face, and his heart thrummed beneath his ribs.

"Matheo." Sebastian halted on the path, staring at his brother's back. His eyes burned along with his chest.

He never imagined that he'd read his little brother so *wrong*. For their entire life, Sebastian had misinterpreted everything about Matheo Riqueti.

Slowly, Matheo turned, meeting his brother's gaze with a guarded look.

Something cracked further in Sebastian's chest.

"You will *always* belong, Matheo. You have a place here. Even the gods themselves have made it known."

Matheo smiled. "I know. And I will forever be grateful to the gods for giving me the purpose I desperately wanted. But ... it's always why I'm just not interested in anything else. I have everything I've ever wanted. Why would I risk that?"

Sebastian met his brother's stare for a long moment. Slowly, he nodded and took the three strides to stand before Matheo. He grasped Matheo's shoulder, squeezing just slightly.

"I understand," Sebastian murmured. "And I'm sorry for pushing."

Matheo shrugged. "Eh, it was only fair. I *did* push you first." He grinned. "I can't wait to tell Trefor and Quentin how right we all were about your crush."

"By the gods, Matheo." Sebastian tossed up his hands, exasperated, before continuing down the path. "I thought you took this job seriously?"

"Of course I take it seriously. That doesn't mean I can't also have a little fun."

Sebastian grumbled to himself, just as the palace stables appeared out of the tree line in front of them. "Annoying little shit."

Matheo chuckled as they passed out of the game park and into the back aisles of the palace stables.

This part of the stables was rarely occupied, only used when the palace was hosting guests and every available stall was needed. Today, it was as quiet and empty as they expected it to be. Only their boot steps on the swept packed earth joined them.

Until something rustled up ahead and hit the wall with a rumbling boom.

Sebastian halted, senses roaring to life. His hand landed on the hilt of his dagger, just as Matheo unslung his bow in a single smooth movement.

The brothers shared a glance. Matheo nodded.

"Who's there?" Sebastian called, voice low but reverberating off the hall.

The rustling paused just before another thump struck the walls, followed by a low groan.

"*Keep quiet!*"

Another groan. "*They've already heard us.*"

Sebastian whipped his head to a stall on his left. The door was closed, and the lights off, but ... He shared another nod with Matheo. The intruders were there.

"If you don't come out in the next ten seconds, we will show substantially less mercy than we are currently inclined."

"Wait! Fuck—Sebastian, it's me. It's Drystan."

Sebastian's jaw slackened, just as Matheo's bow sagged.

That was, indeed, Drystan's voice.

"Drystan?" Sebastian took a hesitant step toward the stall. "What are you—"

The stall door swung open, and out tumbled a rather rumpled

looking Drystan, straw stuck in his golden hair, shirt and trousers askew.

And behind him followed an equally disheveled Feran, shit-eating grin on his face.

Sebastian's shock struck him across the face just as Matheo burst out laughing.

"I fucking *knew it*!"

Drystan glared at Matheo. "Knew what?"

Matheo wiped a finger under his eye, still bent over in hysterics. "This! I knew there was something happening here!"

Drystan shifted his stance. "And this is funny to you why?"

"Alright, easy, Drys," Feran said, coming up to stand beside Drystan. His hand brushed Drystan's, and the golden-haired warrior relaxed. Just a touch.

And Sebastian still gaped like a fish.

"I think you broke my brother," Matheo said, still chuckling.

That finally shook something loose in Sebastian, like netting being cast aside. He cleared his throat, more heat clawing up his neck.

"What is—" He tried. He cleared his throat again. "How did —" Again, the words wouldn't come.

Drystan and Feran shared a look. Feran nudged him with a bare shoulder before turning to Matheo.

"Come on, little Riqui. I'm hungry. Let the adults speak."

Matheo rolled his eyes. "You know, I *hate* that nickname."

"Nickname?" Feran furrowed his brows. "Is it not just ... your name?"

"Riqueti. Our family name is Riqueti."

"That's what I said. Riqui."

"Doesn't that mean 'rabbit' in Kreah?"

"And that's what you are. Little rabbit."

Matheo's response was lost to Sebastian's ears as he and Feran disappeared down the hall, leaving Drystan and Sebastian there, staring at each other.

Drystan smiled, somewhat sheepishly. "I am ... sorry you had to find out like this."

Sebastian took a deep inhale, slowly breathing out through his mouth. He ran a hand through his hair, brushing out the tidy brown strands.

"I didn't ..." He swallowed. "I didn't know you ..."

"Preferred men?" Drystan shrugged. "I didn't either, for a long time. I thought I was just different from the rest of you. Women are beautiful, of course, but they just ... were never for me, I suppose."

Sebastian nodded. "Why didn't you ... I don't know, tell me?"

"You know how it is in Onita," Drystan murmured. "This is just one of those things no one talks about. For all our technology and advancement, we still can't accept people loving who they love."

Sebastian knew. It was why he so adamantly believed in Mariah. It wasn't just women she could help; the change she wanted to bring could impact people of all kinds across the entire kingdom.

But that wasn't what bothered him.

"I understand, Drystan. But ... why not tell *me*?"

It was Drystan's turn to flush. "I don't know. I probably should have, shouldn't I?"

Sebastian barked a laugh, and it was like the tension was broken. He strode forward, clasping Drystan on the shoulder. "Yeah, you should have." He met his friend's golden stare. "I'm happy for you."

Drystan smiled tentatively. "While I am still a little embarrassed you found us in a stall ... thank you."

Sebastian glanced around the quiet stables. "That reminds me," he said. "What about Feran? And how long?"

Drystan cast his eyes down, golden hair falling into his face. "Feran's mother is Kreah. He spent the first part of his life raised very differently than a typical Onitan. He has never been ashamed of himself. Which is someone who enjoys the company of women ... and men.

"As far as ... well, us," Drystan continued, adjusting his shirt. "It started shortly after Mariah went missing. With everything falling apart, we became the only thing to hold each other together."

Sebastian's mind raced, flashbacks of a dozen little moments circling. Times when Drystan and Feran volunteered for battlement duty together, or always seemed to appear places together, or the time Drystan had shown up to breakfast wearing a shirt a lot like the one Feran had worn the day before …

"I feel like an idiot," Sebastian finally said, smiling.

Drystan cocked his head. "You do?"

Sebastian nodded. "Yes. Because now that I know, I cannot believe I didn't notice sooner."

Drystan smiled. "You had a lot on your mind. We all did."

The two men—friends, brothers, warriors—shared another long look, their smiles growing stronger.

"I'm happy for you, Drystan," Sebastian repeated before taking a step back. "Truly. I'm glad you and Feran found something together that made you—and us, as a whole—stronger."

"Thank you, Seb," Drystan murmured warmly. "Care for lunch? I'm starving."

Sebastian grinned. "Oh, I'm *sure* you are."

The punch Drystan landed on Sebastian's arm stung far less than the burning in his chest. Drystan had found someone he could truly share forever with.

Sebastian couldn't let himself think about how much he craved exactly that.

CHAPTER 42

Mariah sat in the conference room alone, staring at the walls, twisting a single thread of silver-gold light around her fingers.

Two weeks had passed since the *allume* snuffed out in the early hours of the morning. Two weeks since Mariah had plummeted inside the *lunestair* pillars and chased away whatever evilness dwelled inside.

And still she didn't know how, exactly, it had gotten there. She only had a few clues, fed to her from a smattering of conversations and her own thrumming instincts. One thing was certain, though.

Something had happened on the Winter Solstice. Something that corrupted the magic she'd brought into their world.

Which after too many sleepless nights, watching the stars from her balcony, had led to her calling this meeting.

The conference room doors swung open.

"Quentin, how anyone puts up with your obscene behavior is beyond me."

"Oh, c'mon, little wolf. It was just a joke."

"I told you." Delaynie glared imperiously at Quentin as she strolled in beside Ciana. "Do not call me that."

"Sure, alright. Whatever you say." Quentin drifted away, heading to the other side of the table, a devilish grin on his face. "Little wolf," he murmured, just loud enough for the room to hear.

Mariah couldn't help her smile as Delaynie flushed a furious shade of pink, ice blue glare biting. Behind them came Sebastian, Trefor, and Matheo, all speaking quietly amongst each other. They were followed closely by Kiira and Rylla, who'd changed back into their Kreah fashioned garb, long paneled skirts fastened by solid breastplates. The last from her court to enter was Drystan and Feran, who shared a lingering look before taking a seat at the table.

Mariah certainly wanted to hear more about *that* look later.

The captains and commanders of the Royal Infantry and City Guard entered next. She hadn't had a chance to formally meet many of them yet, despite so many being her own non-Selected Marked. Sebastian had told her how vital they'd been to the defense of the city, and Mariah figured it was time to bring them into the fold.

They knew the most about the city, anyways. Who better to help her puzzle out their latest threat?

"It's an honor to finally meet you, My Queen."

A young captain had circled the table to stand before Mariah, bowing his head and placing his fist over his heart.

Mariah turned to him and smiled. "You as well, Captain ...?"

"Orryn, my queen. Call me Orryn."

"Orryn," she repeated, flattening her hand on the table. "You were one of my Marked."

Orryn nodded. "I like to think I still am, even if I wasn't Selected."

Mariah tapped a finger. "I like to think that, too." She glanced at the rest of the table, the group watching her expectantly. "Please, everyone, sit."

Everyone slowly settled themselves, chairs scraping across marble floors, when a final shadow lingered in the doorway. The room fell silent as attentions whipped toward the newest arrival.

Mariah slowly stood from her chair, meeting his tanzanite gaze, and nodded, the hint of an assuring smile on her lips. And to her shock, not an ounce of fear or dread filled her veins, although her magic did snap to attention and twist in her gut.

Mariah knew, in her soul, that the person who'd hurt her was not the same man who now stared at her with a glimmer of shadowy hope in his brilliant blue eyes.

So she'd asked Drystan to make sure Andrian knew about the meeting. To tell him that he was welcome to attend, if he desired.

That his queen would appreciate his presence and his counsel.

Qhohena had asked her to learn to trust him again. Zadione had told her to make love her retribution.

So she would try.

A wooden chair creaked as Sebastian shifted uncomfortably. He gripped the arms with white-knuckled fingers but, to Mariah's relief, remained seated. Ciana pinned him with a glare before shooting an encouraging look at Mariah.

Mariah turned back to Andrian, holding his stare. After a heavy pause, she glanced at the last open seat opposite her at the rectangular table.

He exhaled heavily, still warily watching the room as he sank into the polished wood, shadows trailing his steps.

At last, Mariah relaxed and reseated herself.

"Thank you all for coming," she said, doing her best to meet every set of eyes. Murmurs of greeting touched her ears, and she settled further into her seat.

My court, she thought. *My court, and I am their queen.*

"First, I wish to thank you for everything you did to keep this city safe. I know it wasn't easy, but Verithians are alive and safe because of each of you."

Murmured acknowledgments swept the room, followed by more nods and bowed heads.

Andrian, though, was still and silent, thoughts carefully hidden behind his familiar mask.

She cleared her throat uncomfortably. "I also wanted to thank you all for ... bringing me home. You risked your lives for me, and I don't think I can ever repay you for that."

"You are our queen," Sebastian said, his voice warm. "Every one of us would give up our lives for you."

More murmurs of agreement.

Across the table, blue eyes watched her.

Mariah smiled. "While I hope that's never necessary ... thank you."

More nods.

She shifted in her seat. *Be a queen.*

"I called this meeting to discuss what's next. I don't intend to sit here, cloistered in my palace, for the pirates to regroup and return to our shores or for the Royals to decide they want me back."

Brows furrowed and hands clenched into fists. Someone grumbled, a noise like a stifled growl.

She could've sworn shadows brushed her skin.

Drumming her fingers on the table, she continued, "Does anyone know why, exactly, the Kizar pirates attacked in the first place??"

A young commander, dressed in the white of the Royal Infantry, sat forward.

"The Infantry's network of spies has heard nothing, Your Majesty. We never heard they were coming until they appeared in the Bay, and their disappearance has been just as mysterious."

Mariah frowned. "I didn't know the Royal Infantry had a spy network."

The commander grinned. "Not many do. If they did, it would be a pretty shitty spy network." There were low chuckles around the room at that, and even Mariah grinned. The commander shifted, his face turning serious. "I am Commander Luan, Your Majesty. My troops are at your disposal."

Mariah nodded, her smile widening. "Thank you, Commander Luan." She turned back to the rest of the gathered captains and commanders. "So ... if we don't have information on the pirates, then what of the Royals? I don't intend to allow them to capture a queen and get away with it."

Rumbles of agreement came from her court, and an actual snarl may have slipped from between Rylla's teeth. They fell silent when an older Infantry commander sat forward, his armor clinking.

"My queen," he began, gruff voice scratching against her skin. "I fear I may bear an unpopular opinion, but I owe it to the kingdom to speak."

Mariah's spine stiffened. Across the table, shadows danced.

"The Royals are fixtures in Onita," the older commander continued. "Their families are old, and their power runs deep. Too much of the country relies upon them—for food, for employment, for safety. We have already seen the issues they can cause with the latest merchant disputes, as I'm sure your ladies know all too well. If you propose to deal with them by uprooting them, then we could face disastrous upheaval."

Silence fell over the conference room. Wisely, no one from her court dared to speak, their eyes darting between her and the aged commander with wariness and apprehension.

Coolness slid across Mariah's skin as she continued to drum a steady beat on the wood. She laid her hand flat and met the commander's gaze.

"Bullshit." Her tone was icy. Magic danced between the fingers of the hand splayed on the table, silver and gold licking across her skin.

Opposite her, shadows did the same.

The commander paled beneath his beard, his brown eyes widening. "I meant no offense, Your Majesty; I only mean to offer counsel—"

"I know you mean no offense, Commander. But I'm telling you that your counsel is bullshit." Her magic filled her, and she reveled in the strength it offered as a part of her remembered what it was like to be a queen.

"I've spoken to my ladies. Those disputes with the merchants were caused by the Kizar presence in the Bay, not because of the

Royals' interference. This country does not need the Royals to survive. The dependency we have on them is a crutch. Our people are stronger than the Royals—and you—give them credit for." Mariah lifted her chin. "I don't intend to allow Onitan citizens to be crushed beneath the weight of that aristocracy any longer. Our people will find their strength and their voice, and we as a nation will become better for it."

The commander snapped his mouth closed as he sat back down. Defeat and anger warred in his expression, but he didn't push the matter further.

Mariah supposed soldiers—even commanders—knew how to take orders and when to stop.

Her attention snagged on the man across from her. Andrian had relaxed in his chair, his shadows still dancing subtly around his shoulders. The barest, faintest touch of a grin tugged at his lips, and when she met his stare, her chest tightened at the pride dancing in his tanzanite eyes.

She almost jolted when she felt that same pride *inside*, tugging on a brilliantly woven bond.

How the *fuck* had he learned how to do that?

Mariah wrenched her gaze away, turning to her court.

"If we can't decide what to do about the Royals quite yet, then perhaps you all can help me with something a bit more ... personal."

Everyone sat up, instantly attentive.

"When I was ... in Khento, I had a very interesting conversation with our beloved High Priestess Ksee."

Quentin's lips pulled back from his teeth, and Feran and Trefor both clenched their hands into fists.

"She seemed to suggest that she—and the Royals—had interfered with my Solstice. I'm not sure how, or what, they might have done, but there are other reasons that lead me to believe she was telling the truth. Which is where I need your help."

The room awaited her next words.

"Was there anything ... unusual reported on the night of the Winter Solstice? Either across Onita or even here in Verith itself?"

Silence answered her, each person glancing at each other, confusion and intrigue on their faces.

Mariah deflated slightly, slumping forward. Why had she been so hopeful that there was something out there she could learn, something she could do?

Until someone cleared their throat.

"Your Majesty." A young City Guard captain rose from his seat, golden cloak swishing. "I ... I might know of something worth looking into."

The captain appeared nervous, almost unsure of himself, as he fidgeted with the pommel of his sword and the edge of his cloak. His light brown hair and hazel eyes reminding her so much of her brother, Ellan, even though this man was at least a decade older.

She nodded, telling him to continue.

"On the night of the Winter Solstice, the Guard received a ... complaint," he said. "Of a disturbance down in the market district."

Mariah straightened. "What kind of disturbance?"

The captain twisted his hands in his cloak again. "They said they heard ... screaming. *Women* screaming. But when a detachment of the Guard reported to the building, they found nothing—for all purposes, it looked abandoned."

"Did the Guard go in?"

He shifted uncomfortably. "Well ... no, Your Majesty. Like I said, it looked abandoned. They reported it as a false alarm and returned home to celebrate the Solstice."

Mariah's mind was whirring, a thousand thoughts lighting and flashing behind her eyes. Her magic whipped and roiled excitedly in response, and she pushed out of her seat in a rush.

"I'm going to look at that building. Inside, this time."

Right on cue, Sebastian shot to his feet.

"Not alone. Please."

She slid her gaze to him, smiling sweetly. His expression turned wary. "Of course not, Sebastian. The good captain will accompany me as he knows where to go." She paused for effect.

"And you're coming too." Sebastian relaxed markedly but still held a tightness in his posture.

He knew she wasn't done.

She hesitated, just for a moment. A slimy sliver of fear and apprehension twisted around her heart. But the words of the goddess wound through her thoughts.

"You need to learn to trust him again."

Pushing down all her fear, every conflicted feeling she harbored deep within, Mariah turned to Andrian. His face was a careful mask, watching her with predatory stillness.

"And Andrian. You'll come with us." His name fell like honey from her lips. She hadn't said it aloud, not in weeks.

She surprised herself at how *right* it felt.

The inhalations she heard across the room told her she wasn't the only one feeling that surprise. She looked back at Sebastian, daring him to challenge her.

To her shock, he stayed silent, although his jaw flexed with the words he forced himself not to say.

She loosened her breath and pulled her magic beneath her skin.

"Ready your horses. We leave in an hour."

CHAPTER 43

Mariah stood in the stable aisles as the stable hands ran to and fro. A few of them stopped and gawked, eyes going wide. She fidgeted in her riding leathers, adjusting the fitted cropped cotton shirt.

"Your Majesty!" A stable hand stopped in the alleyway, heels digging into the packed earth. He glanced over his shoulder. "Would you ... Do you need me to ready your horse?"

Mariah smiled. "Actually, I was hoping you could just show me to his stall and then to the tack room."

The boy cocked his head, brow twisting. "Your ... Majesty? Are you ... don't you want our help?"

"I know you are all fantastic at your jobs and with the horses," she assured him, twisting her hands together. "But I think I need to saddle my horse. On my own."

The boy nodded. "Alright," he said, though his brow was still furrowed. "I'll take you to his stall."

Mariah followed the stable hand through the rows of inquisitive faces, ears pricked and eyes bright. She knew the stable masters moved where the horses were stalled, depending on the current capacity. If she had tried to find Kodie herself, she might've wandered for hours. The stable hand led her around a corner and Mariah caught sight of a familiar golden head, black forelock spilling over his face.

She touched the boy's shoulder. "I've got it from here. Just show me the tack room, and you can go help the others ready their horses when they arrive."

The boy nodded, pointing to a rolling door to the left of Kodie's stall before wishing her well and disappearing back the way they'd come.

Mariah's smile lingered as she turned back to her horse. That one last trace of home she had left. She stepped forward, holding her hand out to him.

"Hi, sweet boy," she murmured, scratching his velvety nose before moving her hand up to stroke his face. "Miss me?"

He nickered to her slightly as if in response, which only tugged her smile wider. Reaching for the halter hanging beside his stall, she undid the latch and slid open the door. She slipped the halter around his head, buckling it behind his ears, and tied the lead to a loop on his stall wall. Sneaking a quick kiss to his snout, she padded out of the stall and across the hall to the tack room.

It was like falling into a familiar routine. She grabbed a brush and his saddle pad, tossing them both onto the swept aisle floor, before finding her old, comfortable black-leather saddle. It was polished and clean, but Mariah couldn't help the flash of images that raced through her head when she saw it.

She and her father leaving Andburgh under the cover of night after she stole her grandfather's dagger from Lord Donnet.

The parade through the city.

Cedoric's dying gasp as he fell from his horse.

Trefor's shout of pain as an arrow pierced his shoulder.

She shuddered, then grabbed Kodie's bridle from where it hung on the wall, slinging it over her saddle horn much the same way she slung out those dark thoughts from her mind. Forcing them back into the darkest recesses of memory.

She had a mission today. A goal. Nothing would falter her feet.

With practiced hands, Mariah brushed Kodie quickly, then

slipped the saddle pad onto his back, followed by the saddle. She cinched the girth across his belly, clipping his chest piece to the ring beneath him and then to either side of the saddle. Removing his bridle from around the saddle horn, she turned to face his head.

She froze.

Leaning against the open stall door, a contemplative expression on his handsome face, was Andrian.

In a movement that was too easy, too painfully familiar, he smiled, hands sliding into his pockets. "By all means." His voice was a little rough. "Don't let me interfere with your routine."

She glowered at him, but there was no bite behind it. It was only to hide the stupid giggle that wanted to burst from her.

He was *flirting* with her. And she wasn't quite sure how to feel about it.

So, instead, she pasted a haughty look across her face and stepped to Kodie's head. Putting her back to Andrian, she slid Kodie's halter off and hung it on the ring where she'd tied his lead. Kodie dipped his head, letting her slide the bridle over his ears, the metal snaffle bit slipping between his teeth.

Mariah felt Andrian as she buckled Kodie's bridle under his jaw. He was thankfully silent across their bond, but his heat was magnetic. He reached out, scratching gently at Kodie's forelock, though she refused to turn to him.

"You know we have stable hands who do this sort of thing for us, right?"

"Yes," she quipped, "but today, I wanted to do it myself."

That seemed to be enough for him because instead of teasing her further, he asked a different question.

"What's his name?"

That pulled Mariah's gaze to him. Andrian's hand still stroked Kodie's face, but his eyes were fixed on hers, his expression unreadable.

She tilted her head, surveying him quickly.

"Kodie. After my grandfather."

He held her gaze, something sharp in his eyes. "That sounds like a story."

She wanted to snap at him, to tell him that they didn't have time and that the others would expect them soon. That she didn't feel like sharing this piece of her past, one of the few cherished memories she had from her childhood.

"You need to learn to trust him again."

With a deep breath, she broke his stare, looking instead into Kodie's soft brown eyes.

"When I was a girl," she said. "I always wanted a horse of my own. But my family couldn't afford another one—we had my mother's mare and my father's warhorse. That was it. My brother and I were still small enough that we could ride tandem with our parents if we needed to go anywhere as a family ... which, truthfully, wasn't often." She stroked Kodie's face, playing with his forelock.

"But I still begged my parents. Prodded and pleaded and poked until they were sick of me. One day, when I was thirteen, I was out wandering around the outskirts of town, moping about the fact that I couldn't go hunting with my father and younger brother. I stumbled my way onto a local farm." She smiled at the memory. She still felt Andrian's eyes on her, but they were warm, no longer a searing heat.

The bond between them was still silent. Mariah bent, inspecting Kodie's front hoof before righting herself and rechecking his girth.

"The farmer had a horse. A fierce palomino mare that he'd used to plow his fields. And that day, he was just ... standing in the field with her, a sour expression on his face. So, being the bold little shit I was, I walked right up to him and asked him why he looked at his horse like that. 'Because,' he'd said, 'she just had a foal.' And there he was, just a scrawny little guy hiding behind his mom."

That errant bond stirred in her chest. Just a flutter, but enough for Mariah to stumble slightly as she slipped around Kodie's rear to stand on his other side, avoiding Andrian's intense gaze. "I asked the farmer what he planned to do with it. He grew very distressed and agitated. 'Do you have any idea how much work a foal is, girl? I'm an old man; I do not have time for this.'" Mariah looked deep into Kodie's eyes.

"The farmer said he had no choice but to put the foal down. His mare would be sad for a time, but he simply couldn't manage it. But, to me ... that was unacceptable. So, I did what any out-of-control, overly determined thirteen-year-old would do." Mariah smiled, scratching Kodie's ear.

"I told that farmer I would take the foal. Bottle feed it, sleep in the barn with it, I didn't care. I would make that foal my own, and he wouldn't have to spend a dime or raise a finger to care for it." She finally turned to Andrian, knowing his eyes would still be locked on her. That bond still flickered in her chest, just a tickle beneath her ribs.

"So? He said yes?" He shifted against the stall doorway, crossing his arms over his chest.

Mariah swallowed. "Of course, he said yes." She fought back a grin and the telltale heat of her flush. She glimpsed his blinding smile just as she turned back to Kodie. More warmth spilled through their bond, going straight to her cheeks.

"In fact, he agreed to let his mare keep the foal, so I wouldn't have to bottle feed, if I helped him on his farm until the foal could be weaned. I accepted in a heartbeat. My parents were less than thrilled, but my father eventually relented, believing the few months spent on a farm would be a good outlet for my need for adventure.

"So, I spent the summer working on that farm. Plowing fields, sowing crops, caring for livestock ... all of it. Whatever that farmer needed me to do, I did it, no question." Mariah grinned again. "Probably the first time in my life *that* has ever happened."

A deep chuckle sounded beside her, much closer than she'd thought it would be. She inhaled on instinct and caught a whiff of his scent: rain and sandalwood, like the forest of her home.

More warmth pulled in her chest, wrapping around her heart.

"And the rest is history," she ended in a rush, patting Kodie's flank. He pawed at the ground, his hoof scraping at straw. "Kodie came home with me when he was weaned, and I spent the next few years training and breaking him. I never met my grandfather, but my mother told me stories about him. A great warrior who lost his life in some dispute in Vatha. He was impossibly stubborn and fierce, but loyal to a fault. I decided to name my little colt after him. Kodie has never really liked most people, but he's always had a soft spot for me."

Andrian chuckled, extending a hand. Kodie sniffed it once before pushing his nose into Andrian's waiting palm.

Andrian grinned triumphantly. "He seems to not mind me."

Mariah snorted and rolled her eyes. "You probably just hid carrots in your pockets."

The second she said it, she knew what he would say.

"Oh, trust me, princess." His voice was all darkness and smoke, liquid heat dumped into her veins. "That isn't a carrot in my pocket."

Mariah slowly turned to face him, ignoring the pounding in her chest or the flames licking down her neck.

"Did you just make a dick joke?"

His face fell, just a touch, the sly smirk slipping at her question. He chuckled nervously. "Can you blame me?"

She studied him, a reluctant smile tugging across her lips. "No. I think I pretty much handed you that one." She turned back to Kodie, adjusting his bridle.

A stableboy rounded the corner.

"Sir," he called, "your horse is ready." The boy dipped his head to Mariah. "Your Majesty," he squeaked, before scampering away.

Mariah stood beside Kodie's head, staring up at Andrian. He held her gaze for a moment before stepping back, letting her lead her horse out of the stall, Kodie's hooves clipping a steady rhythm across the floor.

"Time to leave, Armature," she called over her shoulder. "Don't make me wait on you."

As it turned out, it wasn't Andrian who kept their party waiting, but the young captain who had agreed to lead them to the abandoned apartment. Mariah, Andrian, and Sebastian all stood, mounted and waiting on their horses in the massive palace courtyard, when the captain rounded the corner, flushed and out of breath.

"My sincerest apologies, my queen," he'd huffed, wiping a hand across his brow. "We had trouble locating the original report. I couldn't be sure of the exact location without it."

"You don't remember it?"

The man flushed deeper. "I-I didn't respond to the call, Your Majesty. I've never actually been there."

Mariah's lips tightened, but she held back her snarky retort. It would do them little good. "Very well." She gestured toward the fourth saddled horse, waiting patiently by the stables. "Mount up. You're leading us."

The man scurried away, swinging himself into the saddle.

Mariah turned to Sebastian. "Seb, you'll ride with him. Make sure he's not full of shit."

Sebastian's lips tightened, hazel eyes darting between Mariah and Andrian, before nodding. "Don't get too far behind," he said softly. His words were clipped, but he said them.

Mariah loosened her breath, thankful that he'd taken a step back.

She had a feeling she had her best friend to thank for that and would be *sure* to pull as much from Ciana about it the second they returned to the palace.

The captain trotted past, still flushed and sweating, and with a soft click, Sebastian urged his mount after him. Mariah squeezed her thighs and Kodie stepped into a steady walk, trailing after the captain and Sebastian.

"You coming, Armature?"

Behind her, she heard hoof steps.

"Always, princess."

CHAPTER 44

"Have you ever been to the market district?"

Mariah glanced at Andrian, riding beside her on a black stallion. Sebastian and Ryland were ahead, the latter chatting animatedly to Sebastian, whose posture was polite yet tense in his saddle.

She shook her head. "Only when I came through with my dad the day before the Choosing. But we stayed the night in the mountain district, and the only other time I've been back down was on the day of the parade."

"Which only leads through the city's main roads," Andrian growled. His hair had grown long and fell errantly into his eyes. He pushed it back with a frustrated movement. "We really should've gotten you out of the palace more."

"It's fine," she murmured. He was dressed in a short sleeve black tee, and when he'd brushed his hair from his eyes, biceps shifting beneath the cotton ...

She swallowed.

"I'm assuming you've been down here before," she said, her eyes wandering around the bustling streets. While the road was clear for their horses, it was also lined with vendors, each desperate to display their wares. The sounds and shouting of bartering rang through the street.

"I've lived in Verith most of my life." His voice was crisp and pointed. "Of course I've been down here."

"Just making conversation, asshole," she muttered under her breath, too quiet—she thought—for him to hear.

With a jolt, she realized he was no longer beside her. She pulled Kodie to a halt, twisting in her saddle. A few paces behind, he'd frozen on his horse, his face fixed in an expression of utter disgust and horror.

"What?" She glanced around, alarmed, which seemed to spark a reaction. He nudged his horse forward, the stallion quickly catching back up to her and Kodie.

"I'm ... just ..." He groaned, again running his hands through his hair. He sighed heavily, eyes lifting to the sky. "I'm sorry," he finally said. "That was a dick thing to say. You were only curious."

Mariah's mouth popped open.

"Are you *apologizing* for being an asshole?"

His eyes met hers. "... Yes?"

"Wow," she said, turning back around. "Maybe Enfara truly has frozen over."

They rode in silence for a few more minutes, kept company only by the sound of their horses' hooves and the crowd around them.

"That's really what you think of me, isn't it?" Andrian's voice was soft, but just loud enough to be heard over the din.

Her brow furrowed. "What is?"

She felt more than saw him tense beside her. "An ass. Foul-tempered." He paused. "Someone who hurt you." His last words were almost a whisper.

It was her turn to pull Kodie to a sudden stop, her glare turning to ice. He wheeled his stallion around to face her, his face unbelievably open.

Raw.

Vulnerable.

With that look, something in her chest cracked wide open.

"Look, Mariah," he murmured fervently, pulling his horse beside Kodie. "I know. I *know* that you can't forgive me for what I've done."

"Andrian," she whispered.

"You have to hear me. I swear. To the goddess, to the stars. Fuck, to *you*. It wasn't me. And I'm just as committed as you are to finding out why the fuck all this is happening, why they are so desperate to end you and your reign."

"Andrian," she said a bit more forcefully.

"What do you want from me?" Desperation creeped into his voice, a wild gleam in his eyes. "Do you want me to get on my fucking knees for you? Do you want me to *beg* for your forgiveness? Because, fuck, Mariah, for you ... I would. I would do anything—"

"*Andrian*." This time, she nearly shouted above the crowd, her voice crackling with a touch of the raw magic in her veins.

He leaned back, blinking as if shaking himself from a daze. She grabbed his horse's reins and pulled them closer, their thighs pressing together.

When they touched, she swore the ground beneath her feet shook, that the heavens above opened, and lightning crackled across the sky. His eyes widened, but she refused to break his stare.

"I don't want you to beg for my forgiveness," she hissed, her voice soft but she knew it carried. Knew he heard it. "There is *nothing* to forgive. I know it wasn't you. I know you were just as trapped as I was." She drew in a deep breath, dropping his reins, but he remained against her side. Even their horses stood skin to skin, ears tilted back as they listened to their riders.

"I want you to beg for something I gave away all too willingly before." She watched the confusion fill his eyes, before she leaned in further, just a touch.

"I want you to beg for my *trust*."

She pressed her heels to Kodie's side, trotting off down the busy street after Sebastian and the captain, leaving Andrian with an expression of wicked determination—and wild hunger—on his face.

THE BUILDING WAS DILAPIDATED, a corner of the roof caving in. Moss and vines crawled up the front, and most of the windows were boarded up or shuttered in.

Mariah stared dubiously at the crumbling brick. "Are you sure this is where the call came from?"

"Yes, my queen. And I'm sure that's exactly what the guardsmen who responded to this call said when they arrived that night."

Mariah hummed, searching for any hints of something more sinister lurking within the decrepit structure. She saw nothing, and even when she sent a simple, slender rope of magic twisting out toward the building, not a single trace of the evilness she'd felt in the pillars clawed back at her.

"Very well," she said, turning to the captain. "Will you help my Armature open the doors?" She gestured behind her at the double entryway, beyond repair and boarded up.

The captain paled. "Your Majesty … I do not …"

"We've got it, M." Sebastian's voice held a hint of amusement as he and Andrian brushed past, each carrying a bundle of rope. While Mariah knew that Andrian's magic could certainly remove the boards—hers could too—she also knew it was good to give her Armature a moment to teach the captain what it meant to investigate a call.

Especially one carrying allegations as serious as this.

Moving as one, Sebastian and Andrian tied their rope to the boards, then led the other ends to their waiting horses. Looping it around their saddle horns, they spurred their warhorses forward, muscles straining against the taut rope.

It only took a few strides from the two beasts to pull the boards free, wood and nails clattering to the ground. They dismounted, retying their horses to the post in the street where Kodie and Ryland's horse stood, and rejoined her.

"Shall we?" She gestured with a flourish to the captain.

His face paled further, but he nodded shakily, pushing back his shoulders as he stepped toward the newly revealed doors.

Sebastian brushed past her. "Stop terrorizing the poor kid," he whispered in her ear.

"*Kid?*" Mariah responded with fake indignation. "He's older than me. Wasn't he one of my Marked?"

"Yes." Andrian stepped to her other side. "His name is Ryland. And he's a good kid, if a little slow on the uptake." Over her head, he and Sebastian shared a grin.

Mariah swung her gaze between the two of them, astonished. "Stop getting along. It's unnerving." Before either of them could respond, she followed Ryland into the abandoned building.

The interior was much the same as the outside. Dirty and crumbling, and it smelled a bit like rotten food. Mariah wrinkled her nose in disgust.

"Gods," she breathed out. "When was the last time this place was occupied?"

"At least five years." Ryland lifted his hand, a small orb of fire cupped in his palm.

Mariah eyed the flame, then let her own light spill from her palms, twisting and winding through the crumbling space.

Andrian flashed a grin, and Sebastian chuckled under his breath.

"Do you know what happened?"

Ryland, watching her light spill and twist throughout the room in awe, quickly closed his fist, snuffing out his flame. He turned to face her again, cheeks a bit flushed.

"I think it was an outbreak of the pox. Swept through the building like the plague. The City Guard eventually had to close it down and evacuate all the residents to different areas of town."

"Hmm. The pox." Mariah looked around again, her magic still searching. "A bit of an unusual disease, isn't it?"

"Now, certainly. But a few years ago ..." Ryland shrugged. "Maybe a bit more common than we thought."

Mariah glanced first at Sebastian, then to Andrian. Both their faces were carefully schooled, held in perfect neutrality. They all knew pox hadn't been prevalent in the kingdom for at least two hundred years; it was allegedly one reason Ryenne had closed the borders at the beginning of her reign. No better way to stop foreign diseases from running rampant through vulnerable communities.

Which meant Ryland didn't know a thing.

"Ryland, you can wait here. Watch the entrance, make sure no one sneaks in after us. My Armature and I will inspect the main floor."

Ryland nodded emphatically. "Absolutely, Your Majesty. My pleasure." With a renewed vigor, he turned to the door, placing his hand on the hilt of his sword and shoving his shoulders back.

Somewhere, wreathed in shadows, Andrian snorted.

Her lips were tugging up into a grin as she let her magic continue to poke and prod through the main floor of the abandoned building, searching for something, anything that felt even remotely like—

That.

It slammed into Mariah, the feeling of wrongness that had her magic recoiling. It came from the western end of the building, just around the right corner of the hallway stretching before them. She pulled back all her magic but for a single thread, watching the silver-gold thrash and vibrate in the air as it fought to get away from whatever it had found.

"There," she whispered.

Without hesitation, Sebastian and Andrian fell into step beside her, the bonds between their souls pulled taut by the distress of her magic. Andrian's burned brighter, a glowing star within her chest, but she was too consumed by the evil she chased.

She followed that lingering thread around the corner, her

steps steady and even, in time with the heavy beating of her heart.

When she pushed into the room beyond, she froze. Her eyes flew wide, magic clawing and raging and whipping inside her chest. Shadows unfurled behind her, and she heard Sebastian swear softly under his breath.

The room ... it dripped with something dark. Something evil. And not just something magical, although that certainly was imbued within the seedy floors and cracked wallpapered walls.

No, it was physically dripping with evidence of the atrocities —dozens, if not hundreds, of them—that had been committed here.

Mariah pushed her magic out further, illuminating the space. She held back her gasp of terror and disgust, just as Andrian growled and Sebastian swore again, this time louder.

On the floors were dried pools of blackish red, spread into pockets every few feet. On the walls, more splatter of the same liquid arched in delicate streaks, dripping down in a morbid mockery of artwork.

Blood.

It was *blood*.

Gritting her teeth, Mariah forced her magic into the room. It recoiled and snapped but obeyed, a piece of it as curious as she was.

An altar sat at the far side of the room. It looked as if it was bathed in blood, just like the rest of the room, deep stains of it spilling rivulets down the raised pedestal.

She took a step toward it.

"*Mariah*," Andrian and Sebastian murmured together, but they didn't stop her.

She had to see.

Mariah inched closer, something deep and integral buried in her soul screaming at her to *run away, get out, do not go closer*.

But ... she had to see. Her rage, the only thing pushing her forward, demanded her to see. To look at what was done in this room on the night of her Solstice. The desecration of the beautiful magic she'd helped to create.

She stood before the altar. On top of it sat a single stone obelisk, its surface so dark she wasn't sure if it was more blood coating it, or if that was simply the stone itself.

A wild impulse seized her. She extended a brazen hand.

"Mariah, no!" Andrian's desperate roar was the last thing she heard before her finger touched the obelisk.

Before her world plummeted into darkness.

CHAPTER 45

Mariah dropped like a stone tossed into a lake, and Andrian's stomach went with her. His shadows whipped and writhed, and he surged across the room.

But he was too late.

She hit the floor just as he reached her, sliding to a halt as his shadows curled beneath her to keep her head from cracking on the filthy concrete floor. Everything in his world narrowed as he threw himself to the ground next to her, searching desperately for the pulse in her neck, the rise and fall of her chest.

When he found the steady thrum of her heartbeat, he relaxed slightly. Until he lifted his gaze to the altar she'd touched, to the stone obelisk sitting atop it.

He swore again, this time much lower and much more vicious.

Sebastian appeared by his side, his own terror wafting from him.

"What the *fuck* was she thinking ..."

Andrian growled, low and deep in his chest. "I have to get her back to the palace."

Sebastian reached for Mariah. "*I* will take her."

Andrian turned his snarl and glare on Sebastian. His brother, his fellow Armature, held his stare, his jaw working and anger sparking in his hazel eyes.

Until his shoulders sagged, conflict still warring in his expression as he leaned away.

"Fine. I'm trusting you, Armature," Sebastian said. "I don't think you deserve it, but I'm going to do it, anyways. Don't make me regret it."

Andrian bared his teeth but said nothing. He only slid an arm behind the back of Mariah's knees, another arm wrapping around her neck and shoulders, and lifted her from the ground.

"Find Ryland. There may be more to learn from this place." He turned on his heel and stormed toward the exit.

Everything about him was sizzling energy, shadows snapping around his shoulders, icy flames igniting in his vision. The only thing that kept him grounded, kept him from exploding and decimating that entire gods-cursed building, were Mariah's soft exhales against his neck, the warm and steady thrum of her heart where she lay curled against his chest.

Ryland started in surprise when Andrian rounded the corner, then backed away as his eyes darted between Andrian and the unconscious Mariah in his arms.

"What ..."

"Find Sebastian. Search the building. Make sure my horse gets back to the palace." Andrian's orders were harsh and biting as he pushed past the captain. He stepped into the afternoon sunlight, the setting spring sun casting golds and oranges across the Bay of Nria just visible beyond the edge of the rundown slums.

Not that he was noticing things like the sunset.

He rushed to the waiting horses. Kodie lifted his head, ears pricking, intelligent brown eyes focusing on his mistress. Andrian stepped to the buckskin's side, shifting Mariah in his arms.

He knew Mariah would kill him if she found out he'd left Kodie behind. And, given what had just happened, he wasn't sure he trusted any other beast to carry them safely back to the palace.

Standing still as a statue, Kodie waited as Andrian carefully settled Mariah into the saddle. Kodie lifted his head and caught her as she slumped forward, her hair falling over her face. Andrian placed his foot in Kodie's stirrup, swinging himself behind her in the saddle. He reached around her, grabbed the reins, and pulled her body back so she rested safely against his chest.

"Back to the palace, Kodie," he whispered, pressing his heels into the gelding's side. "Quickly."

The horse tossed his head and surged forward, hooves clipping on the ground as he leaped into a gallop.

They flew down the streets, now significantly less crowded as the evening hours crept nearer. They left the slums, twisting up and up through the colors and rows of the market district. Andrian's fear was still ice in his veins, and when the rise of the orderly buildings of the mountain district rose before them, he quietly urged Kodie faster.

They had just rounded a bend in the golden-cobbled street when he felt Mariah shift. Her head rolled to the side, just slightly. A soft groan spilled from her lips.

Once again, everything in his world stood still.

He pulled back on Kodie's reins, pushing his seat into the saddle. The horse slowed, his gallop dropping into a steady walk, before he stopped, snorting and tossing his head, sides heaving and drenched in sweat.

Mariah groaned again. She lifted her arm, running a hand over her eyes and down the side of her face. Andrian watched, everything still frozen, a bit of disbelief coursing through him.

If what she'd touched was what he thought it was ... she *really* shouldn't be awake right now.

And yet ...

"What happened?" Her voice was low and groggy as if she'd merely been taking a nap.

"Are you alright?" He was still holding her, one hand wrapped around her midsection. Slowly, he leaned around her so he could see her face, his hand moving to the juncture of her hip.

He tried, desperately, not to think about how his thumb grazed the sliver of flesh on her stomach.

He also tried not to think about how when he saw her face, she wasn't looking at him but at that same hand.

"Yes," she said, somewhat slowly, before lifting her gaze to meet his. They were so close, too close, and he was sure she would pull away. There was something unreadable in her forest green eyes, but ...

"What happened?" she repeated. Still not moving away. Still not pushing his hand away.

Not pushing *him* away.

He watched her for a moment longer, scouring her face for something, anything. When she gave him nothing, he answered, "There was an altar. Back at the apartment. With an obelisk atop it. You touched it and collapsed."

Her brow furrowed. "That's it?"

He reeled back, just slightly. "That's ... it? Mariah, do you have any idea what that was? Why did you feel the need to touch that *thing*?" He tried not to think about the way her name tasted on his lips.

He was trying very hard not to think about a lot of things. Every single one of them were inappropriate at that moment.

That fucking bond in his chest, leaping beneath his ribs as his adrenaline faded, wasn't helping.

She watched him, then shrugged. "No, I didn't know what it was. But I wanted to know. That's why I touched it."

"Gods," Andrian breathed out. "That was *aberrant*, Mariah." Her name again.

She blinked. "What is *aberrant*?"

"Something that shouldn't fucking exist. Especially not in the middle of Verith. They say it's a conduit, between ... Between our realm and Enfara."

Silence. He looked at her again, and that same quizzical expression twisted her face.

"So why is it here?"

"I don't know. Like I said, it shouldn't be. I had only ever read about it; I didn't think it was real."

There was another brief pause. He could nearly see her mind working behind her eyes.

"Hm," was all she said, turning away from him.

"'*Hm*?' That's all you have to say? Mariah, it could have *killed* you—leeched you of all your magic and life until you were nothing but an empty shell—"

"Yes, well." She lifted a hand. Light danced and twined between her fingers, her usual trick. "Seems like there was nothing to worry about. I'm fine."

Andrian stared at her, exasperated. And she stared back, unperturbed.

She shifted again in the saddle. Leaning forward, she ran a hand down Kodie's black mane.

Pressing her hips further into his own.

He swallowed, holding back his groan.

Fucking gods. He regretted not taking his own horse.

"How are we on Kodie? How are *you* on Kodie?" She settled back against him, relaxed and pliant.

Andrian clenched his jaw.

"When you collapsed, and I realized it was *aberrant*, I knew we had to get you back to the palace. And I knew you would likely kill me if we left Kodie behind."

She hummed, and the sound traveled through his chest. Where they touched. "Finally, you do something smart."

"Excuse me? I'm not the one who touched the dangerous, forbidden, cursed rock on top of an altar covered in blood."

She waved a hand in front of her face again, clicking her tongue to Kodie. He started forward, settling into a relaxed walk. She shifted against Andrian with each step, her body moving with the sway of the horse.

Gods, save him.

"I mean, how did he let *you* on him?" She twisted in the saddle, her face again dangerously close to his. Her eyes sparkled still, but this time, he could read what was in them.

Mischief.

He narrowed his eyes. "What do you mean?"

Her gaze dropped to his lips, just for a heartbeat, before she turned back around. "He just doesn't let anyone other than me ride him. That's all."

Andrian knew the game.

"Perhaps you're not as special as you thought, princess."

"I highly doubt that's why."

"This confidence is unbecoming."

"Ah, but that's where you're wrong, Andrian." She purred his name, shooting him a glance over her shoulder. "I think you, of all people, should know that this confidence is *earned*."

"Careful," he said, his voice low, far rougher than he intended it to be. Every single place where they touched was ablaze, the bond between their souls awake and alive and burning. The same fire he felt was reflected in the green of her irises. "Don't start something you're not ready to finish, *nio*."

She stiffened, turning away from him.

He didn't know why he'd said it. She'd told him not to. But it meant more—gods, so fucking much more—than he could ever express to her. And he couldn't stop calling her it. It was the only piece of his past that he still clung to, a piece he hadn't meant to impart to her but that she now owned, even if she didn't realize it.

But he could feel the way she changed. The way she shut down. All the heat he'd felt from their bond only a few seconds ago cooled to marbled ambivalence, solid stone closing him off from her once again.

His hand fell from where it had rested at the juncture between her hip and thigh. She shifted forward, just a touch, no longer pressed to his chest.

"I'm sorry," he murmured, a barely-there whisper spoken to the back of her head.

She didn't speak to him again as they rode through the palace gates. Didn't glance at him as she slid from her horse, leaving Kodie with Andrian and the two stableboys who sprinted from the shadows. She strode away, heading for the palace, her hands clenched into fists.

Even with the coldness Mariah had left him with, Andrian couldn't shake the heat of his memories. Of her against his chest, of her body between his thighs. Of her breathy laugh against his cheek and the wicked gleam in her green eyes.

The way she'd glanced at his lips, if for only a second.

The way she'd leaned forward, pressing her ass into *him.*

The way she shifted and moved with the rocking of the horse, with him, as if her body had been fucking *made* for him.

Fuck.

He rolled his shoulders, running his hands through his hair. Too long. His hair was too fucking long, and the way it fell into his eyes and curled against the back of his neck made his skin crawl. He ran his hand through his hair again, this time grabbing onto the ends and pulling, hoping it would shake the tension ripping through him.

The feeling brought back a memory. Memories. Of bare skin under his hands, smaller hands in his hair, pulling much the same way he was now—

He dropped his hands, clenching his jaw and fists, and pushed his steps faster toward the game park.

He'd nearly sprinted to his room after their arrival back at the palace, quickly changing into training clothes and heading right back out the door. Outside once again, the setting sun warm against his skin, he hoped a run through the park would clear his head. Release some of this energy desperately trying to claw its way out of him.

His feet pounded the packed earth, and each step jolted his teeth.

Fuck, that bond between them ... He'd thought it was bad enough just having it exist. Feeling so connected to her, always knowing what she felt or wanted or needed. That was the real reason he'd drowned himself in booze during those initial days after discovering the truth about what had happened to her in Khento; it was the only thing that dulled the onslaught, numbed the reminder of *her* embedded in his fucking soul.

But then he'd *touched* her.

Not just touched but had her *there*. So close to him that he could feel every inch of her, could breathe in her intoxicating jasmine and cedarwood scent. It turned that bond between them into a live wire, a *thing* with too much power and charged energy that wrapped around his chest to where he could barely breathe.

That they'd found *aberrant* in the city, that she had *touched* it, made his restless energy even more unbearable.

He pushed his pace faster. His lungs were burning, sweat forming on his face and at the back of his neck.

But the energy from the bond kept licking down his spine, eating away at his control.

He stumbled a step, catching himself with a growl.

Andrian ran until the sun had set behind the mountains, only the faintest rays of orange and red still streaking the sky. By the time he returned to the side entrance to the palace, he was winded and drenched in sweat.

And still, the energy in him *clawed*.

He stormed into the palace. Down the winding stairs. Into the subterranean levels, where the palace staff scurried about as they attended to their tasks. Many of them shot him curious glances, giving him a wide berth.

Andrian stormed into the long dining room neighboring the kitchens, the smell of freshly baked bread and roasted game enough for him to notice but not enough to loosen his thoughts. In a corner at one of the long benches sat Drystan and Feran, smiling as they talked with several empty plates of food around them. Feran's head tilted slightly toward Andrian.

Andrian ignored him, moving to the buffet line that was set up each night as palace occupants came and went. They could cook and eat in their rooms, of course. But this was always an easy option on nights like tonight when Andrian couldn't focus much beyond putting his left foot in front of his right.

He blindly scooped food onto a plate, not even sure what he

was grabbing, before moving to the nearest table and slamming his body onto the bench. His ears were ringing, the pressure on—and in—his body suffocating.

He was sure his food was delicious.

He couldn't taste any of it, though.

No, with every bite he forced past his teeth, all he could think about was the way that dark hair had brushed his cheek. The tightening of the muscles in her stomach, still too fucking thin, as his thumb traced her skin.

His tastebuds exploded with his next bite of food. But it tasted like something *very* different from the lamb chops he was eating.

His fork clattered to the table as he dropped his head into his hands, rubbing his eyes. He fought to control his body, breathing deeply through his nose and out through his mouth.

This was not good.

Appetite—for food, at least—gone, Andrian rose from the table, leaving his tray with the dishwasher before striding from the room. He could feel Feran and Drystan's eyes on him, watching him with abject curiosity, but he didn't care.

He needed a fucking cold shower and a shot of whiskey.

CHAPTER 46

Mariah had never been so uncomfortable in her life.

Everything was on edge. Every part of her body was tense and too sensitive. She could see everything, hear everything, *feel* everything.

Especially *him*.

A shiver raked down her spine as she tipped another sip of whiskey down her throat.

"You alright, lassie?" Mikael looked at her over a sizzling pan, concern pinching his brow.

Mariah set her glass down on the island, straightening her shoulders. "Yes, sorry. It's just been a long day."

Mikael nodded, looking unconvinced, but said nothing further as he turned back to the meal.

The ride back on Kodie was ... well, fun. Exciting. For just a moment, she'd somehow forgotten what had happened, who she was and what she was after. The *aberrant* was pushed to the back of her mind, the slimy feel of its dark malignance nothing more than a shallow memory. She was just Mariah, the girl who always knew how to get men to do exactly what she wanted, and *he* was just another man who'd fallen into her beautiful trap of saccharine smiles and subtle touches. It was a game they'd played before, but this time she had more power, and she'd fucking *loved* it.

She hadn't noticed how it affected the bond stretching between their souls. Hadn't paid it much attention, not as his smell of rain and sandalwood wrapped around her, scooping her up into an embrace that was so terrifyingly familiar.

She hadn't noticed how far she'd gone into that game until he'd said it.

That word. That *name*. That one thing she'd told him not to call her because it was the last thing she'd asked him to tell her before her world was shaken apart. Even if it hadn't been him, she couldn't be sure. And she never wanted to hear it from him again.

A plate appeared before her, piled high with steaming buttered bay scallops and seared spring vegetables. The rich aroma wafted up, her stomach rumbling.

"It looks delicious, Mikael. Thank you."

"You're welcome, lassie." The chef hesitated, toying with the strap of leather holding back his hair. "Are you … sure you're alright? Do you want company?"

Mariah forced a smile. "I'm fine. I promise. Like I said, just tired."

Mikael gave her one last lingering glance, before he turned to tidy the kitchen and excused himself from her suites.

Mariah ate in silence, forcing the delicious food down her throat, hoping—*begging*—that it would help settle some of the ache pulling at her gut.

She didn't want to think about how it felt like the tug of a bond, one that wrapped around her like shadows and cooled her fire like ice.

None of her other Armature bonds felt like this. The others were strong but easily malleable, tangible things she could grab and turn on or off. This was too intense, too vexing, too infuriating.

Just like its source.

With a final pull of her whiskey, she set her now-empty glass on the island counter and stormed to bed, desperate to end this day and hoped these feelings ended with it.

SOMETHING YANKED her from sleep no more than an hour or two later.

Not a thing. That *feeling* again. But this time, it was hotter, blazing and uncontrollable, and was sitting far lower in her core than before.

Frustratingly, dangerously low.

She couldn't stop the groan that slipped past her lips as she pressed her thighs together, desperate—for friction, for pressure, for *anything*. Desire, heavy and suffocating, coursed through her, the type of want that in the past always led her to doing something wild and reckless and a little eyebrow-raising. Her hand skimmed down her bare thighs, the hem of her oversized tunic riding up as she twisted her legs together. She traced the source of that desire, down and into her soul ... then following it out ...

Her eyes snapped open.

Her mind sharpened onto a bridge of ice and shadows, the bond that connected her to the source of all this.

Several images flashed through her head.

The strike of a metal-tipped whip.

Him, furious and frustrated with her antics today.

The brush of his thumb acoss the skin of her abdomen.

Anniliese Hareth curled in his lap in a castle dining hall, ball gown hitched and lips pressed against his.

All that hot desire ignited into burning, intense rage.

She knew it hadn't been him in those moments in Khento, not really. But her fury coursed through her like a volcano, untamed and uncontrolled, and everything she'd shoved to the deepest corners of her soul came roaring to the surface.

Fuck him. Fuck him for hurting her, for scarring her, for breaking her.

With a low growl of rage, Mariah pushed from her bed,

swiping her grandfather's dagger off her nightstand as she headed for her door.

She stormed across the hall on instinct, bursting through the doors. When she was greeted by darkness and slightly stale air, she remembered.

He'd moved to a wing on the other side of the palace. Until she could decide what to do with him.

Well, she'd fucking decided.

Her grip tightened around the dagger as she padded off, slinking through the shadows of the palace, following the pull of the bond. That desire—*his* desire—still tugged low in her core, and each step was its own kind of agony. She'd neglected to slip into pants, only the silk of her underwear and thigh-length tunic guarding her against the cool spring air wafting through the palace.

Mariah didn't see a soul as she stalked through the halls. She passed courtyards and stairways, gilded halls and archways wreathed in shadows. It wasn't long before she stood in a hallway lined with doors to guest suites.

That bond kept pulling her forward, to the second door on the left.

Her insides were set ablaze, rage and heat and want racing uninhibitedly through her veins. She was panting, chest heaving, palms slickening her grip on the dagger as she placed a hand on the doorknob.

And twisted.

Her eyes found his the moment the door swung open. Tanzanite blazed in the dimness, ice and fire and light and shadow dancing between them.

Her rage, though, was still an unstoppable force.

"What the *fuck* are you doing?" Her words were hissed, gasped through clenched teeth, her vision fuzzy, and her ears ringing.

But as she held his gaze for a few heartbeats longer, something briefly settled, before snapping into place. A wave of clarity washed over her, lifting the fog and replacing it with a predatory focus.

The first thing she noticed was that he was most certainly alone. No one was in the small room but him. And her.

The second thing she noticed was *him*.

Frozen, slouched back on the couch. Hair messy and tousled, cheeks flushed, and eyes much too bright. Shirtless, his only clothing a pair of dark-gray cotton pants.

The waistband pushed down. His hand—

She snapped her gaze back to his. Where he was still as a statue, watching her.

Waiting for her.

Her grip on her dagger tightened as she swallowed, blood flushing to her cheeks, to her chest, all that rage and heat dropping right back to her core.

"*What*," she repeated, this time much lower, "are you doing?"

Andrian's throat bobbed as he, too, swallowed.

"What are you doing here?" he growled, his voice so deep, husky and warm.

"What am *I* doing here? I could fucking *feel* you. All the way across the palace. I couldn't *sleep*."

He watched her, eyes narrowing, something she recognized twisting his mouth. "So ... you came to pay me a visit?" He glanced at her hand, still clutching her dagger.

She felt the path his eyes took as they skimmed her bare legs before returning to her face.

"Good to see you came armed, at least."

"Gods, you're an asshole." Mariah whirled. She was frustrated, and her blood raged. She couldn't do this. Not with him. Not right now. Not yet.

She heard rustling behind her. "No—shit. Mariah, wait." Just as she took a step towards the still-open door, a hand wrapped around her free wrist, yanking her back into a chest of hot, solid muscle.

Despite the wave of want that ripped through her, she whirled on her toes, her dagger whipping up and pressing into the hollow of his throat.

And, of course, Andrian was grinning, the side of his mouth cocked up into a smile, white teeth flashing as his eyes blazed.

Mariah locked him with a glare, but she worried the heat licking at her spine, the flush she knew saturated her neck and face, softened its burn.

"Gods," he murmured, leaning into her. Her dagger bit further into his neck, a wordless warning. He froze but didn't draw back, that cursed smile still on his face.

"I forgot how pretty it is when you blush like that."

More flames surged into her cheeks. "I'm not *blushing*."

His grin widened. "Sure, you're not."

She inhaled once, through her nose, eyes fluttering closed before snapping open and pinning him with her stare. "Let go of me."

"I'm not touching you, princess. That's all you."

She blinked, taking stock of her body. He stood close to her— far too close—but he'd let go of her wrist, both hands hanging loosely by his sides.

The only places they touched were where her dagger met his throat ... and where her left hand had wrapped around the back of his neck, her fingers winding into the messy lengths of his hair.

She released him with a gasp, stumbling back. Her chest heaved, everything buzzing in her ears, lightning whipping across her skin. Threads of magic crackled and popped, silver and gold sparking off her fingers. Heat flared in his eyes as she fought to control herself.

Fought ... and failed.

"I could ... feel you," she repeated, her words a hoarse whisper. Everything was too bright, too dark, too much.

"Felt what, princess?" He took a small, hesitant step forward. His eyes, burning even brighter, dropped to her lips. "Use your words."

Mariah knew her flush deepened. She couldn't stop it. Couldn't even try.

She gritted her teeth. "You. I could—can—*feel* you. Gods, it's like you've burrowed under my skin, and I can't fucking shut you out."

He cocked his head. "You can shut the others out?"

She nodded.

"But you can't shut me out." A slow grin spread across his face.

A muscle in her jaw tightened, but she didn't answer him.

"Can you feel this?" His voice was husky, but he held his grin as he lifted his hand and laid it across his chest. "Can you feel the way everything in me aches for you? What your presence here, right now, does to me?"

Gods, she could. That bridge between them was so bright; she could see it when she closed her eyes, pulsing and shimmering. Everything he felt, every feeling and desire he harbored for her, crashed down their bond, slamming into her with so much force she worried it might buckle her knees and slam her to the ground.

She closed her eyes. Forced herself to breathe deep, searching inhales and expelling exhales. Not that it helped. Nothing helped.

But she had to try. Deep inside her, somewhere, buried beneath layers and layers of lust and desire and heat, was pain. Distrust. Insecurities she was working to repair but weren't yet mended.

Mariah was terrified of what might happen if she gave in. How much it might shake loose all those things she'd buried.

She was also terrified of what would happen if she forced herself to walk away. To return to her rooms, alone and heated. What that sort of crash might do to her.

Gods, what a fucking mess.

She cracked her eyes, her lids heavy, to find that Andrian had inched closer, and now stood so near that she could still feel his heat radiating off him in waves. He panted, his hands shaking, his eyes whirlpools and his shadows curling around his shoulders.

A dam was broken when she met his gaze.

"Do you know what I had to see back in that place? What I had to endure?"

A shadow flickered across his face. "Mariah, I ... I would trade everything about myself to go back in time. Just the thought that I was the one who hurt you like that ... those scars—"

"Not the fucking scars." Her fury twined with her aching need, washing through her so she didn't know where one ended and the other began. "*Her.*"

This time, it was confusion that passed over him. "Her? Who are you talking about?"

She gritted her teeth, still lost to herself. "I could survive the whips and starvation. Bodies heal. But do you know what truly broke me?" He blurred, and she angrily wiped away her tears.

"When I had to see you kiss another woman. I was holding on, until they convinced me—for one fleeting, horrible moment —that everything you'd ever told me was a *lie.*"

Mariah didn't just see the horror spreading across his face. She could feel it, could *taste* it, thick and slimy and bitter as it washed down that infuriatingly beautiful bond. Andrian's stunning eyes widened as his jaw slackened, taking a staggering step back.

"I ... Mariah, I have no memories of that place. I don't even know who you could be talking about. I would ... I would *never.*" His voice cracked at the end. "I know—I know I said some terrible things to you. Before. In the library, on that balcony. But they were just the words of a scared and desperate man. The moment you stepped out of that carriage, you were it for me. Even if this world lost its moons, you would still be mine."

Everything in Mariah's world narrowed to this moment. This confrontation.

Those words.

Her rage slipped away, dark memories retreating to the hidden corners where they belonged. All that remained was that burning, insatiable heat, an unquenchable desire blending across a bridge of shadow and ice. A demanding pull from a neglected bond made from necessity but screaming for release and acknowledgment.

"I am trying. To forgive you." Her voice broke, and she sagged where she stood. "I know ... I know it wasn't you."

His relief was palpable, a physical thing that snapped in the air. He surged further, closing the distance between them.

And halted when she shrunk away, back meeting the wall behind her.

"You can't touch me," she said in a rush. She took a steadying breath. "I'm not ready for you to touch me."

His chest heaved as he slowly tilted his head. "You are trying to forgive me ... but you still don't trust me." Not a question. He could read the fear, the hesitation in her eyes, could read between her words.

Mariah nodded.

He growled, low and deep in his chest. It was a sound of frustration, and it vibrated down their bond. But he took a step back, until he hit the small dining table in the center of the room. Leaned himself on it, hands braced behind him.

He closed his eyes, taking a deep breath. When he reopened them, he smiled.

"Okay," he drawled, the words like honey on his lips. "Then if I can't touch you ... can *you* touch you?"

The world stood still.

Then everything moved again, blood and wind rushing past her ears. Heat sparked and crackled in her veins, settling low in her core, crawling lower until there was an ache that almost had her whimpering against the wall. Their bond danced so bright she swore she could see it there, stretching between them.

Andrian's forearms tensed, jaw working as his throat bobbed. "An answer, princess. I need an answer."

"Yes," she croaked. "Yes, gods. I can ... I can touch me."

"Good girl." He almost whispered the words, standing up from the table, straightening his spine as he fixed her with a *look*. A hungry look. A *devouring* look.

"I understand. I wouldn't trust me either." His voice was like smoke and shadow. "I promise I won't touch you. Not again, not unless you want me to. But you have to agree to do something for me."

She swallowed, shifting on her feet against the wall. "What?"

His grin shifted into something dark and feral. "For tonight, your hand is mine. For tonight, wherever I say you go, you go. Whatever I say you do, you do. You keep your ability to stop, to walk away, but if you give me just a sliver of trust ..." He pushed from the table, walking not to her but to the still-open door. He stopped beside her, grabbing the handle, his scent wrapping around her like something dark and dangerous.

Probably an accurate instinct. Everything about this was dangerous. She could feel it in her bones, but she couldn't turn away. Their bond thrummed between them, the energy ancient and wild and unleashed.

"If you give me that sliver, I will give you everything you need. All you have to do is say yes."

They watched each other, hearts pounding, beating in rhythm, though neither knew it. After what felt like an agonizing eternity, Mariah nodded.

The look that crossed his face sent a fresh wave of heat through her veins.

He closed the door with a snick before locking her with a stare. Everything about him was commanding and dangerous and, despite the conflict raging through her, exactly what she needed.

"Go stand beside the bed."

At first, her instincts had her resisting the command. Pushing back against the authority woven into his words, she shot him a glare.

Andrian only lifted a brow, the side of his mouth quirking up.

Her nostrils flared, but she straightened her shoulders, shifting on her feet. With every drop of seduction and bravado she could muster, she pushed off the wall and swayed across the room. She still lacked her curves, that soft firmness she'd loved so much, but she was still her.

And even after everything ... like *fuck* would she forget that.

When she reached the bed, glancing once at the dark, twisted sheets, she whirled to face him. He'd taken a few steps forward, moving back to the dining table in the middle of the room. With a movement that tightened her chest, her thighs pressing tighter together, he snagged a chair and swung it around, settling onto it with a lazy grace. He sprawled out, legs spread wide, resting a hand on the table. He was still several feet from her, but the way he watched her made her feel as if he was *right there.*

As if the hand toying with the hem of her tunic could really be his.

His eyes dropped to that hand, as if he heard those thoughts, before lifting back to her own. His jaw tightened, fingers clenching.

"Take off your tunic. Slowly."

Her breath hitched. Her lungs constricted.

But she obeyed.

Her fingers curled into the soft cotton as she lifted her shirt, the material rising over her torso. A brief, wild pulse of self-consciousness flashed through her—she was so thin, her ribs too visible, her collarbones stark beneath her neck. But when she pulled the material free from her body, discarding it onto the floor at his feet and meeting his gaze again, all those thoughts vanished.

Andrian's bright blue eyes had darkened to near black, and the look he fixed her with was ravenous. Desperate. Consuming.

He lifted a finger; what could've been a lazy gesture ... or all he could do without leaping from his chair.

"Now the underwear."

Her heart was pounding. Hammering. The steady beat of a drum. Everything sizzled and cracked as she did what he asked, hooking her thumbs into the hem of her silk undergarments and peeling them down her legs. She kept her gaze fixed on his, desperate to swallow down every raised eyebrow or tugged lip or bob of his throat.

She was now bare before him. Just as she'd been dozens of times before, but never like this. Never in this new, scarred body, its thinness and weakness still unfamiliar to her. He must've seen the hesitation flash in her eyes because he met her gaze again, attention hardening into steel.

"You are fucking perfect. Every inch of you." Andrian paused. "Repeat that back to me."

"What?" she squeaked, voice high and breathy.

"Repeat what I said. That you are perfect."

She stuttered for a moment, twisting her hands together. Nervous. She was never nervous.

But ... She obeyed.

"I'm perfect."

"Yes. Fucking perfect," he growled, hands clenching back into fists. "Now, remember: your hand is mine. Your body is mine. Everything I say, you do. You can stop whenever you want, but I promise—I will take care of you."

Mariah nodded. She was past the point of thinking, anger and jealousy and hesitation forgotten.

"Good." He leaned back in his chair. "Now. Get on the bed."

The backs of her knees brushed the comforter. With a smooth movement, she hoisted onto the soft blankets, the mattress dipping beneath her weight. She sat there, hands resting behind her, thighs clamped tightly together.

Andrian studied her for a moment, running a hand through his messy hair. "Grab the pillows. Put them behind you."

She did as he asked, stealing the pillows from the head of the bed and arranging them behind her. Once done, she looked back at him expectantly, trying to paste a look of boredom across her face.

Mariah was far from bored. She remembered the fun of this game. The thrill of wielding power as only a woman could.

Her expression was enough to pull a grin from him. "Be patient, princess." He tsked. "We're finally getting to the fun part."

Her insides went molten as he rested his arm across his lap, drawing too much attention to the strained gray cotton. He noticed her stare and made a sound in the back of his throat, low and heated.

"Lie back on the pillows."

She did. She had one leg curled up, the other stretched in front of her, thighs clamped together.

He fixed her with a wicked grin.

"Now spread those legs for me, princess."

She hesitated. Just for a moment. The longer she held his stare, the greater the inferno in his eyes grew.

She drew up her other leg. And let them fall apart.

From where he sat, he could see all of her. Every single inch. Nothing hidden, nothing shadowed. But for their agreement that he would not touch her, she was utterly at his mercy.

He watched her, his rapt attention nearly burning. "Just like you told me, princess," he whispered, leaning back in his chair. "So fucking *perfect*." He licked his lips, the tip of his tongue darting out to swipe along the seam of his mouth.

"Now, your hand. Whose is it, Mariah?"

Gods. The way he said her name. "Yours. It's yours." She almost choked on the words, how quickly she forced them past her teeth.

"That's right. *Mine*." His eyes were shadowed. "Your right hand. Show it to me."

She lifted it without hesitation. The fight had left her, replaced by this indescribable burning need.

She'd had her fair share of sexual encounters. Had her fair share of encounters with him.

Not one had made her feel quite like *this*.

"Start at your throat."

She touched her fingers to the column of her neck, brushing them back and forth. Her heartbeat hammered beneath her fingertips, heat pouring off her skin.

"Now move down. To those perfect tits. Show me how good it feels to touch you there."

She obliged, her hand drifting down her chest before circling her breast. She closed her eyes, her inhale sharp as her fingers found her nipple, pinching and pulling, her body responding as her back arched off the bed.

Andrian groaned.

"Open your eyes, Mariah."

She forced her lids open, blinking against the heaviness, the weight of her desire.

She found his stare easily, a glowing blue lighthouse against the dark.

"I want you to watch me for this next part."

She nodded.

An answering growl.

"Move your hand down."

Mariah did, her fingers dancing across her stomach, inching closer to her center. Where she really wanted them, where his attention was now locked, watching her every move with a scalding intensity.

His eyes flashed as she grazed the soft skin of her center. Felt her wetness there, the madness he'd forced upon her since seating her between his legs as they rode her horse through the city.

Since long before that.

"That's it, princess," he praised. She held his gaze steadily, even as her own fingers began to move in and around her, dragging that wetness up to circle her clit. Even as his own hand, the one that had rested on his lap, slipped beneath the waistband of his pants, grabbing hold of his length. "Show me how you find your pleasure, Mariah."

Her fucking name. It sounded like a mixture of a prayer and a curse, something both saintly and sinful, whenever he said it like that.

And because he had, she had no choice but to oblige.

Mariah didn't break from his stare as she used her fingers to inch herself higher and higher, pushing herself toward the cliffside waiting for her. His hand matched her rhythm, chasing after his own release. Sweat beaded their brows, breath hitched in their lungs, but they refused to break.

Even when she pushed herself over the edge, her back arching from the pillows, she held his gaze. Even when he followed soon after her, breath hissing through his teeth with her name panted between jolts of his body, he held her gaze.

It was only when they collapsed—her back onto the bed, him into that chair—that their stare finally broke. Magic, light and shadow, curled and drifted around them, much like it had that first night, so many months ago.

But this time, they were six feet apart. A gap that suddenly felt too far, too detached.

The distance tugged a low, foreign ache in Mariah's soul. An urge to sit up. To stand from the bed.

To close the space.

But just as she was about to move … something stopped her. Something she was coming to hate, something she was becoming more determined to stamp out from her life, once and for all.

Fear. It was a low, slimy whisper of fear wrapping around her heart that had her staying still. That kept the distance where it was, even though everything in her body and mind and soul called to close it.

She sat all the way up, dropping her gaze to her lap and her hands. The boiling tension from their bond was extinguished, but a new sort of frustration rose in its place.

Frustration at herself. At this terror. At these feelings that were so unlike her, were so foreign to everything she was.

The chair in front of her creaked.

"Mariah?" His voice was different now, too. Softer, lighter. More cautious, unsure if he had crossed some sort of line.

She hated that she made him feel that way. He'd been a prisoner, just as much as she. And she only continued to treat him as such, even after being freed.

Mariah lifted her head. Met his gaze. And gave him a sad smile. He answered with his own, so much hesitation on his beautiful face.

"Are you … are you okay?"

She nodded. "Yes. I'm fine. Better than fine." She looked down at her discarded clothes. "But I think I better get back to my own rooms, now."

Andrian nodded, running a hand through his hair. Gods, he really needed a haircut. The thought gave her a streak of amusement, which was quickly washed away by muted sadness.

She wanted to stay. More than she'd ever wanted to do anything.

But she needed to conquer this fear first.

"Let me walk you back."

"No," she said quickly, standing from the bed. His nostrils flared, throat bobbing, as she realized she was still starkly naked. She scrambled for her tunic, slipping it over her head before fumbling with her underwear. "That's okay. I can make it back on my own. Besides," she said, tugging her lips into a forced grin. "I came armed, remember?"

He hesitated, instincts obviously warring inside him, before dipping his head.

It pulled her heart. Shredded it. To see him so muted, so unsure around her. Despite the confidence he'd exuded moments ago, this was the man she'd created.

Perhaps they were each now creatures of the other's creation, even if they hadn't known it.

A headache pounded behind her skull. Her body begged for her bed, for sleep. To fall into unconsciousness and figure all this out another day.

"Yes," he murmured. "You did."

She brushed past him, swiping her dagger from where she'd discarded it on the countertop by the door. Just before she grabbed the door handle, she turned on her heel, finding him watching her with so many questions and not enough answers in his face.

"Andrian?" she whispered, her voice hoarse. She loved the way his name felt in her mouth. The way it rolled off her tongue, as if it had always belonged there.

He brightened, just slightly. "Yes, Mariah?"

Her chest squeezed. "Tomorrow, you can move back into your rooms. But don't forget; I sleep with this dagger under my pillow."

The answering smile he gave her was blinding. "Oh, princess. I wouldn't dare forget."

CHAPTER 47

The palace was quiet.

It was always quiet that late—or early. Mariah didn't often make it a habit of roaming the halls during the deepest part of the night, during those early morning hours over which the stars and moons claimed ownership. Though she'd found herself out during this time more in recent days, whether due to sleeplessness wrought by nightmares or just too many wandering thoughts.

This night felt different. As she passed beneath an archway in the hallways leading into a courtyard, the open sky visible above, as she stepped through a pool of waxing silver-gold moonlight, something rubbed against her skin, tickling her senses with awareness and energy.

Mariah was positive it had nothing to do with what she'd just done. Her fingers twitched against the hem of her tunic as she quickened her steps, eager to vanish back into the comfort of her rooms.

She tried to keep her mind from wandering back down those hallways. Back to the man she'd just left.

To the words he'd said.

To the bitter fear she'd felt, but also the energy to squash it.

She knew, without a doubt, that she still loved him. Didn't think it was possible for her to stop loving him despite everything that happened in Khento. A piece of him belonged to her, something that was made even more apparent by the shimmering bond bridging their souls.

Mariah shivered, hurrying down the smooth marble hall. At least tonight had dulled the sharp bite of that bond, if only a little. She felt a bit more like herself, not like she was about to burst through her own skin.

And as much as it had hurt, it felt good to confess the things she'd been forced to endure in Khento. Not the physical wounds, but the ones that cut deeper than her skin.

Her mind snapped away from her musings as she rounded the final corner, senses flickering to alertness.

A figure leaned against the wall beside her door. But when it moved, stepping into the light, she relaxed, releasing her grip on her dagger.

"Drystan," she murmured, rubbing her face. "You scared the shit out of me."

Drystan chuckled. "Sorry," he said quietly. He stopped a few paces from her, a pensive look on his already-stoic face.

Mariah raised an eyebrow. "What?"

He shrugged. "Nothing. I was on guard duty tonight. Just doing my job." His golden eyes glinted in the pale *allume* light. "Noticed you sneaking out of your rooms not long after you went to bed. Had to make sure you were okay."

Blood rushed to her face. If he saw her sneaking out … "Did you … um … follow me?"

The slight twitch at the sides of his lips was all the answer she needed. She groaned, running another hand down her face.

"If it matters, I left and came back here once I realized you were … cared for."

She peered at him from between her fingers, warmth blooming across her face. "Don't tell Sebastian, okay?" she grumbled. "Let me talk to him first."

Drystan's lips pulled into a full grin. "Don't worry, Mariah. As long as you're safe, it's not my business." More amusement flashed in his eyes. "Besides, I like to think I was a facilitator here."

Her hands dropped from her face as she eyed him. "What do you mean?"

He winked at her, and she couldn't stop her mouth from popping open with shock. "Someone had to break him out of his little pity party. Wasn't doing anyone any favors. I'm just glad he listened."

What?

"What pity party?"

"Oh, don't worry about it, My Queen. But do tell him to send me a new bottle of whiskey as a thank you. It'll piss him off, but he'll do it."

Bewildered, Mariah only blinked at Drystan, shocked at her usually serious Armature. He chuckled again, a soft, low sound, before turning back to her doors.

"It's late, Mariah. Go get some sleep. I'll keep watch."

She nodded, a bit dazed, and brushed past him to her rooms. She swung open the heavy wood door, hinges silent as always.

"Oh, and Mariah?" She turned on her heel, meeting Drystan's stare over her shoulder. He once again lounged against the wall beside Andrian's door. His gaze was soft, understanding, compassionate.

"No one faults you, you know. You went through so much—more than any of us can ever understand. And he did, too. Do what makes you happy, whatever helps you heal. All of us will support you, no matter what. Even Sebastian. *Especially* Sebastian."

She smiled at him, his words soaking through her skin, sitting within her chest. She still wasn't sure what she'd done to deserve men like him. It was a very different love than what she felt for Andrian; it was the love of a brother, a warrior soul who would lay down his entire life, everything he had, while demanding nothing from her in return.

"Thank you, Drystan."

"Goodnight, My Queen."

She pushed through her doors, escaping into the comfort of her rooms and the soft bed waiting for her.

Mariah only slept for a few hours before something woke her.

A power brushing against her skin. The whisper of a night breeze through her room, despite the closed windows. A brightness glowing behind her closed eyelids, shimmering and pulsing.

But when she shot awake in bed, everything in her stilled. Even the eddies of her magic were banked.

Standing at the foot of her bed, hands folded peacefully, long, gilded hair sweeping across her full figure, stood Qhohena. She was ringed in golden light and a crown of snowdrop blossoms, so brilliant they made the crown of Onita look like a cheap mimicry, rested atop her brow. An easy, warm smile graced her lips, her eyes twin aureate pools.

"Hello, Mariah."

Mariah gaped in response.

"Am I asleep? Is this a dream?"

An answering snort sounded from the other side of the room. Mariah whipped her attention to its source.

Now, she was certainly convinced she was dreaming.

Zadione leaned against the closed window, her silver light just as brilliant as her sister. She looked as she did when she first appeared to Mariah in her dream, and again in that cell in the bowels of Khento: dark, silver-dusted skin, waves and waves of silvery hair, a crown of animal bones woven into the thick tresses across her brow.

"No, you are not sleeping. You are very much awake. And we are very much here." Zadione shot a quick glare at her sister. Qhohena only sighed, eyes closing for a moment before resting again on Mariah.

Who could still do nothing more than stare, slack-jawed.

"I told you the last time I visited, my child, that the more we connected, the more I could speak to you. The more corporeal I could become." Qhohena unclasped her hands, spreading them before her. "You did what I asked. You are learning to trust again. To love again. And because of that, I can be here now."

"And *I* am here because I have been speaking to you for your entire life, and you have always listened to me." Zadione stepped closer to the bed, eyes narrowing. Mariah watched the goddess warily; she knew that predatory look filling Zadione's expression.

She'd worn it far too many times herself.

"Except for now, of course. *Now* you decide to ignore the one warning I always gave you and listen to my older sister instead."

Mariah swallowed. "I seem to recall you telling me that since I had fallen into weakness, I would need to learn to make it my retribution."

Zadione stiffened. "Yes. I did say that, did I not?" She stalked even closer until she stood beside her sister at the foot of Mariah's bed. The two of them were something out of a painting: silver and gold, light and dark, life and death. Sisters in every way, but opposites too, flipped sides of the same coin.

"So, dear little queen," Zadione said, folding her own hands, mimicking her sister. "How do you intend to seek your retribution from your current situation?"

"That's enough, sister," Qhohena murmured. Her voice was so soft, so quiet, yet held so much power. A reminder that while Zadione was the goddess of wildness and strength, Qhohena was one of stability and might.

Zadione didn't acknowledge her sister, but she closed her mouth, opting instead to lock Mariah with her sharp, silver glare.

Mariah swallowed down every ounce of apprehension she had and stared back.

Despite her shock, she felt no fear before these two beings. They were immortal, and wielded powers far beyond what her mind could comprehend, but she knew they cared for her in their own way.

"We did not come here to scold you, Mariah." Another quick glance at her sister. "Despite my sister's words, she agrees with me that you are doing well. Remarkably well. She will not admit it —not aloud—but she knows you need him. What he can offer you."

Zadione held herself perfectly still, but Mariah couldn't miss the way her eyes flashed. The way dark memories seemed to fill her gaze, reminders of a love that could've been great but was lost to control and selfishness.

Mariah straightened. "Andrian is … many things. And I know he keeps his secrets. But Zadione, he is not evil."

"No. He is not." Zadione sighed. Mariah wondered if it was an instinct, much like her human impulses. Whether she needed to breathe, even on this plane, in this body. "But he could be. It is in his blood. And with the wrong influences … I fear what he could become."

Mariah went cold. "What do you mean—"

"That's enough, sister," Qhohena interjected, her voice sterner than before. The golden goddess softened her gaze on Mariah. "If you stay by his side, then you need not worry about my sister's warnings. Any darkness that might dwell in him will always be outdueled by your light. Trust in yourself, trust in him, and trust in your strength."

Mariah tried desperately to read for more between the planes of Qhohena's smooth golden skin. She nodded, just once, but couldn't deny the way her stomach still turned, her mind and magic unsettled.

"Did you come just to warn me about him? Or is there more?"

"There is more." Zadione's words were clipped. She ran a hand through her long silver hair, brushing through the ends. They shimmered like whispered starlight. "You realize, I trust, that something occurred on the Winter Solstice."

That got Mariah's attention. She pushed out of bed, planting her feet on the ground as she glanced between the sister goddesses.

"I found an abandoned apartment in the market district.

Destitute, uninhabitable. But there was a room coated in blood, and an altar of *aberrant* at its head." Mariah had only learned of the substance yesterday, but Zadione hissed at the mention of the cursed stone. Mariah stifled her flinch and continued, "Something evil happened in that room. Something vile."

"You felt it in the *allume*, didn't you? After the Solstice?"

Mariah nodded. She could still feel it rubbing against her skin, an unwelcome toxic sludge. "I fixed it."

The goddesses stilled before sharing a furtive glance. "You ... fixed it?" Qhohena's question was quiet.

Mariah's jaw worked. "It was draining the *allume*. The lights went out. I did what I had to."

Qhohena straightened, pushing back her shoulders. "Good. We felt the poison, too. In our realm. When the walls between the paradise of the gods and this world were down, another barrier was dropped. The barrier between this world ... and Enfara. That is what the *aberrant* was used for."

Shock rattled Mariah's mind, replacing the revolting anger at the memory of the dark magic. She blinked as her light unspooled through her gut, whispering through her veins, oblivious to its former ladies.

"He *defiled* our night," Zadione hissed. "That monster turned our sacred gift into something *foul*. He is using it for something. Something that will help him get to me."

"Calm, sister. We do not yet know his intentions." Qhohena turned back to Mariah. "But ... we do know that he pulled something through that barrier. More than just planting the darkness in our *allume*. He is still trapped in Enfara, but ... perhaps a tether. An anchor of some kind. It is hard to tell." Qhohena frowned. "Everything about his power is blocked from me. When I try to look, I am met only by darkness."

"Wait. Just to clarify. This 'he' you refer to ..." Mariah glanced at the sisters. "It is *Flétrir*, right? The Scourge?"

"That is what you know him as, yes," Zadione whispered, her eyes icy and glazed.

Mariah tilted her head, turning to the Goddess of Death. "Have *you* tried? Looking for him?"

Zadione's light snapped around her. "No. If I did, it would reveal everything. He knows me, the feel of my power, too well. And if he reaches me..." The goddess's silver eyes drifted down. To Mariah's chest.

Where that essence of Zadione dwelled, hiding within Mariah's soul. The source of the silver half of her magic, that gift she'd carried all her life without even realizing it.

"You have no idea the value of what you carry, Mariah. The weight of the world, the survival of everything, depends on you."

"Do not trouble the girl, Zadione," Qhohena intervened sharply, snapping the tension that had slowly been filling the space between Mariah and the silver goddess. Mariah blinked and leaned back, a little dazed but her mind whirling. Qhohena's expression was still soft, but with an urgency in her gaze.

"You must discover what happened on the Solstice, Mariah. What they did. Who did it. And, most importantly ... what they brought through."

Qhohena's voice grew fainter as she spoke, and when Mariah blinked, the golden goddess faded to a shimmering silhouette.

But Zadione still stood there, as strong as ever, silver gaze burning with the fires of unending death.

"When was the last you heard from your family, little queen?" Zadione's words were biting and clipped, dark and foreboding. "What makes you think they are safe away from your palace and your Armature and your magic?"

Mariah's heart dropped to her feet. Her skin pebbled, cool sweat coating her brow. "What do you mean?" she croaked, throat tight.

"Protect your blood—all of it. It is more valuable than you realize." The goddess's voice was fading along with her body, whispering away into nothing.

"Wait!" Mariah lurched forward, reaching out. "That's not enough, I need to know more! I don't even know where to begin!"

"Follow your instincts. They have never failed you before; they will not fail you now."

Zadione's shadowy words were the last thing Mariah heard before the goddess blinked out of existence, plunging her room back into the weak darkness of early morning.

CHAPTER 48

The reflection looking out at Anniliese Hareth was that of a stranger.

Beautiful, yes. The same face she recognized, pale skin beneath rosy cheeks, dark brown hair delicately curled into ringlets down her back. Her gown was a deep royal blue, the honey of her eyes enhanced by the gold shimmer across her lids.

Everything about her was the same. And yet, there was so much she didn't recognize.

The flatness behind her gaze. The bags beneath her eyes. The sickly pallor of her skin, and the lack of shine in her tresses.

She couldn't remember the last time she'd slept. Ever since she'd stupidly confronted Lord Shawth about the *thing* dwelling in this castle with them, she'd felt haunted. Followed. Watched. As if something hung over her head like a storm, eager to snatch her in its clutches and drag her into that darkness, kicking and screaming.

She'd refused to meet Lady Beauchamp for tea. Refused to join her father for dinner. Refused to do anything but sit by the window in her room, trying desperately to soak up the weak rays of the spring sun. Too scared to leave, too scared to fight, too scared to move. Wasting away in the safety of her rooms.

Until today.

Her father himself had delivered the invitation. Handed it to Anniliese, her fingers curling around the fine paper, with a stern warning that she would attend, as would he. Their host had summoned them, and it was not an invitation she could refuse.

After all, Lord Shawth had something to show them. Something Lord Hareth claimed could secure the power of the Royals in the kingdom forever. No more bothersome queens, no more relying on mysterious, finicky magic to choose unworthy, clueless women who could not make hard choices. To do what needed to be done.

Anniliese didn't want to see it. Didn't want to know. She wanted to be excluded from these petty power plays. Wanted to be forgotten by Lord Shawth and her father, wanted to be ignored by the queen and her little court who played at ruling in the palace.

Anniliese wanted to melt into the walls and never be seen again.

Of course, she would not be lucky enough to get her wish. Not today.

A knock sounded on her bedroom door. She straightened. Ever the well-bred and well-trained lady of a great Onitan Royal house.

"Come in." Her voice was soft. Muted. Polished.

The handle twisted, and her father stepped through the door. His eyes quickly traced down his daughter's silhouette. His mouth tightened, and he nodded once, a terse movement.

"Good. You're ready." He picked a piece of lint off the lapel of his jacket, the only sign of his nervous energy. "It is time to go." He extended his arm to his daughter, the invitation to escort her clear.

If Anniliese were stronger, more independent, she would've refused him. Would've spit in his face for being weak, for allowing a man like Lord Shawth to do as he wished.

She was not that woman. Not the woman Mariah had asked her to be. Not fit to make such a stand for herself. She'd tried once and had been left weak and embarrassed.

Life was easier without such questions, anyways. Much simpler to fall into place where she was told to go, to let the men in her life lead her through the steps. To make those choices for her.

So, Anniliese Hareth gathered her heavy skirts and faced her father. She strode to him, placing her hand in the crook of his elbow, and let him lead her into the dark, cold halls of Khento.

EVERYONE in the castle was in attendance.

They were outside in the castle gardens, the same ones Anniliese had let Mariah and her Armature escape from all those weeks ago. Lord Shawth lounged upon a black and gold throne arranged on a temporary dais, his watery blue eyes watching as his guests filed into raised stands.

The center space of the gardens was bare, a great empty area circled by those risers, yet a buzzing sort of energy pressed on Anniliese's skin. A gentle wind brushed from the south, sweeping around her and tugging at her perfect curls.

She fiddled with her choker necklace, the delicate black stone cool against her fingertips. Her gaze fixed on the chairs beside Lord Shawth, five similar thrones of dark mahogany on the raised dais.

A jostling beside her tugged her attention away. Her father pried her fingers from his arm, patting her hand once before stepping back.

"I must join our host," he said. "Stay here with the rest of the ladies of the court."

Anniliese nodded, her mind still quiet.

As her father moved off, following the procession of the other Onitan Royal lords—Lords Beauchamp, Campion, Laurent, and Cordaro—Lady Beauchamp filled the gap Anniliese's father had left by her side.

"I heard we are in for a real treat tonight, my dear. Are you not excited?"

"Yes," Anniliese murmured, still playing with her necklace. "Very excited."

Lady Beauchamp turned away with an empty smile on her face. The other ladies of the court wore similar expressions, all pretty pets to watch their husbands and fathers and uncles convince each other of the superior power they held.

A few other lesser lords and their families were also in attendance—Lord Donnet, of Andburgh, the most vocal of them. A smile spread wide across his bullish face, and he had a feverish gleam in his eyes.

"You are all going to love this," he said, voice loud as always, carrying easily to her place on the risers. "I haven't seen it yet, of course, but Lord Shawth informed me of what to expect last night over glasses of his finest whiskey. That little whore queen will never see our next move coming."

Anniliese's attention wandered back to the Royals now gathered on the dais. They had each taken their seats beside Shawth, expressions ranging from barely concealed nervousness, to excitement, to the stoic coldness of Lord Laurent.

That hardly meant anything, though. That was the only expression the Lord of Antoris seemed to wear these days. Despite the fire magic Anniliese knew he carried in his veins, magic he rarely ever used, he was all but made of ice and stone.

"My esteemed guests." Lord Shawth's voice boomed across the gardens, and the chatter and whispers tinkling around Anniliese in the risers faded away. The Lord of Khento rose from his mock throne, tugging on the buttons of his embroidered red and black cloak, chest puffed out and a grin plastered across his face. He took a few steps forward, gaze fixed across the gardens, on the doors leading into his castle. He halted on the top dais step before turning to the risers, still wearing that foxlike smile.

"My guests," he repeated. "I thank you all for the honor of joining me this evening. Tonight, we shall usher in a new age of Onita, one in which those who are best suited to power will freely wield it."

Cheers echoed around the risers. Anniliese kept her hands

folded in front of her, expression blank and empty. The perfect porcelain doll as the men around her celebrated.

"Too long we have suffered beneath the control of a goddess who never paid us any heed. When was the last time any of you asked Qhohena for a favor, and she answered your prayer?" Mumbles of disgust answered Shawth.

"I was robbed several months ago," Lord Donnet grumbled, "and despite all my prayers and offerings, the culprit has still not been brought to justice."

"I say," continued Lord Shawth, "it is time for a change. Why should the gods decide our fate? And better yet, why should we hand our loyalty to a deity who does not deserve it?" He lifted his hands up, as if in exaltation. "No more! Qhohena is not the only god in this world. It is time we, as the leaders of our great nation, choose a new patron." Lord Shawth turned his hands to the castle doors across the gardens, gesturing feverishly.

"And I am not alone in this thought! High Priestess Ksee, if you would join us, please."

Anniliese whirled, along with the rest of the gathered court, as the castle doors swung open.

A figure strode into the gardens, clothed not in the pale gold robes Anniliese expected but in a gown of brilliant white. The material extended all the way to the figure's wrists, the high neckline wrapping around the column of her throat, the train spreading behind her across the path. Even her head was hooded, hiding her features, a demure picture of purity and submissiveness. Behind her, six other women followed, all dressed the same, all subdued and obedient.

Anniliese couldn't help her gaping mouth as she watched High Priestess Ksee walk the length of the gardens before dropping to her knees, head bowed. Her priestesses followed her lead, a pretty, white picture as they knelt before the Royals.

"We are honored to join you on this marvelous day, My Lords." Ksee's voice was the same—still grating, still too nasally —despite the change in her appearance. "We pray the God of the Stars accepts our plea and bestows his favor to us all."

Anniliese's skin prickled. *God of the Stars?* Did Ksee mean Priam?

"Has our Lord Priam spoken to you of late, High Priestess?"

Well, that answered Anniliese's question.

"Yes, My Lord." Ksee lifted her head, and the change in angle cast a bit of her face in the sunlight. She looked about the same, but there was something muted about her. Something slightly off about the pallor of her skin.

"The great god Priam speaks to me in my dreams. He tells me he is ashamed of his Consort, of Qhohena, to whom I previously dedicated my life. She has abandoned him, as she has abandoned us, and has forged her own path away from that of righteousness and good. She has even pulled her cursed sister, the wicked goddess of death, from the depths of Enfara itself and now rules in the heavens with Zadione by her side."

Shocked whispers and outraged shouts echoed through the gardens. Anniliese stilled, her blood rushing cold.

Tales of the goddess of death were whispered to all Onitan children. They were warned to hide all thoughts of the goddess, to ignore her existence, lest she learn of theirs.

Lest she use her dark powers of pain and death to snatch them from their beds and drag them down to join her in the cursed pit of the gods which she'd made both her prison and her sanctuary.

"I know, I know, my people." Ksee's voice rang out louder as she rose, turning to face the gathered crowd. The slight wrinkles in her face were more pronounced, her pale skin washed of color in the setting sun. The shouts died down with the priestess's movement; the crowd's attention was ensnared, fear thick in the air.

"It's a troublesome thought indeed to realize that our goddess has abandoned us. But as I said, Priam has spoken to me. He has shared how we might still save our country and our families."

More silence answered Ksee as she paused. Anniliese's heart thudded in her chest, her fingers back to playing with her black stone necklace.

"Priam has long hidden behind his Consort, hiding his true strength from us. But no more. Tonight, we will beseech him for his blessing and call forth the truth of his power. We know him as the one who escorts our dead, but he is so much more than that. With his power, we will become unstoppable, regardless of whatever pretty gifts Qhohena and her cursed sister may throw our way."

Fear—true, sickening, twisted fear—wormed its way into Anniliese's gut, settling low, just beneath her lungs. It clenched tight, wrapping around her insides, even as the gardens erupted into cacophonous cheers.

A slow smile spread across Ksee's face. She turned back to Lord Shawth, dipping her head to him once more.

"We are ready for you, My Lord."

Shawth nodded, and the other Royals rose from their seats as he took his first steps down the dais. The six Royal lords of Onita followed him down the garden path to where Ksee stood in the center, patiently waiting with her six white-clad priestesses kneeling behind her, each as still as a statue.

Nothing about this felt right to Anniliese. Nothing at all. But there was nothing she could do but watch.

Ksee turned to her priestesses. "Rise, followers of Priam."

They rose as one, heads still downcast.

From a pocket concealed deep within her gown, Ksee withdrew an object. A flat bit of shining black stone, inscribed with runes and letterings in a language Anniliese did not understand. The Royals strode past Ksee, each moving to stand behind a priestess.

A priestess for each lord.

When Anniliese saw the glint of six steel knives appear, it took every bit of her control—every single year of court training, every brutal slap across her ribs and thighs, every night sent to bed without dinner for speaking or acting out of turn—to keep herself from crying out. From breaking right there. From doing anything other than what she did.

Which was ... nothing.

Ksee turned to the first priestess, Lord Beauchamp standing behind her. The High Priestess murmured a few words over the stone, either too quiet or in a language that Anniliese's ears refused to register.

The girl's hands trembled beneath her white robes.

"Thank you for your sacrifice. Be with Priam." Ksee's prayer rang out across the gardens.

Just before Lord Beauchamp slit her throat.

Air choked in the priestess's lungs, her hands grappling to hold in the fluid as her lifeblood poured from her neck. It dumped over Ksee's hands, over the object she held.

Beneath the blood, the runes pulsed a strange orangish gold, like the color of a dying sun. A ringing started in Anniliese's ears, and she swore the sky darkened, just a touch.

Ksee moved to the next priestess. This time, it was Lord Cordaro who was to end her life. Those runes pulsed brighter, the air buzzed, the sky dimmed.

Again, with Lord Campion.

It was soon Anniliese's father who held a blade to a young woman's throat. The girl couldn't be much younger than Anniliese herself, and yet her father pressed cold steel to her pale neck and drew it back, spilling ruby blood across the stone in Ksee's hands.

Anniliese feared she might be sick. But she held her back rigid, her hand wrapped tightly around the choker at her neck. As if desperate to know that it was not her throat, not her blood.

Not her.

It didn't help much.

Next, Lord Laurent. His cut was deep and brutal, and the girl's head nearly split from her body as she collapsed to the ground.

By the time Ksee arrived at Lord Shawth, the grassy garden floor was slick and seeped with blood, the High Priestess's white gown stained ruby-red. The strange stone pulsed brilliantly, and above them, blotting out the setting sun, gathered a dark mass of writhing shadow.

It felt the same as the hallways of Lord Shawth's family wing.

Vile and evil and wrong, something that shouldn't exist in this world but was filled with wild glee to be here.

Shawth brandished his weapon. Ksee lifted her voice.

"Send us your might, great Priam! Bless us with the power to vanquish your enemies and emerge as the victors, forever protected by your grace."

Shawth dragged his dagger across the final priestess's throat.

The moment the priestess's blood washed over the dark stone, Anniliese screamed.

She wasn't the only one. The pressure cracked through the gardens, a whirlwind of smoke and shadow and orange-gold light. It licked and grabbed her skin, too-greedy hands desperate for more to take, take, take. Possession and control, hunger and want.

Above them, the mass of shadows split open and nightmares poured forth.

Creatures made of cracked, scaled skin and taloned feet. Creatures with maws filled with massive yellow teeth, forked tongues tasting the air, yellow poison dripping from their jaws. Leathery wings and spindly limbs, bat-like ears and glowing red eyes.

Anniliese knew them. Their depictions had been drilled into her since her schooling, plucked straight from the histories of the First War.

Mudae.

"Demons!" someone yelled.

"Monsters!" shrieked another.

Shawth lifted a hand to the crowds in the risers, even as the devils of history continued to pour forth from the sky.

"History has been a lie! These are not the demons of Enfara, but the warriors of Priam!" A beast landed beside Shawth in the blood-soaked grass, its lips pulling back into a terrifying snarl.

Shawth smiled.

"They are here to protect you. And to bring us our victory."

The crowd quieted, voices snuffing out in terror. Shawth faced the *mudae* beside him.

"Bring me what I need to break her. Bring *them* to me. As your master promised."

With a bone-chilling shriek, the demon spread its wings and launched skyward, its brethren close behind.

Anniliese could do nothing but watch them go. Everything in her was so cold, so twisted. Fear made its home in her chest, freezing her from the inside out.

Her hands wrenched hard at her choker, a desperate impulse against the thrum of the demons' wings.

The delicate jewelry snapped, the black stone falling to the grass.

She didn't look to see where it landed.

CHAPTER 49

The soft rap of a knuckle on glass pulled Mariah's attention away from the Attlehon Mountains. She twisted in her chair, grinning.

Quentin and Matheo waltzed through her balcony doors carrying two bottles of wine each, shit-eating grins spread across their faces. Mariah lifted her glass of crisp white wine, nodding for them to join her. She turned back to the long stone table where she sat, the one piece of furniture on her balcony that she'd hardly ever used. She'd chosen a seat directly in the center—not at the head—and smiled into her glass as she took another sip.

"Mariah, you'll never believe it; Matheo and I found the good wine down in the storerooms. The kind they only bring out for the balls and parties." Quentin rushed to her side, settling into the chair on her right, Matheo sitting beside him. Behind them, more figures moved through her living room, their voices drifting outside.

She eyed the bottles. "Found it, or stole it?"

"Psh." Quentin waved a hand. "Semantics. As if anyone is going to miss them."

"You would be surprised by how much the kitchen staff notices, Quentin." Delaynie sat down across the table, lovely as

383

ever in a flowing lilac gown. "I am sure they will send you a bill for those bottles shortly."

Ciana, laden beneath an overloaded platter of fruit and cheese, snorted as she set her offerings on the table, seating herself beside Delaynie. Behind her came Sebastian, carrying a similar tray, and he placed it next to the first before sitting on Ciana's other side, just across from Mariah.

Mariah took another sip from her wine as Quentin leaned forward in his seat, a wicked grin on his face, something sparking in his bottle green eyes. "Is that so, little wolf? And are you going to help me pay for them?"

"Absolutely not." Delaynie sniffed. "I won't be drinking them."

"Not even if your queen asks you to?"

Delaynie faltered slightly and quickly darted her gaze to Mariah before returning it to Quentin, a scowl twisting her sharp face.

"*My queen* can drink as much of the palace wine as she wants. You, however, are not her."

Quentin chuckled. "Oh, you've got me there. And thank the gods for that. No offense of course, M." He rolled his head to the side, tossing Mariah a wink before returning his grin to Delaynie. "But could you imagine the uproar in this city if I were a woman? What would all the ladies do without my magic coc—"

"That's enough." Mariah laughed into her wine.

It had been two days since the goddesses' visit. The first, she'd spent in a panic, fear for her family and confusion over her next task crushing her chest with every breath. The second, she'd finally been able to return to her routine—training with Trefor in the game park before seeing what she could glean from the library.

Which was, of course, nothing.

Today, she'd decided to *do* something.

Delaynie flushed a bright pink, her back rigid and hands twisting in her lap. Ciana snickered as she bit into a piece of cheese, and the remainder of Mariah's court who had settled around the table—Feran, Trefor, Kiira, Drystan, and Rylla—all tried desperately to fight back raucous laughter.

"As much as you love to talk about it, no one wants to hear about your magic cock right now, Quentin," Mariah said.

Someone—probably Trefor—gasped a laugh as Mariah set her now-empty glass on the table in front of Quentin. "And thank you for defending the staff, Delaynie. But you can tell them the wine is on my tab." She shot a glance at Quentin, pointing at her glass. "Now, be a good boy and pour your queen some of this *good* wine."

The group snapped. Quentin released a roaring laugh, Matheo doubling over with him. The entire table erupted into hysterics, Ciana nearly spitting out her bite of cheese and crackers. Trefor almost slipped out of his chair to the floor as Rylla let loose great howls of laughter. Even Sebastian chuckled, rubbing his eyes, and Delaynie shot Mariah a grateful glance as she giggled.

"Don't tell me; Quentin made a joke about his dick." A deep voice echoed across the balcony, a brush of shadow against Mariah's skin, and the laughter dropped away.

Well ... almost. Ciana still sniffed, wiping tears from her eyes, and Quentin, Trefor, and Matheo still chuckled involuntarily as Andrian stepped through the balcony doors and onto the patio.

They knew he'd be coming; she'd informed everyone as much earlier that day, just as she'd asked Drystan to invite him. He'd moved back into his room across the hall, as she'd asked, but still kept his distance.

Andrian's eyes found Mariah's, darting behind her once before resting on her with a question in his expression.

Realization struck Mariah like a lead hammer.

All the seats opposite her at the table were filled. Drystan and Kiira sat at the two heads, and Quentin had taken the chair on her right. She'd chosen this table because it had exactly twelve seats, one for each member of her court.

With Andrian being the last to arrive ... That meant the only chair left available was the one on her left. Beside her.

What would it convey if she asked Sebastian or Feran to move and sit beside her, allowing her some distance from Andrian?

She almost scoffed. Her fear was speaking to her, whispering darkness in her ear. Trying to decide her life and her future.

She refused to spend any more time bowing to her fear.

The smile that spread across her lips was mostly genuine. "Thank you for joining us, Andrian. Please, sit." She did her best to ignore the way their bond thrummed when she said his name as he dipped his head in answer and moved toward the table.

She raised an eyebrow expectantly at Quentin. "I wasn't kidding about the wine, you know."

Quentin chuckled, Matheo still grinning beside him. "As you wish, My Queen."

Mariah's smile relaxed into a grin as Quentin uncorked the bottle, pouring Mariah a glass before filling his own and passing the bottle down the table for everyone who wanted it. She focused on their small talk, taking a sip of the delicious white, even as she felt Andrian brush behind her. Her hair shifted against her neck, and she gripped her glass just a little tighter as he slid into the chair beside her. Several inches separated them, but heat still radiated from him.

For someone who acted so cold, he was always so *hot*.

Sipping her wine, she snuck a glance at him.

He was watching her, of course, leaning back in his chair, fingers drumming lightly on the table. Setting down her glass, she turned to face him more fully. She briefly hesitated before leaning across his space, reaching for the plates of cheese and meats and fruits Ciana and Sebastian had brought.

When she did, her leg brushed his, and it took every ounce of self-control she possessed to keep from gasping. Sparks danced across her skin, igniting the magic in her blood. She hurriedly gathered up a few grapes and slices of cheese before settling back, shrinking just slightly into herself.

It was wishful thinking that the other night would dull their bond. The sharp edge was relieved, but it was a momentary reprieve. The thrumming, magnetic energy was back now, stronger than ever, set alight by the graze of her skin against his.

Mariah popped a few grapes into her mouth, sweetness bursting across her tongue. Taking a swig of wine, she cleared her throat. The chatter around the table fell away, eyes turning to her expectantly.

"Thank you for coming—"

Sebastian chuckled. "You do that every time. Thank us." His face turned serious. "You need to stop. I don't think any of us would rather be anywhere else." Murmurs of agreement swept across the group, nods and smirks and giggles with them. Even Andrian's mouth twitched, his eyes shining with something too bright, too real.

She looked away quickly.

"I know I don't have to, but I want to," Mariah muttered and took a bite of cheese. It was creamy and delicate, almost like butter.

"Anyways," she said after swallowing, "as I'm sure you all remember, I went into the city a few days ago to inspect the location that received a strange call on the night of the Solstice. And we ... found something. Something I only wanted to share with my court, and not the rest of the captains and commanders currently in service of the crown. At least, not yet."

Mariah glanced around the table, being sure to hold every set of eyes that met hers.

"The building was an abandoned apartment, long since put out of use. It looked innocuous enough from the street, but inside ..." Mariah drew a deep breath, flexing her fingers beneath the table.

Andrian shifted beside her, surely feeling the rage and fear thrumming through her at the thought of what she'd seen, what she'd felt. What the goddesses had said to her after.

"Inside, something truly terrible happened. Violence. Trauma. Pain. So much pain." Mariah shuddered. "There was blood everywhere. In pools on the floor, splattered on the walls. And at the front of the room, on a pedestal, was a piece of stone."

She cut a quick glance to Andrian, meeting his stare, and he nodded. Reassurance. Her anger was justified, and so was her fear. She could—needed to—share this with the rest of this table.

"It was *aberrant.* I'm told it's used as a conduit to Enfara. And it, too, was drenched in blood, so thick I could hardly see the substance beneath. And when I touched it ... I collapsed."

"Wait, wait." Drystan leaned forward, holding a hand in the air. "What do you mean, you *touched* it?"

"Just that. I put my hand on it. And then I passed out."

Drystan's bright gold gaze bore into Mariah for several seconds before darting between Andrian and Sebastian. "And you two just *let* her?"

"I honestly didn't even realize what it was—"

"I tried to stop her, but that never works well—"

"*Excuse* me? No one *lets* me do anything—"

Sebastian, Andrian, and Mariah all spoke, their voices running together before all halting.

They shot glances at each other, Mariah glaring at everyone. Andrian cut the tension with a chuckle and leaned forward, resting his forearms on the table. His leg again brushed against Mariah's, and her sharp inhale earned her another quick glance and grin.

"I think we all agree that she shouldn't have touched it." Andrian's voice was soft, yet commanding. Mariah suppressed an urge to roll her eyes. "However, she did, and she's fine." He turned to her, black hair falling messily across his forehead. "Isn't that right, princess?"

"Yes," she grumbled, crossing her arms. "I'm perfectly fine. Can I get back to what I need to tell you all now?"

"Wait, there's more?" Feran leaned forward in his seat. "You have more to tell us than finding a crime scene and *aberrant* in the city?"

"How did everyone know what that shit was but me?" Mariah rubbed her eyes. "Yes, there's more."

Silence fell around the table again, eyes once more turned expectantly her way.

Mariah twirled the stem of her wineglass between her fingers. She felt the weight of her court's gazes, but Andrian's scorched her the most. His brow was twisted slightly as if unsure about what she was about to say next.

About how much she might be about to share.

"Early the next morning, I received a visit. From ... the goddesses." She held Andrian's stare as she said it, watched first his confusion, then his realization, and then ... more puzzlement.

A glance around the table, at the rest of the confused glances she found, told her he was not alone.

"Mariah," Delaynie spoke slowly, icy blue eyes sharp and calculating. "What do you mean, you received a visit from the goddesses?"

"I mean," Mariah said, her tone even, "that Qhohena and Zadione appeared in my bedroom. Both of them. And they spoke to me."

More silence. So silent that Mariah swore she could hear wingbeats in the air around her. She whipped her head up, scouring the skies.

Nothing.

"But that is ..." Delaynie pulled Mariah's attention back to the table. Her friend's face was still contorted, watching Mariah too closely. "That's impossible. The goddesses ... they don't have a physical form. They exist on a different plane, and no queen has ever recorded a time when they appeared to her. In *this* world."

"There have been over five thousand years of queens, Delaynie," Mariah said softly. "Who's to know what didn't get written down in Xara's day or in the centuries after? Who knows what knowledge has been lost to time?"

The group settled back into silence. Mariah could almost feel them thinking, the churning of thoughts, the unsettled feelings filtering to her from the six bonds she normally kept closed.

From the seventh bond, though, she felt something different.

Instead, it was something like ... *awe*? She locked her stare on Andrian, and while his features were carefully schooled, that usual icy mask in place, she could see it.

He believed her, and he wasn't scared or bothered or worried.

He was awestruck.

"Mariah." Drystan's soft voice pulled her attention away from Andrian. "What did the goddesses say?"

Mariah inhaled a steadying breath. "They told me that whatever I'd found ... whatever had happened ... I needed to find out what. Someone did something on the night of the Solstice. Something so terrible it could be felt in the realm of the gods, something that shook the foundation of the world. Something that poisoned our *allume* so thoroughly it caused our lights to flicker and go out."

Silence met her words. She took a sip of her wine and sat back in her chair.

The group was quiet for several heartbeats. Quentin fidgeted with his daggers, and Kiira cocked her head like a cat, the gold jewelry in her hair tinkling. Drystan rubbed his chin, and Ciana took a deep sip from her wine.

A breeze picked up and lifted the strands of Mariah's hair, brushing it across her collarbones. It had grown, just a bit, aided by a healthy diet and sleep. It was also shining again, catching her subtle golden highlights in the setting sunlight.

She was feeling more like herself for the first time in months. Herself, but ... harder. Tempered, like steel.

"Mariah," a soft voice said beside her. Calloused fingers gently brushed her forearm, heat blazing across her skin. She jerked her head to Andrian, meeting his brilliant blue gaze.

"What do you propose?"

"For what?" Her mind was blank. The feeling of his fingers on her skin ... Everything had emptied.

Two nights ago, she'd told him she wasn't ready for him to touch her.

But now, she didn't feel even the slightest hint of fear at his caress.

Could things truly change so quickly?

His answering grin was too wicked and carried too many

knowing promises. "A solution, princess. How do you propose we deal with all this?"

"Oh." She pulled her arm back, setting her wine glass on the table. "Well," she started, fidgeting with the stem. "That's why I brought you all here. For ideas. Because while I know I must do something, I don't exactly know what."

"I might have an idea."

Mariah turned to Matheo. He was leaned back in his seat, half-empty bottle of wine in front of him, a contemplative expression on his face. He scratched his chin. "What about that priestess? The one who told us where you were being kept? She spent so much time with Ksee and the others; perhaps she might've heard something."

Mariah sighed. "I've already spoken to her. She wasn't privy to the conversations about the Solstice."

"And you trust her?" Andrian's voice was quiet. "You believe she was telling you the truth?"

"I do," Mariah answered unwaveringly. "She doesn't know anything."

More silence followed. The group settled into their thoughts, the only sounds the occasional sip of wine, bite of cheese or crackers, and the wingbeats of those damn invisible eagles.

"There was one more thing." Mariah spoke again, more slowly. Attentions turned to her. She swallowed down the rush of her fear, the thick sludge that raced over her skin.

"Zadione mentioned one other thing. Something that's been bothering me for weeks—months, even—but that I've been too afraid to confront."

Sebastian leaned forward. "Mariah? Is everything okay?"

"I ... don't know." Her voice wavered, and she swallowed again. "When I was in Khento, Lord Donnet was there. Of Andburgh. My family's home. And since then, I just ..." She shook her head. "I worry about my family."

"But with Donnet in Khento, wouldn't that make Andburgh safer?" Trefor sat forward in his seat.

"That's what I thought, too," Mariah said. "But Zadione ... she said that my blood is more valuable than I realize, and I need to protect it."

"If you want us to go to Andburgh and bring them here, all you need to do is ask." Nods echoed Sebastian's words, but Mariah shook her head.

"No. We're not to that yet. And besides, my father will probably send you away. It would need to be his idea—or my mother's —to leave Andburgh and join us here."

"Sounds like we now know where you get your stubbornness from, princess."

Mariah scowled at Andrian, but it didn't meet her eyes. Not with the way humor danced in his expression.

"Perhaps a letter, then," Sebastian said. "You write to them, invite them here. We'll make sure it's sent."

Mariah nodded, relaxed. She liked having a plan. The weight of her fear lifted from her chest, just enough for her to take a full breath.

"If we may, My Queen, my sister and I will look further into the report from that apartment on the night of the Solstice." Kiira straightened in her seat, tapping the table with a painted nail. Beside her, Rylla nodded. "Surely, someone must have seen or heard something. We'll see what we can find."

"Don't terrify the poor city-folk. There are good people down in the market district," Feran said with a laugh, a smile spreading across his warm face.

Rylla grinned, her canines elongating, her nails lengthening into short claws. "I have no idea what you are talking about."

That drew chuckles and laughs from around the table, and Mariah smiled into her wine.

"That sounds good to me. I'll write the letter to my family tomorrow. The rest of you, help me research. Do what you can. Any information, no matter how trivial, could be important."

Nods answered her.

"Well ..." She set down her glass. "I suppose that's everything."

Quentin shot up, slamming his hands on the table. "I think it's time for a game."

Delaynie groaned. "A game? Seriously?"

"Oh, come on, little wolf." Quentin leaned across the table, grinning wickedly. "Two truths and a lie? Of course, you've lived such a sheltered little life up here in this big old palace; maybe you don't want to play because you know you'd lose—"

Delaynie pushed to her feet. "Fine. But only one round, and only if Ciana goes first."

"Ya—wait, what?" Ciana tossed the rest of her wine into her mouth before standing. "Why me?"

"Because," Delaynie said, already moving across the balcony and toward the doors leading to Mariah's living room. "You always give the most outrageous lie, and it's so easy to guess. If I'm going to lose, I'd rather not lose first."

Mariah smiled as her court rose from the table, filtering back inside and settling themselves on the couches, their friendly banter drifting to her on the early evening breeze. The sun had slowly set during their meeting, and Mikael was now there, busying himself in the kitchen, frantic at the number of people who'd joined her but still wearing his usual cheerful grin.

A shadow lingered by her side, even as the others moved inside. Sebastian also still stood at the table, eyes darting between Mariah, Andrian, and the rest of the group. A muscle in Mariah's jaw twitched as she leaned back and met Andrian's gaze.

"Go inside," she said, her voice soft. "I need to talk to Seb."

Surprise lit Andrian's expression, and a glance at Sebastian revealed the same. Andrian hesitated, before he flexed his jaw and nodded. He brushed behind her again as he left, walking too close, and the feel of his arm whispering across the back of her neck sent a shiver down her spine.

Another sip of wine promptly chased that chill away.

"You want to talk ... to me?" The hesitation in Sebastian's voice stung. She knew she'd been withdrawn, pulled away from him for quite some time. Certainly since she'd returned from Khento, and perhaps even a bit before that.

But then again, he was not entirely blameless for that. His anger, the aggression he'd wielded against Andrian ... She'd let it happen because she was too numb and too cold to do much beyond holding herself together. But it wasn't like him, wasn't like *her* Sebastian, and in all truth, she'd waited far too long to have this conversation.

She set her glass of wine down on the table and met his hazel stare. "When was the last time we just talked? Like we used to? Has it really been since before the Solstice?"

"When you asked me to stand in as your consort?" He slid back into his seat, leaning heavily onto his forearms, and peered up at her through thick lashes. "When I asked you if that was what you truly wanted, and you lied to me and said yes?"

"I don't think I actually said anything."

"And I think you're avoiding my point."

She smiled and sat forward, mimicking his pose. She extended a hand across the table, and he reached his to greet hers. His fingers were warm when they brushed, comforting and familiar and steady.

Her rock. Her foundation. Her friend.

"I miss you, Seb." She drew in a deep breath. "I miss you so gods-damned much. And these past few weeks, since I got home, I feel like neither of us has really been here. Not the way we used to."

He was silent for a moment, and he twisted his hand and grasped her fingers in his. There was nothing romantic about the way he touched her, the way he held her hand. Perhaps they'd been together in that way once, when wild magic had rocked her sideways, but that part of their relationship was long since put to rest. Now, he was just ... Sebastian.

"I've missed you too, Mariah." His words were shuddering. She tried to catch his gaze, but he hid it from her. "And, gods, I am so, so sorry." Another deep inhale, and she knew.

Knew he was crying. That he was hiding his tears from her.

"I'm sorry I wasn't there. That I couldn't protect you. I'm sorry that they touched you, that they got to you. I'm sorry that I *failed*."

"Sebastian." She tightened her grip on his fingers, pulling his arm toward her. It yanked up his attention, forcing him to meet her gaze. His eyes were rimmed in tears, his handsome face wrought with devastation and rage and terror and failure.

Everything he'd felt since that night in the courtyard. It was all laid out, so plain for her to see.

This was why he'd reacted the way he had. Sebastian had always demanded perfection of himself, and nearly always succeeded.

But this time, with his most important job, he thought he'd failed.

"You didn't fail. Do you hear me?" She dug her fingers into his palms, opening the bond between them just enough to feel the twinge of pain with him. "There was nothing you could have done to stop them from getting to me that night. *I* am the one who pushed them too far. I'm not saying I'm at fault for my capture—that was always the Royals—but the decisions that led to it were my own. I know you strive for perfection. That you are afraid of failing me. And I'm here to tell you, as your queen, that you have done anything but."

She was crying now too, thick tears running hot and heavy down her cheeks. "Sebastian, you are the one who saved me. Without you and our friends, I would still be trapped in that fucking pit. So do not for a second think that anything was your fault."

Mariah dropped the wall between their bond fully. Waves of emotion pushed and pulled across that bridge between their minds—anger and pain and regret and grief and sorrow and love. So much shared and traded, passed between two souls as if they were one.

Mariah had always thought the Armature would offer her nothing more than physical protection, a means of deterrence from those who might wish her harm.

But in that moment, it was so much more. It had always been so much more.

A gentle, steady smile pulled across Sebastian's lips.

"I'm so glad you're home."

"I am, too." She squeezed his hand once more before dropping it. She slowly closed the bond between them, the tide of their emotions withdrawing back into themselves.

"There's one other thing."

Sebastian pulled his own hand back, gaze inquisitive. "Oh?"

Mariah smiled, taking a final sip of her wine. "Can you leave Andrian alone? Please? I know he's an ass, and I know his … involvement. But I need to work through that with him on my own. And I need you to trust me that I can make the right decision for myself."

Sebastian stiffened for a moment before relaxing, slightly deflating as if weights lifted from his shoulders. He dropped his gaze into his lap, staring at his hands.

"I never meant to isolate him. I'm sorry if that was the wrong decision."

"You know how you told me to stop saying 'thank you?'" She leaned forward again, catching his gaze. "Well. I'm now telling you to stop apologizing. We're past that. Just trust me. Please."

Sebastian drew in a deep, shaky inhale. "I'll always trust you, Mariah."

"I know. It's just nice to hear you say it."

His lips quirked at the sides. "So. Nothing that happened is my fault. I need to back off and forgive Andrian. Anything else?"

Mariah smiled—a genuine smile—and stood from the table, the chair scraping across the floor. "You can get another glass of wine with me, and you can have some fun with everyone. And tomorrow, we'll get to work on figuring out how to save this kingdom."

She snatched her glass and walked toward the sliding balcony doors, Sebastian meeting her at the end of the table.

Inside, teams were being formed, more wine was being poured, and Mikael was depositing platters loaded with steaming food on the tables. Andrian leaned against a pillar near the doors, and her gaze found his. Something flickered in his eyes, something that spoke of more than they could discuss tonight.

More than she was ready to discuss that night. One emotional conversation per evening was enough for her.

The sound of voices greeted her when she pushed inside. Ciana's tinkling laugh rang out, a chime amongst the clamor.

"Seb!" Ciana called, her hand waving in the air. "Get over here. You're on my team."

With a last glance at Mariah, Sebastian joined the group.

Leaving Mariah beside Andrian. He stepped closer to her, warm against her shoulder. She turned, tilting her head up to meet his gaze.

She opened her mouth to speak, not sure what would come out, but he beat her to it.

"Join them," he murmured, voice low and quiet. It warmed her belly, made heat flush to her cheeks.

He smiled and leaned closer. Just a touch.

"You know how much I love that blush, princess," he said, words just for her, "but you deserve this night. We'll talk later. I'm not going anywhere."

He pulled back, and she swallowed. The wild blue of his eyes was so warm, almost on fire, and familiar shadows danced in their depths.

With a final nod and a smile, she joined her court—her friends, the first she'd ever had—as laughter echoed off the mountains.

Outside on the balcony railing, a golden eagle watched on. A black butterfly floated past the eagle on its perch before soaring up on the night winds and joining the stars above.

CHAPTER 50

"May I come in?"

Andrian twisted in his chair, glancing over his shoulder at the figure standing in the doorway to Mariah's study.

He wasn't quite sure why he was in there; she wasn't in her rooms, instead down training with Trefor and Matheo in the game park.

He was even less sure how Sebastian had found him and was halfway to forming a scowl before he noticed the way the other man stood. Anxious and slightly uncomfortable, hands stuffed in his pockets and eyes downcast, a muscle in his jaw working.

Andrian swallowed his building retort and nodded. "Sure." He slammed his book shut and set it on the white wood table as Sebastian stepped into the study and settled in the chair beside Andrian.

The two men sat there, the air a little tense. Andrian studied Sebastian, resting one hand on the armrest, the other brushing a finger across his tightly closed lips. Ever since their return from Khento, Sebastian had been hostile, aggressive, and angry, especially toward Andrian. But that talk he'd had with Mariah last night, that quiet moment they'd shared while the others had been making teams and settling into their night of revelry ...

Andrian had always known Mariah was magic. That she had powers extending far beyond just the silver-gold light in her veins. But the way she'd drained Sebastian of his rage in just a few minutes was a shock even to him.

None of that gave him any clue what *this* talk could be about, though.

Sebastian leaned forward, eyes focusing on the book Andrian was reading. His brows pushed together even as he smiled.

"'*A History of Dragons?*'" He looked at Andrian. "Again?"

Andrian grunted, shifting in his seat. "What? It's a favorite."

"Oh, trust me. I know. I remember that being the one item you brought with you when you moved to the capital. How you read it every night for eight years. Often aloud and to the rest of us, whether we wanted to listen or not."

"Of course, you all wanted to listen. They're stories about dragons." Andrian shot him a weak glare out of the corner of his eye. "What boys aren't obsessed with dragons?"

Sebastian chuckled. "Fair," He settled further into the seat. "They say the stories are true. But they're all so old, they feel more like fiction now."

"I still believe in them."

They fell silent. For the briefest of moments, Andrian let himself fall into the idea of dragons walking the earth again. Three decades into his life, and he didn't think he'd ever give up those boyhood dreams of one day hearing one roar.

Andrian almost scoffed at himself. He might believe in the stories, but to think dragons could return? Those were the wishes of a child.

The dragons were gone, and they were never coming back.

"Did you need something, Sebastian?" Andrian's tone was almost bored as he turned to fully face Sebastian. The other man's brows were knitted in contemplation, and he shook his head slightly before running a hand through his hair.

"Yes," he began, his words slow. "I have ..." He drew a deep breath, rubbing his palms across his thighs. "I've come to apologize."

Well … of all things, Andrian certainly hadn't expected *that*.

Andrian blinked. "Apologize?"

"Yes. Apologize." Sebastian turned away, looking at the marble fireplace on the other side of the room. "I was an ass … after. I've known you my entire life, and the moment that was tested, I treated you like an enemy. And I'm … I'm sorry."

Andrian kept his expression schooled into neutrality, a skill he practiced far too often. "I was an enemy. You don't have to apologize for treating me like one."

"No. No, you weren't. And we all know—knew—that. But I was so angry at myself for failing that I didn't even care."

A heavy silence extended between them.

"She wouldn't have been taken if it hadn't been for me," Andrian murmured, his voice too soft, too quiet, too empty.

Sebastian whipped his head. "But you don't remember any of it. You have no memories until she woke you up with the bond." His eyes narrowed. "Right?"

Andrian's jaw worked. "No, I don't remember any of it. I've tried; trust me. I spent those early days back from Khento drowning myself. Both in whiskey and in my memories. But no matter how deep I tried to go, nothing came up. It's like it never even happened." He scratched at a frayed thread in his chair.

"But even without my memories, I know, in my *soul*, that it was my hands who took her. It was this body that tormented her. And for her, it *was* me. He might not have been me, but he wore my face, and spoke with my voice." He refused to meet Sebastian's stare, too afraid of what he might find there.

Andrian drew in a shaky inhale. "I keep people distanced from me because I don't want to see them hurt. To lose them. To be the one who causes those things. It happened first with my mother, and I swore to myself, never again." He clenched his hands. "But I was too fucking weak. I let Mariah in. And it happened again."

He finally risked a glance at Sebastian, whose eyes were now wide, expression open. "I don't want your pity. I don't want your apologies. You treated me the way I deserved. You treated me the way I would've treated myself, had the roles been reversed."

The room was quiet and still. Understanding—something the two men hadn't shared with the other in a long, long time—passed between them. The understanding of two brothers who knew each other too well and were now bound by something more than just an oath or a mark on their chest.

Love made things weak, but once tempered, it could be forged into something indestructible.

Even love between brothers, even if they shared no blood.

Sebastian broke the stillness with a great, drawling inhale. "Okay, then. No apologies." He smiled. "Acknowledgment, then?"

Andrian leaned back and nodded. "Yes. Acknowledgment."

Sebastian smiled tentatively. "Good." His gaze drifted around the room before returning to Andrian. "So, what do you plan to do now?"

"What do you mean?" Andrian ran a hand through his hair.

It was too fucking long.

"I mean," Sebastian said, something like humor in his hazel eyes, "Mariah has obviously started to forgive you. I can see it on you; how desperately you need her to. So, I'll ask again: what do you plan to do now?"

Andrian tensed. He'd been taking things with Mariah one day at a time. They hadn't been alone together since she'd confronted him the night they'd returned from the market district, and he'd been too cautious to try seeking her out.

But nothing had made him happier than when his skin brushed hers at the meeting, and she hadn't shied away. When she'd leaned into him instead, the hint of that blush creeping into her cheeks.

He swallowed. "I've been trying to give her space. I want her to tell me when she's ready for ... more. From me." Gods, this was uncomfortable. He'd shared stories with Sebastian in the past—all young men did, growing up hot-blooded and stupid with a city at their disposal—but about Mariah? Something about that made him defensive, a primal instinct roaring awake.

"I know. That's good." Sebastian grinned. "But I think she may also be waiting for you."

"What?" Andrian bit out, astonishment and surprise like coils of lightning in his veins. "Waiting for me to do *what*?"

Sebastian waved his hand, exasperated. "I don't know. Make some grand gesture." His grin widened. "Trust me, Andrian. Last night, none of us saw a woman afraid. Perhaps her fear is still there, lingering, but she is conquering it. As she does most things. I think she has a lot of emotion bottled up and is just waiting for an offering of trust so she can let it all out."

Andrian remembered last night, vividly. The group was rowdy, drunk, and happy. And despite everything, despite the tension that still existed between them, Mariah had sat beside him, the warmth of her body pressed against his thigh. She'd lost so much weight in that hellhole, but she was putting it all back, and the sight of the healthy flush to her cheeks, the tan glow of her skin ... Fuck, it had taken all his strength to walk away. To go back to his rooms when the night was over and not linger there in her threshold like a lost puppy, waiting for her to either let him in or slam the door in his face.

Perhaps Sebastian had a point. He was so fucking gone, and the only way either of them would get past this was through an act of trust. Something he could offer to show her that he was hers in every way he could be.

Andrian tapped his finger against the armrest, feeling the annoying brush of his hair on the back of his neck.

"I think I have an idea."

CHAPTER 51

"You almost had me there on that last move. I'll give you that much."

Mariah cast Matheo a sidelong glance as she panted, smearing sand across her sweat-drenched skin. His face was streaked with sand and dust and dirt as he sprawled across the grass outside the sparring pit, grinning broadly. "'*Almost?*' I had a dagger to your throat."

"Yeah, well ..." Matheo's grin faltered as he shrugged, grumbling, "you weren't supposed to have the dagger, anyways."

"Oh, dear Matheo." She leaned over, clasping a hand to his bare shoulder. "I *always* have my dagger."

Behind them, Trefor snickered, his laughter turning into a cough with the glare Matheo shot over his shoulder.

This morning was one of many like it before. Always Trefor, usually Matheo, and sometimes the others, meeting in the game park to train. The build felt slow, but Mariah was feeling strong again.

She was still underweight, but when she looked in the mirror her cheeks were no longer sallow and sunken, her bones no longer jutted out at odd painful angles. Her curves were filling back in, muscle forming in her arms and legs.

That morning, she'd picked up her favored twin short swords for the first time since being freed.

Mariah grinned, releasing Matheo. "Either way, it was a good spar. Thank you for joining us."

Matheo sagged into the soft grass, messy brown hair falling across his forehead. "Of course. I'm so proud of you."

She smiled but didn't answer.

She was proud of herself, too.

"C'mon," she said. "We need to get to the aviary before today's hawks are sent out." She reached for the pocket of her training leathers, feeling the outline of the small, folded letter.

The letter to her family.

Matheo sprang to his feet. Trefor brushed his shoulder against hers, a playful shove.

"Lead the way, queenie," Trefor said with a grin. Mariah chuckled, adjusted her dagger on her thigh, and set off down the forest trail.

The woods were quiet, save for the chirping of the birds and the rustling of the leaves. Mariah tilted her chin skyward, savoring the sun's warmth on her cheeks. It was past the Spring Equinox now, when the moons vanished from the sky. She'd been born on an Equinox—the Autumnal Equinox—but always felt the most uncomfortable during those nights. The darkness of the night left her feeling wary and nervous.

She was always glad when the moons emerged the next night and only grew more at ease as they waxed through their next cycle.

Which, in this case, would be the Summer Solstice. As much as the thought of that magic energized her, she wasn't ready to deal with how it would be handled. Not with the schemes of the Winter Solstice still lingering.

The stables appeared through the trees and Mariah paused on the path, glancing around.

"Mariah? Everything alright?"

Mariah shook her head, brow furrowed. "I just realized I've never actually been to the aviary before."

Matheo chuckled. "It's just around the stables. This way." He veered right down the path, heading away from the palace. Mariah followed, Trefor at her side.

They passed by the sprawling stables, the low-roofed buildings replaced by taller, multi-story facilities. They were still within the palace gates, but Mariah had never been this far from the main courtyard. Her brow creased as she studied the simple structures with their unadorned windows and plain doors.

"It's the barracks."

Mariah turned to Trefor. "What?"

He nodded at the buildings. "The barracks. City Guards stationed at the palace stay there while on assignment. It was also where we—the Marked, I mean—lived and trained for twenty-one years."

"You lived here? All of you?"

"It's nicer than it looks," Matheo said over his shoulder. Trefor grinned.

"It is," he said. "It's really not bad. When we were young, we all shared a large dormitory together, but we were given our own rooms as we grew older. But it was nice to have a place that was ours, away from the sophistication of palace life."

Mariah snorted. "Sophistication. Right."

Trefor bumped her with a shoulder. "Things only got debaucherous after you arrived." Their laughs rang out into the clear morning.

"The aviary is just up ahead." Matheo pointed at a domed structure tucked against the wall ringing the palace land. It was made of woven metal, a solid barrier against the outside world, but one that still allowed light and air to pass through it. Towering roosts sat in a corner and the screeches of falcons and hawks cut through the air.

A middle-aged man pushed through a hinged gate, his weatherworn face twisted into a scowl. His shoulder-length gray hair was pulled back in a low bun, revealing a savage scar across his left cheek. In his gloved hand, he carried a hooded falcon, the bird quiet and calm.

"What do you boys want? I'm busy," he called out gruffly. The falcon jostled its neat pewter feathers.

Mariah stepped out from behind Matheo, grimacing as her hand shot up in an awkward wave. "I need to post a letter. To Andburgh."

The man's eyes widened, his mouth popping open. "Oh— Your Majesty, I—please forgive me—"

"It's fine." Mariah smiled. "I often have the same reaction when these two come around."

"Hey," Matheo said indignantly. "What do you mean—"

"Can you help me? Post the letter, that is?" Mariah interrupted, her smile sweetening as Matheo crossed his arms and huffed.

The man nodded. "Of course, Your Majesty." He whispered something to the falcon on his arm, just before removing its hood. With a shake of its head, it spread its wings and launched into flight, soaring up through the trees and vanishing from sight.

The man turned. "This way, Your Majesty."

Mariah followed him through the gate and into the domed aviary. Birds were perched on tall limbs, soaking in the sun's rays, while a few roosted quietly in their nests.

"What's your name?"

"Aldric, Your Majesty."

"It's nice to meet you, Aldric. Please, call me Mariah."

Aldric smiled. "I thank you for the kindness, but having lived most my life on the outskirts of the palace, I prefer to give our queen the respect she is owed."

Mariah liked this man.

He turned back to his birds, trilling softly. A medium-sized red hawk landed on his glove, and Aldric quickly slid a hood over its eyes before setting it on a perch. He tied a small leather cylinder to its leg, just large enough to carry a handful of rolled letters.

"To Andburgh, you said?"

Mariah nodded. "Yes."

Aldric extended a hand. "If I may have the letter? It should arrive in two days. Shaye here is one of my swiftest flyers."

"How do they know where to go?" Matheo asked curiously, leaning against the roosts, fingers dangerously close to the beak of a sharp-eyed falcon.

"I assume, lad, that you're familiar with Onita's system of post."

"Well ..." Matheo shrugged. "I know there are aviaries just like this one all over Verith and through Onita. I know each city, town, and castle has a roost, and they can distribute letters quickly throughout the kingdom. But how do they do it? The birds, I mean?"

Aldric huffed indignantly. "Because they are bred to do it. They are trained to. The messenger hawks and falcons of Onita are no ordinary hawks and falcons. Maybe it's our goddesses' blessed magic or just the paths of nature, but they are born knowing where to fly when asked. Some are more stubborn than the others, but they know this land better than we do."

"Okay, but ... do they need a special language? Or do they speak the common tongue?"

Trefor's question, and Aldric's exasperated response, faded from Mariah's ears as she withdrew the folded piece of paper from her pocket. She stared at it, heart hammering in her ears, before slowing unfolding the cream page and reading the words she'd spent hours agonizing over.

Mother, Father, & Ellan:

I hope all is well. I miss you. More than anything. The capital is magical and everything I hoped it would be, but ... I need to see you.

Please consider a visit to Verith as soon as possible. There is so much I want to share with you, and I am bursting at my skin to speak to you again. I can have an escort sent to you within the week.

Write back when you get this.

I miss you.

Love, Mariah

P.S.,

Mom, I read the diary. Please come—we have so much to talk about.

"Your Majesty?"

Mariah glanced up at Aldric, mild concern etched across his face. The aviary had fallen silent but for the trills of the birds and the flaps of wings.

"Sorry," she murmured. She refolded the letter, rolling it into a cylinder, before handing it to Aldric. The aviarist gave her an assured smile as he slipped it into Shaye's scroll carrier, binding the ends securely.

"Shaye will take care of your message, Your Majesty. You can place your faith in her. She has never let me down."

The hawk fixed a fierce yellow eye on Mariah, and Mariah could've sworn that she dipped her head.

She swallowed. "Thank you, Aldric." Before any doubts could set in, she whirled toward the exit. "Matheo, if you get any closer to that bird, it's going to peck your fingers."

"Hey, we're friends—ow!"

Trefor laughed. "No one's fault but your own, idiot."

Matheo glared. "Why don't you go fu—"

"Please, for the love of the gods, can you stop bickering? I need a shower." Mariah cast one final glance towards Aldric and Shaye, who both still watched her with too-sharp gazes.

She nodded once and pushed through the gate, walking back towards the palace before she could see if they nodded back.

Mariah tossed a light farewell to both Trefor and Matheo before slipping inside her rooms, the heavy white wood closing behind her with a *snick.*

She took a few steps into her rooms and froze.

"You're an idiot. Nothing is better than Sacalan whiskey. And aren't you from there?"

Mariah would know that deep, shadowy voice anywhere.

"You're right, I am. That means I know full well its shortcomings. As much as I hate those pirates, there is nothing sweeter than Kizar rum."

Andrian and *Sebastian?* In her study? Together?

Set alight with confusion—and more than a little interest—she moved to the glass-paneled door and watched them.

They both sat in comfortable chairs, weapons leaned against a wall, their postures almost mirrors of each other. Sebastian was relaxed, in a way he hadn't been since she'd arrived home.

Andrian, however ...

He'd always been beautiful. She'd seen it the moment their gazes had met in the palace courtyard all those months ago. But now, to see him sitting with his friend, an easy smile spread across his face, eyes sparkling in the light of the *allume* lamp sitting on the table ...

Something had lifted from him. No shadows clung to his shoulders; no darkness plagued his gaze. He looked as he probably should've been, if his father hadn't used him in his desperate grasps for power and his mother was accepted in this kingdom despite her northern heritage.

So much about Andrian's darkness was forged by his fate, and Mariah's heart broke to see what he could've been. As bright and brilliant as the sun, instead of tragic like a falling star.

Andrian's attention drifted away from Sebastian and snagged on Mariah through the glass doors. He held his smile, but it softened, settling into his usual smirk. Something tugged in her mind, feelings of warmth stretching into her soul.

The bond.

He had figured out how to grab into their bond and *pull*.

Good goddess.

She raised her eyebrows but said nothing as she pushed through the doors. Sebastian quickly took in her appearance before a similar, easy grin stretched across his face.

"Good morning, Mariah. Looking beautiful as ever."

"Why, thank you, Seb." She wore a grin now, unfamiliar—but not unwelcome—lightness bubbling in her chest. "I always feel my best when I'm a little bit dirty."

"Careful, princess." Andrian leaned back in his chair, settling against the suede. "You keep talking like that, and we'll start to think you're flirting."

"Hm," she hummed, tilting her head. Something surged in her —something hot and wild and desperate. "But what if I am?"

"And on that note." Sebastian cleared his throat to mask his laugh and stood. "I should get going. I hear you're to be coronated in two days."

Mariah stiffened. She'd forgotten; or, at least, she'd forgotten as best she could. Delaynie was working with Ryenne's ladies and Liliane, the young priestess, to arrange Mariah's coronation. It was to be a small affair, something quiet and intimate, as all coronations were. This was not a ceremony for the people, but a moment shared between queens. The opposite of Mariah's Winter Solstice, but just as powerful in its own way.

And with Mariah's ascension, with the rise of a new queen … her predecessor would return to the stars. Mariah refused to dwell on what that would mean. She hadn't seen Ryenne since the day she'd visited Mariah after her return and, in truth, had been too afraid to call on her again.

The thought of a world without Queen Ryenne, the one guiding force she'd had since arriving in Verith …

It was paralyzing.

Mariah plastered a smile on her face. "Yes. Exciting times." She glanced at them both one more time. "I need to go shower. I'll see you both later?"

Sebastian smiled and nodded.

Andrian, however, said nothing. He simply sat and watched her with an unreadable expression, running a finger across his lips.

Mariah swallowed and left the room, dashing to her bathroom and the shower waiting for her like something chased her.

THE WATER WAS SCALDING, dust and sand and dirt sleuthing off her skin and down the drain, and all it had done was boil her blood more than it already was.

Mariah quickly dressed in a pair of leggings and a mustard yellow cotton blouse, staring at her reflection as she toweled off her short hair. While she missed the length and was looking forward to it growing ... This cut suited her. The *new* her. The one that was dragged through Enfara itself and spit out the other side, damaged but stronger.

Setting the brush down, she squared her shoulders and strode from her bathroom and through her room into the living and kitchen space beyond.

And halted.

Sebastian had left, as he'd said, but the room was not empty.

Andrian sat at her dining table, leaned back too-casually in a chair, arms folded across his broad chest.

Watching her.

A nervousness sparked in her belly, fluttering about like butterflies. "Something I can help you with?"

His lips twitched. "Yes, actually." Andrian sat forward, pushing back from the table. "I have a favor to ask of you."

Mariah eyed him cautiously. "A ... favor?" She shifted from foot to foot before crossing her arms herself. "What do you need?"

"Well, now that's a complicated question, princess." He now wore a full smirk, but it faltered, just slightly, as he took a step from around the table. He walked to her slowly, as if afraid she might flee.

She hated that she'd made him feel that way. That she was a flight risk, too afraid to stand near him.

She'd decided to no longer be a slave to her fear.

So she took her own step forward, meeting him halfway. His eyes widened, and his nostrils flared, but he said nothing.

They stood no more than a foot from each other, gazes locked.

"What do you need, Andrian?" Her repeated question was pitched low, her voice rough.

He'd spoken those same words to her, too, once. In this very room.

He smiled down at her. Reaching a hand into his pocket, he pulled out something long and shiny and ... metal? Her brow twisted, and he opened his hand to reveal a delicate pair of scissors.

The kind Ciana had used on her, just a few weeks prior.

The kind used for cutting hair.

She met his brilliant blue stare. His smile was soft and hesitant, something so unlike him yet so painfully beautiful.

"I need you to give me a haircut."

CHAPTER 52

"Okay. Sit."

Mariah gestured to the cushioned vanity chair in her bathroom, waving the scissors in her hand impatiently. Andrian's lip pulled back into that familiar smirk as he slid smoothly into the seat. He met her gaze in the mirror, humor flashing in his marvelous eyes.

"Nervous, princess?"

Mariah scoffed. "No. Of course not." She stepped closer to him, close enough to feel his warmth. "I've cut plenty of men's hair before. Yours is no different."

"Oh, is that so?" His smirk stretched into a grin. "Care to elaborate?"

"Nope." She popped the "p" in her response. Her hands were clammy.

A heavy pause filled the room.

"Just your brother's, then?"

She shot her gaze back up to meet his in the mirror. His smile had softened, as had his expression.

Mariah only hummed low in her chest and turned back to his hair. It was quite long, the longest it'd been since she'd met him. It had always fallen a bit errantly but there was a sort of reason to the madness. Messy, yet polished. Tousled, yet groomed. Never past his ears, never reaching his brow.

Now, the onyx strands brushed against his neck. His ears were nearly concealed behind black, and it fell into his eyes.

"Who normally cuts your hair?" She didn't ask what she really wanted to. She looked in the mirror, flinching away when she found him watching her.

Why ask me *to cut it?*

"Since moving to the palace? There are plenty of barbers in the market district; they aren't too hard to find."

"And why didn't you go find one before today?"

A shrug. "Not sure, princess. Maybe I was looking to change some things."

Her chest squeezed. There was so much behind that statement. So many unspoken words, so many unasked questions. She nodded, not meeting his gaze.

"You were right, by the way."

Out of the corner of her eye, she saw an eyebrow lift. "Oh? About what?"

She cleared her throat. "About my brother." She dared a glance. Held it. Let herself fall into his stare. "He's the only one whose hair I've cut. Our mother worked long hours at the clinic, and our father would've tried, but ... that was a terrifying idea. So I learned to cut Ellan's hair, and he learned to cut mine." She squeezed her fingers around the scissors, the cool metal slowly warming in her palm. "Although I hardly ever let him take any off mine. I loved my long hair."

She could feel him in the silence, weighing what to say next.

"I love the short hair, too."

Mariah smiled. "So do I."

She took one last half-step closer to him. The tips of her slightly shaking fingers brushed against the black strands of his hair.

His forearms clenched. A muscle feathered in his jaw.

A smile tugged at her lips. Emboldened, she dove her fingers deeper into his hair.

It was softer than she remembered. Like strands of silk. Black as night, dark as the shadows that exist opposite every bright light. She ran her hands through its length, pulling it back from his face and away from his ears. She stood behind him, tapping the scissors against her palm as she met his gaze in the mirror.

Pained. His expression was *pained*. And desperate. Holding so much back.

Something surged in her.

Something like … excitement.

She gripped the scissors loosely, the metal now familiar. Flashes of memory painted her minds' eye: sitting outside by the firepit with her brother, snipping bits of dark auburn hair as he spoke of his friend's antics, or told a story about finding a quiet brook deep within the Ivory Forest. Of wanting to bring the pretty girl with yellow-blonde hair who lived down the road there with him. How the wildflowers that grew along its bank would look so lovely woven into her curls.

"Mariah." Andrian's soft voice pulled her from her thoughts. She blinked, her hand still wrapped around the scissors.

He met her gaze with a smile. "I trust you. I … I just want you to know that."

She smiled at him a little shyly, nodded, and with a deep inhale made the first cut.

"You know, princess, it doesn't look half bad."

"'*Half bad?*'" Mariah scoffed, setting down her scissors. She stepped back and rested her hip against the bathroom counter before crossing her arms and cocking her head, a faint smile on her lips. "I don't think you've ever looked better."

He froze, a hand in his hair, eyes blowing wide. His shock was … almost humorous, and she didn't stop the laugh that slipped free from her chest.

Besides, she meant it.

She'd gotten quite skilled in her life at cutting her brother's hair, and it wasn't a skill she shared with many. But she knew what she was doing with a man's haircut, and even with time and lack of practice, she hadn't lost it.

She'd trimmed most of the length around his ears and neck and cut back his bangs so they no longer fell haphazardly into his eyes. But she'd still left a good portion of the length on top, enough for fingers to dig into.

Enough to grab.

Mariah swallowed, giving her head a slight shake, and brushed away those thoughts.

She'd also found a sharp-edged razor in one of the drawers—where it had come from, she had no idea—and had used it carefully to trim around his ears and neck and face just a little closer.

The result was polished yet roguish.

Perfect.

And standing that close to him while doing it …

She uncrossed her arms, rubbing her sweaty palms on her leggings. He dropped his hand from his hair at the same time, relaxing in his seat.

"Never looked better?" A touch of a smile on his lips. "Tell me more about that."

"Alright, now you're pushing it." She pushed off the counter, striding for the exit. She didn't know where she was going, but just had the feeling that this moment, whatever this was, was nearing its end.

"Mariah … wait."

She halted less than a foot from her bathroom door and closed her eyes, clenching her eyelids so tight she saw spots. Mariah drew in a deep breath and held it for a moment before expelling it through her lips.

"A haircut isn't all you wanted, is it?"

There was a shuffle and the scraping of a chair on marble floors.

"I … No. Well, it was. I needed a haircut. But there's more." A pause, his voice closer to her than before. Then, quieter: "With you, there's always more."

Mariah drew in another shuddering breath before turning slowly to face him.

Andrian stood in the middle of her bathroom, tall, imposing, yet subdued. Open.

Vulnerable.

He drew in a deep breath of his own, shadows flickering around his shoulders.

"I know you said I didn't have to beg for your forgiveness. That there was nothing for you to forgive. And maybe you're right. Maybe there is nothing to forgive. But those scars on your back and the shadows in your eyes say something different."

Her stomach twisted and knotted around itself. "Andrian—"

"I'm not finished." His eyes flashed with intensity and desperation. "You say that instead of begging for your forgiveness, I should beg for your trust. So, that's exactly what I'm going to do. With a story." He sagged as a bit of heaviness left him. He raked a hand through his hair. "A story ... about my mother."

Mariah blinked, shock spiking through her. *His mother?* The one he spoke of in the past tense?

The one his father had mocked in that last meeting before their world had flipped upside down?

"I told you that my mother was Leuxrithian. It's where I got ... *this.*" He lifted a hand, shadows dancing around his fingers. "Growing up, she was—she was all I had. Antoris is a cold place, and you've met my father." He nearly spat the word, lip curling into a grimace. "She was the only thing I loved about living there. The first person I loved." He met Mariah's gaze. "The *only* person I loved ... until you."

Mariah's heart hammered against her ribs. Her hands clenched into fists at her sides. Magic rippled through her veins.

Andrian took a small step closer.

"You asked who usually gave me my haircuts. I told you that after coming to Verith, it was always some barber in the market district. But before that ... it was my mother. And during those moments, when it was just me and her, she would teach me bits about her culture. Her language, her legends, the magic of her people." More shadows danced around his shoulders. "My father hated it, of course, but that didn't stop her. I think it was her version of rebellion against him, in a way."

Mariah's throat tried to close around her words, but she pushed them out anyway. "Why are you telling me this?"

"Because," Andrian said, his voice thick. With a slow, measured movement, he lowered himself to his knees. His head bowed, and he laid a hand flat on the white marble floor.

"Because you told me to beg for your trust, and this is the only way I know how. Yes, others besides my mother have cut my hair. But since her, I've never let myself be touched like that by someone I love. Because I haven't loved *anyone* since her. Don't you understand?" He looked up at her, peeking through stray strands of his hair. "My love got her *killed*. And it will do the same to you. That's my deepest secret, my darkest truth. I'm fucking terrified because I love you more than I love myself, and that means I will always be destined to lose you."

Her hands shook at her sides. Tears brushed against the back of her eyes and settled in her throat.

"I'm not sure this is convincing me to trust you."

He laughed—a sorrowful, bitter sound. "I have nothing left to give you other than my honesty, Mariah. I warned you long ago I would bring you nothing but pain. That my love for you was selfish." He shook his head. "And it will never not be selfish, but if this is my fate, then I accept it now."

Her mind spun. This felt so much like before, when he had come to her with his grand confessions. But that was before they'd been taken. Before he'd been captured, along with her.

This man kneeling on the floor before her was broken, just like her.

With a racing heart and clammy hands, she took a step toward him. Then another.

"Why?" she whispered, the breath hoarse as it left her lungs.

He glanced up, confusion twisting his brow.

She took another step.

"Why ... me? Why love *me?*" She bit her lip. "Why did this happen?"

The hint of a smile touched his lips. "I don't know, Mariah. I don't think anyone does. Perhaps only the gods know."

"No. The gods have nothing to do with it." She remembered her conversation with the goddesses. "That much, I'm sure of."

Andrian narrowed his eyes, his mouth tightening. "Fine. Not the gods. But perhaps something. Or maybe nothing at all. It doesn't matter. I don't think there's an answer to that question. There is no 'why.' *I love you,*" he growled, voice pitching lower near the end. "And I don't care if you don't want to hear me say it. Because it's true, and I know you feel the same."

She held her breath, counting each beat of her heart in her ears. It thudded against her chest like a war drum, a march toward a fate she'd always tried to fight.

Love would be your retribution.

She lifted her chin.

"You're right," she said, taking one more step to him.

He held her gaze, the tanzanite steady and blazing.

"I do feel the same. I do love you, Andrian Laurent, and despite the part of myself that's terrified, that hates this weakness, I can't stop it. Can't fight it. But," she said, breaking from his too-bright stare to look at her hands. Her callouses were reforming, each mark and scar and imperfection a reminder of her strength. Of what she'd endured.

Of what she *would* endure.

"But," she repeated, dropping her hands.

He watched her with so much intensity, she was amazed he still knelt on the floor. Energy crackled around him, shadows winding down his arms.

"There is only one way you can earn back my trust."

"Anything," he ground out, his voice a hoarse whisper. "Mariah, I would do anything. Even if you asked me to journey to Enfara itself, to face the Scourge alone, I would do it."

She smiled gently at him, heavy sadness filling the cracks in her chest. "I know you would. But that's not it. I need you to answer one very simple question. Tell me the truth, and I think ..." She drew in a great breath, lifting her gaze quickly to the ceiling before returning it to him. "I think I can learn to trust you again."

He nodded. "Okay. Ask your question. Whatever it is, I'll answer it."

She met his stare, and for just a moment, a surge of fear—anxiety, nervousness, trepidation—washed over her.

But instead of pushing it away, she let it exist. It rolled through her before receding, washing away as a wave returns to the ocean. With a final, deep inhale, she spoke.

"Andrian, what does *nio* mean?"

CHAPTER 53

"Andrian, what does *nio* mean?"

Andrian's heart dropped to his feet.

It wasn't the question that panicked him—not exactly. And it wasn't the thought of answering it, either.

It was hearing *that* question, *that* word, from her lips. After all this time. When she'd told him so clearly not to call her it anymore, after he'd slipped up and done it anyways and she'd retreated from him.

And yet, there she was. Standing a few feet from him as he knelt on the cold marble floors in her ridiculous bathing chamber. Asking him the meaning of a word that had slipped from his mouth many months ago. A word he'd tried to convince himself he meant as an insult, a dig at her and her power.

A word he'd always known meant so much more.

He lifted his head, lips curling into a sad smile.

"Really? Are you sure you want to know?"

Her brow furrowed, a mark of her hesitation. But silver-gold light flickered in her forest green eyes as she lifted her chin and nodded.

Always so defiant, even to her fear. He huffed a desolate laugh and dropped his gaze to his hands, where they rested on his thighs.

"*Nio*," he began, "is an old Leuxrithian word. My mother always told me it was special—that for her people it held special meaning, special powers." He chuckled, shaking his head. "I hadn't thought of it in years. Not since that day she first taught it to me. I couldn't have been older than eight years old. But then, for some reason, when I met you it just … slipped out. I couldn't control it, just like I couldn't control any other gods-damned thing about myself around you. I tried to convince you—convince *myself*—that it was some sort of insult, something you should be disgusted by. But I think eventually, I could no longer fool myself and therefore could no longer fool you."

He knew he was rambling. The meaning was just there, on the tip of his tongue. But it was catching in his throat, and he couldn't quite push it out.

Until she took another step closer, standing so near that her eucalyptus and jasmine scent wrapped around him. He could've leaned forward and rested his head on her hip if he wanted.

But he didn't. He remained immobile, waiting for her. As he always had and always would.

"Andrian," she repeated hoarsely. "What does *nio* mean?"

He exhaled. A long, steady release of breath. A weight unfurled from his chest.

The answer spilled from him.

"It means 'moon.' Specifically, 'my moon.' The Leuxrithians have stories about the moons, about how there may be two now, but that wasn't always the case … and that wouldn't be the way of it forever." He looked up at her and felt his heart crack in his chest.

"It was always a word of worship, *nio*. It always meant I was worshiping *you*."

Tears filled those magnificent eyes. The silver-gold living within the forest pulsed like a heartbeat, pushing up from her skin with each rasping breath. She lifted her hands, and they trembled slightly.

He didn't shut his eyes until the calloused skin of her palms met his cheeks, when her fingers slid along his face and curled into the now-short strands of his hair. Her hands tightened and her scent grew stronger, heady and crisp, like a forest at night.

He couldn't stop his sharp inhale the moment her forehead met his, her skin hot and burning against his. Her exhale brushed gently across his skin, carrying more jasmine with it.

"Andrian." Her voice was a soft, shuddering whisper.

He smiled. "Mariah." He hesitated and then spoke again. "*Nio.*"

She shivered, the movement traveling through her body and into his own. He forced his eyes open and found his vision filled with a forest.

A tear splashed against his cheek, and he wasn't quite sure whose it was.

"I love you," she murmured.

They were the most beautiful words he'd ever heard.

"I love you too. Until the stars blink out of existence and the moons fall from the sky."

She huffed against him, a breathy laugh, and pulled slightly away.

"Do you remember the last time you said that to me?"

"I do." He grinned. "In the gallery."

"Yes. In the gallery." She released his face and stepped back. The loss of her was like a punch to his gut, but a look danced in her eyes. Something that kept him planted in place, still on his knees.

Something that made his pants feel a little bit tighter.

"In the gallery," she repeated, "when you told me you would never be crazy enough to show me how much I drove you insane. Not until 'the stars blinked out of existence and the moons dropped from the sky.'" She kept walking back, taking short, shuffling steps away from him and through the bathroom door toward her bed in the room just beyond. His gaze was locked on her as she moved, marking her every step.

But he didn't speak.

"I take it," she continued, hips reaching the edge of the bed.

She leaned back, stretching out her long, lithe legs. "That those two things must've happened, hm? Or perhaps you just ... changed your mind?"

"Let's just say, *nio*, that I had a spiritual awakening of sorts." His cock was hard between his legs. His body begged to go to her, the discomfort of it all bordering on painful.

But he didn't dare move.

Not when she stood there, looking like that, after having just told him those three little words he would rip the heavens apart to hear every single moment for the rest of his days.

In the other room, she hummed. "A spiritual awakening. I like that. Or perhaps ... a religious one?" She cocked her head.

His usual smirk broke free. "I don't consider myself very religious."

"Oh? I seem to recall someone just a few moments ago admitting to calling me a name that was always meant to worship. To worship *me*." She rested her palms on the down duvet.

His body twitched. He clenched his hands into fists. "What do you want, Mariah?"

She smiled, slow and wicked.

"I want you to prove it. Show me what it means to be worshiped by you."

Gods.

Blood pounded in his ears as breath panted from his lungs. His hands still clenched, his cock still hard, as he picked up a foot, moving to step it in front of him.

A sound—a click of a tongue—froze him in place.

"Ah ah." She tsked. "I haven't been to the temple in some time, I'll admit. But I do know that when we worship, we do so *on our knees.*"

Her eyes blazed, her cheeks and neck flushed that beautiful shade of pink, as his smirk morphed into a wicked grin. Every inch of him was on fire; all his ice melted away.

"Not sure how you expect me to worship you from all the way over here, *nio*."

"I guess you'll just have to figure out how to get to me, then." She leaned back further, lips twitching. "Crawling might suffice."

He debated pushing her. Giving her a biting retort, some stinging reply. He didn't think he'd ever crawled before in his life.

But, then again, he didn't think he'd ever kneeled before, either.

He knew what this was. Another way to prove himself. Another way to show that she could trust him, that there was no part of him he was scared to keep from her.

So, he lowered his knee back to the floor. Dropped his hands to the cool marble.

And crawled, one agonizing movement at a time.

Her eyes blazed brighter, and her skin sparked and glowed with each step he took. His hands hit the rug beneath her bed, warm and soft, his knees following.

He didn't stop until a bare foot on his shoulder halted him in his tracks. He raised an eyebrow, the place where their skin touched too hot and burning.

She smiled down at him, a dark queen illuminated by glowing power. "Who would've thought you could be such a good boy following my orders like that?"

A growl started in his chest. He sat back on his heels, snatching her foot before she could wrench it away.

"Yes, I'll follow your orders." He tugged on her ankle, the sound of her soft gasp as she slid across the bed shooting straight to his cock. "But only until you get in my way. Once that happens …" Andrian slid his hand up, wrapping it around her calf. He shuffled closer, hand gliding up the curve of her leg. He brushed his nose along her thigh, exhaling as he moved to the gap of bare skin between her leggings and her simple sweater.

His hand slid behind her back, thumb grazing her skin, just as his breath whispered across her stomach. Gods, her skin. Everywhere they touched, it was like lightning crackling. Raw energy and power, lust and love and heat and magic.

When she jumped at his breath, biting her lip, he smiled.

Sliding his other arm around her body, he hooked his thumbs

into the waistband of her leggings. His body shook, but he at least held his hands steady. He glanced up, her gaze locked on him, raw desperation and need written across her ethereal face.

But he still needed to hear it. From her.

"Do you trust me?" His words were whispered, but she heard them. He suspected with the way their bond was singing a wild song, the raw magnitude of the moment thrumming between them, he could've simply thought the words and she would've heard.

She hesitated for a moment—just one, pausing moment—before that familiar strength, that beautiful power, retook control, and she nodded.

He nodded in return, his breaths still panting against her skin. Digging his fingers into her flesh, into the material of her leggings, he gave her a single, simple command.

"Raise your hips, *nio*."

CHAPTER 54

Mariah couldn't have resisted his command even if she'd tried.

She did as he asked and raised her hips. Andrian slid her leggings and underwear off in one smooth movement, discarding them behind him on the floor.

He still hadn't broken his stare from hers. Not even as he picked up her foot and placed a painfully gentle kiss on the inside of her calf.

And then her thigh.

His breath was hot as he skimmed his lips across her skin. Her core tightened; her entire body too sensitive. Their bond sang between them, freed from the restraints she'd wrapped so tightly around it—ever since it'd been formed out of necessity and desperation. He pressed in closer, rising to his knees, hand moving up her back and beneath her sweater.

She waited for the fear to come.

But as she stared into his tanzanite eyes, it never did.

He paused when his gaze was level with hers, his heat wrapping around her. She was bare from the waist down, and frustration bolted through her, hot and wild, at the fact that he was still so clothed.

He must've read that frustration because his smile faltered, his eyes dimming. His burning heat was replaced with something far more serious, far more urgent.

"Are you okay?"

Gods. Of course, after everything, he misread her exasperation as something darker. Her heart squeezed. Tears—more tears—pushed behind her eyes.

She leaned forward, wrapping her legs around him. She stroked her fingers across his brow before burying them in his hair. Her body trembled, months and months of buried feelings and pain and need coursing through her, fueled only by their neglected and ravenous bond. In her soul, in that place where her magic dwelled, that bond sang as if each touch of his skin made it brighter.

It was as if all the feelings of the bonding, feelings she'd suppressed in the aftermath of her capture, were rushing back. Stronger than they'd been with any of the others, more vibrant, more alive. Something *more* than an Armature, something fated beyond the power of the gods.

"Yes, Andrian," she whispered. Again, she rested her forehead against his. "I'm okay." She inhaled once, energy thrumming across her skin. "But if you don't fuck me right now, I might kill you."

Even from her angle, she could just make out his answering grin.

"What happened to your patience, princess? What happened to being worshiped?"

A soft whine slipped past her lips. "Fuck being worshiped. I just want you."

When she slammed her lips to his, the world stopped.

Her magic ignited, lighting up her blood. The way he tasted, mixed with that familiar, beloved smell of rain and sandalwood. The way he growled against her, pressing into her as he bit her lip, his tongue pushing into her mouth ...

Gods, she'd missed this. Missed him. So much anguish, regret, and pain these last few months.

No more. She was done.

She wrapped her hand around the back of his neck and pulled him even closer. And bit him back.

"*Fuck.*" Andrian chuckled into her mouth. In a too-fast movement, he slid his hands around her hips, lifting them both up and pushing back onto the mattress. His hands were under her before her back hit the comforter, lifting her sweater and tossing it away. His fingers snapped the clasp of her bra, and just as quickly, that was gone, too. He settled over her, his lips moving to the sensitive skin beneath her ear, traveling down her neck.

"Why are you still dressed," Mariah growled, that aggravation back, teeth clenched as she dug her fingers into the corded muscle of his forearms.

Andrian chuckled against her collarbone, shifting above her. Just enough so she could feel *him* pressing against her core, hard and hot and thick.

"I'm worshiping. Remember, princess?" He peered up before propping an arm on either side of her. He bent down and licked a smooth line between her breasts and up the column of her throat.

Mariah almost choked on her breath, gasping as his lips settled against her ear.

"I'm already yours, Mariah. I've always been yours. Let me make you *mine.*"

His claiming kiss swallowed a half-hearted retort resting on the tip of her tongue. Her heart jolted at their clash of hot breath and teeth, a desperate search and devouring of the other.

When Andrian pulled away, she was panting for air, her chest heaving with her thundering heartbeat. He slid to the column of her throat, peppering kisses and stinging bites down her neck and across her collarbone. He traced a path back between her breasts, across her stomach, settling between her legs.

His breath fanned across her bared center, and she writhed on the bed. He pinned her in place with an arm across her stomach. A soft chuckle had her opening her eyes.

He stared at her, something ravenous and consuming in his gaze.

"Time to learn another word."

She clenched her fists around the sheets.

"Is now really the time?" she gasped.

Andrian's smile broadened. "Oh, yes." He shifted, freeing his other arm. Slowly, possessively, he pressed a finger against her—not into her, but *on* her, right against that collection of too-sensitive nerves.

Mariah broke, her eyes fluttering closed as she tilted her head back into the mattress, body shuddering.

"Hm." He hummed. "So fucking wet for me, *nio*. Do you know what else you are?"

She couldn't answer him. Only shook her head, one quick jolt to the side.

Andrian chuckled again. He removed his finger and replaced it with his mouth, his hand now digging into her thigh.

"*Svass, nio*." He groaned against her. "It means *sweet*. And you taste like the sweetest nectar the gods have ever dared to make."

And, as if it were Andrian's last meal, he devoured her.

Mariah lost herself to the feeling of his mouth on her. The heavy, urgent swipes of his tongue. The gentle nipping of his teeth against her clit.

She felt as if she were floating. Lifting into the heavens, rising to join the stars. Magic and power and love crackled around her, around them, and it wasn't long before the rising tide of her climax swept toward her.

As it washed over her, pulling a shuddering moan from her lips, something in their bond changed. Snapped into place, shifted and grew more solid. A thundering, ancient, magnetic power, intoxicating in its strength.

Andrian's lips against her thigh, and then beneath her navel, yanked her back into her body. Back to the present. Her eyes flew to his, the brilliant blue wide and blazing and hungry.

Fast as an adder, she pressed her hand against the column of his throat. He froze, eyebrow lifting.

"Your turn." Her voice was hoarse, low and husky in her throat.

Andrian gave her a dark and feral grin.

"My turn for what?" He answered her with shadows and smoke.

She sat up, pushing him with her. He stood, backing away from the bed. She followed him, standing before him, bare as the day she was born.

Not long ago, she'd been unable to stomach him touching her.

Now, she couldn't stop.

She snaked her hands beneath his shirt, lifting the hem. He met her halfway, pulling it over his head and shoulders and tossing it aside. She paused for a moment, staring at the Mark on his chest. Jagged scars now bisected it, the results of a bond made with a too-dull blade and a shaky, malnourished hand.

"Hey," he said, pulling her attention back to his face. Some of the heat had dimmed, concern now filling the depths of his eyes. "Are you okay?"

Again. That gentleness. He was the same Andrian, still sour and angry and brooding, but with a new layer of softness, a vulnerability that broke her and built her back up again.

She lightly brushed her fingers across his Mark and scars. "Despite everything that happened, I wouldn't change it."

He blinked. "You wouldn't?"

"No." She drew in a breath, her hands tracing a path across his chest, down the tightened muscles in his stomach. "Because without it all, without everything we went through, I wouldn't have you. Not like this." She reached into her mind and tugged on their bond. He jerked in response, hands flexing and eyes widening. "Not the way I have you now."

"I was stupid for not doing it sooner. For letting my father intimidate me. Blind and pathetic and selfish." His words were growled, low in his throat, rumbling through his chest.

Mariah only smiled. "It wasn't just you. I was a fool for letting those men dictate my life. But ... I don't want to talk about that tonight." She stepped closer, her hands reaching for the waistband of his pants. "Instead, I think you deserve a reward for your worship."

The softness left him, his eyes hooded and darkened. "Did you not just beg me to fuck you?" He nipped at her bottom lip.

She tsked. "I changed my mind." Still holding his stare, she popped the first button to his pants, sliding her hand into the fabric. He inhaled sharply, nostrils flaring as she wrapped it around his cock. Her mouth watered at his hot thickness, at the bead of moisture gathered at the tip that she swiped away with her thumb.

With a slow, teasing movement, she dropped to her knees.

Andrian's trousers followed, and soon they, too, were discarded across the room.

Without breaking his stare, she took his length in her hands and licked him once from base to tip. He tasted salty and sweet, with that hint of rain and sandalwood beneath it all.

His head rocked back with a groan, eyes fluttering closed, as she took him fully in her mouth.

"Gods ... *nio* ..." His fingers wound into her hair, gripping onto the roots. The pull was painful, but she welcomed it as she took him deeper, swallowing him down her throat even as tears burned behind her eyes. Her hands reached up, over the hard lines of his stomach and across his hips, nails digging in and scratching as they went, making her own type of claim.

His grip on her hair tightened. He pulled back on her head, tugging her away from him, his cock sliding from her mouth with a wet pop. She tilted her head up to meet his gaze, a protest on her lips, only to find his expression devastated and absolutely pained. His hand gripped the back of her neck as he yanked her from the floor, a yelp slipping from her throat.

Andrian pushed forward, and she stepped back in surprise, her shoulders meeting the wall behind her. He crowded into her, breath hot and desperate against her skin.

"Enough of that, *nio*," he growled, hands gripping her thighs. In an easy movement, he picked her up, wedging her against the wall. She felt his cock between them, hot and thick and wet from her mouth, and her magic danced along her skin. He glanced at it, sighing and resting his forehead against hers as his own shadows brushed her cheek.

"Andrian?"

He smiled at her, enough joy in his eyes to shatter worlds. "Mariah," he whispered before he claimed her lips again in a kiss.

Her hands wound into his hair, gripping the soft strands as he snaked a hand between them, fisting his length and lining himself up with her.

Their magic danced together as he finally pushed into her, filling and forgiving and claiming.

She gasped for breath. "Fuck, Andrian—I am … you are …"

He rested a hand on the wall behind her, arm shaking. "I know, Mariah." He held her gaze, so much unsaid whirling behind the blue. "I know."

Then he *moved*.

At first, his thrusts were slow and steady, almost hesitant.

But it wasn't long until that bond between their souls burned hotter, shimmering with silver and gold and shadow and smoke. It rippled with the song of the moon and the sun and the stars, ancient powers greeting each other after so many millennia apart.

Their control snapped.

The wall behind her rattled and shook, their blended breathing ragged and desperate. Mariah rose again on that tide, their bond and the heavy expression in Andrian's eyes carrying her up, higher and higher.

He pressed his forehead against hers, sweat dampened hair brushing across her face.

"Blind me, *nio*."

The same words he'd used on the balcony. So many different times he'd told her exactly how he felt, but neither of them were ready to be truthful.

She whispered back words she'd doled out too sparingly the last time.

"I love you, Andrian."

Together, they dropped over a bridge of light and shadow, their souls entwined as magic danced in the air around them.

CHAPTER 55

The bright spring sun was warm on Ryenne's pale cheeks. She tipped her head, ignoring the stiffness in her neck and the pain in her back, closing her eyes against the glare.

She was always so cold now. Every muscle and joint in her body ached. Her skin sagged, her once-lovely blonde hair now grayed and thin. Most days, she could hardly get out of bed or leave her rooms.

Of course, that had nothing to do with her age. She'd been a shell of herself for months, ever since her seven Armature were brought down to six.

Other queens in the past had lost Armature before the end of their reigns. It sometimes happened; lives were often claimed by conflict long before old age had its chance. But those queens were young, at the height of their reigns, and could continue with the full power of the goddess in their veins.

Ryenne had no such luxury. Already weakened, already lost, Cedoric's death had stolen the last of her fight.

Today, though ... today, she'd forced herself from her bed. Had asked one of her ladies, Seiren, to help her dress and escort her down to her favorite courtyard garden. It was filled with cherry

434

blossoms and azaleas, the latter's floral blooms filling the air as butterflies flitted from flower to flower. She'd wanted to enjoy the palace, the beauty of her kingdom, one last time.

Because tomorrow was Mariah's coronation. The formal beginning of the life of the eleventh Queen of Onita.

And with the beginning of one life, the other had to end.

"My Queen?" A familiar, beloved voice rumbled above her.

Ryenne cracked open her eyes, meeting Kalen's deep brown gaze. He was just as aged as her, just as tired, but he'd always been stronger. He left their rooms every day and kept his presence in the palace known. But he always returned to her, never asking questions, only holding her close as her exhaustion drowned her.

Over three hundred and fifty years of life, and she was so, so tired.

She smiled up at him, invigorated by the sun's warmth. "My love. Sit with me."

He nodded, bracing himself heavily on his cane as he settled on the bench beside her.

She leaned against him with a sigh, resting her head on his shoulder.

"It is such a beautiful day today, don't you think? With the azaleas blooming and the butterflies out in the gardens."

"Yes. It is beautiful. But none of it compares to you."

She wheezed a laugh. "Oh, Kalen. All these years, and you still try to make me blush."

"Try?" He shifted, turning so he could meet her gaze, fake shock on his face. "Does that mean it didn't work?"

Ryenne smiled. "Of course it worked, my love. It always works."

Kalen answered her with a warm grin of his own before settling back against the bench, Ryenne's head again resting on his shoulder. They remained like that for a long moment, an old queen and her consort, watching the butterflies dance in the air.

More footsteps sounded from the hallways leading to the courtyard. Five more figures emerged, stepping into the sunny flowering glade, each one as aged and tired and quiet as the couple on the bench.

Ryenne lifted her head from Kalen's shoulder as her Armature approached. More smiles, more than she'd had in days. Weeks.

And yet, they were still missing one. Cedoric's loss pricked at her like a knife, the wounds still not healed. Never healed.

But soon, those wounds would no longer matter.

"How did you all find me?" The comfort of their familiar presence surrounded her like a fortress. Her fortress. Their bonds remained, but they were so weak now, the magic bridging her soul to theirs diminishing with each new bond Mariah made. That, too, was the way of things. They had enough to stay by her side until the very end. But she could no longer feel them, could no longer trade presence and emotions like others might trade friendly words and embraces.

Orryn stepped forward, his once-long, dark hair now dull and gray. She looked up at him as he rested a hand on her shoulder. "Even without the bond, we will always know where you are, Ryenne. We will always find you."

Tears pricked behind her eyes. With a delicate sniff, she quickly wiped them away. "Even ... even after tomorrow? Even after it is done?" She didn't need to finish those words. They all knew what she meant.

"Even then. Our souls are yours, and we will follow you until we are nothing but forgotten specks of dust between the worlds." Warren's words were soft, just as he was; he had always been the most lyrical of them.

Ryenne felt more tears forming, but they did not fall. She was too old to spare more than a few.

She was just so ... tired.

"Steven." She turned to a tall man whose auburn hair had always set him apart. Now it was as faded as the rest, stripped of life by the passage of time. But his eyes were as bright as ever, just as icy blue and fierce as they'd been the day he'd sworn his oath at her Selection.

"Have you had a chance to ... to say goodbye to your family?"

A hush fell upon the small group. Steven smiled, expression pensive and quiet and only a little sad.

"Yes," he said. "We are having dinner tonight. We've always known this day would come, ever since Briella became pregnant. I knew one day the magic keeping us here would fade, and they would be left without me." He paused, and Ryenne dared not speak.

She didn't think she could.

"But," Steven continued, "I am glad. While not all has gone to plan—far from it—at least this part did. At least I will not have to see myself outlive my daughter. We raised Delaynie to be strong, for just this moment. Knowing that we leave this kingdom with her, with Lady Ciana and Queen Mariah, soothes the sting of loss."

There were murmurs around the group, more than a few wiping tears from their eyes and coughing emotion from their throats.

Somehow, some way, Ryenne found her voice, aided by a gentle squeeze from Kalen around her hand. "Yes. The goddess has blessed the kingdom with strength to see Onita through the coming years. Although, I still do wish that Mariah did not have to suffer through what she did to get here."

More murmurs of agreement.

Ryenne drew in a deep breath. "Regardless, my time—our time—is over. We've fulfilled our service. It is time to rest."

"What do you most look forward to? On the ... on the other side?" Ryenne smiled at Warren's quiet question. None of them knew quite what awaited them after tomorrow, but she had her faith.

After all these long centuries, even when she'd lost so much and gained so little, she would always have her faith.

"Cedoric," Ryenne said, his name catching in her throat. "I will look forward most to seeing Cedoric. It has not been the same since he left us." She glanced around at this group of men who'd spent several lifetimes by her side and had never wavered, never faltered.

Ryenne prayed Mariah would have the same. That she had the same now. Ryenne believed she did, from what she'd seen, but every queen was different, and every Armature unique.

She rose from the bench, her joints aching. Her hand shook as she rested it heavily on her cane, but she met each set of eyes, as much love and devotion in them as there was on the day hundreds of years ago when they'd sworn themselves to her forever.

"I look forward to being whole again. To being complete. United with the gods, and all seven of you by my side, for eternity."

Hundreds of years, and she was ready to rest.

CHAPTER 56

Andrian had always thought the bathtub in the queen's chambers was a bit ridiculous. Far too large, far too indulgent.

But as he sank further into the decadently warm water, he could feel his opinion on the matter change.

Especially when the sound of soft footsteps had his eyes cracking open. His queen walked into the bathroom, shedding her silk robe and stepping into the tub, settling herself across from him.

Much too far.

That wouldn't do.

He knew hunger consumed his expression. His cock hardened beneath the surface of the water; his fingers twitched on the armrests.

Mariah simply smiled at him, a wicked little expression, before closing her eyes and dunking her head beneath the surface. Her legs brushed his, and it took every ounce of his control to keep himself from latching onto her, from dragging her to him.

But he refrained, and she reemerged a few moments later, pushing her wet hair from her face and wiping the water from her eyes. She blinked at him, lashes heavy with droplets of water, and grinned.

"Oh, please," Mariah purred. "Don't look at me like that. Am I not allowed to enjoy a bath in peace?"

"No. You're not. Not anymore."

She pouted. "And why is that? Just can't get enough?"

He growled, leaning forward as he braced his arms on the ledge. "No. I'll never get enough of you. I feel like a man starved, and even if I indulge on you every single day for the rest of my life, I will never be sated."

It was true. A day had passed since he'd asked her to cut his hair. A day since he'd gotten down on his knees and begged, pleaded that she find it in herself to trust him again. A day since he'd shared the last little pieces of himself, the only ones he had left.

A day since he'd told her that all along, he'd been worshiping her, even when he hadn't known it.

Her eyes widened for just a moment, bottled emotion flashing behind the forest green. It didn't drop away, not quite, but it shifted into something more playful, more teasing.

More ... *Mariah.*

"Isn't that sweet," she said, another smile twisting her lips. "I might feel the same. But, as much as I love you, I still love my baths more." She leaned back. "And right now, I desperately need to wash my hair."

He watched her for a moment, deciding his next words. "Let me do it."

She stilled. "What?"

He swallowed, his blood hotter than the water around him. "Let me wash your hair."

Her eyes darted between his before she shrugged. "Fine. I suppose."

Andrian huffed a laugh. *Brat.* "Turn around. And grab the shampoo."

Surprisingly, she did as he asked. Swiping the bottle off the ledge, Mariah turned and slid back. She handed him the bottle, tucking herself between his knees. He squeezed a coin-sized amount into his palm before clipping the bottle closed, setting it behind him, and ran a finger down her arm. His lips twitched as goosebumps rose along her flesh.

No matter what she tried to hide from him, her body would always betray her.

"Lean back," he murmured. She did, and he slid his hands into her hair, working the shampoo into a rich lather. A high-pitched groan slipped from her throat, and his grin widened.

"Why history?"

Her question surprised him, his hands still tangled deep in her hair. Despite the shortened length, it was still thick. Easy to get lost in. "What do you mean?"

"You've always spoken of history differently than you do other things. You read, but not the fictions that Sebastian does. It's always some old text, legends from a time long passed. So ... why? Of all subjects to be drawn to, why that one?"

He hummed as he resumed his ministrations, massaging the skin of her scalp. "I think that answer is far more complicated than the question, *nio*."

She twisted, meeting his gaze over her shoulder. Her expression was open and vulnerable, and it squeezed something in his heart.

"I have time."

He chuckled. "Alright." Placated, she turned back. He ran a handful of water over her hair, rinsing out the suds.

"When I was a boy ... life was not simple. Or easy. I was a lord's son, an heir to a Royal house, but that guaranteed me no luxuries. I had to be the strongest, the most well-spoken, the best. Perfect. I started training at eight with the armsmaster. That was when I got my first blisters, my first lashings. They were never terrible, never enough to permanently mar me, but just enough to cause lasting pain." He took a breath. "I had lessons with the librarians every day in the afternoon after training. And even though every muscle in my body hurt, I still loved those lessons. Especially the ones on history."

The memories washed over him, some of the only good ones he had of his childhood, and he smiled.

"There was one book. *A History of Dragons.* It was the subject of our lesson one day, but I never wanted it to stop there. It was the first time I truly escaped that castle, lost in the past when great dragons walked the earth, epic battles waged and terrible enemies defeated."

He gripped her head between his hands, tipping her back until her hair met the water and her eyes stared up at him. Her gaze searched his as he rinsed out the shampoo before letting her sit up. Still running his hands through her soft hair, unable to stop, he continued.

"When I was Marked, I kept the habit. Brought my favorite books with me when I moved to Verith. Our lessons continued, and history was always my favorite. I would spend my free time in the library, lost in the dustiest, most ancient texts I could find."

Slowly, begrudgingly, his hands untangled themselves from her hair. She twisted, her hip pressed against his leg, her arms folded in her lap beneath the surface.

"I wish I had known you then," she said quietly. Those eyes were still so open. So painfully brilliant.

He chuckled, low and dark. "No, *nio*. You don't. I was moody and standoffish."

"Right." Her words were dry. "Because you're so bright and bubbly now."

She had a point. Still, he let his jaw drop, pasting his best attempt at an aghast expression on his face. "*Me?* I am an absolute delight, princess. The life of every party."

She giggled, and the sound was light enough to lift his soul, cracking it in half, just a bit more.

If there was any part of Andrian that didn't already belong to her, it disappeared with that giggle.

He smiled and brushed a hand down the side of her face. Water dripped across her cheek, splashing onto her shoulder, her green eyes shimmering with the silver-gold of her magic.

"What about you, *nio*?" His question was barely more than a whisper. "Beyond the horse and the dagger, what did younger you find happiness with?"

Mariah smiled, a little shyly. "You mean, before I turned eighteen and found the taverns?" That smile faltered, and she glanced away.

"Yes," was all he said. She looked back at him, and he elaborated. "Your past doesn't matter to me, Mariah. I know you were unhappy in that place, so you did what you could to create a semblance of freedom for yourself. I could never fault you for that."

That shy smile returned. "If you say so," she murmured, shifting against him.

Mariah hesitated again, but another brush of his fingers across her cheek, down her arm, was all the encouragement she needed. She leaned back against him, tucking the top of her head beneath his chin. She heaved a contented sigh.

That unfamiliar place in his chest where his heart resided squeezed painfully, enough to hold his breath in his lungs.

"Well," she began, her sweet breath tickling his chest. "I loved —love—Kodie. And I loved the Ivory Forest. Most of my days were spent lost between the aspen and spruce trees, watching the birds overhead or trying to chase the rabbits through the underbrush. But I think most of my happiness, my *true* happiness, was found with my family."

That wasn't a surprise to Andrian. He remembered those nights, just a few months ago, when she'd told him stories from home. All stories of her family—her healer mother, her soldier father, and her younger brother who was still learning his place in the world.

"I had no friends in Andburgh," she continued, "mostly by choice. So, my only real companions were my family. Mornings on the training pitch with my father. Afternoons hunting in the woods with my brother. And stolen moments with my mother sprinkled between the two." She drew in a heavy breath. "I wish ... I wish I had asked her more questions. Had learned more from her. She left me that book, that journal she said would hold all the answers, but ever since ... since we got back, I've only been brave enough to open it once." She shuddered, and a twinge of curiosity picked at his mind.

"Never again, though. Whatever answers it might carry, I don't want them. But I think about her. Far more often than I probably should. And I know there are things only she can tell me, things that might help us figure out all the bullshit that happened on the Solstice. But ..."

"Fear," he finished, reaching for her hand. She looked up and he met her gaze. "But you're afraid of what you might find."

Her answering smile was tight. "I've been afraid of a lot lately." Frustration twisted her mouth into a frown. "I've never been afraid before. I don't know how to deal with it." Her eyes flickered. "But ... I faced it with you, so perhaps I'm learning."

Andrian's throat closed. It took him a few seconds, but eventually, he found his voice. "They'll receive your letter. They'll come. And I look forward to meeting them when they do."

Her brow furrowed, amusement dancing in her eyes. "Really? You do?"

Andrian smiled and pressed a kiss to the soft skin beneath her ear. "I do, My Queen." Another kiss and an inhale of the ever-present jasmine on her skin. "I think you'll find it all particularly mortifying, which sweetens it a bit." He drew away with a laugh just as she swatted his arm.

He was still laughing when she faced him fully. She cocked her head, wet hair brushing her collarbones, and watched him.

And he simply watched her back, his stare unwavering.

After what felt like an eternity, she smiled. A slow, coy smile, something far more wicked than before.

"You know," she started, her voice gravelly. His hand clenched into a fist on his knee. "I think this might be my new favorite thing."

"What?" he said, his voice rough. "Talking about your parents?"

She shook her head, smile widening. "No." She leaned

forward, laying her hands flat on the bottom of the tub. "I mean, taking baths ... with you in them."

Fucking gods. He couldn't stop his body's reaction to this woman, even if he tried. He shifted slightly, lifting an eyebrow. "Is that so, princess?"

She bit her lip, slipping her right hand across his hip and pressing it to the porcelain behind him. "Oh yes," she purred, leaning into him until her lips brushed his. "It makes things *far* more interesting."

He groaned. But just as he was about to lean forward and capture her lips with his own, a boom reverberated through the bathing chamber. Mariah froze, eyes darting to the door, but she didn't move or draw away. Her bedroom door clicked open, and footsteps smacked across the marble floor.

"Mariah? Where in the Goddess's name are you?"

Andrian recognized the voice instantly, but there wasn't enough time to react before the sliding bathroom door was pulled open and Ciana burst in, her cheeks bright with a flush of exertion that morphed into something far more mortified.

Mariah glanced over her shoulder at her best friend.

"I think knocking is appropriate when entering one's bathroom, Cee."

To her credit, Ciana didn't back down. Still flushed a brilliant pink, she instead locked her hands on her hips, tossing her golden curls over her shoulder.

"So, this is where you've both been for the past day. I thought you hated him?" She turned her glare to Andrian, but then flushed harder, and looked away.

Mariah turned back to him, amusement and warmth and joy dancing in her eyes.

All things that made him so unbelievably happy.

"No," Mariah murmured. "I don't hate him."

"Ugh," Ciana groaned, spinning away. "Just ... get out here as soon as possible. In case you forgot, you're getting coronated tomorrow, and we have to decide on your dress." Ciana stomped from the room, shouting to whoever she'd brought with her.

Which was Sebastian, if Andrian had to guess.

"Well," he said, tucking a loose strand of hair behind Mariah's ear. "I expect to hear shit about *that* from Ciana for the next fifty years or so."

Mariah's bright, answering laugh was swallowed by his kiss, and he showed her just how much better baths could be.

"How about this one?"

Mariah's eyes flashed as she pushed through her bedroom doors into the living room, spinning the skirts of the burgundy and gold gown. It hugged her curves, her skin glowing with a healthy tan. Her gaze settled on Andrian when she stopped moving, lips curled into a smile.

She was so beautiful, he worried his heart would stop in his chest.

He cleared his throat, leaning forward. "It's—"

"It's not the one."

Attentions turned to Feran, who sat stoically on the couch. Curiosity brushed away Andrian's mild annoyance.

Despite the years together, Feran had always been quiet, preferring the company of the horses to people. But Andrian knew he was from a town near the Kreah border. His mother had come from a family of importance in Kreah but had thrown it all away for a handsome Onitan rancher.

Even knowing all that, Andrian could not have predicted Feran to be the one amongst them that was the most outspoken on royal fashion.

Ciana peered around Mariah, eyes narrowed and hands on her hips. "Care to explain, Feran?"

Feran shrugged. "The color is wrong. Red isn't Mariah's family color."

"I don't know if you're aware of this, Feran," Mariah drawled, her expression bored. "But I don't *have* a family color."

Somewhere, Quentin chuckled, Matheo and Trefor echoing him.

There was silence for a beat.

"Not yet," Feran answered. "But you could."

Mariah froze. Andrian cocked his head, watching her. He leaned forward, resting his forearms on his knees and clasping his hands. Slowly, she turned to him, her eyes sparkling with her thoughts.

He met her look with a grin.

"Got any ideas, princess?"

A slow smile spread across her face.

"Yes. I do." She turned back to Feran. "Actually, let me change what I said. I don't *currently* have a family color ... but I used to. My mother's family used to." She twisted on her heel to Ciana, Delaynie behind her. Waiting just beyond was Brie, the young palace seamstress.

Andrian's chest swelled with pride for his scarred queen. For his Mariah.

"Silver," she said. "My family's color is silver."

CHAPTER 57

The dress made of moonlight swished around Mariah's feet, brushing across the glistening marble floors. She toyed with the ends of the sleeves, the lace soft against her wrists.

Warm hands wrapped around her bare shoulders as heat enveloped her back. "Stop fidgeting," Andrian murmured in her ear. "You look beautiful."

She leaned into him, almost an instinct. "Oh, I know." Twisting in his arms, she tipped her head to meet his gaze. "And I'm not fidgeting."

He smiled, a hint of that smirk peeking through. "Of course you're not."

Mariah chuckled and stepped out of his arms, turning to the foyer mirror. She cocked her head at her reflection.

She'd pulled the front pieces of her hair back with two delicate silver clips. Her makeup was simple, only a feathered dusting of shimmer across her eyelids and her cheeks. It brought out the silver glowing behind her eyes, ethereal and vibrant.

But it was the dress that was the true work of art.

Mariah didn't know where Brie had found it—or made it. But the young seamstress had heard Mariah's proclamation and, with a quiet smile on her lips, disappeared from Mariah's suites, entering again nearly thirty minutes later bearing the silver gown in her arms and that same wordless smile.

Mariah knew it was the one the moment she stepped into it.

The sleeves were long, tapered to her wrists, but they were sheer and delicately laced with something that sparkled, covering her body like fallen stars. A fitted bodice, beaded with more bits of starlight and a sweetheart neckline, scooped across her chest and hung off her shoulders. The rest of the dress dripped down her body, flaring slightly around her legs to accommodate a slit to her thigh before it brushed around her feet and pooled behind her in a train of silver moonlight.

It was the dress of her mother's family. A dress for the last Silver Priestess, the last Ginnelevé daughter. Over the past months, while she'd struggled to hold the shattered pieces of herself together, she'd forgotten those ties. But wearing that dress, clothed in those colors, it all came rushing back.

She was not just Chosen of Qhohena, but a daughter of her mother's family. Gold and silver, life and death, Qhohena and Zadione.

She swore she could feel the brush of those beings against her mind. Her magic stirred, winding down through her limbs, and in the mirror, her eyes glowed.

Mariah held the gaze in her reflection for two more heartbeats before turning away.

Brie had also somehow found attire suitable for her Armature in less than a day. They all wore a dark, regal gray, delicately embroidered with patterns of silver and the faintest lacings of gold. Their weapons were on full display—short swords crossed across their backs, longswords sheathed at their hips, daggers and knives in baldrics across their chests. The ladies of her court were also there, each wearing a gold dress so pale that it almost looked silver.

And beside her stood Andrian, no weapons in sight except for the faint shadows twining down his arms. Mariah knew his black-bladed dagger was on him somewhere, hidden beneath his jacket.

Hopefully, though, there would be no need for that tonight.

Everyone was gathered and waiting. Her court, her friends, her family. Andrian stepped closer to her side, and she inhaled deeply.

"I don't have much I need to say that hasn't already. I wouldn't be standing here, right now, if it weren't for every one of you. I'm happy to be home, but I'm ready to fix the things that are broken in this world. And with your help, I know I'll be able to." She drew in another breath, expelling it through her nose. "So ... let's go make me a queen, shall we?"

Feral grins and wild smiles answered her. She placed her hand on Andrian's waiting arm and stepped out of her rooms and toward the next part of her future.

THE THRONE ROOM was quiet and dim, lit only by the *lunestair* pillars at the front of the room, and the candles scattered in a circle around the throne.

And on that throne sat Ryenne, wearing her usual gown of crushed red velvet, the snowdrop crown of Onita on her brow.

Mariah bit her cheek to hold back her gasp of surprise. She'd known her rise into her power would weaken Ryenne, had remembered how old and frail the queen was when she'd visited Mariah after her return from Khento. But nothing could've prepared Mariah for Ryenne's appearance now, for the way her skin sagged around her face and her body curled in on itself on the throne as if lacking the strength to even remain upright. Beside her sat her own Armature, looking as frail as their queen, and at the foot of the dais steps stood the last ladies of her court, ladies who likely never imagined they would somehow outlive their ageless queen.

Mariah's gaze swept over Delaynie's mother. And her father, a member of Ryenne's Armature. Her heart squeezed in her chest at the realization that no more than twenty years after finding each other, they would be separated by the same gods who'd made their daughter's life possible.

Swallowing her sadness, Mariah strode down the long throne room, heels clicking against the marble floor. Her court flanked her—Andrian on her right, Sebastian to her left, the rest of her Armature and ladies following behind. Their footfalls rang eerily through the nearly empty cavern, heralding a melody of change.

Kalen, seated beside Ryenne, pushed to his feet as they neared the dais steps. His face pinched with exertion, his once-youthful body now hunched and frail. Mariah halted, the rest of her court fanning out behind her.

With all the strength he had left, Kalen set his shoulders and lifted his chin, representing his queen as her consort, one final time.

"Who approaches the throne of Queen Ryenne of House Shawth, Chosen of Qhohena, Protector of Onita and Lady of Verith?"

Mariah paused before the steps, hands tightening around her skirts as a wave of apprehension and fear and sickening dread washed over her.

She knew she wanted to be queen. Knew in her soul, in the place beside those silver and gold threads that twined and danced together, that this was an inescapable destiny. But her hesitation came from a dark place born in a cold and lonely cell in the bowels of a loathsome northern castle. From a desire to change her kingdom for the better after it was so twisted by foul greed and a wicked sense of possession.

It came from the crack of a whip, the sundering of her skin, the slow drip of blood down her back. From sweaty hands on her skin and in her hair, touches she'd locked away from herself—until now.

She was lost to those memories for too many tense beats of her heart. Lost in herself, at the magnitude of what she'd endured, the realization that despite this being her fate, she would never succeed. Not like this, not as damaged as she was.

Until the faintest of touches across her spine brought her back. A touch from a warm, calloused hand, skin she recognized as well as she did her own. It swept across her scars, revealed by the open back of her gown and the short length of her hair. She twisted her glance over her shoulder to meet a pair of tanzanite eyes with shadows dancing in their depths.

She almost—*almost*—swore she heard his voice whisper in her head, the stroke of his consciousness down the one bond that she could not close.

"Are you alright, nio?"

She wasn't, but with him ... maybe she could be.

So, she let her lips turn up into a soft smile and nodded. Something small but enough for him to see.

There were more words there, but she didn't know if they were from the bond or her memories.

"Show them what moonlight really looks like."

Still smiling, she returned her attention to the dais, where Kalen stood and Ryenne sat, their expressions regal and expectant.

"I do." Mariah drew in one more breath, pushing back her shoulders. "I lay claim to the power of Qhohena, the throne of Xara, and the kingdom of Onita."

Silence answered her. Kalen turned, glancing down at his queen. Offering his arm, Ryenne laid her hand on his, and with shaky legs rose from her great golden chair.

Despite her weak appearance, she was steady once she stood, head held proud and ocean-blue eyes shimmering with centuries of life. She leveled that stare on Mariah, heavy enough to make Mariah's skin itch and her throat tighten.

"And who are you, daughter of the moon, to claim such things?"

"I am Mariah Salis, born of Wes Salis and Lisabel Ginnelevé. I come from Andburgh. I carry Onita in my blood, and the magic of the goddesses in my soul."

Goddesses.

Not goddess.

The room stilled at her change to the words. She'd told Ciana and Andrian of her plan, to claim her throne not just under Qhohena, but Zadione as well.

Mariah hadn't warned Ryenne, though. She'd told the queen about the other magic she bore, but that wasn't this. And for a moment, she feared what Ryenne might say.

The old queen stepped forward, her hand lifting from Kalen's arm. She laid that hand across her chest, above her heart. Her fingers clenched into a fist as she uttered words that stopped Mariah's heart.

"Then by Qhohena and Zadione's grace, may you claim your throne."

When Ryenne's head dipped, gray hair falling around her face, Mariah's heart beat again.

Those beats turned into a pounding drum as Ryenne's Armature bowed their heads, mimicking their queen. When her ladies knelt into curtsies.

The young priestess—Liliane—stepped out from between the pillars, a shy smile on her face as she dipped her head, pale gold robes brushing the floor.

Ryenne lifted her head at the priestess's arrival, meeting Mariah's stare with warmth in her eyes before turning to Liliane and reseating herself upon the throne. "With the absence of our high priestess, Liliane will assist in your ascension."

Liliane gave another small nod and smile, standing beside Ryenne as Kalen seated himself on the dais.

With one final, deep inhale, Mariah gathered her skirts and ascended the dais.

Every step felt heavy, weighted with the burdens of her past and future.

Whore.

Sister.

Unworthy.

Daughter.

Murderer.

Queen.

She reached the top of the dais, where Ryenne waited for her.

The old queen smiled. A real, true smile, perhaps the first Mariah had seen on her face in a long, long time.

"I am so proud of you, Mariah. Do not let this kingdom make you into anything other than what you are."

Mariah swallowed. "If I end up as half the queen you are, Ryenne, then I will be happy enough."

"No," Ryenne answered, her smile softening with sadness. "You do not want to be half the queen I was. I was not a good queen. You will be much, much greater."

Mariah wasn't sure she could answer without tears, so she only clenched her jaw and nodded once.

Ryenne turned to Liliane. "We await you, priestess."

Liliane dipped her head, a fresh blush on her face. Mariah remembered how young the priestess was—barely out of girlhood and yet thrust into a ceremony that had only happened ten other times in Onitan history.

It brought Mariah great happiness to know that Ksee would live—and die—without such an honor, but this young woman who had risked everything to stand for what she knew was right had it now.

"Stand beside the throne, Mariah."

Mariah nodded, obeying Liliane's direction. Ryenne had mentioned briefly what this ritual might entail, but also informed Mariah that this was something the priestesses guarded close. While a queen and her court knew, no others did.

Hence the small crowd there tonight. There would be a more formal celebration later, when no weaknesses could be exploited.

For that was the secret.

Ryenne still held a piece of Qhohena's magic—a meager, miniscule drop. Enough to fight off the infirmaries of time but not enough to heal wounds inflicted by more nefarious actors.

And if something were to happen to either queen before this final ritual could occur, the queen's full power would be lost forever.

Mariah's magic writhed awake as she met Ryenne's stare.

Liliane stood before them both, and from within her pale gold robes she withdrew a slender, wickedly sharp dagger.

"Your palms, Your Majesties," Liliane said, voice timid.

Mariah flashed her a reassuring smile as she extended her right hand, just as Ryenne raised her left.

Liliane lowered the dagger to Mariah's palm. "With these cuts," she said, slicing the delicate blade across Mariah's skin, the sting of pain hardly registering even as ruby blood burst free. Some splashed on the armrest of the throne, and Mariah's eyes widened as it disappeared, seeping into the shimmering gilded stone.

"With these cuts," Liliane repeated, mimicking the cut on Ryenne's palm, "we bridge the light between two queens. One whose time is setting, and the other who is rising. Waxing and waning, just as the moons in the sky. May their blood bind them to the realm, and to each other, for eternity." Liliane bowed her head and stepped back from the throne, bloody dagger still clutched in her hands.

Mariah and Ryenne's palms were still outstretched, nearly touching as their blood dripped, soaking into the seat that held the power of a kingdom.

Her arm shaking, Ryenne drifted her bleeding hand closer, fingers brushing Mariah's. A single, delicate drop of gold shimmered in the open skin of the cut.

The final drop of magic.

An eighth and final bond.

Mariah met Ryenne's gaze. One last time.

"Take it, Mariah," the queen whispered. "I am ready."

The world held its breath as Mariah turned over her palm, placing it atop Ryenne's.

The second their hands clasped, palms meeting, the doors at the end of the throne room burst open.

CHAPTER 58

Mariah's eyes whipped to the lone figure sprinting into the throne room, his face red with exertion and his eyes blown wide with fear, even as the magic flowed from Ryenne into her, that final drop of gold reuniting with her own well of power.

She couldn't stop the way her hand tightened around Ryenne's, refusing to release.

Her Armature moved before she even gave the order.

Drystan had his sword drawn, Quentin palmed his knives, Matheo and Trefor had unslung and notched their bows, and Feran swung his short swords in a slow arc. Sebastian moved toward the newcomer, hand on the hilt of his longsword, just as Andrian took a single step up the stairs, shadows unfurling down his arms.

"That's close enough." Sebastian met the messenger in the middle of the hall. He was young, hardly a man, his face dripping in sweat as his limbs shook.

"I ... I have ... a message ..." he wheezed.

"How did you get in here?" Sebastian's voice was harsher now, more clipped. His grip on his sword hilt tightened.

"Let me in … City Guards …" the messenger panted. "Message … for the queen."

Everyone froze. Mariah still gripped Ryenne's hand in hers, squeezing tight.

"Which queen?" Andrian's growl was filled with dark, unending malice. Shadows leaked across the floor, weaving between the feet of Mariah's Armature.

The messenger's face lifted, his gaze settling on Mariah.

"Queen Mariah." He gasped. "The message is for you. It's urgent."

Andrian spun to Mariah. She blinked at him, just once, before looking back at the boy.

"Speak."

The boy sagged with relief before he remembered his task. He drew himself up, face still flushed, fear shining in his brown eyes.

"I come with a message from Khento."

Mariah's blood turned to ice.

She'd prayed dozens of times in her life. To Qhohena, to Zadione, to any god who would listen.

This time, she sent a prayer to every last one, a desperate plea and cry for help.

Not them. Please, tell me I wasn't too late.

Not them.

Please.

But of course, gods have no control over the actions of men.

"The Royal Lords of Onita have taken the Salis family. They are being held at the castle in Khento, the seat of Lord Victor Shawth. The Royals hope the Queen finds the urgency in this situation and comes willing to reach an amicable solution."

The boy's words were robotic, memorized. They flowed through Mariah's mind like a river, meandering and bathing and drenching her in fear the likes of which she'd never known.

Mariah dropped Ryenne's hand. The old queen slumped forward in the throne, Kalen rushing to her side to catch her before he too collapsed, sprawled across his queen's lap. The rest of Ryenne's Armature followed, sagging into their chairs upon the dais.

The room erupted into chaos, but all Mariah could hear was the steady drip of her bright red blood against the gold stone of her throne.

PART 3

FREED

Xara says she was given a gift,
But I fear for her.
The freedom of her power
Is nothing more than the chains of the gods.

—Excerpt from the Ginnelevé diary. Authored by
Marielyn Ginnelevé, the first silver priestess, in the first
year of Xara's reign.

CHAPTER 59

"The Royal Lords of Onita have taken the Salis family. They are being held at the castle at Khento, the seat of Lord Victor Shawth. The lords hope the queen finds the urgency in this situation and comes willing to reach an amicable solution."

Andrian heard the words, but his eyes never left his queen.

Mariah's hand gripped Ryenne's. Their blood—still glowing with the last drops of Ryenne's power—dripped onto the golden throne. It wasn't until the last of the messenger's words rang out through the room that Mariah finally moved.

She dropped the old queen's hand, sparks and magic and power glimmering in her eyes and along her skin. She lurched down the dais just as Ryenne sagged into the throne, Kalen rushing to catch her.

Before he collapsed, too. Before the rest of Ryenne's Armature collapsed, frail bodies slumping into cushioned chairs.

Andrian didn't need to test their pulse to know what had happened.

Mariah took another slow, jilting step. Ryenne's ladies rushed to their queen and the Armature they'd served for most of their lives. A scream pierced the veil of silence, but Mariah didn't flinch.

Instead, her light pulsed brighter, coiling around her fingers and up her arms in shimmering silver-gold ropes.

It woke Andrian's magic, shadows slithering through his veins. They branched off his shoulders, some twisting into his hair while others reached out for his queen with desperate, hungry fingers.

The bond between them was still open, but from it ... he couldn't read anything. Her mind was a vicious storm, a whirlwind of too many emotions snapping like animals against their chains. All he could do was latch his mind to hers, squatting amongst the chaos, and stand by her side.

She took another step down the dais.

"What did you say?" Her voice was whisper-soft, dangerously quiet.

The messenger boy paled, despite the exertion still panting from his lungs. "It was just a message, Your Majesty. I was told to deliver—"

A silent snap of gold and silver, the rope of magic wrapping around his throat, cut his words short.

Sebastian pitched forward a step, eyes wide, but froze when Andrian fixed him with a pointed, jabbing stare. The rest of Mariah's Armature settled defensively around her, hands gripping their weapons, eyes flickering with all the rage and suspicion Andrian felt himself.

But everything he felt ... it was *nothing* compared to what seethed across the bond.

Mariah's lips pulled back in a snarl, fingers twitching at her side. The magic around the boy's throat tightened, his eyes bulging slightly in their sockets.

"*Who?*"

The messenger gasped like a fish. "Majesty ... I don't ... can't ..."

Andrian inched closer to Mariah. He brushed a tendril of shadow down her arm, tracing across the exposed skin of her collarbone.

He leaned down, whispering in her ear, "Not here. There are

always eyes, even in the most secure of places. Release the boy so he can speak."

Another stroke of shadow over her skin. She shivered, goose-bumps rising on her arms, the distraction of his touch calming some of that rage burning down their bond, around her soul.

Somewhere, in a faraway place, he was elated that he could do that for her. That he could calm her, just for a moment, even if it was simply a distraction.

Andrian turned to meet the wide, terrified expression of the messenger. It took a few heartbeats, but slowly, the silver-gold noose around his neck loosened, the rope of light falling away and slinking back beneath Mariah's skin. The boy sagged, his hands wrapping around his throat, coughing and sputtering as he gasped for air.

Mariah lifted her gaze to meet Andrian's own.

When he saw what shined in those forest green depths—rage and regret and anguish and disbelief—his thoughts left him, animalistic instinct taking hold.

The messenger was just regaining his breath when a new rope wound around his neck. This one, though, was made of onyx shadows, the opposite in every way from the light it replaced. Andrian's pulse raced through his magic as if it were his fingers wrapped around the boy's thin throat. Could feel hands scratch and claw at the shadowy bindings, even as they lifted the messenger into the air, feet swinging wildly beneath him as he struggled helplessly.

But that look in Mariah's eyes, the same one she still wore, reminded Andrian of something he'd always known about himself.

He was not a good man.

He sometimes pretended to be, when that was what she needed. But for her, he would always be willing to let his darkness loose.

His shadows tightened around the boy's neck. The boy's face turned purple, lack of oxygen streaking his eyes red.

"Your queen asked you a question." His words were growled,

but his shadows made sure they carried. "I'm going to set you down, and you are going to answer her. Understood?" Somehow, the boy blinked, his head barely nodding.

Good enough.

He dropped the boy, letting him fall heavily to the floor, his coughing and sputtering echoing harshly off the glass-ceilinged hall. Andrian's shadows lingered close, vipers waiting to strike.

Mariah pushed her shoulders back, light dancing at her fingertips.

"Why did the City Guard let you past the palace gates?"

Andrian froze.

The entire room froze.

It was a question he hadn't thought of, and he cursed himself for it.

Tonight was a private ceremony. Meant only for the members of Mariah's and Ryenne's courts. The City Guard was instructed to keep the gates closed, all entrances protected.

And yet this messenger had burst through, unimpeded.

The boy's face was still flushed, but his eyes widened. "I-I don't know. The guard at the gate," he croaked. "The guard at the gate. He let me in."

"Which guard?"

Sebastian stepped forward. "Mariah, I doubt he knows the name of the exact guard—"

"I do. Know it. I ... I've met him before." The boy still struggled with his words, but he forced them past his teeth.

Sebastian's hand returned to the hilt of his sword, lips turning down into a scowl. Mariah took another step forward, a predator stalking her prey.

"Who?" she growled again.

"Ryland," the boy whispered. "His name is Ryland."

Fuck.

Andrian's magic snapped forward again, this time wrapping around the boy's wrists, binding them together in front of him. Not that the messenger would try anything—his eyes were wide and terrified at the shadow magic holding him—but it was enough time for Trefor and Matheo to surge forward, each grabbing one of the boy's arms.

Once he was secured, Andrian pulled his magic back to him, just beneath his skin. He turned to Mariah, light tremors of her rage washing through her frame.

"*Nio?*" he said gently, barely more than a whisper. She darted her gaze up to him, an unearthly wildness still blazing in her eyes. "What do you want to do with him?"

Her jaw worked. "Take him to the meeting room. I have more questions for him." She raised her voice. "The more forthcoming he is, the less this will hurt."

Matheo and Trefor hoisted up the boy, dragging him from the throne room, heading toward the meeting room they'd used so many times over the past few weeks. The boy had pissed himself in his fear, a dark stain spreading across the front of his pants as his sobs sputtered through the cavernous space, pleading for his innocence, that he was only doing a job.

The boy had to learn the lesson at some point. A job for the wrong people would get one killed.

"Mariah." A feminine voice rang out, hesitant yet clear. Mariah was rigid as she turned, her beautiful face cold and brimming with power.

The power of an ascended queen.

Pride—dark and vengeful and eternal—swelled within Andrian, even as his knees threatened to buckle before her.

Ciana stood with Liliane, the latter pale-faced as she stared at Ryenne and Kalen's bodies. Behind them was Delaynie, slumped over a male form as silent sobs wracked her body, her mother beside her.

Ciana swallowed. "Mariah ... they need to be taken to Priam's Antechamber."

The room was still. So still, an unearthly quiet that raised the hair along the back of Andrian's neck.

Mariah's gaze was focused on Ryenne's lifeless body, now pale and empty of the magic that had given her long life.

"I know." She cocked her head. "It's all been arranged. Liliane will see to it." The sound of her name roused the young priestess, raising a wide-eyed stare to Mariah.

"Give honor to our departed queen and her court, priestess. The rest of you, we meet in the meeting room. Now."

"Mariah." Ciana's voice was firmer now. The tone was not of a queen's lady but of her best friend. Mariah's gaze snapped to Ciana's, and Andrian could feel the battle of wills clashing between them.

Without another word, Mariah stepped back toward the dais. Up the steps. Past where Ryenne and Kalen lay, where Liliane had bolted to gather the assembled assistants who would help her take their bodies to the antechamber and begin the death vigil.

Mariah stopped above Delaynie, kneeling with her mother beside her father, tears streaking her high cheekbones. She turned up to face her queen, auburn hair shifting across her back.

Mariah bent, resting a hand on her friend's shoulder. "Stay, Delaynie. Mourn your dead. Join us when you can."

Delaynie nodded, and out of the corner of Andrian's eye, he saw Quentin tense, as if he might spring up those steps. But he didn't move, simply remained standing beside Andrian, bouncing subtly from foot to foot.

Mariah rose and turned to Ciana, who gave a tight nod. Mariah's face was still blank, empty of all except that deep, unending fury as she started toward the dais' steps.

She stopped again, right beside Ryenne's prone body. Her eyes flickered downward.

With a slow, drawn-out movement, she knelt beside Ryenne, the old queen's gray hair splayed around her head. Mariah's fingers wrapped around something, a surge of wild desperation clawing down their bond.

When Mariah stood, she had the golden snowdrop blossom crown of Onita clutched in her fingers.

She considered the crown for a moment, tilting her head like an animal regarding its next meal. With that same slow movement, she lifted the crown, resting it atop her head.

When she raised her gaze to Andrian, her eyes sparkled and cracked with something that wasn't quite human.

Without another word, she turned on her heel, stepping down the dais and striding from the throne room. Andrian fell into step behind her.

It was time for her to plan her vengeance, and he would do everything in his power to help her capture it.

CHAPTER 60

H*er family.*
Her family.
Her family.

It was a taunt that ran through her head on a loop, laughing at her as it wound its noose tighter and tighter.

They have her family.

It was like her worst nightmares had come to fruition. All the reasons she'd been so hesitant to mention them, to visit them, to ask them to visit her. She'd kept her distance on purpose ever since that first meeting with the lords that had resulted in the death of Lord Beauchamp. She'd created powerful enemies who'd made their commitment to her destruction more than clear. Her fear grew with Donnet's presence in Khento, but that same fear kept her trapped in stasis, too broken to send word.

And when she finally summoned her courage to send that short, unassuming letter, it was too late.

She should've known. Despite the goddesses she felt breathing down her neck, any higher power had abandoned her long before tonight.

The tip of her dagger, the one that had belonged to her mother's father, the same one she'd stolen back from that greedy lord along with a sack full of repossessed coin, dug into the messenger boy's slender neck. A bright red bead of blood dripped down his skin, splattering on his soiled trousers.

"What's your name?" Her voice was too soft, too quiet for her ears. She was detached, not present in her actions.

That same beast she always knew dwelled beneath her skin had taken over, just as it had the day of the parade, on the rooftop with the assassin. She'd given into it then, surrendering to the sweet bliss of its anger and power and vengeance, and she gave into it now.

Vengeance was a drug; she lost herself to it.

The messenger boy blubbered. "Pl-please … Your Majesty … I was just doing a job—"

"Shh. That's enough." She tsked. "Yes, you were doing a job. But doing a job doesn't excuse you from what you know. And you *will* tell me what you know." She pulled the dagger back, twirling it against her thumb. "I'll ask one more time. A name?"

The boy's lip trembled. "Finn, Your Majesty. My name is Finn."

Mariah hummed. "Finn. Pleasure to meet you." She dropped her dagger again, leveling it with the crook of his neck, right where she'd previously drawn blood. "Now, Finn. I need you to tell me exactly who sent you and where you came from."

The boy swallowed. "Your Majesty, I don't understand. I told you, I was sent from Khento."

"Yes, yes. I know. Khento." She sighed. "But I recall at least a half dozen lords currently residing in Khento. So, which one sent you? Who is your employer?"

The boy's eyes were light brown and blown wide with his terror. "Lord Shawth, Your Majesty. I work for Lord Shawth."

She cocked her head. "Did he not want you to tell me that you work for him?"

More tears sprang to the boy's eyes. "Please. Your Majesty, please. I don't know anything—just what I was told."

Her dagger pressed further into his throat. More blood dripped over the blade onto his stained trousers. The animal beneath her skin watched it fall, fascinated by the metallic scent filling the air.

"I don't believe that, Finn."

The boy was shaking harder now. "Your Majesty?"

Mariah nodded, more to herself than to the boy. Her Armature shifted on their feet behind her, hands readied on their weapons.

But she had no need for them. Not right now, not at this moment. Not when the full power of the queen hammered through her veins, not when immortality wrapped itself beneath her skin.

Not even the figure who stood closer than the rest, the shadow at her back. She could feel him, feel where his soul connected to hers. Felt her same anger blazing through him, the same need for revenge.

Mariah knew a few of the others likely shied away from her holding a knife to a boy's throat.

She was thankful that at least the one her soul had wound itself closest to did not.

"I think you know far more than you think you do. I think you saw things in the castle at Khento. Things that you're ready to share with us." Mariah pushed back, standing, her dagger hanging loosely between her fingers.

Finn looked up at her, eyes still wide, terror still flushing his cheeks.

"I'm going to ask you some very specific questions, Finn. And how you answer them is going to determine whether you live to breathe the fresh air again or if you will die in the bowels of this palace, doomed to live the rest of your days with only the company of the rats. Do you understand what I'm offering you?"

Finn nodded fervently; more blood from the wounds at his neck dripped onto his filthy pants.

"Good. Now." Mariah tightened her grip around the hilt of her dagger. The dragon wings on the pommel dug into the skin above her thumbs. "When you were in Khento, before you were sent here. Did you see them?"

The boy's lip quivered. "See who?"

The wing bit deeper. "The people the lords took, the ones being held captive in Khento." She knelt again, this time leveling the tip of her dagger at the boy's belly. "*My family.*"

She'd heard Finn's delivered message; his dreaded words still rang through her ears, clattering against her skull. But she could not deny the part of her clinging to some foolish hope, that this was just a trick, some ploy to draw her away from Verith.

She could hold herself together, at least until her nightmares were confirmed.

All the blood drained from the boy's face. "I ... don't ... I don't know, Your Majesty—"

Silver-gold magic rushed from her skin, wrapping around the boy's arms. They bit with her fury, and Mariah could feel the tiny cuts and slices they made across Finn's skin like thousands of teeth attacking his flesh. Finn yelped in pain.

Somehow, she could taste it. His blood. The tang of his fear. The salt of his desperation.

"You know, Finn. I know you do. Who did you see?"

The boy shuddered, his eyes closing, another tear slipping free.

"There was ..." He gulped down a sob. "There were three people brought in. The day before I was sent here with my message."

There was a roaring in her ears, the beast in her chest thrashing wildly. But she was still, emotionless.

Empty.

"What did they look like? The people you saw?" Her voice was icy and detached. It didn't sound like her own.

"There was a man," Finn said, voice shaking as he reopened his eyes. "He was tall but old. Older. A soldier, or he was one at some point. His hair was gray, but not too bad."

More screaming stillness. "And the other two?"

"A kid. Boy. Older than me? I don't know. He had auburn hair. And he must've had magic because they had the cuffs on him." Finn's eyes widened as if realizing what he'd just said. He quickly deflated, sagging in his chair. "They only use the cuffs when someone has magic."

The stillness was fracturing into a storm, crescendoing towards something uncontrolled.

She knew far too well what those cuffs felt like. The way they bit into the skin, the way they erected a wall between a person and their soul.

"And the third?" she whispered, deadly and quiet.

"A woman," Finn said, still sagging in the chair. "The same age as the man. Curly dark hair, but it was going gray. She looked very kind and gentle. Like a healer. All the healers I've ever known have been kind."

He has no idea.

Mariah snapped her magic back as she stood and whirled from Finn. The boy released a sob, but Mariah didn't hear it.

Not when her eyes clashed with a familiar tanzanite glare, shadows and death whispering around him.

It was only then, in the safety of that glare, that she let herself falter. The animal whimpered, sidling away, relinquishing control back to her.

With control came the pain, washing away the blessed numbness.

"They have them. They have my family." She staggered a step forward. Andrian surged, catching her in his arms. His scent of rain and sandalwood wrapped around her, the only comfort in a dark and dim world.

There was movement behind her. Murmurs and shuffles, a soft whine from the boy's throat and trudging steps as Finn was hauled from the room.

She didn't know where they were taking him.

She didn't particularly care.

A hand rested on the back of her head. Brushed down her

neck, over the short length of her hair. Across the exposed scars on her back, the low scoop of her dress.

"We'll get them back, *nio*. I swear to you." Andrian's words were a rumble against her cheek. She still felt his fury, his simmering thirst for blood that was answered in her own soul.

Mariah did not doubt his conviction.

She only doubted his ability to make it a reality.

CHAPTER 61

Mariah's rooms belonged to a stranger.

These rooms belonged to a girl whose family was safe, enjoying a night by the fire in a quaint cabin nestled in the Ivory Forest.

To a girl who thought she might see that family again one day. Would visit them there in that cabin and enjoy a night of peace and smiles and cold whiskey. Would watch the man she loved meet them, would watch her father shake his hand, watch her mother wrap him in an embrace, watch her brother pester him about his strange, foreign magic.

What a fool she'd always been.

Mariah sat on one of the many couches, slumped against the cushions. Empty. So empty. Even the press of Andrian's thigh against her own wasn't enough to shake the numbness.

She'd cried as they'd walked through the halls to her rooms. The tears slowed as she tossed her bloodied dagger on the bed, stopping completely as she changed out of her coronation gown and into her familiar leggings and tunic.

She emerged from her bathroom to Andrian, waiting, her dagger cleaned and polished in his hands. He offered it to her without question, and she took it without a word.

It was back against her thigh, her fingers toying with the hilt.

Mariah would slit Shawth's throat with this dagger, would ensure she did not leave this world until she felt his life drain out from beneath the blade.

There were murmurs around her living room. The rest of her Armature—besides Matheo and Feran, who had dragged Finn away—were perched around her, exchanging tight whispers and shooting her concerned stares. Sebastian, especially, sat close, brows pulled tight as his concern stretched across his face.

She didn't bother getting their attention before speaking. They'd all hear her, anyway. "I need to get them back."

"We will, Mariah. We promise, we'll get them out." Sebastian leaned forward, reaching for her hand.

Mariah didn't offer it to him but didn't pull away, either. She simply remained motionless, devoid. An empty shell of vengeance and anger.

More lurked beneath the husk of her rage. But she was too afraid of it, of the way it looked back at her with slitted eyes and burning death in its maw.

"You misunderstand me, Sebastian." Her voice was biting. "I don't want to get them out, *eventually*. I want to get them out *now*. They can't spend a single second more in that miserable pit." She shivered, the scars on her back itching.

Mariah remembered all too well what they did to visitors in that castle.

Andrian tensed beside her. Sebastian's jaw worked, frustration in his hazel eyes.

"I know, Mariah. We understand. But we can't just go now—"

"Of course we can," she interrupted. "I'll go alone if I must. But I will not sit here, waiting in safety and comfort, while my family rots in a cell in that fucking castle."

Silence answered her. A hand rested gently on her thigh, warm and familiar.

"*Nio*. Look at me."

She slowly turned to Andrian. Shadows danced in his blue eyes, twined down his shoulders, brushed against her cheeks. She leaned into them, just for a moment, before snapping herself back.

"We will get them back. As soon as we fucking can. But we can't take down a whole castle without a plan."

He was right, even though the beast in her gnashed its teeth and raked its claws across her soul.

Matheo and Feran burst into her rooms, followed closely by Ciana, Kiira, and Rylla. Their footsteps were tense and clipped as they strode through the foyer. Ciana pushed and shoved past Quentin and Drystan until she stood by Sebastian, her normally bright face tight. She dropped to her knees, resting a hand on Mariah's forearm, amber eyes flickering.

Mariah hardly recognized the feeling of her friend's hand on her arm, but she met Ciana's gaze. Did her best to acknowledge her, to feel something other than her rage.

A memory tickled at the back of her mind, a reminder of something else that had happened that night.

"How is Delaynie?" Mariah croaked as her mind filled with images of her friend bent over the body of her father. Of her sobs echoing through the throne room.

Her rage greeted her guilt like an old friend, both settling in her chest.

Ciana's hand tightened on Mariah's arm. "She'll be alright. They always knew this day would come."

Mariah grimaced. "Knowing something is going to happen doesn't make it any easier."

"No, I suppose it doesn't." Ciana shook her head and inhaled a deep breath. "She's going to stand vigil with her mother and Liliane. She hoped that would be okay with you."

That guilt twisted tighter, wrapping around Mariah's throat. Her anger suffocated, still itching and raging to leave for Khento. But she wasn't the only one to lose someone tonight.

She didn't even know if she *had* lost anyone. Her family was only taken, if Finn's message was to be believed. They were not dead.

Not like Steven, Delaynie's father.

"Of course it's okay." Mariah felt tired. So very, very tired. She hung her head, her chin meeting her chest. "I'm sorry. I was selfish."

"No, Mariah." Andrian's hand brushed her hair off her cheek and tucked it behind her ear. "You're not selfish, and nobody here thinks you are." There were nods around the room, but Mariah's attention remained focused on him. On his tanzanite eyes and the bond of light and shadow stretching between them. "Your family was taken. And we're going to figure out a way to get them back. *All* of them." He growled the last few words, shadows dancing between his eyes.

Mariah drew in a breath and let it out slowly between her teeth. She curled her hands into fists, nails digging into her palms.

"I need to get them back." She turned to Ciana, still kneeling on the rug. "But ... I also need to be here for Delaynie. For Ryenne. She deserves as much."

Ciana nodded, tears forming behind her amber eyes as she gave Mariah a sad, heartbroken smile.

Mariah turned to Sebastian. "Is three days enough time?"

Hesitation flashed across Sebastian's eyes, but he wasn't who answered her.

"Yes, *nio*. Three days is more than enough." Mariah nodded but kept her attention on Sebastian.

"Do you disagree, Sebastian?"

He pressed his mouth into a thin line. "No. I don't. I just don't want you going with us."

Mariah's rage came roaring back.

"I would rather die," she whispered, venom on her tongue, "than stay here, in the comfort of this ridiculous fucking palace, while my family is held captive in an enemy's castle. I will never let someone else fight my battles for me, especially when the fight is for people I love."

She caught Andrian's subtle smirk out of the corner of her eye, something close to pride shimmering in his gaze and down their bond.

Sebastian shook his head, lips tight. "It's just ..." He breathed a heavy sigh. "It feels like a trap. You must see that."

"Of course it's a trap." He blinked with shock. "But that's not a good enough reason to stay behind. To not do what I can for them. They were taken because of *me*."

Sebastian's jaw still worked, but he said nothing.

"I have a question." Drystan's clear voice rang through the room as he leaned his hands on the back of the couch. "Did anyone else catch that the messenger boy said that a City Guard named Ryland is who let him into the palace tonight?"

"Yes," Andrian responded, his eyes flashing. "And I'm going to fucking *kill* him."

Mariah didn't object. She only met his stare, feeling his anger.

This was a man Andrian had grown up with. Had regarded as a brother for over twenty-one years. Mariah didn't know Ryland —not beyond the few meetings they'd had and the trip they'd made into the market district. His deceit stung, but the pain of it was mild, inconsequential. For Andrian, though, and the rest of her Armature, this betrayal meant something else entirely.

"I wouldn't be surprised if he has left the city. Regardless, we need to find him and talk to him." Everyone around the room murmured their agreement to Mariah's words.

"I'll find him." Feran crossed his arms across his chest. "Tracking down animals is something I'm good at."

Mariah nodded. "Good. Can you do it in two days?"

Feran's answering grin was savage. "Respectfully, M, I think I'll have him back by nightfall tomorrow." He chuckled. "Ryland is many things, but the smartest of us ... he is not."

"Then it's settled." Sebastian rose to his feet. Ciana watched him stand, her brows twisted together. "We'll leave in three days, in the morning." He glanced down at Mariah. "Who all is to go with you, My Queen?"

His rigidity would have bothered her had it not been for her numbness—her anger and guilt.

"All of you. I need you all close. We're stronger when we're all together." It was the truth; everything felt whole like all the pieces of her soul finally fit together when they were near. The thought of going into a place like Khento, a place haunted by the darkest of her memories, without them ... She couldn't stomach it.

She turned her attention to the women of her court. "Kiira and Rylla, you'll both remain here in Verith. As will you, Ciana. Stay with Delaynie and her mother. Keep the palace safe until we return."

All three women nodded. Kiira and Rylla's eyes hardened and flashed, reflective like a cat.

Mariah turned to her first friend, the golden girl who had taught her that a life of responsibility and power might not be so bad after all. Ciana's amber eyes were rimmed with tears, her lips quivering as she held back a sob.

Mariah gave her a gentle smile and felt something other than the emptiness of anger and guilt. She extended her hand to Ciana. Gripped her friend's fingers with her own. "I need you to promise me something, Cee."

Ciana sniffed, a single tear falling from her eye. It landed on their clasped hands, rolling off their skin.

"Anything, Mariah. You know that."

Mariah drew in a breath, raising her chin. "If things go poorly —if you get word that things have gone poorly—you need to get out of here. If I'm gone, and the *allume* fails again ... the wards will fall, and you won't be protected here. You need to promise me that you'll get everyone out—Delaynie, Mikael, Brie, Ryenne's ladies, Liliane. Everyone who might have sympathy for me. Get them out and get them somewhere safe."

Ciana's eyes widened. "That won't happen. I know it won't."

"Of course it won't. But ..." Mariah's voice turned pleading. "Just promise me, Ciana. Take care of them. Get them out."

Ciana opened her mouth as if she had more to say, but snapped it closed. It took a few moments, the mind behind her eyes working, before she nodded.

"I will. I promise," Ciana said, her voice nearly a whisper. She cleared her throat. "If I do, where should I go?"

Mariah stared blankly.

She hadn't thought that far.

"To Kreah." Kiira stepped forward. She still wore her silver-gold gown, styled after Mariah's own. Her deep brown eyes glowed behind gold dusting on her eyelids, her skin warm against the lightness of her dress. "If we have to flee, we should go to Kreah."

Mariah straightened. "Kreah is a long way away."

"It is." Kiira nodded, folding her hands. "But it would be safe. I know you—and all those in this room—would be welcomed there without question." Kiira's gaze sharpened on Mariah, a hint of the predator beneath shining through. "Rulene has always been a friend to Qhohena—and to Zadione."

Something stirred in Mariah at the mention of the Kreah Goddess. Confused glances were shared between her Armature, but she ignored them as she stood, extracting herself from Andrian's hold. It only took a few steps before she stood before Kiira, searching her friend's fierce expression.

"I trust your people more than I trust my own. If it comes to that, please keep them safe."

Kiira regarded Mariah with a curious, unreadable look. She slowly bowed her head, dark braids shifting around her shoulders.

"With my life, My Queen."

CHAPTER 62

Mariah hadn't been to Qhohena's temple since the day after the parade.

Since the day she'd visited Ryenne, standing vigil over the shrouded corpse of her fallen Armature, Cedoric. When the shadowed glass of the Antechamber of Priam had hidden the sunlight, casting the space in comforting darkness.

Now, she stood in the main temple, pews lined on either side of a narrow aisle. Candles burned around the dais at the front of the room, their wax dripping onto the floor.

The priestesses—now, just Liliane—led weekly services in the temple, the one time when those from the city were welcomed past the palace gates. Mariah had never been; that sort of group worship wasn't for her.

But she hadn't had it in her to tell the priestess no. Even with the threats crushing them from all fronts, they still opened the gates once a week. Citizens were allowed through, allowed a chance to stand in the temple and rest lit candles on the altar, hoping to gain Qhohena's favor.

It was said that if your candle burned all the way down, leaving only a puddle of wax on the floor, then your plea would be answered. But if your candle extinguished before the wax burned out, then the gods had found you unworthy.

For the moment, at least. Just until the next service, when you could try again.

Mariah stepped forward, boots clicking across the polished floor. She knelt before the flickering candles, the sheath on her thigh tightening around her padded leathers.

She dressed for war most days now. The only time when she wasn't armed was at night, when she hid her dagger beneath her pillow.

And she knew Andrian also had his own blade tucked beneath his own.

It was the only way she was able to fall asleep; curled against his chest, the familiar scent of rain and sandalwood chasing away her nightmares. Her fears for her family hit her hardest at night— where they were, how they might be treated. What they might be enduring.

Because of her.

She held her hand above the dancing flames. The heat burned her palm, but she didn't draw back.

Was this you? Is this all part of your plan, Qhohena? I was already doing as you asked. I was looking into the Solstice. I was trying to work through what happened. And now ... Her throat constricted around a choked sob.

There was no use trying to speak to the goddess. She hadn't felt even the slightest brush of otherworldly power against her skin—from either Qhohena or Zadione—since that night they'd visited her in her rooms. Even at her coronation, they were silent.

Her magic thrummed in her veins, silver and gold dancing along her fingertips. It steadied her, somehow.

The gods would not answer her, so she would make her own fate.

Become her own god.

Footsteps that wanted to be heard sounded behind her. She lifted her chin and looked over her shoulder. Andrian stood a few paces away, wreathed in shadow, the silver hilt of a longsword peaking over his left shoulder. She turned back to the candles, casting one more glance at the weak golden flames.

How silly they all were, lighting candles to gain the attention of a goddess.

As if the gods controlled this world.

Mariah stood, stepping back from the dais altar and turned towards the hallway to Priam's Antechamber, Andrian falling silently into step behind her.

<hr>

THE SCENE before her was too like Cedoric's vigil. Clouds shielded the summer sun, hazing the room in a layer of darkness, the black and gold marble gleaming.

The difference, of course, was instead of one shrouded body resting on a moveable pedestal, there were seven. Six large frames, all pointing toward the smaller shape in the center of the room.

Even in death, Ryenne's Armature stood guard around their queen.

Beside the shrouded body of one of Ryenne's Armature was Delaynie, her black gown harsh against her pale skin, dark auburn hair falling in ringlets down her back. Her mother stood at her side, hair only a few shades darker and beginning to streak with gray. Their faces were solemn, their postures tired, leaning into and on each other as they stood in a silent wake.

Mariah had expected to see them there, saying goodbye to a father and a partner, one last time.

She hadn't expected to see the man standing behind them, a baldric of knives strapped across his chest, bright red hair pushed back from his face. A face that wore an uncharacteristically open expression, the concern and sympathy on his features clear as day.

Quentin's bottle green eyes drifted toward Mariah as if sensing his queen. He blinked, almost in surprise, glancing once more at Delaynie before pulling away, walking quietly to Mariah and Andrian. Andrian subtly lifted a brow, the hint of a smirk playing on his lips.

"Feeling pious, Quentin?"

Quentin shot Andrian a brutal glare. "Fuck you, Andrian. I'm just being a good friend."

Mariah tilted her head. "Since when were you and Delaynie friends?"

Quentin shifted uncomfortably. "She just lost her dad. I figured she could use some extra support."

Mariah felt Andrian's growl begin in his chest—felt his surge of indignant anger down their bond. "And your *queen* just had her family cap—"

"It's okay." She rested a hand on Andrian's arm. Turning back to Quentin, she let a gentle smile play across her lips. The movement felt off, uncomfortable, not something that fit against the pieces of her rage.

But she tried.

"I'm glad you're there for her. Someone should be."

Quentin blanched, expression softening. "She knows you're there for her, M. I didn't mean to make you feel guilty."

Mariah's smile turned sad, morphing into something more authentic. "I know you didn't. And I don't. I'm just saying—thank you. For being there for her."

Quentin opened his mouth before closing it, dipping his head. "Of course."

Mariah's gaze wandered away from his, trailing until it landed on Delaynie and her mother. Continued until it reached the small body lying prone in the center of the room.

"Stay here," she commanded softly.

Andrian's fingers brushed across the back of her hand, a whisper of a caress, as Quentin dipped his head again.

With quiet steps, Mariah walked first to Delaynie and her mother, Briella, silent beside Steven's shrouded body. Just a few paces from them, Mariah paused. They wore simple yet elegant gowns of black lace and tulle, their skirts hanging in layers around their legs.

She looked so savage when compared to these women, these ladies. In truth, she'd always felt a little savage beside Delaynie, with her moon-white skin and poised demeanor. Mariah had seen that elegant exterior slip more than a few times now, but the Delaynie that now stood before her fallen father was the same one raised to hide her emotions behind a mask so no one in this court of vipers could learn her secrets.

Mariah took another step, letting the heel of her boot scuff across the marble floor. Delaynie slowly lifted her gaze from her father and turned it to Mariah.

That mask was there, to be sure. All her emotions carefully cloistered behind a face of polished beauty. But deep in her blue-gray eyes, Mariah saw the truth—the pain, the heartbreak, the guilt and sadness and rage.

That rage surprised Mariah the most.

Mariah shifted on her feet.

"I'm so sorry for your loss, Del. Nothing I could say could make this better, but … I'm here for you. I need you to know that."

Delaynie blinked. Briella turned, smiling sadly at Mariah and dipping her head, just once, before returning to her silent vigil.

"You are … sorry?" Delaynie said, her brows lifting with muted surprise.

Mariah tensed. "Yes. I'm sorry. I want to know if there's anything I can do." Her words felt rigid and forced.

All that had happened—it was too much. She wanted to be there for her friend; a friend who'd fought for her when she hadn't, who'd reminded her what it meant to be *her*. But she couldn't.

No. She could. Mariah gritted her teeth.

And faltered when she found Delaynie looking at her with tears in her eyes, grief and pain written across her face.

"Mariah," Delaynie whispered, reaching a hand for Mariah's. Mariah let her take it, blinking once.

"I don't need you to apologize to me. Especially not now. Okay?" More tears filled Delaynie's eyes. "Yes, I lost my father. But I always knew that for you to ascend the throne, he would have to leave us. We came to terms with it long before we ever met you. And even then ..." A sad smile played across Delaynie's lips. "Even then, I could never blame you for this. He told me once that he was happy to see his kingdom being left in the hands of a queen who truly deserved it. And he asked me to always be there for you —to help. So, please. Do not apologize." Delaynie's stance shifted, her mask of composed grief faltering, revealing a fire burning beneath it.

"But you ... Mariah, they have your *family*. A family that is still very much with you, not one you've spent years knowing you would have to part from. *I* should be the one asking *you* if there's anything I can do." Her gray eyes flashed, more fire peeking through. "If I could burn those lords alive myself, I would."

Mariah was stunned, lips parting with her shock. Whenever she thought she knew Delaynie, had figured out her quiet friend who clothed herself in perfect facades and tailored dresses, she surprised Mariah. Would say something so painfully true that it felt like a knife driven through Mariah's chest, a jolt that would wake her from the depths of her anger and pain.

She remembered the name Quentin had called Delaynie no more than a week ago, when her court had gathered on her balcony over wine and companionship. Before she knew her family was taken, before she'd donned the crown of Xara. Before her world had descended into chaos.

Little wolf.

Despite the depthless chasm of her rage, a subtle smirk played its way across Mariah's lips. Fitting. She hoped Delaynie let Quentin keep using it.

"I know you would, Delaynie. And trust me—I intend to burn them myself for what they've done. But I'm still going to apologize to you. And you don't have to accept it, but let me say it, anyways."

More blue flames flickered in Delaynie's eyes before she nodded once, a slight dip of her head.

When she did, Mariah noticed something.

There was a delicate necklace around her friend's throat. The chain was so thin that Mariah had never noticed it before, especially since her friend so often wore heavier jewelry that masked the simple adornment.

But today, Delaynie's neck was bare, her collar exposed. Mariah's gaze lingered on the simple necklace ... and then narrowed on the small black stone resting in the hollow of Delaynie's throat.

"Del," Mariah whispered, alarm racing through her, magic flooding her limbs. "What is that necklace?"

Delaynie's hands flew to her throat, her brows furrowing. "What, this little thing? It's my *sautoire*. One of the lord's wives— Lady Cordaro, I think—gave it to me at my first *debutante* when I was thirteen. It's a traditional gift for a high-born or wealthy girl." Delaynie's voice faltered as Mariah's expression fell, then twisted into something furious and a little sick.

Her magic writhed and thrashed in her gut, begging to be freed, to wrap around that delicate chain and rip it from her friend's throat.

"Mariah," Delaynie said slowly, still running her fingers along the necklace. "What's wrong?"

Mariah took a slow, shaky step forward. "What is that stone in the center?"

"I don't know." Delaynie's response was slow, hesitant. Her hands dropped from her neck. "It's just what is in every *sautoire*. It's always the same stone."

"A *black and gold* stone." Mariah's words were a growl. Her bond with Andrian snapped taut, her sudden anger racing through the air between them. She was distantly aware of him pushing off the wall and striding across the Antechamber, Quentin on his heels.

Delaynie's eyes were blown wide. "I don't understand, M—"

Mariah's hand snapped out, her friend's words halting in her throat. Faster than a viper, Mariah slid a finger under the delicate silver chain and yanked. With a silent pop, it broke against the back of Delaynie's neck, masked by her friend's sharp gasp of shock.

"Mariah! What are you doing?"

Mariah didn't answer. She could only glare savagely at the necklace in her hand, at the black and gold stone shimmering back at her. It burned where it touched her skin, her magic hissing and recoiling through her veins.

This was the same stone that had cuffed her wrists when she'd been taken. The same stone used to sever a magic user from their gifts.

The same stone now wrapped around the wrists of her baby brother, if that messenger was to be believed.

"Do you know what this is?" Her voice was still and quiet, only a whisper. Andrian appeared by her side with a gentle brush of shadow down her arm and a rumble of fury from his bond. Quentin wasn't far behind, but he moved around the side, standing between Mariah and Delaynie.

Delaynie blinked. "It's just ... the *sautoire* stone. Every *debutante* gift has the same stone in it. It's just tradition."

"Tradition," Mariah spat. She inhaled deeply, desperately trying to rein in her fury.

This wasn't Delaynie's fault.

Her friend was yet another victim of her kingdom's fucking *traditions*.

"This," Mariah said, "is something I didn't know existed until very, very recently, when I was forced to become painfully familiar with it." She met Delaynie's stare. "It's called *deistair*. It's Old Onitan for sunstone. It's the same substance they used to cuff my wrists to lock away my magic when they *took* me. That's what it does, Delaynie—it locks away magic. Severs your connection to the gods, to their gifts, to the very earth and *allume* in the ground around us."

The room was quiet. Delaynie's mother stepped forward, standing beside her daughter, her eyes wide.

"I ... This is ..."

"Impossible. I know. But here it is, and I can promise you—this is *deistair*. You said every high-born or wealthy girl gets these *sautoires* on their thirteenth birthday? Their first *debutante*?"

Delaynie and her mother nodded, their eyes still wide with shock and confusion.

It settled around Mariah then. The gravity of what that meant. She'd always found it odd how so many boys had magic but hardly any girls. And how when it was a girl, she was always from one of the poorer families, those who wouldn't have been able to afford a gift like this ... or even knew it existed. Mariah wouldn't be surprised if this was a closely held secret guarded by those who could afford it. A method to suppress the magic in every girl they found worthy of being a wife, to keep them docile and tamed and obedient.

Mariah's gut twisted, and she feared she might be sick.

"Wearing this ... it would mask all magic, if you had any. Especially if you wore it before any gifts manifested. They've been suppressing magic in girls—in women—for a long, long time." Mariah's voice was hollow and low, the depth of her anger sinking deeper into a never-ending pit, clawing and screaming against the evilness of the world that even after showing her its hand, still surprised her.

Her gaze snapped to Ryenne's body, shrouded in gold. Mariah gripped Delaynie's ruined *deistair* necklace tighter in her palm and stalked toward the raised table. Light shimmered off her skin, coils of silver-gold snapping between her fingers like snakes. The vile stone in her palm was just enough to make her magic hiss and twist, but as a fully ascended queen, it would take much more than a small morsel of it to lock her power away.

It was plenty to unleash the unearthly rage lurking beneath her skin, though.

Mariah stood for a moment beside Ryenne's corpse. She pinched the end of the shroud, pulling it back just enough to reveal Ryenne's face, peaceful and still in death. Her eyes were closed, gray hair brushed away from her face. Her skin sagged, but the magic of this room held her in stasis until the vigil was complete.

"Did you know?" Mariah's whisper was so quiet, she doubted none other than the gods could hear her. "Did you know what they've done to their girls to keep them weak and suitable as wives? How many girls could be running through the kingdom with flames in their palms or the winds on their heels, free from either the confines of an unfulfilling marriage or a lifetime of servitude?" A tear streaked down Mariah's face, her voice breaking as it landed on the golden shroud.

"*How many*, Ryenne?" Her last words were raised, almost a shout as she let her tears fall upon her predecessor's body. A queen who'd had a good heart but was too weak to protect those who needed her most.

Mariah stepped away from Ryenne, glancing down at the burning stone in her palm.

With a growl that morphed into a scream, she funneled all her magic into that stone. It burned against her palm as the black heated to orange, the gold crackling with power before it shattered, vaporizing into thousands of tiny pieces scattered into the air.

Mariah sank to her knees in the antechamber, her shoulders sagging, chin hitting her chest.

Footfalls echoed behind her. A large, familiar shape lowered to his knees before her. Andrian leaned into her space, forehead resting against hers, a hand slipping behind her neck.

"You will end them, *nio*. You will end them all for this."

Mariah raised her head, meeting that beloved tanzanite stare. That face that she'd once despised so much, had tried to resist but was drawn to, nevertheless. The tortured soul inside that was still so full of anger and grief and self-loathing but was learning to put it aside for her. A soul she was determined to help mend, with each day he stood by her side.

Which, she hoped, would be a long, long time.

"*We*, Andrian. We will end them, and we will scatter their ashes like dust on the wind as we build this world anew."

CHAPTER 63

"Please. *Please.* I didn't do anything—"

Sebastian's jaw clenched as a terrible cry of pain cut Ryland's plea short. The tip of Mariah's dagger dug deeper into the sensitive skin beneath the nail on his forefinger, a trickle of blood leaking onto his stained City Guard uniform.

It took Feran two days to find Ryland. The young captain was hiding in the market district, hoping to disappear into the constant movement and activity.

If someone other than Feran had searched for him, perhaps it would've worked. Perhaps Ryland would've vanished into the heart of the city or even boarded a ship heading south to Idrix.

But no one tracked their quarry quite like Feran. When he'd dragged Ryland from the seedy tavern, thrashing and angry, he'd worn only a look of grim satisfaction.

Feran stood somewhere behind Sebastian now, that same look still on his face, arms crossed, the black braids of his hair pulled back at the nape of his neck.

"I'm going to ask you. *One* more time." Mariah's voice was low and vicious as she twirled her dagger in her hand. "Who ordered you to let the messenger past the palace gates on the night of my coronation?"

Ryland's body shook. "I didn't—I don't—"

Mariah paused the twirling of her dagger and pointed it at his next finger. Ryland's eyes bulged, arms and legs struggling against the ropes of light and shadow binding him to the chair.

"W-wait." His face flushed red, eyes fluttering closed, and he released a sob.

"Any day now, Captain." Sebastian's blood chilled at the coldness in Mariah's voice.

"I'm so sorry," Ryland whispered. "I didn't want to, but it was such an innocent request. I figured … no real harm."

Mariah tsked. "I need a bit more than that, Ryland."

He took another shuddering breath. "The … the lords. Lord Hareth. He told me … told me that if a messenger ever came with an urgent message for the queen, I was to let him in, no matter what."

Andrian stepped out of the shadows. "You spoke to one of the men who held your queen captive, and you kept that to *yourself?*"

Ryland was shaking again. "Like I said, it … it seemed harmless. And …" He hung his head.

"And *what?* Speak, Captain." Mariah raised her dagger again.

Ryland winced as the binds around his body tightened. Sebastian shifted from one foot to the other, keeping his face a careful mask, even as the beat of fury thundered through him.

"And he promised me something I would never have anymore. Not as a Marked, non-Selected guard. He offered me recognition and value. He told me I could be someone important. And since that's all he was asking for … I said I would."

That frayed the last edges of Sebastian's patience. "Someone *important?* What about being a captain of the City Guard? Is having a seat at the queen's counsel table not *important* enough for you?"

"It's alright, Sebastian." Mariah rose from her crouch, smoothly slipping her dagger into its sheath on her thigh. With the short chop to her hair, the padded and fitted dark clothing, and the short swords crossed behind her back, she looked the picture of a vengeful queen.

He understood. Gods, he understood; he was just as enraged. Could feel her rage sneaking across their bond whenever she forgot to fully close their connection.

But there was also something cold and dead behind her forest eyes. Something glimmering with otherworldly power, a magic like the silver and gold of her throne, but also ... different. Wilder. More ancient.

He couldn't deny that it terrified him.

"So that's really all you wanted? Recognition?" Mariah leaned against the table, watching Ryland with a masked expression.

"Yes," the captain said, his head still hung. "That's all I wanted. I wanted to be more than just another captain. I wanted to be valued." He lifted his chin, eyes flashing.

Sebastian took a step forward, as did Andrian, their hands resting on the hilts of their weapons.

"You could've given me that, you know. First, you passed me over at the Selection. Which is fine; I could survive that. But then I tried to show you something that I thought would have value to you. Something that would make you *appreciate* me." Despite his still flushed face, his bleeding hands, and the bindings that held him, Ryland's lip lifted in a snarl. "I am permanently Marked because of you. Branded like cattle. The least you could do is give me a simple 'thank you.' Especially after I gave you *exactly* what you were searching for."

Sebastian's fury was hot in his veins. Andrian took another step forward.

"What do you mean," Andrian said, voice deathly low, "that you gave her exactly what she was looking for?"

For the first time, something besides pitiful terror flashed in Ryland's gaze. He fixed Andrian with a stare that was full of anger and hate and disgust.

"Gods, you were always such a dick. Do you know that? Always sulking around, thinking you were better than us because you had cursed *reykr* magic. As if that made you *special*." He spat the last word, his face flushing red. "I knew what you'd find in that building. I was the one who had it boarded up after the

Solstice." His attention swung to Mariah, who stood still as a statue a few paces away. His expression turned pleading. "I just wanted to make a name for myself. To give you something that you were looking for. To make a difference—for *you*."

The room was silent, so still that Sebastian could hear Ryland's heavy breaths and the pounding of his own heart. His fingers twitched against the hilt of his sword. Ryland let out a sharp yelp as the shadows binding his arms and legs tightened, Andrian's mouth parting in a snarl.

Sebastian rarely envied Andrian for his gift, but at that moment he would've traded anything for the ability to hurt Ryland, even in just some small way.

Andrian's growl tore through the room.

"I am going to ki—"

"Andrian." Mariah's command was sharp as she moved, resting a hand on Andrian's arm. The man instantly relaxed, his face dropping all hints of his wrath and settling into his usual ambivalent mask. He shook his arms loose and rested back against the table. Sebastian blinked at his change, still touched by a hint of surprise.

He wasn't sure he would ever grow used to that. To an Andrian who was still Andrian—still an ass, still insufferable— but was no longer ... lost. An Andrian who was saved from himself and was learning how to trust.

An Andrian in *love*.

Sebastian's fear and shameful regret had driven him to rash decisions after rescuing Andrian and Mariah. But now, seeing them, seeing the way he was to her ... He couldn't deny there was something between them that no one could understand. That not even the gods could touch.

Mariah chuckled lightly.

"My, my, Ryland. Is that really it? You just wanted my attention?" She took a step forward, cocking her head. "So, you've known about that apartment building ever since the Winter Solstice?"

Ryland nodded, keeping his eyes downcast.

"And correct me if I'm wrong, but it is now, what … the middle of spring? Early summer?" Mariah glanced around at her Armature and was answered by grim nods and dark chuckles. "If I'm understanding you, that means you knew about that building and what happened there for *months* before bringing it to someone's attention."

Ryland paled, his eyes going wide again. "I didn't—you didn't—"

"What? *I didn't ask?*" Mariah surged forward, the tip of her family's dagger appearing beneath Ryland's jaw.

"Do you know what they did in that building? Do you know how many people were hurt, how many people were *killed*? On the goddess's most sacred night, do you know how many were there to *pollute* it?"

Ryland gasped like a fish, more terror flashing in his eyes.

"I should do it. Kill you for that, I mean." Mariah's voice was so flat, so emotionless, it raised the hairs on Sebastian's arms. "It would be so easy. I'd only have to push, just a touch, just enough to hit an artery. That's all it would take for you to choke on your blood."

Ryland whimpered, his eyes closing as he panted, pulling against his bonds of light and shadow.

They stayed like that for a moment. Mariah, with her dagger against Ryland's throat. Ryland, shaking with his fear. Andrian, Sebastian, and the rest of her Armature tense and alert, waiting with wide eyes and clenched fists.

After what felt like an eternity, Mariah released a breath.

"But I hardly think killing you will do any good. Not yet, anyways." She dropped her dagger and took a step back.

Ryland sagged against his bindings, sweat dampening his hair.

"Trefor, Matheo," Mariah called, turning on her heel. Trefor and Sebastian's little brother stood a little taller.

"Take Ryland to the dungeons. He'll wait there until we get back. If my family is found safe and we return here with them, then we can revisit his sentence and what exactly we're going to do with him. And if we can't ..." Mariah glanced back over her shoulder. "Then I hope you give him a comfortable cell because he will rot down there." Mariah strode for the door at the other end of the meeting room, Andrian following her. The bindings around Ryland fell away just as Trefor and Matheo reached him, securing him between the two of them.

"Wait," Ryland croaked, lifting his head weakly from his chest.

Mariah paused, turning halfway. "Yes?"

Ryland swallowed. "What do you plan to do about them? About the lords? You can't ... You can't beat them." His head dropped again. "None of us can."

"I don't believe there are any men in this kingdom who are that powerful. Anyone can be beaten. And I assure you, Ryland." Her voice dropped into a low, deadly promise. "They *will* meet their end. I will burn the entire kingdom down to see it done if I must."

Sebastian lingered in the room as Mariah and Andrian continued out through the back door and Ryland was hauled away. Quentin, Drystan, and Feran traded low whispers as they slowly followed Mariah and Andrian, presumably back to their rooms to finish packing for their journey. They were set to leave tomorrow, just after daybreak.

Sebastian stayed in that room for many long minutes, alone. He stared at a swirl in the wood of the meeting table, the reds and golds of the mahogany gleaming.

And as he stood, he realized he was afraid.

Sebastian was also angry, of course. He wanted to rip the world apart by Mariah's side as she searched for her family, wanted to burn the lords where they stood. Never once had he doubted his faith in her, to the world she wanted to build, to the future she could bring about during her reign. He'd already fought for her, had stood by her even when so many in the kingdom turned their backs.

But he was afraid of what might happen if they failed. If they couldn't rescue her family. If the lords sprang whatever trap they'd laid.

He was afraid for Mariah. For what was happening to her. For who she might become.

He was afraid that if they failed, she might actually burn the kingdom down as her vengeance.

"The moons are setting, and the sun will rise."

He still hadn't told her about that strange encounter he'd had in the city. And now, with everything happening, he was glad he hadn't and wasn't sure he ever would.

As Sebastian stared at that swirl in the wood, he wondered how far he could follow his queen.

CHAPTER 64

Mariah hardly felt the scalding water beating a drum against her skin.

She didn't know how long she'd stood in the shower. She'd walked straight from Ryland's interrogation to her rooms, Andrian a silent ghost on her heels. The moment she strode through the doors, she'd begun peeling layers of clothing from her skin, desperate to relieve the itching and burning of her rage.

It was mostly a dull flame now, a steady roar at the base of her skull. Ryland's confessions had reignited it, the beast in her chest clawing at her skin and scraping against her mind.

Mariah didn't know what was happening to her. It felt like those days before she'd been Chosen, when her magic was stirring. Some other awareness had stirred awake with it, but for so long she'd thought it all the same.

She still thought it was connected to her magic, somehow. Some unintended consequence of carrying the grace of two goddesses in her veins. But it pressed against her control every day, feeding off her fear and her anger, growing more potent with each second she spent dwelling on the terror of her situation.

Of her family's situation.

Mariah inhaled a quick gulp of air, water streaming down her face. She leaned her forehead against the steam-warmed marble wall and closed her eyes, forcing herself to take deep, measured breaths.

She couldn't control it, this rage. The more she focused on it, the more it grew, clamoring for more of her attention. She needed to be rescued from it, to be distracted from it. A part of her worried that if she couldn't claw back to sanity, she would lose herself to this. And if she did … there would be no hope of ever getting her family back.

A blast of chill air hit her back, the steam rushing out as the glass shower door opened and then closed.

She felt him there, behind her, before the water changed. Before a hand brushed down her side, her skin tingling in its wake.

"Talk to me, *nio*." Andrian's words were just loud enough to be heard over the roar of the showerhead, his mouth close to her ear.

She slowly lifted her head from the wall, turning around and leaning her back against the marble. Andrian had one arm braced above her, partially caging her in, but the water still rained in on them from above. It dripped through his hair, droplets catching on his lashes, the crushing blue of his eyes vibrant in the soft *allume* light.

He was so beautiful; it made her chest hurt. Even that beast calmed itself and curled up as she admired him, sinking into the feeling of his finger as it traced idle circles on her hip. She scanned his face, the strong shape of his jaw, the barely there stubble shading it. Down the column of his neck, across his broad shoulders, her gaze resting on the Mark on his chest.

The roaring dragon, with the jagged scar running down its center. It was so much more brutal than the bonded Marks of her other Armature, but for him … it fit.

Together, they were not clean or simple or ordinary.

They were jagged and messy, but somehow, each other's broken pieces fit together perfectly.

Apart, they were shattered.

Together, they were forged.

Mariah skimmed her fingers across his scar. Andrian tensed, the press of his hands on her hip gripping her just a little bit tighter.

"A long time ago," Mariah started, still tracing circles around his Mark, "I asked for a distraction, and you promised me that was all you would ever be." She stopped, lifting her gaze to his. His eyes glowed beneath a furrowed brow. "Do you remember that?"

He nodded, a brief movement that sent more water dripping across his face. "That failed promise is one I'll never forget."

She smiled at that—a sad, slow smile. "Do you know why I asked it? I had just been attacked by an Uroboros. A demon that shouldn't even exist, sent by a lord I was expected to rule beside. And yet … all I wanted was a distraction. From *you*. Do you know why?"

He blinked. "I might guess, but I'd prefer it if you tell me."

She sighed. "I've always sought things that could help me … forget. Things that got me out of my head, just long enough to ignore the fact that this world would always force me into some role I had no desire to play. At first, it was horses. Then, it was training. And then, when I reached early adulthood … it was sex." She didn't shy away from his stare. She had nothing to hide—not from him.

Mariah suspected he already knew all this, anyways.

"After the Uroboros, I needed a reminder that I could feel something again. It wasn't really a distraction—not in the sense some might think. I just needed something to remind me that I was *here*, that I was alive."

Andrian was still for a moment before he nodded. "And now?"

Mariah snaked her hand around his neck before sinking it into his hair. It was still short on the sides, but she was glad he'd let her leave some of the length on the top. The strands were like black silk, even beneath the water. With a gentle tug, she pulled his head down so his forehead rested against hers.

"I feel like I'm losing myself, Andrian. I'm just so fucking *angry*. Delaynie just lost her father, and I could barely find it in myself to show her any sympathy. I have so much rage and fear that I can feel myself losing the ability to ... well, *feel*. It's numbing me, drowning me out from *me*."

Andrian squeezed her hip. He dropped the hand above her head, sinking it into the hair at the base of her scalp. He pulled back from her, just a touch, so he could meet her gaze.

"So, what is it, *nio*? Do you want me to help you feel again? To remind you that you are Mariah Salis, Queen of Onita, daughter of a soldier and a healer?" His grip in her hair tightened, eyes dropping to her lips.

"To remind you that you are my moon, and that no matter what they take from you, they can *never* take your strength?" His murmur was so low, she was shocked she could hear it.

But even without words, the feelings pulsing down their bond ... she would've known what he was saying, even if all her senses were stolen from her.

"Yes, Andrian," she murmured. "Gods, yes. Remind me." Her breath hitched. "*Distract* me."

Those final words snapped something between them, a tether of energy unleashed.

With a growl, he claimed her mouth, her back flattening against the wall as he crowded against her. He still held her head, but the hand at her hip had gripped her thigh, hitching it around his waist.

Her entire body was set ablaze, but not with the flames of rage.

Currents of energy buzzed along her skin, and she gasped for breath when his tongue met hers and his teeth nipped her lips. Her hands sank deeper into his hair, pulling him so close that she could no longer tell where she stopped and he began. Heat pooled in her core as his cock pressed against her stomach, hard and ready.

Something soft and familiar slid across her arms. Andrian drew back, leaving her panting and desperate. Her eyes flew open, meeting his gaze, a wicked grin spread across his face. His shadows wound around her arms, the water passing through them harmlessly. He leaned back in, hot breath tickling her ear, sending a shiver down her spine and a fresh wave of heat to her belly.

"Trust me, *nio*. I hope I've earned it." His shadows tightened around her arms and wrists, and before she could resist, they yanked her hands out of his hair, pulling them up and securing them above her head.

Her chest heaved, but she didn't speak. Not as he leaned in, pressing a painfully gentle kiss to her lips, then to her jaw, then to the hollow of her throat.

His lips left a trail of flickering, burning flames down her body. He dropped to one knee, lifting her left leg over his shoulder before planting a kiss to the sensitive skin on the inside of her thigh, followed by a nip that had her hissing and jolting against her bindings.

"Stop playing." Her voice was husky and low.

Andrian smirked at her. "Oh, princess. You should know by now. The playing is my favorite part."

She inhaled sharply, straining against the bindings. His grip around her hips tightened, and his eyes darkened as shadows flooded his gaze.

"Listen to me, my queen. I am going to make you come until the only thing you know is how much I worship you, and the only thing you can think is how good I make you feel. I won't just distract you from your rage; I will *replace* it."

Any response she had died in her throat as he brought his mouth to her core, water falling like stars around them.

Sparks danced across her skin. A groan slipped past her teeth. He devoured her, consuming like a man starved, teeth nipping and biting at her clit as his tongue greedily drank from her. She struggled desperately against her bindings, fighting to sink her hands into his hair, to push him deeper, to chase a release that could wash away the weight on her soul.

Instead of letting her free, though, he only chuckled, the rumble of his breath jolting against her sensitive flesh.

"Give me your control, *nio*. Stop fighting. Surrender to me."

Mariah didn't want to. Losing control, with her frayed emotions ... Her wounded soul bellowed in agony.

But she'd told him she would trust him. And the more she struggled, the more he slowed, refusing to give her what she sought.

Mariah forced her body to still. She gripped one bound wrist with the other hand, squeezing tight to keep from struggling. Forcing a breath, she leaned her head back against the wall, feeling every single drop of water bead down her too sensitive skin.

"Good girl," Andrian murmured against her. She sucked in another breath at the praise, at the feel of his words against her core, heat rushing through every inch of her skin. A whine peeled out of her, unbidden and desperate.

He chuckled again and resumed his worship. But this time, he was just as frantic and gave her exactly what she chased.

Mariah shot up, then came crashing down, her shattering release wracking through her as she writhed against the bindings. Unintelligible words spilled from her throat, her entire body shaking when he didn't stop until the final waves of her orgasm had washed away.

He pressed a single kiss to the soft skin of her thigh before slowly rising, moving up her body with predatory purpose. Her head was still thrown back against the marble, chest heaving with her gasping breath.

"*Goddess*," she groaned as his mouth fell to her shoulder, then her neck, making his way to the hollow of her ear.

He chuckled again, breath tickling against her wet hair. "No, *nio*. I'm not sure who you pray to, but as far as I'm concerned, the only goddess here is you."

She dropped her head and opened her eyes, lids heavy with lust. "If I'm your goddess," she crooned, "does that make you my god?"

He pulled back from her, just a hair's breadth, just enough to meet her gaze. A slow, wild smirk pulled across his lips.

"Only when you scream my name."

She clamped down on the whimper that tried to claw from her chest. "Maybe you should stop talking, then."

His eyes flashed with challenge just before he slammed his lips to hers. She opened beneath him, letting him sweep in and claim her.

As if there were any part of her left for him to claim.

The bindings around her wrists loosened, and she tugged her hands free to grip his shoulders, nails digging into his skin. Blood rushed back into her fingertips, the sensation setting her entire body ablaze. His shadows curled around her legs, wrapping around her thighs, before his hands gripped her and lifted her farther up the wall.

Her legs settled around his hips, pinning his cock between them, his hard length gliding across her arousal. His shadows continued to twist around her legs before tightening around her left, hoisting her leg higher, opening her further to him. His hand rested against the inside of her leg, thumb dangerously close to her center, just as he broke their kiss to burrow his face into her neck as she gasped for air.

"The shadows are hardly fair," Mariah whimpered, a hand sinking into his hair and pulling as her nails dug into his shoulder.

Andrian didn't answer her. Only nipped at her ear, down her neck, and with a growl, lined himself up. He sank into her, slow and deep until he was buried to the hilt. Another groan escaped her throat as she was stretched and filled, and he landed another biting kiss on her neck, right over the sound.

"Fucking made for me, *nio*. Every single time." He pulled out, just halfway, before thrusting back in, her body shoving up the wall. "You take me so fucking well."

"*Gods*," she whispered, her mind lost to a haze of lust and love and desire.

"That's right." Another thrust. "I am your god." Thrust. "But you are my goddess."

Those were the last words they traded before they were swept away in each other. The water rained around them, each droplet like lightning on her skin. Mariah lost herself to him, to the feeling of them together, to the way their bond shimmered and sang and burned, light and shadows dancing together in a place that transcended time.

Shadows snaked between them, sliding to where they were joined. Mariah whined when they touched her clit, brushing in time with the rhythm of his thrusts. Andrian's hand slid up her back and into her hair, cradling her head as he whispered into her ear.

"I love you, Mariah. Until the moons fall from the sky." Her body tightened, her world narrowing to the sound of his voice, the rough grip of his hand, the way he moved inside her. "Come for me, *nio*. Let go."

Her release shattered through her as she cried out, clawing for him as if she could meld him to her forever. He came with her as she shuddered apart, her name on his lips like a prayer, a call for salvation.

They collapsed against each other beneath the falling water, panting and shaking in each other's arms. His shadows loosened around her legs, vanishing back beneath his skin. She was glowing faintly, the light in her veins dancing around them.

It took several long moments for their breathing to slow, for their hearts to stop racing. Andrian pulled away from her just enough to meet her gaze. His usual mask was gone, and he looked at her with that raw openness she'd seen only a handful of times. It was an openness he reserved only for her, a blend of love and wonder and awe and just the smallest hint of sadness.

Pressing a heartbreakingly gentle kiss to her forehead, he slipped himself out of her. She gasped at the sudden loss but found herself scooped into his arms, legs still wrapped around his torso as he held her to him with an arm around her back. He turned off the shower before pushing through the glass doors.

Snagging two plush white towels hanging on a rack, he set her down gently on her feet, keeping a steadying hand around her.

Mariah let him wrap her in the towel, groaning at the softness of the cotton against her still-sensitive skin. Her body felt heavy, and her mind felt calm, the magic bridging their souls still wrapped tight around her and holding the beast of her rage at bay.

Andrian led her to the bed and together they sank into the down comforter, the sound of the night breeze outside brushing in through the open window. They both succumbed to sleep, their momentary comfort fighting off the dread they harbored deep beneath their current happiness.

Dread that tonight, this feeling of contentedness and bliss, might be the last one they ever have.

CHAPTER 65

Mariah woke to the darkness of early morning before the sun's rays had peaked over the mountains. She was warm beneath her down comforter, limbs tangled with Andrian's, the gentle rise and fall of his chest telling her he still slept.

She wanted to go back to sleep. Knew she would need it. She had plenty of time to rest; they weren't planning to leave until midmorning when the sun had fully risen. Their bags were already packed and only the gods knew when she would get her next chance to really rest.

Mariah squeezed her eyelids closed, trying to slow her breathing. Focused on Andrian's skin against hers, the steady beat of his heart, the rhythm of his breaths.

But none of it chased away the racing thoughts beginning to take flight. The momentary peace from the night before was forgotten, replaced by panic and fear and anxiety.

She didn't know which was worse: the fear or the rage.

Slowly, Mariah untangled herself from Andrian. It took nearly all her strength to pull her skin from his, craving his warmth, but she couldn't stay lying there. Her heart was racing, her mind spinning, and she needed to be outside.

Andrian grumbled, rolling towards her as she moved. She stilled, placing her hand on the side of his face. He nuzzled her palm, sighing into her skin.

It made her smile to see him so happy. So content. Something that she wasn't sure she would ever see in him.

His darkness was still there, but despite all they'd endured, she was glad they'd found this again. That she had learned to trust and heal herself, and he had learned to find joy.

The bond stretching between them danced and shimmered. Mariah pushed as much of the love and gratitude she felt for him across it, along with four words.

Sleep. I love you.

Mariah wasn't sure if he heard them or why she tried. But this bond felt so different and changed every day.

Maybe one day, they really could trade words across it. She still didn't know what to make of it—if it was just because he was her consort, the one Armature she'd always been drawn to over the others, or if it was something ... more.

Her consort. She didn't doubt it. In truth, she'd always known what he was to her. But there was something about it that felt almost too inconsequential, a too simple title to describe this thing burning between them.

With a sigh, she pulled her hand from his and turned to the bathroom. She grabbed a warm cotton robe hanging on a hook, wrapping it around herself before silently padding through her suite and to the glass balcony doors. She lingered there for a moment, staring out at the mountains, breath fogging on the glass. Clenching her jaw, she pulled the handle and stepped out into the early morning air.

Mariah walked across the patio, the wide space outfitted with tables and chairs beneath the roof. She left the covered area, striding out into the open, her feet crossing the very place where she'd bonded with six of her seven Armature. The winter snows and spring rains had washed away all traces of those nights, any droplets of candle wax long since scrubbed from the tile.

Mariah wondered if she would ever feel so clean. If she could one day stand beneath those rains and have every mark and stain and scar washed from her body, sluicing off like that wax from the ground.

She doubted it, but it was nice to dream.

Reaching the edge of the balcony, she leaned against the chest-high railing circling the space. The drop was devastating. The valley beneath the palace so far, she could hardly see the brush of the mountain wind through the treetops. She lifted her gaze to the Attlehons, to the streaks of pink and orange beginning to spread behind them. The sun would be up soon, its triumphant light sending them all not to celebration but to something that was as close as she'd been to war.

A breeze floated past her, brushing her cheeks and lifting the ends of her hair around her face.

She thought of herself, no more than half a year ago, as the girl who wanted nothing more than to be free of a society that despised her. But that girl, the one desperate enough to abandon her family and vanish into the edges of the world, was dead.

All who remained was the woman with scars across her back gifted to her by the hand of one whom she loved, a woman who now ruled a country of people who didn't know she existed. A queen who was prepared to tear the world down in order to keep those dearest to her safe.

Mariah drew a deep inhale, holding the air in her lungs. She closed her eyes against the rising sun, its rays warming her cheeks and the exposed skin of her neck. Her fingers tightened around the railing, grounding herself against the dawn of the new day.

A new day that could bring with it so much change.

Hope that she might rescue her family.

Belief that the love she'd found would not fail her again.

Power that she would assert as her own, squashing those desperate and hungry lords once and for all.

But somewhere, far away from that balcony nestled between the mountains and the sea, Mariah could feel it. Could feel something dark festering in the world. She didn't know what it was or how she felt it brushing against her with vile and greedy fingers, but it was there.

That beast shifted beneath her skin. It was not angry, did not claw for freedom. It only watched, looking back at her with burning eyes of silver and gold and forest green.

Mariah's own eyes shot open, heart hammering against her ribs. The sun had risen higher as she'd stood, its light bright across her face. She gasped in a lungful of the warm morning air, beads of sweat running tracks down her temple.

Something fluttered above. Her attention darted up as a black butterfly floated and fluttered through the air mere feet from her balcony, dipping and swirling in the breeze.

Each time she'd seen it, she'd been convinced it was not the same butterfly. It was impossible; insects couldn't fly that far or live that long.

But now … she couldn't be sure. Something settled in her soul, that beast calming with her, as if it, too, watched the butterfly's delicate dance through the sky. It floated across her vision, her head following it from left to right.

She lost it when she turned all the way, but not because it vanished from sight.

A golden Attlehon eagle was perched beside her on the balcony railing. So close that if she wanted, she could reach out and touch those gold and white feathers, the filaments still shifting as they refracted the morning light.

The eagle was massive, nearly three feet tall. Mariah met its unblinking golden gaze, its stare intense and probing as it watched her.

As she watched it back.

Mariah didn't know how long it lasted. How long she watched the eagle, unsure which of them was the beast, and which was the queen.

Perhaps, Mariah thought, *it's one and the same.*

Her fingers twitched and she lifted her hand. With a massive gust of air, stirred by powerful wings, the eagle launched itself into the sky, shooting over the edge of the balcony. Mariah only caught the barest glimpse of her black wingtips before her feathers opened fully, blending into the sky above and the valley below, vanishing her from sight.

She didn't search for the eagle after that. It was futile.

But she did tilt her head to the sky, past the rising sun. She stretched her awareness up to the moons disappearing behind the light of day, to the two goddesses who frustrated her beyond belief, but she still knew, without a doubt, were with her. Always.

"Thank you," she whispered into the morning wind, just as a tear laced with silver-gold light fell from her eye and splashed on the railing, rolling off and falling to the valley below.

CHAPTER 66

Ciana twisted her hands, her nerves like the brush of hot coals beneath her skin.

The main palace courtyard was a frenzy of movement—stable hands ran to and fro, lugging tack and bags and food to the line of waiting horses. Mariah's Armature, expressions tense, weaved amongst the horses and stable hands, tightening cinches and securing weapons. Sebastian was in a quiet, strained conversation with Drystan and Feran while Delaynie stood to Ciana's left, her friend even more quiet and pale than usual.

Something had happened between Delaynie and Mariah during Ryenne's vigil. Not wanting to overwhelm Delaynie, Ciana had left before Mariah had arrived, giving her friend and her queen time together alone. Delaynie had looked like a ghost ever since and even now clutched her arms across her chest as though she might float away if she let herself go. Every so often, Delaynie's fingers would brush across her throat as if seeking something that was no longer there.

Ciana's face tightened into a scowl. She opened her mouth, about to ask what was wrong, when a presence yanked her attention away.

"Hey, Cee."

Mariah wore all black—leather-lined leggings for the ride, a sleeveless tunic, a reinforced jerkin fitted snugly across her chest. Her twin short-swords crisscrossed behind her back, dragon-winged dagger holstered at her thigh, her dark, shoulder-length hair tucked behind her ears.

She looked more like a warrior than a queen. But Ciana supposed she was. Queens didn't always need to wear their crowns.

Especially not on missions to rescue their families.

Ciana answered Mariah's greeting with a forced grin, pushing aside her fear and frustration. "Hi, M."

Mariah's mouth lifted into a hesitant smile. "Are you ... Do you have everything you need? For while we're gone."

Ciana waved her off. "Yes, yes. Everything's fine. Don't worry about me." She scanned Mariah. "But you, though ... How are you?" She whispered at the end, unable to hide her worry.

Mariah glanced away, looking across the courtyard toward the movement by the stables. Feran now stood beside Kodie, checking over the tack and Mariah's bags.

"I'm ready." Mariah's answer was terse and short. There was a tightness to Mariah's jaw, her throat bobbing as she swallowed. Light danced around her fingertips, the way it always did when she was feeling something so strongly, she couldn't contain it beneath her skin.

Someone else stepped around Mariah's shoulder. The one person still missing from the courtyard, appearing out of nowhere like the annoying shadow he was.

Ciana focused on Andrian. He, too, was dressed in all black, a longsword slung across his back. He watched Ciana with a disin-terested mask, eyes darting between her and Mariah.

Despite the ambivalent facade, he couldn't hide the emotion in his eyes. Not when he looked at their queen.

Ciana's hands tightened into fists. Mariah took a surprised step back as Ciana stomped around her, not halting until she was chest to chest with Andrian.

Except … she was so much shorter; the top of her head barely reached his chest.

Swallowing her grumble of annoyance, Ciana twisted her brow into a scowl, tilting her chin up to meet Andrian's stare. He regarded her with mild curiosity as she crossed her arms over her chest.

They glared at each other for a few heartbeats as Ciana organized her thoughts. Long enough for Mariah to shift uncomfortably from foot to foot.

"You know," Ciana began, staring hard into his bright blue eyes, "I never really liked you much. You've always been a bit of an asshole and a dick, and grumpy whenever there was no reason to be. You're rude and stand-offish and sometimes say things just to hurt other people. Plus, the shadow wielding has always kind of freaked me out."

Andrian arched a single brow, the corner of his lip twitching.

"But," Ciana continued, her tone settling into something more serious. Just a little sadder. "I've also watched you change. You're still all those things, but it's more tolerable now. And I don't blame you, either. I think it's something we have in common."

Andrian still didn't speak. Only shot a quick glance at Mariah before returning his gaze to Ciana, blinking once.

Ciana smiled and nodded. "I, too, came to this palace broken and in need of saving. And I get it. I know the way she can heal someone. The way she healed me. And I think … the way she healed you, too."

"Hey, wait—I'm not some healer, I didn't—"

Ciana held up a hand to her queen. Mariah let out a soft yelp of surprise but fell silent.

"Listen to me, Andrian Laurent. I know you don't value much in this world; I sure didn't. Not before I met our queen. But I know you treasure her. This kingdom needs her—more than either of us knows. So if you don't bring her home to us, I swear to all the gods that I will chop off your balls and feed them to you. Do I make myself clear?"

"Ciana, calm down. Don't be dramatic—"

Mariah's protest was cut short when Andrian moved.

He took a step back from Ciana. Without ever breaking eye contact, he lifted his right hand, curling it into a fist and resting it over his heart. Over his Mark.

In a slow, measured movement, Andrian lowered his knee to the ground, still not looking away.

"Ciana Visseau," he said, voice low and darker than his shadows. "I swear to you, by all the gods of this world—and of the worlds beyond—that I will bring our queen home. I will give my life for hers. Not just because she is my queen, but because she is more precious to me than the moons and stars themselves. You have my word; her reign will not end with this journey."

All movement in the courtyard halted at the dark Armature kneeling before the golden lady. The final words of his vow echoed off the cobblestones, falling like stars.

Ciana swallowed thickly. Out of the corner of her eye she saw Mariah standing, mouth agape, a single tear tracking down her cheek. Locking her stare back on Andrian, Ciana nodded.

"I accept your vow, Armature. And I intend to hold you to it."

Andrian dipped his head before rising to his feet. He closed the gap between himself and Ciana, and with an almost-hesitant movement, rested his hand on her shoulder.

"I know you never liked me much, Ciana," he said, his words just for her. "But I always admired you. And I've always been grateful to you for being there for her when I wasn't ready to be."

Tears pricked behind Ciana's eyes. She nodded again, a short, sharp movement.

She understood now what Mariah saw in him. She hadn't fully comprehended it before, but with that honesty, she got it.

With a smile cast her way, Andrian stepped back from her, rejoining his queen. Ciana turned as he went, and with her tears choking her throat, hurtled herself into Mariah's arms, nearly knocking her off balance.

"I'm sorry," Ciana whispered as she gripped her friend tight.

"I didn't mean to cause a scene. I just … We all need you to come back to us."

Mariah pulled back from her embrace and smiled. "I know, Cee. Don't worry. I'll come back. And I'll have my family with me, and we'll be ready to take on whatever else those fuckers try to throw our way."

Ciana chuckled, the sound thick with her tears. "Good."

They were quiet for a moment, two friends watching each other.

Mariah's face fell slowly. Shifted into something more serious, more masked and composed.

"Cee," she began, her voice measured. "Do you … Were you ever given a piece of jewelry with a black and gold stone in it? Maybe around the time of your first *debutante*?"

Ciana started. Of all the questions, that was not one she'd been expecting.

"Well, yeah, I guess," she said, confusion spiking in her gut. "My …" She swallowed. "My stepfather gifted me a ring on my first *debutante*. It had a small black and gold stone in the center."

Mariah glanced down to her fingers, and Ciana watched her heave a great sigh of relief when she saw Ciana wasn't wearing it.

"Why, Mariah? What's happening?"

"You don't wear it anymore?" Mariah ignored her question, glancing between Ciana's hands and her face.

Ciana shook her head. "Not really, no. It was never my style. I wore it every day back home because my stepfather would've been furious if I hadn't. But since I've come here, I haven't put it back on."

"Good. Don't." A strange urgency was in Mariah's voice, a feverish light igniting behind her eyes. "I'll explain everything when I'm back, Cee. But there is so much more going on in this kingdom than we ever knew. Just whatever you do, don't put that ring back on. In fact, it's probably best if you don't even touch it until I'm back."

Ciana nodded slowly. "Okay. I won't. But I'm confused as shit."

Mariah chuckled. "I know, Cee. I promise, it will make sense after I explain. Just wait a few more days for me, okay?"

Ciana nodded. "Okay. You have my word."

Mariah gathered Ciana up into another great hug. Her scent of jasmine and cedarwood washed over her, as if lifted by a breeze. Something else stirred in her chest, something she'd been ignoring, and continued to ignore.

Too many goodbyes. Now was not the time for any nonexistent revelations.

Mariah pulled back, eyes brimming with tears. "Take care of my kingdom while I'm gone, Ciana."

"As if she were my own, My Queen," Ciana answered.

They separated, and with a final glance, Mariah and Andrian strode toward the waiting horses, shoulder to shoulder, looking as if they'd already spent a lifetime walking by each other's sides. Ciana watched them go, a soft wind lifting her golden curls around her face as she again twisted her hands together.

She'd said her goodbyes. She'd made—and received—her orders. Her best friend would come back to her. And she had the promise of the one person in that palace who loved Mariah more than she did to guarantee that.

But there was still one goodbye she had yet to make. One she didn't particularly want to do, because she wasn't sure she knew how.

"Second time we're leaving you in charge, and I like it even less than last time."

A familiar voice behind her—a voice belonging to the one she'd been dwelling on—answered all her questions. Ciana froze, then slowly turned, meeting Sebastian's hazel gaze. He stood a few feet from her, hands crossed behind his back, the picture of the perfect Armature. He must've seen something on Ciana's face because his good-natured smile faltered, and his brows furrowed.

"Not that I don't think you'll be wonderful. The leadership suits you, Cee. I just ..." His cheeks lightly flushed. "I just don't like all of us being separated. I need to go with my queen, but I don't like leaving you here. Without ... us."

"Without us," Ciana repeated, her voice quiet.

Sebastian nodded, still wearing a confused expression on his handsome face.

"Do you think all the others mind leaving me here?"

His flush grew. "Of—of course. You are a lady of the court. You're important to Mariah, so you're important to all of them. All of us."

Ciana shook her head. "That wasn't my question, Sebastian."

Sebastian glanced away, taking a deep, heaving sigh. When he looked back at Ciana, his expression was pained.

"What do you want me to say? That *I'm* the one who doesn't like leaving you here? That I can't stand the thought of leaving you alone in this palace without me?" He choked on a bitter laugh, running a hand through his hair. "What good would that do any of us?"

Ciana wasn't sure her heart was beating. Her lungs froze in her chest, tightening as if the weight of a thousand bricks had landed there. Her hands had stopped wringing together, now just clasped in front of her, knuckles white.

"What good would it do?" she whispered, taking a step closer to him. "Sebastian ... Mariah is the reason I chose this palace as my new home, but you ... *you* are the reason I stayed. You reminded me that no matter what terrible men had done to me, I still had *me*. That after all they'd taken from me, they could never take that. I still had choices I could make for myself. I could still *choose*." Her voice broke at the end, more tears welling in her eyes.

"And, Seb, despite everything we have working against us, despite your bond and my past and the Royals and everything ... I would still *choose you*. Every single time." She hung her head, staring at the cobblestones beneath her feet. "I just ... needed you to know that. Just once."

Silence passed between them, a stillness shared only in the microcosm that existed in those few feet of the palace courtyard.

It was broken by a shuddering groan, a desperate plea.

"Ciana—"

That was all it took.

Ciana lifted her head, eyes clashing with Sebastian's before she closed the distance between them.

His arms wrapped around her waist as she threw hers around his neck, crashing her lips to his.

His body tensed in surprise, just for a moment, before relaxing against her. Sebastian was so warm, so familiar, so safe. He tasted of mahogany and parchment, like nights spent wrapped beneath a worn quilt with stacks of books and a raging fire glowing in the hearth.

He felt like home. A home she'd never known but was so desperate to find.

Ciana tangled her fingers in his hair, aching to pull him closer. To remember as much of him as she could, to soak in all he was so no matter what happened, she could never forget. His hands brushed through her curls, fingers digging lightly into her back.

After what felt like forever, she pulled away. They both breathed heavily, his cheeks as flushed as she knew her own to be.

"Ciana," he whispered, eyes bright, pupils blown wide. He lifted a slightly shaking hand, resting it on her face, pushing back the tangled mass of her hair.

She smiled up at him. "Sebastian."

He searched her face. "I never ... I never knew. That you might ..."

"Might what? Want to be with you? I may be damaged, Sebastian, but I'm not broken."

Sebastian flushed again. "That's not what I meant." He opened his mouth, about to say more before a shout shattered the moment.

"Seb! Lover boy! It's time to go. Get your ass over here."

Fucking Quentin. If they all made it back, Ciana would rip out his tongue herself.

Sebastian sighed, resting his forehead against hers. "When I'm back, we'll talk. About ... everything. All of this. I promise."

She nodded against him. With the gentlest of movements, he

tipped her chin up just enough to kiss her; one more time, a sweet and delicate touch.

Ciana searched his face when he drew away from her. "Come back to me, okay?"

Sebastian smiled. "And leave this unfinished? There's not a chance under the moons I'm letting that happen, Goldie."

CHAPTER 67

Manic energy chased Mariah from Verith, leading her Armature west on Xara's Road with an urgency that crawled beneath her skin.

The sun was setting when they reached a small town on the road, just before it branched and they would take it north. Mariah's body was stiff and, despite the anxiety swimming in her gut, her exhaustion weighed heavily on her bones.

"What do you think?" Mariah nodded at the small inn and tavern, speaking to no one in particular. "One more sleep in a bed before braving the woods?"

"I don't like it. It's not safe." Sebastian appeared at her side, pulling his warhorse to a halt. His brow was furrowed. "What if someone recognizes you?"

Mariah frowned. "Why would they recognize me? Because I'm a queen they don't know?"

It was true. While she was coronated and the full power of the queen flowed through her veins like intoxicating threads of silver-gold power ... none but those in the palace knew. Normally, a formal ascension celebration would've been held days after the coronation to present the new queen to the people.

But Mariah would not sit idle for another antiquated tradition while her family rotted in a prison cell.

Sebastian made an exasperated sound. "They have *seen* you before. At the parade, for example. And it's not exactly common to see a young woman traveling with seven men."

Mariah fell silent as she stared at the inn. The quaint little town was quiet, and only a few horses were tethered to the posts lining the road. A few stable boys lingered around the inn doors, bored as they waited for patrons, their presence indicating the existence of a proper stable behind the inn.

"*Nio?*" Andrian's dark presence enveloped her as his horse stopped beside Kodie. "It's a risk, but if you want to stay here, we will."

Mariah held his gaze, sinking into the brilliant, sparkling blue of his eyes, before nodding.

"This is the last town we'll pass before reaching Khento," she said. "And it was a hard ride today. The horses—and us—need one last rest." She tightened her jaw. "My family is strong, and I need to arrive strong for them."

Andrian's eyes glittered in the hazy dusk light as she pressed her heels into Kodie's flank, trotting to the waiting stable boys and the glow of the tavern doors.

"Fuck," Andrian murmured in Mariah's ear. "I take it back. This might be too much of a risk."

Sebastian hmphed. "Finally, some sense."

As much as Mariah didn't want to admit it, they *did* have a point.

While the inn had looked quiet from the street, boisterous chatter and a wave of warm, malted heat greeted them. The room was nearly full, patrons packed shoulder to shoulder around the bar or sprawled around wood tables and benches. A lively band at the back of the room played a jig, and several couples danced and laughed across a makeshift dance floor.

It was loud and bright and so *alive*.

Something about it all stirred a drifting piece of Mariah's soul. Hooked a string around it, dragging it back to her through all the pain and rage and hollowness.

She'd spent so much time over the past months staring death and despair in the face. It was a beautiful, wondrous shock to see so much overflowing happiness and life.

Their horses needed the rest. They needed the sleep.

And Mariah needed ... this.

Mariah shook her head. "No. If they have rooms for us, we're staying here."

Andrian groaned, the sound of it rumbling through her. "Of all the times you could choose to be social ... why *now*?"

She shot a glare over her shoulder. "I'm not *choosing* to be social." A young man bent down at the table in front of them, asking a blushing girl for a dance. "I'm choosing to enjoy one last night in a comfortable bed." A group of weather-worn farmers clinked their pint glasses together, crows' feet cracking at the corners of their eyes. "I'm choosing a night of *normal*. I don't want to be ..." She glanced around before loosing her breath.

"I just want to be Mariah. One last time." She straightened her spine, meeting her Armature's stares. "And if you don't like it, you can sleep in the stables."

They grinned at her, a few of them chuckling. Even Sebastian took a step back—still on alert but conceding for tonight.

Andrian, however, held her glare.

"Fine." He leaned in closer. The corner of his lip twitched. "But only because I would be a madman indeed to turn down one more night in a bed with you."

She tightened her features, desperately holding onto her glower, even as the flames of her blush licked up her throat and cheeks. "Control yourself, Armature. Besides, I refuse to believe there won't be many more nights to come."

He pulled back from her, just enough for her to see his lifted brow, a smirk spreading fully across his face. "Many more nights to *come* seems incredibly accurate—"

Mariah whirled, shouldering through the crowd as heat crept higher on her cheeks, his soft chuckle following her.

"Excuse me," she half-shouted, leaning over the sticky lacquered bar. A dark-skinned, gray-haired man tended the bar, his tired, crinkled eyes swinging to Mariah.

"How can I help ya', miss?"

Mariah flashed him her sweetest smile. "I'm traveling with my fiancé and his cousins to Ettervan. We need accommodations for the night. Is there any way you could help us?"

The innkeeper gave her a sharp-eyed once-over. "How many?"

"Eight, including myself." She rushed out the words, delivering them with another brilliant smile. If he recognized the significance of a woman traveling with seven men ...

But the innkeeper only grunted. "Large party. We're quite full tonight. Let me see what we have available." He shuffled away to a pile of books and ledgers tucked into a shelf above the bar, sliding a pair of glasses onto his wide nose.

A warm shadow wrapped around her back; just as actual shadows danced around her hips. "Fiancé?"

She shrugged, even as her skin prickled. "I needed something convincing to keep him from asking questions. Don't tell me it triggered your commitment issues."

Andrian's breath huffed across her cheek as he laughed. "Far from it, princess. Maybe I liked it a little *too* much."

Mariah's eyes widened, and she was about to whirl on him just as the innkeeper returned, glasses still sitting on the bridge of his nose.

"Good news," he rumbled. "We have two rooms that should fit your needs. Bunk rooms, four beds in each room."

"Perfect. We'll take—"

"You don't have any single rooms left?" Andrian leaned around her, forearm resting on the bar. The innkeeper flicked him a glance.

"I have only one left, but it's my smallest. It has a private bathroom, but the bed ... it is quite cramped." His dark gaze pinged between Mariah and Andrian, and more warmth bloomed across Mariah's cheeks.

"That's quite alright—"

"We'll take it."

Mariah shot Andrian a glare at the second interruption, only to see him giving the innkeeper a blinding smile. The aging man nodded, giving them their total for the three rooms before helping another patron to a refill. Andrian finally glanced at Mariah, eyes wide with feigned innocence. "What?"

She grumbled, digging a hand into the satchel strapped across her chest. Her fingers brushed against the coin she carried, pieces of silver and copper and gold. Some of it was from the palace coffers, but …

As she placed what they owed on the bar top, the innkeeper swiping it up as he handed them their keys with a nod, she couldn't help but smile at how far Donnet's stolen coin had traveled.

"The food should take about twenty minutes, but I will be back with ale shortly." The young serving girl smiled at their table, a soft blush staining the apples of her cheeks before she rushed away.

"Did we make her nervous?" Trefor frowned after the girl, ruffling his pale blonde hair as he scratched his temple.

Mariah stifled a giggle, the sound instead coming out as a muted snort. She settled further into her chair, leaning into Andrian's warmth. His arm rested on the chair-back, his fingers tracing idle circles on her shoulder. "It may be hard to believe, Trefor, but I think the group of you would make anyone nervous."

Trefor's frown deepened. "Why? I think we're nice." His sea-green eyes slid to Andrian for half a heartbeat. "Mostly," he finished, his mouth lifting a little into a grin.

Andrian's fingers stilled, and this time Mariah did not try to muffle her laugh. "It's not so much about being *nice* but more about how *many* there are of you. I just happen to be stuck with you for life and therefore had to get over it quicker than most."

They chuckled, grins stretching across faces, as the serving girl reappeared with a tray laden with ale. Even Andrian smiled softly and shook with quiet laughter, his fingers resuming their circles on her skin.

Trefor turned to face the girl as she set the last glass on the table. "Do we make you nervous?"

The girl blushed even more furiously this time, her entire face flooding with color. "I—no, of course not—"

"Because we're nice. I promise!"

"Very convincing, Trefor." Feran turned to the girl with his gentle, easy smile. "Don't let him trouble you, miss. He's seen twenty-seven years, but we don't really let him out much. For obvious reasons."

It was Trefor's turn to flush bright red, muttering under his breath as the serving girl nodded her head and rushed away.

Mariah laughed again, leaning forward and resting her forearms on the lacquered wood. The loss of Andrian's fingers was immediate, but his warmth still pressed against her side, solid and sure.

"I guess," she started, meeting the stares of each of her Armature, "that this is our last night for some lightheartedness. I think, after this journey ... everything might be different."

Despite the noisy rabble of the inn dining room, the silence at their table was deafening.

"How are you? With everything, I mean," Matheo asked from his seat across the table. Mariah's smile faltered, shifted into something tinged with sadness.

"Better, now that we're out of the city. And I'm glad I'm not alone, that I have each of you." Warm smiles and nods answered. She cracked open her bonds, just enough to feel: affection, pride, fear, sadness, all woven together in a tapestry of emotion that seeped into her soul.

She wasn't exactly sure when, or how, these men had become her family. Closer to her than brothers. The love she carried for them differed from the love she carried for Andrian or even her blood.

To be known so deeply and be accepted without question anyways was a special thing.

"Gods, you know what would be great, though?" Quentin leaned forward, palming the hilt of a throwing knife strapped to his chest. "If our bonds gave us the ability to use some of your magic. I mean, we each carry a piece. Why can't we cut people in half with some light magic, like you can?"

Sebastian snorted, Andrian grinned, and Mariah laughed.

"First of all," Mariah said, "I have never *once* used magic to cut someone in half."

"Yeah, but you could. You put a cut in a mahogany table and stopped a lord's heart with just a flash." Quentin shrugged. "I'd like to do those things, too. That's all."

"I'm sure you would." Mariah rolled her eyes, chuckling. She took a long sip of ale, the cool bite of the hops welcome on her tongue. "Unfortunately—"

A familiar woman walked into her line of sight.

She was dressed in a simple gray tunic and black pants, a far cry from the strange silver robes she'd worn the last time Mariah had seen her. But Mariah would recognize her distinct features—and telltale violet eyes—anywhere.

The Leuxrithian priestess who'd first found Mariah at her *Porofirat.* Who she and Andrian had seen fleeing through the game park, escaping a pack of Shawth's soldiers. Who had appeared in the palace library before the Winter Solstice and given Mariah so many answers but left her with just as many questions.

The priestess stood in the center of the tavern, glancing around as if searching for someone. Mariah laid her palms flat on the table and slowly stood from her chair.

"Mariah?" Sebastian stood with her, alarm in his voice. Even Andrian straightened in his chair, hand dropping from her back.

But Mariah ignored them. The priestess met her gaze across the sea of crowded tables. A slow smile spread across her ageless face, slightly up-tilted eyes twinkling with mischief in the warm tavern glow.

"You," Mariah murmured breathlessly. So quiet, it should've been impossible for the priestess to hear her.

But the priestess's smile stretched wider, and she wove her way through the tables to where Mariah and her Armature had settled in the back. She halted across the table from Mariah, standing between Drystan and Sebastian, the latter still standing as her Armature watched her warily.

The priestess dutifully ignored them. Instead, she met Mariah's gaze, dipping her head in the smallest of bows. "It is good to see you again."

The confusion that pummeled Mariah through the bonds she'd left open had her sucking in her breath. She slammed the mental doors closed; all but one.

But Andrian was not confused or suspicious. From him, Mariah felt only pointed curiosity.

"What—what are you doing here?" Mariah's shock coursed through her. Bluntness was all she knew.

The priestess shifted, smile faltering. "That is a complicated question." Her eyes darted quickly around the crowded room before returning to Mariah. "The gods make strange requests of their servants."

Mariah scoured the priestess's face. She clawed back through her memories; something the woman said was familiar.

The revelation struck Mariah like a blow.

The gods ... The priestess chose her words carefully. Because she served no Onitan god but one from Leuxrith. Callamus, God of the Night Sky.

A god no one in Onita knew. The knowledge this priestess carried—that there were other gods who kept to other kingdoms, hidden behind closed borders and centuries-old embargoes— could shatter the foundation of many Onitan's beliefs.

But Mariah couldn't help but wonder if that foundation needed to be destroyed.

"Mariah," Sebastian said, his controlled voice cutting through the thick silence. "Care to introduce us to your … friend?"

Mariah frowned, still holding the priestess's stare. "I would, but—"

"You can call me Signe." The priestess turned her smile to Mariah's Armature. "And fate has crossed our paths before, though most of you do not know it." Signe lingered on Andrian, her violet eyes flashing. "Except for you, *madr*."

Andrian chuckled softly. "I thought you looked familiar. Glad to see those woods didn't give you too much trouble."

Signe dipped her head again.

"It's great to see you again, Signe, and to finally make your acquaintance," Mariah said, voice slightly sharp. "But why are you here?"

Signe's humor fell away, something depthless creeping into her face. "As I said, the gods make strange requests. But I am hardly one to question them." She sharpened her gaze on Mariah, that same scorching stare that peeled back too many layers.

"You ride toward great danger and darkness. I would try to stop you, but I know it would be futile." Signe pitched her voice lower, masking her words from the din of the crowd. "If you are willing to pay the price, then you will change this world forever."

Mariah's stomach plummeted to the floor, her heart racing as a buzzing ignited in her ears. "So, it *is* a trap."

"I do not know. Everything is shrouded, and not in the familiar darkness of the night."

"What about my family?" Mariah swallowed, panic clogging her throat. "Will we all survive this? Where are you going?"

Signe glanced around again, as if to remind Mariah of where they were. Even now, a few curious glances were cast their way. Mariah did her best to relax, to calm her racing heart.

"I cannot say more," Signe answered. "I have my task, and you have yours. Our paths lie before us, and regardless of where they lead, I am glad to have seen you as I walk mine. I can only hope they cross again soon in the coming days."

Mariah held Signe's violet stare for a long moment. They

exchanged no more words, but something passed between the two women. Something ancient and nameless. Something ready to be unleashed. Something indescribably *female* and filled with undiluted rage.

"Thank you, Signe."

"You are welcome, Mariah." Signe took a step from the table. "Stay strong and be the light against the darkness." With one final, fleeting bow of her head, Signe whirled on her feet, vanishing through the thick crowd.

The tavern door opened, then closed, and Mariah knew she was gone.

"What the *fuck* was that about?"

Mariah slowly lowered herself back into her chair, not answering Quentin's question. She fought back her nausea mounting higher with her fear.

As if on cue, the serving girl reappeared, bearing heavy trays laden with food. Mariah stayed quiet as their dinner was passed around—roasted vegetables, rice, and stewed mutton, all warm and inviting and hearty.

Her stomach still rolled, but she picked up her knife and fork and cut into her first bite. Her Armature shared a concerned glance, before following her lead and burrowing into their food.

Judging by their mumbled words of appreciation, she was sure it was delicious. But she tasted none of it.

Andrian leaned closer to her. His breath brushed against the shell of her ear. "Are you alright, *nio*?"

Mariah nodded, taking another bite. She washed it down with a sip of ale. She tasted only ash.

"I will be."

"That innkeeper wasn't kidding. This bed is small." Andrian stood in the doorway, arms crossed as he scowled at the small wooden bed tucked into the corner.

He had a point. The mattress looked soft enough, but it was barely larger than Mariah's childhood bed.

"I think you're just spoiled," Mariah said with an affectionate grin, stepping around him. The meal had settled her some, but she was still on edge from Signe's appearance. She craved a semblance of normalcy and was desperate to create some for herself.

Andrian grumbled. "I might be too tall. And you're a bed-hog."

And thankfully, Andrian somehow always knew *exactly* what she needed.

"*I'm* the bed-hog?" She scoffed. "I thought we agreed to this a long time ago, Andrian. No more lies."

He chuckled. "Fine. Maybe we're both lying." His eyes were bright and warm. "As long as you shower, I'm sure it won't be too bad."

"What are you insinuating? That I stink?" She knew, for a fact, that she did. One couldn't spend the day riding hard in warm spring weather without picking up a certain scent. She strode further into the room, turning to the small, attached bathroom. She cast a look back over her shoulder at Andrian, who lifted his brow with a smirk.

"I would never dare say such a thing, princess. But also ..." He shrugged.

Mariah laughed. "You're an asshole. You stink too, you know."

Andrian pushed off the doorframe with a brilliant smile—one of those smiles he seemed to share only with her—and closed the door behind him with a soft *click*. He chuckled and followed her into the bathroom, landing a kiss on her temple as he joined her.

The shower was small, the water barely more than lukewarm, but they still washed the grime of the road from their skin. The cramped quarters forced them together, every move a brush of skin, and it didn't take long for Andrian to push Mariah up against the tiled walls, taking her hard and fast. Raw desperation fueled their joining, mixing with a fear they tried their best to ignore during those few blissful minutes, even though it lingered just below the surface.

Half an hour later, Mariah was dressed in one of Andrian's shirts and sitting cross-legged on the tiny bed, toying with her grandfather's dagger. She threaded light between her fingers, her body clean and sated but her stomach still twisted into knots.

The door hinges whined and Andrian slipped back into their room. He'd gone to check on the watch order for the night, and the floorboards groaned beneath his weight as he padded to the bed, dropping to a knee before her. He slipped a finger beneath her chin, lifting her gaze to his, taking the dagger from her and setting it on the tiny bedside table.

Andrian searched her face before brushing back her hair, tucking a strand behind her ear. "They are strong, *nio*. Just like you. We'll get them out."

Mariah swallowed. "I'm glad I made everyone stop. But now that we have, I want to be back on the road. I don't want to be here, comfortable and resting, while they're in that place."

"I know. But your gut was right; we needed this. It'd be useless to them if we arrive tired and drained." He dropped his hand from her chin. "Try to sleep tonight, Mariah. Then tomorrow, we can ride like the Scourge himself is chasing us."

Mariah blinked and he stood, pulling off his boots before sitting beside her on the bed. She drew her magic back beneath her skin, sliding up the bed and slipping beneath the covers. Andrian followed her, wedging himself between her and the wall.

The moment he settled, she twisted into his chest, wrapping her arms around his middle as his hands brushed down her spine. His breath brushed the top of her head as she burrowed into his neck, taking a deep inhale of his rain and sandalwood scent. The smell of the Ivory Forest, of a quiet cottage in the woods, of the only home she'd known for the first twenty-one years of her life.

"Sometimes," she whispered, "I worry because I think he might be."

Andrian didn't answer. Only tightened his hold, fingers

tracing patterns along the scars on her back as she eventually faded into sleep.

CHAPTER 68

The woods were silent during the starlight hour. The insects had retreated into the ground, and it was still too early for the birds to wake.

Beside Andrian, Mariah sat up on the bedroll they shared, drenched in sweat and panting as she clutched at her chest. He could feel her roiling emotions down their bond—panic and fear and rage. He reached for her, but before his fingers met her skin she stood, padding away from their camp. She sat beside Feran, who was on watch and curled her legs under her chin.

Andrian watched her, not yet ready to stand. She needed this, he realized. Needed this moment alone, with one of her Armature who was least likely to ask questions.

They'd left the inn early that morning, riding hard north through the day. They were now only a half-day's ride from Khento and had taken shelter in the small glade, one last chance to find rest.

He laid on his bedroll in the grass until night fell away and the birds chirped. The first rays of dawn and the anxious, charged energy still churning from Mariah pulled him to his feet, and he joined them there on the edges of camp.

Feran gave him a short nod, which Andrian returned, but

Mariah didn't move. Not until a few long minutes after he sat, when she reached out a hand, resting it atop his in the grass. His fingers curled around hers as they watched the sun rise over the woodland canopy above.

"We need to go," Feran murmured. Mariah turned to Andrian, and they shared a look that said more than they could ever speak. Andrian tightened his grip on her fingers.

He'd never been very good with words, at least not the ones about how he felt. But this? This he could do.

Mariah gave him a slow nod and a tight smile, and then they were packing their camp and mounting their horses, ready for the last stretch of their ride to Khento.

The woods were darker this far north. Even on the cusp of summer and the sun bright and shining overhead, there was a biting chill in the air. The shadows of the trees seemed to nip at their heels, a pack of rabid wolves chasing them as they galloped.

Mariah pulled Kodie to a stop beside a bubbling spring running through a quiet dell. She glanced at Feran, who nodded. "Here," he said.

She faced the rest of them. "This is where we leave the horses. Untack, but make it organized. Like we discussed."

They swiftly set into action. Their silence was tense and heavy, broken only by the clinking of metal and leather and the thud of packs and saddles to the ground.

This part of their journey was planned in detail. The horses would be left here, untacked and untied; as warrior horses, they were trained not to leave their area, even without fencing. Not unless something chased them away.

They were only a short distance from Khento now and needed to move undetected, so they would finish their journey on foot. Once at the castle, Quentin, Trefor, and Matheo would split away to create a diversion—which was part of the reason they needed three days to prepare—while Sebastian, Andrian, and Mariah would sneak in through the gardens and down into the dungeons. Drystan and Feran would stand watch just beyond the walls, their bonds with Mariah staying open to alert her of any approaching danger.

It sounded so simple, yet something nagged at Andrian. A hidden instinct, perhaps.

Or just the feeling that whatever they were walking into ... there was nothing any of them could do to prepare for it.

Minutes later, they all stood around Mariah. She was a warrior-goddess, dressed in her dark fighting leathers, twin short-swords crossed behind her back and her red-sheathed, dragon-winged dagger at her thigh.

It filled Andrian with a dark, feral sort of pride. *His* goddess, *his* moon, *his* woman.

His.

"I don't know what we'll face in there," she said softly. "But I do know that I'm thankful to have all of you by my side while I do."

"We are with you, Mariah." The words passed Andrian's lips without a thought. The others murmured their agreement, and Mariah's lips tilted up in the hint of a smile.

"Let's go rescue my family."

Andrian's anger was a cool fire as he stared at the spires of the castle at Khento from behind the tree line, the stone piercing the bright cloudless sky. The eight of them knelt together in the dense underbrush, scanning the castle in silence.

The parapets lining the castle walls were empty. No guards walked alert with bows and arrows. Just as it had been when they'd escaped the last time.

Everything about it made Andrian's skin crawl.

"Alright," Quentin said, shouldering his pack. "Matheo, Trefor, you know the plan—"

"Wait."

Quentin stilled, and they all turned slowly to Mariah. A mask of cold determination was painted over her intoxicating features.

"I'm changing things. I'm going up to the front door and knocking."

Sebastian made an exasperated sound, and Drystan blanched. But Andrian …

A smirk twitched at his lips. Mariah had never been one for hiding in the shadows, always opting to embrace the light. Of course she would want to walk right in through the front gates.

That's my girl.

"Mariah. Absolutely not. That is a terrible idea." Sebastian shifted, his knee dropping to the moss-covered ground. Mariah faced him slowly, blinking with mild disinterest.

"We have a plan for a *reason*. Let Quentin and the others lay their diversion while we sneak in through the gardens. Just because we suspect a trap doesn't mean we need to walk right into it."

"They didn't just take my family for no reason, Sebastian. They took them to get to *me*." Mariah's words were so low they were almost a growl. "I want those lords to look me in the eye and tell me why they thought they could get away with threatening my own. I have the full power of the queen, and I'm blessed by two goddesses. Who in there can stop me?"

Sebastian made a frustrated groan. He glanced at Andrian. "Please, Andrian, tell her this is a bad idea."

Andrian prickled, brows pushing together in a scowl.

Of course he despised the idea of Mariah putting herself in danger. But she was right; who could stop her?

And he never wanted to be the man who told her to stand by while others fought her battles. She could burn the whole world down herself, and he'd be there proudly at her side.

"Actually," he said in a low voice. "I agree with Mariah."

Mariah watched him with a feverish brightness in her forest green eyes and a slight tilt to her head.

"I agree that she should not be afraid to make her presence known. But the rest of us still need to split up." He met Sebastian's hard glare. "Here's our new plan …"

Andrian braced his feet, hands shoved deep in his pockets, as Mariah's fist connected with the massive castle door.

His idea hadn't exactly been well received; not at first. But the more he'd explained, the more Mariah's eyes had sparked, her mind working to catch up with his.

By the end, even Sebastian couldn't argue against the logic.

They'd split into three groups. Sebastian, Drystan, and Feran would slip in through a servant's entrance by the stables while Matheo, Trefor, and Quentin went through the gardens. Sebastian's group would comb the castle for Mariah's family, and the moment they found them, they would alert Mariah through their bond. Quentin, Matheo, and Trefor would set off their diversion in the gardens—which Andrian still wasn't sure what it would be, exactly, but was ensured it would guarantee their escape.

Meanwhile, Mariah and Andrian would walk in through the front door. No matter what chaos Quentin created, nothing would cause as much commotion as the queen herself appearing on the doorstep. The focus would be on them and away from the three men searching the castle.

And once Mariah's family was out and safe, well ... hopefully Quentin's diversion, and their own magic and swords, would be enough.

That was the part Sebastian had liked the least. But even he couldn't deny that unleashed, Mariah and Andrian's magic together—light and shadows—would be unstoppable. Even against other wielders.

Footsteps and shouts rang behind the door. Mariah glanced up.

Back.

He didn't know how he'd heard it. It wasn't the first time, either. Every so often, their bond would flare with light, and he could hear words pushed across to him.

He wondered if it was the same for her. If he could speak to her in return.

Before he could try, he was following her backward steps, hurriedly rushing away as the door gave a heavy groan and swung away from them. The hinges shrieked and cried, as if they hadn't been used for centuries.

A guard stepped through the open doorway, clothed in Shawth's blood red livery. His face was familiar in a way that made Andrian's shadows dance down his arms and roil with agitation through his blood.

The sickening grin the guard gave Mariah certainly didn't help.

"It is so wonderful to see you return to us, Your Majesty," the guard sneered. "We missed you so *dearly*."

Anger and terror pulsed down the bond.

Mariah *knew* this man. From her time here before, she knew him. And not in a good way.

Andrian's fingers itched toward the pommel of his broadsword strapped across his back. But a pointed look from Mariah had him holding himself still.

The guard shifted his attention to Andrian, sneer tightening. "And if it isn't the little lordling. What a waste you were. A pliant little queen placed right in your lap, and you decided to deprive us of a treat. Shame." He tsked, expression shifting into something sinister as he raked his gaze down Mariah's body. "I would've liked a chance to show her what it's like to be with a *real* man for once."

Andrian saw only red and darkness. A low growl rumbled from his throat, shadows spilling from his palms.

A hand met his arm. Light and warmth danced across his skin, pulling away his shadows. Andrian's attention sharpened on Mariah as she took a step toward the guard.

And chuckled.

"It is so nice to see you again, Ellis," she said, voice low and carrying a hint of poison. Her smile widened, light winding around her fingertips. "Glad to see you're just as desperate for pussy as you were the last time I saw you. Or maybe you can only get it up when the girl is drugged?"

Everything around Andrian stilled.

Had this man ... he couldn't even finish the thought.

But before he could spiral down into his rage, before he stalked forward and cleaved this man's head from his shoulders right then, Mariah sent him another message down their bond. No words this time, only a feeling.

Calming. Comforting. Assuring.

He exhaled through his nose, masking his relief.

She was merely playing a game.

Ellis took a staggering step back. "You insolent little *bitch*—"

"Ah, ah," Mariah scolded, lifting her hand. Her magic shimmered in the sun. "That's no way to speak to your queen. I might not be wearing my crown, but that's only because it doesn't travel well; I'd hate to lose it. You understand."

Ellis froze as if remembering where he was. He straightened, fixing his face back into a condescending sneer.

"Of course, Your Majesty. I assume you are here to meet with our honorable Lord Shawth?"

Mariah lifted her chin defiantly. "Your *honorable* Lord Shawth took my family. I demand answers and will exact my punishment, if necessary."

Andrian tried to hide his smirk of pride, but it died as he watched Ellis's face.

No flicker of surprise. No flash of fear. Only that same insolent smirk, the same sniveling smile.

"Of course, Your Majesty. Lord Shawth has all the answers waiting for you, just inside." He stepped back through the doorway and into the entry hall beyond. He gestured to them, welcoming them inside. "Please, follow me."

Alarm bells again rang through Andrian's skull.

"Mariah—" He tried to whisper to her, to capture her attention.

But she was too set on her mission. She strode toward the doors, passing beneath the arching entrance, following too closely behind that ferret of a man who Andrian wanted nothing more than to sink his blade into his gut.

And, of course, because he would follow her into death itself, Andrian had no choice but to stalk after her, shadows clawing at him to go anywhere else but into that castle.

The heavy doors closed behind them with a thud. Ellis faced them, hands clasped behind his back, a sneer still plastered on his face. "Your weapons."

Andrian's hands tightened into fists. Something felt off within the walls of the castle, as if there were unfamiliar shadows grasping at his own.

He really, *really* fucking hoped Mariah didn't turn over her weapons. Because that would mean he would, too.

Mariah regarded the contemptuous guard with her own icy expression. "No."

Andrian's shoulders sagged with relief. He watched Ellis, waiting for his reaction.

But none came. Ellis merely shrugged, almost nonchalantly.

It only added to Andrian's feelings of wrongness about this place.

"Suit yourselves," Ellis said, giving them a cool smile. "Follow me, please." He turned on his heel and strode away, not bothering to see if they followed.

Mariah shot Andrian a glance, her mask slipping for a moment to reveal her confusion. He gave her the slightest shake of his head.

He didn't understand it either, but what choice did they have? At least they still had their weapons and their magic.

They were led down long, winding corridors. A well-decorated receiving room. A spacious meeting hall. They walked and walked and walked.

Andrian's trepidation crept in further with each step. It lurked over his shoulder, his shadows whispering against the back of his neck.

This wasn't right. Something wasn't right.

He felt for the bond. Latched onto it, like a lifeline.

When he did, he received one feeling back.

Dread.

Not terror. Not panic. Only a deep, grating sense of foreboding, an awareness telling them something was wrong. That it should not have taken so long to reach their destination.

Andrian pulled back from the bond and glanced around the hallway. He'd been to Khento before. Just a few months ago, yes, but he hardly remembered those days.

No, most of his memories of Khento were from his childhood. From the few trips his father had made to visit Lord Shawth, the few times Andrian had glimpsed more of their kingdom, paraded around like a prized horse for his father to flaunt before the other lords.

And this hallway ... it was familiar. Not just from his childhood, either.

They'd walked this way before, only a few minutes ago.

His mind reached blindly for Mariah, the warning that raced through him shoving its way down the bond. She faltered—a small misstep, slight enough to be masked by a shortened stride. She glanced at him, a question in her eyes.

"Been here before." He mouthed the words and forced them across the bond.

Mariah scanned the hallway, and he knew she'd gotten the message. She leveled a hard stare at the back of Ellis's head, her body tense with fury.

Fast as lightning, she drew her short-swords, magic dancing around her fingertips and down the blades. Ellis stopped at the sound of steel slipping free from sheaths. He turned slowly, looking bored.

"Your Majesty?" His tone was so insolent, it took all Andrian's control to not rip his vocal cords from his neck.

"Stop fucking around, Ellis. You're leading us in circles. Take us to Shawth. Now."

Ellis regarded her for a moment, and then with another sneer, chuckled. He took a step closer to the corridor wall. There was a single recessed door, the wood unassuming. It looked to be nothing more than a coat closet.

"Relax, Your Majesty. We're here." Ellis gripped the handle and pulled, gesturing to Mariah and Andrian.

Andrian watched Mariah, her chest heaving as she slowly slid her blades back into their sheaths and straightened her stance.

She reached for him, just a slight flick of her fingers, and together they rushed past Ellis through the door.

Andrian had to blink against the sudden, blinding light.

Sunlight.

As his vision cleared, he realized they now stood outside, at the very edge of the castle gardens. The flowers were in full verdant bloom, blossoming trees dripping with yellow and purple and blood red. Risers were built around an open, central space, filled with Onita's upper echelon: lords and ladies, wealthy merchants, anyone either born to power or with enough coin to make it for themselves.

Nearest to Mariah and Andrian was a dais adorned with six chairs, and seated in each was a man. The Royals, Lord Shawth and Lord Laurent in the center. Andrian's dread cooled, settling into true, unadulterated fear.

Because kneeling on the dais steps below them ...

Andrian's throat went dry, his lungs constricting around his heart.

Trap.

The other six of Mariah's Armature were there, bound and gagged. Around each of their wrists were cuffs of a familiar black and gold stone.

Deistair. Even though they had no magic of their own, they'd been cuffed with it. To keep Mariah from knowing what was happening. To keep her from being warned.

Had she felt their bonds go silent? Or had she kept them closed to avoid the distraction, until she knew they would be able to escape?

On a second platform, in the middle of that open space and on display for all to see, was Mariah's family. Andrian knew them from Mariah's stories. Wex, the loyal soldier, a deep cut on his face oozing dark blood. Ellan, the gentle and kind brother, his hands cuffed in *deistair* and his face streaked with tears. Lisabel, the wise and mysterious healer, chin still lifted defiantly despite the bruise forming on the side of her face.

Terrifying monsters—humanoid demons straight from the darkest histories of their world—held serrated claws to their exposed necks, tongues snaking past deadly maws, vicious teeth begging for a chance at death.

It was the last thing he saw before he was rushed from behind. Before more *deistair* was locked around his wrists, his shadows snuffed out.

It was the last thing he saw before he realized how badly they'd all failed.

It was the last thing he saw before Mariah's cry of rage pierced the air, a sound far more animal than human.

CHAPTER 69

Mariah's rage, her terror, was a living, breathing monster.

That beast in her soul was awake; its hot exhales tickling the back of her neck as it wrenched control from her, pushing a roar of anguish into the air.

Her Armature. Her family.

She was too late.

No wonder the bonds in her mind were so silent. She didn't know when they'd been captured, but it must've been mere minutes after they'd entered the castle grounds. Mariah had kept the bonds closed, wanting to wait until escape was feasible before checking in. Not wanting to feel *distracted*. She hadn't even bothered to check on them.

What a fucking fool.

There was still one bond blazing in her mind, the only one she couldn't close. But just as hands grabbed her from behind, it too was snuffed out, its sudden loss pulling a mangled cry from her chest. The familiar weight of *deistair* cuffs snapped around her wrists, that vile black and gold wall severing her from her magic.

But that beast ... the *deistair* did not cage it. It was still free, floating and clawing and raging beneath her skin, at the back of her mind, whispering for freedom.

Not yet, Mariah whispered back. It calmed, curling around itself with angry, slitted eyes.

Mariah turned her own wrathful, broken glare to her family, bound and bruised and bloody on the central platform. To the creatures straight from nightmares holding serrated claws to their throats.

Too late.

Her family was captured by demons, all because she'd been too afraid to confront her own.

Lord Shawth rose from his seat on the dais near Mariah. He faced her, pushing his hands into the pockets of his embroidered black and red suit. His pale blond hair was greased, and his watery blue eyes shone with excitement.

"Ah, Your Majesty!" He clapped his hands, silencing the chatter from the risers.

Rough hands on Mariah's shoulders shoved her forward between the gallery stands and the lord's dais. More of the garden came into view; guards and more demons lined every exit, the men shooting the monsters nervous glances. Below her family's platform squatted a mound of black stone, its vileness tangible even from the distance.

She knew that stone. Had touched the same substance in that abandoned apartment, the one where horrible atrocities were committed on the gods most sacred night.

Mariah's world went quiet, narrowing like a predator on her prey. The beast prowled beneath her skin, watching, feeding her rage.

"I am so glad you could join us!" Shawth boomed, cheeks flushed an excited shade of cherry red. "I was sorry to have to interrupt your coronation—congratulations, I suppose—but this day has been many months in the making. Maybe even years; it is hard to say. I wouldn't want you to miss it." He chuckled, grinning darkly, showing too many yellowed teeth.

"My esteemed guests!" Shawth faced the galleries. "You are

representatives of Onita's finest. I assume some of you have met her, but I would like to be the first to introduce you to the eleventh Queen of Onita, Mariah Salis!"

The attendees in the galleries hissed and booed and jeered. Shawth's grin widened.

"Now, now! That is no way to greet a queen. Especially with her family in attendance. They deserve our respect!" He turned halfway to Mariah. "Isn't that right, little queen? Why don't you tell us all how deserving your healer mother and soldier father are of our deference?"

Mariah could nearly taste the venom in Shawth's words.

"Let them go, Shawth." The earth trembled at the darkness— the threat of broken violence—in her voice.

A gasp rippled through the crowd. Shawth exaggerated his surprise, leaning back on his heels and splaying his fingers across his face. But he couldn't hide the morsel of doubt and fear that flickered in his eyes.

"Oh ... my, is that what you truly want, Your Majesty? I did not think their presence would bother you." His ruthless smile returned. "I find it hard to believe that you ever truly cared for their well-being. In fact, I find it hard to believe that you truly care for anyone other than yourself."

He tapped a finger to his chin, a mockery of a pensive expression. "How often did they cross your mind after you were Chosen to live in your pretty palace? All that time, and you only wrote them *one* letter, and a sad excuse for one at that."

Mariah wanted to feel more anger. Wanted to give herself to her rage, to her blind fury. Wanted to let the beast in her soul take over and loose her sword and dagger upon this crowd of rotting, jealous monsters.

But she couldn't do it. Not even as the galleries grumbled and whispered, not even as Shawth's smile turned smug.

Because Shawth had confirmed her worst fear. That her letter —that short, pitiful, desperate excuse for a letter—had never made it to its destination.

That she had failed the only people who had never let her down.

Shawth's words fell around her like coins tossed into a well, and she was pulled down with them. Her shoulders sagged with the weight of her guilt, her head hanging with her shame.

"What do you want?" Her words were a hoarse whisper. The crowd fell silent. A light breeze rustled the leaves of the flowering trees and the sweet-smelling blossoms.

"What do I want?" Shawth laughed, his head tipping back before stepping down the dais, hands still in his pockets. He passed Mariah's Armature, ignoring their baleful, hateful glares. His cool, watery gaze slid down Mariah, mouth curving into a sneer.

Beside her, Andrian strained against the hands holding him. Mariah stilled him with a quick glance, his brilliant eyes wide with panic and fear and rage.

She blinked slowly and turned back to Shawth.

"Just tell me what you want. Tell me what you want and let them go."

Shawth chuckled. "My dear, little queen. If only it were that simple." He lifted a brow. "I don't want anything you can give me. I want *everything*. Do you not understand?" He spread his arms wide, and something cracked in Mariah's chest.

"I want your throne. Your crown. Your magic. I want your *power*. I want all of it. Why should you be the only one amongst us who carries the might of a god?" He snorted. "It has all been promised to me by someone far stronger than your little moon goddess."

He gestured behind him to the platform with her family. To the creatures who held them, leathery wings shifting in the warm air.

"Do you see them? They are gifts from my new benefactor. That is strength, to be sure, but it is not power. Not like what you have, just by being the right slut born in the right year."

Mariah's gaze darted helplessly between Shawth and her

family. Her father's eyes blazed with fury, but he gave her the smallest shake of his head.

He wanted Mariah to stand strong. To not give in. To not give this man what he asked.

Beside him, her mother lifted her chin. The stoic rage shining in her eyes was enough to wrench a small, choking sob from Mariah's lips.

Wex and Lisabel Salis were strong. The strongest people Mariah knew.

But Mariah ... was not. Not like them. The demons tightened their grips, pressing claws closer to her family's throats. Her Armature was chained and bound before her, raging and helpless.

Her guilt, her shame, her empty rage pounded through her until everything around her drowned.

Selfish.

Pathetic.

A shameful daughter.

An unworthy queen.

Something cracked deep in the darkest crevices of Mariah's soul. Something that had remained strong, even when she was held captive. Something even the strike of a metal-tipped whip couldn't break.

Shawth saw her fracture. He leaned forward, still grinning, foul breath brushing her cheeks.

"Do you know why we let you go?" He chuckled. "I'll admit, we had fun sending our friends from the Kizar Islands to torment your Armature during your stay with us. But we soon realized that we could never break you here. As much as we did not wish to admit it, you were too strong. You care very little for your well-being and your body. Which I suppose we should have known, given your reputation."

Mariah was numb to the laughter that rose around the gardens.

The whore queen.

"I will admit, we were stumped for a time. Until Lord Laurent helped us make an invaluable realization."

Andrian's father sat in his chair upon the dais, expression a careful, solid mask. But despite his efforts, the wicked delight that glimmered in his eyes was impossible to ignore.

"You have a weakness, Mariah: your ability to love. You don't love many, but once you do ..." Shawth glanced once at Andrian, then to her Armature, then finally to her family. "Once you do, you would tear the world down and spit upon its ashes to keep that love safe."

Mariah's heart thumped against her chest. Had she really been so easy to read? She'd said almost those same words to Andrian before they'd left.

She'd tried to make love her retribution, but it all turned out to be her weakness.

"We knew about your Armature and the Laurent heir; your ties to them were obvious. But it was our esteemed Lord Donnet, who reminded us of all you'd left behind in Andburgh. With a little help from the *true* god of Onita, we had them brought here. For safekeeping, of course."

"What do you mean by true god of Onita?" A force beyond her control yanked the question from Mariah's mouth. Likely that beast still crawling beneath her skin, growing more agitated as the seconds ticked past.

She contemplated giving over control to the beast of her rage. But she clung to the last broken pieces of herself, if only for the hope that she might, somehow, be able to bargain her way out of this.

She'd gladly toss herself, her magic, and her crown at Shawth's feet if it meant her family—both those of blood and those she'd selected for herself—could leave this place free.

Shawth blinked down at her, brow twisting with curiosity. His empty eyes flashed, and something dark and sinister slid across his features.

"Patience, little queen." He tsked. "You will meet him before the day is done."

The beast in Mariah's skin stilled.

Something was very, very wrong. Mariah wrapped herself around the beast, begging for just a few more moments.

Please. Please, I have to try to get them out. Please.

"Whatever you want, Shawth, I'll give it to you. Partake in any ritual, swear any oaths, drain my entire body of blood. Just ... please. Let them *go*."

Muffled bellows of revolt rolled through the gardens, even as the risers fell into a still, breathless silence. Mariah slumped her head, chin hitting her chest.

She fell to the grass, knees meeting the soft ground with a quiet thud.

Somewhere, she heard Andrian's roar of fury. The guards struggled to contain him, dragging him away from her as he cried her name. Her Armature thrashed against their bindings. Their desperation leeched into the air; desperation to escape, to claw their way to their queen, to pull her up from her knees.

But Mariah was done fighting. Her family had given her everything. Taught her how to be strong in a world that would try to keep her weak. She could not pay the price her defiance now demanded.

Shawth had won.

Shawth crouched down before her, groaning slightly as he wobbled on his balance.

"Whatever I want?" he whispered. "So, you offer to me your blood by your own free will?"

"Yes," Mariah breathed. "Whatever you want from me, I'll give it willingly. But only if my family, my Armature, and my court can go free. Let them go to Kreah. They will leave the kingdom and will never bother you again." She didn't dare raise her gaze. Her words were steady and sure, but she didn't trust herself. Didn't trust her resolve if she looked anywhere but at her knees.

The gardens were silent, and her heartbeat thundered in her ears. The beast in her chest was snarling and thrashing. She did her best to soothe it, desperate to quiet the rage. She had no magic to push it back, so it raged against her, and she weathered it as rocks weathered the waves of the sea.

For her family, Mariah could do this. For as long as it took to get them out, to get them to safety, she could do this.

Shawth rose. Mariah's gaze followed him, and he stared down at her, puzzled.

"Hm," he said, crossing his arms. "How disappointing. I had expected you to fight harder than that."

"You've won. What's the point of fighting?" She glanced at her mother.

She shouldn't have.

Lisabel's expression almost tore Mariah in two. There was no disappointment on her mother's face, only heartbreak. Pure, terrible, awful sadness glistened in Lisabel's golden-hazel eyes.

"I'm sorry." Mariah blinked, a single tear falling from her cheek, before she stilled.

She'd spoken those words out loud.

Shawth watched them, and his puzzlement faded away to wicked delight.

"You have all heard it," he said, raising his voice so it carried across the gardens. The sun burned down on them, far more intense than it should have for the late northern spring. "An ascended queen has offered her blood to us willingly. Our god shall have his offering, and the curse will be lifted." Raucous cheers answered him, even as cruelty sparkled in his eyes.

Dark cruelty. Inhuman cruelty. Otherworldly cruelty.

"Of course, our god needs the pretender queen alive. But she has offered her blood, and her blood, he shall take."

The beast roared in Mariah's ears. Her heart hammered in her chest. Her lungs froze, fingers curling into desperate, reaching claws. Her muscles strained against the hands holding her. She lurched to her feet, throwing herself forward, taking a single, feeble step.

Toward her family. Toward her mother.

The demon holding Lisabel tightened its grip, its serrated claw digging further into her neck. A scream she did not hear pulled itself from Mariah's throat.

The journal. The dagger. Our family. I want to know, I need to know, I need you—

So many thoughts and memories and dreams and hopes slammed into Mariah. Bitter regret and frantic rage pummeled her, battering her broken soul. If she could just get to her mom, could just get that monster away from her, then she could understand ...

Lisabel's mouth opened, a single tear sliding down her bruised and bloodied face.

My light, she mouthed. *It's okay, my light. I forgive you, my light. I am so proud of you ...*

Over and over and over. More tears landed on Lisabel's swollen lips. The demon behind her parted his maw in a ravenous growl.

Shawth turned to the creature, his eyes alight.

"With the blood of the usurper, may the true god be set free."

The demon snarled in feral delight.

My light—

The words were frozen on Lisabel's lips as the demon's serrated claw pulled a jagged line across her throat, biting deep into the delicate flesh. Dark, ruby blood burst from the wound, splattering the *aberrant* below the platform in a violent, macabre waterfall of death.

When her mother's lifeblood met the cursed stone, Mariah erupted.

CHAPTER 70

The beast consumed her.

It tore through Mariah's skin, unleashed by her rage, her pain, her regret and anguish and love. A thing of light and fire, scorching through her veins, turning her blood to molten lava and her bones to ash.

Once everything within her was burned and destroyed, the beast began to build and change.

There was pain. So, so much pain. Her bones reformed into pillars of steel, shifting and cracking and changing beneath her skin. Her flesh hardened, stretching across those new bones. She was dipped into fire, forged into something *other*.

Her hands lengthened, extending out across the gardens, the cuffs on her wrists snapping easily. Her neck elongated, turning serpentine as she arched toward the sun blazing high above. Light burned her, burned *around* her, as she shifted. Talons took the place of her feet, leathery membranes unfolding down her arms and connecting to the skin along her sides.

Mariah thrashed in pain as her tail erupted from the base of her spine and scraped across the grassy footing. Behind the pain, the gardens grew small, the tang of blood and fear filling her nostrils. She stretched, and her arms—wings—nearly spanned across the gardens, shadowing the gathered crowd.

She gave herself further to the beast, losing herself to her heartbreak and the burning pain.

When the blinding agony stopped, the roar of a great silver-gold dragon tore across the Khento castle gardens, and the earth shuddered.

***

Everything was so much brighter. The world more vibrant. Sounds echoed against her ears; smells inhaled through deep, powerful lungs.

The smell of her mother's blood was the worst of it. Sweet, tinged with a trace of silver moonlight, that single drop of magic Lisabel had carried and hid from the world for so long.

As terrible as the smell was, the sound of it dripping onto the vile, black stone was worse.

Mariah's claws scourged deep rivulets into the soft soil beneath her. She reared up on powerful hind legs, her body crashing into a riser. Her great, leathery wings, shimmering with silver and veined with gold, spread wide. Her lips pulled back from wicked sharp teeth, and with all the anger and pain in her heart, she roared again, so loud it shook the walls of the castle behind her.

The people quaked. Cries of terror and pain filled the risers, and the crowd rushed to escape her wrath. Those in the riser nearest her were crushed beneath the weight of metal and stone, the tang of their blood mixing with her mother's sweet scent. A few still cried meekly from the rubble, left for dead by the other fleeing attendants. Guards—both human and demon—raced to block the exits, filling the air with more panicked shrieks.

Mariah paid no heed to any of it.

She was still focused on the slow *drip, drip, drip* of her mother's blood against the stone.

She took a lurching step, the soft earth giving freely beneath her talons, her wings crashing more of the risers to pieces. A black-haired man appeared before her, gazing up at her with a look of awe and pity and devastation.

Mariah knew him. Would always know him, no matter the form she took. He was as familiar to her as the silver-gold magic whirling freely through her new body, set free from invisible chains, unleashed from the confines of mortality.

She was still here, but she was also no longer the same. Everything had changed. She still felt that mortal part of her, buried deep within. But the woman had retreated, content to let the beast decide the fate of her world.

At her feet, the familiar, beloved man—Andrian, her mind told her—was speaking. He gestured at the cuffs on his wrists. On instinct, Mariah reached for the bridges in her mind, the ones meant to bind her to this world.

And was met by black and gold adamant.

Renewed fury flooded her, and with a snarl, she sent a burst of magic down those bonds, smashing the walls holding them from her to bits.

That substance was made to bind mortals; it was never meant to withstand whatever she was now.

The cuffs on Andrian's wrists snapped. His bond roared to life, along with six others beside it. They filled her mind, shouting and roaring and calling her name.

Mariah lowered her wings to the ground, the talons at the apex digging into the grass. She snaked her head down, facing a raised dais with six large chairs.

Her Armature knelt before the dais, their faces wearing mixed expressions of awe, desperation, and terror.

Not terror of her. As she sent back the best assurances she could and closed their bonds, she sensed they were not fearful of her.

They were fearful *for* her. Of what was done to her, to someone she valued more than she could ever value herself.

Scared of what she might do to the world because of it.

Only one bond remained in her mind—the one she couldn't

close, even if she wanted to—as she lifted her head, bringing all her new, deadly focus and instinct to the sad, angry little man with watery blue eyes and wheat blond hair.

His fear was the sweetest. So pungent, so vile, so intoxicating.

Shawth scrambled up the dais steps, stopping before his false throne. The other lords cowered there with him, their fear a thick blanket around them. Even Lord Laurent, his normally fixed expression now slack-jawed, his golden eyes filled with alarm.

Mariah lifted her head and parted her maw. Something hot and ancient and deadly stirred in her chest, churning as it crept up her throat. She tasted ash and moonlight on her tongue as she drew in a breath, flames building and unfurling around her fanged teeth.

If she could smile in this form, the desperate cries for mercy from those lords would have brought one to her lips.

Something hot and vile and wrong sliced down her side, pain shooting deep beneath her skin.

"*Mariah!*" That familiar, beloved voice roared her name.

Flames died on her tongue, were pulled back down her throat. She whirled, instincts older than the world itself taking over.

A demon was latched to her side, serrated claws digging into her scaled skin. But her hide was stronger now, far more durable than soft human flesh, and with a bucking leap, she dislodged the demon. Leathery gray wings unfurled from the demon's side, lips curling back from its distorted face as it hissed, low and vicious. It launched into the air, hovering just above her. She twisted to meet it, growling low in her chest.

"*Welcome,* dragaina," the demon whispered, its words falling not from its mouth but into her mind. She blinked with momentary shock, double lids sliding across her eyes before her bloodlust resumed its grasp.

She spoke back on instinct, her mind reaching for the foul, twisted mess of the demon's soul. "*Go back to the miserable pit you crawled out of, and I'll let you live.*"

The demon chuckled. "*Do you really think me that lacking in intelligence?*" It lifted a serrated claw to its mouth, a long, forked tongue flicking out from between its teeth, licking the blood still there.

Mariah's blood, and another's, layered in. She shuddered, and her eyes focused, a predator narrowing on its prey.

"*Your mother tastes so sweet,* dragaina," it hissed, wings flapping as it held itself suspended above her. "*And her blood mixed with yours?*" The demon inhaled again, closing its slitted yellow eyes. "*Divine.*"

Mariah was done with this foul creature, mocking her with the taste of her mother's blood.

Her muscles bunched beneath her scaled skin, and with a great push, she leaped from the earth, launching at the demon. The demon hissed a laugh as it shot to the right, its body narrowly avoiding the devastating snap of her jaws that crunched through the air, right where it just was.

Its body evaded her ... but not its wing.

Foul blood burst across Mariah's tongue, her razor-sharp fangs shredding the delicate flesh. The demon's screams piercing the air around them were sweeter than any song. As her hind legs hit the ground, the demon was plummeting to the floor, cracking against the risers with a sickening crunch.

As its body slumped to the gardens below, the earth shook.

The demons holding her father and brother on the central platform backed away, retreating to the edges of the garden. The crowd was still screaming, sharing glances of abject horror as the world rumbled beneath their feet. The bitter tang of their fear pulled Mariah's lip back from her teeth, the demon's black blood dripping to the grass and soaking into the soil below.

Something—a hand—touched her side. She glanced down wildly, meeting a stare of crushing tanzanite blue.

"*Mariah.* Nio. *Come back. Come back to us.*"

The woman inside her stirred.

The words—in that same, familiar voice—were not spoken, at least, not out loud. But Mariah heard them all the same as if they were threaded into her soul, the silver-gold bond flaring brighter than ever before.

The beast rumbled, and the woman took a hesitant step forward. Retook some control.

And clarity slammed into her.

She cautiously opened the other bonds. But instead of feelings and emotions rushing to greet her ... she *heard* them.

She'd heard them before, too, when she'd blasted the *deistair* from their wrists. But only with the beast now sharing some of her mind, and not all, she understood what that meant.

As her Armature's thoughts pummeled her, six jumbled voices all panicked and roaring in her head, she knew.

Those bonds were not for any mortal purpose. They'd never been to simply serve a queen trapped in a human form, limited by the confines of a body unable to access magics far deeper and more ancient.

It was for *this*. For this beast dwelling in the heart of the queen's power. So that when it was unleashed, she would have seven carrying a trace of that power to understand her fully. Seven who could be a voice to a world that would see only a monster, a legend come to life.

Their voices ceased when she spoke to them, down all seven bonds.

"Get my brother. Get my father. And get the fuck *out of here."* The ground shuddered again. Those wild instincts roared at her, an instinct she couldn't ignore even if she tried.

"Something is coming. I can feel it in the earth. I need them safe." Her gaze found Andrian's. *"I need* you *safe."*

Hard rebellion flared across his face. But Andrian nodded and sprinted for the central platform, shadows spilling from his hands as he unsheathed the broadsword from his back. Sebastian raced after him, followed by Quentin and Feran. Drystan, Trefor, and Matheo drew their weapons, forming a semi-circle around her, searching for an exit.

It was sweet of them to still be seeking to protect her. But she had no use for it now.

She snapped her jaws and ignored the pang of guilt when

Trefor and Matheo jumped in surprise. *"I told you to leave me. Get my family and find a way out."*

Drystan met her stare fiercely. *"If you're staying, then so are we."*

Mariah hissed in frustration, swinging her head to the central platform as the earth shuddered again. The four warriors had reached her father and brother. Sebastian and Quentin grabbed Wex by both arms. Their touch shook something loose in him and he roared, struggling against their grip. His gaze was locked on his wife's body, her blood still dripping onto the *aberrant*. They gritted their teeth and dragged him down the platform, back across the garden.

Ellan still stood there, expression shocked and broken. Feran rested a hand on his shoulder, shaking him, and Mariah's brother stumbled forward, emptiness shrouding his soft green-gold eyes.

They gathered behind Mariah, eyes searching for a way out, a path that wasn't guarded by demons or blocked by the screaming crowd. Mariah lifted to her full height, unsteady as she continued to adjust to this massive and cumbersome form, scanning the gardens.

"Escaping? Really? How unlike you. Even like this, I would have hoped you'd put up more of a fight."

Shawth's shaky voice from her right scratched against her skin. Her head swung to the dais, flames once again bubbling deep in her chest.

Another shudder wracked the earth, this time somewhere deeper.

Somewhere, in a long-forgotten realm sunken deep beneath their feet, Mariah heard a terrible, furious, murderous roar.

Ignoring the sniveling lords on the dais, she whipped back to the central platform. To the block of *aberrant* still being fed by the slow drip of her mother's blood. The gardens were suspended in tension, the air stilling as ancient, terrible, forgotten power trembled around them.

With a sigh, the tension snapped, and a crack split through the deep black stone.

Every instinct in Mariah recoiled. A feeling of wrongness wrapped around her, screaming at her to fight or fly.

But she was held still, rooted to the ground, planted between the stone and her family as shadows leaked from the crack in the *aberrant*.

They were not unlike the shadows she loved with all she was. Even the way they moved, dancing and winding through the air, was reminiscent.

But where Andrian's shadows were cool, delicate whispers of ice against hot skin, these were scalding, their heat permeating the air as they seeped into the bright, cloudless day. The already warm temperature rose as more shadows poured forth, snaking around themselves like billows of cloud and smoke.

Slowly, the shadows pulled together. Formed into a great, massive writhing shape. A shape as imposing as Mariah, and just as similar.

Black wings burst from the shadows, the membranes veined with gold, the dark twin to her own. A body followed, smoke solidifying into gleaming onyx scales. A tail snaked and swished across the ground, followed by an arching neck and scaled head crowned with four horns so red, they looked to be dipped in blood.

The fiery, red-gold eyes of the dragon burned back at Mariah with the intensity of the sun as it opened its jaw and roared.

This roar shook the castle behind them. Shook the earth beneath them, made the sun pulse brighter against the shadows, made the sky tremble.

A dark consciousness brushed against hers, and Mariah could only pull her lips back from her teeth and snarl.

"Well, well. What a treat it is to meet you in the flesh, little goddess. I have watched you for so very long."

His voice ... it was far from unpleasant. As much as Mariah wished to recoil, a part of her struggled, wanted to lean into the voice instead. Wanted to wrap herself around it like a cat, to lose herself in the unusual cadence and soft, sinful darkness.

She fought against that part of her, warring deep in her soul.

"Who are you?"

She swore he made a sound like a tsk. *"Really, little goddess? Do you not recognize me? I know there is a part of you that does. A part of you that will always know me."* If dragons could grin, he gave her what could only be described as such. *"A part of you will always be mine."*

A growl rumbled from her chest. *"I belong to no one. Only myself."*

"Are you so sure of that, little goddess?" The dragon flicked his tail, wings rustling. *"I can feel her in you. And she has always been—and will always be—bound to me."*

Something clicked in Mariah's mind. Her power, this new form. The part of her that ached for this other beast that had crawled out from the blackest of pits yet took a form of beauty and magic and whispered to her in a voice of dark, tantalizing secrets.

All their stories were wrong. The dragons were not summoned by the gods.

The dragons *were* the gods.

And this god ...

"You're him." She trembled, but whether it was from fear or anger or wild energy, she couldn't be sure. *"You're Flétrir. The Scourge."*

The black dragon's lip curled back from his teeth. Wickedly sharp fangs gleamed against his scales. *"Those are not names I chose. I am not a scourge upon this earth. I was one of its creators, and I was locked away for daring to believe we should be worshipped as such."* He stood back on his hind legs, wings stretching wide. The crowd screamed again; the air thickened with their fear.

"My true name, my forgotten name, is Kol. I was once the God of Sun and Shadows. Until I was betrayed by Zadione and her cunt of a sister for the crime of loving too much. I was thrown from my throne for wanting more for this world than what it was. But now, little goddess ..." He drew in a deep breath. The center of his chest glowed, as if he held the sun itself.

"Now, thanks to you, I am free."

CHAPTER 71

Everything in Mariah's world tilted, instincts wrapping around her like soft hands.

"That's ... impossible. I would never ..." She released a devastated, frustrated rumble.

"Impossible, or simply forgotten?" Kol's dark voice chuckled. *"Some stories are true. I was cursed from this world, bound to a prison in Enfara by the magic of all the gods. And Zadione used her blood as the key. But that meant she had to be imprisoned as well, her essence as tied to Enfara as mine."*

Mariah's tail twitched against the rubble of the risers. *"No. You kidnapped her. Zadione is free."*

"Her prison was not the same as mine." Kol's lip curled, smoke billowing from his nostrils. *"She found a way out. But she is far from free.*

"None of the gods are free, and they know it. Because the magic they used to bind me had a flaw. If they returned physically to this world, then my bindings would fail. Freed, all I would need is the right key, and I could return."

A hand touched her side. *"It's a lie,* nio. *There is no god of the sun."*

Mariah speared her mind for Andrian's. "*You can hear him?*"

"*Yes. Of course.*"

Waves of confusion and fearful anger washed over her from her other Armature. "*I think you might be the only one.*"

Kol stretched, burning eyes fixed on them. "*Of course he can hear me. He is one of mine.*"

Mariah ignored him, ignored the way her stomach dropped at the possession in his voice. "*The gods haven't returned. If what you say is true, you can't be here.*"

"*Are you so sure they're gone?*" Red-gold eyes flickered with shadows. "*Because I am looking at one right now.*"

"*I am not—*" But she stopped herself. Dug her talons into the ground. Her wings quivered, her mind racing.

It was impossible.

It was ... *impossible.*

Kol growled a laugh. "*Yes, little goddess. You are Qhohena's— and Zadione's—little hidden creation. That light magic you flaunt so brazenly. Have you never wondered why it's so different from all the other gifts of your world?*" He shook his massive head, more smoke and shadow drifting around him.

"*Qhohena's line of queens was her worst-kept secret. She gave that first queen her grace—all that made her a goddess—and spelled it so it would be passed down to a new bearer every few hundred years. The real golden moon goddess has been hiding in plain sight this whole time. And when Zadione followed her sister, as she always does ... well, they were always foolish.*"

A dull ringing filled Mariah's head. The scent of blood and fear and her broken family still swirled around her. "*Why—why would Qhohena do that?*"

Kol's wings rustled. "*To remove the temptation from herself, I assume. With her grace hidden in a mortal, she could not be tempted to return. To break my prison and free not only me but her sister.*"

"*I don't understand,*" Mariah murmured. "*But Zadione escaped.*"

Behind Kol, his demons—*mudae,* as they'd once been known —sidled out of the gardens, claws gleaming and jaws dripping. The crowd they'd been holding at bay shouted their panicked relief, sprinting for the castle. Her Armature brushed into her closer, finding their weapons and unsheathing them. Their alarm at the advancing demons brushed her mind down their bonds, and Andrian's gaze swept over her with concern.

Instinct pulled a growl from her throat, her body shifting around powerful hind legs.

"I told you—those sisters are foolish. Zadione just as much as Qhohena. I mean." Kol chuffed. *"She spelled the key to my prison to her own blood and then made an entire line of priestesses with that same blood. When I discovered the newest bearer of not only Qhohena's grace, but Zadione's as well, was of that same line?"* The black dragon rumbled in vicious, terrible delight.

"They made it all too easy. All I had to do was manipulate those easily swayed lords to kill the right bitch, and I'd have the key unlocked and the god's curse broken. Take your mother's blood, force you to shift, and my return was solidified."

The world fell away from Mariah. That ancient beast of fire and light and moonstone wrapped around her, spreading great, opalescent wings.

Kol reared up, his wings of smoke and shadow stirring the air in great beating strokes. *"Over five thousand years in a prison and I have dreamed of this day for every single one of them. The day I would rise from the ashes and take my place once again, as the great ruler of this land. All people shall kneel, all people shall serve. For what is a world without its sun?"*

Mariah's gaze dropped, ignoring the risen god and falling to her mother's body, still leaking dull black-red blood into stained and scourged grass.

The heavens held their breath.

I'm sorry. Sorry I wasn't strong enough. Sorry I failed you.

Mariah leveled her forest green eyes at the fallen god of the sun. *"The world has existed without its sun for five thousand years. I'm sure we can manage many more without it still."*

And she launched herself with a mighty roar, snapping gleaming white teeth at Kol's exposed throat.

Kol's orange-red eyes narrowed and flashed. He ducked his

head, protecting the vulnerable flesh. But he couldn't evade Mariah's powerful leap, and as her body collided with his, chaos erupted.

The demons hissed and vaulted into the sky, flying past Mariah. Drystan gave a wild cry, echoed by Quentin and Trefor before the clash of steel against serrated claws filled the gardens. Mariah snapped her teeth, lashing at Kol with razor talons. He snarled below her and they fell, crashing into more risers, toppling stones into the blooming trees and garden flowers.

With a powerful shove, he forced her back, hind legs raking down her side. She roared into the air, leaping away, her tail sweeping a path of destruction across the gardens behind her. Her Armature battled the demons as she lifted her lip in a snarl.

Mariah might've had the advantage of surprise, but Kol was larger and accustomed to this form after eons spent in it.

Kol shook dust and bits of shredded plants from his black scales, eyes still blazing. *"Do you truly wish to challenge me here, little goddess? You hardly know this form. And think of your family, so exposed."*

But her pain and her rage and her heartbreak blinded Mariah. *"You took something irreplaceable from me. You will die for it."*

Digging into the darkest, most festered parts of her soul, she pulled on the heat churning in her belly. Let it claw its way up her throat until it rested behind her teeth.

With a breath that was almost like a sigh, Mariah opened her mouth, and silver-gold flames spewed forth.

They pummeled Kol, wrapping around him with a lover's embrace. He screamed into the air and jumped into the sky with a mighty beat of his wings. Mariah closed her mouth, swallowing the rest of her flames.

The gardens around her were now nothing more than piles of smoking rubble. Shouts of concern filled her mind and she shoved them back. A battle still raged behind her, but her focus was on the sky.

On the black dragon circling above, a shadow in the light of the sun.

"If you want me, little goddess," Kol taunted, *"you must go where dragons dance."*

Mariah lifted her lip. Spread her wings across the gardens.

"Mariah—"

Her Armature's desperate cries were lost in the great down sweep of her wings. She shoved against the ground, lurching into the air.

Muscles she'd never used screamed in agony. Instinct took over as air filled and grazed the sensitive membranes of her wings. She clawed against the sky, releasing a mighty roar. She was off balance, but she surged up with each great flap of her wings.

Above her, Kol hovered. *"You are bold, little goddess. I will give you that much."*

Mariah snarled, urging her wings faster. He grew closer with each burning down beat. Almost there—

She opened her jaws, lunging again for his neck.

He dove, nimbly swooping away from her despite his size. A laugh echoed in her mind. *"Do you want to know why those lords let you go?"*

She twisted, fighting the wind, muscles in her back barking in protest. Kol banked below her, a slow-moving shadow, and she tucked her wings and dove.

He again snapped away, moving too fast for her to even react.

"I suppose it hardly matters to you," he murmured. He sounded almost relaxed, as if she wasn't fighting her body and the winds to claw him to pieces. *"But when I first gave the order to have you captured ... I thought you were already ascended. Only a queen could shift, you see. And I very much needed you to shift."*

"Fuck. You." Her lungs burned beneath her ribs as she again bent her body in the sky, scanning the clouds.

There. A massive shadow lazily cut in and out of the bright rays of the sun. She snarled, pumping her wings.

Kol sighed into her mind. *"Imagine my disappointment when you arrived here. Just a single bonding short!"*

Mariah was beneath him now, catching her breath on an

updraft, focused on the soft scales of his belly. Just one good lunge, and if she got her claws there ...

"That's when I ordered you released. I needed to give up my little plaything to do it, but ... we all make sacrifices for what we want. Isn't that right?"

She shook her head. His voice had a way of wrapping in her mind, circling and looping her thoughts.

Enough.

She gathered her body, and with a great beat of her wings, shot through the clouds.

Mariah slammed into his underside, a surprised roar sawing from his chest. She sank her teeth into his leg, her own claws flipping, desperate for purchase.

Beneath the rays of the setting sun, its fallen god screamed. Hot blood, like liquid shadow and brilliant flame, burst across her tongue. She clenched her jaw tighter, trying to crunch the bone.

A furious, burning pain tore through her abdomen. Her jaw loosened, wingbeats faltering.

Far below, an agonized bellow echoed.

Kol twisted away from her, hissing in pain as his leg leaked blood. Mariah tried to hold herself aloft, fighting against the wind.

But the *pain.*

With her own desperate cry, she plummeted to the earth, her wings catching her at the last minute. She slammed into the ground, talons sinking deep, as she heaved breath into her lungs.

The pain, the pain, the pain ...

She swung her head, searching her body, but ... she was unharmed.

"Feran!" That same cry rang out again. Mariah's blood cooled.

Her Armature still fought desperately, savagely. The bodies of demons lie around them, some still twitching in the grass. Dirty and haggard and covered in blood—mostly black, but some red, too. Behind them crouched her father and brother, the former holding a short-sword and wearing a fierce, broken expression.

The guilt hit Mariah like a crushing, impossible wave.

They'd formed a ring against the encroaching demons. And in the middle of it, sheltered from the fighting, lay Feran.

The tang of his blood struck Mariah first.

He'd been cut, from chin to hip. A long, devastating slice, deep and deadly. His chest still rose and fell, his face scrunched in agonized, staggering pain.

The same pain Mariah felt coursing through their bond snapped open the moment he'd been struck.

Drystan was bent over him, blood-streaked golden hair hanging loosely around his face. His cries still filled the gardens, even as the battle raged.

Even as Kol drifted down from above, a descending shadow upon the world.

He landed heavily, favoring his uninjured leg. Dark blood dripped from the other, smoking as it hit the grass.

Despite the broken carnage around her, that sight brought Mariah some grim satisfaction.

"Enough!" Kol's roar shattered the bloodshed. His demons halted, retreating into the rubble of the gardens.

Mariah didn't give her Armature a similar order, but they did not follow. They bunched in tighter, hardened concern and terror and rage wrought across their faces.

"That is enough," Kol seethed through sharp teeth. With a hiss, he lifted his injured leg, pushing it into a ray of sunlight speckling the grass.

Dread joined the turmoil in Mariah's gut as she watched his skin knit back together, as the pain left his face, as that wicked gleam returned to his eye.

"You have had your fun, little goddess. But I grow weary of these games."

A figure stepped out of the circle of her Armature. A figure carrying a broadsword in one hand, and wielding shadows in the other.

Andrian was defiant and furious as those shadows curled, brushing against the sensitive membrane of her wing. His fury, his fear, his love was so tangible, so potent, she could *taste* it.

Kol cocked his head, his gaze turning curious.

"It's you. How interesting."

Andrian's jaw tightened, his fist clenching as more shadows brushed her wings. "I know you."

The world tilted beneath Mariah.

Kol only chuckled. *"I'm glad you remember."* He swung his formidable head to Mariah.

"I will make you a deal, little goddess." Flames and shadows flickered in the depths of his eyes, the brightest light of the sun casting the longest of shadows.

"I will let you live. Take yourself, your wounded, your Armature, and your family, and leave. I will grant you temporary safety from my wrath. And in exchange ..." Smoke curled from Kol's nostrils. *"I keep him. The last of the reykr. My greatest creation."*

Mariah's world had stilled many times that night.

This time, though, her heart truly froze.

Everything dulled. Her bright senses narrowed and focused, her world becoming only herself, Kol, and Andrian. Those heart-breakingly beautiful tanzanite eyes turned to her, and she could read his answer in them.

Too bad that, despite her failures, she was still his queen. That was not an answer she would allow him to give.

They'd only just found each other again. This *monster* would not be what tears them apart. She would rather cleave the world in two, would rather shred apart her body and her soul before she denied herself this single morsel of happiness. Not after everything, not after what she'd already lost.

"No—"

"I accept."

"NO." Mariah roared, both across the bond and into the air, the castle shaking behind them.

"No. I will not leave you. Not after everything." She broke at the end, pain shuddering through her.

"There's no other choice. Feran needs a healer, and fast. Your family needs to get out of here. You either choose me, or you lose them." Andrian glared at her. All his love and heartbreak and anger

poured into those miraculous eyes. *"And I … I am not worth it. Not worth all of that."*

"No. You are worth everything." But even as she said it, his words landed their mark. She glanced over his shoulder.

Her Armature, bloody and bruised, leaning heavily on weapons. Drystan crouched beside Feran, whose blood still soaked the grass, his breathing growing shallower.

Wex and Ellan behind them. Her father, sword outstretched despite the brokenness in his eyes. Her brother, shattered and shadowed, black and gold cuffs still clamped around his wrists as he huddled behind Wex.

It should have been an easy choice. Eight lives in exchange for one.

But she was dealing in games and trades of love, and love would always be her weakness.

Andrian rested a hand on her wing, his warmth seeping below her scales, racing straight for her heart.

"And you are worth everything to me, nio. *My moon, my stars, every light that has ever graced my life. Let me be the one to ensure those lights keep shining."*

Dragons could not cry. As her grief and anguish and rage and fury heaved in her chest, scratching down her throat, Mariah realized it had nowhere to go. So instead she unleashed another roar, tilting her head back to the sky. More silver-gold flames burst from her maw, and the sound of her despair and fury clawed its way to the stars. Across the continent people turned skyward as impossible heartbreak washed over the lands.

Kol simply watched, humor glinting in his orange-gold eyes. As if he was drinking in her pain, feeding the sickness in him that had festered for five thousand years.

Mariah swallowed her flames and her pain, turning to Andrian one last time.

"I will come back for you, Rhoi. *I am Queen, but without you, I will rule over ashes and dust."*

Andrian smiled. A soft, sad smile.

"I would have gladly ruled by your side, even over a kingdom of

rubble, until the gods called us back to the stars. But please, nio. *No matter what.*" His smile fell, grim hardness tumbling over him. That mask going up, the wall of ice freezing him in.

"*No matter what, do not come back for me.*"

Mariah snarled.

"*We will finish this conversation. When I see you again.*" She lowered her body to the ground, sending a blind tug out to her Armature. They leaped into action, Sebastian and Matheo falling beside Drystan. Together, the three men carefully lifted Feran's limp form. Drystan face was wrought with the worst type of devastation as he cradled Feran's head.

Something in Mariah both warmed and chilled. She'd been so wrapped up in her internal struggles, she hadn't noticed ... hadn't seen ...

And now, Drystan might lose something precious. All because Mariah was too broken to stop herself from becoming a monster.

As her Armature and her family climbed over her wing, onto her back, she fixed Kol with a world-ending glare.

"*I will* end *you for this.*"

Kol tilted his head. "*I have no doubts you will try, little goddess, even though this destruction today has all been caused by you. Driven by so much emotion, you moon goddesses. But remember—*" His wings rustled as he shifted, testing the weight on his healed leg.

"*No matter how bright the moons shine, the sun always burns them away.*"

Her family was now all settled across her back. She hadn't realized how large she was; not truly. Not until she rose, and barely felt their weight between her wings. Her muscles were sore and tired, but she extended her wings regardless, gritting against the pain.

Mariah cast one final, heartbroken glance at Andrian, whose shadows had withdrawn beneath his skin.

"*Stay alive,* Rhoi. *I will come back for you.*" She cracked, heart splitting. "*I love you, Andrian.*"

"I love you too, Mariah." He spoke aloud, tears lining his eyes. "But, *nio* ... don't come back."

Mariah latched onto his bond with all her might as she cast a final snarl towards Kol, arched her wings, and leaped into the air.

She stayed latched onto that bond for as long as she could, until the distance between them stretched too thin, and his words vanished behind her on the evening breeze.

CHAPTER 72

The gardens were silent as Andrian watched his soul fly into the sky. Her roar tore through the heavens, their bond pulling taut in his chest before fading with her disappearing form.

"Don't come back for me."

He kept repeating those words, over and over, even after he was sure she could no longer hear them. But only because he had to be sure.

She had to listen. She'd never been good at listening, but by all the gods, he hoped she would now.

He wasn't worth her rescue. This one act may have bought him true redemption for the pain he caused her, and he hoped she would let him have it.

"I think we both know she will come back for you, son of shadows."

The rays of the setting sun gilded the edges of the great black and gold dragon, aureate eyes glowing like twin suns. Shadows danced between the membranes of his wings, just as light had twined through Mariah's.

And to Andrian's bitter disgust, he felt his own shadows *reaching.* Desperate to leak from the dark place in his soul, curious to investigate this being who was so much like him in so many ways.

But Andrian had known for many months now: his shadows might have been cast by the sun, but they'd grown stronger beneath the silver-gold light of the moons.

"You know nothing about her."

Kol chuckled. *"Maybe not the woman she is. But I know her. The grace she carries is a part of her. It will never allow her to leave you behind. Not forever."*

His words grated against Andrian. *"You don't know what you're talking about. She is not her magic."*

"Are you so sure about that?" Kol lowered his massive head. *"All people are nothing more than their power. Power determines their place in this world. And magic is but a manifestation of power."*

Andrian gritted his teeth, holding Kol's gaze with a defiant glare, but said nothing.

The dragon chuffed, snaking his head back to the sky. The shadows around his wings wove thicker, caressing his onyx scales. They leaked from his body, soon shrouding him in a rush of darkness, opaque clouds billowing around his form. The air crackled and the shadows snapped together, condensing into a size a fraction of the beast.

Into the size and shape of a man.

They peeled away slowly, revealing the figure beneath.

Andrian's breath left him in a rush. He staggered backwards, knees buckling, almost sinking to the blood-stained grass.

The man—Kol—wore a dark, fitted jacket, black pants tailored to a powerful and imposing frame. His skin was warm and tanned, his hair black and shimmering with traces of gold.

But his face ... his face was Andrian's. Only his flaming red-gold eyes and their slightly more upturned shape set the two men apart.

They could have been brothers. Far more alike than Andrian was to his actual brother, Gabriel, whose absence from Khento was something a part of him noted and stored in the darker corners of his mind.

Kol looked enough like him to shred through Andrian's wall of ice, fear and confusion slipping past his careful mask.

The dark god brushed a hand across his shoulder. His face lifted into a familiar, cocky smirk. "Surprised by something, *reykr?*"

Murmured gasps washed through the gardens as the court members reemerged from where they'd hid amongst the rubble and behind the castle walls. But Andrian couldn't tear his gaze from Kol.

From the face that might as well have been his own.

His words failed him, so his mouth stayed closed, all his resolve pouring into his limbs to keep his body standing and steady.

Kol laughed. "There is so much you do not know. Which reminds me ..." His laughter died as he shifted his attention behind Andrian.

To the dais with its six mock thrones that somehow still stood. To the six lords who were hunched and hiding behind their chairs, just now emerging, eyes wide at the carnage.

Kol's smirk morphed into a hungry grin. "My Lord Laurent!"

Andrian wavered as his father hesitantly stepped around his chair, an uncharacteristic panic visible in his golden eyes.

"It is so very good to see you! And in the flesh, this time. I always knew we'd see the day." Kol was the image of courtly charm, yet something dangerous danced in his eyes. "All of our carefully laid plans, executed almost to perfection. But tell me ..." Kol tapped a finger to his chin. "Why was I not told that my dear *reykr* was unbonded? I lost a perfectly good vessel—and soldier— all because that little *bitch* of a moon goddess could burn me out." He snarled his last words, the suns in his eyes flashing.

But Andrian's world felt colder than ice.

Colder than it had been as he'd watched Mariah fly away from him. Colder than those weeks when she'd refused to be near him because of the trauma and pain his body caused her. When he'd been imprisoned in his mind, unable to recall any memories beyond flashes of nightmares woven with his past.

Imprisoned, by …

Julian Laurent sank to his knee and bowed his head. "Your Holiness," he began. "I—I did not realize whether he had bonded to the whore queen was important to you—"

"*Important* to me?" Kol snarled. Shadows lashed out, gripping Julian by the throat. The lord's eyes bulged in terror, clawing at the rope of darkness.

"If you had given him to me after he was bonded, as we had *agreed*, I could have returned before the season changed to spring. I could have used their little bond to *break* her from the inside out."

Julian's eyes darted to Andrian. "He is here now, Your Holiness," he spluttered. "You can take him again, *use* him again. It's not too late."

"Sniveling *fool*." Kol released Julian, the lord falling forward with coughing chokes. "Don't you see? She not only burned out my presence; she scorched my *essence*. The very piece of him that made him useful." Kol turned his sneer to Andrian. His face softened a fraction, even as his words fell upon Andrian like stones into water.

He'd always known his shadows were a curse.

His father slowly rose to his knees, throat red.

"What are you talking about?" Andrian said with deadly softness, his quiet rage and dread and fear wrapping around him, consuming him.

Kol's mouth twitched with the beginning of a smirk. "So many shocks for you today. I'll answer your questions, but tell me, did Lord Laurent ever tell you to withhold the bond from your dear little queen? I saw so many interesting things in your mind, but I think I'd like to know the truth."

But Andrian had no interest in answering Kol's questions. "It was you," he murmured, almost to himself. His shadows, though he hated it, danced with his rage.

"It was you in my mind," he said louder. "You forced me to *hurt* her."

Kol shrugged. "Not *exactly* me, but close enough, I suppose.

Everything you did was on the order of our dear Royal friends here, not me. I only wanted our queen broken, so she would shift and my prison would be broken. Though I hear you struggled quite a bit against it, especially when she was involved." He frowned. "How curious. Or, perhaps, not curious at all."

Andrian decided then that he would kill this god. No matter if it was impossible, he would find a way.

With a snarl, he lashed his shadows out, his aim for Kol's neck true.

But shadows far more ancient swatted him easily away. His magic dissipated like smoke, vanishing into the air.

Kol tsked. "Now, there is no need for that. I understand you're upset, but we're simply wasting time here. You can't hurt me, and you know it." His glowing eyes crackled. "Answer my question, Andrian. Did Lord Laurent tell you not to bond with the queen?"

Andrian hesitated, darting his father a glance. Still on his knees, golden hair disheveled, face twisted into terror.

Before he knew what he was doing, Andrian nodded.

Kol sighed. "How disappointing." He snapped his fingers, and two demons emerged from the rubble, serrated claws still dripping. "Take him to the dungeons. Until I decide what to do with him."

The demons obliged, gripping Julian between them and hauling him to standing. The lord didn't speak, his face too blanched with terror. A pair of *deistair* cuffs were clamped around his wrists, even though the fire had long since left his eyes.

"And send word to Antoris," Kol called after the demons. "I'd like the Laurent heir to join us here. I don't like that his father has kept him out of the fold."

"*No,*" Andrian growled, but it was hollow with his defeat and rage.

The dark god smiled. "Oh? Feeling protective? You never have before. I've seen your memories, remember?"

Andrian's hands shook. "Leave him out of this. Please."

Kol frowned. "I don't understand why you care."

"He's my blood. Of course I care."

"Oh, but is he?" Kol's grin now ... it raised the hair on Andrian's arms. Made his shadows quake in his soul.

"Have you ever wondered," Kol said, folding his hands behind his back, "why you look nothing like them? Why you didn't get the golden Onitan hair and the ability to wield flames? Why you took so much after your mother, as if her Leuxrithian blood was all you had?"

"I favor my mother. That's never been a secret," Andrian rasped.

Kol's smile was villainous. "And what if I told you that you favor her, because the man you thought to be your sire does not share blood with you?"

The earth tilted.

"What are you saying?" Andrian whispered.

Kol stalked a step closer. "The truth of the *reykrs* arrival in this world was always my best kept secret. I may have been trapped in Enfara, but my influence ran deep. You can take the sun from the world, but you cannot take the world from its sun." Shadows curled off the lapels of his jacket.

"I *made* the *reykr*. With the pieces of my magic that lingered here, I created them. Quickened them in their mother's bellies. There were always communities in Leuxrith who favored me; in a country so cold, they craved the sun's heat. The first generation was always the strongest. They carried so much of me, and when raised by loyal mothers, it made it easy for me to wield their minds and shadows as my own. Their offspring made good soldiers, too, but they were more difficult to control. More corrupted by humanity." He scoffed.

"My magic was not infinite, though. After a thousand years, it all but ran dry, and my *reykr* faded with it. Weakened with each generation they bred into until they were all but extinct."

Kol stood too close to Andrian now, his golden stare level with Andrian's own. Something in Andrian—something deep and buried and woven into the very fabric of his being—called out in recognition. As if knowing the truth of Kol's words and knowing what more there was to come.

Andrian, though, simply rooted himself to the bloody grass. His dread and loss and heartbreak was all he had left.

"Until your beautiful, brilliant, loyal mother found the last cache of my power, stored away in her ancestral home." Kol sighed, almost dreamily. "I did not give it to her; not right away. I used the influence I had stretched into Onita to encourage a marriage between herself and a powerful Royal. Told that lord what was expected of him; he would allow his wife to bear me a *reykr*, the last of its kind. To raise it as his own, a member of his family—his heir, even. If he did that, I would raise his house to unimaginable heights."

The gardens were silent. The lords and guests watched on, fascinated, horrified, but if they spoke, Andrian did not hear it.

Andrian heard nothing but the racing of his heart and the crushing, knowing agony of his soul.

"And now, here you are." Kol ran a hand down the side of Andrian's face. Andrian could not stop the way he flinched at the touch, at the way Kol grinned like someone delighted that what he was doing, what he was saying, was ruining the man in front of him. "It's interesting that Priam Marked you, but it was but a small hiccup. He has always been an annoyance." His hand fell from Andrian's face, and he took a step back.

"The last of the *reykr*. A once-perfect specimen, Marked by a pest and corrupted by that stupid little goddess. But it is no matter. You were made with the last of my earthly power, the most powerful drop I hid. I think there is time yet for you to reach your potential."

Andrian begged to be released from this hell, begged for some sort of mercy.

But the gods, as he'd always known, were as selfish as men. They would not listen to his prayer.

"It is time to welcome you back into the fold ... my son."

CHAPTER 73

Anniliese Hareth walked amongst the rubble, ragged skirts catching on charred plants and scorched stone.

Khento's gardens were destroyed. They'd always been lovely in a cold, detached sort of way. But now they were gone, destroyed by nightmares and legend made flesh.

Night had fallen and Anniliese still could not comprehend the past day. When Shawth had ordered them all down to attend another ceremony in the gardens, she'd felt only dread. Dread that was replaced by terror, then sickening, puzzling rage.

A breeze swept through the gardens, bringing with it the smell of burnt flowers, charred flesh, and lingering dragonfire. She tightened her cloak around her shoulders against the chill of the night, shuffling forward. Wisps of her dark hair that had fallen out of her coiled braid brushed her cheeks.

Anniliese stepped over a large piece of stone, once part of the risers lining the garden's central space, and halted in her tracks.

The temporary wooden platform was still there in the middle. Despite the destruction, it still stood, almost untouched.

And atop it, laying behind that mass of foul black stone, was the body of Lisabel Salis. Forgotten, discarded, abandoned.

Something deep in Anniliese's chest cracked.

She'd been trained and used and manipulated her entire life. Such was the way for women in her world. She never saw it, never knew anything different. Not until Mariah had snatched her future from her. Anniliese's eyes were forced open, and the rage of thousands of generations of women rang in her soul.

Lisabel deserved better than this.

With purpose, Anniliese strode to the platform. She fixed her gaze on Lisabel's white face, her open, unseeing eyes, the brutal gash across her neck as she unclasped her cloak. She swung the thick velvet, draping it across Lisabel's form. A modicum of dignity; the best she could do.

Anniliese sank to her knees in the burnt, blood-soaked grass, staining her already ruined gown.

"Lord of the stars," she whispered, tilting her head to the sky, "take this soul. Guide her into the heaven's sweet embrace. Show her true peace and let her know the Goddess' light."

Anniliese hadn't spoken Priam's prayer since her mother's vigil. A rite reserved only for the closest loved ones, a plea to Qhohena's Consort to carry dear departed souls into eternal rest.

She was far from Lisabel's loved one, but she hoped her words would suffice.

Bowing her head, she twisted her hands into the ruined fabric of her dress. "I'm sorry," she said in a choked whisper. Tears burned behind her eyes, so much sorrow and rage and regret wrapping around her, swallowing her.

Beneath the stars, kneeling amidst blood and ruin before the body of the queen's dead mother, Anniliese cried.

She should have listened to Mariah. Should have fled with her when she had the chance. She'd been lied to and manipulated; everyone in that castle had. Her instincts knew something was wrong, and in her fear, she'd ignored them. She hated—*despised* —the part she'd played, even unwittingly, in bringing about that day.

She hated herself for not being strong.

The tears ran down her face, mixing with ash and dust and smudged makeup. And as each one fell, something wild stirred awake, deep inside. Something forgotten and bright and *burning*.

Burning, burning, burning. Heat washed through her, consuming her, tugging at her chest as a caged animal begs to be set free.

Anniliese was too exhausted to hold it in.

That feeling burst from her chest, and light flared against her closed eyelids, splotching her vision with searing gold. Warmth crackled in her hands, along her skin, and her eyes flew open in wild shock.

Her hands ... they were on *fire*.

Sobs caught in her throat as a scream threatened to crawl its way out. Fear—anticipation of the pain, of the searing of her flesh —heaved through her chest. But before her terror could consume her, she realized something.

That fire ... it wasn't burning. It danced on her skin, wrapped around her fingers, but caused no pain. Nothing but glorious, freeing warmth bubbled all around her.

"What ..." she whispered breathlessly, horror dying in her chest as she watched those glowing golden flames dancing in the moonlight.

These flames were hers.

This was *magic*.

Which was impossible. Anniliese did not have magic. That's why she'd attended the Choosing, why she was eligible to marry, why she wasn't garbed in a priestess's golden robes.

A ringing started in her ears. Her chest heaved as her hands began to shake. "I can't be. I can't be. I can't—"

The flames twinkled at her, as if in laughter.

They were ... they were *beautiful*. Wild and dangerous and terrifying, certainly. But they were hers. And as Anniliese watched them, she felt a piece of herself shift, clicking into place.

She'd been taught to be meek and quiet and perfect. But that was not who she was, not really. She was fire and light and rage, and she would not be contained again.

The night breeze shifted around her, catching sparks from her skin. They illuminated Lisabel's dark, covered form, still there on the wooden platform.

And Anniliese knew what she needed to do.

On shaky legs she stood, hand still wreathed in flames. She reached out, holding her breath, her golden flames shimmering.

Anniliese touched her palm to the dried wood of the platform. *Go*, she whispered to her magic.

Burn. Cleanse. Free.

Her flames obeyed.

They hungrily leaped from her hand, gobbling up the wood. Within seconds the platform was ablaze, a great torch ignited against the quiet night. Lisabel's body lay within the flames, Anniliese's cloak burned to nothing, the horror of the day swallowed by the cleansing fire.

A makeshift pyre. One last, small thing Anniliese could do. She would never earn true forgiveness, but she knew, in her heart, that this was right.

Perhaps the first truly good thing she'd ever done.

"Well, well. Now isn't this intriguing, Ms. Hareth."

Anniliese's stomach bottomed out with panic and fear. Her flames snuffed out, even as the platform kept burning up the night.

Slowly, her feet barely loosening against the ruined grass, she turned to face High Priestess Ksee. The older woman wore a malicious smirk upon her face, white robes splotched with ash and blood.

"I truly did not think you had it in you. I always suspected you of having the gift, but with your station and *sautoire*, you were of better use to us as breeding stock." Ksee frowned. "Speaking of … where is your necklace, girl?"

Anniliese trembled. All that newfound power vanished with the breeze. The flames of the pyre were warm behind her but no longer felt like hers. No longer felt connected to her. Returned was the trained and perfect Royal lady, bred for perfection.

Her fingers brushed her neck, the column of her throat,

searching for the slender necklace she always wore. Her *sautoire,* the traditional *debutante* gift for a high-born or wealthy lady.

But it wasn't there.

A memory flashed behind her eyes. Of watching the sacrifice of the priestesses, when the first demons had cracked from the earth. Watching her father slit the throat of a girl no older than her.

Of her fingers at her neck, yanking away that necklace with its small black and gold stone. Of the way she'd tossed it at her feet, lost amongst the chaos and death.

Her panic consumed her. "I-I don't know," she whispered softly, voice wavering.

Ksee shrugged. "Shame. We had such high hopes for you." The darkness behind Ksee rustled, and more white-robed priestesses melted from the shadows, heads bowed.

"But it is no matter," Ksee continued, frown tilting up into a sinister smile. "Replaceable is all you ever were. And replace you at court is what we will do."

Cold, scaled hands wrapped around Anniliese's arms. Hands tipped with sharp, serrated claws, still coated in dark, cracked blood. Voices hissed in her ears.

She screamed, a sharp pierce against the night.

Ksee's smile broadened, the light of the fire carving her with shadow.

"And now you, dear Anniliese—you are *mine.*"

CHAPTER 74

The muscles in Mariah's back were an agonizing ache. Her chest burned, the fires long-extinguished, energy leeching from her body with each powerful stroke of her wings.

And still, she flew.

Maybe one day, she could fly whatever distance she wished. But it was all so new, so uncomfortable. She gave herself to instinct, but faltered each time she was pummeled by an updraft or when the winds shifted to drive her back.

Those instincts had at least guided her away from Khento. East would've taken them to the Mirrored Sea, where the only haven would be the same cutthroat pirates of the Kizar Islands who'd threatened her city not long ago. Idrix and Vatha to the south were too much of a mystery for the refuge they sought; despite occasional trade, no Onitan had seen or heard from any southerner in thousands of years.

Which left her only option to head west. Just where she'd told Ciana and her court to go if things went horribly wrong.

Mariah could only beg the gods that they'd left. That by some miracle they heard of Mariah's failure and fled. She pleaded desperately that they wouldn't be trapped in Verith, vulnerable and alone.

All she could hope for was that they were waiting for her in the west or were on their way there now.

To Kreah, the desert nation just over Onita's western border.

The sun was scorching as it beat against the gleaming silver-gold scales of her back. It grew stronger as they flew toward the rust-colored sands looming just over the horizon.

A hot updraft bludgeoned the undersides of her wings, rocking her violently to the side. The cargo she carried shifted precariously across her back, surprised cries reaching her ears. More warm liquid pooled between her shoulders. Blood.

Feran's blood.

Mariah unleashed a guttural roar and beat her aching wings, fighting against the wind to right herself.

It was a battle between a beast of the skies and the wind itself. With more effort than she had left to her, Mariah twisted her body, correcting herself. She leveled off over the increasingly arid land, trying to ignore that sticky warmth sinking beneath her scales.

Her wings faltered with the next beat, and the ground grew closer.

A hand pressed against the armored skin at the base of her neck just as a steady presence brushed over her mind. Like rocks beneath the waves, unmoving and strong. She cracked open their bond at the request.

"You need to rest, Mariah. We've flown far enough; take us down."

She gritted her teeth against Sebastian's words. *"No. We still aren't to Kreah. We have to make it—for Feran."* But just as she thought the words, a small splattering of buildings appeared in the hazy distance. A small village or trading outpost on the Kreah border, a resting place for weary travelers braving the barren lands bordering Onita and Kreah.

Her eyes sharpened on a well in the center of the ring of structures. And despite her pain-fueled resolve ... she wavered.

This place must have a resident healer. Someone who could stabilize Feran, at least until they could get him real help.

More minds brushed her own. They must've seen the outpost, too.

"You must rest, Mariah. Don't push yourself too hard," Trefor said, repeating words he'd said to her in all those training sessions.

"M, it's hot! You have to land. And this form is badass, but I'm starting to chafe." Mariah chuffed at Quentin. Not quite a laugh, but as close as she could bring herself.

Her resolve broke with the third voice.

"Please, Mariah. Feran—he is so cold. He's lost so much blood. We need to get him help, now, while we can." Drystan paused, fear and heartbreak and pain washing down his bond. *"And don't forget your father and brother. They're not well. They need water and rest, and they need you. Your family—all of us—need you."*

With a shudder, Mariah angled her wings toward the village, and let the hot winds spiral her down to the burning sands below.

PEOPLE WATCHED from the stoops of their stone houses as Mariah's taloned claws met the sands, their jaws slack as her exhausted body slammed heavily into the ground.

"We need a healer!" Drystan bellowed, sliding from her back. "Do you have a damned *healer?*"

Stunned silence greeted them. Mariah lifted a lip and snarled, shattering fatigue pulling her into the sand.

She supposed there was no better way to announce the return of the dragons than one on their doorstep. But still, she needed these people to fucking *move.*

Another growl rumbled low in her throat just as the crowd parted.

"Out of my way!" A rather bedraggled looking man shoved through his neighbors, head wrapped in a scarf to combat the blistering heat. The rest of Mariah's Armature and her family slid from her back, Drystan catching Feran with Matheo's help. The healer's already wide eyes bulged in his face, but he swallowed down his shock as only a healer could.

"This way," he commanded. "Get him this way, to my clinic." Drystan and Matheo hurriedly followed the man, Feran limp between them, and disappeared into the crowd.

Mariah finally allowed herself to breathe.

She closed her eyes. She was cracking, breaking. There'd been no moment of rest, no moment of grief, because she'd feared *this*. This collapse. When her losses would become her identity, and she'd drift like a star far from home.

A warm hand pressed against her cheek. She lifted a heavy, scaled brow and met a familiar handsome face and concerned hazel eyes, brown hair tousled from the wind.

"It's okay, Mariah. You can let go. We've got you."

She tried to hold herself together. To breathe in the hot desert air, to relax the tense muscles of her wings.

Another figure appeared beside Sebastian. A face that looked so much like her own, albeit older, bearded, and notably male. Wex rested a hand on Sebastian's shoulder, and her Armature quickly stepped aside.

When her father placed his hands on her cheek in the same place Sebastian's had been, when he looked at her with the same brokenness that dwelled in her soul, she crumpled.

The beast retreated, shuddering back as quickly as it had burst forth. The human, the mortal who hid away inside, curled tight like a child, was reluctantly dragged back to the surface. Silver-gold light swirled and sparked and wove, and though the excruciating pain of the shift burned and broke her body, it was nothing compared to what wracked her soul.

Within moments, the dragon was gone, replaced by the simple girl who once, long ago, had simply wished for an adventure.

The girl, who was trained by her father to defend herself and was molded by the careful guidance of her mother. A mother who'd always known what her daughter was and what she would become. A mother who'd kept hundreds of generations alive in a simple diary, knowing that one day her daughter would right a wrong made five thousand years ago.

A mother who was murdered because of her daughter's mistakes, sacrificed on the altar of a dark god ready to exact vengeance on a world he long believed to be his.

Wisps of Mariah's dark hair brushed across her face, human once more. She sagged against her father as a true, gut-wrenching sob tore from her chest and crashed to the sands.

Wex said nothing, only wrapped her in his arms and returned her sobs with his own.

Mariah lifted her head at the approach of a third figure. Ellan's normally lighthearted face was shadowed and broken as he stepped into their embrace.

And together, the Salis family mourned an unfathomable loss.

THE DESERTS GREW cold in the evenings.

Three days had passed since they arrived in the village, which they'd learned was just over the Onitan border into Kreah; from the air, Mariah had missed the border markers, whatever they might be. The healer, by the grace of the gods, had stabilized Feran, but he was in no condition to travel. Word had been sent to Kreah, in hopes that an envoy would come.

Mariah sat beside a crackling fire, wrapped beneath a fleece blanket, eyes blankly watching the flames. Somehow, when she'd shifted, the magic of the transformation had restored her clothing and her weapons, but she couldn't stay in fighting leathers for long. She now wore clothes borrowed from a woman in town— soft leather breeches and a flowy blouse, both designed to combat the heat of the scorching deserts.

And while she no longer carried her twin short swords, her dagger was still strapped to its familiar place on her thigh.

Her father and brother sat on either side of her, their warmth a welcome comfort. Her Armature was spread around the fire, shooting her concerned stares as they talked quietly amongst themselves. All except Drystan, who refused to leave Feran's side.

A wall had slipped into place inside her after she'd fallen to pieces in her father and brother's arms. An aching coldness unrelated to the chill of the desert at night seeped in, a blankness settling over her as she spiraled into places of true darkness.

She'd dwelled on it all for days.

Her mother, gone. Never to come back.

And Andrian. A love who'd betrayed her, then saved her, then reminded her that she was worthy of happiness and worship, regardless of those who might wish her dead or weak. She'd tried, once, to reach for their bond. Her soul frosted over when nothing but dreadful silence answered.

She tried to tell herself it was only the distance. But she always was a terrible liar, even to herself.

A week ago, Mariah was ready to burn the world down to save her family.

Now, with one of them gone and her heart taken captive …

There was no limit to what she might do.

Across the roaring fire, Matheo shot to his feet. He scanned the pitch-black desert and skies, an arrow already notched in his longbow. Sebastian stood, moving to his brother's side.

"Something's out there," Matheo murmured.

A faint glow appeared on the horizon. Her Armature slid smoothly into action, drawing weapons and settling around Mariah and her family.

A figure on horseback emerged from the darkness, carrying a glowing torch. And another. And a third.

Two great prowling cats—one black panther, one golden leopard—followed, gleaming eyes reflecting the firelight.

Mariah rose slowly to her feet, something unfamiliar spreading through her limbs, softening the ice encasing her.

Hope.

She padded around her Armature, her blanket falling to the sand. The two big cats broke into a jog and then a run, sprinting towards her.

To their queen.

Mariah sank to her knees as Kiira and Rylla slid to a halt before her. She threw her arms around them both, their purrs rumbling from beneath soft fur.

"You're here," Mariah whispered. "You made it." She kept repeating those words, so many times, until the figures on horseback had neared. Kiira and Rylla drew back, glancing over their shoulders as the first rider halted and slid from her mount's back. She sprinted across the sands, blonde curls flying behind her.

Mariah had thought herself empty of tears, yet she still choked out a sob.

"Ciana," she said, the sound broken and soft as her best friend slammed into her, small body hitting Mariah with the same fierceness dwelling in her heart. Behind Ciana, a second woman with long auburn hair raced across the dunes. Mariah barely had time to open her arms before Delaynie crashed into her and Ciana, the three girls collapsing as their tears fed the sands.

"We're here, Mariah. We made it." Delaynie's whispers were soft and calm, but she gripped Mariah with a desperate viciousness.

Mariah pulled back, scanning them both. They wore comfortable clothes—those meant for traveling. Clothes that Delaynie in particular would never be caught dead in outside the safety of her rooms.

"What happened?" Mariah asked quietly, instincts prickling.

Her friends shared a glance.

"It is ..." Ciana started.

"Quite unbelievable," Delaynie finished.

Mariah frowned. "I think I can handle it."

"I'm just ..." Ciana swallowed. "I'm not sure it's our place to say. So much has changed, Mariah. All the legends and stories—"

"I know. Trust me, I know." Mariah's voice wavered. "Was it just you? Who got out?"

Delanie smiled softly. "No, Mariah. Not just us. We all got out."

"We?" Mariah didn't dare let herself be too hopeful.

"Everyone who cares about you. Me and Ciana. Kiira and Rylla. My mother, Ryenne's ladies. Even Brie and Mikael and a few other palace staff we knew to be wholly loyal to you."

Mariah released a heavy, broken sigh. She was still cracked, still shattered, still hungry to tear the world apart, but something loosened in her soul. A heaviness at knowing that those she cared for most had at least been bought a momentary safety.

Although a part of her wondered if they would ever know true safety again. Not with Kol returned to the world.

"I brought something else, too." Ciana's amber eyes crackled in the firelight. "You told me to keep it safe and hidden, and I didn't want to leave it there. Not with us all gone, and the future uncertain."

Mariah dropped her gaze to Ciana's hands. Where she was reaching into a satchel on her side and pulling out a small, gray leather book.

A journal. With *Ginnelevé* etched on the cover in silver foiled script.

The pain, the loss, the heartache swept over Mariah, and she did not fight it.

With trembling hands, she took her mother's journal from Ciana. Tears streaked her face and stained the sands, her magic quiet and shuttered.

"She's gone," she whispered into the night breeze. "I failed, and she's gone."

"Oh, Mariah," Ciana whispered back, arms wrapping back around Mariah. "I am so—gods, M, I—"

"We mourn your loss with you, Mariah," Delaynie said, tears thick in her own voice. "And we will do so properly once we get you and everyone safe. Right now, there is someone you need to meet."

Mariah met Delaynie's fierce, icy stare. From anyone else, those words would have been harsh. Callous. Cold.

But from Delaynie, they were necessary. A reminder of strength when Mariah had none left.

She nodded, and the three women stood, Mariah clutching

her mother's journal as if it were the only thing keeping her rooted to the earth.

Another figure had approached. They dismounted their horse, stepping forward into the firelight. The townsfolk who'd gathered at the new arrivals gasped, a few bowing their heads, hands fisting over their hearts.

The newcomer was regal and poised, sky blue robes flowing around a tall and androgenous frame. Their black hair was cropped close to their head, gold jewelry adorning a viciously beautiful face. More gold dusted their umber skin, highlighting their arching cheekbones. They smiled warmly at Mariah, hands clasped together, more gold upon their fingers.

"Mariah," Delaynie said, nodding respectfully. "I would like to introduce you to Amasis, High Counsellor of Kreah."

The High Counsellor bowed their head, the portrait of regal grace. "I wished to be the first to formally welcome you to Kreah, Your Majesty. You are most welcome here, for as long as you need refuge. I cannot imagine the journey you have made or the trials you have endured." Amasis's voice was as warm as their smile, their shockingly blue eyes glowing in the light.

Mariah blinked in surprise. "That is—thank you." She remembered herself and dipped her head. "You didn't need to come all this way yourself."

Amasis cocked their head. "Perhaps not. But this is a special occasion. Thousands of years have passed since a Queen of Onita crossed into our lands, and not because we have wished her to stay away."

Mariah understood. Onita was distrustful of outsiders and had been for far too long. A distrust, she realized, that was likely fueled by Kol's subtle influences upon the kingdom's powerful men who had long grappled desperately for control.

"Well ..." Mariah glanced at the group by the fires. Wex and Ellan, her court, her Armature. Even the townspeople, Kreah citizens who hadn't hesitated to help a foreign queen arriving on their doorstep in the form of a dragon.

"I am honored to be the one to break the drought, then."

Amasis's eyes sparkled. "There is one more who has traveled with us. One who is most desperate to meet you."

Something stirred in the dark, and Mariah knew.

At first, it was nothing but a gentle rustle, like the shifting winds across the sands. Then louder, like the beat of a butterfly's wings, growing deeper until it whooshed like the Attlehon eagles.

A roar tore through the desert night, and a dormant part of Mariah's soul sang in answer.

They were buffeted by a surge of winds, the sands whipping and stinging their cheeks, as two taloned legs landed heavily on the desert floor, a familiar reptilian shape illuminated in the firelight.

Even in the flickering dimness, Mariah was not afraid. This dragon was not black and gold, like the one she feared. Instead its scales shone a delicate blue, fading to white at its wingtips, the horns atop its head the color of soft white clouds on a brilliant summer day.

When the dragon's mind brushed Mariah's, it felt like open skies and changing moments, as lasting and fleeting as nature and the heavens themselves.

It was also unmistakably female.

"Welcome to Kreah, my sister. I have waited many long years to meet you." Her pale-yellow eyes glinted in the firelight. *"Or, perhaps, I have waited a long time to see you again."*

"Who are you?" Too stunned to voice back through her thoughts, Mariah spoke out loud. Confusion and alarm and awe danced down her bonds, chasing away some of her broken coldness.

The dragon lifted her long neck, shifting her great wings.

"My name is Rulene, and I am Goddess of the Day Sky and the Changes of Nature. You have endured so much, and have done so well, sister. But I fear this is only the beginning. War is coming, and we will need all our powers if we wish for this world to remain standing by the end."

. . .

To be continued...

Mariah, Andrian, and the rest of the gang's story will continue in *SHATTERED,* Book Three in The Solstice Cycle, expected in 2026.

In the meantime, head to https://www.tayrosebooks.com to join Tay's newsletter and be in the know about the latest updates. You can also find the links to Tay's reader Discord server, where you can chat directly with Tay and other readers of The Solstice Cycle.

Follow Tay Rose on Instagram and TikTok @tayrosebooks.

Thank you for reading! I would so greatly appreciate it if you take the time to rate and review *Scourged* on Amazon, Goodreads, and any other platform of your choosing. Your reviews are invaluable to indie authors and mean the world to us!

Acknowledgments

Wow. So, anyone who told me my second book would be easier to write than the first? Yeah, liars. All of you! (Just kidding).

In truth, this book took a lot from me. And not just in time and sacrifices; emotionally, it both drained and filled me up. Broke something in and healed me. And without my circle of supporters, I'm not sure I could have finished it.

First, to Mom and Dad: I may not say it enough, but you are my rocks. The way you have never once batted an eye or wavered in your support of me and this crazy, silly, outrageous passion project of a dream. Mom, I sincerely apologize for the events of this book, but please understand: it's nothing personal. I love you more than words can express (and Dad, too, of course, but I didn't kill off the father character, so ... Dad, you get it).

Next, to my author girls (affectionately known by many as "the coven"): Authoring is such a lonely business, but you all make it a little less so. All the late night trauma-bonding, commiserating, idea-bouncing, art-sharing ... it got me through the loneliness of writing this book. We all know how much I hate getting sappy (yuck), but I love you guys. Thanks for being there and always lending support when it's needed.

To my editor, Brit: How are you not sick of me yet?! Jokes aside, you have no idea how much I appreciate your experience, advice, humor, and encouragement. You have an eye for focusing a rather chaotic thought-jumble into something that says what I needed it to and that I'm proud of. This baby wouldn't be what she is without you!

To my alpha and beta readers: gods-bless you girls. You read this bad boy when she was in the roughest of states and loved her anyways. Your feedback was so impactful for helping me turn this book into what it is now. Thank you!

To Les: I won't embarrass you too much, but I sure am glad to call you a friend. Thanks for being the number one champion of me and this series. I swear, you know Mariah and Andrian better than I do at times. Truly terrifying! (In the best of ways).

To Libby: I can't say much without crying, BUT. Thank you for all you do for me and for your unwavering support. You have brought so much goodness into my life. The Discord would be nothing without you (especially since you literally own it), and I would similarly be missing a bright, shining light from my life. Don't leave me; I fear I wouldn't survive it.

To the cabana girls: Yeah, so, chapters 53-54? Those were for you. Thanks for being the goodest girls out there.

To all my friends in Discord: I'm so thankful for the space we have created. I can only hope it continues to grow and shine, and we always have a safe place where everyone is welcomed and feels comfortable being themselves!

And finally, to you, the reader: None of this would be possible if it weren't for you, being here, reading my books. Words can never express my gratitude. Thank you, and show them what moonlight really looks like.

xo, Tay

ALSO BY TAY ROSE

The Solstice Cycle

Threaded

Scourged

About the Author

Tay Rose is the author of The Solstice Cycle, an adult high romantic fantasy series, and loves to draw inspiration from the natural world in crafting tales of magic and love. A lawyer by day, author by night, she lives in Nashville, Tennessee with her sweet pup and way, way too many books.

A Capricorn and an Enneagram Type 8, she's never known quite when to stop or even the concept of "giving up." Writing has always been an escape for her, and despite a far too busy schedule, she always makes time for her stories. She's been inventing tales since the days she got her first computer, and while they were mostly either about dragons or fanfiction, everyone has to start somewhere.

When not reading or writing, Tay loves live music, being outside, and daydreaming about even more stories that she hopes to bring to life one day.

https://www.tayrosebooks.com

instagram.com/tayrosebooks

tiktok.com/tayrosebooks

threads.net/tayrosebooks

amazon.com/author/tayrose

goodreads.com/tayrosebooks